The Boxer

A Novel

by Christopher Conley

Note: This is a work of fiction. The characters in this novel are entirely the product of the author's imagination. Any similarity to actual events, locals, or persons, living or dead, is entirely coincidental.

Library of Congress registration number: TXu1-688-828

1st edition published through CreateSpace

ISBN-13: 978-0692406076

ISBN 10: 0692406077

The Ghost of Tom Joad by Bruce Springsteen. Copyright © 1995

To Rob Lawrie

Also by Christopher Conley:

• The Tree

• The Rains

• Billy's Curse

• A Collection of Work (chapbook of poetry)

Acknowledgements

Firstly, I have to give special thanks to Rob Lawrie who, not only is one of my best friends, but also was the backbone to the character of Shawn Calloway. Most of what you see in these coming pages of Shawn is as a direct result of Rob. There are several scenes in the story that he directly contributed and many more in addition that he collaborated on with me. Without him, this story would not be what it is today.

Secondly, I would like to give thanks to a number of things which have influenced another or me in one form. I list them here alphabetically rather than in order of importance:

-        *Cinderella Man*, a film by Ron Howard, written by Cliff Hollingsworth and Akiva Goldman. Based on the life story of heavyweight boxing champion James J Braddock;

-        *Million Dollar Baby*, both the book, which is a collection of short stories by F.X. Toole, and its movie form, directed by Clint Eastwood and written by Paul Haggis;

-        the *Rocky* franchise, written by Sylvester Stallone and directed by both Sylvester Stallone and John Avildsen.

Finally, I would like to thank my parents for their constant support over the years.

C.C.->

Introduction

I believe I first came up with the idea of this early in the fall of 2004 while I was working at Cazenovia College in their horse stables. While trying to nail out the details of this at work, I was working on another story of mine, Billy's Curse. It would not be for almost another year after this before I would start putting pen to paper in an effort to write the story you now have in your hands.

I had this story based around two guys, both best friends who were almost like brothers. I figured I would have the story set in today's times with both guys as adults but also incorporate flashback scenes to their youth to bring the reader up to speed on their history. The two main characters I wanted to be very different, from different sides of the tracks. One of them, Christian, I imagined being quite similar to me and, as a result, I loosely based him on myself. The other, Shawn, I based loosely on my friend at the time Rob Lawrie. Since I felt he had a real good imagination, I asked if he wanted to help me write this story. He did so by helping me define what, and who, Shawn was as well as the relationship between him and Christian.

The biggest piece of advice I feel I got from him, outside of whether or not I was staying on track, was simply not to have the flashback scenes at all. Rather, he suggested why not just simply start at the beginning of their story and move forward from there. For me, this gave us the opportunity to explore more of their past and tell the story of the two main characters. With this, I am extremely happy he had mentioned it to me since I feel it ultimately gave the story more depth to it overall. Anyway, here is my story and I surely hope you like it.

C.C. ->

Prologue

"Death and rebirth; and as I die, so shall I be reborn!"

With the onslaught of torture the champ was taking, all Christian Eaton could do was fumble back against the ropes in a vain attempt to defend himself.

"Ooh, that was a slick combo the challenger just delivered," Lou commented in the microphone. "The left hook he followed it up with was huge! I don't know how much more the champ can take!"

Whatever happened, Shawn was on autopilot with eyes hungry, mouth frothing, and fists blazing. After a slight pause from the challenger, the champ's hands soon became too heavy to hold up. Once they dropped, the fury began again. A flash of bright, blinding, white light soon followed it.

"My God! Goes down Eaton! Down goes Eaton!" Tom yelled into his mic as the crowd exploded around him.

"1...2...3...," counted the ref as his right hand whipped out to signal the number he was on.

"I don't believe it! The champ is down! My God!" Tom continued to yell. "For the first time in his illustrious career, the champ, Christian Eaton, has been knocked down!"

"...4...5...6...," the ref continued.

"You know, Tom, this doesn't look good for the champ," Lou said while rubbing his chin and shaking his head. "To think that Eaton may lose his retirement match against his brother and former best friend is unfathomable."

"...7...8...9...!"

For the first time during the count did the champ stir. The ferocious combos and the killer hook that followed felt like he had been mowed over by a train. By the time he managed to roll over to one knee, it was too late. All he could do was look up to see the ref finish the ten count.

"...10!" the ref shouted while waving his arms in front of him. "You're out!"

The crowd exploded as Shawn Calloway danced around center stage with his arms held high. The ring announcer made his way to the middle of the squared circle to meet the microphone on its decent down. When he had it in his grasp, he cleared his throat before speaking into it.

"The winner by way of knockout with one minute and thirty-eight seconds of the fifth round and nnneeewww Undisputed Cruiserweight Champion of the Wwwooorrrlllddd, Shaaawwwnnn Callllloooowwwaaayyy!"

While quickly grabbing the four world belts, he put two over one shoulder, one of the other, before holding the WBA world title high in the air. He was happy with delight as a look of ridicule came over his face. He looked with a glance over to the now former champion to see him being helped to his corner. One of Eaton's men soon began waving smelling salts under his nose. Smiling with contempt, Calloway grabbed the microphone from the announcer.

"In light of my easy and recent victory, I just want to say one thing," he paused long enough for Christian to look up at him. "It's about time the undisputed championship was in the hands of a worthy and superior fighter. Everything comes to those who wait, and I have waited so very long for this moment!"

With that said, Shawn dropped the mic before fighting his way to his corner for his robe before heading back to the locker room.

All Christian could do was sit in his corner as his face lay in his hands. Dominic, his trainer, and Tony, his cut man, made a failed attempt at keeping the media away.

Minutes later, Christian entered his own locker room before sitting on a padded examination table. With his face back in his hands, he began to slowly move them up and down his face. His eyes were closed.

"Hey, kid. Ya alright?" Dom asked with concern in his voice while hobbling over to see his beaten pupil.

Christian jumped a little from surprised when he heard his voice. "Yeah, I guess," he answered while putting his head back into his hands.

"Ya guess?" asked the trainer with a confused, rough, unsophisticated voice. "What'cha mean by that? Is something wrong with ya, kid?"

"My head just hurts a little, Dom. That's all," Christian softly said.

"I'm sure it does hurt from the beatin' ya just took."

"No, not that. It's, um, hard to explain."

"Then what is it, kid? What?"

"It's, um, just," Christian started though he found it hard to get the right words. "You know the feeling your arm or leg gets when they're asleep? That's how my head feels."

"Hell, kid. I could tell your head was asleep by the ways ya fought tonight." Dominic sighed with a chuckle.

"No, it started feeling, ah, weird a short time ago." Christian placed his right palm on his temple to help ease the pain.

"So, your head feels all tingly as a result from the abuse ya just took." Dom put his hand on Christian's shoulder "Ya see, kid; Shawn was on a rampage to prove to the whole world that ya was nothin'. He set out to destroy ya from the first second of the first round. Ya took a hell of a beatin' and ya gave him all ya had, but he just kept comin'. It's a wonder ya're still breathing, kid. He's not the type of fighter ya go toe-to-toe with. Yeah, ya're a great fighter, but ya're smoother, more fluent, and smarter than he is.

"All he knows how to box is by being a brawler or a bruiser. Ya ain't like him; and he ain't like ya, either, kid. No one should be allowed to take the beatin' that ya took this evening. If ya fought him like ya did in your first two matches, ya would have eventually worn him down and won. But since ya fought his style of fight, ya were no match no matter how valiantly ya did. No offense, but it's no wonder your head feels a little fuzzy," Dom softly whispered with tenderness before sitting down next to him. When he was finished talking, he looked to his fighter to read his reaction.

"Dom," Christian moaned while now using both hands to push on his temples.

"Hey, kid, what's the matter? What is it, kid?"

At that, Christian lay back on the bench while being on the verge of passing out. Dominic got up and hobbled to the door while yelling to it the whole way there.

"Hey, you bums!" the elderly man yelled while opening the door. "Get a doctor in here! Hey, we need a doctor in here!" He paused long enough to look down the hall at a group of people. "Hey, don't just stand there looking at me! Move your asses! Christian needs a doctor right away!"

Within minutes, a pair of paramedics rushed in with their needed equipment and started assessing Christian. While doing a few needed procedures, Christian lost consciousness to the sounds of muffled voices, grunts, and pressures of CPR, and the sight of white, blinding light.

Part I

The Beginning

The beginning of the end;

The beginning of the rest of our lives;

The beginning of a beautiful friendship;

The beginning of something extraordinary.

Chapter 1

It was a typical warm mid-August day, though it seemed hotter. The sun was bright, the sky blue, and a warm breeze shown itself to relieve the stress that any weekday could bring.

Through the trees on the hillside, a valley opened up to reveal a housing development in the distance. On the outskirts, there were meadows, fields, and farmland with cows grazing. The development itself was your typical white suburbia in middle-class Americana. It had a couple of trees with well-maintained lawns, children playing or riding bikes, sprinklers sprinkling, and a lawn mowers mowing.

In one part of the development, the smell of apple pies was in the air; while in another, chocolate chip cookies dominated. The people that weren't busy baking were busy attending a wide range of hanging flower baskets decorating their porches.

In the midst of all this, a chunky, over-weight boy was playing in his front yard while working on some science project. While trying to perfect his experiment, he hummed the theme song to his favorite TV show. When he was just about finished, he suddenly hears a loud, cruel voice. Turning, he sees the five punks, who are on either bikes or skateboards, glaring at him from the street.

"Yo, Lardass!" Wesley, the leader of The Hoods, mocked. "What the hell you messin' with now?"

"Another one of your stupid experiments?" Eric, of the other cronies, yelled out.

"You know you're such a geek," Wesley yelled from the street while not getting off his bike. "Don't you know no one likes a geek?"

"Ya, you're such a geek!" shouted Kyle, who was second-in-command, as he picked his skateboard up.

These five kids were the terrors of the town. Even at the age of ten, they already had a reputation for vandalism, mouthing off, and getting anyone and everyone pissed off. They showed no respect to anything and got away with everything.

Not only was he the leader, Wesley was also the oldest and biggest. He also seemed to have the knack of getting in the least amount of trouble while his comrades ended up being the scapegoats. Everyone knew that he was pulling the strings but was never actually caught in the act. It was never clearly explained what exactly Wesley's problem with the chubby boy was, but maybe it was simply because he was just a weaker species. Wesley probably just needed to feel better about himself as low self-esteem was a genetic disorder in his family.

"Why are you always messin' 'round with that stuff? It's stupid and it's queer and nobody cares! You gonna say somethin' or has your neck got so fat that it's making you get a speech impalement?" he questioned while trying to puff himself up the best he could. Wesley wasn't very smart and had a tendency to prove this fact over and over again by continuously letting his mouth do the talking.

Overall, the intelligent, overweight boy didn't usually talk back to Wesley but at that moment, he felt unusually brave.

"You know something, Wesley," he softly said with a muffled chuckle. "You're about as stupid as you are ugly."

"Ah, is that so?" questioned Wesley as the color drained from his face.

"Yes, as a matter of fact, it is." He shook his head "It's 'impediment,' not 'impalement.'"

"Oh, that's it fatso!" Wesley said as his face reddened. He slow got off his bike while puffing himself up. "You're gonna get it now. C'mon boys, let's get 'imp!"

Then, just like that, the five hoodlums began taking turns beating on the chubby child. It lasted only a minute or so when all of a sudden Stan fell down with a "uuuggghhh!" When the other four turned, they saw a scrappy ten-year-old standing there looking at them.

"Why don't you give the kid a break? How about you beat on me for a while?" he asked coldly.

"That's not a bad idea," Wesley told him. "Two for the price of one."

After taking a couple steps towards the scrappy child while swinging his right hand, the dirt boy sidestepped and tripped him with his left foot. He watched as Wesley went down face first in a cloud of dust. Kenny and Eric looked on in amazement as Stan finally got up. Kyle, second-in-command and second toughest, made a half-hearted lunge at the stranger before finding himself spinning upside down in the air.

"Hey, you three want some?" the stranger asked the three remaining bullies.

"Uh, no. No way, man," came the reply as Kenny, Eric and Stan all bolted.

"This isn't over, jerk-off!" Wesley shouted while bending over to pick Kyle up by the collar. They each soon ran off to catch up with their retreating posse.

"Whatever," the dirty kid said while turning to offer a hand to the chubby boy. "You alright, kid?"

"Yeah, I'm a-a-a-all r-r-right," stuttered the chubby boy.

"What the hell's wrong with you? You got a fat lip or somethin'?"

"No. T-t-that's just how I t-t-talk."

"Well, you sound weird, kid. Are you stupid or is it 'cut of the beatin' you just got from those jackasses?"

"It's not that. I have a speech impediment that gets w-w-worse when I'm n-n-nervous."

"Right," the stranger said while giving him a bewildered look with a sarcastic, raised eyebrow. "You gonna be ok? I'd hate to come back in an hour or so to save your butt again."

"Y-y-yeah, I'm ok. Thanks for helping me."

"No problem, bro," the dirty boy said before turning to leave.

"Hey," the chubby boy suddenly blurted out. "You wanna come in and maybe get a soda or something? I mean, I do owe you that as least. Right?"

"Look, kid. You owe me nothin'," he said before stopping to think for a moment. "But I am thirsty."

The chubby boy's home was placed smack dab right in the middle of suburbia Americana. The yard was neatly landscaped with a well-tended flowerbed in front. A swing-bench decorated the wooden wraparound porch. In back, a mid-sized tree house was a few yards from an in-ground pool. The house itself was two floors with an attached two-car garage. It was the color of snow with charcoal trim. The front door opened as the two boys went to the kitchen.

"What kind of soda would you like? If you want something else we have milk, water, iced tea, and lemonade."

"Root beer if you have it."

"Eww, let's see. Oh here we go. Last one," he said while handing the can to the stranger. "Oh, I'm sorry; I'm Christian. What's your name?"

"Shawn," he simply stated while taking the can and opening it. "Name's Shawn."

"Nice to meet you, Shawn."

"Yo, are you always this perky?" Shawn asked.

Christian shrugged before saying, "Well, normally I am a happy little trooper."

"You can't be happy all the time. That's downright impossible."

"Well, my ma says that happy people are the best kind." Christian smiled.

"Your *Ma* say's that?" Shawn smirked as his sarcasm was mixed with rudeness. "What other advice does your *Ma* give you?"

"What's wrong with me listening to my mother?"

"Nothin' is wrong with it. I'm sorry. It's just been one of those days." Shawn shook his head and rubbed his face. "It's the kind of day you wouldn't wish on your closest enemy."

"Is it anything you wanna talk about?" Christian asked while sitting down at the kitchen table.

Hearing this, Shawn's body posture stiffened while shooting him a cold, icy glare. "With you? I don't think so!"

"Look, I was trying to be nice since you helped me out," Christian returned the stare with a little agitation.

"Look, Chris. I didn't help you because you're my friend," Shawn told him. "I did it 'cuz I don't like bigger people pickin' on those more small than them. That's all."

Christian smiled slyly. "Don't you mean 'smaller'?"

Irritated, Shawn asked, "What the hell are you, an English book?"

"English? Well, you can say that. I'm also part Spanish book to, just to let you know."

"You're something else, you know that, right?"

"Yeah, I'm kind of special or something. My parents say I'm their special little dictionary."

"Aye carumba," sighed Shawn while rolling his eyes.

Hearing this, Christian smiled. "You know a little Spanish, too?"

Shawn just closed his eyes as he shook his head. "I gotta get going now. My dad will be home soon," he told him before finishing his soda. "Hey, I'm gonna be at Deeley's Market around, say, elevinish tomorrow. If you wanna come, that's cool."

"Really?" Christian smiled with excitement. "You're asking me to hang out with you tomorrow?"

"I'm not asking you anything," mocked Shawn. "I'm just sayin' if ya happened to be there at that time, I'll be there too."

Christian smiled with a nod. "Oh, yeah. Sure. I got'cha. In that case, I may be there then."

With that, Shawn walked out the front door. "Yeah, whatever. Later, kid." The screen door slammed behind him as he started walking down the street.

Looking out the window after him, a twinkle came in Christian's swollen eye as a smile rose on his bloody lip.

Chapter 2

Deeley's Market had been in the middle of town for as long as Christian could remember. It was one of those mom-and-pop shops where the actual market was an extension of the owner's house. Mr. and Mrs. Deeley where an elderly couple who owned and operated it.

Mr. Deeley was a medium-sized English man with thinning grey hair, hazel eyes, and a nose almost as big as his smile. He always seemed to be in a good mood no matter the occasion. For some reason, Christian was surprised to find that he didn't smell like other old people he had encountered and found it funny that every few steps Mr. Deeley would have to pull up his grey, sagging slacks to stop them from falling to his ankles. He always wore a well-worn, brown, leather belt that was obviously too big for his frame and claimed to wear it in remembrance of how big and strong he used to be in his prime.

His wife, on the other hand, was just the opposite. The very eccentric Mrs. Deeley was an older Jewish woman with the age and build that equaled that of her husband's. She wore thick glasses that seldom stayed on her nose without a little assistance from her fingers. It seemed like she was always pushing them up whenever possible. Unlike her husband, she always wore clean, freshly pressed housedresses with a white apron covering her front. Her hair was always disheveled no matter how well she brushed it. Of the two, she definitely was the talker. What Christian found entertaining about the way she spoke was not how she spoke but, rather, what didn't come out of her mouth. She never had a shortage of arm mannerisms to elaborate her stories; and always seemed to have an endless supply of Oy's that seemed to equal every other word. Christian liked her because she was always very nice and complimentary to everyone.

"Oh, Timothy," she said as Christian came in while adjusting her glasses. "It is *so* good to see you again. It's been awhile since your last visit. How are you doing today, dear?"

"I'm doing very well, Mrs. Deeley. And, yes, it's been awhile," answered Christian while giving her an inquisitive but confused look. He noticed that her husband was giving him a look from the ladder he was on that was a combination nod, roll of the eyes, and chuckle all in one as he went back to stocking the shelves. "Sorry I haven't been in a while; I've been working on my science project for the school fair."

"Oh, the young Einstein's at it again, huh?" Mr. Deeley commented while stepping from the ladder to get a towel to wipe off his hands; a twinkle was in his eyes and a piano key smile on his face. "Is this going to be like your last two successes?"

"Harold!" his wife exclaimed. "Don't pick on the poor boy because they didn't turn out as he had planned."

"Didn't go as planned? Didn't go as planned?! Gee, I should hope not!" he retorted dryly in mock jest.

Taken slightly aback, Christian asked, "Hey, what's that supposed to mean?"

"Well, considering your last project, what was it, some sort of missile? From what I heard, that thing exploded so loud that no one could hear properly for a day or two afterwards."

"That wasn't my fault," Christian said in his defense. "The guy sold me bad wiring or something. It wasn't supposed to explode until after it was outside!"

Mr. Deeley leaned in a little while looking at the young lad before him in the eye. "And the time before that? Hmm? You built yourself a regular volcano, didn't you? Which one did you name it after?"

"Mount Saint Helen, sir," Christian meekly answered.

"I should say you did. And, if I remember correctly, it did it's rendition of its world famous 1980 eruption. All over the gymnasium. Ha!" the elderly shopkeeper laughed heartedly. "Outside of having to replace the majority of the floor, it took them almost two weeks to get all the ash, soot, and smell out."

"Well, that is true," Christian admitted with a look of thoughtfulness. "That was just a slight miscalculation on my part. If I had put in the extra carbon instead of substituting it for lead, I would have for sure gotten the desired results."

"Oh, I'm sure this will be the year," Mrs. Deeley politely told him. "Don't give up on it, ok dear?"

With this, she went to the cooler to remove one of her homemade apple pies. She cut a good-sized piece and put it on a plate on the counter before giving it to Christian. Gladly accepting it, he began eating it. He soon was moaning and groaning with pleasure as he chewed it. It was gone in a total of four bites.

"Umm, that was good. Thank-you, Mrs. Deeley. You sure do make the best pies."

She smiled when she heard this. "Not a problem, dear. So, tell me, Timothy, what can I do for you today?"

"Damn it, Ellen!" her husband bellowed from the back storeroom. "The boy's name is Christian!"

"I know what his name is, Harold. You don't need to shout at me."

While making his appearance from behind the curtain, this time carrying an unopened box to shelf, he said, "If that's the case, why on earth did you just call him Timothy for the second time?"

"I did?" she asked in a honest and confused tone.

"Yes, you did," the acid response came as the box was opened.

"Oy! I'm so sorry, Christian," she quickly apologized as her hands went to her cheeks. "I don't know where my mind's been. I don't what came over me."

"Don't worry about it, kiddo," Mr. Deeley looked at Christian with a slight smile on his lips. "We've been married over 50 years and she still has trouble remembering my name."

"Harold, don't be telling the boy that," she stated with a feistiness Christian hadn't seen before. "He'll actually start thinking I have Alzheimer's or something."

"See what I mean, kid?" the old man said with a straight face. "Over fifty years of marriage and she still thinks my name is Harold. After about the first ten, I stopped trying to tell her my name's actually Stanley."

"Men! Oy!" She exclaimed before laughing and waving her arms in the air before fixing her glasses again. She soon calmed down enough to go behind the counter to do some cleaning.

"So, Einstein, I don't think you answered the misses' question," Mr. Deeley said while wiping the sweat off his brow. He then went to a little stand-up cooler near the cash register, withdrew two sodas and waved over Christian. He soon sat down on a bench before handing his visitor one of the sodas and opened the other. "What's the reason for such a nice lad as yourself to come visit two old timers such as us on your summer holiday?"

"I'm here to meet a friend," Christian told him while cracking open his soda and gulping down about half of it.

Mr. Deeley was interested when he heard this. "Oh, a friend you say. And we thought you came for the pleasure of our company." He smiled at this.

While adjusting her glasses from behind the counter, Mrs. Deeley said, "If you're here to meet a friend, I should really like to meet him, seeing how you picked him out especially. What is your friend's name, dear?"

"Shawn," Christian told her before letting out a soda-flavored burp. "Excuse me."

"Shawn? Not that damn Calloway boy, is it?" Mr. Deeley gasped when he heard the name. "That trouble maker from the other side of the tracks?"

"I'm not sure," Christian admitted. "I only know his first name. I'll let you know when I find out, ok?"

"There's a Shawn that frequently hangs out here out front every so often," the eldery man stated while pointing a bony finger at his much younger counterpart. "I'll tell you one thing. That boy's nothing but trouble."

"How do you know that, Mr. Deeley?" Christian was surprised to hear this since he had never heard the old man say anything negative or derogatory about anybody.

"Because their hooligans. All of 'em!" Now visibly agitated, Mr. Deeley waved his arms and wrenched his face.

"Dear, you think all young boys are hooligans," Mrs. Deeley commented while putting some loose change in the cash register.

"Well, ain't they?" snapped Mr. Deeley.

"I don't think he is," whined Christian.

Mr. Deeley eyed him suspiciously. "How long you known him?"

"I just met him yesterday."

The shopkeeper waved a finger at him. "You should have known by looking at him that he's no good."

"That's not fair, Mr. Deeley. My mommy said that you shouldn't judge a book by its cover," Christian told him with a little whine in his voice as he tried sticking up for his new friend.

"Boy, I never had enough time in the day to read a book," he told Christian while looking at him dead in the eye. "You even know what an honest day's work is all about? I've worked sixty hours a week for over fifty-five years without a single vacation. Not a one! That's working sick, holidays, weekends. You name it and I've worked it. I even worked when she had two of our kids," he said matter-of-factly while throwing a thumb towards his wife. "Until you've achieved that, then don't you tell me how to judge anyone. You got me?"

"Yes, s-s-sir," Christian sheepishly said while avoiding eye contact.

"Oh, hun, will you stop you?" Mrs. Deeley said from the counter as she came to Christian's defense. "You shouldn't be so hard on the boy. After all, he just told us that he met the lad yesterday."

"Anyway," her husband stated while trying to calm down. His fingers rubbed his forehead in the process. "I think his dad is some type of laborer at the factory here in town. Isn't your dad a boss or something there? Maybe he knows him."

"I don't really know what my dad does at the factory. He does go there with a tie on," Christian said while thinking for a better answer before realizing what he heard. "Hey, you know my dad?"

"Sure I do," Mr. Deeley answered before standing to pull up his pants. For a moment, it looked like his pants were going to be in his armpits. "He comes in every so often. Mostly he gets some little nick-knack for his projects. The apple doesn't fall too far from the tree."

Until then, Christian hadn't realized that his dad had come there for supplies. He always assumed he went to a bigger store that specialized in hardware. Sure, Deeley's Market was a small town market where you could go to buy groceries, but it was also more. The market was also one of the few places in the area where most of the produce they sold was locally grown, either by farmers or by those with the love of big gardens. The misses ran this part, and she ran it tight. A number of kids would try to cheat her out of something like soda or candy, but not many succeeded. Though they looked at her as she were a harmless old woman, almost like their grandmother, but she acted more like a mother who was always ready to dish out punishment when it was needed.

Mr. Deeley, on the other hand, ran the store's hardware department, though it wasn't actually a department. In reality, it was more of a side room in reality. There was nothing fancy or state of the art about it. The room was about the size of a bedroom and consisted equally of tools on the wall and catalogs on a shelf to order from. He had been running this for as long as Christian could remember and it had never been bigger than what it was then. Mr. Deeley always said he wanted to stay small with his business and small is how he kept it. He wanted to know what he had in stock while also being able to talk with the customers without having to worry about the business be just about selling things. He said the way he did it kept him up on preserving things the costumers would respect most; things like honesty, quality, and loyalty. If he got any bigger, he said, he felt he would suffer any of those three basic standards he had. He felt everyone was better off in a long run with the way he had it now.

Before they could get any further in their conversations, Shawn walked in while chewing on some bubble gum and listening to his Walkman. Upon seeing him, Mr. Deeley huffed a bit before walking towards the storage area and acting like he was doing something important.

"Hello, Shawn," Mrs. Deeley cheerfully said. "How are you doing today?"

"Fine, I guess," Shawn muttered.

"Good good," she replied while slowly turning away to go back to her work while yet again fixing her glasses.

When Christian had his chance, he quickly approached Shawn. "Hi'ya Shawn. How's it going?"

"Fine," Shawn answered while giving him an irritated look. He kept heading back to a get a soda from the bigger cooler. He reached in, grabbed a can, and let the door slam behind him.

Christian, meanwhile, was in the process of reaching in when the door closed in his face. He gave a look of dismay before shaking it off and reopened it to grab himself a Pepsi.

Shawn headed over to the candy section to grab himself a small bag of Twizzlers while drowning out the world to the music coming from his headphones. Christian, meanwhile, was slowly following behind trying to catch-up as he soon found himself following Shawn to the comic book rack up near the door. Shortly thereafter, a recent Superman comic was selected before Shawn proceeded to pay for his stash of goodies. He walked out the door after paying before sitting on the bench out in front to start reading his newly purchased comic.

Christian, meanwhile, followed not knowing what else to do expect to just stand there staring at him as he wondered if he should say something.

After a minute or so, Shawn took off his headphones and looked at him. "You wanna sit down?" he asked while briefly pointing to the vacant space next to him.

"It that alright with you?"

"I offered, didn't I?"

"Oh, gee. Thanks," Christian happily said while sitting down before cracking open his can of soda. After guzzling half the can and letting out a gut-wrenching belch, he looks over to Shawn to ask, "What'ya readin'?"

Slowly looking at him from the corner of his eye, Shawn slowly turned the comic book so Christian could see its title.

"Oh, cool. You like Superman?"

"Yep."

"Have you read that one before?"

"Nope."

While tapping his feet, Christian asked, "What's it about?"

"I don't know," came the reply while its speaker was immersed in the pictures.

"Then how do you know that you haven't read it before?"

"I just know," answered Shawn with growing frustration in his voice.

"Well, you don't have to be mean about it. I was just asking," Christian whined while hanging his head as Shawn went back to reading his comic. "Did I do something wrong?"

"Look! I just want to read my comic. Ok?!" exploded Shawn.

"Sorry to upset you," Christian quickly apologized. "I didn't mean anything by it."

At which point, Shawn realized the damage he had caused. He soon put down the comic while turning to Christian.

"Look, Chris, I'm sorry," he told him. "I look forward every month to read the new Superman comic and I'm not used to anyone being with me. I'm sorry if I yelled at you. I can read it later. Ok?"

Sniffing and wiping his nose, Christian said, "It's ok with me if it's ok with you."

"I have an idea," Shawn told him while quickly changing the subject. "You wanna go down to the train tracks with me? I have to go home to feed my dog and the tracks are on the way."

"The train tracks?" Christian asked with a gasp. "I'm not supposed to go there without my parent's permission."

"You have my permission. Besides, what's the big deal? Ain't nothin' gonna happen to ya."

"Are you sure we won't get into any trouble?" Christian hesitantly asked.

"Well, you could get your foot stuck in the rails and the train could run you over and smash you into a million pieces with your blood going everywhere,"

"Really?!" Christian freaked as his eyes got as big as saucers.

Sighing while rolling his eyes, Shawn said, "No, not really. I was joking. Dude, relax. Come on, let's get outta here."

Minutes later, Christian was following Shawn down the road on his bike while trying not to hyperventilate. He was also really worried about the tracks, afraid he'll either get hurt or in trouble. When he thought about it, he wasn't exactly sure where the tracks were.

"Hey, Shawn! How much further is it to the train tracks from here?"

"I don't know. About two more miles I think," answered Shawn while still dominating the lead.

"Wow! I've never been that far from home by myself before. How 'bout you?"

Shawn couldn't help but look at him with raised eyebrows as a sarcastic smirk rose on his face. "All the time."

"Really?" asked Christian with surprised.

"Really really."

"So, um where do you live? Near the tracks?"

"Ahhh, somewhere around there. Like a few minutes away."

"How far?"

"I don't know exactly how far. I've never actually measured it," Shawn said before pausing long enough to look at Christian. "What's up with all the questions?"

"Sorry, I just like to ask questions. If you don't know something, then all you gotta do is ask."

"You don't get out much, do you?"

"I work on my science projects outside in my yard all the time. Why?"

Shawn could feel his blood pressure starting to rise when he felt he had to explain himself yet again. "That's not what I meant. Let me ask you something. Do you have any friends?"

"Well, I have you. Does that count?" Christian said while feeling embarrassed that he couldn't name off more.

Rolling his eyes again with a sigh, Shawn told him, "Yeah, I guess. Hey, let's take a left here. It's a short cut."

"You mean through the woods?" Christian asked while slowing down his bike.

"Yep, through the woods."

"Well, alright, but I hope there's no poison ivy or anything," Christian reluctantly agreed. "I'm allergic to poison ivy, and poison sumac, and..."

"Aye carumba!" muttered Shawn while retaking the lead into the woods.

Shawn, who by now was peddling at a moderate and deliberate pace, turned to chuckle as he watched Christian twenty yards behind struggling to keep up.

"Are there any wild animals out here?" Christian called out.

"There may be some."

"Really? Like what? Deer?"

"Deer, skunk, squirrel, fox, bear…"

"Bears?!" Christian asked while quickly scanning the surround landscape. "Did you say bears? Are there really bears out here?"

"Yep. Big, black smelly ones with huge claws and rabid teeth," explained Shawn calmly with a hint of sarcasm. "Ones that like to eat small whiny kids who ask a lot of questions."

Becoming extremely nervous almost scared, Christian asks, "You aren't being serious, are you? You'd better be joking! There hasn't been any reports of bears in this area, has there?"

Hearing this, Shawn couldn't control his laughter any more. He burst out with laughter which distracted him to the point where he ran off the path and into a tree. Swerving sharply to miss it, he hit instead a pothole to send him flying over his handlebars.

"I thought you were being serious," Christian said while pulling his bike up next to a sprawled Shawn, who was trying to get up. "You got what you deserved for scaring me like that. Are you alright?"

"Of course I'm alright!" he answered angrily while springing up and quickly getting on his bike. "Does it look like I'm not?!"

"That was a pretty nasty fall. You sure you're alright?"

"I said I was fine!" Shawn shouted while turning around to glare at him. " Stop asking me, alright?!"

"Sorry, Shawn. I didn't mean to upset you. I was just worried you got hurt, that's all," whined Christian while trying to avoid eye contact.

"Chris, listen. I just don't like being asked if I'm alright. If I wasn't, I would have said something. Also, I'm sorry I said that there were bears in the area. I just had to pick on you because you seem so gullible."

With this said, things seemed to be back to normal between them and, moments after that, Shawn took off down the path on his bike with Christian trying to catch up. For a moment, Shawn felt sorry for him because he was overweight, didn't have a clue on what was going on, didn't have any friends, and, worse of all, was smart. The sentimental moment quickly passed when he realized he was actually thinking about someone other than himself. He soon saw the train tracks before coming to a stop near them. Looking at his right arm that he scratched during the fall, he took any dirt from it that he could before turning back to Christian.

"You alright, Chris?! Need some help back there?"

"No, I'm alright. Thank-you, though," he answered while coming up the remaining distance to rest besides Shawn. When he stopped, he used his hand to wipe off his sweaty brown and flushed cheeks.

"So, here are the tracks." Shawn nodded his head towards them before pointing further down. "My house is off that way. If you take the trail here on the right, it'll lead you to the high school." With that said, Shawn turned his bike and started pedaling for home.

"Hey! Where'ya going?" Christian asked with total shock in his voice.

"I told you already. To feed my dog, remember?"

"What, I can't go with you?"

"It doesn't take two people to feed a dog. Besides, he doesn't like strangers," Shawn told him indifferently. "I'll see ya around."

"When? When will I see you again?"

"I don't know," Shawn said flatly. "Maybe when I'm done feeding my dog."

"Are you coming back to play?" Christian asked in hopes of getting an answer.

Without answering or acknowledging ever hearing the question, Shawn went straight over the tracks and continued down the dirt path. Christian was left to ponder whether or not the bear story was real and, more importantly, whether or not Shawn was coming back.

Chapter 3

"Christian, time for dinner!" called his mom, Sally, from the kitchen. "Hurry up and get washed!"

"Coming, Mama," he answered while putting down the rocket he was working on.

The smell of pot roast and potatoes were in the air, and the aroma of freshly brewed coffee was also present. Upon entry to the kitchen, the table was set with his dad and grandfather in their usual spots, both reading the newspaper; his dad, David, with the Business section, his grandfather, Joe, with Sports. His mother, meanwhile, was cutting up the rest of the roast before putting it on the table.

"Goddamn it!" an irritated Joe yelled.

"What's wrong, Gramps?" Christian asked while taking his usual seat next to him.

"Those freaking Yankees!" he replied with frustration. "They beat my team again!"

"Dad, you know you shouldn't read that with your blood pressure," Sally warmly said. "Wouldn't want you to have a heart attack or anything."

"I know, I know. I just don't know how they can be so Goddamn lucky all the time," he snapped back.

"Luck?" David asked. "Is that what you call it? Maybe they won because your team isn't playing very well this year."

"Excuse me?" Joe eyed his son. "Not playing very well? That's blasphemy! It's not my fault they lost their two best players. They could have taken those bastards if they hadn't gotten hurt."

"Can you believe this?" Christian's dad asked while shaking his head. "The price of our stock went down again for the third straight week. I don't even know how much more of this I can take if it keeps up."

"Come on, boys. Put those papers away," Sally instructed while putting the finishing touches on the table before finally sitting down herself. "This is time for family. Your papers can wait a half hour or so."

Both did as they were told before looking at the table laid out before them. Gramps did so with a shake of his head while muttering something under his breath.

"Did you say something, Dad?" asked Sally.

"No, I didn't say anything," he retorted. "Still irritated about those damn Yankees. I can't believe how they…"

"Dad, you should take it easy. It's only a game," David commented as he passed around the steaming plate of meat.

"Only a game? Only a game?! Only a game he says," Joe stated hotly while looking at his grandson. "You hear that? Baseball most defiantly is NOT a game. It's way of life. Just like boxing! You remember that, ok boy?"

"His name is Christian, not boy, Dad," David corrected.

"I know what his name is." Joe shot his son a glare before soon turning his attention back to his grandson. "So, you remember what I just told you, ok? Baseball AND boxing are both a way of life. Alright?"

"Alright, Grandpa," Christian told him in between mouthfuls.

"So, sweetie, what did you do today?" Sally asked while patting his arm.

"Oh, nothing," came the reply that was mixed in with sounds of chomping meat.

While fixing her plate, she said to him, "Nothing? You were gone for several hours today."

"I just met someone at the market this morning."

"You say you met someone?" Joe asked over his glasses while raising his cup of coffee. "Who did you meet?"

"Remember that boy I told you about yesterday? The one who stuck up for me?"

"Ah, yes," Grandpa Joe said while looking to his son. "And you say children today do not have any morality."

"There are exceptions to every rule," Dave replied without looking up.

"Well," Christian continued with a grand smile showing his excitement. "He asked if I wanted to hang out with him today."

"We'd like to meet your new friend, dear," Sally told him. "You should invite him over for dinner."

"Yes, I'd really like to meet your new friend," Joe stated while clearing his throat. "He sounds like boxing is in his blood."

"Dad, you think everyone who fights has boxing in their blood," David said with a hint of sarcasm while finally looking up.

Leaning back in his chair, Grandpa Joe carefully thought for a response. "No, not everybody," he soon stated. "Just the ones that feel they have too for a good reason." Sitting for a bit longer with a look of thoughtfulness while reflecting on what he just said, he finally was satisfied with his answer while nodding his head. He then leaned forward to start eating again.

"So, dear, tell us what you did with your new friend today," Sally asked her son while taking a sip of her tea.

31

"Oh, I don't know, stuff," Christian happily responded. He then took a massive mouthful of potatoes while tapping his legs to a song in his head.

"I think what your mother meant was," David said patiently while looking at his son from under his brow, "was for you to actually tell us what you two did. That is, if it's ok for us to know."

Hearing this, Christian suddenly became very sullen while quickly looking down to his lap. He sat there with his head held low while trying to avoid eye contact with his father.

"Oh, dear," Sally said while trying to play peacemaker as she rubbed her husband's arm. "If he doesn't want to let us know, don't force him. Ok?"

"Christian," Joe said softly while leaning forward and trying to lower himself to his grandson's height. "We are interested in what you did today with your new friend. Why don't you hare those grand adventures of excitement that you had with him?"

Christian nodded his head while sitting there worrying for a little more; wondering where to begin.

"It's ok there, young man," Joe assured him softly. "Take your time and start when you're ready."

Christian physically relaxed when hearing this and after a beat or two, he began. "Well, we met at Deeley's Market around eleven this morning. I got there first and visited with Mr. and Mrs. Deeley for a while until he showed up."

"What did you say his name was again?" his dad asked while chewing on some bread.

"Shawn," Christian answered bubbly as he continued on with his adventures. "I told them about my new science project I'm working on. She gave me a piece of her apple pie. She said she made it fresh last night. He gave me a soda to drink."

Smiling at her son, Sally asked, "Ooh, how did you like that?"

Christian quickly returned the smile with sparkling eyes and a few quick nods.

"Did Mr. Deeley say whether or not my order had come in yet?" David inquired.

"Um, I don't know. I don't remember him saying anything about that."

"Oh, dear. The Deeley's said they would call you when your supplies came in," Sally chastised. "Let Christian finish his story."

During that brief moment that she spoke to her husband, Christian had switched thoughts to something else entirely while enjoying his meal. While grabbing the bowl of pork gravy his mom had made, he poured some on his potatoes before putting some butter on the butternut squash she had mashed. He was in the process of filling his mouth with a spoonful of potatoes, squash, and peas while tapping his feet on the floor to a song he had heard on the radio earlier in the day. He managed to hear some talking in the background which caused him to come back to reality and look up. His parents, as well as Grandpa Joe, were looking at him like they were waiting for something. He honestly, at that moment, didn't have a clue what it was.

"What?" he asked when his mouth wasn't full.

Without hesitation, Joe started laughing at his grandson's expense while shaking his head. Tears started to form in his eyes.

"What's so funny?" he asked while swallowing the rest of his fool. Narrowing his eyes, he tried to figure out why they were staring at him and why his grandfather was laughing.

"Didn't I tell you two that your son lives in a world of his own?" Grandpa Joe said in between bursts of laughter while looking at his scowling son. "That comes from my side."

"Dad, you think any little quirk that I or he has comes from your side," David commented. He shook his head with a scowl before taking a sip of his coffee. "That's starting to get really old."

"And what's wrong with that? You make it sound like that's a bad thing. And who do you think you two got it from, your mother? God rest her soul. Not her, I'll tell you. You got that from me!" Joe told him with still a hint of a chuckle in his voice and a glint in his eyes. Leaning back in his chair while drifting off in thought to think about his deceased wife before quickly changing his posture to look at Christian. "What your mother had asked was for you to carry on with your story."

"Ah, ok," responded Christian quickly, again drifting back to the sound he had in his head, which set his feet tapping almost immediately. "Well, like I said, I visited with the Deeley's for a while before Shawn got there. He got some stuff and then we went outside to talk for a while."

"Is that all you two did, talk outside of Deeley's?" Sally asked when he stopped to eat a little more.

He shook his head. "No. We were there for a little while so he could read the comic he got. Then he had to get home to feed his dog."

"He had to fed his dog at eleven o'clock in the morning?" his father asked with a hint of skepticism.

"That's what he said," Christian confirmed.

"Did you go with him?"

"Well, he lives by that tracks. That's as far as I went with him."

"You went to the tracks today?" A hint of irritation was heard in his father's voice. "Christian, what have we told you about going down there? You could have been hurt."

"I know and I'm sorry, but he said it was ok. Besides, he does it all the time he said," Christian protested with a whine.

"He may have said it was ok but we didn't," David told his son sternly. "You shouldn't have gone without our approval. Don't go it again, alright?"

"I won't. I promise. I don't want to get eaten by the bears in the woods anyway."

"Bears? What on earth are you talking about, dear?" his mom asked with a confused laugh.

"That's what Shawn said, Mama," Christian explained. "That there's bears in the woods that likes to eat kids. He said that they are big and smelly with big claws and teeth and would…"

"Sweetie, there aren't any bears in the woods. Never have been. He was just trying to scare you," Sally told him warmly while putting a hand on his forearm. "So, once you got to the tracks, what did you two do?"

Christian merely shrugged at this before taking a drink of his water. "Nothin'."

"Nothing?" Gramps injected. "You two went to the tracks to do nothing? I don't believe that that little quirk comes from my side."

"As soon as we got there he left."

"What do you mean he left?" David asked. Obvious bewilderment was on his face.

"Well, he said he had to feed his dog so he went home. I couldn't go because his dog doesn't like strangers. I waited almost an hour there for him to get back before I gave up and came home."

"You were there almost an hour after he left and he never came back?" his mother asked in a confused tone. "Why on earth would he do that?"

"I don't know." Christian shrugged while cleaning off his plate. "He just left and didn't come back."

"Did he say where by the tracks he lived?" his dad asked with a great interest.

"No, but he did say it was a few minutes away."

"Which way did he go?"

"Ah," Christian thought back to earlier in the day. "We went through the woods near Deeley's Market until we came to the tracks. He then crossed them and took a path to the left that he said would take him to his house. To the right came to the high school."

"Yep, just what I thought," David said with an irritable shake of the head while running a hand through his hair. "The Calloway's. They live in a rundown trailer by the tracks. Bruce, his dad, is one of the laborers I oversee at the plant."

Christian nodded his head while pointing to his dad. "Yeah, yeah. Mr. Deeley said something about his dad working for you, but I wasn't sure what he meant."

"If he's anything like his old man, then he's bad news," David informed him. "I'd rather not have you hanging around with that family if you can help it. I'm not so sure they'll be the best..."

"Honey," Sally interrupted softly while taking hold of her husband's hand to hold. "You shouldn't judge every book by its cover. Maybe he isn't the Calloway's son; and, if he is, maybe he isn't like his father. He could be more like his mother."

"Dear Lord! That's even worse," commented David with closed eyes while putting his face in his hand to rub his forehead.

"If Christian calls him a friend, isn't that good enough?" she gently asked as David finally looked up to meet her gaze without responding. Sally soon turned her gaze to her son. "Why don't you invite your new friend over for dinner one evening next week, ok?"

"Ok, Mama," Christian answered bubbly while starting to tap his feet again, only this time to a different song than before.

"There. We'll see him next week so you can put to rest your worries," she stated confidentially to her husband while nodding her head.

"As for me," Grandpa Joe started with a smile and a clear of the throat. "I'll finally get to see what kind of boxer this new friend might have to potential of being."

In an effort to officially close the subject on Shawn for the evening, Sally got up. "Now, if the three of you are all done eating, why don't we pick up so I can do the dishes?"

There was nothing further that needed to be said. Within moments, the table was clean and Christian's mom was filling the sink with dirty dishes. His dad and grandfather took their usual places at the table and got back to reading the newspaper they had started earlier. Christian, who felt like joining them, grabbed the Entertainment section and immediately flipped it to the funnies before burying his face in them.

"So, Christian, how is your rocket coming along?" Joe asked without looking up for his section of the paper.

Christian laughed at one of the comics before answering. "It's ok, I guess. I still have a long way to go before I can show it at the science fair."

"When is it again?" Gramps asked while looking at the MLB standings.

"What's what?"

"The science fair."

"Oh, um, November sometime. Around Thanksgiving, I think," he told his grandfather with a brief moment of thought before immediately going back to reading his comics.

"So, Dad, what time do the fights start tonight?" David asked.

"I think around 9:30 or so," Joe told him after checking the time in the paper.

"Are most of the fights still on the card for tonight?"

"Says here they are. It looks like the champ is going to have a hard time defending his belt. Even though he is a three-to-one favorite to retain, I sure hope he doesn't lose. I have money riding on him."

"Dad, you shouldn't be gambling like this," Sally chastised with a sigh. She looked over her shoulder to her father-in-law while continuing on with the dishes. "It sets a bad example for Christian."

"It's just another way to make money," Joe told her. "If I shouldn't be doing it, then they wouldn't allow us to do it. Isn't that right, Christian?"

"Don't bring him into this," Sally said. "He's way too young to even begin hearing things such as this."

"The boy's going to learn about it sooner or later. It's better if he learns it in the safety of his own house."

By the tone of this grandfather's tone, Christian assumed he was doing this to get his mom going but he couldn't be sure. He just kept sitting there reading his papery trying to act like he wasn't listening to any of it.

"So, Gramps, can I watch the fights with you tonight?" he soon asked with a little bit of excitement.

"No, you may not young man!" his mom answered before his grandfather could. "I don't want you watching that kind of violence. It's not good for you."

"It's not that violent," Joe informed her while looking up from his paper. "There're movies you let him watch on cable that're more violent in half an hour than all of these fights combined. Why is it ok for him to watch those but not these?"

"True, but still. I don't want him watching them," Sally admitted while still standing her ground before looking to see what time it was. "Oh, dear! I'm running late. I have to get going if I want to make it on time."

"Where are you going tonight, dear?" David asked while looking at her.

"Tonight is bridge night. Mary Beth is having us over at her house for the evening," she informed him while drying her hands. She soon left the kitchen to go upstairs to get ready. Half hour later she came back down to finish getting ready. While grabbing her purse, he put her car keys in her pocket, grabbed a pen and some paper, and wrote something down. She gave it to David while saying, "Here's Mary Beth's number should you need to contact me for any reason. I should be there until 11.30 or so and ought to be home my midnight at the latest. I'll see you all soon."

She then kissed each member of the family and walked out the door. The sound of her car was heard exiting the garage as it drove off down the road.

"So, you still want to watch the fights? Joe asked while looking at Christian from over the top of his newspaper.

Looking at him in disbelief, Christian said, "Mom said I couldn't."

His grandfather returned his gaze. "But your mother isn't here, now is she?"

All Christian could do was look at him with wide eyes. He couldn't believe what he just had been asked. He looked to his father to find him still submersed in his paper. Either he didn't hear it or was merely ignoring the situation.

"Yeah, I'd love to, but wouldn't my mom find out about it?"

Joe sighed while putting down his paper. "How's this, if you're in bed by the time she gets home and you don't say anything about it, how would she find out? I won't say anything because I don't want her mad at me. I doubt your father, who's trying very hard not to hear this conversation, will say anything for the same reason."

At that, David let out a muffled chuckle and half grin.

"So," Joe continued, "that leaves only you. If you agree to what I just said, then how will she find out?"

Smiling at the prospect of this actually working, Christian asked, "If I do, may we get pizza? Possibly with wings, barbeque style?"

"Well, we'll see. But you'll have to agree not to tell her and to also be in bed when she gets home."

"I won't say anything if you won't. What time do they start again?" Christian quickly answered while barely able to control his feelings. Nights like his he really enjoyed; being able to do stuff with his grandfather while his mom was out of the house.

Chapter 4

A couple of days later, Sally called Christian down for breakfast. The smells of which emanated from the kitchen had filtered upstairs to help with the wakeup call. The aroma of eggs, sausage, and bacon were mixed with cherry pie, chocolate chip cookies, and freshly brewed coffee. Christian came stumbling down moments later while yawning, rubbing his stomach, and scratching his head through his mop-like hair.

"Morning, Mama," he said while sitting in his usual spot. He yawned again while his arms stretched out as his body arched.

"Morning, sweetie. Did you sleep well last night?" she asked while taking her finished pie out of the oven while noting the cookies had a few minutes longer.

"Good, I guess. Same as the night before," he told her before taking a deep breath of the delicious smells. His mouth salivated in the process. "Everything smells so good, Mama."

"I'm glad you think so." She smiled at her son before getting a plate and silverware for him. "So, tell me, what would you like to eat?"

"Eggs and sausage sound good to me, please. Can I have some toast with that too, please?"

"You sure can. And what do you have planned for today?"

"Well, I was thinking about going to school or someplace open enough to try out my rocket," Christian said as his mother brought over the plate of steaming food for him. His eyes widened when he saw it. "Oooh, thank-you, Mama. That looks really good!"

"Hope you like it. Would you like some orange juice with that?"

He nodded his reply while cramming a load of scrambled eggs into his mouth.

"Is your rocket all done?"

"I think so. I just need to see if it'll fly. I also wanted to see if I wired the remote correctly."

"Couldn't you do that here, dear? In the yard that is?" asked Sally while bringing him the juice. By this time, her cookies were done which she removed from the oven.

"I guess I could but I really wanted a big open area without anything getting in the way," Christian told her while gulping down the rest of his food. After doing so, he got up and put his dishes in the sink before turning his attention to the cookies. "May I have one, please?"

"Yes you may, but only one. I know how you are; you're just like your grandfather," she said with a smile while wiping the flour off of her hands. "One will turn into three and before I know it, half of them are gone. Save some for later, alright?"

He quickly agreed while taking a single cookie before running upstairs to his room. It didn't take him long after that to get ready for the day. He was soon packed and running back down stairs while saying good-bye to his mom.

"Oh, sweetie!" she called out to him until she turned to look back. She soon walked over to him to try and arrange his hair with her fingers. "Would you do me a favor today while you're out? Would you go to Deeley's and see if you're father's order has come in yet?"

"Sure can, Mom. I'll be my first stop. Anything else?"

"No, that should be it, dear," she told him before bending over to kiss his forehead. "Thank-you. You have a nice day. Don't forget to invite your new friend over if you see him today."

Within moments, Christian was on his bike and riding down the street with his backpack swinging side to side. His first stop, as he told him mom, was to Deeley's. Unfortunately, it was a wasted trip. Not only was his dad's order not in yet but also because he didn't even get a piece of candy or soda for his trouble. Any other day if he went to visit he would have gotten both. Today he got nothing. So, much to his chagrin, his mouth was leaving as empty as it had arrived.

Upon leaving the market, Christian saw Stan and Eric, two members of Wesley's entourage, approaching from a distance on their bikes. He could tell it was them by Stan's long hair and Eric's heavy frame. He didn't stay there long enough to see where they were going. Quickly straddling his bike and peddling off in the opposite direction towards the woods, Christian hoped to get to one of his proven hiding spots for situations like this. He only got a yell from Stan demanding for him to stop. Christian just pretended to not hear.

Soon after entering the woods, he followed his favorite path through: a crevice by the creek, a creek that could be heard all around him. After a few minutes of riding on his bike, he changed his thoughts as easily as his bike changed paths. Once his bike was on the path that led to the school, his thoughts changed to his rocket. He had spent the better part of the summer building it from scratch so it would be ready for the science fair. If anything went wrong that day, he still would have three months to get it ready.

Being deep in thought when he came out into the clearing behind the school, he hadn't noticed the time it took to reach the playground. He thought this would be the perfect place for his rocket when he noticed Shawn shooting baskets over on the playground. While remembering his mom wanted him to invite Shawn over for dinner; he figured this would be as good of a time as any to ask. With that, he left his bike and bag in the clearing before walking over.

"Hey ya, Shawn," he happily said without receiving a look from Shawn. "You play basketball?"

"Yep," Shawn simply answered without looking.

While looking up to see the blue sky, Christian asked, "Nice day to play, isn't it?"

"What do you want?" Shawn asked while finally stopping long enough to look at Christian. A black right eye was evident on his face.

"Well, my family, they, uh, wanted me to..."he started before realizing Shawn was irritated by him being there.

"Come on, Chris. Spit it out. I don't have all freakin' day," Shawn said as he started dribbling his basketball.

Christian's mouth dropped. "You said the F word. You're not supposed to talk like that. Only grownups are."

"A lot of people say that, kid. And besides, I'm more grownup than most in the area. Including you," Shawn stated bluntly while trying to be as mature and adult-like as possible. "Are you goin' to stand there whining about this all day or are ya gonna tell me why you're bothering me?"

"Well, my family wanted me to invite you over for dinner one night. But, since I'm bothering you, I won't." Christian turned with his head down to walk away.

For the first time since he met Shawn, it appeared Shawn was finally taken off guard. "Dinner? Your place?"

"Yeah, they wanted you to come over because you stuck up for me that day. But since you don't seem to like me, just forget I said anything about it. Ok?" Christian said while stopping briefly before continuing back to his bike. He soon found himself smiling slightly in the process. He wasn't sure why he had smiled, but maybe it was because he felt he knew Shawn well enough to know he'd feel guilty about the way he acted. Sure enough, after eight or nine steps with complete silence, Shawn cleared his throat to speak.

"Hey, um, Chris? If it's not too much trouble for you, coming over for dinner sure does sound good. Do you guys make it homemade like or will it be TV dinners?" Shawn asked while looking around to see if anyone saw them talking to each other.

"TV dinners?" Christian asked as a look of confusion rose on his face while blinking two or three times. "No, it'll will be homemade."

"So, ah, will Monday be ok for me to come over?" Shawn asked with an obvious nervous edge to him. "That's the day my dad has friends over at the trailer, I mean, over at the house to watch the games. They do that while drinking a lot of beer, smoking bad cigars, and playing cards."

While surprised by the sudden expression of sincerity on Shawn's part, all Christian could do was nod and mumble an "ok." He then watched Shawn turn his back to shift his attention back to shooting baskets. He soon found himself taken back at the ease that Shawn was able to change his focus so easily. How Shawn was able to be nice and sincere for that brief moment then turn back to how he was before without so much as a blink of an eye totally dumbfounded him.

Christian debated about leaving before making a few more unsuccessful attempts at small talk. These attempts eventually led to a game of one-on-one. Christian soon found himself out manned, out gunned, battered, and badly bruised. Shawn showed a hidden source of aggression that seemed to show itself a little with the potential for more. Christian thought this would have been a friendly match, not *War of the Worlds* as it turned out to be. During the first few minutes, Christian only had the opportunity to shoot the ball once, which didn't even come close to the basket. Shawn seemed to find something gratifying in making this game as lopsided as possible.

"Hey, Shawn. Would you ease up on me a little, please?" Christian asked while gasping for breath and bending over to hold his side. "I haven't really played this before."

"What'ya mean you haven't really played?" Shawn asked while stopping dead in his tracks. The ball bounced away as his jaw dropped.

"Well, I've played in gym. Does that count?" he admitted while feeling a little embarrassed and somewhat belittled.

"Aye carumba," Shawn muttered as a look of contempt came over his face.

"What's that look for?"

"What look?" Shawn asked defensively while being surprised not that Christian actually noticed, but that he actually said something about it.

"When I said I only played in gym, you gave me a weird look while muttering something. I was just curious what that look was for."

"No, you're not," Shawn answered coldly while giving Christian a dark stare.

"No I'm not what?"

Shawn continued to stare at him. "You're not curious what the look was for. You don't wanna know."

"Actually I am," Christian happily said while not noticing either Shawn's glares or tone, or the fact he wanted to be left alone.

"What difference does it make what it was for? Why do you have to know?"

"Well, that's what friends do."

Shawn raised his eyebrows at that. "Oh, do they now?"

"Well, that's what my mom says. She said friends should always..."

"Hey, listen Chris. I'm sure your mom gives you real good advice, but what's the deal with you?"

"What deal? What're you talking about?"

"I mean, what difference could it matter what the look's for? It's just a look! It doesn't matter!"

"I guess it doesn't" Christian whined while now holding back tears. "If it was important enough for me to know, you would have told me. Besides, I want to get back to my rocket. You have a good game with yourself, Shawn."

"Rocket?" Shawn suddenly asked when Christian was walking away. "What rocket?"

"The one I'm making for the science fair?"

"What science fair?"

"You know, for school? The one in three months, a couple days before Thanksgiving."

"You're working on your science project during summer vacation?" Shawn was highly confused by this thought.

"Yes."

"Why?"

"Because I really want to at least get some kind of ribbon this year," explained Christian. "What project are you doing for it?"

"I ain't doing no stupid project for no stupid fair," Shawn stated. "Only dumb-assed geeks and nerds do that kind of stuff. I got better things to do with my time then mess around with a stupid, dumb-ass science fair project."

"That's not true. My mom says that geeks and nerds are gonna run this country someday."

"That's the stupidest thing I ever heard!"

"Is not," Christian said while starting to tear up.

While realizing what he had just done, Shawn softened his tone while saying, "Rocket, huh? What sort of rocket?"

"Uh, you know, a long slender one with a remote control to it," Christian told him while trying to sound smart while hoping it would make him feel a little uncomfortable.

"You're making a remote controlled rocket from nothin'?" Shawn asked with a hint of awe.

"That's what I said, wasn't it?" Christian said bubbly with a smile as he turned to trot off while leaving Shawn behind him.

"Hey, Chris!" Shawn called from behind him. "Could I watch?"

"Nay, that's alright. I wouldn't want to bother you or take up your valuable time," was the reply as Christian turned to leave Shawn where he found him.

***

"Mama?" Christian said out roughly three hours later when he walked into his kitchen at home. "Mr. Deeley said that Dad's order wasn't in yet."

"That's alright, sweetie. He did say it would take a little while for it to come in," Sally replied as he took Christian's bag from him and put it aside. "So, tell me, dear. Where you able to see your new friend today to invite him to dinner?"

"I saw him at school," Christian confirmed while thinking back to earlier in the day.

"Oh, really now? Did he help you with your rocket?"

"No, he was, ah, busy doing something else," he said with a heavy sigh while hanging his head.

"What's the matter, dear?" his mom asked while putting a hand on his shoulder. "Did your rocket not go as you hoped?"

"No, it's not that, Mom. The rocket was fine. Well, it almost did fine. I just need to work on the remote control part of it a little bit more," he answered, again with a heavy sigh.

"If it's not your rocket, then what is it?"

At times like this, when his mom was merely being herself, being completely open, honest, and sincere, Christian found it impossible to withhold anything from her.

"It's Shawn, Mom. You know, the kid we've been talking about?" he asked while on the brink of tears.

"There there, dear. It's ok," his mom reassured him while hugging him and patting his back. "What did he do to you?"

"He was mean to me today, Mama."

"What mean things did he do?"

"He was rude to me and he yelled at me and he made fun of me. I thought we were friends. Friends aren't supposed to be mean to one another. Right, Mama?" he asked as his tears started flowing out like a waterfall.

"Was it something you did or was he like that when you first saw him?" Sally asked while wiping Christian's eyes.

"Well, he did seem irritated and rude a little when I first saw him. All he wanted to do was play basketball alone."

"So he was rude and irritable from the start? And he wanted to be alone?" Sally repeated. "It wasn't until after you approached did he start being mean and rude to you? Is that about right?"

"Uh-huh," he nodded with a sniff.

"Well, did you ever consider that maybe he was having a bad day up until that point? Maybe he went to school to be alone and to think? Maybe he wanted to shoot baskets to vent some of his frustrations or whatever he had to get rid of. Did you ever think of this, sweetie?"

He looked at her as she wiped his eyes before shaking his head. "No, I didn't."

"If this is the young man that your father thinks he is, he sounds like he might not have a very good home life," Sally told him while running her fingers through her son's tangled hair. "That might be the reason he was rude to you today and also the same reason he didn't want you to help feed his dog the other day. Try not to think he doesn't like you. Try to get to know him if you can. Ok, sweetie?

"Oh, Mama, I will," Christian agreed with a smile.

"So may I assume you didn't ask him over for dinner?"

"Oh, I asked him."

"And what did he say?"

"He said he'll be here Monday."

Smiling broadly when she heard that, Sally asked, "Really? See, he doesn't hate you as much as you might think. Did you two set a time?"

"No, I forgot. He'll be here Monday, though."

"Do you have any idea what he'll like to eat?"

"No, but I think as long as it's homemade and not TV dinners that he won't mind."

"TV dinners?" she asked with a smile. "Why on earth would I make that?"

"I don't know, but he did ask if it'll be homemade or TV dinners. And when I said it would be homemade, he seemed happy 'bout that."

"Your friend seems like an interesting young man," she commented while trying to understand what was just said. "How's this; I was planning on making a nice home cooked meal for all of us. You know the type when we get together for the holidays?"

"Really?" Christian asked with excitement as a smile from ear to ear appeared on his face.

"Now, I can always change it to TV diners if you and your friend want me to."

"Nah, that's alright, Mom. That'll be fine. I love your holiday meals."

Smiling, she said, "I know you do. Speaking of meals, I should start making dinner soon. Your grandfather is in the garage trying to clean out that storage room above it. Would you be so kind as to out help him out for me, please?"

"Ah, Mom!" Christian protested. "Do I have to? I really wanted to work more on my rocket."

"No, you don't have to but it would mean a lot to me if you did, sweetie. Besides, I know he'd like to spend some time with you."

"I suppose I could work on my rocket later," he reluctantly agreed with heavy disappointment.

With a trademark tap on his cheek, she said, "Thank-you, sweetie."

Being a typical nine year old, Christian disliked the thought of house work, especially when it came to physical labor. He also detested the fact that he had to do physical work with his grandfather, a person whose idea of retirement meant rocking in a chair on the front porch while sipping lemonade and grump how fast people drive past the house. He thought a person like that would work less than him and want him to do the bulk of the work. When Christian did make it out above the garage, he was not at all surprised to see Grandpa Joe sweating and out of breathe. What he was surprised to see was how much more organized the room of chaos was. Though it was far from what he would call organized, it was a vast improvement over what it was before. Since his grandmother had died earlier in the year, all his grandfather wanted to do was to keep busy. And though how unfortunate for Christian, today's project was the garage. It was being cleaned out after a random thought David had had about a week ago to convert it into an apartment for Grandpa Joe to live in.

Christian's dad had mentioned it in passing, which went roughly like, "Since Dad's over here practically every day, he might as well sleep here too." But since David was too busy with work and his own projects, and being too cheap to hire anyone; and that Sally didn't go up there enough to know what they had, let alone do anything about it; and Christian being only nine; the task of cleaning it out fell squarely onto Joe. With this in mind, the idea seemed reasonable to Christian because his grand-father was going to be living there so he might as well clean it out. But what confused him was the fact that his grandfather was an old man and who in their right mind would let an old man do this kind of work? However, upon seeing Joe work, Christian was surprised not only how fast and efficiently he did it, but also how strong and agile he was. Though he was big in stature, Christian never thought that a person of his grandfather's age would be any of these.

Two hours and several talking points later, Christian felt he could continue chatting away with him for the rest of the night and on into morning. Even though their conversations had morphed from one subject to the next, they always seemed to find themselves back to life; and the part of life they were on was Grandpa Joe himself.

The more they talked, they more he learned about him. He had moved here to upstate New York when he was no older than what Christian was now after Joe's dad got transferred to open up the town's factory. The summer before he graduated high school, he got a job at the factory alongside his old man which, unfortunately, went nowhere. He stayed there until the next summer before enlisting in the U.S. Army. All Christian got out of this was that his grandfather was something in the Intelligence field, flew with Airborne, did two tours in World War II with the infantry, and two in Korea with the Rangers. He served close to twenty years before retiring at the rank of Sergeant Major, whatever that was. After he got out, he went back to the job he had before jumping out of airplanes and eating MREs and stayed there until Christian's grandmother got sick three years ago. Christian also found out that his grandfather was an amateur boxer in his youth up until the time he had enlisted. Joe had tried taking it up years later after the Army life but had found he lost the magic.

Since Christian's grandmother had been dead these several months now, Joe had supplemented his time by helping with the yard work, taking up outdoor activities such as hiking and fishing, and volunteering down at the local YMCA. He always said he's meet his next wife there, though everyone knew he was joking.

At this point, the sound of David's car pulling into the drive signaled that he was home from work. When Christian came back to reality, he found himself in the corner surrounded by boxes of toys he had forgotten he had had. He was playing with them while listening to Gramps ramble on about his life that he didn't even know that two hours had vanished in a blink of an eye. He heard his dad pull into the garage, turn the car off, and get out. This was soon followed by heavy footsteps up the stairs until his dad's head came into view.

"Aren't you done yet up here, Dad?" he questioned with a disappointed look. "You've had all day to do this. And, Christian, why are you doing in the corner? Shouldn't you be helping your grandfather rather than getting in his way?"

"Yes, Dad," Christian meekly said while proceeding to stand and put his toys back in their boxes.

"He's not in the way and he's doing just what I told him to do," Joe informed his son while turning to look at him.

"Yeah? And what is that?" David questioned while returning the stare.

"To act like a kid. He's nine, not nineteen," the elder Eaton stated while putting his hands on his hips while holding his own with his son. "He has the rest of his life to act like an adult. Until he gets to be an adult, let the boy act like what he is, a child. That is, if that's ok with you."

"Fine. Whatever you want, Dad. You're the boss," David stated irritably while shaking his head before turning to go back down. "This room better be cleaned out tomorrow night because by the morning after that, I have some people coming over to give me a quote."

"Have you ever known me not to finish something once I started it? Well, have you?!" Joe yelled down but, by then, it was too late. His son had already gone in the house. With this, he turned to see Christian sulking in the corner. "Hey, don't worry about your dad, ok kiddo? He just had a bad day at that office I bet."

"He always has a bad day at the office," Christian whined. "It seems like he doesn't want me to have any fun. He wants me to be like a grownup and not have any fun at all. I can't do anything right to make him happy."

"Oh, that's not true," Grandpa Joe told him with a sigh before wiping his sweaty brow with a dirty forearm. "You can do a lot of things right. And as far as your father is concerned, he never had what I would call a normal childhood. Moving around from Army life isn't what most children would want. As a result, he found more comfort in playing the stock market than baseball. Can you picture that? An American boy not wanting to play ball? Ah, enough of this. Break time. How does a glass of lemonade sound to you?"

"Sounds good, Grandpa," Christian replied before realizing that the room they were in really was warm. The time he had been there looking through the box of G.I. Joe's and Transformers, mixed with his grandfather's working and the lack of proper ventilation were all good conductors for the late summer's heat to make itself at home. He wiped his sweaty face off with his shirt before following his grandfather outside for some ice-cold lemonade in the evening's shade.

Chapter 5

"So, Christian, when is your friend coming over for dinner tonight?" Sally asked during breakfast Monday morning.

"I think around 6.30, Mama," he answered while stuffing a massive amount of toast in his mouth.

"Don't take such a big bite, sweetie. We wouldn't want you choking. Remember what happened to Mrs. Wilkins?" she told him while sipping her tea.

"Toast killed her? I thought she died from a ham sandwich?"

Sally put down her tea and morning paper. "She did, but you missed my point. The point it she died because she choked to death. And she choked because she put too much of her ham sandwich in her mouth. We wouldn't want that to happen to you, now would we?"

"I don't know about we, Mama, but I know I wouldn't want it too."

Taking a bite of her own toast, she said, "Well, now that we have that settled, what do you have planned for today?"

While opening the paper to the comics, Christian said, "I finished the modifications to my rocket and it's remote. I wanted to see if it works."

"Let me know how that turns out, ok? And if you see your friend while you're out, ask him what he'd like to have to eat tonight. I was planning on pot roast, mashed potatoes, and all of the trimmings. I was just curious if that was ok with him."

"Ok, Mama," he quickly responded while engrossed in one of his favorite comic strips. "I'll ask if you want."

Sally, meanwhile, got up from the table. "Thank-you, sweetie. Now, if you excuse me, I have a few errands to attend to. Make sure you pick up after yourself."

"Ah, sure. Ok, Mom," he answered absently as his mom left the kitchen.

Roughly ten minutes later, Christian was picking up after himself before running off to his room to get ready for the day. Fifteen minutes after that, he was biking through the woods on his way to school to test his rocket. As he neared the creek running through it, he saw Shawn sitting on a giant rock throwing pebbles into it.

"Hi'ya, Shawn. What'ya doing'?"

"What the hell does it look like I'm doing?" he rudely responded without looking at him. "I'm throwing rocks in the water."

"You swore. You shouldn't talk like that. Only grownups can," corrected Christian.

"You should know by now I don't give a damn." Shawn's icy tone was highly evident as he hurled another stone into the water as hard as he could.

As Christian approached, Shawn turned slightly to his right to keep his back to him. When Christian finally did get a good look at Shawn's face, a fresh black left eye was prominent.

"Hey! What happened to your eye?" Christian asked with concern.

"I fell. This morning."

"You did?" Christian asked while looking at Shawn's hands, which didn't appear to be damaged by the fall. "Then how come you didn't hurt your hands?"

"Don't you ever go two minutes without asking questions?"

"Well, yeah. Why?"

"Why don't you do it know, then?" snapped Shawn.

Standing is disbelief as he jaw gaped open, Christian came back to reality before starting to count off the 120 seconds.

"One…two…three…" Once he got to forty seconds, he asked another question. "So, um, how long have you been here?"

"Awhile." While answering this, Shawn's posture stiffened with obvious annoyance at Christian's lack of understanding. "Don't you have anything else to do?"

"Well, yeah," he answered before thinking about where he had left off counting before continuing. "…41…42…43…"

"Why aren't you doing it then?" Shawn asked while finally turning to look at him.

"'cause I'm talking to you," Christian told him while he stopped counting. "I was on my way to school to see if the modifications I made on my remote works."

"Oh, that. You still working on that damn thing?" The coldness to the question chilled Christian as Shawn turned his attention back to the stream and his rocks.

"As a matter of fact, I am," Christian said in an angry tone which surprised him. He so rarely spoke like that that he paused momentarily from embarrassment. During that same moment, he noticed Shawn had also paused before finishing throwing his current rock into the stream. "I did tell you I wanted to win a ribbon at the school fair this year. I thought the best way to do that was to spend as much time on it as needed. Don't you agree, Shawn?"

"Yeah, sure. If you say so," he replied barely above a whisper.

"Anyway, I'm off to try my rocket," Christian told him before stopping to look back over his shoulder. "Hey, Shawn?"

As expected, no response came from the young Calloway except for the rock exiting his now open palm to land in the water with a plunk sound about ten feet away.

"Shawn?" Christian repeated without prevail. "While I'm here, I just wanted to tell you that I told my mom you'd be at our house tonight about 6.30 or so. Is that alright with you?"

"Whatever," a cold replied was retorted.

Standing there for a moment, Christian was waiting, hoping even, that Shawn would turn to acknowledge him. While Shawn was being Shawn, he went right back to throwing rocks into the stream. When the silence and waiting got to be too much, Christian spoke to break the tension.

"I'll be at Deeley's Market after I get done to get a soda and stuff if you want to join me. We could go to my place after that if you want. If not, maybe I'll see you later at my place. Alright?" he told him while shrugging his shoulders. He hopped back on his bike and finish his delayed journey to school.

A few hours later, Christian arrived at Deeley's Market.

"Hey, Einstein! How's the young genius doing on his fine, glorious afternoon?" Mr. Deeley yelled from across the market when Christian entered. His piano-key smile was there even before he finished his question.

"Great," Christian told him with high energy while the screen door slammed behind him. "I just got done trying my rocket at school and it works great and everything and I think I'll finally win a blue ribbon and..."

"Whoa, hey, slow down there," Mr. Deeley interrupted with a hearty chuckle. "Do us both a favor and take a couple of breathes before you pass out. So, your rocket's finally done?"

"Yes sir, it is," the young boy answered with so much excitement that he practically was jumping up and down. "I just came from school where I was testing it most of the day. It works better than I had hoped and it might go further than the 100 yards I had planned."

"Good job. Ellen, did you hear that?!" the old shopkeeper yelled back into the storage room while pulling up his ever sagging pants. To his dismay, his wife didn't answer. "Ellen?!"

"Yes, for Christ's sake, Harold! Yes, I heard you," she yelled back while coming into view from around the corner. She came with a clipboard in hand while adjusting her glasses. "I just wanted to finish up what I was doing first."

"Then how come you didn't answer me?"

"Because I was counting, that's why. Oy! You know I can't talk while I'm counting or I'll lose count," she told him while placing the clipboard on the counter. She walked around it to join her husband. Smiling, she patted Christian on the shoulder. "How are you doing today, Timothy?"

"Like I told Mr. Deeley, I'm doing good," he answered, again with enthusiasm before eyeing her husband who had let out a laugh.

"What's so funny?" she asked. "Did I say something funny?"

"No. No you didn't outside of the fact you called him by the wrong name again." Mr. Deeley laughed very loud at this while attempting to pull up his pants.

"I did?" Oh, I'm so sorry, Timothy. It won't happen again," she apologized with great embarrassment while both hands went to her cheeks.

"Damn it, Ellen! You did it again. The boy's name is *not* Timothy. It's Christian!"

"Yes, I know his name is Chri... Timothy? I called you Timothy?" she asked in disbelief while staring at the two of them.

"Yes, *you* did. Twice," her husband told her with a hint of annoyance while shaking his head. A soft chuckle escaped his lips.

"I'm so sorry, Christian," she apologized again. "I don't know what came over me."

"It's ok, Mrs. Deeley. Mistakes happen," Christian assured her.

"So, like I asked while you were busy counting," Mr. Deeley asked with a loud clear of the throat, "did you hear Einstein here say his rocket is finished?"

A smile quickly formed on her wrinkled face. "Why, no dear, I hadn't. That's wonderful, dear. Do you have it with you now?"

"Well, not on me now, no. It's in my bag next to my bike outside."

"Would you mind letting us see it, dear? Maybe show us how it works?"

"Well, um," Christian started while stopping to think for a moment. "Yes and no."

"Yes and no to what, dear?" she asked with an obvious confusion.

"Yeah I can show you the rocket; but no, I can't show you how it works," Christian told her while suddenly feeling slightly embarrassed. "I used it too long at school today. Batteries wore out."

"Ah, that's alright, Einstein. What type batteries do you need?" Mr. Deeley asked while slapping a hand on the boy's shoulder.

"I'm not sure. I always get the sizes mixed up."

"That's alright," the old man assured him. "I always get them mixed up too. Why don't you go on over there and pick out the batteries you need. Once you have the right ones, why don't you go out there and show the misses and me your award-winning rocket?"

Hearing this, Christian merely stood there looking absently up at him without moving at all. Just stood there and stared.

"C'mon, boy. Let's get a move on. I don't know about you, but I ain't got all day. Now hurry up before I change my mind!" Mr. Deeley smiled.

At that, Christian thanked him with a broad grin before running towards the batteries. Once he got the right size, he made a run for the screen door before letting it slam behind him. Within a couple minutes, he had his rocket in the air as the elderly couple watched nearby in amazement.

After what seemed like eternity of being in his own little world as he showed off his rocket, Christian noticed Shawn walking down the road towards the Market. While making the rocket do a few more laps in the sky, Christian landed it a little ways away.

"Ah, Christian, is that it?" Mrs. Deeley asked with disappointing eyes.

"Yes, ma'am, it is," answered Christian while walking over to pick up his rocket. "I was hoping to not wear out the motor. I wouldn't want to replace it again. The batteries also wear out fast in this. I'd like to keep both without replacing them until after the school fair."

"We understand, dear. You should bring it back afterwards and give us a longer presentation. Yes?" she asked with eagerness.

Always eager to show off one of his projects, Christian quickly said, "Sure, if you want me to. I'd be more than happy to."

"When you do come back, be sure to bring that ribbon of yours, alright?" Mr. Deeley told him with a glint in his eye while pulling up his pants. Before anyone could say anything further, he saw Shawn approaching from down the road. "Goddamn it! Look who's coming. That damn Calloway boy!"

"I told him I'd be here, Mr. Deeley," Christian told him in an apologetic voice. "I said if he wanted to do anything to meet me here. Do you not want him here?"

The old man rubbed his face in annoyance. "I'd rather not if I can help it."

"Ok. I'll go tell him for you." Christian shrugged while turning to walk towards Shawn. "We can do something later."

"No, no! Don't you dare do that!" Mr. Deeley stated in a harsh tone he rarely exhibited.

"Why not? If you don't want him here, then he shouldn't be. It's my fault he's here, so I should take care of it. Right?"

"Wrong. That's the last thing I want. Granted, I don't want him here, but I don't want him to know that. I don't want the pleasure of dealing with his hot-headed, alcoholic father if he ever found out. I don't want any more of that ignorant, trailer trash family here if I can help it."

"Harold!" his wife exclaimed. "Don't say such a thing! It's not Shawn's fault what kind of family he comes from. And, besides, if Christian likes him, then there has to be some good in him. Just give the boy a chance!"

"I have, Ellen. The more chances I give him, the more and more he's like his old man," her husband bluntly stated while watching Shawn approach. After pausing momentarily, he turned his face to Christian. "Now, remember, not a word about this, you hear? Not one word! If you need me, I'll be inside."

"Where ya going, Mr. Deeley?"

"I'm going inside to make sure your new friend doesn't try to steal anything," he answered foully before vanishing behind inside.

Once the door slammed shut, Mrs. Deeley and Christian turned to see that Shawn had narrowed the gap between them quite a bit. He had the same expression on his face as every other time Christian had seen him, so it was impossible to tell how much of Mr. Deeley's griping had had heard, that is, if he actually had heard anything.

"Hello, Shawn. How're we doing today, dear?" Mrs. Deeley asked when he was a few feet away.

"I don't know about we," he told her while continuing to walk. "But I'm doing fine."

"Hey, Shawn. Did you see my rocket?" Christian asked with excitement.

"Yeah, I saw it."

"Well, what'ya think of it?"

"It's ok. I've seen better," Shawn responded acidly while watching Christian's excitement fade away while walking up to Mrs. Deeley. "Have you gotten any more Superman comics?"

"Why, yes dear, I do believe we have. But they're all older issues. I believe the last time you came in you purchased the newest issue," she told him while pushing up her glasses to take a better look at Shawn's face. "Oh, dear, what happened to your face?"

"Nothin'. I just fell by the stream this morning."

"You fell by the stream?" she questioned while looking him all over to see if he was alright.

"That's what I said, wasn't it?"

She gave him a hard questioning look before finally speaking. "Reason I asked was the location of your fall. I'm surprised you only suffered a black eye. The rest of your face, as well as your hands, don't seem to have any other marks. You'd better be more careful, dear. I wouldn't want to lose one of our better customers," she said before relaxing a little while waving her hand. "Ah, enough of that. You go on ahead and look at the comics. You know where they are."

"Yeah, ok," he said without so much as a side glance while walking past her and Christian towards the front door of the store.

"Mrs. Deeley, can I ask you something?" Christian asked before waiting to continue. He waited until Shawn went inside before continuing.

She smiled at him while adjusting her glasses. "I think you just did, dear."

While biting his lip, Christian thought about how to word what he wanted to say. "I'm curious about Shawn, ma'am."

"I think we all are," she commented while noticing him blink with a misunderstanding look. "You see, given how he was raised and how he is and all, it's understandable that you might be curious. So, that wasn't your question, was it?"

"Ah, no ma'am, it wasn't." he shook his head. "Do you know why he doesn't like me?"

"Who he doesn't like you? Shawn?" she asked in confusion while Christian nodded his head. "What makes you think he doesn't like you?"

"I don't know. He didn't say that he doesn't; it's just the way he acts," he replied with a sigh. "He always acts mean and rude and seems to like making me feel bad. I don't think that it's me, but... Do you know whether it's me or not, Mrs. Deeley?"

"Of course it isn't you, dear," she quickly replied with a soft smile. "You have to understand, Shawn's a loner. Always has been. He's never really been a people person. It's no wonder given his home life. Just seeing him here after you told him you would be here is quite surprising. You must have or did something that caught his eye. Just give it time, ok dear?"

"I know, I know, but I just can't help feeling this way. To think that my parents wanted him to come over tonight for dinner might be a mistake. I'd feel weird knowing he was coming over if he didn't really like me. Mrs. Deeley, what do you think? Should I feel this way?" Christian asked while looking up right into her eyes.

She quickly smiled at him while taking a moment to think of an answer. "Well, dear, from your point of view I can see how you might feel that way. He isn't the most loving or talkative person in the world. He is rude, blunt, inconsiderate, and, up until today, I thought he was invulnerable to any outside influences but his own. Considering he's here after you told him he'd be here, let alone accepting your dinner invitation, oy!, I believe you must have done something for him to take an interest in. But, then again, given his background and home life, don't be surprised if his coming tonight isn't for a free meal. It's how he acts to you tomorrow that'll be your answer."

Meanwhile, commotion and an angry Mr. Deeley were heard from inside the Market that drew the looks from both his wife and Christian from outside.

"What's going on in there?" Christian asked.

"I don't know," she told him while starting to walk towards the door. "Let's go find out."

As they neared, Mr. Deeley's voice bellowed out like a lion's roar. "Don't be lying to me or take that tone with me, boy! I saw you. Either pay for that stuff you pocketed or put it back. Then you can get the hell outta my store!"

"Harold, what's the meaning of this?!" his wife demanded when she entered.

"This little thief was trying to rob us blind!" he yelled while pointing a shaky finger at Shawn.

"What are you talking about?" she asked.

"See those sunglasses he's wearing? The tags for them are in his pocket, right next to the candy bar he very smoothly slipped in when he thought I wasn't looking! Then he had the gall to walk right on by me on his way to the door," he stated angrily while using his arms to gesture. He stopped long enough to catch his breath and pull his pants up.

"I was making my way to the comics. I wanted to see what other Superman comics you had," Shawn rudely told him while staring at the old man, almost daring him to say something.

"You where, huh? Then why didn't you do that first seeing that it's the first think you pass? And you being as big of a Superman fan as you lead us to believe, it's hard for me to believe that an eight-year old boy would walk right by them for a cheap pair of sunglasses and a candy bar," Mr. Deeley told him while coming within a few feet of Shawn before putting his hands on his hips. "Why'd you walk past the comics when you always look at them first? Where you trying to see what you could pocket first without me knowing? Then either look through the comics like nothing happened or keep walking right on out the door?"

"Eight? Who you calling eight?!" Shawn hotly asked him. "I just turned ten!"

"Whatever," Mr. Deeley replied indifferently. "Are you going to pay for those or are you going to put them back?"

While fixing her glasses yet again, Mrs. Deeley cleared her throat. "It's just a pair of sunglasses and a candy bar, Harold."

Her husband firmly shook his head. "'Just a pair of sunglasses and a candy bar' you say? If it's a pair of sunglasses and a candy bar today, then what will it be tomorrow? Or the day after that? What'll it be next week? You above all people, Ellen, should know what I'm doing here. If we let him walk out of here with those glasses and candy, why type of example are we setting? We'll be telling everyone here that it's alright to steal from us and then lie to cover it up. No sir! You and I have worked far too hard for far too long to build this store up with our own two hands to simply let it slip away piece by piece to people like him!"

Hearing this, Mrs. Deeley sighed heavily before turning her attention to Shawn. "Shawn, dear, is any of what he's saying true?" she asked softly. The tone of her voice, mixed with the look in her eyes, had a very motherly effect that was difficult for anyone to lie to. "Are those our sunglasses that you're wearing? Is its tag in your pocket? Is there also one of our candy bars next to it?"

Shawn simply shrugged his shoulders at that. "Yeah. So what?"

His reaction to this whole ordeal conveyed a certain sense of coldness and inconsideration which took Christian completely off guard. Meanwhile, Mr. Deeley had a slight grin on his face as he appeared happy Shawn had admitted to it.

Mrs. Deeley leaned in to eye him closely. "And where you just going to walk out of the store without paying for them?"

"No, I wasn't. Honest."

"Then why did you put the candy bar in your pocket and take the tags off of the glasses?!" Mr. Deeley demanded while trying to control his temper while his face was now a lighter shade of red. "Why do that if you weren't going to steal them?!"

"'Cause," was all Shawn said to this.

"'Cause? Because why?!"

"'Cause I wanted to. Is that alright?!" Shawn yelled at him while finally showing some emotion for that first time that day.

"No, Shawn, it's not alright," Mrs. Deeley told him before walking to her husband to wipe off his sweaty brow. "Oy! And you! You should try to calm down. I won't want you to make me a widow. Ok?"

"Fine, have it your way," he told her hotly. "You take care of him, Ellen. When I come out of the storage room, I don't want to see him here. And, Christian, remember what I said. After the school fair, be sure to bring your rocket over with the blue ribbon it won. Ok?" With that, he put his head down, turned, and proceeded to walk into the back storage room.

After he left, the inside of the store was quiet for several seconds before Mrs. Deeley turned to face the two boys. "Shawn, I'm sorry to say this, but you'd better leave. Ok?"

With this, Shawn looked at her for a brief moment, shrugged his shoulders and turned to leave before being called back.

"Oh, Shawn? The glasses and candy. Did you want to finish paying for them or would you like me to put them back?"

"Oh, I forgot," he quickly answered while going to the comics. He paused long enough to look at the recent Superman comics before selecting one. He carried that to the counter while reaching into his pocket to take out the glasses' tag and the candy bar. "I'm all set. I'll pay for these."

"Sure, if you want to. Is there anything else you would like?" Mrs. Deeley asked while noticing the only answer he was going to give her was a blank stare. "In that case, your total is $3.94."

Shawn gave her four $1 bills before collecting his purchase and walked to the door without waiting for his change. He brushed Christian's shoulder on his way by.

"Oh, Christian?" Mrs. Deeley said when he turned to follow Shawn out.

"Yes, ma'am?" he replied while turning and walked over to her.

"Would you tell your father, dear, that his order has arrived, please? It came this morning," she said while walking around the corner towards him. When she got to him, she straightened both her glasses and apron.

"Sure, I'll let him know tonight when he gets home."

"Thank-you, dear. Oh, while I'm at it, I'll need to ask a small favor of you if it's not too much trouble."

Christian shrugged. "Sure. What's your favor?"

Looking uncomfortable, she went on to say, "Would you be so kind as not to encourage Shawn to come around here for a while? I know he's your friend and all, but we've been having some problems of late. I don't want to be pointing any fingers, you see. Merely just trying to eliminate some suspects is all."

After some mild coaxing, Christian reluctantly agreed. He got a smile, a pat on the cheek, and a 'thank-you' from her before leaving the Market before trying to catch up with Shawn.

"Hey, Shawn! Wait up!" he called while riding his bike while pedaling faster and harder to shorten the distance.

Shawn, who was on foot, had walked a considerable distance from the Market within a short amount of time. It didn't take Christian much longer to pull up next to him and coast.

"Hey, how come you didn't answer me or wait up? Didn't you hear me?

"Oh, I heard you," Shawn answered while continuing to walk in a vain attempt to ignore Christian for as long as possible.

"Then why didn't you stop or wait or answer or something?"

"Because I didn't want to. Alright?"

"Are you trying to be mean and rude and hurtful? Or are you always like this?"

"I do what I want and say what I want to say when I want to do and say them," Shawn bluntly told him. He glanced to Christian who was having a hard time reading his expression due to his tinted sunglasses. He looked back to the road before saying, "If you call that mean or rude, then, yeah, I'm always like that. If you don't like it, then leave me the hell alone. Later, you nerd."

"Hey! You still coming to dinner tonight?" Christian asked as he watched Shawn pick up his pace to a light job while waiting for an answer or an acknowledgement that never came.

Christian simply sat on his bike, sulking, to watch Shawn vanish into the woods and disappear among the trees. Staying there a bit longer to decipher what had just happened, he became disappointed and upset with himself that he allowed himself to become friends with Shawn and soon wished they had never met. Wished that Shawn never stuck up for his against Wesley and his friends. Maybe Mrs. Deeley was right, he thought. Maybe tomorrow he'll find out if Shawn is really a potential friend or is just using him. Tomorrow will have the answers. Tomorrow.

Chapter 6

Later that night when they were all sitting down to dinner, Christian's father was eye-balling Shawn.

"So, you're Christian's new friend?" he asked.

"Yeah, guess so," Shawn said vaguely while looking around the table to see what sort of food was available before grabbing the bowl of mashed potatoes just as Grandpa Joe placed a hand on it to pick it up. Looking at him from over his glasses, Joe just sucked his teeth while watching Shawn mound the potatoes up high on his plate like there was no tomorrow.

"Might I ask what you mean by you guess that you're his new friend?" David asked as he made eye contact with his father.

"D'I stutter?" Shawn asked while finally putting the bowl of potatoes down, totally ignoring Sally's interest in it, before practically lifting the plate of pot roast out of Christian's hands like it was offered to him.

While accepting the potatoes from Sally, David said, "No, you didn't but why wouldn't you know if his new friend or not?"

Pausing long enough to look up at him before going back to finish taking more than a quarter of the meat, Shawn informed him that it's "Because we just met."

"It just amazes me that after, what?, a couple of weeks and multiple visits, Christian has already voiced repeatedly that you two were friends."

"Why?" Shawn asked while grabbing the cabbage salad and scooped it onto what little room on his plate he now had.

"Why does it amaze me?" David question in a serious tone. "No reason. Just that you two apparently have different thoughts on the matter, especially after you two met specifically after you stuck up for him."

"I ain't Christian," Shawn bluntly stated in between massive mouthfuls of food.

David merely leaned back in his chair while looking fully at Shawn. "Why no, no you're not. That actually is quite evident to all of us that you're not."

"So, this food is homemade or what?" asked Shawn while not addressing anyone while in particular inhaling his food.

"Why, yes Shawn, it is," Sally told him. "I made it myself. Do you like it?"

He shrugged. "Ah, it's ok."

A huge smile appeared on Grandpa Joe's face. "By the way he's eating, it looks like it's more than ok. Either that or he hasn't had a decent meal in quite some time. Hell, maybe both."

While giving Joe a side glance, Shawn filled his mouth with more food before turning his attention back to it.

"You know, Dad, you shouldn't swear in front of the children," his daughter-in-law told him.

"Oh, I'm sure they've heard worse."

While clearing his throat, David began eating. "So, Shawn, I've a question. Do you always make it a habit of walking into a person's home, like you did here today, without knocking or being invited in first?"

"Door's open."

"Sorry? I don't understand what you mean by that."

Shawn looked up at him, swallowed his food, and repeated. "I said your door was open."

"Let me get his straight," David said through hard eyes and gritted teeth. "You came into our home without knocking or waiting to be invited in because our door was open?"

"I was invited," Shawn told him while meeting his eyes.

"By whom?"

"By Chris."

David leaned forward. "How could he have invited you in through the front door when he was in the garage with me?"

"He invited me last week."

"That was last week and for dinner. But who invited you in tonight when you arrived?"

Simply shrugging his shoulders, Shawn focused his attention back to his food.

"Just so you're aware," David said with a hint of irritation in his voice, "that if you happen to be over here again, we all would greatly appreciate it if you were to knock first and then wait to be invited inside before simply walking in. Of course, if that's alright with you."

While rubbing his arm, Sally said, "Oh, David, leave the poor boy alone. Let me him. Can't you see the poor boy's hungry?"

"I ain't poor!" Shawn quickly correct while shooting her a glare before going back to eating. He failed to notice the looks either David or Joe had given him.

"So, young man," Joe said in a soft tone. "I just wanted to thank-you for sticking up for Christian a couple of weeks back. It takes a real selfless person to put someone else's well-being on the line ahead of theirs."

"Yeah, whatever." Shawn shrugged while devouring the rest of the food on his plate.

"So, Shawn, where did you say you lived again?" Shawn asked.

"I didn't say."

"Christian mentioned something about that you lived out by the tracks."

"If that's what he said," Shawn nonchalantly told her before filling his plate up a second time.

"It appears you don't want to answer the question," David stated before taking a bite of pot roast. "Do you live near the tracks? If not, then where?"

"Not far."

"Not far from where? Here or the tracks?"

"Both."

"You can just come out and say you do live near the tracks," Joe commented with a sly grin. "There's nothing wrong with that. Is it really so hard to say or admit?"

"Ok boys, that's enough," Sally told them while getting up to refill everyone's drinks. "It's obvious he doesn't want to tell us where he lives. So, Christian, how's your rocket do today, sweetie?"

"It did real good, Mama," he answered bubbly while inhaling a big wad of potatoes.

"Is it ready for the fair, then?"

He confirmed this with a nod and massive smile before remembering something and turning to his father. He soon swallowed his food before speaking. "Oh, that reminds me. Dad, Mrs. Deeley said your stuff came in."

"Really?" his dad asked which drew a nod from Christian. "About time. I wonder what took it so long."

"Didn't he say that it'll take a little time?" asked his wife.

"Yes, but he always says that. They always seem to arrive in about half the time then what I'm told. This shipment took the entire time, if not more."

"What'ya get?" Christian asked.

"Never you mind," his dad bluntly told him.

"Is it a surprise?" he persisted with a surprise.

"Never *you* mind," David repeated only to include a smile this time around.

While catching the smile, Christian moved with excitement in his chair. "It *is* a surprise! Is it for my birthday? I wonder what it could be." This made everyone in the room laugh from his excitement, everyone except for Shawn.

"You shouldn't talk to your father that way," Shawn informed him with a certain edginess in his voice.

"What way?" Christian asked with a look of confusion.

"You questioned him."

"Yeah. So?"

"You shouldn't do that. Not unless you want to get beat on," Shawn explained with a stern, melancholy look.

"Is that what your father does to you, Shawn?" Sally asked softly with a shiver. "Beat you if you question him?"

"My dad does NOT beat me!" he snapped while glaring at her. "He's a great man!"

"There's no reason to get upset, Shawn. It was just a question."

"If your dad doesn't beat you," Grandpa Joe injected softly while leaning forward to place a hand on Shawn's forearm, "then how did you get your black eye, son?"

While jerking his arm away, Shawn states, "I fell and I'm *not* your son!"

"I know you're not my son," Joe said softer still. "Where did you fall?"

"In the woods this morning down by the stream."

"Oh, I see. That would explain it. Explains a lot of things," Joe thoughtfully replied while sitting back in his chair and running his fingers across his mouth. "That would explain your black eye there. However, there is one question that it does not answer for me."

"Yeah? And what's that?" Shawn asked defiantly while also sitting back in his chair to return Joe's stare.

"Your hands."

Stiffening slight as if in anticipation, Shawn asks, "What about my hands?"

"They weren't damaged from your fall," Joe informed him directly. "No cuts, scrapes, or bruises. As a matter of fact, neither your hands or arms show any sign of injury as a result of your fall where you say your fell."

"Why should they?"

"Well, given that you have a black eye would suggest you fell face first. Usually, by instinct, you would raise your arms and hands up to protect yourself to help block the fall," Joe explained while looking down at Shawn to make eye contact. "The way your eyes looks, I'm surprised you don't have any other marks on your body."

To this Shawn gave no response.

"Shawn, honey, did your dad give you your black eye?" Sally asked.

"I fell."

"Yes, dear, you said that. If he hits you, we can help."

"I said I fell and I don't want any help, especially yours!" Shawn rudely states while lowering his head to continue eating. "Don't wanna talk about this anymore."

"Sure, Shawn, whatever you want." Joe sighed while looking to his son and daughter-in-law before returning his gaze back to Shawn. He soon passed the rest of the mashed potatoes over to him while asking, "Would you like more?"

Without answering, Shawn simply took the bowl and put whatever was left in it on his plate before giving the bowl back. After that, he proceeded to take the remainder of the pot roast, as well as the last traces of gravy. A big helping of cabbage salad soon followed.

Smiling, Joe commented, "It's good to see he has an appetite."

"He seems to feel comfortable here enough to make himself right at home," David sarcastically said while turning to his wife. "Good thing you made enough to eat, hun. So, Shawn, what did you say your last name was?"

"I didn't."

"It wouldn't by any chance be Calloway, would it?"

"What if it is?"

"Just as I thought," David said. "You must be Bruce's boy, then."

"Yeah. What's it to ya?" Shawn defensively asked.

David leaned in to get a good look at the defiant boy. "Ah, no reason. He's just one of the guys I oversee at the plant. And, yeah, you're Bruce's boy alright."

"You don't over see him," Shawn told him with surprise. "How can you over see him when he's the boss there?"

"Enough of this talk. You two will make him uncomfortable if you haven't already," Sally said in a tone she usually had after a fight or argument. "So, tell us Shawn, are you looking forward to school next Monday?"

"Nope."

"That's too bad, dear. School should be fun and filled with experiences that you'll cherish for the rest of your life," she said as a smile came across her face. "I remember this one time in tenth grade, Margaret Kinney and I decided to skip biology. That Mr. Thompson was always such an old frog; we just didn't want to have to worry about his class. Anyway, what we did that period would make a nun blush. Oh, dear me. I haven't thought of that in nearly twenty years. How time flies. What we did…"

"Sally, dear, I don't think the young man is interested in anything here but the food," Joe told her with a hearty chuckle. "He's kept most of his attention on that and very little to anything else since he's gotten here."

David laughed at this. "Hell, I don't blame him. Not only is this probably the best meal he's ever had, but the most food he's eaten at one time. Compared to what I imagine he normally gets, he probably just ate equivalent to a week's worth of food at home. If I thought for a second he cared anything about us, I'd consider having him over more often."

"So, what happened, Mama?" Christian asked with a mouthful of food.

"Happened with what, sweetie?"

"With you and your friend Margaret Kinney. When you skipped biology."

"Oh, that. What we did was silly. No one wants to hear what we did twenty years ago," she told him with a childlike laugh.

"I do," Shawn told her with interest while looking up at her.

"You do?" Sally asked with obvious surprise in her voice and on her face. "You're interested in what we did?"

To this, Shawn nodded.

"Wait. What?" David asked skeptically. "You're actually interested in what she did?"

"I wouldn't of said it if I didn't."

For a moment their eyes met before Shawn broke contact to continue eating.

"I want to apologize for my son, Shawn," Joe said softly while leaning towards him. "What he was trying to ask was, perhaps if someone were to ask her nicely, maybe she'll continue on with her story. Isn't that right, David?"

"Correct. That's exactly what I meant to say," David answered while clearing his throat as he made eye contact with his dad.

"So, Sally…" Shawn started to say before being interrupted by Christian's dad.

"Mrs. Eaton," he injected.

"What?"

"Her name. It's Mrs. Eaton."

"It is?"

"Yes. It is."

"Then why did you and the old man here call her Sally?" Shawn asked while nodding towards Grandpa Joe.

"Because that's the name we adults call her," David informed him with authority in his voice and a glint in his eye. "And since you are not yet an adult, her name to you is Mrs. Eaton. Understood?"

Shawn sat there in silence while going from person to person as he waited for someone to come to his defense. When it was obvious that no one would, he fidget a little in his chair before speaking. "So, ah, Mrs. Eaton, what happened with you and your friend?"

"Funny you should ask, Shawn," she said with a smile. "We went down to Deeley's market, bought two dozen eggs, came back to school, and redecorated Mr. Thompson's care with them."

"Really? You did that, Mama?" Christian asked in awe.

With how her son asked that, Sally soon burst out laughing. "Yes, unfortunately we did. Funny thing about it was that we were never caught." She soon went quiet as her eyes drifted off before coming back to reality. "So, tell me honey, are you all set for school to begin?"

"Oh, yes," Christian answered happily. "Fifth grade will be a lot of fun this year.

"Who did you say your teacher was again?" his grandfather asked him.

"Miss Johnson, I think her name is," he said with a thoughtful expression. "Though her name is spelled different than that."

"Do you mean Miss Johansson?" his grandfather inquired.

"Yeah, that sounds right." Christian nodded while pointing a finger at him. "How'd you know that, Grandpa?"

"I worked with her grandfather at the plant the last few years I was there. He immigrated here when he was a kid with his parents. Germany, I think, but I don't remember exactly. Came over here during the war; World War 2 that is," he said while his fingers stroked his cheek and chin as the thought back. "He was a good guy. Family man."

Christian gulped his food. "Was?"

"Christian, you shouldn't make those noises at the table," his mother scolded.

"Sorry," he quickly said before returning his gaze to his grandfather.

"Yeah, he was a good guy. Got killed a few years back."

"How?"

While giving Shawn a glance, Joe answered, "Muggers. He was coming out of the bank here in town when he got stopped by two teenage boys, 'bout 16 or so. They both pulled knives on him and demanded his money or any other thing valuable he had. When he refused, they attacked him. He was able to whack one of 'em pretty good before the other one stabbed him. Once he went down he didn't get back up. They kicked him repeatedly just for the hell of it. Took everything of value; his money, the new watch his wife had given him, and car."

For a minute or so afterwards no one spoke. The only think that spoke was silence and that was deafnifying. During which time, Christian thought he saw both his dad and grandfather eye each other before looking at Shawn.

"Did they get caught?"

"You want to know how?" Joe asked while his grandson nodded. "The kid I said he was able to whack, well, he broke that kid's nose. The two punks didn't know what to do so they went to the hospital to get it fixed. They even drove his car there. Parked it right outside. They didn't realize that there was a policeman there checking on a friend or family member or something like that," he said with a wave of the hand. "To make a long story short, the policeman got a call on his radio about the attack. Once he saw the two kids, he approached them since they fit the description. That's how they got caught."

"Whoa, bummer, dude." Christian let out a long sigh while trying to sound like one of his favorite characters on a current Saturday morning cartoons.

Grandpa Joe agreed. "Bummer is right."

"Excuse the conversation, Shawn," Sally told him sweetly. "We usually don't have such morbid conversations during dinner."

"Good," he soon replied in a satisfied tone while finishing his food.

"So, Shawn, what grade will you be in this year?"

"Fifth," he muttered before drinking the last of his milk.

"Oh, how wonderful! You and Christian will be in the same grade together. Who's your teacher?"

"Don't know." Shawn got up and went to the refrigerator before reaching in for the milk. He proceeded to fill his cup with most of what they had left. What was left he drank right of out of the container before resealing it and putting it back.

"You're welcome," David told him with annoyance.

"For what?"

"The rest of our milk."

Confused by this, Shawn asked, "Ok...? Why'd you say 'you're welcome' when I didn't thank-you for it?"

"Just to let you know young man, if you ever decide to come over here again..." Joe started before being interrupted.

"What makes you think I won't be back over?" Shawn asked.

"So you will be over again?"

"I didn't say that."

"Just asking in case you decide *not* to come over again for dinner," Grandpa Joe said while looking at him. "Like I was going to say earlier, if you ever decide to come over here again and would like something, we would all greatly appreciate it if you were to ask first before helping yourself to it. And if you happen to finish something off, like you did with the milk right now, there's honestly no need to put it back. Just putting it on the counter would have sufficed. Ok?"

"Whatever." Shawn shrugged before letting out a loud burp. "So, Sally, um, I mean, Mrs. Eaton, what'cha have for dessert?"

"Apple pie," she responded.

"Homemade?"

"Yes, dear, homemade. Why do you ask?"

"No reason. Just never had homemade apple pie before."

"Have you had apple pie before, Shawn?" she inquired.

"Of course I am. I'm an American, ain't I?" he angrily asked.

"There's no need to get upset, Shawn. She wasn't trying to insult you," David told his young dinner guest. "So what's your favorite type of pie?"

"McDonald's."

"Come again?"

"McDonald's is my favorite pie."

Pausing for a moment, David quickly regained his composure. "McDonald's is your favorite pie?"

"Yeah, their apple pie. Somethin' wrong with that?" Shawn asked while almost wanted someone to say something.

"No, dear. There's nothing wrong with that," Sally told him. "We just never knew McDonald's had an apple pie, that's all."

"It's Shawn," he quickly corrected with a glare.

"Excuse me, dear?"

"My name's Shawn," he repeated through gritted teeth. "Not dear, or honey, or sweetie. Just Shawn."

"Are you saying you don't want to be called any of those or you don't want me calling you those?" Sally asked while getting up to get the pie she had made earlier.

"Both!"

"Why is that, if I may ask?"

"'cause."

"Oh, ok," she said while turning quickly to hide her smile.

"Because why, Shawn?" Joe asked with an open grin while drinking his coffee.

"Because they're girlie names. I ain't no girl." he told him while taking a piece of pie before sitting back down. He soon inhaled the pie in roughly four bites. "I think you make better apple pie than McDonald's, Mrs. Eaton."

"Thank-you, Shawn. That means a lot." Sally smiled broadly at that before turning to her son. "Christian, sweetie, would you show Shawn your room after dinner, please?"

"Do I have to, mom?" he protested. "I was hoping to show him my tree fort."

Obviously not interested, Shawn asks, "Yeah, does he have to?"

"You can always go home instead," David said while holding back a smile. "I know how you must be anxious to get home to your dad and his beer chugging buddies as they get drunk playing cards and watching baseball."

"Will you stop? He probably isn't interested in doing that with his dad or his friends," Sally asked him with a slight smile before looking back to Shawn. "He may have plans later with friends. He's just here as a dinner guest."

"Nah, that's alright," Shawn said in a surprisingly pleasant tone. "I have a little more time before I need to get going."

"David and Sally," Joe said, "why don't you let the boys decide what they'll do later? It seems like Shawn's not going anywhere for at least a little while."

After dinner was completed, and while there was still enough light outside to do things, Christian showed Shawn his tree house and surrounding neighborhood. Christian found it increasingly difficult to hold Shawn's attention for anything longer than a minute or so. Once they did get back to his house, Christian was hoping to hold his attention long enough to show him his room, which wasn't what one might expect to find for a boy his age. Rather than finding it covered with posters or memorabilia of various sports teams or some other action-based theme, it was filled instead with something that invoked some level of intelligence.

Various sized bookshelves lined the room that were filled with books and models. The books were vast and consisted of many topics including, but not limited to, astronomy; zoology; air dynamics of airplanes; various volumes on mythology ranging from Greek, Roman, Celtic, Norse, and Native American; the entire Sherlock Holmes collection and most of The Hardy Boys.

The models he had were not as diverse, yet equally impressive. They included a miniature human skeleton, which Christian made himself; a collection of replica talons from most of the birds of prey New York State had to offer; another display consisted of the eggs, in replica form, of the more common state birds; and a number of rockets and space ships that he built. The ceiling had a number of different stars scattered over it, which were placed in the manor of different constellations he enjoyed looking at. In the ceiling's corner, Christian had a kite fastened there which displayed the image of a dragon. He also had a few models of airplanes that he made that were hung from the ceiling as well.

Against the wall and under the window was a wooden desk with its accompanying chair. On it was a desk light; a coffee mug from some science competition he had won filled with an array of pens and pencils; and a number of field guides. Nest to the desk, in the same corner as the dragon kite, was a mid-sized telescope on a tripod. A black, padded box lay on the floor next to it which was labeled telescope lenses.

"Hey, Shawn, I was thinking," Christian said to him.

"Aw, great. The genius has something on his mind," Shawn sarcastically replied in an irritated tone while rolling his eyes. "What are you planning on doing now, build a car outta toothpicks or something?"

Hearing that, Christian squinted his eyes at him while wondering why he was asked that. "Ah, actually no. I already did that. I was going to ask what you thought if I became the first person to create a time machine, that is, if you really care," he said while noticing Shawn blankly staring at him. "I thought it would be great but I can tell you could care less."

"Why would that be great? It's stupid," commented Shawn.

"Wha...what? Stupid? No it's not. It's a good idea."

"Yeah? What's so good about it?"

"Well, we'd be able to go and time travel and see places and things that we'd only see in books and stuff."

Scowling, Shawn asks, "Why would you use it if you already know how it'd turn out? I'd rather go to the future and see how great I'll turn out."

"You won't be able to do that."

"Says who?"

"Einstein's Theory of Relativity," Christian told him. "He said time travel to the past is possible because the future doesn't exist yet."

"In English, nerd ball."

"Have you ever heard of Albert Einstein?"

"Of course I have! Get on with it."

"Through his studies in math, physics, and whatever, he determined that if time travel came to be, then we couldn't go to the future because it doesn't exist yet. It doesn't exist yet because we haven't gotten there yet," Christian explained as best he could. "But we could go to the past because we've already been there."

"In that case, how would you get home if you go to the past then?"

Staring absently, Christian asked, "What?"

"You said that the future doesn't exist yet, right?"

"Actually Einstein said that."

"Ok, fine. But how would you get home should you go to the past?" Shawn asked. "You call this the present, but to the past the present if their future. And if the future hasn't happened yet, then you'd be stuck in the past. Right? Wouldn't your chubby ass just be stuck there?"

Blinking several times before catching on to what he was being told, Christian finally admitted, "I never considered that."

Rolling his eyes, Shawn stated, "Well, yeah, that was obvious."

Meanwhile, Christian had moved on to showing Shawn a number of other things in his room while trying to get his interest and attention before soon realizing it was eventually useless for him to try. When he was about to give up Shawn suddenly asked him about his family.

"What about them?"

"Are they always like this?" Shawn asked.

Being confused by the current conversation, Christian asked, "Like what?"

"Like this," Shawn stated while waving his arm towards the door. "How they were at dinner."

"Yeah, I guess so. Why?"

"Well, they seem a little bossy, don't they?" Shawn asked with a certain directness.

Shrugging, Christian said, "I don't know. Maybe. They always seem to act like that to me."

Just then, noises filtered upstairs from the living room. David seemed to be grumping as Grandpa Joe was yelling at the television. The TV, however, seemed to have cheers emanating from it.

"What the hell is that?" Shawn asked while looking out in the hall.

"Monday Night Fights."

"Huh?"

"Monday. Night. Fights," Christian repeated, this time louder and deliberately slower.

Shawn shot him a glare. "I heard you the first time."

"You seemed confused and incoherent when I did tell you the first time."

"I'm never confused," Shawn told him in as deep of a voice as he could muster while puffing himself up. "I'm alert like a cat. Sharp as a tack, too."

"But you're incoherent?" Christian asked with a sly smile.

Shawn sighed irritably and shook his head. "Whatever. I'm going down stairs."

Following Shawn to the living room, Christian watched him take a seat in the corner with a clear line of site towards the TV.

"You still here?" David asked Shawn while reading an article in that day's newspaper.

Christian had always been amazed at his dad's ability to know who walked in or out of a room without having to look up.

"Looks that way," Shawn answered.

"I thought you would have left just as soon as dinner was over."

"It's not bad here."

"Really? Then that's probably a step up from your place."

"Hey! What you talkin' 'bout?!" Shawn demanded while standing.

"Oh, nothing," David told him while continuing to read. "Forget I said anything."

"You tryin' to say *where* I live is bad?!"

"I didn't say that."

"You tryin' to say *how* I live is bad?!"

"Didn't say that either," David calmly informed him while changing pages.

"Yo, man! You don't even know me," Shawn angrily explained. "Where I live is a great place. My parents are the best people you'll ever meet!"

"Yes, I know that. You seem to forget I work with your dad. So you need not tell me about your home life."

"What's that s'pose to mean?!"

"Since I already mentioned at dinner that your dad works for me, then you telling me what a superior home life you have is a waste of our time," Christian's dad said while giving their visit a side glance.

Shawn smiled arrogantly and nodded his head when he heard that. "Yeah. That's right! Great home life."

"I am curious about two things though, champ," David voiced before clearing his throat and trying to think about how to word his next thought.

"Yeah? What's that?" Shawn asked with a cocky swagger.

"If you have such a great home life with great parents, great home, the works, then why aren't you in a hurry to get back to it?" he asked while finally looking to Shawn.

As his cocky smile faded, Shawn asked, "What?"

"It just stands to reason that your home life being what it is, being so much greater and far superior to what you would ever find here, then why didn't you leave hours ago to return to what most people would consider heaven?" he asked while folding his paper neatly before moving on to the sports section. "You just don't seem to be in any hurry to go back. I was just curious about that, that's all."

"It's not bad here."

"That's right. You *had* mentioned that," David told him.

In an attempt to change the subject away from him, Shawn nervously asked, "What're you guys watchin'?"

"Monday Night Fights." Joe smiled. "But you already knew that."

"No I didn't. That's why I asked."

"Then I'll assume you didn't hear my grandson tell you twice before in his room what we were watching a few minutes ago."

Not sure how to respond to this, Shawn merely remained silent while staring at him until David spoke again.

"The second thing that concerned me is your brother," he continued following the interruption.

Hearing this, Shawn stiffened. "What 'bout him?!"

"How's he doing?"

"What's it to you?!" Shawn asked with a hint of anger. "You writin' a book?"

Turning the page of his paper, David said, "Oh, no reason. Just that your dad hasn't mentioned him in a while at the plant and, since you haven't either, I thought something may have happened to him. I was just wondering about Daryl. That's all."

"He's doin' great," replied Shawn while relaxing a little while sitting back down.

"He is, is he?" David jested while turning to look at Shawn from over his paper and thought for a moment.

Shawn shot him a stiff glare. "I just said he was, didn't I?! I wouldn't have if he wasn't!"

"No, I guess you wouldn't have." He turned back to his paper. "I'm glad to hear that."

"David, you make it sound like the young man here is lying to you," Grandpa Joe said while looking at his son before transferring his gaze to Shawn while continuing. "Why would he intentionally lie to us about his brother's, or even his family's, well-being? Or, should I ask, why would he knowingly lie to us? Considering he stuck up for Christian, he accepted our dinner invitation, he's still here in our house, he's watching our TV, and all the while the food we made for him is digesting gin his stomach. Given all of this, you suspect that he would have the nerve to lie to us in our own home?"

"You know, you're absolutely right, Dad," David admitted innocently. As he finished the article he was reading, he put the paper down, took his glasses off, and looked over to Shawn. "Please forgive me, Shawn. My deepest apologies to you if I made you feel like I didn't believe you. I really am sorry. Given what my father just said, I admit you wouldn't lie to us."

While sitting there defiantly, Shawn looked at Christian's father and grandfather while they all waited for him to respond. On the TV behind them, a commercial for the new Ford pickup came on. He thought about when he could drive. He would get a truck like that; a truck like his old man's. A truck tough-as-nails, just like him. He soon looked back at everyone who were still waiting for his reply before he spoke.

"Right, no need for me to lie to you. Whatever you say," he lied effortlessly with a shrug as he went back to watching the TV. "Is Tyson defending the championship?"

"Maybe, maybe not," Joe told him while turning up the volume to hear better. "If you're curious, maybe you'd better stay and find out."

"Just be quiet if you *do* decide to stay," commented David while focusing on the upcoming match.

Chapter 7

Shawn stayed until the fights were over before leaving just after eleven that night with a turkey sandwich for company. He left well after David had gone to bed at 9pm and Christian who followed his father twenty minutes later. For the better part of the last two hours before finally going home, Shawn planted himself next to Grandpa Joe and didn't leave his side.

Maybe it was Joe's patience or tolerance of him. Maybe it was because he didn't judge Shawn like everyone else had before. Perhaps, maybe, Shawn felt like he could be himself around the older man without any preconceived notions on how to act or behave. Hell, maybe all of the above, but whatever Grandpa Joe did or didn't go, Shawn felt comfortable.

Over the next two weeks Christian and Shawn didn't see much of each other. On the two occasions that their paths did cross, Christian felt Shawn was nicer to him. And by being nicer simply meant that Shawn wasn't nearly as blunt, rude, or insulting as he normally was.

That Thursday, Ed, the contractor that Christian's dad had hired finished the room converting the room above the garage into a small apartment for Joe. While grumping again that night at dinner, David once again voiced his disapproval it had taken the contractor far too long to complete the task at hand, though failed to mention that it was only one man doing all the work. In the end, the room's dimensions were roughly 30 feet deep-by-30 feet wide-by-8 feet height and it had basically everything done to it to ensure it was its own self-contained living environment. During the fortnight worth of renovations, the room got a complete facelift and then some.

Ed was a short spit-fire of a man with a humorous comment about everything. He insulated and sheet rocked the interior; put in electrical wires, plumbing, and plush carpeting. He installed a small kitchenette in the back left corner, while also converting the back right corner into a small bathroom. The back half had hardwood floor while the front half had plush carpeting. In the end, it was an excellent apartment for a single man to have. There was a window overlooking the backyard; a built-in bookshelf next to a bed that could rise up into the wall; recess lighting; a ceiling fan; and most importantly for Grandpa Joe: heat in the winter and air-conditioning in the summer.

The next day, Christian's dad took the morning off to help move Joe's belongings from a local storage unit into the now finished apartment. Christian went more for the fun of it and to be with both his father and grandfather then for the actual experience of physical labor. After a couple of hours, the unit was empty and its contents now spread sporadically throughout the garage's former storage room.

By which point, it was lunch time in the Eaton household and once again David and Joe couldn't see eye-to-eye on something. The subject in general this time was where to have lunch. David wanted to make something to save the money, whereas Joe wanted to go out for food.

Shaking his head, David commented, "You know, Dad, you going out to eat is just a waste of time and money."

"But it's my time and my money that I'm wasting, now isn't it?"

"Well, it may be your money, but it's also my time you'd be wasting." David looked to the floor while putting his hands on his hips. "You now I didn't have to take the day off of work to help you, right?"

"I'm well aware of that, son, and I do appreciate the help you're giving me. But you can go back to work anytime you want if you feel like I'm wasting your time."

"What are you saying that for, Dad?" his son quickly asked while shooting him a hurt, confused look.

"Considering all of my belongings are now in the apartment, it just stands to reason I can now take care of things from here if you want to go back to work," Grandpa Joe said while looking at his son in the eye before turning to walk back to his truck. "You know, pizza sounds good right about now. How's that sound to you, Chris?"

"Pizza? Really?" Christian asked with both confusion and excitement while looking at both this dad and grandfather. Although his dad didn't seem pleased by this, his grandfather, on the other hand, appeared totally serious by this while waiting for his answer. "That sounds great!"

"Well, come on then and get your ass moving!" his grandfather told him while climbing behind the wheel of his old, blue pickup while starting it all in one motion. "You won't be gettin' any by just standing there. Let's get a move on; I'm hungry."

Without further ado, Christian quickly got in next to his grandfather as the truck started out of the drive before the passenger side door was completely shut. As always when he drove, Grandpa Joe was flipping between three stations on the radio. The one he played most of the time was music from when he grew up in the 1920s and '30s. The other two, which he played equally, were rock-n-roll from the 1960s and '70s, and country. Although jazz from the '20s was his favorite to listen to especially it was from Louis Armstrong, and everything else was secondary next to this; he had a wide range of musical tastes. If he didn't know what to listen to, Joe would always find what he labeled as "the old standbys," which usually meant jazz, Patsy cline, Dolly Parton, George Jones, and any of those Motown doo-wop groups from the '60s. For an old man, Christian was surprised at the current music his grandfather listened to although it was still old by Christian's standards. Current to Joe were The Doors and CCR, while current to Christian meant Springsteen, Mellencamp, and Adams.

Before he knew it, they were pulling into the local pizza shop while hearing his grandfather comment on it wasn't as busy he would have thought for lunch time on a Friday, especially given how this place in particular made good pizza and wings. Even before they finished parking, the smells emanating from the pizzeria filled the cab of the truck. Christian soon found himself thinking of the possible combinations of toppings quickly filled his mind as he let out a hmmmm.

Laughing at this, Joe glanced over to his grandson to simply ask, "Hungry?"

"Uh-huh."

"Know what you want?"

"Ummmm," Christian thought for a moment before quickly deciding. "Yep. Sausage."

73

His grandfather smiled at that. "Sausage what?"

"Sausage pizza!"

"Ah, that does sound good. Unfortunately, none for me since sausage always gives me heartburn," the older Eaton said reluctantly while noticing a look of disappointment on his grandson's face. "But no one said you couldn't get it," Joe soon explained that immediately perked up his grandson.

As they smiled at each other over this, they left the truck, slammed the doors behind them, and proceeded to enter the pizzeria. When they entered, they saw an older man at a table reading a newspaper with a sandwich next to him and Mr. Deeley jawing with Bobby, the worker behind the counter.

"Hey, Joseph, Einstein! How the hell are you two doing?!" Mr. Deeley exclaimed as a smile came to his face. His arms went out wide with job before quickly going back to his pants to hike them up. The noises that he made made the man at the table jump with surprise while shooting him a glaring glance.

Grandpa Joe simply nodded. "Harold."

"Hello, Mr. Deeley" Christian said while running up to him while returning the smile.

Mr. Deeley patted Christian on the head with one hand while shaking Joe's hand with the other.

"So, how are you two doing today?" he asked.

"Oh, we're doing fine, Harold, just fine. Thanks for asking."

"Good, good." Mr. Deeley nodded a few times from hearing this. "Oh, young David came in last night for his order and said in passing that your apartment was done. That true?"

"It is. Finished it yesterday around one," confirmed Grandpa Joe.

"Wow that was fast. What was it, week and a half?"

"Two, actually."

"So who'd you have do it for you?"

"Ed Thompson."

"Ed Thompson?" Mr. Deeley repeated while thinking who it might be. "Isn't that Jacob's son, the old farmer from the next town over?"

"The one in the same," Joe answered.

"How is old Jacob doing? He hasn't been in the story last year or so."

Hearing this, Joe let out a hearty laugh. "He isn't. He's dead."

74

"Really?" Mr. Deeley asked in disbelief. "From what?"

"His wife killed him." Joe told him while continuing to laugh. "Apparently she found him in bed with another woman. Caught in the act; literally. From what I heard, the other woman was Ed's age. I don't really blame Jacob for what he did, considering what he was married to and all. Anything is better than that, even death."

"What happened to his wife?"

"She's doing life downstate somewhere. From what Ed said, this is the happiest she's been in years," Joe told him with a thoughtful look. "Funny thing is that in order for her to be so-called happy she'd have to commit murder."

"Poor bastard. At least he died happy." Mr. Deeley smiled before a thought came to him, bringing a laugh from his mouth. "Great way to go, huh? Sure beats cancer."

The laugh caused the other gentleman with the paper and sandwich to jump again while looking at both Joe and Mr. Deeley.

"Will you two please be quiet?!" the elderly customer demanded with obvious annoyance. "I came here to a nice lunch and would like some peace and quiet!"

"Sorry about that, sir. We'll be quiet," Grandpa Joe said to him.

"Like hell we will! You be quiet, Joe, but not me," Mr. Deeley said as he turned towards the other man before smiling. "I'll be peace." With that, he let out another long lasting, loud burst of laughter like there was no tomorrow. He laughed and laughed until he was red in the face and tears streamed down his face. The only thing Grandpa Joe could do was stand there with crossed arms, smile, and shake his head.

The man, obviously more annoyed than before, folded his paper, wrapped up the remainder of his sandwich, and left.

"Have a good day, Mr. Smith," Bobby said from behind the counter without as much as a glance from the leaving patron after taking the order Christian had given him.

"Well I'll be a monkey's play toy," Mr. Deeley commented while being confused by Mr. Smith's reaction. "What the hell kind of bug crawled up his ass?"

"His wife did," Bobby answered.

"Sorry? Come again?"

"His wife is the bug that crawled up his ass."

"I don't follow."

"I think the conversation you two were having hit a nerve with him," Bobby commented as he started to make Christian's and Joe's pizza order. "Rumor has it, his wife found out he had a girlfriend of sorts on the side. I don't remember her name, but they've come in here a few times before; him and his girlfriend that is. She just graduated high school this year. I had her in a few of my classes. Let's just say she's not the sharpest tack in the world. Anyway, his wife hit him pretty good with divorce papers as a result."

Hearing this, Mr. Deeley chuckled. "Huh. Who would have thought? That reminds me, how's Ed doing from his parents' rather sudden separation?"

"Who knows with him? Reading a door is easier than reading him," Joe replied simply.

"That's true. And, speaking of doors, how'd he do on your apartment?"

"Great!" Grandpa Joe quickly told him. "Once he got going, he moved like hell; though David thought he should have been done that first week." He shook his head. "We just got done moving my things in there this morning. Thought I'd bring my grandson here for lunch. Which reminds me, Christian?" he called to his grandson.

"Yeah, Grandpa?" he answered from behind an arcade fighting game he was currently playing.

"Did you order yet or should I do it now?"

"I already placed it."

"What'ya get?"

"Ah, oh. Large pizza, half sausage, half peppers; twenty barbeque wings; and two large Pepsi's. Is that ok?"

"Oh, that sounds great. Thank-you." Grandpa Joe smiled before going back to Mr. Deeley. "So, how's business been?"

"Oh, it's been great. If it keeps up like it has been, the wife and I should be able to retire in about twelve years or so," he answered while following it with his trademark smile. "You should come in some time and see the renovations we've done the last few months."

"I'll be in when I can," Joe promised. "How's Ellen?"

"Not bad. I've been trying to get her to go to the doctors. She's been getting more forgetful in her old age. Just want to make sure she's alright."

"Give her my best, would you Harold?"

"Oh, I sure will. I'll let her know once I get home."

"Mr. Deeley," Bobby stated while sliding a box of pizza on the counter to him. "Your order's ready."

"Thank-you, Bobby. That was fast as usual," Mr. Deeley said while taking the box while handing the young man a five dollar bill. "Here's a little something for you for being as quick as my order."

76

"Mr. Deeley, I can't take this," Bobby answered while trying to give back the money.

"Yes, you can," Mr. Deeley said while cramming the money in the young man's shirt pocket. "Take that girlfriend of yours out for me, ok?"

Finally giving in, Bobby reluctantly accepted the money with a smile. "Gee, thanks, Mr. Deeley."

"Anytime, young man. Anyway, I'd better get going or the misses will think I have a girlfriend," Harold explained while grabbing his order. He then walked to Joe to shake his hand before walking to the door. "Joseph, I'll be expecting a visit from you sometime soon. And Einstein, I'll be expecting one from you as well as soon as you win that school fair of yours. Ya hear me?"

"Yes, Mr. Deeley," Christian said while not taking his eyes off of his game.

With that, Mr. Deeley was gone out the door as it closed behind him. In the same instance, Bobby trayed up a pizza and some wings before carrying them to the front counter.

"Mr. Eaton, your order is ready. Will you be sitting in your usual spot today?"

"Yes, Bobby, I believe we will. Thank-you," Joe told him while paying for the food. He took the pizza to the corner booth, as Bobby followed with the wings, before coming back to grab the drinks. "Come on, Christian, time to eat."

"Ah, Grandpa! I'm on the sixth guy now, Sgt. Blister. I've never gotten this far before," Christian whined.

"Well, hurry up then. The pizza won't be any good cold."

A minute or so later, Christian finished up the game before coming over to sit opposite of his grandfather.

"Wow, I've never made it that far before," he told his grandfather bubbly while loading his plate up with both pizza and wings. "The furthest I've ever made it was to the fourth guy, Soulless Piper. I made it to the sixth guy this time, Sgt. Blister."

"Good job. Maybe next time."

The next few minutes they sat there in silence while they ate. Christian bobbed his head while humming a song from one of the various TV shows he watched. Joe, on the other hand, watched Bobby clean up while getting ready for his next order.

A few moments later, Shawn walked in with earphones on while heading to the fighting game Christian was on minutes earlier. He and Joe exchanged a nod as he passed. Christian, still being in a world of his own, hadn't noticed Shawn had entered. While guzzling the last of his soda, he got up to get a refill before finally noticing Shawn.

"Hey, Shawn," he said while filling his cup with soda.

No response.

"Hey, Shawn," he repeated while walking over to stand next to him.

Again his salutation was met with silence as Shawn played the game.

"Shawn?" Christian asked before reaching out to tap him on the shoulder.

"It would appear he doesn't want to be disturbed," his grandfather told him.

"Then why doesn't he just tell me then?" Christian asked in a whiny tone. "It isn't that hard to do. Is it?"

"Maybe he can't hear you given the fact that he has his earphones on," Grandpa Joe said while waving his hand towards the seat opposite him. "Why don't you come on over and finish your lunch?"

"Yes, Grandpa," Christian said while hanging his head while sulking back to his seat.

When his back was to Shawn, Shawn looked over to Grandpa Joe, shook his head slightly, and went back to his game.

With this, Joe got up to get a refill of his own. While passing the arcade playing boy, he says, "You know, Shawn, if you really didn't want Christian talking to you, it would have been a lot easier and more polite to come out and tell him rather than ignoring him like you did."

"Why are you talkin' to him, Grandpa? He can't hear you," Christian mumbled while munching on a piece of pizza crust.

"Oh, he can hear me."

"He can? I thought he's listening to his music."

"It would be a little hard for him to do that when it's not even on," Grandpa Joe said while nodding towards the Walk-Man attached to Shawn's belt. "He probably has the earphones on to give the impression he's listening to something when he's really not."

"Why would he do that?"

"I'd imagine so no one would bother him. Isn't that right, Shawn?" Joe asked while looking at the boy in front of the arcade.

Outside of looking at him from the corner of his eyes, Shawn didn't acknowledge the question any other way.

"Yeah, just as I thought." Joe laughed while continuing to look at Shawn for a few more beats before going back to sit down with his grandson. "Is there anything else you want to do today, Christian?"

"Um, I don't know. Why?"

"Well, since all of my crap in now in the apartment, there really isn't any reason for us to get home right away. I can always take care of it late on," he said while rubbing his cheek. "I'm not really in a hurry to go home just yet so I was wondering if there's something you'd want to do."

"Well, the park is always a good spot to go." Christian shrugged while munching on a wing. "We can always see the ducks and geese at the pond there. I know they wouldn't mind eating pizza crust. We can always go walking on the trails they have there in the wood if you wanted to."

"Hmmm. That sounds like a great idea. I haven't been to the park in quite some time." Joe nodded when he heard that. "You can grab your rocket and how it to me there if you want. You know I haven't seen it yet."

"That might wear down the batteries," Christian told him. "I don't have any more and I want to save them for the fair."

"What if I were to get you more batteries? Would you do it then?"

Smiling broadly, Christian quickly nodded his head.

"Good, then it's settle," Joe said absently. "We'll swing by the house on the way to pick it up. Afterwards, we can swing by Deeley's. Kill two birds with one stone."

"Is that possible to kill two birds with one stone?" questioned Christian.

"Yes, in this case it is. I've been meaning to stop by the Deeley's for a few months now to visit them. While we're there, we can grab the batteries for your rocket. Hence the 'two birds with one stone' comment," Joe told him while getting up to get a carryout box from Bobby. He and Christian soon put the leftovers into it. "Go get a refill if you want, Christian. We'd better hurry up if we want to do all this at the park while it's still light out."

"Can do, Grandpa."

After they were done doing that and on their way to the door, Joe turned to say something.

"Hey, Shawn. If you're interested, you're more than welcome to join us at the park if you want. Also, since my apartment above our garage is done, you can come by any time and watch the fights on Monday nights, alright?" With that said he turned back around and walked the remaining distance to, and out, the door.

Moments later, they were pulling out of the parking spot to head for home for Christian's rocket. With any luck, they'll be at the park within twenty minutes after that.

Chapter 8

School started that following Tuesday and Christian was so excited from it that that first week quickly faded to the end of October. Though he and Shawn weren't in the same class that year, they did share the same recess where Christian would often see Shawn off by himself. Whenever he would go over to see him, more often than not, Shawn would make some rude comment before walking off. Pretty much all the insults that Shawn would throw at him didn't quite make much sense, almost as if he were trying to repeat what he had heard on TV. After a while, Christian took that as Shawn wanting to be left alone while trying to sound more adult-like in the process.

During this same time, as well as the next two months, Shawn had been coming over to Christian's home more and more, but it was mainly on Monday nights to watch the fights with Grandpa Joe. Christian would go up and visit before soon feeling like he was an unwanted fifth wheel. During these visits, Joe and Shawn seemed to be more and more in a world of their own that Christian wasn't sure exactly how to get to. However, he had noticed, Shawn was much nicer to him during these interplanetary visits than he had once been.

During a few of these fights on Monday nights, a number of the boxers seemed to have been promoted by a new comer to the boxing realm by the name of Duke Snyder. Duke was a man with a lot of intelligence and wit, as well as a thesaurus for a mouth. He was able to speak for as long as he was allowed to with seemingly much more to come. What he lacked in concern for his fighter he made up for it in charisma. Grandpa Joe called him a peacock without the feathers, who made up for his lack of feathers with fancy three-piece suits while seemingly only wore the finest clothes that money could buy. At times, Christian would watch the Monday Night Fights solely for the chance to see Duke Snyder in action. And the nights he did get to see him, he was never disappointed.

***

"Christian? Oh, Christian!" Sally called from the kitchen on Halloween.

"Yes, Mama?" he answered while popping his head out of his bedroom.

"Are you going out trick-or-treating tonight?"

"Don't I always?"

"I was just making sure. Do you know what you'll be yet?"

"Nah, not yet. Thought I might go down to Deeley's to get some ideas," he answered after coming down with his backpack.

"Just don't be late for dinner tonight, ok sweetie?" she told him before kissing him on the forehead.

"Ok, Mama," he answered before walking out the door.

After straddling his bike and taking off down the road, he soon disappeared into the woods to take the path to the village market. Minutes later, he saw Shawn in his usual spot with a fishing pole in hand.

"Hi'ya Shawn. What'cha doin'?" he asked while pulling up next to him.

"What's it look like? I'm fishin'," Shawn bluntly answered without turning to look.

"Isn't it past fishing season?"

Shawn shrugged. "I don't know. Maybe."

"You might get into trouble if it is."

"Might."

"Aren't you worried?"

"Nope. Why would I be? I won't get caught."

Looking at him for a moment while trying to figure out what to say before he remembered the reason for his trip, Christian shrugged off Shawn's normal indifference while asking, "So, anyway, would you like to go out twick-or-tweatin' with me tonight?"

"Do I what?" Shawn asked while blinking his eyes in disbelief while turning to look at him. "Do I want to go *twick-or-tweatin'* tonight? What type of question is that? No, I don't want to go *twick-or-tweatin'*!"

"Well, why not?"

"Because *twick-or-tweatin'* is for kids," Shawn mocked with a scoff.

"Well, that's why I asked you," Christian told him with a confused tone.

"What are you sayin'? That I'm a kid?" Shawn demanded with a glare while standing to puff himself up.

"As a matter of fact I am. You're a kid, just like me."

"What?! Do I look like a kid? Do I act like one? Huh?!"

"So, is that a no?" Christian asked as his eyes started to fill up a little.

"Ah, hell yeah that's a no!" Shawn stated rudely. "I already told you I didn't want to go. So just stop askin' me, will ya?!"

Gasping when he hear this as he started to cry, Christian asked, "Why are you always so mean to me, Shawn? What did I ever do to you? I just wanted to know if you wanted to go twick-or-tweatin' with me tonight. A simple yes or no would have been fine. You didn't have to be mean about it."

"You know, Chris, I'm sorry," Shawn said with a surprisingly amount of softness. "Trick-or-treating is just not for me. Would you wanna do anything after that when you get back?"

"Ah, sure, if it's not too late," Christian answered while trying to hold back what tears he had while drying his cheeks.

"I'll be at your window then around 9:30, ok?"

"9:30? 9:30 tonight? I have an 8 o'clock curfew."

"Hey, do you want me to come over or don't yeah?" Shawn questioned while spreading his arms.

"Yeah."

"Ok, then. I'll be around your window about 9:30 tonight. Ok?"

"What will we be doing?" Christian asked while looking around to see if anyone might be overhearing them.

"I just wanted to drop some eggs off to a couple of your neighbors," Shawn told him with a shrug and smile while turning to walk away. "Just be ready when I come a'knockin'."

At 10:05 when Christian had just climbed into bed, there was some banging outside his bedroom window. When he looked, he saw Shawn standing outside throwing rocks up to get his attention.

"Hey," he said after opening his window.

"Hey," Shawn responded back. "You ready?"

"I thought you said you'd be here at 9:30?" Christian asked before looking towards his door to see if his parents were coming.

"I did."

"That was almost forty minutes ago," Christian told him. "It's after 10 o'clock now."

"I got sidetracked." Shawn's tone indicated he didn't want to be questioned about it. "Ya ready to go."

"It's time for bed."

"It's time for *bed*?" Shawn mockingly repeated. "You just said it's ten."

"It is. And, like I said, it's time for bed."

Shooting a glare up to Christian's window, one masked by the surrounding shadows, Shawn soon revealed a plastic bad from behind him. "You said you'd come with me tonight so I could drop some eggs to a few people. As you can see, I have the eggs. Now, let's get a move on or I'm leavin' without you."

"You also said you'd be here forty minutes ago," Christian whined while looking back to his door. "You go on without me then, Shawn."

"What did you say?!" Shawn demanded while puffing himself up in his trademark way.

"I said for you to go on without me," Christian repeated. "I'm sorry but I'm a little tired. I wanna be awake for school tomorrow."

"So you ain't comin' with me then?"

"Not now. I'm sorry. I would have if you were here earlier," Christian timidly answered.

"Great! That's just great. You expect me to pass out these eggs without you?"

"Why are you doing this now when it's so late? Wouldn't it be easier to pass 'em out in the daytime?"

"C'mon and find out," Shawn answered with a mischievous grin while nodding his head towards the road.

"I'd better not now," Christian softly said while making another look to his room's door. "It's late. Besides I don't wanna get in trouble if my parents found out."

"You're going back on your word then, huh? Just like that?"

"I guess I am. I would have gone if you were here when you said you would be. Besides, you never said why you're late."'

"I told you I got sidetracked."

"Sidetracked doing what?"

"What's it to ya?" Shawn defensively demanded. "Are ya comin' or what?"

"What," replied Christian.

"What?"

"Right."

"Huh?"

"I answered 'what' to your question," Christian told him.

"To what?" Shawn was obviously confused by the current conversation.

"You asked if I was coming or what and I said what. In a more simple way, I'm not coming." Turning sharply to face his door, Christian looked back to whisper, "Someone's coming. I gotta go."

With that, Christian shut the window, pulled the shade, and turned off his bedroom light before hopping into bed. Shawn, meanwhile, stood outside in the darkness for a few more moments before leaving.

Over the next week, Christian heard from various neighbors about eggs being splattered on their houses and cars that Halloween night. Even though he had his suspicions, he kept them to himself out of fear that Shawn would get angry with him. After that, the few weeks transpired exactly how the last few had; Christian saw Shawn either at recess or on Mondays for the fights. However, during these weeks, Shawn seemed calmer, less insulting, and not as rude as he once had been.

His grandfather, meanwhile, purchased a speed- and punching-bag, put them up in his apartment, and used them constantly to help regain some of the skill he lost from his youth. Shawn, consequently, appeared at the house more often after this. He began receiving regular instructions on the basics of boxing and Christian's dad insisted that the last thing to do was to teach a future criminal how to fight. Joe would listen to his son's objections but politely said he would keep showing Shawn the basics so long as he remained genuinely interested, tried to do what he was told, and hopefully trust them enough to possibly open up. The first two Shawn did very well at, although the third was taking its time to surface.

The day before the school fair, Christian's mom helped him paint his rocket. It ended up being silver with a yellow lightning bolt at tip and red flames at its base. All day leading up to the fair, he felt like he ate a double helping of butterflies for both breakfast and lunch. He was so nervous he couldn't concentrate during school. He found himself fearing the curse that had plagued him the previous two years would resurface but he would find out that the curse had run its course. Something about the third time being a charm or something or another. The only think that did any plaguing was Christian's rocket. It easily won first place by unanimous decision. He not only received the blue ribbon but also a lot of congratulations, a few pats on the back, one firm handshake from Grandpa Joe, and one big sloppy kiss from his mother.

"I wish Dad had been here to see this," Christian stated in a disappointed manner when it was over.

"He did wish he could be here, sweetie," Sally said while kneeling down to his eyelevel. "He wanted me to say he was sorry for him. Just some of his current projects were talking longer than expected. He just had to stay late at the office to finish them. You understand, don't you honey?"

Hearing this, Christian hung his head and sulked. "Yeah, I guess. Just wish he was here, is all."

"I know, but your father will be so proud of you."

Later that night when Christian showed off his blue ribbon to his father, it didn't garner the response he was hoping for.

"Good job, Christian," his father told him with a pat on the shoulder. "But just remember, it's easy to get to the top. Staying there's the hard part." Then, after saying that, he went to bed.

And, that weekend, as promised, Christian took both his rocket and blue ribbon over to the Deeley's to show them both off. For his efforts, not only did he get a glass of milk and a big piece of apple pie, but he was able to show off his rocket for much longer than he was able to last time.

Thanksgiving came and went without incident. Sally, as usual, made a traditional dinner with all the trimmings. Shawn arrived late, as usual, to the family well into the meal.

"How come you didn't want for me?" he complained in an almost demanding tone when he finally did show up.

"We did wait. Twenty minutes," David told him with obvious annoyance. "If you got here when you told us you would, you would have started with us."

"Something came up!" Shawn stated while shooting him a glare before quickly changing his tone when he realize that David would have no problem throwing him out of their home.

"Something always seem to come up with you. You should have called. You guys have a phone, don't you?" David asked while looking at him from the corner of his eye.

"Yeah, we do, but my dad didn't pay the phone bill again," Shawn told him with a little less defensiveness.

"What the hell does he do with all his money?!" David demanded while getting a disappointed look from Sally as she shook her head. He relaxed a little before continuing. "How many times have I told you to knock before you walk into our house? Do it again and you'll find you won't be able to walk in so freely. And while you're at it, have a seat and fix your plate. The food won't be any better than it is right now."

Other than that, Thanksgiving for the Eaton's went quite smoothly, and for one young Calloway it was as if he had been dreaming the whole day.

The first frost came that night and the first snowfall that following Sunday. Christmas came as fast as Thanksgiving had and, as usual, Sally outdid herself. She also insisted that Shawn come over the night before for dinner. When Shawn arrived, he came precisely at the time he said he would. This brought a comment from David about how Shawn arrived early.

"What do you mean early? I'm right on time," Shawn told him.

"Yes, I know," David replied with a smile. "That makes you early given you're always late."

Within minutes of Shawn's arrival, dinner was served. Ham, mashed potatoes, string beans, fruit cocktail with Jell-O, yams, and anything else associated with Christmas dinner. Dessert included banana crème pie, cherry pie, and chocolate pudding. And, unlike most families who open their presents on Christmas Day, the Eaton's did this the night before after they ate dinner. Sally usually put on Christmas music for the occasion but that night they had TV on because Christian was begging to watch *A Miracle On 34th Street*. Shawn, feeling like he wasn't part of the family yet, made his way to the door in an attempt to leave at this point.

"Where the hell do you think you're going?" David asked him.

"I'm leaving," Shawn told him.

"No you aren't. You think you can just leave after you ate dinner? You're not getting out of here that easy. If I have to stay and open presents, then so do you. Go plant yourself down somewhere and we'll start opening them soon." David sternly pointed back to the living room. Though he made a good attempt, he still wasn't able to conceal a smile on his face. "And, Christian, turn that down so we can hear ourselves think, will you please?"

"Sure thing, Dad," Christian said while obeying his father's command.

Christmas at the Eaton's was something Shawn only saw on TV. There was a big fir in the corner with all the trimmings; decorations spread throughout the house; electrical candles in every window; lit candles in the living room filling the house with the aroma of cinnamon; and all the while a good comfortable heat emanated from the crackling fireplace. This was the first time that not only did Shawn have a Christmas he had always dreamed about, but it was the first Christmas he ever had. Among the gifts he received that night were a new jacket, knit hat, gloves, socks, and other clothes from Sally; a handful of how-to books and magazines, and a new pair of boots from David; and a new gym bag and a pair of boxing gloves from Grandpa Joe. In the bag, Joe had put in a few G.I. Joe's and various boxing magazines.

Christian, on the other hand, had to be pried away from the television. He got clothes from his mother; model kits from his dad; and the best presents from his grandfather: toys. Transformers mostly, but there were a few G.I. Joe's and something he never thought he would get, a VHS copy of *A Miracle on 34th Street*. His mother, being a charmer that she was, was able to get him to finally turn off the TV so she could start playing Christmas music.

After the joy and excitement of opening presents wore off, Grandpa Joe took Shawn up to his apartment so he could try out his new gloves. Sally, meanwhile, cleaned up the wrapping paper and ribbons which now littered the living room floor. Christian turned the TV back on to watch the rest of the movie. His dad gathered his things, gave Sally a kiss, and went down to his workshop in the basement.

When it ended up being just Christian and Sally in the living room, a loud banging was heard coming from the front door. The house seemed to shake in the process. When Sally answered it, a big, burly man was revealed with shoulder length dark hair, dark eyes, and a scraggily, half-filled in beard. He appeared to be very drunk.

"I'm Bruce Calloway, Shawn's old man," he announced with slurred speech and unfocusing eyes. "Where the hell is my boy?"

"Shawn's with my father-in-law in the apartment above our garage, Mr. Calloway," Sally informed him. Tears began to fill her eyes as her hand went to her nose once she got a scent of the booze rolling off of him. "Shall I go get him for you?"

86

"Like hell you will! I'll get him myself," he told her with slurred anger while elbowing his way past her on his way into the house while making his way to the garage by way of the kitchen. "What the hell is wrong with you people?! Keeping a boy from his family at Christmas time. Christmas! Besides, what the hell is your father doing with my boy out there, anyway?"

While staggering his way towards the garage, the stench from sweat and booze overpowered the candles scent. Standing there for a moment longer, Sally soon came back to reality as she quickly went to the basement to get her husband. Meanwhile, Christian shrugged it off the unusually late visit while going back to his movie and toys. When David and Sally came up from downstairs, a commotion from the garage was heard. Christian went out with his parents to see what was going on.

Bruce was just inside Grandpa Joe's apartment pointing his finger at something just inside. "Listen, old man! I don't wanna kill ya and ya don't wanna be dead. Just get the hell outta my way and we'll be outta here real soon," he was heard saying with slurred speech while moving further into the apartment out of view.

After he disappeared fully from view, a loud smack was soon heard as Bruce came staggering back out the apartment's door and down its stairs. While landing on the concrete floor, his head banged hard enough to render him unconscious. Blood was seen flowing from his mouth. Grandpa Joe soon came out of the apartment with raised fists and crazed eyes before realizing there was nothing left to worry about. While quickly shooting a concerned look towards this family, cries from Shawn were heard from behind him.

"David, Sally, call an ambulance! Shawn's hurt up here," he told them before turning to disappear back into his apartment to attend to hurt and crying Shawn.

Chapter 9

"Hi, folks. Are you the ones waiting for Shawn Calloway?" a young, freshly shaven doctor said while approaching them. He appeared to be in his early thirties, had neatly trimmed hair, wore green scrubs, and had massive bags under his eyes. He was carrying a clipboard with what looked like a file or something on it.

"Yes we are," Grandpa Joe said. "How's he doing?"

"He's doing fine. He just had a dislocated shoulder, which you seemed to have set before he came in," the doctor explained while looking at them behind suspicious eyes. "We gave him a sedative to help him rest."

Hearing this, Joe smiled softly as he nodded his head. "Good, good. And his father?"

"Oh, you mean Bruce?" The doctor chuckled while making it sound more like a statement than a question. "Outside of a concussion and a couple of teeth being knocked loose, he'll live. Cockroaches like that are hard to kill." At that moment, there was a momentary pause as the doctor looked at each of the Eaton's while acting like there was something he wanted to say. "So, um, what really happened tonight?"

"Well," Sally said after clearing her throat. "Mr. Calloway came to our home looking for his son. He went to get him from the apartment he have above our garage for my father-in-law. When he went out there, I went to get my husband who was in our basement workshop."

Hearing this, the doctor merely turned his attention to David.

Returning the look, David picked up the story where his wife left off. "When I got upstairs we heard an argument coming from the garage. When we got out there, Bruce Calloway was in the process of falling backwards from the above apartment. Him landing on the floor is what knocked him out."

When he finished, everyone turned their attention to Grandpa Joe, who remained silent.

"And what happened in the apartment, sir?" the doctor politely, but firmly, asked.

"I had given the boy a new pair of boxing gloves for Christmas," Joe simply stated before clearing his throat and looking at the floor. "We were in my apartment trying them out when a man claiming to be the boy's father barged in and demanded that Shawn go with him. When the boy refused to leave, his father grabbed him by the arm and pulled him hard towards the door. This is what dislocated his shoulder. The sound when that happened was awful."

When he said this, Joe went silent and continued to stare at the floor. When it was evident he wasn't going to say anymore, the doctor spoke.

"Then what happened, sir?"

"I asked him to leave."

"You asked him to leave?" questioned the doctor before going quiet. A small smile soon appeared on his face. "May I assume you didn't ask nicely?"

"Yes, you may assume that." Joe returned the smile. "As a matter of fact, I punched him in the face which he apparently wasn't expecting. This is what sent him down the stairs and out of my apartment."

"I should say I'm sorry about what happened to him but I'm not. Not for the father, anyway, but I am for Shawn, though," the doctor stated while flipping through the file he was holding onto. "This is the first time I've actually seen the father and the first time I've seen Shawn since late August or early September."

"What do you mean, Doctor?" Sally inquired as she briefly looked to David.

While continuing to look through Shawn's file, the doctor answered. "I shouldn't say anything with the whole patient-doctor confidentiality thing, but Shawn's been here before. Multiple times in face. So has his mother, Karen, though a few of her visits were different."

"What sort of visits?" Grandpa Joe asked while still looking down to the floor.

"Both have been here on several occasions over the past eighteen to twenty-four months or so for various scraps, cuts, bruises, broken bones, dislocations, blackened or swollen eyes, that sort of thing. You name it and they probably came here with that as an injury."

"What were the reasons for these visits?" David asked.

While finally looking up from the file, the doctor met David's gaze while sucking on his teeth before answering. "Their favorite line has always been that they fell."

"Off the record, what do you think happened?" Joe inquired.

While looking at them from under his brow while once again flipping through the file, the doctor says, "Honestly? That their full of shit. That, or they're brain damaged. Probably both for all I know. Off the record of course."

Christian, at this point, finally woke up from his half asleep slumber when the doctor swore. Like his grandson, Joe looked up while Sally started sniffing a little. David did his best to console his wife.

"I'm sorry for my language but I'm tired and it's been a slightly busy shift," the doctor apologized while rubbing his eyes. A yawn soon escaped his mouth. "I mean, they come in here with hand prints around their necks and arms and yet they say they got them from a fall. I don't know, maybe it's me."

"Doctor, you said that a few of the mother's visits were different. How so?" Grandpa Joe probed.

"I'm sorry, but I can't get into that. Doctor-patient privilege. I'm sorry," the young doctor simply said while looking around to see if anyone was listening.

"It wouldn't have been drugs, would it?" David questioned while the doctor looked back to meet his gaze with a weary smile. "What's her drug of choice now, cocaine?"

"Heroine, actually, but you didn't hear that from me. Some people are lawsuit happy, you know."

"What's going to happen to Shawn, Doctor?" Sally asked.

"Since no one's answering at his home, I guess he'll have to stay her for the night," the doctor replied in an offbeat tone that seemed to mean more of a hint than an actual comment. "Too bad there isn't someplace safe and warm he could go."

Looking at her husband with pleading eyes, Sally says, "David, could he come home with us tonight? After all, it *is* Christmas."

"Where would we put him?" her husband asked in a tone saying he didn't want Shawn to go home with them. "It's not like we have an extra bed ready for him."

"He can stay with me," Grandpa Joe told him. "In my place."

"Well, if it's ok with the doctor then it's ok with me," David told him. "But just remember, he'll be your responsibility. Ok?"

Grandpa Joe merely nodded to that.

"So, Doctor...?" Sally started but left the ending open.

Smiling, the doctor said, "I'll need to ask you folks to fill out some release forms up at the nurse's station for him when you can. You know, the whole legal thing."

"Um, Doctor? What about his dad, you know, Mr. Calloway?" Christian asked nervously. "Will he be released tonight, too?"

"No, son, he won't. Not tonight anyway. The police will want to talk to him when he wakes up, which should be soon. They've been waiting to talk with him shortly after he was brought in. Shawn will be ready to leave once you're done filling out the paperwork, ok? And I hope you folks have a good Christmas." When he was done talking, the doctor closed Shawn's file and turned to leave before vanishing into a crowd of loners, drunken has-beens, and other cases in need of medical attention.

The Eaton's left about a half hour later with an added member to their party.

The next morning Christian woke to the smells of food his mom was fixing. Joyous sounds of Christmas music and laughter from his parents were heard. The sound of his dad laughing was almost an oddity, but, being Christmas morn, always brought out his more carefree side.

As Christian entered the kitchen, he asked, "Where's Shawn?"

"He's still sleeping, dear," his mom told him while bringing over a plate of food for him. She shook her head a little with that comment before going back to what she was making. To Christian, it appeared to be some kind of soup or something.

"Poor thing. He passed out last night as soon as he got here." "Yeah and your grandfather's not here if you're wondering," David added with a smile. "He's been gone for quite some time. Left early this morning."

"Where'd he go?" Christian asked while cramming a wad of scrambled eggs into his mouth.

"Shawn's place. Apparently to pay his parents a visit." David chuckled to himself while getting himself some coffee.

"Really? Aw, man!" Christian complained. "And he didn't wait for me? I would've gone with him."

"You'll get your chance one day, I suspect. Given your grandfather's mood when he left, it may have been best he went alone."

Once Christian was done with breakfast, he went into the living room to watch the movie and play with the toys that he had gotten the night before. Roughly halfway through, Grandpa Joe came home in a fiery mood rarely seen.

"Goddamn it! Those sons-of-bitches!" he exclaimed foully while removing his coat. He threw it on a kitchen chair before continuing on with his rant. "People like that should think long and hard about getting abortions as part of their insurances plans!"

"Dad!" Sally said. "Don't say such horrible things."

"Well, it's true!" Joe sat down at the table with a shake of the head.

"It went that well, huh?" David asked while sitting down next to his father.

"Worse," Joe told him while looking around the kitchen for the first time. "Oh, where's Shawn?"

"He's still sleeping," Sally told him. "I checked in on him a little while back."

"Still in bed?" Joe questioned while looking at his watch. "It's almost 11:30."

"Let him be; he's had a long night. And, besides, it's Christmas."

"I know, I know, but his family is, you know…?" Grandpa Joe grumbled while rubbing his face in annoyance.

"A waste of space?" his son asked while flipping through that morning's paper.

"To say the least," Joe muttered behind his hands which were still rubbing his face. "I spoke with Shawn's mother, Karen I think her name is. Apparently his father, Bruce, hadn't come home yet from last night. All she knew was he left last night for Shawn and he didn't come back. She didn't seem too worried about him. My impression was that he's done this sort of thing before, you know, left and been gone all night that is."

"At least she's having a good Christmas so far," his son commented sarcastically from behind his paper.

"What happened while you were there, Dad?" Sally asked while sitting at the table with a pot of fresh coffee and an extra mug.

"Well, I went there just to talk to his parents for what it's worth, though I knew most likely it would be a waste of my time. When it was just Karen there, I gave her an overview of last night's events. What pissed my old, wrinkly ass off the most was that the just didn't seem to care." Pausing, Grandpa Joe was both annoyed and irritated as he looked off out the window. "Didn't seem to care that her husband hurt their son. Didn't care that her husband was hurt. Didn't care that Bruce hadn't come home yet. Just…didn't care. She just seemed to be off in her own little fantasy world there in that rundown, condemned pigsty they call a trailer."

Once again, he paused long enough to get his thoughts together while pouring himself a cup of coffee. He sat silent so long that Christian thought he was all done talking until he cleared his throat to continue.

"You should have seen that place. If I had passed that place under any other situation, I would have assumed it was vacant. There was more furniture outside than in; and what furniture they did have inside was covered with beer bottles and ashtrays. It reeked of alcohol, cigarette smoke, and dog shit. The dog that they had was this timid little pit-bull that was way underfed. Karen had puncture marks on the underside of her arm by her elbow," he said while pointing to the same area on his arm to show where he meant. "Some of them where fresh, recent, but most of them were bruised over. I can't believe Shawn lives in that shithole."

"No wonder he's always over here with you, Dad, especially in this colder weather," Sally said to no one in particular.

"Hey, David, how much does his old man make there at the plant?" Joe asked his son.

"I don't know, 30, 35 thousand I think."

"$30,000? Where the hell does it all go to?"

"You just answered it," his son told him while finally lowering his paper to drink some of his coffee. "Beer, cigarettes, and drugs mostly. Hospital visits are also another expensive hobby they seem to have."

"Can't child services do anything for Shawn?" Sally asked.

"Apparently not." Joe got up to stretch his back before walking towards the garage. "I'm going to see how he's doing."

A minute or so later, he reentered the kitchen only to stand there in silence with a perplexed look on his face.

"What's the matter?" David asked him.

"He's gone."

"Who's gone? Shawn?" his daughter-in-law asked him.

"Yep. Shawn. He's gone," Joe replied while remaining to stand there with his hands on his hips. He thought for a moment before sitting back down to finish his now cold coffee. "He's gone and so is the stuff we gave him last night. The only thing that he left were his boxing mitts, which were left where we put them last night."

"Looks like your adopted son left in a hurry," Christian heard his dad say. "Speaking of which, do you still have the receipt?"

"The receipt for what?"

"Those boxing gloves."

"I should. Why?"

"So we can return them," David told his father.

"Return 'em? Why would I do that?"

"He's the one that left them, not you," David patiently explained. "Just makes sense that if he wanted them, he would have taken them with him."

"No, he wants 'em," Joe informed his son.

"How do you know that?" questioned David. "Did he tell you he did?"

"No, he didn't tell me. You know Shawn. Besides, that's not what we should be worrying about at the moment."

While putting down his paper, David sighed before looking at his father. "And what should we be worrying about? Trying to find that kid so he can screw us over again?"

"You're goddamned right we find him!" Joe bellowed with anger in his voice while his hands went through his hair. "We own him that much."

"We owe him that?" his son questioned him with raised eyebrows. "He's not our responsibility. Hell, he's not even your responsibility. We don't owe him anything."

"David, how can you say that?" Sally asked him in shock. "It's Christmas!"

"Christmas has nothin to do with it! And Dad's not his father," David grumbled while attempting to go back to his paper.

"I'm more of a father to him than his old man is; and I'm not going to stop now to make you happy," Grandpa Joe told him bluntly before getting up to go to the living room.

"Have it your way, Dad. Have it your way," David said while opening the business section.

"Hey, Christian," Grandpa Joe said while approaching his grandson who was still immersed in front of the TV watching his movie. "Shawn's gone. Do you have any idea where he might have run off to?"

While waiting for a response, Christian had fast forwarded the movie to the climatic courtroom scene at the end while watching it intently.

"Hey, did you hear what I just asked you?" Joe asked him with an edge to his voice.

"Yes, Grandpa," Christian mumbled absently while not taking his eyes off the TV screen. "He might be out at his spot by the stream."

"What spot?"

"In the woods."

"Alright then. Let's go," Joe told his grandson while walking back to the kitchen.

Hearing this, Christian's eyes finally blinked while coming back to reality as he focused his attention to this grandfather. "Go? Go where?"

"To the stream, of course," Joe patiently told him. "We're going to go find Shawn. Grab what you need and meet me in the garage."

"Aw, Grandpa! Do I have to?" Christian whined. "The movie's almost over."

"Do as your grandfather says," David scolded while looking at his son. "You can watch the movie later. Besides, you've seen it countless times."

"Yes, Dad." Sulking, Christian got up, turned off the television, and went up to his room to get ready for the winter's cold.

When Christian was upstairs, David got up. "I'd better get to work now; I only took the morning off," he told them before putting on his coat. After kissing his wife, he went out to his car and left.

Five minutes after this, Christian and Joe stepped outside to embark on the journey of a lifetime, one that would change their lives forever, although they didn't know it at the time – the journey to find Shawn.

When they finally arrived to Shawn's usual spot at the stream, Grandpa Joe pointed to recent tracks marking the snow.

"Looks like someone was here recently," he said while pointing to them with his hand. While taking a closer look at them, he realized they were fresh and one track looked roughly the size of a duffle bag. Turning his gaze as he used his hand to follow the tracks upstream, he saw them turn down an adjacent path. "The tracks look roughly the size and shape of the boots we gave him last night. Where do they lead, Christian?"

"That way goes to the train tracks, " he said while going over to a big indentation near the stream. " It looks like he sat here for a while."

"Didn't you say something about having to pass the tracks to get to his house from here?"

"Yeah, but I was just repeating what Shawn said, Grandpa," Christian told him while finding something on the ground that he pawed at with his foot. "Look, yellow snow."

Smiling, Grandpa Joe asked, "Did he pass?"

"Pass what?"

"His drug test."

"Huh?"

Shaking his head and trying not to laugh, Joe simply shook his head. "Nothing. Never mind. Let's go; it looks like he went home. Come on, let's get this over with. Your mom would skin us alive if we're late for dinner."

Kicking away the rest of the yellow snow before following his grandfather, they continued on the path before disappearing into the trees towards the tracks. Several minutes later, they reappeared by the tracks roughly in the same spot Shawn had taken Christian months earlier. They took the way Shawn had before soon coming upon a colony of rundown trailers. There were a dozen or so broken-down things sporadically spread over a couple acres of land. It looked as if a tornado had been through, picking up and casually throwing them back down to let them fall where they will. The appearance of each indicated people were at the end of their ropes.

Christian remembered being told multiple times how lucky and fortunate he was to have the kind of life that he had, especially after he complained about something being unfair. He had also been told to count his blessings because there were people who would do anything to have a life like his. He knew he had it good, that he honestly had no reason to legitimately be upset, and knew he was comfortable with all the necessitates his family had provided for him. He had everything he currently needed and most everything he wanted.

However comfortable and nice his family was to him, they did have one flaw, though that one flaw was out of love and respect for him. This flaw failed to give him one important gift that he never had until now. Ironically, it wasn't his family who gave him this gift in the end. In a manner of speaking, the Calloway's were the ones who were generous enough to give it to him. This gift in question was to see people living in a situation much worse than his own. A way of living that would be unfit for even the worse criminals. Christian simply would have passed them for being desolated if it wasn't for cars or other vehicles parked next to them or smoke rising out of what chimney's they had.

Christian kept walking on the path past the neglected trailers when he finally noticed he was the only one still walking. He turned to see his grandfather standing in front of one of the empty, unwell trailers. Confused, he approached to inquire what might be the matter. As he neared, a small puff of smoke rose from a pipe coming out of the roof; apparently its version of a chimney. Every window appeared to have been broken before then being covered with thick, clear plastic that was either stapled or nailed around it. There was no porch, front step, or railing; only a big concrete block lay in their stead. The roof was two big pieces of sheet metal, one for each side. A makeshift doghouse sat next to that as a scrawny pit-bull lay inside. It barked a couple of times at them but didn't bother to get up. She shivered endlessly in an effort to warm herself.

"Hey, um, Grandpa? Why'd you stop?" Christian asked him when he walked up to him. "Weren't we going to Shawn's place?"

"Yeah, we're going to Shawn's alright," Grandpa Joe answered him somberly while looking to his grandson with an extremely serious look upon his face. "This is it. This *is* Shawn's place."

Before Christian could say anything to this, a child's cry for help came from inside. Without hesitating, Grandpa Joe came to attention, sprinted to the door, and forced his way inside. When Christian entered the trailer seconds later, and was finally able to catch up to his grandfather, he saw a sight he wished he had not seen.

There, before his kneeling grandfather, Shawn lay on the floor with a woman's upper body on his lap. Christian wasn't able to tell if she was alive or not, but was able to tell that she was definitely wasn't conscious. Shawn, meanwhile, caressed her head while massive tears fell on her face while he pleaded to her.

"Momma, please, wake up. Wake up, Momma," Shawn continually begged as his tears streamed down his cheeks. "Please, Momma. I'll be a good boy, I promise. I'll be anything you want, just wake up. Please, just wake up, will you? Wake up, Momma…"

He continued pleading while shaking her until her left arm slide off her body and onto the floor. Looking at it, Christian saw a syringe coming out of its bruised forearm.

Chapter 10

"It looks like you guys are having one helluva Christmas this year," the same young, freshly shaven doctor who spoke to them the night before said as he approached. He looked wearier and more sleep deprived then he had before. "I hope this won't be habit forming for you folks."

"Doctor," Grandpa Joe said with a brief nod. "This visit of ours, I assure you, isn't by choice."

"That makes me feel better." The doctor smiled slightly while shifting his attention onto Shawn. "How are you doing, young man?"

"I'm fine," Shawn answered through dried tears while trying to act tougher then how he felt. He avoided any type of eye contact by looking at the floor.

"Are you now?"

"Yeah, I am! Why wouldn't I be?!" Shawn demanded while shooting a glare up at the doctor.

"Easy, Shawn," Grandpa Joe softly told him while putting a hand on Shawn's shoulder which was immediately shrugged off. Joe soon looked back to the doctor. "I'm sorry about that."

"That's alright," replied the doctor while returning his gaze back to Shawn. The file which he held was closed in the process. "The reason why I asked how you were doing was because you've had two very traumatic days; last night as a result of your father and then today when your mom almost died in your arms."

"They were nothing. I've had worse days at home. These are some of the better ones," Shawn said cockily before realizing what he had just been told while looking up at the doctor. While trying hard to fight back the tears, his eyes soon widened as a smile appeared on his face. "Did you say *almost* died?"

Returning the smile, the young doctor stated, "Yes, as a matter of fact I did. It was fortunate your friends showed up just shy of too late."

"So my mom's alive?!" Shawn asked while whipping his eyes in disbelief.

"Yes, yes she is, though only just."

"How's she doing, Doctor?" Sally asked.

"It's still too early to tell," he responded while flipping back through the now open file. "Shawn, do you have any other relatives at all?"

He answered only with a shake of the head.

"Don't you have a brother you'd want to notify about this?"

"He's busy," Shawn answered quickly while looking at the floor.

Hearing this, the doctor quickly looked to Shawn. "Busy? May I inquire what he's busy doing?"

"Twenty to life the last I heard."

Hearing this, Christian quickly shifted his attention to Shawn with confused eyes and gaping mouth. He was about to say something when he looked to his grandfather, who was looking back at him while shaking his head.

"Now's not the time to be asking about his brother," Joe quietly told his grandson. "I'll explain later when we have a chance."

"I'm sorry to hear that, young man," the doctor said with compassion in his voice. "You don't have any other family for us to inform?"

"Doctor," Grandpa Joe spoke then, "it would appear that we're the closest thing to a family that he has at the moment. What you've got to say, you can say to us."

Initially silent and thoughtful on the subject, the doctor soon nodded before pulling a nearby chair over to sit down on. After he was comfortable, he skimmed the file in his hands while clearing his throat to speak.

"Ok, let's see where to begin," he said while pausing momentarily. "Alright. Shawn, as you know, your mother was in very bad shape when she arrived. She was unconscious, as you were also aware, as a direct result of a drug overdose. We were able to revive and stabilize her, as well as sedate her to help keep her calm. From the years of hard living, she's very, very lucky to be alive. The drugs and alcohol, combined with an extremely poor diet, has taken a very heavy toll on her body and organs. We've contacted a number of rehab centers in the area in search of help for her. There are two in the Syracuse area that are good that I'd recommend she go to when she's released from here."

After saying that, the doctor nodded his head while closing the file, placed it on his lap, and looked to Shawn before continuing to speak.

"Do you have anywhere to stay temporarily until this mess is taken care of?" he sympathetically asked.

Hearing the question at hand, Shawn wasn't able to control his melancholy emotions any further. His tear ducts slowly opened up as tears dropped into his hands.

Seeing this, the good doctor quickly turned this attention to Grandpa Joe. "Joe, ah, as far as you know, does the boy have any place he can stay for a while?"

"He'll be staying with us for the time being until this affair is over with," Joe softly informed him.

Hearing this, Christian became very excited at the prospect of having Shawn stay with them. He started anxiously moving about in his chair which drew the looks, and smiles, from the doctor and his grandfather, as well as a teary side-glance from Shawn. Christian, however, noticed Shawn went back to staring at the floor while trying hard to fight back his tears.

"Alight," the doctor said with a satisfied nod while looking back to Shawn. "Now, if you need or want someone to talk to about this, we have a number of really good people here at the hospital that can help you out."

"I'm fine," Shawn softly stated.

Smiling, the doctor said, "That's right, I do apologize. In that case, would you like to see your mother?"

Perplexed by what he had just been asked, Shawn instantly looked up the doctor before him. "Can I?!"

"Of course you can," the doctor confirmed. "I wouldn't have asked if you couldn't. Mrs. Eaton, would you mind taking him to see his mother?"

"No, not at all, Doctor," she immediately said while standing.

"Thank-you. She's right down the hall. Third door on the right past the nurses' station," said the doctor while waving his tired hand in the general direction.

With that, Sally led both Shawn and Christian down the hallway to search for Karen Calloway's room.

"And, Joe," the physician said when they were out of earshot, "while they're doing that, may I have a word with you, please?"

"Of course. Please lead the way," Joe answered while standing to follow.

Christian was the one who found Karen's room first, but was immediately pushed aside by Shawn when he made his way inside. At first, Christian felt like Shawn didn't recognize the woman but, once he determined that it was his mother, he opened cried.

The woman, Christian noticed, was fairly slender with long, matted brown hair. Her face was pale and had large, dark bags beneath sunken eyes. The inside of each arm were heavily bruised; and there were wires and tubes coming out of every possible part of her body. There was a heart monitor, a ventilator to help give her air, three IVs he saw that each pumped some sort of fluid into her malnourished body, and a handful of other things he didn't recognize.

When focusing back onto Shawn, Christian noticed he was saying basically the same thing to hear as he did earlier in the day at their trailer. He was begging her to wake up and pleading any possible deal if she did so. Christian, feeling embarrassed for witnessing such a private moment between the two, looked around to see his mom sitting in the corner. He walked over to her before sitting on the floor. They each watched Shawn briefly as he cried what remaining tears he had inside him.

***

Roughly an hour later, after several depressing hours, Shawn, Christian, Joe, and Sally finally left the hospital. On their way home, they had stopped off at Shawn's place for him to pick up whatever essentials he would need for his stay with them. He grabbed what clothes he had, his Walkman, several cassettes of music, miscellaneous items, and Lucky, the scrawny pit-bull who was still shivering in her doghouse. Despite what Shawn said about his ferocious beast of a dog, she quickly jumped into the back seat, curled up, and fell asleep between the two boys. Their next stop was the grocery store where Sally bought several bags of groceries and two bags of dog food. When they finally did get back home, Lucky was so excited at the new environment she began running around the garage and barking at the top of her lungs.

Hearing the commotion, David stuck his head out into the garage before demanding, "What the hell is going on out here?"

"Shawn's moving into my place for a little bit," his father calmly explained while removing Shawn's belongings from the trunk.

While taking a step out into the garage, David stated, "What do you mean he's moving in? I didn't say he could."

"No, you didn't," his father told him calmly. "Sally and I did."

"This is still my house. Besides, isn't there any friends or family he could stay with?"

"Yes," Joe said while continuing to unload the car. "He has us."

"Besides us. Isn't there anyone else?"

At this point, Sally grabbed two bags of groceries from the trunk and walked past her husband into the kitchen. "Take it easy, dear, please. It's only temporary and he won't really be moving in with us. Shawn will be staying with your father. The doctor had hinted at us taking him in since we're the closest thing to family he's got."

"That's it then? He's staying here because the doctor hinted at it?!" David demanded while following his wife back into the house and watched her put the groceries on the counter.

"The doctor said that since he didn't have any other friends or family in the area, the only choice would have been foster care," Sally informed him while putting the groceries on the counter before starting to unload them. "Oh, dear, would you please go out and grab the bags of dog food for me, please?"

"Yeah, him staying here probably would be better than foster ca...wait. Did you just say dog food?"

"Yes, dear, I did. There should be two bags out in the trunk."

"Why is there dog food in the car?" David asked while quickly looking back out into the garage to see Christian petting Lucky. "And why is there a dog out in the garage?"

"Her name is apparently Lucky and she's Shawn's dog. You wouldn't want them to have just left the poor thing there, would you?" Sally innocently asked while coming over to give her husband a kiss. "Don't worry. It's only temporary. Both Shawn and Lucky will be staying with your father."

100

"There's no use arguing about this, is there?" he said while looking at his wife who was smiling sweetly at him. "Goddamn dog! It better not make a mess or there'll be hell to pay. I'm going to hold you to your word, you hear me? Only temporary." With that, he walked out into the garage to get the dog food. After that, he helped his father finish moving Shawn into the apartment while Sally started making supper.

At dinner, Grandpa Joe informed his son of the day's events starting with what happened after David had left for work. According to Shawn, he came down for breakfast and overheard them talking about him. While getting upset at the fact they were talking about him behind his back, he left soon afterwards to go home. Joe chimed in here to say that Shawn took that as a form of betrayal. At that, the Eaton's all assured Shawn the best they could that they were worried and cared about him, even David. Sally picked up here by telling her husband that Karen would be staying in a local rehab center until she got clean. A number of family members had been notified of the Calloway's situation, but none had been willing or able to take in Shawn for the time being. Bruce, on the other hand, was released from the hospital sometime in the night and was spending Christmas in a dry, warm jail cell. The police were holding him for trespassing and assault. They would hold him until his drunkenness wore off and, at which point, he could post bail. His court date was set in two weeks.

"I guess I'll have to have a talk with him come Monday at work," David commented out loud. "I'll tell him what happened if he does show up. In the meantime, I think it's safe to say that you'll be staying here with us, Shawn."

"What about Lucky? Can she stay, too?" Shawn immediately asked while smiling at his current change of living situation while absently rubbing Lucky's ear.

"Oh, alright. If you insist," David said with feigned hesitation while chuckling, rolling his eyes, and shaking his head all at once. "But if she makes any kind of a mess in the house, I'll hold *you* personally responsible. Deal?"

"Alright. Deal." Shawn smiled before going back to eat.

"What do you say to him?" Grandpa Joe asked while looking over to Shawn.

With a confused look, Shawn asked, "Huh? What was that?"

"Times like this, saying thank-you would be an appropriate response for him letting both you and Lucky stay. So, again, what do you say to him?"

"Why would I thank him? It was you and Mrs. Eaton that said I could come here, and it's you that I'm staying with, not him," Shawn said while flicking a thumb to David. "I don't need to thank him. If I do have to thank anyone, it's you and Mrs. Eaton."

"Well, that is true," Grandpa Joe reluctantly admitted while attempting think at how to word what he was about to say. "But Mrs. Eaton just got you here and it's me that you're staying with tonight. However, this is still my son's house. It came down to what he had to say should you and Lucky stay any longer after. After all, we all have a say. And your say should be thank-you."

"And if I don't?" Shawn angrily asked.

"To some people that could be misinterpreted as an insult," Grandpa Joe tactfully worded his response.

"And those people that might take it as an insult might have you find another spot to stay," David injected while looking at Shawn from under his brow.

"Come on, Shawn," Sally said softly while leaning in to put a hand on his forearm, which was quickly jerked back. "Just a simple thank-you to him, won't you please? It'll make him think that you're not trying to use him."

"Well, um, in that case, thank-you Mr. Eaton," Shawn finally said with much reluctance.

"Thank-you for what exactly?" Grandpa Joe pressed with a smile.

"Ah, thank-you for lettin' me and Lucky stay here for a while," Shawn said while hanging his head in embarrassment while feeling ashamed for almost being forced to say that, almost as if he was submitting everything to someone else but him.

"That wasn't that hard to say, was it?" David asked. "And you're very welcome."

"Not hard for you. You weren't the one who had to say it," Shawn grumbled before eating the rest of his meal in silence.

The rest of the meal quickly faded to the end of the week. Everything went with the usual formalities in the Eaton household while Shawn was soaking it up. He joked to Grandpa Joe that it had been awhile since he and his dog had slept in a dry, warm place though it was obvious he wasn't. Sally had commented that weekend that she was glad Bruce hadn't stopped by. Upon hearing that, David quickly seconded it.

That Monday after David came home from work, he appeared more agitated than he normally did. He seemed to grumble more at things but, strangely, kept his comments to himself. During supper he was also excessively quiet; a part of the day that he himself often encourage the rest of the family to say what they had done during the events of the day. After dinner was concluded, David suggested that Christian and Shawn go up to his dad's apartment and get ready for the fights later in the night and that Grandpa Joe would soon be up. When Shawn protested because he wanted to stay with Joe, the elder Eaton said that they just needed to talk a bit before he did go up.

"Don't you mean you want to talk about me and my family behind my back?" Shawn demanded.

"That's one of the things we were going to discuss, yes," David admitted. "But there were also a number of other things we needed to talk about as well."

"Why do you always talk about me when I'm not here, huh?!" Shawn questioned while standing up in anger. "Is this what Christmas is all about? A chance to make someone feel good about themselves only to then find a way to talk about them behind their back?"

"Shawn, please, take it easy," Grandpa Joe softly said while raising his palms as he tried to calm down Shawn. "No one here is trying to upset you. David, Sally, and I were going to discuss your situation for a little bit to try to decide what we should do before we…"

Backing up when he heard this, Shawn's eyes got really wide. "My situation?! What do you mean by my situation?"

"The situation with your parents and where you may be staying for a while, dear," Sally informed him as gently as possible.

"Shawn, I have an idea," David said while leaning back in his chair as he put his chin down to his chest in thought. "If you want, why don't you and Christian go into the living room and watch the fights in there rather than up in my father's apartment? That way, you get to hear a little bit of what we're saying and you still get to watch boxing at the same time. After we're done here, we'll then tell you a condensed, formal overview on what we'll plan on doing. How does that sound?"

"I still don't know why I can't stay here," Shawn told him.

"Let me put it to you a little differently, Shawn," David told him while leaning forward to look at him straight in the eye. "We'll be able to concentrate better if you weren't in the room with us and we'll come up with a decision a whole lot faster. Meanwhile, you'll be in the next room watching the fights while being able to hear what we're saying. Alright?"

"Sounds like a win-win situation if you ask me," Grandpa Joe added.

"Yeah, but no one's asking you," Shawn quickly told him before looking back at David. He soon resigned while shaking his head before saying, "Fine, have it your way." He left the kitchen as a sigh of frustration was heard. He went to the living room, sat down next to Christian, and started watching the beginning of the fights.

Although Christian wasn't able to hear what Shawn was saying, he did hear him mutter something all the way there. Once Shawn had sat down next to him, Christian came back to reality. While glancing over to him, Christian noticed Shawn held his head down and had gloomy eyes. His dad, meanwhile, was hiding behind the Business section of that day's paper, a section he already read, while his eyes would periodically pop around to look at them on the couch. Grandpa Joe, on the other hand, was the only one of the three that was looking at them. He was slouched over the table as his left arm rested on the table as its fingertips gently rubbed his brow which covered thoughtful, emotion filled eyes. His right arm laid on the table as its hand held a steaming cup of coffee.

"…and in the blue corner weighing in at an even 168 pounds…" the ring announcer's voice stated from the television which drew Christian's attention back to it. Almost immediately afterwards, conversations in the neighboring room started.

Over the next hour or so, the family talked amongst themselves. David started by informing them of his encounters with Bruce that morning. Bruce had come into work late and immediately went to David's office to confront him about what he and his family were doing to Shawn. Bruce accused him of keeping his son from his family, brainwashing him against them, and the added stress was what caused Karen to overdose, which he only found out about that morning.

While trying to explain to Bruce that Shawn was merely spending time with his father, Bruce quickly interrupted David with the accusation that Grandpa Joe was some dirty old man who wanted to get his rocks off by committing unnatural sexual acts with his son, if he hadn't already. David did his best to assure Bruce that wasn't the case. He told him that Shawn was over mainly to watch the fights on Monday nights, to get help with school work occasionally, and to get boxing lessons, all of which were provided by Joe. And on the nights Shawn was there late, he would also have dinner with them.

David seemed to laughed when he then informed the family that Bruce said he had noticed a change in his son's demeanor since he had been spending time with them the last several months. He claimed that Shawn wasn't as aggressive, was more polite, and had been getting letters from school saying what an improvement he'd made that year. Bruce went on to accuse him of turning his son into a brainy, cowardly pushover. Bruce finished his tantrum by demanding that Shawn return home that night or else he'd have the family arrested on grounds of kidnapping.

"Is that what he said?" Sally asked in a stunned manner. "Can he actually do that? And do you think he'd actually try?"

Laughing at that, David got up to fix himself another cup of coffee. "That is what he said, but it's anybody's guess on whether or not he'd actually attempt it. I'm thinking he's just all bluster, but there's still a chance."

"What did you tell him?" Joe asked.

"I told him I'd be more than happy to oblige but he would have to start acting like a father if we did," David told his father as he return to the table and sat down. "Of course he didn't get the point so I was obliged to inform him on a few things of what the courts would look for. Things such as adequate shelter, heat in the winter, a good supply of food in the kitchen, access to a phone for emergencies, and, most important, sober adult supervision who takes a positive, active role in Shawn's upbringing and development. I went on to say that he, Bruce, would have to meet all the required things to give Shawn a healthy home life or else child services might be informed on his shortcomings. In which case, they would take Shawn from him and place him into foster care, foster care in which he would be required by law to financially contribute to. To make a long story short, Bruce wasn't happy and he cried blackmail. He left shortly thereafter but not before making a mess of my office."

"What do we do in the meantime?" Sally ask while getting up to go to the counter. Once there, she grabbed the coffee pot, brought it back to refill both David's and Joe's mugs before pouring the rest in her cup. She sat back down after this.

"There's nothing much we can do. Legally, Shawn's not our responsibility." David shrugged with a sigh. "If Bruce did go to the police, most likely Shawn would go back to his parents and we would be ordered not to have contact with him again. But, on the other hand, once Shawn was back home and child services were to get a call informing them of his living situations, chances are he would be removed and placed into foster care."

"Could he live with us should he ever get placed in foster care?" Grandpa Joe asked. "That way he's not really at home, but yet we won't get into trouble either."

"I'm not really sure how that would work," his son admitted as he leaned back in his chair in thought. "However, one of my old employees, Brian Bise, is in that line of work now. Child care, foster care, something like that. I have his number at the office. I'll try to give him a call tomorrow."

"Before we even talk about that, maybe we should ask Shawn to see what he wants to do," Joe suggested before rubbing his face.

"I agree. We should give him that much," Sally added.

"Would we have enough room for him if he were to stay here on a more permanent basis?" David asked as his eyes filtered up to focus on a spot on the ceiling.

"We'll make the room!" his father exclaimed. "Shawn has a lot of potential and deserves better than that. He's just starting to take an interest in things. There's no way I'll let him go back to that shithole if I can help it."

"I'm sorry, Dad, but it's not really your decision," David told his father as mildly as he could.

"Shouldn't it be Shawn's choice, though? Shouldn't we ask him about this?" Sally probed.

Then, out of nowhere, a voice came from the living room doorway. "I'm staying."

Turning, the three Eaton adults saw Shawn there in the doorway looking at them.

"What was that, Shawn?" asked Sally.

"I said I'm staying, here," he repeated in a firmer, more confident tone. "That is, if I have any choice to it."

"You sure?" David asked directly.

"Yep."

Hearing that, Grandpa Joe nodded while looking to his son. "Then it's settled."

"And I guess that means I'll be giving Brian a call tomorrow," David announced while looking at Shawn. "Tomorrow night we'll all know if this is something we can, or want to, pursue."

Chapter 11

As January waned, Shawn was making himself quite at home with the Eaton's. As promised, David called his former employee, a one Mr. Brian Bise, regarding his situation. To his surprise, the longer Shawn stayed, the more he felt part of a family for the first time in his life, and the more he was also beginning to enjoy Christian's company. However odd and quirky Shawn found him to be, Christian was slowly becoming one of his first, true friends. Christian, on the other hand, was still at the same high intensity as he was a month ago when he learned Shawn would be staying there for the time being; and finally felt he was getting a friend he badly desired.

Brian Bise, after receiving David's phone call, went and inspected Shawn's living conditions. Well before leaving, Brian had made his mind up to pull Shawn from his family in hopes of placing him in a more proper home life. Since Shawn had been staying with the Eaton's, and they had all the necessity requirements that child services were looking for, Brian didn't see any need to pull him from that household as well. While speaking to the Eaton's at length over dinner one evening, Brian told them that if they were serious about this, the first thing they would need to do was apply for legal guardianship over Shawn, which they did that very same week and Brian signed off on it that next day. The hardest thing after that was the waiting, which the courts, they found, were very generous with at times. It could happen as soon as a month or be as long as three. By the beginning of February, the courts had not yet made a ruling.

Shawn's mother, Karen, had went to rehab the week after Christmas to a center outside of Syracuse. Joe and Sally would take him nearly every day after school to see her. Occasionally Christian would go, but soon would wind up exploring to pass the time.

Physically, Karen appeared to look better but the withdrawal process was the most difficult and challenging part. The physical and psychological dependence the drugs had over her was more than she could bear. The doctors, however, expressed to them that if she was able to make it through the first week, then she would be on her way to a good recovery. For Shawn, the hardest thing he went through while visiting his mother were the empty promises to get well so they could be a family once again.

Bruce, on the other hand, came to visit his wife once that first week but due to his less-than-friendly and not so sober attitude, was asked relatively firmly not to come back. And Bruce being Bruce, wasn't willing or able to accept the fact that the problems he and his family were having had been a direct result of their own doing, believed that it was as a result of someone, or something, else. In this case, that someone or something else were the Eaton's. He did come by David's office a few times at work during that week to voice his illegitimate concerns, but always left just shy of too much.

After two weeks of being in rehab, Grandpa Joe received a phone call he never thought he would receive: Karen Calloway was dead. Apparent suicide by hanging, which had happened sometime during the night. The only explanation he got for this was that she had worse problems coping with the withdrawal process than previously thought. Her funeral was held that coming weekend and, outside of the Eaton's, no one attended. Not even her husband. Christian did hear his father say in passing, "That it was more important for Bruce to help keep a local bar in business then to come to his own wife's funeral."

Shawn obviously took the death of his mother hard, which came to a head at her actual burial. Joe did his best to console him but, other than simply being there for him, there wasn't much he could do. When the service was over it seemed Shawn's so was grieving process. Christian found it odd that Shawn's emotional state got worse with his mom's failing health and ultimate death, but once it was said and done, he went on with his life as if nothing had happened. Outside of this unfortunate incident, the rest of the month went pretty well for the Eaton household.

Christian and Shawn started walking home together; and on days that Shawn wasn't with Grandpa Joe, he was with Christian. Joe happily admitted one night during dinner that Shawn's boxing was coming along better than he had expected. He mentioned in passing that if Shawn kept up like he had been, that there would be no reason he couldn't start some amateur boxing in a youth program somewhere. David had been against it from the start while constantly expressing it would eventually lead Shawn to criminal acts. Sally was also against it but for different reasons; she was saying it more for the health reasons than criminal. Christian didn't care either way as long as it didn't interfere with his cartoon shows. The only one of the group that was serious about it was Joe. He openly stated that even though their concerns were nice, they were unwarranted because Shawn was off the streets, was receiving better grades in school, and was no longer fighting in general.

While expressing his interest to Shawn that he worked hard at both school and boxing, then he, Joe, would see about the youth boxing program that summer. Soon after this, Christian noticed a more definite change in Shawn, one where he actually tried to do better, especially in school. This seemed to be the first real opportunity Shawn had had to actually strive to do better rather than merely coasting through.

At the end of February, Christian and Shawn received their report cards. Christian, once again, received straight A's, an 'excellent' in every subject, and was on pace to be valedictorian, again, for his class. Shawn, on the other hand, didn't fare as well but did say that his grades for the first time ever were all at least a 75%. He also said that since staying with the Eaton's, this was the longest he had gone without being in some sort of a fight. Shawn was worried that his classmates would think he was turning into some sort of nerd or something worse as a result.

On that particular day while walking home from school, and midway through Shawn giving himself a handful of over-complimentary comments, Wesley and the rest of his juvenile delinquent friends crept out of the wood works to surround them.

"Yo, Callow-punk!" Wesley stated as he walked up to stand five feet from Shawn. "We've got a bone to fry with you after what you done to us last year!"

"You have a bone to fry with us?" Shawn mocked with a confused smile.

"That's what I said! Got a problem with your hearing, little man?!" Wesley laughed while looking to his entourage, who were also laughing.

"No, I heard you the first time, fat boy, but I think you have a little too much fat upstairs clogging your brain," Shawn told him while pointing to his head. "What you should'a said was that you have a bone to *pick*, not *fry*, with us, you freakin' retard!"

"What'cha just say?!" Wesley demanded while looking around with a mocking smile and arms held out. "Yo, Eric, did he just correct me? Did this punk just call me a retard? *Me*, a retard?"

"That he did, Boss, that he did," Eric confirmed with a nod of the head. He paused long enough to cram the rest of his Twinkie in his mouth before going back to his previous head nodding.

"I'm surprised you would say that to me, especially when you're outmanned." Wesley sneered while puffing his fat body up while taking a step forward.

"Me? Outmanned?" Shawn defiantly asked while looking at each of the five boys in front of him. "By who? Besides, it surprises me when some stupid, fat assed, retarded wannabe such as you thought they couldn't be surprised. It's the story of your life, brother. Better get used to it or better start doing something about it!"

"Yo, guys, did this loser just try and insult me?" Wesley asked his friends.

Kyle, Eric, and Kenny all quickly confirmed this. Stan, on the other hand, was just standing there, posing, while chewing his toothpick and running his hands through his long hair.

"Stan!" shouted Wesley.

"Aw, yeah, sure boss, whatever you say," Stan quickly said when he heard his name being called.

While stepping a bit closer to Shawn, the Hoods leader said, "Hey, punk! There's a rumor out that you're doin' good in school. And considerin' you're living' with this chump here," he said while pointing to Christian with a sneer, "You should'a enough smarts to know you're in a no-win situation. If you wanna get out of this without gettin' hurt, I suggest you do as I say."

"Maybe you don't remember last summer when I not only kicked your fast ass, but I also kicked theirs as well," Shawn told him while pointing to each of Wesley's cronies.

Hearing that, Wesley mockingly pointed to Shawn. "Like the Mellencamp song says, you got lucky. Thunder doesn't strike the same place twice, just remember that Calloway." He laughed before having the other four join in with their own laughter.

"Thunder? What the hell you talkin' 'bout, you stupid tub of lard?" Shawn asked through a laugh while he spread his arms. "Lightning! Lightning, *not* thunder, doesn't strike the same place twice, you putz! And it was Petty, not Mellencamp, that sang *You Got Lucky*, you freakin' moron!"

"Aw, that's it, little man! I was just gonna take your fine lookin' jacket there but, before we do, I think a little payback is in order." Wesley, unable to tolerate Shawn's disrespect any further, took a step forward while raising his clenched fists.

While mirroring Wesley's actions, Shawn was about to engage him when Christian got in between them.

"Now, S-S-S-Shawn, this i-i-isn't a g-g-g-good idea," he stuttered as a look of fear was seen on his face. "R-r-r-remember what G-g-g-grandpa said about fighting. Besides, we'll g-g-get in trouble."

"Why don't you listen to your chubby friend here, Calloway?" Wesley sneered. "There's no sense the both of you gettin' hurt. Just give me your jacket and we'll call it even Steven."

Through clenched fists, Shawn tells him, "Like hell I will!"

"C'mon, Wesley! Teach him some manners that that the do-gooder Eaton couldn't," Kenny yells in the background while fixing his tinted sunglasses. "That'll show him not to mess with us!"

"C'mon, Calloway!" Wesley arrogantly called while his four friends closed ranks around Christian and Shawn. "You have one of two ways outta here: either give me your jacket and whatever else you have that I want or leave as a bloody mess."

While noticing Shawn's anger building up inside me, anger that desperately wanted to be released, Christian feared they'd get in trouble if he didn't forfeit his jacket. He also knew Shawn could take care of himself, but could he against the same five boys that have been terrorizing over kids all across town going on three years now?

"S-S-Shawn, it's not w-w-worth it. It's not worth g-g-getting hurt or in t-t-trouble over. R-r-remember what Grandpa said," Christian pleaded as tears came in his eyes. "Just let him have your jacket. Please!"

Just then, right when Shawn was beginning to take into consideration what Christian was telling him, Wesley had to open his mouth.

"What's wrong, Calloway? You yella?!"

"What'cha just say?!" Shawn demanded while his anger came back to him.

"Nothin' that ain't true," Wesley mocked with a cocky chuckle. "Ever since you've been with chubby here and his family, you've been avoiding fights. I think that streak down your back finally matches your true color inside. Yella! Ha ha ha!"

"Nobody calls me yellow." Shawn announced while stepping around Christian to get a clear shot at Wesley. "Nobody!"

Since Wesley and his entourage had only picked on people they knew wouldn't put up a fight or not much of one if they actually did, they honestly didn't expect either Shawn or Christian to fight in this case. So when Wesley saw Shawn go for him, it totally took him of guard. He quickly shot a punch in vain as he attempted to hit him, a punch that hit Christian instead. On the impact, Christian's knee's faltered slightly before giving way while he collapsed on a roadside snow bank. He immediately raised his hands to hold the spot on his face where he had gotten hit before starting to cry.

When Christian was able to focus enough on the situation long enough, he noticed Shawn had already dismissed Kenny form the mix. Though Kenny had heart, he by far was the shortest and weakest of the bunch and, consequently, didn't stand a chance. Eric was soon thrown aside who soon seemed to want to get sick; most likely from all the junk food he ate for lunch. Stan left voluntarily while saying something about not wanting to get his hair messed up. This left Kyle and Wesley to worry about. Wesley, being the fearless leader that he was, told Kyle to take care of Shawn. When Kyle made a go for him, Shawn simply side stepped him before doing a nice combination of two jabs before following it with a hard left hook. Kyle was soon thinking about what had just happened as he spun around into the same snow bank Christian was in.

"You probably thought they were easy, Calloway, but wait 'til you get a load of me!" Wesley threatened before attempting one last time to intimidate him before finally taking a failed imposing step or two forward.

"Go for it!" Shawn said before adding "fat boy" to the end of it moments later.

Wesley attempted a lunging right hook towards Shawn's head, a hook that was easily blocked. It was quickly followed by a string of blows to Wesley's gut and ribs in a quick, orderly fashion. When Wesley composed himself to make another attempt at hitting Shawn, Shawn sidestepped that attack to interlock his left arm with Wesley's right before proceeding to give him four or five hard kidney shots. After the last one, it looked like to Christian that Shawn was going to stop but, after a momentary pause, he saw Shawn continued with five more. Shawn released Wesley after this second set of punches.

"If you don't stop this, Tubby, you'll be peeing blood." Shawn smiled while looking over Wesley with great satisfaction.

"Me, quit? I'm just getting warmed up," came the response before being followed by another failed attempt to harm Shawn.

When Wesley lunged, Shawn stepped back out of range before quickly moving in with a forceful straight smack dab into Wesley's nose, breaking it on impact. It appeared to Christian that Shawn was actually enjoying himself by this point. Whatever pent-up emotions that Shawn had had since Christmas all seemed to be coming out at this very moment. Unfortunately for Wesley, they were all directed towards him. The other four bullies seemed to be the smart ones by not wanting any part of this. Christian, however, thought if Wesley and his gang really wanted to hurt them, they all could simply have rushed them instead of doing it one at a time.

After Wesley's nose was broken, he stepped back in shock before realizing Shawn wasn't done and was coming to what appeared to be to finish it off with a right uppercut to Wesley's jaw. This last shot sprawled the bully out in the middle of the snow-covered road. While looking up at Shawn, Wesley couldn't believe what had just happened as he watched with wide eyes and bewildered look as Shawn walked towards him.

As Shawn neared, Christian got up and quickly put himself in between of him before putting a hand on his chest.

"Shawn, it's over," he told him. "C-c-come on, Shawn, let's go home."

With that, Shawn came back to reality from whatever faraway land he just visited. He saw the fear in Christian's eyes and a bloodied Wesley on the ground before him. While looking down to his hands he noticed the blood on them. He merely nodded before looking back to Christian.

"Sure, alright," he said, barely above a whisper. "That does sound good right about now. And my hands seem to hurt."

"W-W-Wesley, maybe you'd better leave us alone from now on, ok? Please? I'm not sure if I can stop him next time," Christian politely asked of him before facing Shawn once more. "C'mon, S-S-Shawn."

***

"Christian, sweetie, what happened to your face?" Sally asked when they came into the kitchen.

"Wesley hit me on the way home from school today, Mama," he told her as he and Shawn sat down at the table.

"Who hit you?!" Grandpa Joe, who was already at the table in his usual spot, demanded.

Lucky, meanwhile, was on the floor chewing on a bone, jumped from the tone of his voice.

"Remember that day last summer when Shawn stuck up for me?" Christian asked him. "Wesley was one of them."

"Why would he hit you, sweetie? Did you do something to him?" his mom asked while bringing five plates as she started to set the table for dinner.

"They were trying to hit me instead," Shawn answered while opening a can of root beer that Sally put in front of him. "He just got in the way."

"They? You mean there was more than one of them?" Joe questioned while sipping the coffee he was given.

"Yeah, there were five of 'em." Shawn shrugged. "Same ones I beat up last year."

"Shawn, why were they trying to hit you?"

Shawn guzzled most of his soda before letting out a loud, long belch. "I guess they wanted to do to me what I did to them, I suppose."

"Why would they wait so long?"

Shrugging, Shawn said, "I think because they were afraid of me. I think since I've been staying here with you guys, they thought they would have had an easier time beating me up."

"So, ah, what happened?" Grandpa Joe inquired as a look of curiosity crossed his face.

"Shawn beat 'em all up, Grandpa. All by himself." Christian smiled before drinking the chocolate milk his mom made for him.

"Was there any way for two could have left without fighting?" Sally asked.

"No, Mama. We tried to leave but they wouldn't let us."

"So you had no other choice but to fight, huh? There was no other way around it?" asked Joe.

"It was either that or Shawn give 'em his jacket," Christian confirmed what Shawn had just said while wiping off his mouth.

"Oh, Shawn. Why didn't you just let them have your jacket?" Sally asked in a disappointed manner. "You and Christian could have gotten hurt."

"I wasn't going to give them my jacket! He already had one," Shawn hotly retorted. "Besides, it's cold out. I'm not gonna walk home cold again."

Grandpa Joe nodded in agreement. "I agree. You shouldn't have to. That's a nice coat you have; warm too. So, um, tell me what happened! Did you fight all five of them at one time or just this Wesley kid?"

"Dad! You shouldn't antagonize them!" his daughter-in-law chastised.

"Sorry, Sally," he quickly apologized without even bothering to look at her before continuing with Shawn. His hands soon began to rub together from excitement. "So, all five or just him?"

"Well, it started out with all five but I quickly got rid of Kenny and Eric. Stan left because he didn't want me to hurt him. So, it was more of two-on-one, really. Kyle wasn't really that hard. I did that two jab and left hook combo you showed me on him." Shawn smiled with a bob of the head while saying that.

"That's my boy!" Joe continued to rub his hands together in anticipation. "And Wesley? What happened to him?"

Shawn just laughed at that. That was one of the few times Christian could honestly say that Shawn felt comfortable around them if he felt he could laugh like he just did.

"Did you do that kidney thing where you lock arms with him?" Grandpa Joe asked during a rare excitable moment.

Shawn smiled, "Yep, yep. I did that."

"How 'bout that straight to the face, jab to belly, hook to the face, and end it with the uppercut?" Joe asked while using his hands to simulate the moves.

'I finished him off with that," Shawn told him with a laugh.

"Yeah, he broke Wesley's nose with that straight," Christian told his grandfather after drinking the rest of his milk.

"You did?" inquired Joe while seeing Shawn nod his head to acknowledge that he, in fact, had. "Well, I guess he had it coming. You did alright, kid. But just remember, you should fight only when you have to. Alright?"

"What's this I hear about fighting?" David asked when he finally emerged into the kitchen from his shop in the basement. He soon took his seat next to his father. "Where were you boys fighting today?"

"Not exactly. It was just Shawn," his father told him while looking like he was choosing his words carefully. "Those boys that beat Christian up last summer, that day Shawn stuck up for him, were back and tried to do it again while they were on their way home from school."

"What happened?" David quickly asked with concern. "Are you boys alright?"

"They're fine. Shawn took care of it," Joe assured his son. "Nothing too serious."

"Did you have any other choice other than fighting?" David asked while accepting the coffee his wife gave him.

"From what it sounds like, no, they didn't, dear," Sally told him.

Nodding, David said with sincerity, "In that case, thank-you Shawn. Thanks for being there for Christian. But I'm sure my father's told you that you should fight only when you have to. Right?"

"Yes, Mr. Eaton." Shawn rolled his eyes when he answered that.

"Come on, boys. Enough of this fighting talk, especially at the dinner table," Sally said while finalizing the current conversational piece. She brought over that night's dinner in the process before placing it on the table. "Time to eat."

"Before we start anything, I have a little announcement I'd like to make," David said while fixing himself a plate of food. "I got a call from Brian Bise today and he said that he got an answer on whether or not we can be Shawn's legal guardians. Apparently, if Shawn wants to stay with us, the courts don't seem to see any reason as to why he can't."

"Really?!" Shawn asked full of excitement. "It went through?"

"Yes, it went through," David told him while turning his attention to Shawn. "We're now your legal guardians. So, now that it's all legal, are you sure you want to stay with us for a while longer? Or would you prefer to live somewhere else?"

Shawn just grinned while filling his plate full of food.

David coughed. "That's what I thought. Brian will be stopping one night in a day or so to finalize this. There'll be some papers we need to go through with him and some other options to discuss. Now, Shawn, if there's any reason you don't want to stay with us, now's the time you really should tell us."

"I wanna stay here if it's still ok," Shawn told him while looking at David with pleading eyes.

"Alright. In that case, we might want to consider getting you your own room. But, enough of that. There's plenty of time to talk about this," David stated while ending the subject. "So, tell me, what have the rest of you been up to today?"

For the rest of the day Christian noticed that Shawn seemed to have a smile permanently stuck to his face.

Chapter 12

Winter soon seem to fade as spring before summer once again started to make an appearance.

"Christian? Oh Christian!" Sally called from the kitchen as the smells of what she was making diffused upstairs alongside her voice. These smells ranged from marble cake, to both apple and cherry pies, to pork roast, and to mashed potatoes.

"Coming, Mama!" Christian yelled while finishing an article on rocket electronics from one of his current science magazines. Once he was finished, he put it on his desk and went downstairs.

Turning when he entered, Sally says, "I'll need for you to do me a big favor if you would, please."

Shrugging, he says, "Sure, ok."

"Today is your grandfather's birthday. Even though he thinks everyone has forgotten about it, your father and I are planning something special for him later," she told her son with a smile while doing one of her hundred checks to the food. "We're planning a little party with some of his friends later. I would like you to keep him occupied for the time being until everything is set. Would you please do that for me, sweetie?"

"Sure, I'll do that," he quickly told her.

While patting her son on the cheek, Sally smiled and said, "Thank-you, sweetie. Now, don't tell him anything. Ok? We want this to be a surprise."

"I won't, Mama. I'll try and talk about boxing or his apartment or whatever. He always can talk about those," Christian said before going outside to meet up with his grandfather, who was currently in the garage tending to their lawn mower after having recently moving the yard. "Why are you doing that, Grandpa?"

"Oh, just something I have to do," Joe answered. "I hadn't a chance earlier in the year and thought I should now while I had a chance to. I was just about to change its oil. Wanna help?"

Since Christian had never seen this process before, he watched intently to learn how it was done. Lucky, on the other hand, played with a new found toy in the corner. Roughly a half hour later, Sally and Shawn came out to the garage. Sally somehow managed to sweet talk her Joe into going to Deeley's for some sort of supplies. Christian simply took this as his mom wanted to get her father-in-law out of the way so they could finish the preparations for the party later on.

"Oh, Dad, while you're at it, would you and the boys take Lucky to the park for a little exercise while you're out? The vet did say she needed to lose a little weight and I was thinking that today would be a nice day for that. Thank-you," she said before turning to walk back inside without waiting for an answer. That only reinforced Christian's idea for her wanting him out.

"You heard her, boys. Will you two go get Lucky, please?" Grandpa Joe told the two young boys.

With that, Christian called Lucky over to his grandfather's truck and helped get her into the truck's bed. Shawn, meanwhile, was looking down the road before gasping and calling out.

"Grandpa Joe! Look!" he shouted while pointing in the direction he was looking.

As Joe and Christian turned to see what Shawn was pointing at, they saw a rusty, old pick-up swerving down the road towards them. While attempting to pull into their driveway, it came up short before taking out the mailbox and coming to a stop, mostly on the yard. Bruce, Shawn's father, got out and attempted to walk up to them in a drunken swagger.

"Dad?" Shawn asked with surprise.

"You're Goddamn right I'm still your father, boy! And don't you fuckin' forget that!" he slurred with unfocusing eyes.

While barking aggressively at him, Lucky's back hair stood on end. Christian got in the truck to help calm her down.

"What are you doin' here, Dad?"

"What am I doin' here? You have to ask me that, boy?!" demanded Bruce while approaching his son. "I've come to take your ass home where it belongs!"

"But I *am* home," Shawn told him while looking to Grandpa Joe, who appeared equally confused.

"Don't be talkin' to me that way, boy!" Bruce stated angrily while giving Shawn a stiff backhand across the face. The force of the blow knocked the young Calloway down as the older version watched as Grandpa Joe approached. Bruce soon focused his drunken attention onto the old man before him. "You stay outta this, old man, if you know what's good for you. And, as for you, boy, get your girlie ass up and plant it in the fuckin' truck where it belongs. Now!"

"The only place he'll be going is inside to call the police," Joe firmly said while coming around his truck as he approached. "Bruce, what's the meaning of this?"

"What the fuck it look like? I'm takin' my boy home!" Bruce replied, once again with slurred speech while he staggered towards Joe. "While I'm at it, what's this I hear about you guys adoptin' him? There's no way in hell I'm gonna let anyone take my son away from me, especially people like you!"

"Christian, why don't you and Shawn take Lucky inside. Have your mom call the police for me, ok?" Joe asked his grandson before turning back to Bruce.

"Yes, Grandpa. C'mon, Lucky. Let's go," Christian said while he and the dog jumped from the truck before going inside with Shawn close behind them. Upon entry to the house, he informed his mom what was going on outside while Shawn, meanwhile, went to the window to watch. He soon opened it to be able to listen to what was happening.

Hearing the news, Sally did what was asked while going to the phone to start making the call.

"Now, Bruce," Joe said softly while planting himself firmly between the unwanted visitor and his home. "I don't want to make a scene here, especially in front of the children. You'd better get back in your truck and move along before the police show up."

"I don't give a fuckin' rat's ass what you say! Let those fuckin' pig coppers show up. I ain't afraid of those bastards! But before they do, there's one thing I gotta say to your ass, old man." Bruce looked around before attempting to throw a hefty right towards Grandpa Joe.

Easily side stepping it, Joe merely pushed Bruce aside, causing the drunken caller to lose his balance and stumble to the ground. When Grandpa Joe looked back to the house, Christian and Shawn were seen staring out of the window at him.

"Hey, boys? Are the police on their way?" Joe asked mildly.

"Yeah, Grandpa, they're on their way," Christian told him without moving away from the window.

"So, what's it going to be?" the elder Eaton asked Bruce while he was getting up. "Are you going to leave on your accord or will you be leaving with the police?"

"Well, hey there, Joe. There ain't no sense in being too hasty," Bruce said slyly once he was able to compose himself while stretching a hand out. "I don't wanna cause any problem. I'm leavin', old man. But, before I go, I want you to remember one thing."

"Yeah, what's that?" Joe asked coldly.

"This ain't over. You might have this little victory," Bruce told him while backing away towards his truck and pointing a finger at him. "But this won't be the last time you'll hear from me. You can count on that. Just remember that, old man!"

No reply was given to this as Bruce entered his truck and drove away. In a matter of minutes, two police cruisers pulled into the drive and the accompanying officers got out to investigate the now nonexistent situation. They took a statement before saying they would keep an eye out for Bruce but wouldn't be able to do anything beyond that. The Eaton's ended by assuring the police they would call should Bruce show up again before the cops themselves got back into their cars and drove away.

When the family was back to normal after their unexpected intrusion, Grandpa Joe, the two boys, and Lucky were barreling down the road in their own pickup while making their way to Deeley's. On the way down, Christian thought back to what had happened to his family the last several months. He had received a ribbon from school for going through his elementary school as valedictorian in each grade. He was currently trying to figure what he would do for that next year's science fair.

Shawn, on the other hand, was just happy he passed the fifth grade so he could finally get out of elementary school. He had a personal best of a 77% overall, and for the first time had at least a 75% in all of his subjects. He had been improving quite well in boxing which was still being provided faithfully by Christian's grandfather.

Joe had bought some new equipment and had placed Shawn in a boxing program to learn what he couldn't teach him. On the down side, when Joe tried to setup some youth amateur boxing matches, he had been told Shawn was too young but could come back once he was twelve.

David was still talking to Brian Bise about various options concerning Shawn and at the moment was contemplating the idea of adoption. He also had Ed Thompson, the man who did his dad's apartment, come back and make a room for Shawn in the cellar next to his workshop. His latest projects at work had made him a little more irritable the last couple of months but since several of them were now finished, he was a bit more at ease.

Sally, as usual, was fine and probably would be for years to come. The only difference to the Eaton household was Grandpa Joe. Over the past couple months or so, Christian felt that his old age was finally catching up to him. He seemed to now be having trouble picking things up and, if he did bend over to pick them up, couldn't hang on to them for very long before his arms would start shaking. This would force him to put whatever it was back down. His body periodically seemed to shake when he walked as well, and Joe would mildly say he was practicing some new dance moves to impress the ladies.

Once they were at Deeley's, Grandpa Joe seemed to take his take his time with Harold, which seemed to span the better part of an hour as they chit-chatted on a variety of subjects. Meanwhile, Christian and Shawn were outside playing with Lucky when the two elderly men finally excited the market.

"I don't mean to cut this short," Mr. Deeley said as he slightly stumbled from his sagging pant before promptly pulling them up, "but I got to get ready to close up shop for the day."

"Closing a little early, aren't you, Harold?" Joe questioned him while looking at his watch. "It's not even six yet."

"Yeah, I know. I was going over to a friend's later for a little get together and I don't want to be late. You know how that is," he responded with a glint in his eye.

"Alright. I'll let you get back to your work. Hope you have a good time tonight," Joe told him while looking towards the woods. "While we're at it, Sally wanted us to take ole Lucky her to the park to try and work off some of her weight."

Confused, Mr. Deeley quickly looked to the dog for an extended moment. "Work off some of her weight? Why in the world would she want that? Earlier this year she was just skin and bones."

"True, but the vet had said she was a little over weight."

"Jesus, Joseph, and Mary! As soon as the dog gets to a good weight, you're told she's too heavy. Vets these days! How come we never had these problems when we were kids?" Mr. Deeley chuckled while shaking his head.

"I totally agree. I think the dog's fine just the way she is," Joe stated in agreement before extending a hand out for his friend to shake. "Well, Harold, I'd better leave so you can close up. See you at the party later."

"Yeah, I'd better get going before Ellen thinks I've got a girlfriend out here." He accepted the hand and shook it with a smile before becoming very serious. "Party? What party? What the hell are you talking about?"

"Oh, never mind. Have a good night, Harold," Joe responded before turning to walk back to his truck with his supplies in hand. "C'mon boys. Grab the dog and load up. We're burning daylight. Time and tide wait for no man."

"Thanks, you have a good one too, Joseph," Mr. Deeley turned then to walk back inside. Once inside, the door was shut, its lock was heard being engaged, and the open sign flipped around to read CLOSED.

Ten minutes later they pulled into the park. The park itself had a relatively decent sized parking lot, and it had a lot of open space that people used to play various sports or just lay out in the summer sun. The further out in the park you got, the more shrubs and trees were visible, which ultimately led to a few nature tails to hike on. Sporadically spread throughout were old, wooden picnic tables and accompanying barbeque grills. The main highlight was a fairly large pond which was regularly stocked for the village's annual fishing derby.

Once they got there, Christian and his grandfather put a kite, one with the likeness of an eagle on it, together that they got at Deeley's. Shawn, meanwhile, started playing Frisbee with Lucky nearby. Shortly after getting the kite in the air, Grandpa Joe let out an irritating sigh.

"What's wrong, Grandpa?"

"Ah, nothing's wrong, Christian. I just hope that not too many people show up tonight."

While trying to act as confused as possible, Christian simply asked, "Show up for what?"

Joe just looked at his grandson while shaking his head. "Yeah, ok. Play dumb if you want but just don't tell me that your mother wanted us to come here was mere coincidence."

Rather than responding, Christian merely chased the kite instead when it took a nasty fall to earth. Just as he left, his grandfather glanced over to Shawn to make sure he and Lucky were alright. On the road behind them, he saw Bruce driving out of sight.

"Hey, Shawn?" Joe called out. "How are you two doing over there?"

"Fine!" Shawn said while playfully tugging at the Frisbee in his dog's mouth. "This is the first time in a long time that Lucky has been able to come here and play. Oh, I've seen my dad drive by about five or six times in the last ten minute or so."

"I saw," Joe commented with a slight hint of concern in his voice. "You two better say close, ok?"

"Alright, Gramps." Shawn shrugged while pulling the Frisbee loose and throwing it towards the pond. Lucky quickly ran after it. After picking it up, she walked over near Grandpa Joe and laid down for a rest while chewing on her toy. Shawn, meanwhile, walked over to rub her ear. Christian continued to fly the eagle kite high in the air as Joe made various unimportant comments about it.

Moments later, a rumbling nearby soon caught their attention. While turning to see, they noticed it was coming from within the park's boundary near the road. Several shrubs and trees were blocking their view to see what it came from but, within a matter of seconds, Bruce

Calloway came around them in his rusty pickup as he drove full speed ahead right towards them.

Christian, who seemed more concerned for his kite, and Shawn, who stood there in shock at what he was seeing, were both pulled sharply out of the way by Grandpa Joe. They happened to move just in time as Bruce zoomed by, barely missing them, before hitting the side of an old oak and plunging nearly full speed into the park's pond.

"Go call an ambulance!" Joe yelled to a nearby woman who was out walking her dog before running into the water to drag a semi-conscious Bruce out of his truck. Bruce simply seemed to want to speak through a face full of blood, a result of banging it against the steering wheel, but all he could do instead was spit a handful of teeth out before passing out.

An hour or so later, Joe pulled into their drive with Christian and Shawn sitting next to him; Lucky was laying in the bed behind them. Catching a movement from the house, Christian looked to catch the last remnants of the drapes moving back to their original positions before quickly looking to his grandfather. Hoping he didn't see what he did, Christian was happy to notice that Grandpa Joe seemed oblivious to this.

"Why don't you two take Lucky inside," Joe told the two boys as they all climbed out of the truck. "I'll be in soon. There's something I want to do out here before I come in, alright?"

"Alright, Grandpa," Christian told him while going inside with Shawn and Lucky.

Entering the house, they found the living room filled with people of all ages. Most were elderly, and most of these had served with Grandpa Joe in the military, but quite a few of the remaining others were a lot younger. Most of them were people that he had either helped or worked with at the Y.

"Hey boys," Sally said when she saw them. Lucky trotted up to her for a pat on the head. "Where's your grandfather."

Shrugging, Christian said, "Still outside. Said he wanted to do something. Oh, Mama, you hav'ta hear what happened to us at the park today!"

"What happened, sweetie?"

"Well, um," Christian started but soon fumbled with his words when he caught a look from Shawn. The glance was a combination glare of anger and a sigh of disappointment. "Never mind. It's not that important."

"Not important? They why did you seem so excited to tell me?" Sally asked while looking back and forth between the two boys. "Oh. I see. We'll talk about this later, ok? In the meantime, go get ready for the surprise party you two. Did your grandfather say what he had to do?"

"No, Mama." Christian shook his head while he waded through the crowd of people to go to his room. Just before he left the now silent crowd, he noticed Mr. Deeley in the corner by the hors d'oeuvre table. His wife, meanwhile, was chastising him for not waiting until the party had started to begin eating. After coming back down from getting ready, which simply meant putting on a clean t-shirt, he found that his grandfather hadn't come inside yet. His mother immediately approached him.

"Are you sure he didn't say anything else of where he might have gone or what he was going to do?" she inquired.

"Yes, Mama," he told his mother with a shrug. "All he said was he had to do something. That's all. Do you want me to go check on him?"

"Would you, sweetie? I would but that might raise his suspicions."

"Alright, I'll be right back."

As Christian was making his way to the door, it suddenly opened as his grandfather finally came through it. The people behind him immediately turned on all the lights while beginning to shout HAPPY BIRTHDAY, but only got about halfway through saying that when they all stopped to stare, stopped to gasp really, at Grandpa Joe. He had come dancing through the door wearing nothing but a pair of boxers, old cowboy boots, and a cowboy-like hat before letting out a loud "YEEEE-HHAAWW!!" while slapping his belly repeatedly with both hands.

"Now that I'm here, we can get this party started!" he playfully yelled while patting his stomach a handful more times.

"Dad! W-w-what are you doing?" Sally asked with surprised while approaching. "Why aren't you wearing any clothes?"

"Isn't this supposed to be a surprise party?" Joe told here with a giant grin. "Well, surprise!"

Most of the crowd stood there in stunned silence while looking at a near naked Grandpa Joe. Meanwhile, Christian and Shawn immediately started laughing at the sight of him. Sally tried to quiet them down while at the same time tried to convince her father-in-law to go put some clothes on.

The only other noise in the room came from Mr. Deeley, who was laughing even harder than the two boys were back in his corner. "Hey, Joe, now that you're here, we can finally eat, right?" he called out while grabbing a small plate before an answer was given, started stock piling food onto it, all the while ignoring the glares his wife was shooting him. "Oh, by the way, nice birthday suit you got going on there."

By this point everyone seemed to have lightened up at the idea of Grandpa Joe standing there in his boxers as a stir of laughter slowly began to spread itself through the house. Joe left before returning shortly thereafter for a more appropriate attire to a now known surprise birthday party. When he did reenter, the party members were finally able to give him a full blessing of HAPPY BIRTHDAY that they failed to give the first time around. The tradition of passing out presents and blowing out cake candles familiar to an American birthday soon came to pass.

Like always, Joe was pleased at the overabundance of people that were there. He greeted everyone personally who had come, but soon wound up finding himself spending a big chunk of the time talking with his old Army buddies that had been invited. Christian and Shawn seemed to shadow him around for a short period of time before he settled back into the likes of Right-Eye Mahoney, Mad-Dog Johnson, Moonlight Jones, and Left-Hook Gordon. Within minutes of joining them, it seemed like they had somehow been magically been transported back thirty years. They picked up to finish conversations started decades earlier while beginning new ones to finish at a later date, whenever that might be. It went well until Grandpa Joe made the mistake of asking about another old buddy of theirs, Brian Leonard. Once this was asked, the bunch got all quiet and looked around to one another.

"You don't know what happened to Goose?" Moonlight questioned.

"No, that's why I asked," Grandpa Joe retorted while looking at his friends. "If I had, why would I be asking? Either someone start flapping their lips or I start breaking bones. What happened to him?"

"We're sorry you have to find out this way, but Goose's dead. Has been going on ten years now. We thought you knew," Right-Eye said with heavy regret and sorrow.

"Dead? How?" Grandpa Joe asked in astonishment, almost not believing what he had just heard.

"Maybe this isn't a good time to be talking about him, Joe," Mad-Dog said while starting to look around. "Maybe we should wait until later...?"

"Like hell we will! I want to know now," Joe informed them.

"Alright Joe, take it easy. We'll tell you," Moonlight told him while trying to calm him down. "Goose was killed in prison; got knifed in the shower. A few guys wanted a few favors from him that he wasn't willing to perform, if you get my drift, so they killed him for it. We honestly thought you knew."

"I never knew. I honestly never knew," Joe said softly while wiping the tears from his eyes. This was not only Shawn's time seeing him cry, but Christian's as well. "You said prison. What happened? Why was he there?"

"He killed some people, Joe," Left-Hook answered.

"Well, sure, we all did. It was wartime after all."

"That's not what we mean," Mad-Dog said. "He was a civilian when he did the killing."

"What?" Joe sat in a nearby chair almost like he was unable to remain standing.

"Shortly after we got discharged, he went back home to Georgia, Alabama, or wherever the hell he came from," Moonlight began.

"Mississippi," Grandpa Joe corrected. "Goose was from Mississippi."

"Anyway, Goose was having a real hard time adjusting to civilian life. Depression set in and all that good stuff," continued Moonlight. "About six months or so after getting out, he went into some roadside dinner for lunch, and Goose being Goose, he went in in full uniform. A group of three young black guys made the mistake of trying to start a fight with him. Calling him a baby killer or whatever other vile crap they could come up with. They spat on him, blew snot at him, whatever they could to instigate something from him. Goose quietly excused himself, went home, came back with his 12-gauge, and filled all three men with lead. Killed all of 'em. He was later convicted of three counts of second-degree murder and got three consecutive 25-to-life sentences. He was inside not even a year when he got knifed."

Hearing this, Joe continued to sit in silence while trying to keep his tears from escaping his closed eyes. Sally had come over twice to see if he was alright before being quickly dismissed.

"We're sorry you had to find out this way. We thought you knew, really we did," Right-Eye said as they tried to comfort him.

They either stood or sat there in silence for a few moments while not knowing what to say or do. Christian was shocked by the fact at how emotional his grandfather got over the loss of a friend he had not seen in what seemed to be a lifetime. Looking around to find Shawn, Christian discovered he was nowhere to be found.

Joe, once he pulled himself together, quickly changed subjects and told them about his hobbies. He focused on what he had been doing with Shawn the past several months, his volunteering at the Y and the traveling he started doing where he would go to neighboring YMCA's, either locally or out of state, and how Christian was valedictorian again of his class for the fifth straight year.

Hours later when most had left, Joe commented that everyone left too early and wished that no one was in a hurry to leave. His Army friends were the last to actually leave but not before exchanging numbers, address, and promises to keep in touch.

"That was a nice party," Joe complimented while sitting down in the kitchen with a cup of coffee. "David, Sally, I just wanted to thank-you two for inviting some of the people that you did today. By the way, how were you able to locate my old Army friends?"

"Oh, we've been in touch with them for a couple of months now," his son told him while getting coffee before heading back to his workshop. "Sally was the one who actually invited them."

"They were the ones who called us first," Sally said while sitting down next to Joe. Christian, meanwhile, came in with a coloring book and a box for crayons before sitting at the table. "We didn't tell you because we thought it'd be more of a surprise if you didn't know they were in the area. "Oh, incidentally, have either of you seen Shawn lately?"

"No I haven't. Why?"

"Because no one has for a few hours now," Sally told him. "I'm getting a little worried. I know he takes off for hours on end without saying anything, but this is the longest he's been gone at one time since he's been here. He's usually home by now. He's not in his room nor is he in your apartment. Any ideas where he might be or why he's been gone for so long?"

Hearing this, Joe laughed somewhat to himself. "I can't answer the former but as for the later, I think it may have something to do with what happened at the park this afternoon."

"What happened this afternoon?" Sally asked while looking at Christian.

Her son stopped humming a song while looking at her. "That was what I wanted to tell you earlier, Mom, when we got home. Shawn's dad tried to run us over at the park."

Stiffening when she heard that, she exclaimed, "He what?!"

"You know how Bruce came by earlier to try and start something?" Joe asked while receiving a nod in return. "Well, later on at the park he came barreling through in his truck at us. I happened to pull the boys out of the way just in time. He missed, of course, but ended up bouncing off a tree and drove head first into the pond they have there." He paused just long enough to shake his head and laugh. "I had someone call the police before hauling his sorry ass out myself. That's why we were late; we stayed long enough to talk to the police."

"You pressed charges, I hope."

"No, not today. I told the police that if he's charged with D.W.I. or D.U.I., then that would have been good enough. He was obviously quite drunk. I told them that if tried any of this crap again, I would press charges then. They seemed satisfied with that. Bruce was unconscious from bashing his head on the wheel, so he wasn't able to respond." Joe shook his head before looking at the time. "Well, I'd better go find Shawn before it gets any later than it is already." With that said he excused himself from the table and left the house.

"Mama?" Christian asked after his grandfather was gone.

"Yes, sweetie?"

Sitting there momentarily looking off into space, Christian was silent before continuing. "Something was wrong with Grandpa earlier at the party."

"Wrong? What happened?"

"Nothing really happened, just that I saw him crying for the first time. I'm just wondering what was wrong with him," he said while still looking off in the distance before finally glancing at his mother.

"That's weird," his mother commented while thinking of what could have been the matter. "What happened leading up to that point that would have made him do that?"

"Nothing. They were just talking."

"Talking about what?"

"Um, his Army friends were telling him about someone they knew died or got killed or something," Christian told her. "Then he started crying."

A hint of recognition appeared in her eyes at this. "Ah, I see. Was it about his old friend Goose?"

"Yeah. How'd you know?"

"Your grandfather told me a little bit ago. With that in mind, I think I know what the matter was with him," his mom told him while her son looked at her with a blank stare. "You see, your grandfather and his friends were such good, close friends that they were almost like brothers, one big family. So if one is lost, it's felt by all of them. Do you understand?"

"No, not really, Mama," Christian confessed as a confused look came over his face.

"Well, you will when you get older," Sally assured him with a smile. "So, do you have any idea where Shawn might be?"

"No, but knowing him he's most likely alone. He might be at his spot by the creek again," he answered while finishing the picture he'd been coloring.

"Perhaps you're right," his mom agreed while finishing her coffee. "We'll find out when your grandfather gets back."

Almost forty-five minutes later Joe finally came back, alone, though he was in a better mood as compared to when he left.

"Well, I found him," he told them.

"Oh, good. Is he ok?"

"He will be," Grandpa Joe answered. "He's not physically hurt if that's what you mean."

"Where is he?"

"He's been in the tree house for a while now." Joe walked over to lean against the wall and look out the window.

"The tree house?" Christian gasped. "What's he doing out there?"

"There's just some things he has on his mind that he wanted to take care of. He'll be in when he's ready."

"So, Dad, what got into him? What I mean is, what happened to make him ant to be alone out there?"

"He left shortly after my friends and I were talking about Goose, the one that got killed." Joe sighed as his eyes appeared to focus on something off in the distance. "Apparently, it struck a chord of the realization of what could happen to his brother."

"His brother? What do you mean, Grandpa?"

"You heard what happened to my friend Goose, right?" Joe asked his grandson. "He was killed in jail. Remember?"

Christian replied with a combination nod and "Uh-huh."

"Do you remember Shawn saying that his older brother Daryl was in jail?"

"No, I don't remember hearing that, Grandpa."

"You're fifth grade teacher, Miss Johansson; remember what happened to her grandfather?" Grandpa Joe asked while briefly looking at Christian before returning his gaze to what lay beyond the window.

"Wasn't he killed by someone who was trying to steal from him?"

"That he was. Unfortunately, it was Shawn's brother who killed him," Joe informed his grandson before turning to see the look of surprise on Christian's face. Before saying anything more, he came over to sit at the table. "That was a couple of years ago. Up until then, Daryl and Bruce were the only role models Shawn had had. Now it's only Bruce. When my friends and I were talking about Goose, it wasn't so much that he did die as opposed to where and how he died.

"Though Shawn's been haunted by the idea that all the people he's looked up to, or that have been there for him, haven't really been one's to look up to. Once he started associating with us, he began getting a way of life he needed but never knew existed," Grandpa Joe continued. "He began finding interests and hobbies; and, for the first time in his life, people began seeing him for who he was. We didn't judge him or, if we did, we kept it pretty much to ourselves. When we did speak our minds, it was out of concern, not anger. No matter how good or loving or positive we are to him, he still has a strong bond and connection to his own family. Though he doesn't have or need to be like that, he has a hard time letting go because that's been all he knew up until a few months ago. Though he's part of our family now, I doubt it'll be any time soon before he feels completely comfortable, welcome, or happy here. But the two things that happened today must have hit home."

"What two things today?" Christian asked.

"First, when his dad tried to run us over at the park and, second, when he heard that my friend got killed in jail."

"And what do you mean by hit home?"

"Are you aware of the saying 'like father, like son'?" Joe asked before pausing long enough for Christian to acknowledge that he had. "Until he started living with us, I doubt Shawn ever realized what a bad influence his home life had been on him. Over the past few months, his eyes were finally able to see his dad for who he really was. Unfortunately, the image he painted of him isn't who he is in reality, which Shawn is finally beginning to see. So, if Shawn now sees Bruce for how he really is, he undoubtedly must feel that part of that is in him. If part of that is in him, then there's a chance he could become his dad.

"On the other note," Joe continued, "what happened to my friend got him thinking that that could happen to his brother. Both went to jail for killing a person. The thought that his brother could get hurt, or even killed, bothers him. Anyway, as a result, Shawn's not really happy right now. The combination of realizing how his family is, mixed with the welfare of his brother, and the possibility of him being like any member of his family really started to bother him."

"Dad, is that what he told you while you were out with him?" Sally inquired.

"Not in so many words, no, but the general jest of it was there." Joe got back up to return to his spot by the window to stare out it once more.

"How long do you think he'll be like this?" Sally asked while adjusting herself in her chair to a more friendly position.

"Depends," Joe replied vaguely while searching for the words. "He has all these pent up emotions that needs to be purged. He has all this anger and resentment that's rarely seen in such a young age.

Sighing, Sally asks, "What can be done? Can we get some type of help for him?"

"With his pride?" Joe scoffed at that. At this, he continued in a voice barely louder than a whisper. "I highly doubt he'd be receptive to it. Probably the best thing to do right now is just keep doing what we're doing and let it ride its course. There's no sense adding more fuel to the fire until we have to. He's shown a lot of improvement since he's been here. I don't think there's any need to worry about him just yet. We just need to give him a bit more time. If we can get him to open up and tell us what's bothering him, what's on his mind, maybe he'll trust us more. But, unfortunately, we might have to do more than we've already done for him to trust us enough to totally open up. Until then, I don't think he'll ever be completely forthcoming with us or totally let us in. Times like this, I can't help but be reminded what Ben Johnson once said. He once called time the 'old bald cheater'."

"Who's Ben Johnson?" Christian asked him.

"An English writer," his grandfather explained. "He was foolish with money and given to flatulence."

"Flatulence? What's that?"

"Never you mind, Christian," Sally told him while looking at her father-in-law who was smiling.

At that moment, Joe looked at his grandson before raising a hand to his mouth and blew hard against it to cause a farting sound. Hearing that, Christian laughed uncontrollably while his mother shook her head at them.

With all that had been said since his grandfather came back, Christian was having a hard time digesting it all. Most of the things he either didn't know or couldn't understand. He began questioning himself at how well he really did know Shawn. Did he really know him? What percentage of Shawn did he actually see? Christian also began thinking that Shawn was similar to a glacier; in both cases, you only saw a small part on the surface while the rest is buried, hidden from view. He liked having Shawn as a friend but wondered if Shawn felt the same about him. If not, would he ever? If so, how long would it take? Maybe Grandpa Joe was right. Maybe if they gave him more time, he'd be willing and able to shed this tough guy routine to expose more of himself underneath. Christian often heard that time was the best healer, but he had also heard that there are some wounds that time cannot heal. He hoped that whatever wounds Shawn had, that they'd be able to heal. But, unfortunately, only time will tell.

Chapter 13

Over the next several months, Christian's interest in science expanded to include nature, wildlife, and animals, though his main focus still had been inventing something for the science fair. With his newly formed interests, he was intrigued and compelled on designing and building a three-foot cube ant house.

The house was going to be made out of some type of durable clear material before being filled with dirt and whatever ants would need. He was hoping to create a real working ant hill, but was worried that he wouldn't be able to have the right plants to keep it going, and was currently without a queen. When it was all done, he had increased the height to three and a half feet so he was able to add grass and other plants to it. The top was screened off to aid in air circulation and watering, and to help keep the ants contained within. Though he was hoping to get the blue ribbon, he only placed second. He was happy about getting a ribbon, but was able to make a long, detailed list of things that could have been improved on or modified to achieve a ribbon color to that of blue.

Outside of that, the first few months of school had been rough on him because he was no longer in elementary school. He now thought he was in the big leagues because he was now in junior high. He complained once at dinner that he had just gotten used to elementary school when he had to change when his dad replied that 'you can't expect to go through life without changes, that it's inevitable.' Christian at that point decided not to complain unless he had a valid reason to.

Shortly after Grandpa Joe's next birthday, he tried keeping his word by signing Shawn up in a couple youth boxing programs. But since Shawn was still a year too young, Joe got him a membership at the Y he volunteered at. The main reason he did that was because the YMCA had just recently incorporated a series of boxing and martial arts clinics that were free for members. And since Grandpa Joe was traveling to other Y's in the area to volunteer, he felt this would be a good way to keep Shawn up on his training when he wasn't home.

These clinics were something Shawn immediately took full advantage of and was there multiple times a week. Though Grandpa Joe had taught him a lot in terms of boxing, there wasn't much else that he knew that he was able to teach without repeating himself. Though the Y itself wouldn't be able to teach him much more than he already knew, the experience he would gain, not only from the clinics but from the actual interaction with other boxers, would equate to a wealth of knowledge.

On days that Shawn went, he would frequently come home late and often missed dinner. On more than a few occasions, he would arrive home banged and bruised from various unsuccessful sparring matches with much bigger and older boxers. On nights like these, he would appear agitated and say he "couldn't wait until he was a little older so he could offer a little payback." Sally often would tell him that he shouldn't think about such things. Joe would often agree with her, saying that the object of boxing is not to wish harm onto your opponents, but to improve on our own skills so you wouldn't get hurt as bad. Shawn would apologize or agree with them, but Christian felt he was just telling them what they wanted to hear.

Christmas soon came to pass and David made a comment in jest that this was the second straight year they had a new member to share it with: Shawn the previous year and Lucky that year. Though Shawn was trying hard not to show his emotions he had had that holiday season, Lucky was another story. This was the first time where she not only got presents, but she also had a family to enjoy them with. Shawn had commented that he had never seen her act the way she did that Christmas, and that something must be wrong with her. When Sally replied that it was because Lucky was happy, had a family that cared about her, and was getting presents, that she couldn't help but show he excitement. Shawn claimed not to believe her, or acted like he didn't anyway, and said that Lucky was just a dog, and dogs don't get excited in that way. Even though he tried to comment after Sally spoke up in Lucky's defense, he had no other explanations to why her tail wagging and mouth smiled all night.

If Christmas was a gift from the gods for them, then New Year's Eve was a gift from Hell. The family had all gathered around the TV on that very cold, blustery night with Dick Clark and several bowls of popcorn for company while waiting for the giant disco ball to welcome in the New Year. As they waited, a great and horrendous disturbance came from outside which was soon followed by hard banging. Incoherent yelling from a very drunken Bruce was heard as the banging continued along the whole front of the house as he made his way to the front door. Every member of the family jumped when hearing this, Lucky got to her feet and growled while facing the door.

"That better not be who I think it is," David said while getting up to look outside. "Yup, just what I thought. Bruce."

"I'll call the police," Sally said while getting up to walk to the kitchen.

"Please, don't," Shawn requested of her with apologetic eyes. "Can we see what he wants first?"

"Is that what you want, Shawn?" she asked before pausing briefly. This pause, Christian gathered, alongside the look that accompanied it, told him that his mother hadn't a clue why he didn't want her to call the police but was willing to do what was asked and trust that he had a good reason for it.

"Yeah," Shawn said while keeping eye contact with her. "Will you please not call them yet? Maybe he isn't here to cause trouble. Maybe he's just here for a visit or to see Lucky or to wish us a happy New –"

"Like hell he is!" David sternly said while peering out the window again.

"David, you shouldn't say such things," his wife chastised him. "Maybe the boy is right."

"Hey, Eaton!" Bruce's voice rang out in a drunken slur while he banged and kicked at the front door with such force the whole house shook. "Open the fuckin' door before I fuckin' break it down!"

Bruce proceeded to kick, bang, and shoulder the door repeatedly for the next several seconds to the point where it looked like the door would be forced open. He stopped short of breaking it down when he was heard falling down on the porch where no sound or movement was heard thereafter. When the silence seemed to last longer than everybody thought it would, David slowly opened the door to look out. All that was seen from the others inside was a large pair of legs sprawled out on the porch.

"Hey, Dad, would you help me out here, please?" he asked while going outside. A cold burst of air entered as he did so.

Grandpa Joe simply followed his son outside without bothering to answer. When they were both on the porch, they picked up the now unconscious Bruce Calloway, who had apparently passed out, and brought him inside to lay him on the couch. They left the now empty whiskey bottle outside, the remainder of its contents colored the surrounding snow. As they carried him, the smell of alcohol, cigarettes, and other foul aroma's came in as well.

"Oh, hell," David grumbled as he rubbed he side of his face while looking down at the unconscious Bruce. "What do you propose we do with him?"

"Maybe we should call him an ambulance?" Sally suggested.

"Maybe, but who's going to pay for it?" he replied while still looking at Bruce.

"Why don't we ask Shawn what he wants?" Grandpa Joe asked. When no one seemed to object, he turned towards Shawn and asked him. "Shawn, what do you want us to do with your father?"

"Could we take him home? Please?" he replied while looking at his father before turning to look up at him.

"Sure, if that's what you want."

"Maybe we should take him to the hospital first; just to make sure he's alright," Sally pressed.

"Can we just take him home?" Shawn insisted. "I know he'll be fine if we do that."

"How do you know that, Shawn?" Sally asked him. "Maybe he needs to see a doctor?"

"He's always like this. He's never needed a doctor before," Shawn told her matter of factly. "Don't see why he needs one now."

"Is this what you want?" she asked. "To take him home?"

"Yes. I just want to take him home," Shawn replied irritably at having to answer the same question for a third time.

"Alright, let's get him up and put him in the car," David grumped as he and Grandpa Joe bent to pick up Bruce.

"Hey Christian, would you mind opening the garage door for us, please?" Joe asked while he and his son dragged their unwelcomed visitor with them.

Christian quickly did what was asked of him, as well as opening the car's back seat. After Bruce was placed in the back seat, David got behind the car's wheel, his father sat next to him, and Christian and Shawn sat in the back seat with the unconscious man propped up against the door.

Once they got to Shawn's place, David and Grandpa Joe pulled Bruce inside. They laid him on his bed and took off his boots and socks before covering him with what blankets they could find. After they did this, Grandpa Joe went to Shawn.

"Shawn, would you do me a favor and turn the heat up a little in her for him, please?" he asked him.

Up until then, Christian hadn't noticed how cold it had been in the trailer. He also noticed for the first time that he was able to see their breath in the air.

"I don't know if I can," Shawn told him with a shrug. "He has a tendency not to pay the heat. He does that to save money, but I'll try." He then left only to come back a short time later. "I did it. Seems like he paid it this month."

"Good. Thanks for doing that, Shawn."

"Shawn," David said before he left Bruce's bedroom. "Is there anything you want here before we go back?"

Shaking his head, he said, "Ah, no, I'm all set."

"In that case, and if it's ok with you guys, I want to get back to watch the ball drop. If we still have time that is," David commented while hesitating a little before walking outside.

The rest soon followed before they all took the same seats they were in on the ride over. Once home, each member of the family assumed their positions in the living room to watch the New Year be ushered in.

Two days later, David came home from work a little more agitated than usual. Christian and Shawn were in the living room watching TV and Sally was making dinner when he walked in. Putting his coat away, he sat at the table with a heavy sigh.

"How was work today, dear?" his wife asked him while coming over to kiss his forehead.

"Ah, good. Fine," he said shortly as a look of frustration crossed his face.

While looking at him, she asked, "Really? Then what's that look for?"

"I had to fire Bruce today," he stated sourly before opening that day's paper that was lying on the table before him.

Hearing this, Shawn immediately perked up and turned his attention to the kitchen.

"Fired him?" Sally quickly asked. " Why?"

"He almost killed someone today at the plant," he told her while flipping through to the Business section.

"On purpose?"

130

"No."

"What happened?"

"He knocked someone against one of the machines," David informed her while leaning back in his chair. "The guy's shirt got caught in the mechanisms which then proceeded to drag him along the conveyor belt to the main part of it. This piece he was on dealt with forcefully attaching multiple pieces of metal together before moving them into a heating section that would basically melt them together."

"Oh dear! How bad was he hurt?"

Shaking his head while going back to his paper, David said, "He did get his arm nailed in a few spots which caused the bone to break a couple of times. He was just about to be dragged head first into the heating unit when some of the other guys got it turned off. He was taken to the hospital after this."

"Why'd Bruce do it? Knock him against the machine, that is?"

"He was drunk," her husband stated with a wave. "From what I heard, Bruce slipped or something and knocked Ted into the machine. It seems like he's been coming into work drunk more and more the last few months."

"Why haven't you done anything about this sooner to ensure that this didn't happen?"

"The union." He scoffed while shaking his head. His voice was filled with disgust while looking at his wife. "We can't do anything without their ok. If it was me, I'd have fired him long ago but the only thing I could do was give him a verbal warning or write him up. Unless something actually happened, firing him was out of my hands."

"Oh, that's too bad. Is this Ted guy alright?"

"Yeah, outside of his arm he's fine." David laughed. "He's one tough little bastard. Thank the good Lord the other guys were quick to stop the machine. If they hadn't, the heat inside it would have killed him."

As the conversation ended, Shawn got up and went to Grandpa Joe's apartment. He would be out there until he was called in for supper. After which, he excused himself early and stayed the rest of the evening downstairs in his room. Though Christian was sure Shawn had heard all of the conversation about his dad like he had, Shawn never said anything about it, nor made any mention to it. Unfortunate for him, he didn't have the luxury of hearing more good news concerning his father.

A little more than a week later, the phone rang late one evening when the Eaton's and Shawn were all watching TV together. Grandpa Joe was the one who answered it and, by his overall reaction to it, the call was not a good one. After hanging up, he called his son into the kitchen to have a brief and muffled conversation with him. They soon got their coats and left. An hour and a half later they came back home looking worse than when they left. While walking into the living room, David turned off the television as Joe sat down next to Shawn on the couch.

"Shawn, I'm not sure how to put this so I'll just come out and say it," Joe told him as a sorrowful look came upon his face. "I've got some bad news."

"Is it about my dad?" Shawn asked while looking up to the older man next to him with a somber expression before looking down to his hands.

"Yes it is. It is about your father."

"What did he do now?"

"Shawn, I'm sorry," Joe started with much hesitation, "but your father was found on a side street in the city earlier this evening."

"Is he ok?" Shawn asked, although by his tone and mannerisms he already suspected the answer.

"No, he's not. Shawn, I'm sorry to tell you but your father died," Joe told him.

Shawn, on the other hand, wouldn't, or couldn't, look back at him. He just sat there looking down at his hands as tears filled his eyes. "No, it wasn't my dad. It was someone else," he said while his head slowly shook back and forth.

"I'm sorry, Shawn, but it was your father," Grandpa Joe told him softly while putting a hand on the boy's shoulder.

"No, you're wrong," he told him, refusing to believe what he was just told. "It wasn't him."

"Shawn, he's telling you the truth," David said while reconfirming the bad news. "He and I just came back from the coroner's office; that was who called before we left. The officer that reported it recognized your father but since he and the coroner needed someone else to make the ID, they called here."

"That's why David and I left," Grandpa Joe injected here. "We went down to see whether or not it was him."

"You could be wrong," Shawn told them while trying to raise up his hopes while tears riddled his cheeks. "It could be someone else that looks like him."

"I'm sorry, Shawn, but no," Joe sadly told him in a more firm tone. "The man that we saw *was* your father."

"No, that's not true," Shawn repeated to himself while still not wanting to believe the bad news he was hearing. When it seemed no one was going to agree with him, he got up to run downstairs to his room, slamming the door close behind him.

"Wasn't it this time last year that his mom died?" Sally asked.

"Yeah, last January," her father-in-law confirmed.

"Not to sound cruel, but January doesn't seem to be Shawn's month," David commented.

At that time, they all sat there in silence for a few minutes before anyone spoke again. Sally was the first to break the uncomfortable silence.

"What's going to happen to Shawn now?" she asked

"What do you mean?" her husband asked her.

"Well, we're his legal guardians but we never actually got the ok to adopt him," she mentioned. "What's going to happen to him now that both his parents are dead? Will he be able to stay here with us? Will we be able to adopt him? If not, will he go to an orphanage or to some family member?"

Rubbing his head, David thought for an answer to this. "We'll be his guardians for the time being but the final decision to whether or not we can adopt him is now up to the state. I know Shawn has some family around who would have first dibs on him, legally that is, but from what I've heard I doubt they'll take him in. The only alternatives I see is either we get the ok to adopt him or he'll be awarded to the state for them to do what they see fit."

"What would we have to do to adopt him?" Grandpa Joe asked while looking off to a far corner.

"I don't really know but, like I said before, it's now up to the state."

"Before we do inquire about this, we should ask Shawn to see what he wants to do," Sally informed them as her voice dictated that the idea wasn't open for debate.

"You want to ask him now?" Joe asked while finally being pulled back to reality. "Can't we give him a day or two to grieve a little first?"

She laughed at his question. "I didn't mean right now. I just meant when the time was ready, we should ask him before we assume anything."

"Don't worry, hun. We'll cross that bridge when we get to it," her husband assured her while rubbing her on her back. "In the meantime, there's a funeral we should be thinking about first."

The funeral for Bruce took place that following weekend and went fairly smooth. Except for the Eaton's and Shawn, only a handful or two of other people came to bid him a final farewell. The people that did come were mainly relatives that Shawn either had never seen before or not in quite some time. Only one nonrelative, a former drinking buddy of the deceased, had shown. The amount of people, or lack thereof, which showed up only seemed to upset Shawn. He previously made it a point to tell Christian several times on how many people he had expected to turn out to pay their respect for his father, but since only a small number in reality actually did turn out, it seemed to hit home with him. He acted surprised at the actual number while saying he expected a lot more.

The family that did come, all six or seven members, had inquired what was going to happen with Shawn. When the thoughts of Shawn's potential adoption was mentioned, none of them were interested in doing that. Instead, they gave David and Sally their approval if they wanted to adopt Shawn themselves.

The next night at dinner did Shawn himself get involved in the conversation when he openly asked about it.

"What's going to happen to me now that my parents are dead?"

"That's up to you really," David told him. "The choices that you have are first to your family. If they agree to it, it looks like you'll be going there to live, probably with your aunt and uncle."

"I don't want to live with them," Shawn bluntly stated without much hesitation. "Why would I want that?"

"You may not have much of a choice, Shawn. Legally, they'll have the right to you. After all, they are your family."

"They aren't my family," he said bitterly. "I don't even know most of them."

Chuckling at that, Grandpa Joe asks, "What would you want?"

"You mean, if I had a choice?" Shawn was taken back with surprise by the question, almost like he wasn't expecting it.

"Yeah, if you have a choice, what would you want?"

"You serious? I'd stay here!" He shrugged as if it was a nonissue while cramming his mouth full of food.

"Shawn, dear, don't put so much food in your mouth at one time," Sally told him for the umpteenth time. "We wouldn't want you to choke."

"Yes, Mrs. Eaton."

"So, Shawn, is that what you really want or are you just saying that because you think it's what we want to hear?" Grandpa Joe asked him.

"Better here than with my own family, or what's left of it," Shawn told him after drinking most of his milk.

While adjusting his glasses, David mentioned, "Shawn, before you actually answer that, maybe you should be aware of the situation you're in."

"What situation? Either I'm staying here or I'm staying with them. Right?"

"Well, no, not exactly," David corrected while clearing his throat to momentarily pause to think. "Technically, it's up to the state what happens to you. Since we're only your legal guardians, we don't have first rights to you. First and foremost, it's your family the state will look at. In this case, your aunt and uncle."

"But I don't want to live with them," Shawn bluntly stated again.

"Yes, you've said that, but that's what the courts may do," David said while trying to continue on with the conversation. "If you don't have any family available, or if the family that you do have doesn't want you, you'll be put into foster care or some sort of orphanage until you're adopted, or until you're 18."

Hearing that, Shawn looked up at him with wide eyes and a look of dread at the thought of having to potentially leave the Eaton household. "Does that mean I can't stay here?"

"That's what we're trying to figure out."

"You telling me you don't want me here?!" Shawn demanded, almost shocked that he may not be welcomed there.

"Shawn, that's not what my son is saying," Grandpa Joe corrected softly as he defended his son. His neutral tone almost made Shawn ashamed of what he had said. "If you just listen to what he's trying to say, you might understand better."

"If you don't want me here, all you gotta do is just tell me. I can handle that," Shawn hung his head as tears began to fill his eyes. He then got up and went to his room.

"We aren't done talking yet, Shawn," Joe told him firmly when Shawn disappeared around the corner. "Please come sit back down so we can finish the conversation."

After a moment or two of silence, Shawn slowly, and reluctantly, reemerged back in the kitchen before sitting back in his chair.

"As I was saying before," David said while giving his father a side glance before focusing back onto Shawn. "Legally, your family has first dib. If they wish not to take you, then you will be put up for adoption. What we're trying to get to is what do you want? Since you clearly stated twice before that you do not want to live with your aunt and uncle, is there any family that you do have that you would want to stay with?"

Shawn remained silent to this. He simply sat there hanging his head. Drops of tears began to fall onto his plate.

"Shawn, honey," Sally softly said while leaning towards him. "Please answer the question, won't you? Is there any other family you would want to live with?"

Again, Shawn refused to answer. He did, however, shake his head a little as if to say "no."

"Is there any place that you can think of where you *would* want to live?" Joe asked him softly.

Shawn nodded to this.

"Where, Shawn? Where would you want to live?"

"Here," he finally said.

"You want to live here?" Sally asked him. " You want to live with us?"

135

"Yeah," he answered softly without hesitating or bothering to think for an answer. "I want to stay here if it's ok."

While looking thoughtfully to his wife, David said, "I guess we could try to arrange that. But before we go through with anything, I need to make sure we heard you correctly. Do you really want to live here? Do you want to live with us?"

Shawn merely nodded his head to confirm that he did.

"If that's the case, do you realize that we will most likely need to adopt you for that to happen?"

Again, Shawn nodded.

"Ok, then it's settled. I'll see what I can do about it this week." David nodded before drinking his coffee. He then glanced at each member of the family to read their expressions. "Before I do, does anyone have anything to say about this before I look into this? If anyone does, now is the time to say it."

Before any of them had a chance to say anything, Grandpa Joe said something that seemed to settle the discussion one and for all. "What kind of idiotic question is that? Of course we want him here and, no, we don't have any problems with it. End of discussion!" he stated to the point while pounding the table with a closed fist before going back to his meal.

"Guess that settles that," Christian said happily before starting to hum a song he liked.

While giving Shawn a wink, Grandpa Joe said, "It better 'cause I don't want to have this talk again."

When Christian looked over at Shawn, he noticed that even though he was still hanging his head, that that was one of the few times he remembered actually seeing him smile openly and actually mean it.

Lucky, meanwhile, seemed to noticed the improved emotions in the room as she went up to Shawn to force her muzzle under his hand for attention.

Chapter 14

It took David, the Eaton's lawyer, and Brian Bise almost two months to get everything in order for Shawn's adoption trail. The day of, Christian went to his mom with a concern.

"Mama, I think something's wrong with Shawn," he told her.

"What's wrong with him?"

"I don't know, but he's acting all weird and stuff," Christian stated while thinking of how to word what he had to say. "He's acting both nervous and happy at the same time."

"Oh, I wouldn't worry too much about that, dear. Shawn's going to be just fine," she told him in a nonchalant way as a smiled crossed her lips. "He's nervous about the adoption, but he's also happy because he knows that after today he'll be part of our family for good."

To Christian, the trial was boring to the point of almost causing him to fall asleep in their town's courtroom. In the courtroom, there were two tables that lay in front of the judge. The table on the right stood Shawn's aunt, uncle, and their lawyer while standing at the left table was David, Brian Bise, Shawn, and their respected lawyer.

Shortly after it officially started, each lawyer had a chance to speak their side before the judge asked them to approach. There, the mouths of those involved were seen moving, but whatever that was voiced could not be heard. A number of hand gestures and nodding occurred before the remaining people involved at the trail were also asked to approach. Each person was asked questions before responding in their own way. This was soon followed by a long silence as the judge bobbed his head back and forth while going deep in thought. He soon nodded again before signing a handful of papers. After the signing was complete, all the participants shook hands before going back to their assigned table. Once there, David, Brian, and the lawyer shook hands while smiling and patting Shawn on the back. Christian, meanwhile, noticed that he had never seen Shawn as happy as he had that day in court. That night they had a special celebration of sorts with each other's newly acquired acquisitions: the Eaton's for getting a new member of the family, and Shawn for a new life and new family. Each member was pleased by their own personal gain but none as much as Shawn.

From that point on, it seemed that Christian and Shawn were doing everything together, except when Shawn was getting boxing lessons from either Grandpa Joe or from the Y. Not only where they walking to and from school every day together, but they also played, watched TV, did homework, and even went as far as trying to press their own interests off onto each other. Christian's interests laid mostly with cartoons and science whereas Shawn's laid in action movies and sports.

Christian had tried to get Shawn into various magazines he had or models he was trying to build but soon stopped after several of several recycled excuses. The real reason behind these excuses Christian didn't know, but assumed it was because Shawn either didn't have the patience for them or they didn't offer enough action or excitement for him.

Shawn, meanwhile, had a little better luck passing his interests onto Christian, such as sports he was into, but failed to realize that Christian's interest laid mainly in the overall mechanics of the sport rather than the actual enjoyment of playing it. Shawn, however, would soon fail at this because of some internal thing he had. That something was about not being beaten if he could help it. Though it was friendly competition, it was only if he himself was winning. This eventually led Christian to come up with some excuse of his own not to be there before going back to the safety of his room.

The only interest Shawn had that seemed to stick to his now adopted brother was wrestling. Not collegiate or amateur wrestling, mind you, but that of professional. The names of Hogan, JYD, Warrior, Jake the Snake, Steamboat, and Macho Man often passed through his lips when the occasion occurred. This professional form of wrestling often helped pass their time together, especially during that cold winter they were having.

As winter eventually faded into spring, they found themselves outside more and more. Out here, the big difference between them was that Christian would want to stay near strategic points of safety such as the house, road, or a friend's place; whereas Shawn liked taking a chance by going off the beaten track. Literally. With Shawn's more vocal and dominant personae compared to Christian's laid back eager-to-please one, it wouldn't take Shawn long to drag him into one of his adventures. These adventures usually meant exploring some uncharted place not on Christian's map. Sometimes Christian's sense of logic and safety deterred Shawn from doing some activities he himself would normally have done, but not very often.

School finished up again in June and Christian once again was valedictorian of his class even though he was disappointed with his grades. To think that someone was valedictorian with a grade average of 95% would be disappointed, it was truly for Christian in this case since it was his lowest grade point average to date. Shawn, meanwhile, beat his previous academic high, which he set the year before, with a 78%.

The Sunday night after the last day of school, Shawn had talked Christian into watching pay-per-view of a wrestling promotion he liked, which was brought to them courtesy of Grandpa Joe. They both watched it up in his air-conditioned apartment as they waited for him to return from another routine trip of his. All of the big names were there including Shawn's Shawn Michaels, who defended the company's secondary belt, and Christian's Bret Hart, who won the tournament that highlighted that specific pay-per-view; and each were upset when Hulk Hogan lost his world championship.

During a less than stellar nontitle 8-man tag team match, Grandpa Joe finally returned home. He had been up in northern New York the past week helping out with a couple of their Y's boxing clinics. He slowly came up the stairs to his apartment, grunting and groaning while doing so, before eventually appearing in the doorway rather looking his age. He was tired and quite a bit soar from his physical activities that he had been in.

"Hey, boys," he said softly when he finally entered. Tossing this luggage on the floor against the wall, he came over to sit on his bed with a heavy sigh. "How's your show going?"

"Great, though this match isn't that good," Shawn told him.

"How was your trip, Grandpa?" Christian asked while getting up to sit on the bed next to his grandfather.

"Good, good. I had fun," he answered quietly with a tired voice and heavy eyes. He soon rose to stretch a number of times to help alleviate tired muscles. "It looks like I'll be going over to Missouri for a week or so next month. A couple of their Y's over there are getting some of these clinics that we have here. Kansas City and St. Louis seem to need some help. I'm not sure which one I'll be going to yet."

"Can we go, Grandpa?" Christian eagerly asked.

Perking up when he heard this, Shawn shifted his attention over from the television. "Yeah, can we?"

Bending over to take off his shoes and socks, Joe replied with a, "Maybe, we'll see. We'll see. Why don't you two go back to your show and enjoy the rest of it? I want to go take a shower; I smell like hell."

"Alright, Grandpa," Christian said before going back on the floor next to Shawn.

With that, Joe went to wash off with the sounds of two young boys cheering and booing their favorite and most hated wrestlers of the show.

The next few weeks went by like any typical summer would for a couple of kids: fast. They sent the time doing a variety of things such as exploring new parts of the woods and surrounding areas, fishing at their spot by the stream, and visiting the Deeley's for their afternoon soda run. Mr. Deeley always seemed to enjoy the visits from Christian, but seemed to be standoffish whenever Shawn was there. More often than not, they would usually come home tired and dirty. Those weeks went so fast that it seemed like only a week after their pay-per-view that Grandpa Joe was going off to Missouri for his volunteer work.

"What can't we go with you, Grandpa?" Christian whined.

"Yeah, why can't we?!" Shawn demanded.

"A couple of reasons, actually," Joe said. "There probably won't be much for you to do there."

Cutting him off, Shawn told him, "There'll be plenty of stuff for me there."

"Well, yes, for you there will be, but what about Christian? He'll be bored as hell for most of the trip. And for you, Shawn, I don't think you'd find stuff at the Y to keep you occupied all day long," Joe explained. "Besides, I'll be there most of the day. Who'd look after you two?"

"We'll look after ourselves just like we always do," Shawn replied in a very matter of fact way.

Grandpa Joe laughed at that while looking down at them. "You will, huh? Just like you always do? You two would get lost. Well, not totally lost anyway. I think I could trust Christian into staying around where he's supposed to, but you, on the other hand, I'm afraid I'd have to send out a search party out for you every night."

"What's that supposed to mean?!" Shawn questioned.

"You know damn well what that's supposed to mean. You have a tendency of exploring places you know you shouldn't, you're gone for hours on end, and we never know where you're off to or when you'll be back. I don't want to have to worry about that with either of you on this trip."

"You won't have to worry about us 'cause we won't do that," Shawn said.

While finishing putting his luggage in the car, Joe closed the door behind it. "That's right. You won't because you're not going."

"What?!" Shawn sharply asked. "We'll stay right where you want us to and not go anywhere else. How's that?"

While looking down at him, Joe retorted, "That might work for the first day or two, but with you being you, you'll get bored and will want to start exploring. And with Christian being Christian, he'll go along with you mainly because he can't seem to say no to you. With that in mind, it's better all-around if you two were to stay home. And, besides, who knows? Something might come up that would prevent me from being there for the two of you."

"So there's no way we'll change your mind?" pleaded Christian.

"I'm sorry, but no, not this time. Maybe next time," his grandfather said before walking up the steps in the garage that led to the kitchen to pop his head inside. "Come on, David, let's go! I don't want to miss my flight!"

"I'm coming! No need to lose your temper, Dad," his son said while coming out of the house. "You still have two hours before your plane takes off."

"I like getting there early."

"Now boys, you behave your mother until I get back, ya hear?" David told the two boys as he climbed into the car.

"Yes, Mr. Eaton."

Christian rolled his eyes. "Yes, Dad."

"What's that look for?" David smiled.

"Just that you always tell us to behave. Have we ever not?"

"I just need to make sure you two won't do anything, that's all."

"What makes you think I'd do anything to get into trouble?"

His dad smiled at him while starting the car. "You'll have Shawn here with you."

"Hey! What's that supposed to mean, huh?" Shawn asked with a hint of anger as David pulled out of the garage with Grandpa Joe sitting next to him. "Hey! You gonna answer me or what?" Shawn continued to wait while spreading his arms.

All David did was back out into the road as Grandpa Joe smiled at him. Shawn followed them out to stand in the drive. No answer was ever given. When he realized they weren't going to answer, he shook his head before walking back into the garage to find Christian smiling at him.

"What the hell you smilin' at?"

With that, all Christian could do was look at Shawn while his smile immediately turned into an outburst of laughter.

Shawn simply waved his arms at him. "Whatever. Forget you, man! I'm going fishing down at the creek." And, with that, he grabbed his fishing pole and gear before leaving. He would not return until almost dinner time.

Christian, meanwhile, went to his room for various toys, magazines, and other items before putting them in his backpack, then went and spent the better part of the day in his tree house.

David came back about four hours later with a bag of knick-knacks he got during an extended visit at Deeley's Market. Once he took care of that, he came back outside to do some yard work it was time for dinner. At which point, he lit up the charcoal grill before throwing on some hamburgers to cook.

"So, dear, how were the Deeley's doing?" Sally asked soon after they were all sitting down for dinner.

"Oh, you know how they are," he told here in between sips of coffee. "She's getting more absent minded as she used to be and he thinks every kid that comes in there is trying to steal something. It's getting to the point where I don't even want to go in. Most of the things they talk about I've heard so much that I could fill in for either one of them during a conversation."

"I know what you mean, dear," commented his wife. "You know my friend Jen, right? Well, all she seems to talk about is her on again off again boyfriend Jimmie. That's all she talks about. 'Jimmie did this' or 'Jimmie did that,' with an occasional 'Jimmie irritates me when he does this or that.' Same thing every time. It's gotten to the point I don't want to talk to her."

"It's gotten that bad?"

"I'm afraid so."

"Tell her then."

"I can't tell her that. It'll hurt her feelings."

"So? Is it better them you not wanting to be around her?"

Sally sighed before taking a few bites of her food. "I guess you're right, dear. I just don't want to upset her or ruin our friendship."

"But that's exactly what she's doing by her repetitiveness of her boyfriend," her husband told her. "The difference is she doesn't know what she's doing to the friendship, whereas you know what you're feeling about it."

"I know, but still." She went silent before soon changing the subject. "Anyway, I haven't seen you boys much today. What have you been up to?"

"Nothin'," Shawn replied with a mouthful of food.

"Really? You must have done something," Sally responded. "And please don't talk with your mouth full; it isn't polite."

When he swallowed his food, Shawn went on to tell her, "I was just fishing by the creek today."

"Well, that's something. Did you catch something?"

"No, not today."

"How about you, Christian? What did you do today, sweetie?"

"I was up in my tree house today," he replied while bobbing his head to a song he was humming.

"*Your* tree house?" Shawn quickly asked.

"Yeah, that's where I was."

"Don't you mean *our* tree house?"

Christian looked at him. "No. I mean my tree house."

"What'd'cha say that?"

"Because it's mine."

"What'd'ya mean it's yours?" a slightly irritated Shawn questioned.

"I meant just that. It's mine."

"Why do you say that?"

"Because I use it."

"I use it too."

"Not very often." Christian shrugged before taking a few more bites of food. "You're usually somewhere else like by the creek or wherever. I've used your fishing pole a couple of times. Would that make them our fishing poles?"

Scoffing, Shawn tells him, "No! Why would it?"

"Because I've used them a couple of times."

"Yeah, you used them, but that doesn't mean they're yours."

"I rest my case." Christian smiled. "You have your fishing poles, I have my tree house."

"Ok boys, enough of that," David sternly voiced while tapping his finger on the table. "None of that at the dinner table. You hear me?"

"But he started it!" Shawn protested while pointing a finger at Christian.

"I don't care who started it, but it's going to end. Now!"

"Alright," Shawn said while looking down at his food.

Christian, meanwhile, had already forgotten about the conversation as he had already gone back to booking his head to some song he had been humming during dinner.

"So, dear, was Dad going to call tonight?" inquired Sally.

"He said he'd try after he got settled in, most likely after dinner."

As predicted, Grandpa Joe called later that evening about 7:30 and was all settled in his hotel in Kansas City. Though his flight experienced a couple instances of turbulence and having a hard time finding the hotel he was booked at, everything went as expected. Tomorrow morning would be his first day that the Y over there though he didn't know what to expect. He would also find out if he'd be there for his two-week duration or if he'd travel to St. Louis at some point to help out there.

On the way up to his room, Grandpa Joe had said he passed a restaurant in the hotel's lobby. The smells that emanated from it, mixed with his lack of an appetite for the day, made him aware of how hungry he really was. The sign going into it stated that the feature for the night was their house sirloin, which he was thinking about getting. Speaking briefly to both Christian and Shawn, he soon got off saying he would call the following night. At which point, they all said their good nights before finally hanging up.

Near the beginning of the week, Joe told the family during their nightly phone call that he would be going to St. Louis the day after next to lend a helping hand there. He also said he still had a good day's worth of work at this current Y in Kansas City and would leave the following morning. The next night he called a bit later than he had the night before, just after 9 o'clock. He had finished everything he had needed to do at about two hours previously before going back to his room to shower, change, and going off to eat dinner once again at the hotel's restaurant. Though he did call later that night, he was still able to speak with each member of the family. That particular night, Christian noticed that his grandfather had spoken a bit longer to each of them than he did before.

"Now, you behave your parents now," Joe told him. "I don't want to hear anything about you causing trouble or anything."

143

Christian sighed. "Grandpa, it's not me you should worry about. Have you ever known me to get into trouble?"

"I know. You're the good one of the bunch," he said with a smile. "I just want to make sure, that's all. Also, if no one has anything else to say, I'll get getting off now to head to bed."

"I don't, Grandpa, but I'll check with the others," Christian said before pulling away from the phone to call out. "Does anyone have anything else to say to Grandpa before he hangs up?!" When no one said they did, Christian went back to talk with his grandfather. "Sorry, Grandpa, but no one has anything else to say."

"That's ok, kiddo. I think I'll get off now anyway. But before I do, I just wanted to remind you that I might not call for a couple of days. I'm going to St. Louis tomorrow for a few days."

"Ok, Grandpa."

"We, you have a good, night Christian. I love you."

"You have a good night too, Grandpa. And I love you, too." With that, Christian hung up before letting his parents know not to expect a call for a couple of days.

Two nights later during dinner, the phone rang.

"Geez, Dad's calling a little early tonight. I thought he wouldn't call for at least another hour and a half if he did," David commented while looking at the time. He soon got up to answer the phone. "Hello...speaking....yes, this is David Eaton...Yes, Joe Eaton is my father...oh, are you serious?" At this point, there was an extended, uncomfortable silence as he let out a heavy sigh. Tears soon filled his eyes. "Yeah, I'm still here...what do you want from me?...Ok, I'll try and catch a plane over later this evening. Where can I meet you?...Oh, you will? That'll be great; thank-you...If all goes well, my dad'll be fine until I get there in the morning....Yeah, thanks for calling."

When he was done talking, he slowly hung up the phone. It took him quite awhile before he was able to turnaround to face the rest of the family. He simply just stood there with his back to them while his hands were at his face, wiping away what appeared to be tears comin down his cheeks.

"David, what's wrong?" Sally asked while looking at him from the table.

"It's, it's...my dad. He, he..." he replied while trying to answer the question before finally turning to face the family. "He was in a really bad car accident in St. Louis this afternoon."

"Is he...ok?" his wife asked.

"I-I-I don't know," he softly told her while wiping his tear-riddled cheeks. "It looks really bad, though. They don't expect him to make it through the night."

The room went morbidly silent for what seemed like eternity for Christian. For the first time in his short life, he found his father having a hard time composing himself. His dad's face was pale,

144

cheeks slightly flushed, and eyes disoriented as tears highlighted them. When he was finally able to, he walked slowly back to the table to sit back down.

"He's dead, isn't he?" Shawn softly asked while looking down at his plate with fork in hand before playing with what food he had left.

"No, he's still alive," a visibly shaken David replied.

Sally, meanwhile, watched her husband for a moment before putting a hand on his forearm in an attempt to help calm him down.

"Honey, it'll be alright," she softly assured him. "What are we going to do?"

"I told 'em I'd fly over there later tonight. After that, we'll play it by ear, I guess." Wiping his eyes for the final time, he brought in a long breath that was soon followed by an equally long exhale.

They soon found themselves eating the rest of their dinner in an awkward silence that Christian had never experienced before. Afterwards, his dad packed a small bag while his mom quickly did the dishes. They were all in the car practically before the dishes had time to fully dry.

Arriving at the Syracuse International Airport roughly 8 o'clock that night and, though it was slightly busy, it felt like a tomb to Christian. Whether it was the shiny marble floors and walls, or the stale air being circulated, it gave the appearance of a giant mausoleum. The many glazed over, stoned-out faces he saw didn't help any which gave the wearers a zombie-like look. Though Christian had to admit it wasn't *Night of the Living Dead*, a movie that scared the crap out of him, he couldn't help but think that the situation they were in would have been a great scene for either that movie or, for that matter, any zombie movie in general.

Christian assumed that once his father had his plane ticket and flight schedule taken care of, that the mood for the rest of them would soon improve. He would soon find that his assumption was wrong. His dad's flight would leave in roughly an hour after that and Sally had decided that she, Christian, and Shawn would wait there until after he had boarded. While taking possession of a bench in quiet, yet random corner near a palm-like tree, they sat there to wait in silence.

Sally soon started to cry softly, sniffing, and blowing her nose while David did his best to console her. He soon stopped this after a little while when it looked like it wasn't doing any good before leaning back against the wall to stare up at the ceiling. He soon seemed to speak aloud while thinking about his flight.

"Leave here...fly into Philly...layover in Cincinnati...then land in St. Louis." He paused briefly in thought before continuing. "I don't know why I make two spots. Why two? Couldn't I just fly directly into St. Louis? With layovers, maybe five hours or so. Hopefully I'll be there no later than 2 am. Yeah, that sounds about right."

His voice seemed to drift off during the last few words before being replaced with Sally's muffled crying. Christian felt numb from all this, a numbness that made his senses muffled to everything around him. The minutes seemed like hours as they waited. The clock on the wall next to them ticked loudly while its second hand went around. The minute hand, meanwhile, would slowly bang occasionally as it went from minute to minute. While focusing on the clock's hands,

Christian almost missed his father talking but happened to catch the last few words of whatever it was he said.

"....time's captives, hostages to eternity," was all Christian was able to hear from him.

Sally, meanwhile, turned to her husband to simply ask, "What was that, dear?"

"I was just quoting something, that's all," he quietly told her.

"What was the quote?"

"'Eternity's own hostage and prisoner to time'," he said while his head, still resting against the wall behind him, turned to look at his wife. "Boris Pasternak said that."

"Who's that, dear."

Shifting his gaze back to its previous position, he casually explained, "Russian writer my father used to like when I was younger. Since we got here, I've been thinking about my dad. Gosh, a lot of things I haven't thought about in years, things that aren't really important are things that I'm remembering. They're just little things. Trivial things."

"You're dad's going to be ok. You'll see," she softly said with a loving tone while patting his thigh.

A tear appeared slightly from the corner of one of his eyes. "I hope so. I really hope so."

That was the last words spoken between them as the announcement was heard over the loud speakers for his flight.

Standing, Sally soon was talking to her husband again as she adjusted his shirt. "You be sure to call when you check into your room, no matter what time it is."

"You know I will," he replied while looking around to see if anyone was watching them. "It'll be really late just to let you know."

"That doesn't matter. I want you to call," she told him while finishing up with his shirt before hugging and kissing him. "It'll be alright. Don't worry too much about your father."

David returned the hug and kiss before patting Christian on the head and Shawn on the shoulder. Picking up his bag, he paused to look at them all before turning to walk down the terminal. He soon disappeared while melting in with the crowd.

The ride home was the longest and quietest car right Christian had ever been on. It seemed to affect both his mother and Shawn equally, and he couldn't help but think of what Shawn may have went through when his own parents had died. Though Grandpa Joe wasn't his dad, he still felt like he was losing a big chunk deep within him.

Shawn, who sat in the back seat, either looked down at his lap or out the window. Sally, meanwhile, focused her attention out the window in front of her as she drove. She did take her gaze off the road once to glance over at Christian.

"What was that?" she asked.

Startled from her speaking to him, Christian looked up at her. "Huh?"

"I'm sorry, but what was that?" his mother asked while she looked over at him again.

"What was what, Mama?"

Sighing, she replied, "Oh, nothing. I just thought you said something."

"I didn't say anything."

The mood for the rest of the night remained somber. Christian and Shawn went to their respected rooms soon after getting home and would not leave until the following morning. The only disturbance in the Eaton household that night was a telephone call around 2:30 in the morning.

The next morning the phone rang when Christian was playing in his room. His mom, who was in the kitchen making breakfast, French toast, scrambled eggs, and sausage filled the air, had answered it. He normally wouldn't have paid any attention to it if it wasn't for his mom's reaction to it. He had heard a gasp from her before she started to cry softly while talking to the person who had called. When the conversation was over, she took the food off of the stove to go out into the garage for an extended stay. Whatever was said on the phone, Christian knew it wasn't good. He was hoping it didn't have anything to do with his grandfather, but he couldn't be sure.

It wasn't until they were at the table eating breakfast did Sally inform them that Grandpa Joe had died during the night. The news hit Christian like a ton of bricks. The air went out of him and he found it increasingly difficult to draw a breath. The news was like a vice grip squeezing down on him as it sucked the life out of him. His blood seemed to boil under the pressure building up inside. He could feel the rush to his head, causing it to momentarily throb massively. His eyes seemed to swell up as he fought back tears.

"Grandpa's dead?" he asked his mother.

"Yes, honey, he is."

"Why?!" Shawn cried out while beginning to sob uncontrollably.

"The car accident that he was in was really bad. He didn't make it through," she said next to him at the table. She soon found herself trying to wipe Shawn's tears from his eyes. "It seems like it was worse than what we expected."

"How b-b-bad w-w-was it?" stuttered Christian.

"Bad."

"Wha...what?" he asked his mother as his crying became harder to control. "You mean h-h-he's not c-c-coming home?"

"Your grandfather will be coming home, you won't need to worry about that," Sally informed him while turning her attention to her son. "He'll be coming home with your father."

"That's not what he meant," Shawn stated. The words he spoke seemed to make him cry a little harder as the realization was hitting him. "We won't see him again, will we?"

"No, sweetie, I'm afraid we won't."

"What about the funeral or whatever, Mama?" Christian asked when he was able to pull himself together enough to ask.

"Your father had him cremated there. We haven't talked about that yet, but I'm assuming we'll have something," she told him while reaching over to wipe the tears from his face. "It's still early for that. We still have plenty of time."

"So, w-w-we're not g-g-gonna see G-G-Grandpa again?" Christian practically choked on his words.

"No, we won't see him again, honey," she answered while running her fingers through his hair.

Once the realization that Grandpa Joe had died finally began to sink into his head, Shawn started crying harder than he had before. Meanwhile, Lucky walked over to him and laid her head on his lap, which only seemed to fuel his anger.

"Stop that!" he demanded while smacking her across the head. "Will you get out of here and leave me alone?!"

Lucky quickly put her tail between her legs and walked tenderly into the next room before climbing up on the couch to lie down.

"Shawn, there was no need for you to do that to her," Sally chastised him the best she could under the given situation. "She was only trying to make you feel better."

"Tryin' to make me feel better?" he repeated in a scoffing tone while trying not to cry. "She's just a dog!"

She merely looked at him before saying, "That doesn't matter. Dogs have feelings too."

Finding it harder to control his emotions, Shawn ran from the kitchen and down to his room to cry out whatever tears he had left in his head.

Christian, wanting some time and space to himself, also left the kitchen to go up to Grandpa Joe's apartment. Once there, he emotionally looked around while trying to find something there among his grandfather's possessions that could possibly comfort him. When he couldn't, he merely laid on his grandfather's bed and cried himself to sleep.

Christian woke a short time later to the erythematic beating coming from somewhere inside the apartment. When he scanned the room with blurry eyes, he saw Shawn hitting Grandpa Joe's speed bag that hung in the corner.

"Oh, hey Shawn," he said while sitting up on bed before rubbing his eyes.

Shawn just gave him a quick look without as much as a break on the bag. Christian had never used the speed bag much, but the times he had he found it difficult to be able to hit it in somewhat of a coordinated fashion. Seeing Shawn hit in the way that he was, Christian had to admit that he was really good.

"You're pretty good at that, Shawn."

"Yup," Shawn told him while hardly acknowledging the compliment.

"How long did it take you to be able to hit it like that?"

"Couple of weeks."

"Too bad Grandpa won't be around anymore to help you with your training," Christian said while getting up to walk over to the heavy bag. It hung from the ceiling a few feet away from the bag Shawn was currently using.

"Yeah, well, get used to it," Shawn told him while finishing off the speed bag with a power shot.

While starting to take a few miserable attempts at punching the heavy bag, Christian asked, "Get used to what?

"People leaving," Shawn sadly informed him.

"Huh?" he asked dumbfounded. "What?"

Looking at him, Shawn repeated himself. "I said for you to get used to people leaving. They always seem to leave when you start needing or wanting them around."

"They who? Who leaves?" Christian asked while continuing to hit the bag. He found that to do so helped resolve a lot of the tension and sorrow he was feeling over the current loss of his grandfather.

"People do. Whenever I've had a person in my life that I needed, they all left," Shawn explained with anger in his voice while starting to tear up.

"Where'd they go?

"I don't know. They just leave! My brother's in jail; my mom and dad are both dead; what family I do have don't want me; and Grandpa Joe just died. That's what I'm saying. Everyone that you have leaves. They go away and never come back."

"Oh, I'm sorry," Christian apologized while continuing to punch the heavy bag. He soon stopped when he was out of breath while looking down at his hands that were now red around his knuckles. "I'm tired. And my hands hurt, too."

"You weren't breathing right," Shawn explained while wiping the tears off his face. "The way you were hitting it was all wrong. Want me to show you how to hit it the right way?"

Christian nodded. "Ah-huh."

"Alright, try and pay attention," Shawn told him while stepping up to the bag before demonstrating the proper way of working it. His feet seemed to flow over the floor as his hands bounced repeatedly off of the bag. After a little bit, he stopped to walk around behind it to hold it for Christian. "Here, now you try."

Striking the bag a few times, Christian tried to follow Shawn's lead. He hit it better than he had before but not as well as Shawn had. A few of the punches stung his hands. He stopped after a bit to look at his hands. They still ached a little while a couple of his knuckles had split open. Droplets of blood were visible in cracks but, overall, he felt good. Punching the bag had made his hands hurt but he was feeling better. He was calmer than he had been and, as he drew in big gulps of air to feed his lungs, he became more clear headed and more relaxed.

Smiling, Christian said, "That felt good."

"You looked good, too," Shawn complimented.

Surprised to hear Shawn actually say something nice about him, Christian happily asked, "Really? I did good?"

"Hey, hey, hey," Shawn blurted out with an open raised hand towards him. "I wouldn't say you actually looked good."

"But you just did."

"What I meant was, I wouldn't say you actually looked good but you do have some potential."

"Ya think so?" Christian smiled broadly when he heard that.

"Yeah, I think so," Shawn reluctantly admitted. "I can help show you some more stuff on the bag if you want."

"Would you do that for me? Really?" he asked while receiving a nod for an answer. "When can we start?"

Shawn shrugged. "Now, if you want."

When Christian accepted with a nod, Shawn walked behind the heavy bag once more and began instructing his adopted brother on some simple boxing techniques.

Part II

The Awakening

"The first shall be last and the last shall be first,

in a cardboard box 'neath the underpass."

(*The Ghost Of Tom Joad*, written by Bruce Springsteen)

Chapter 15

In the middle of a crowded arena, a boxing match was under way. A lean black man was in the process of forcing his white counterpart back with a series of sharp, strong punches until they reached the corner. Sensing that he was about to be trapped with more yet to come, the white pugilist made a comeback with a string of jabs and crosses, helping to enable him to take several steps out of the corner before his opponent came to his senses and retaliated.

The black man soon punched his counterpart back against the ropes after a brief exchange of jabs and hooks before landing a well-placed elbow square in his opponent's face. The force of the blow broke his opponent's nose on impact, who, after making several faces at once while letting out an agonizing grown, quickly dropped to a knee. He raised a glove to cover his face in the process like someone trying to hide a deformity.

The ref immediately got between the two fighters. He moved the dark-skinned man to a neutral corner.

"What the hell you doin'?!" the ref demanded.

"What?" The black man stretched out his arms as a confused look came upon his face.

"You know damn well what I mean! The next time you try and pull that crap in my ring again, it'll cost you a point! You hear me?!"

"Whatever!"

"Hey, kid," the ref said while focusing on the injured fighter who by now was in the process of standing up. "You alright?"

While bleeding out of both nostrils, the injured boxer had a terrified look across his face after noticing the amount of blood on his glove.

"Kid, you alright?" the ref repeated.

"Um, yeah. Fine, ref."

Before the ref could have him go to his corner to be looked at the bell rang signaling the end of the round.

"Alright, go to your corner, kid," the ref told him. "Go get checked out."

Approaching his corner, he saw his spit man bring a stool into the ring for him to sit on. His aging trainer, a short, old, white-haired Italian man, also came through the ropes. He looked like he was going to explode.

"What the hell was ya doin' out there?!" he yelled at his boxer sat on the stool. "What was ya thinking', huh?!"

"I don't know."

"Well, it's showin'." The old man bent over to take a look at his boxer's bloody nose.

Taking the boxer's mouth guard out, the spit man, a lean, muscular, young man with a not-so-trusting eye about him, gave his fighter a drink of water that was soon spat out into a gray metal pale.

As the trainer continued to look at his nose, the boxer looked past the old man's face to see an attractive woman walking around the inside of the ring. She was holding up a giant white sign with a big, black six in the middle of it.

"Sixth round," he softly said while seeing this.

"Yeah?" his trainer muttered. "What 'bout it?"

"We're gonna start the sixth."

"With the way ya fought last round, I'm surprised ya made it this far." The trainer stood to signal he was done looking at the bloody nose. "I've got some good news and some bad, kid."

"Yeah, what's that?"

"The good news is I know what's wrong with it," he said before briefly pausing. "The bad news, kid, is it's broken."

"Broken? You serious?" the boxer asked while receiving a quick nod of confirmation. "Man, it doesn't hurt that much. Can you fix me up, Dom?"

"If I do, bloodily be spraying outta yer nostrils like a damn gusher. Match'll be called."

"Come on, Dom! Fix me up," the pugilist pleaded. "I know I can win if you do."

"If I do, ya'll have less than a minute to pull whatever magic ya have left outta yer ass before this fight'll be called," Dom firmly told him while still having a pair of pleading eyes ask for him for help. "Alright, kid. Hang on. This'll hurt a little," he finally said before turning to the spit man. "Would ya grab a towel or something to cram in his mouth? He may want to bit on something."

The request was quickly answered with a nod as a clean towel magically appeared in the boxer's mouth.

"Here goes nothin', kid." With that, Dom bent over and proceeded to snap the nose back into place.

It took a few tries and a couple good yanks before his nose snapped back into place. The sound it made as it went back made the spit man cringe slightly. The boxer, on the other hand, stiffened up while biting hard on the towel in his mouth and let out an agonizing moan.

At this point, a well-dressed, middle-aged man came over to look at them.

"How's your man doing?" he asked.

"Fine, fine. He's doing fine," Dom told him while wiping the blood off of his boxer's nose and lip before glaring over to their unwelcomed visitor.

"You sure about that? You wouldn't be lying to me to keep your man going, would you?"

"Doc, for Christ's sake! He's fine," Dom angrily retorted while throwing another glare at him. "Now, if ya don't mind, I'm trying ta work here."

"Alright, but any sign of trouble and I'm calling it," the ring doctor said while pointing a finger at him before walking away.

"Ok, kid, now I hav'ta stop the bleeding," Dom said after looking back to his boxer. He soon grabbed two long cotton swabs, soaked the ends with adrenaline hydrochloride, and forced each one up his fighter's nostril while using his free hand to pinch the nostrils closed. "Now, breathe deep."

"Wha...?"

"C'mon, damn it!" the old man growled. "Breathe in!"

Doing what he was told, the boxer felt a burning sensation in the middle of his head. The now bloody cotton swabs were taken out before being tossed aside. A small piece of cotton was crammed up each nostril to help absorb any access blood.

"Guys," the ref said while walking up to them. "If your man's not out here in ten second, I'm gonna call it."

"Yeah, yeah. Hold on. Almost done," Dom shot over his shoulder while finishing what he was doing while removing the cotton from his man's nose. "Ok, kid, you're set. Remember, less than a minute tops. Get it done."

Nodding, the boxer rose to receive a pat on the back from the spit man and a scowl from his trainer. The bell sounded as he walked to the middle of the ring to signal the beginning of round six. His head was still a little dizzy but was fully away of his opponent coming towards him. By the way he moved, his opponent gave the impression he was going for a quick knock-out.

A moment later when they met in the middle of the ring, his opponent started a combo that proved the white guy right. He let fly a couple of strong head shots, which were blocked, before attempting to work on the body of his adversary. When he stopped to catch his breath, the white man saw his opening and struck immediately.

Knowing that this may very well be his last chance at victory, the Caucasian man hit fast and hard before the opening closed. He began with a series of well-placed head jabs and straights before landing several hard body shots. He soon ended his string of punches with a hard, fast hook across his opponent's face to send him to the canvas.

While going to the neutral corner, he watched the ref to start counting. By this point, he noticed his nose was beginning to bleed again. Looking to his trainer for some silent help, he saw him nodding his head softly while pumping his hand; his way of telling him to calm down and take it easy. The boxer did what was asked before going back to face his opponent who was still face down on the mat.

"...9...10...!" yelled the ref while waving his hands. "You're out!"

Excited about being able to pull out a victory, the fighter pumped his fists before quickly returning to his corner. Standing against the ring post with is arms draped over the ropes, his spit man, along with Dom, got in the ring next to him.

"Good job," the spit man told him while taking the boxer's mouth guard out.

"Took ya long enough," grumbled the white haired man.

They watched as the ring announcer made his way to the middle of the ring to grab the microphone as it was lowered down out of the rafters above.

"The winner by way of knockout, 42 seconds in the sixth round," he said as his voice echoed throughout the arena, "Chriiiistiiiaaannn Eeetttooonnn!!!"

The crowd gave a modest applause to Christian's name being called. The other boxer, who by now was in his corner talking to his trainer, hung his head while shaking it slightly side to side in disbelief. He and his trainer both seemed shocked at the sudden lose they just suffered. Christian made his way over to touch gloves with him before making his way out of the ring to go back to his dressing room.

"Good fight," his spit man, who was walking next to him as they made their way back, complimented.

"Thanks Shawn; glad you liked it," Christian told his brother.

"Took ya goddamn long enough, though," his spit-fire trainer exclaimed.

"What do you mean it took me long enough?" Christian asked.

"Just what I said! Took ya long enough."

"Yo, leave him alone, Dom," Shawn told him while mounting a defense for Christian. "He did good for his first fight."

"I don't care if it was his first," Dom growled. "He had a chance in the third and twice in the fourth to put him away."

"But weren't you the one who said I shouldn't try for a quick victory?" Christian reminded him. "That I should take my time, to wear him down, and look for the right time?"

"Yeah, I did, but I didn't think you'd actually listen to me," Dom explained while entering the dressing room. "Hurry up and get ready. I wanna go somewhere to have your nose checked out."

"Can't the ring doctor take care of it?" Shawn asked.

"Probably, but I wouldn't trust him."

"Why not?"

"If he was a real doctor, one that *actually* practices medicine, what's he doin' here?" the old man answered. He waved his arms at them before sitting down. "If he's a real doctor, he'd have his own practice or be at a hospital or something. So, hurry the hell up! I don't wanna be here anymore than I hav'ta."

Christian and Shawn quickly showered and dressed before Dom took care of Christian's nose one last time before going out, got in their car, and drove to the nearest hospital.

After sitting silently in the waiting room for about five minutes, Shawn started getting antsy before getting up to start pacing around the room. Almost immediately, Christian started laughed while Dom scowled at him.

"Don't start, kid," growled the old man. "Don't even think 'bout it."

"So, um, Dom, you wanna take care of it now or later on?" Christian asked while looking at him with a large smile.

"Take care of what?" Shawn asked while turning towards them without receiving an answer. "Take care of what, damn it?!"

"Never ya mind!" Dom told him with a look. "And ya keep yer head back, damn it. Ya wanna stop the bleedin', don't ya?"

Putting his head back like he was told, Christian let out another long winded laugh.

"Will one of you tell me what in the hell's going on?" Shawn demanded.

"Dom and I had a little wager on how long it would take before you weren't able to sit still anymore." Christian laughed while trying to look at his brother with his head back.

Dom nodded towards Christian. "Yeah. He won."

"A wager?" Shawn repeated with a slight chuckle. "For how much?"

After a momentary pause among the three of them, Dom took out his wallet, removed a crisp one dollar bill, and raised it for Shawn to see it.

"A dollar?" Shawn question while watching Dom put the bill into his brother's hand. "You two bet against me for a dollar?"

"Hey, we would've bet more but this was all we could afford." Christian smirked while taking the money.

"I can't believe you two made a bet like that," Shawn told them while immediately going back to his pacing. He shook his head in the meantime as a smile appeared on his face.

Looking at him, Christian asked, "What's that? You and I make bets like that all the time about Dom."

"Kid, what I tell ya 'bout keeping your head back?" snapped Dom.

"Sorry, Dom," Christian quickly apologized while immediately putting his head back.

Moments later, a nurse came down the hall with a clipboard in her hands before calling for Christian. He got up and followed her down the hall.

"Don't worry about him, Dom," Shawn said while coming over to sit down. "Every good boxer has their nose broke sooner or later; even a wimp like Christian. Besides, broken noses don't really hurt that bad."

"I'm not worried about him. I'm worried about the bill. Do ya know how much this could cost?" Dom asked while rubbing his nose. He soon stopped to look at Shawn. "And how would ya know a broken nose doesn't hurt that much? Yer face is so calloused over from yer lack of interest in the blocking department that half ya face could fall off before ya'd notice."

"Lack of blocking?" Shawn repeated in a slightly insulted tone. "If I don't block, why haven't I been knocked out yet?"

"For starters, kid, boxers generally try not to block punches with their faces. Ya do it either 'cause ya want to save yer arms from tiring out or ya just don't wanna spend the extra second or two it would take to properly defend yourself. Hell, knowing ya, maybe both, kid," the old man said while glaring to the young, cocky fighter sitting next to him. "And secondly, ya haven't been knocked out, or down, yet because I haven't put ya against anybody that couple capitalize on that flaw yet."

"What the hell do you know anyway, huh, old man?!" Shawn angrily asked before getting up to walk down the hall.

***

The next morning, an alarm clock was heard beeping for about fifteen seconds.

"What the hell?" Shawn mumbled. He rolled over and immediately slammed his hand down on top of the clock to shut off it off. After a few more seconds, he laid back down to his original position with his eyes closed while trying to go back to sleep. After about ten seconds, he opened his right eye to shoot a glance towards the clock.

"8 a.m.," he said while pushing a sigh out of his mouth. After another minute or so of lying there motionless, he looked back at the clock before finally deciding to get up. He swung his legs over the side of his bed before stopping to sit on its edge. He sat there with his head in his hands, elbows on his knees. His face was crumpled and looked as if he was in the worse pain of his life.

"Goddamn it," he groaned while rubbing his temples.

While slowly getting up, he winced as his knees cracked and back snapped. He limped across the room and out the door straight into a jolly, wide awake Christian, who was reading the Wall Street Journal in the kitchen.

"Morning, Shawn," he greeted with a smile when he saw him.

Ignoring him, Shawn made his way to the coffee maker. He got a cup from the sink before pouring himself some coffee.

"How'd you sleep?" Christian asked with even more enthusiasm than before. His eyes were blackened and his nose swollen as he smiled to Shawn. A fresh bandage covered the bridge of his nose.

Turning around with raised eyebrows, Shawn sipped his coffee. He quickly spat it back into his mug as a look of distaste came over his face.

"Goddamn it, Beeker!" he exclaimed. "This coffee if fuckin' horrible! How many times have I told you have to use this goddamn thing? I even went as far as to give you a demonstration on the very aspect of making coffee and you still make the worse fuckin' coffee on the entire east fuckin' coast. For the life of me, I can't understand how a 160 IQ disqualifies you from making something as simple as coffee. What the fuck is your malfunction, man?"

Christian, while taking all this in with supreme concentration, sat for a several seconds while deciding on how to respond.

"I'm sorry, Shawn, but my IQ is actually 152, not 160. And I don't like coffee; therefore I don't know how to make it to your standards. May I make a suggestion, though?" Christian asked as Shawn shrugged. "If my way of making our coffee isn't up to your standards, then my suggestion would be either doing it yourself, or going two blocks to the Gas-n-Save to pay $2.75 for a cup of their gourmet stuff. If you choose the latter, keep in mind you'd be paying $19.25 a week for coffee. You'd be spending money, mind you, which you've been saving for those new boxing gloves you've had your eye on. So, unfortunate as it is to be you right now, you have to decide what's more important: 'Should I make the coffee instead of Christian? *Or* should I spend my hard earned money that I've been saving for a brand new pair of gloves, on a cup of coffee two blocks down?'"

Staring at his brother for a moment before simultaneously pouring this cup's contents down the sink's drain, Shawn soon said, "Dude, you're such a fuckin' nerd."

With that, he went to the bathroom and shut the door behind him. He came out twenty minutes later before going to his room. While sorting through a pile of dirty clothes he had on the floor, Shawn picked out the cleanest ones before putting them on. Once dressed, he came out and saw Christian putting on his shoes.

"Are you r-r-ready, Shawn?" he asked while lacing up his shoes.

"Yeah, Beeker. Let's rock."

159

Waiting for Christian to finish, Shawn looked around their small, yet modest, apartment. As you entered, you first came into the living room. It's floor was covered with a shag brown carpet that had gone out of fashion years ago. It was furnished with a sofa, chair, and coffee table of sorts Shawn had bought at various garage sales. A fish tank against the back wall and a big screen TV with surround sound was next to it, something that Shawn was proud of and would show off whenever possible. These two were by far the most expensive items in the entire apartment. Behind the living room was the eat-in kitchen whose linoleum floors were peeling, cracking, and in dire need of replacing. To the right of the apartment's door was a closet. On the other side of the closet was Shawn's room, with Christian's room in the back left corner. The bathroom was in a small space in between the kitchen and Christian's room.

The apartment itself was located in the back right-hand corner on the second floor of Dom's building; and was the second one out of four apartments. The door leading in and out of it was located on a landing atop a flight of stairs that led down to two doors, one that went outside to the street and the other that went into Dom's gym. Dom's gym made up the entire first floor of the building they were in.

Christian was the first one out of the apartment with Shawn close behind, who slammed the door shut behind him. They walked down the narrow hallway for about fifteen feet before going down a flight of stairs. At the bottom of them was a door which led into an enclosed porch. In the porch was the main door that led outside; five mailboxes on the left wall, four for the upstairs apartments, and the fifth for the gym; and a door on the right wall which led to the gym they trained at. Christian stopped momentarily to pick up whatever mail there was for them and also for the gym.

"C'mon, dickhead. Let's go!" Shawn yelled while unlocking the door that led to the gym. They walked down a narrow hallway before going through a door that took them to the locker rooms. "Hey Beeker, you wanna be my sparring partner today? I've got that fight on Saturday in Glens Falls and I need some practice."

"What was that?" Christian chuckled while leaning forward with his eyes open wide. "Did I just hear Shawn Calloway say that he actually needs to practice?"

"Yeah, I need to practice on how *not* to kill the guy," he quickly shot back.

"Nah, I can't today. I've got some paperwork to do this morning for Dom and then I have to be at work later at the restaurant. Besides, the doctor said I should take it east and to give my nose a rest."

"Man, fuck that place! Dude, why do you work in that shithole anyway?

"How else am I supposed to pay my bills, Shawn?" Christian asked while sitting down by his locker. "I've got credit card bills and college loans to pay for. Unless by some stroke of luck I win the lottery, I'm going to have to work to pay them off."

"Yeah, I guess you're right, bro. It's just that I hate seeing you struggle when you can make a helluva lot more money knocking people out than you can by flipping burgers."

"What the hell is all this jabberin' 'bout?!" Dom demanded as he came gimping around the corner towards them. "Are we ready to get to work, ladies, or do we still need another minute or two to freshen up?"

"Hey, wazzup Dom?" Shawn nodded his head at him. "Nah, I'm ready. In fact, I've been trying to leave but old flap jaw here was talkin' my ear off."

"Then get your ass out there and warm up with Tony," Dom told him with a hard look while pointing to the door. "I wanna talk to your brother for a minute."

"Yes, sir!" Shawn said while coming to a mock stance of attention as he gave him a poorly executed salute with the wrong hand before slamming his locker door shut. He then left the locker room.

Dom, meanwhile, walked over to Christian to hand him a piece of paper which his young fighter read.

"Now, kid, here's a list of things I want ya ta do today. They're not necessarily in order or anything, but what I want first thing this morning is for ya ta go to the bank and get that account straightened out so we can pay the electric," he said with a hint of frustration in his voice. "How can I suppose ta run a business without any proper power, huh?"

"Y-y-yeah, sure Dom. I'll get right on that," Christian said before pausing briefly. "Is the bank open yet?"

"If they ain't, they'll be open at nine. Now, I want ya ta take care of that stuff before ya work out today." Dom jabbed Christian's chest a couple of times with his finger. "I don't wanna see yer mug anywhere near a ring until that list is done. Capisce?"

"Yeah, sure Dom, anything you want," Christian replied while squinting a little before rubbing his right temple.

"What's the matter with you, kid? Sick or somethin'?"

"No, just a headache, that's all."

"Another one?"

"Yeah, but I think it may have to do with my nose. It's been bugging me all morning," Christian told him before focusing back on work. "Anyway, I'll get this stuff taken care of as soon as I can."

"Good, kid, real good." Dom patted Christian's shoulder before pulling a folded newspaper out from his hip pocket and opening up the sports section. "Here, I got ya something."

"What's this?" Christian asked while taking the paper.

"It's last night's garbage," Dom retorted sarcastically while drawing an agitated look from his young pupil. "It's a brief review on yer fight last night."

"I-I-I had a review? R-r-really?" stuttered Christian while quickly opening up the paper.

Sure enough, in the lower corner in amongst the other miscellaneous boxing articles, a head line caught his yes: *Local newcomer makes a statement in his debut.* Christian read it several times, each time with a more obvious smile then the time before, before glancing at the name of the article's author.

"Hey, th-th-this was written by D-D-Dave Mercer."

"Don't get too cocky, kid," Dom retorted while pointing a gnarly finger at him. "Just be lucky he was in the same arena as ya was last night. While I'm at it, be grateful he noticed ya enough ta give yer match a review."

Pupil and teacher looked at each other briefly as a smile rose on each other's face.

"You knew he'd be there in the audience, didn't you?" Christian accused.

"Well," Dom hinted while shrugging his shoulder and spreading his arms. "I might'a been told he'd show up at some point."

Christian smiled. "Thanks, Dom."

"You're welcome, kid," Dom said while patting Christian on the shoulder before leaving the locker room.

While watching him leave, Christian turned to his locker when Dom was out of sight. He reached in back and pulled out a bottle of prescription pain pills before taking two of them. He placed the bottle back where he had it before sitting on the bench next to him. Sitting there for a few minutes while closing his eyes, he waited for this head to stop throbbing before heading out for that day's events.

Chapter 16

A sweaty and out of breathe Christian came through the apartment door just before 9 a.m. to a waiting Shawn, who was sitting at the kitchen table with a can of root beer.

"Hey, Shawn. How's it going?" he asked while getting a drink of water.

"How's it going?" A slightly agitated Shawn asked with raised eyebrows. " You ask me how it's going?"

Christian gulps down his water. "Yeah. Why wouldn't I?"

"You really want to know how I'm doing?!" Shawn asked in a little more agitated tone then he did before.

"I did."

"What's that supposed to mean?!"

Sighing, Christian knew Shawn was in a rare form and looking for a fight. "It means just what I said. I did want to know how you were doing, but I don't know."

"Yeah? And why's that?"

"Because I can see how you're doing. You're pissed off and looking for a fight," Christian said while putting his cup in the sink. "I don't have the time, patience, nor inclination to dick around with you and one of your petty disputes."

"You think all my problems are petty disputes?!" Shawn angrily demanded while shooting Christian a nasty glare.

Sighing again, Christian responds with, "I don't say that. And, no, I don't think they all are. But the dispute you have now is petty."

"So you know why I'm pissed?"

"Yes, I have a feeling. You're pissed because I didn't continue waiting for you this morning so we could go out running together."

"Continue waiting? Dude, you didn't even wait for me before you left!"

Hearing that, Christian turned sharply to look at Shawn. "I didn't wait for you this morning? And how would you know that, huh?" He cocked his head while waiting for an answer. "Before you gracefully answer that, would you be able to tell me what time we agreed to go out this morning for a run?"

Shawn didn't answer. He just sat there searching for an answer as his temper rose.

"Six," Christian told him while Shawn's eyes focused on him. "We agreed to go out running at six. As in six a.m. Three hours ago."

"Yeah, and you didn't wait for me, you dickhead!" Shawn angrily told him while standing up to point at him. "When I got up, you were gone."

"And what time did you get up?" Christian asked while pausing for an answer that never came. "I left here at a quartet to seven. Quarter to seven. As in 6:45 a.m. I waited forty-five minutes for you and you're upset because I didn't wait for you? I'm sorry that I didn't wait for your ass to sober up before I left."

"Listen here, jackass. I had a long night, so back off!" Shawn shouted with a glare while taking two steps forward.

"Oh, a long night, huh? Is that what it's called now?" Christian chuckled. "You came stumbling in drunk, again, a little after three this morning. You woke me up, again, probably also woke up the other guys down the hall as well. You then spent the next ten minutes or so puking whatever alcohol you had left in you. At six, your alarm went off and continued for the next ten minutes before I went in to turn it off. I then tried to get you after that, but you just rolled over and pulled the covers over your head. So, pardon me all to hell if I didn't want to wait any longer than forty-five minutes for your drunken ass to get up."

With that said, Christian stopped talking and started walking down the hall.

"Where you goin'?!" Shawn asked in an angry voice.

"If it's any of your business, I'm going to take a shower," he answered while going into the bathroom and closing the door.

"Take your time, dickhead," Shawn commented to himself before going to his room and grabbed a sweatshirt before leaving the apartment.

A half hour later, Christian walked through the door of the gym and quickly caught the eye of Dom, who was in the ring arguing with Shawn on how he should think under different situations.

"C'mon, kid! Get yer head outta yer ass and think, will ya?!" Dom said with a scowl while poking Shawn in the chest. "Ya're a light heavyweight, not a damn heavyweight! Ya can't go around thinkin' ya can go balls-to-the-wall in every situation lookin' fer yer knockout punch. Ya need ta learn patience, ta look for an openin'. The way ya wanna fight, ya'd be lucky ta go four rounds."

Shawn scowled. "But I haven't had the need to go that long yet, Dom."

Christian wasn't sure if Shawn was still irritated at the argument they had earlier or if he was not irritated at Dom for telling him he needed to change something. Christian just shrugged it off and assumed that it was a mixture or both with Shawn while heading towards the locker room.

Dom simply glared up to his argumentative student. "That's because the fights ya've been in, ya've knocked 'em out by the second."

164

"What's wrong with that? I won, didn't I?" Shawn demanded while glaring back with harms held out before going to his hips.

"Yeah, ya won, but keep doin' that and nobody'll wanna put their fighters in the same ring asya."

"That's because they're afraid of me," Shawn explained with a cocky stance. "They're all afraid of me."

"They're afraid ya'll embarrass them. No one wants ta see their fighter embarrassed. Once that happens, ya'll be outta damn job!" Dom yelled before briefly with a glint in his eye. "And who're ya ta be telling my job, huh?"

"What do you mean?" Shawn questioned.

"Ya know damn well what I mean. Just in case ya've had too many blows to the head, let me refresh what memory ya have left. Ya're paying me for my services, ya see. And my services are ta try ta teach yer blockhead how to box. Ya're payin' me ta teach ya how ta box. If ya know what ya're doin' and if ya continue knockin' people out the way ya've been doin', then ya don't need me 'round. If that's the case, please feel free ta tell me so I can stop wastin' my time on ya. That way, I can concentrate my efforts on someone who'll actually listen ta me," Dom told him with a glare while glancing over to Christian who was still inside the doorway. "Now, when ya're thinkin' about yer decision on that, I'm gonna go in the locker room ta have a word with yer brother. At least I know he'll listen ta what comes outta my mouth."

Upon hearing this, Christian quickly ducked into the locker room before Shawn was able to respond. He opened his locker, undressed, and sat down while dressing into his training attire.

While entering, Dom asks, "Hey kid, how ya doin' today?"

"Not too bad," he answered with a sigh while getting a pat on the back from his aging trainer. "How are you doing?"

"Aw, ya know. I'm still here. The air keeps wantin' ta go in and out." Dom chuckled while sitting on a bench. "I think the good Lord above wants me ta keep livin' so people like yer brother can make my life a livin' hell."

"You know that old saying, don't ya Dom?" Christian asked while giving Dom a side glance.

"Yeah, what's that, kid?"

"Things that don't kill you only make you stronger."

"Yeah, that is what they say, ain't it?" Dom said while looking down at the floor while rubbing his knees. "So, kid, what's eatin' at yer brother today?"

"What do you mean?"

"What I mean is he's more irritable today than normal. He doesn't want ta listen, he insists on doing crap his own way, and seems ta wanna argue with everythin' I say. That's what I mean."

"And you think that there's something wrong with him?" Christian jokingly asked.

Dom smiled. "That's true, kid. That *is* true."

"Well, we did have a little argument upstairs this morning before we came down."

"Yeah, what about?"

"Usual stuff. Nothing important. Well, it wasn't important to me anyway."

"Oh, one of those, huh?" Dom asked as he eyes the novice boxer for his reaction while walking over closer to him. "Ya did good in yer first fight, kid. Did real good."

"Thanks, Dom, but you over exaggerate." Christian bent over to lace up his boots. "At best, I'd say I did alright."

"Just alright?" Dom contemplated the response while bobbing his head back and forth. "Well, yeah, overall you did alright, but considering it was your first fight and all, you did good."

Christian smiled while looking at him.

"Ya're welcome but, listen, don't let it get ta yer head, alright?" Dom's eyes went wide while holding up a hand. "We don't need another young, cocky fighter round here. Ya hear?"

"Yes sir, I hear you," Christian told him.

"Ya'd better if ya wanna be good. So, kid, ya think ya're ready fer another fight?"

While standing there for several seconds thinking whether or not the little old man was being serious or not, he finished putting his clothes in his locker before pulling his gloves out before closing and locking his locker. Turning to face him, Christian wanted to see Dom's expression before giving an answer. When he wasn't able to read his trainer, he decided to play it safe.

"No, I don't think so, Dom," he finally said which seemed to be the wrong response. His trainer seemed somewhat deflated after that. "I think I'll need a little more time training, if that's ok."

"Ya're not ready? What ya mean ya're not ready?" Dom asked with quite a bit more surprise than what Christian had anticipated.

"Just what I said." Christian shrugged. "I'm not ready. I felt I was ready for my frit fight two months ago, the fight I just had a week or so ago. On the other hand, who am I to say whether or not I'm ready? That's why I have you here for me, to tell me when I am ready. And since you're also my manager, you also tell me who I fight, when I fight them, and where I'll do the fighting. So, if I was actually ready for my next fight, I'd know because you would have already scheduled it for me. Right?"

"Yeah, right kid," Dom said with a smile while patting Christian's shoulder. "It sounds like ya've got it easy around here. Hell, with me doin' all the work, would ya mind tellin' me so much what exactly it *is* ya do here?"

"Well, let's see," Christian said thoughtfully while bowing his head to think. "I can think of only two things. First, I pay my monthly dues here; and, second, I do whatever you tell me to do. That sound about right?"

"Ya know, kid, that was beautiful. Just beautiful. Like music ta my ears," Dom smiled broadly while slightly out-stretching his hands.

Christian smiled. "Really? You think so?"

"Yeah, kid. That was real poetry, real sweet," Dom said before turning his smile to a scowl before yelling at his young apprentice. "While we're at it, what the hell ya doin' in here?! Ya're not paying me to be some sort of babysitter, are ya?!"

Christian shook his head. "Not that I'm aware of, Dom."

"That's precisely what I thought. Now, what I want ya ta do is to get yer ass out there and start trainin' fer yer next fight," the elderly spitfire stated while pointing to the door.

"Kind of hard for me to train for something I don't know anything about," Christian said while walking out into the gym.

"Ya've got a fight this Saturday." Shrugged Dom. "That make ya feel any better?"

"This S-S-Saturday? I was gonna help Shawn with his fight over in Glenn Falls then."

"Don't worry about that, kid. Ya'll still be able ta," Dom assured him. "Ya're on the same undercard as him. Ya both will be workin' each other's corner."

Still slightly shocked at the announcement, Christian stood there with his mouth gaping open. "R-r-really? I've a fight this Saturday?"

"That's what I said, wasn't it? I didn't stutter, did I? If ya don't shut up 'bout it and start yer trainin', I just might have the mind ta pull ya outta it. Understood?!"

"Yeah, sure Dom. understood."

"Good! Now, get yer ass over ta the speed bag and start warmin' up."

"A-a-alright. Sure. Right away, Dom." With that, Christian immediately left to walk to where the speed bags were located. On the way there, he saw Shawn standing outside of the right getting a drink from a water bottle he had. Once Shawn saw him, he put it down and walked over to him.

"What was that about?" he asked him.

"What was what about?" Christian replied.

Shawn nodded towards Dom, who by then was walking back into his office. "That."

"Nothing. Just curious if I was ready for another fight."

167

"What'ya tell him?"

Christian shrugged before getting into rhythm on a speed bag. "That I wasn't ready."

Shawn scoffed in disbelief when he heard that before leaning in towards him. "You're not ready?! You told him you weren't ready for your next fight? Dude, why in the hell would you tell him a thing like that?"

Christian stopped at the speed bag so he could focus on Shawn without the distraction of the speed bag. "You know how Dom is. Hell, you're the one who told me that he's purposely put a match off several weeks just to show people he's in charge. I figured if I told him what he'd most likely tell me, I might actually get a match sooner than if I did tell him I was ready."

Nodding in agreement, Shawn said, "Yeah, good thinking."

"What the hell ya two girls doin' over there? Why ain't ya two doin' what I told ya ta do?" Dom asked them as he walked over.

"Talkin'." Shawn shrugged.

"Talkin' won't help ya two win your next fight."

"What do you mean by 'you two'? Don't ya mean it won't help *me* win *my* next fight?"

"No, I meant *ya two*." Dom told him while flicking a thumb towards Christian. "I scheduled his next fight with yers so ya two can work each other's corner." Hearing this, Shawn quickly looked at his brother with a scowl as he went quiet for a few moments to brood.

Catching the look, Christian shrugged. "Sorry, I hadn't gotten that far yet."

"Then when the hell were you going to tell me, bro?" Shawn asked while watching his brother go back to the speed bag he had been working.

"Dude, it's just my second fight. It's not that important. I probably would have told you once training was done."

Shawn, still agitated at not being told of his brother's upcoming fight, just stood there shaking his head as a smile came across his face.

"C'mon, damn it! Ya're not paying yer dues here ta stand 'round and talk all damn day. Get yer asses ta work!" Dom growled harshly as Shawn merely shrugged before going back to the ring. "We'll talk 'bout yer fight later, alright?"

"Yeah, whatever," Shawn commented with a wave as he entered the ring.

Christian laughed slightly at this while continuing to work the speed bag. Dom, meanwhile, walked off to talk with some of the other boxers who had entered the gym.

Chapter 17

In the middle of the ring the ring announcer fixed his tie while clearing his throat. "And now for the light heavyweight match of the evening. Introducing in the red corner, wearing white trunks with red trim, and weighing in at 169 pounds, Maaaaxx Trammell!" he stated in the microphone while pointing to Max.

"And his opponent," the announcer continued, "in the blue corner, wearing black trunks with red trim and weighing in at an even 175 pounds, Shaaawwwnnn Callllloooowwwaaayyy!!!"

Shawn, who was focused and immune to the couple thousand attending fans, started out of his corner before Dom reached in to pull him back.

"Don't spend too much time showing off, ya hear me? Save some of your energy for the fight."

Hearing this, Shawn put his arms in the air for about two seconds before going back to moving his arms, shoulders, and head in quick, rhythmic motions to keep his muscles loose.

"You're telling him not to show off too much?" Christian asked while putting Shawn mouth guard in. "Why would you do that?"

"I think he's confusing me with you, bub," Shawn commented.

"I ain't confused," Dom said firmly with a faint chuckled. "Don't let this go ta yer head, kid, but get in there and take care of this guy ASAP. Got it? I want ta go back and talk ta yer brother about his fight later."

"You want me to what?" Shawn asked while turning sharply to look at Dom while not believing what he just heard.

"Ya heard, me so don't pretend like ya didn't," Dom told him with a snarl. "Get yer ass in there and unload on this chump. Can ya handle that?"

Shawn answered with only a grin and a quick nod as Dom and Christian left his corner to head back to the locker room.

The bell ran soon thereafter and Shawn came out swinging. Two right body shots and a hard left hook were followed by an even harder right uppercut to send Max to the mat face first. Blood and mouthpiece were jediscent in the process. After the uppercut, Shawn casually walked back to his corner to wait for the ref to count his opponent out.

"…8…9…10. You're out!" screamed the ref while waving his arms in front of him. The ref then went over to raise Shawn's left arm in victory.

Raising his right arm, Shawn flexed his muscle and kissed his bicep as the ring announcer came out to announce him winner by knockout. The ref and Max's trainer went over to where Max was sitting to check on him.

Shawn, meanwhile, looked over at him with a definite swagger and supreme confidence while climbing out of the ring to walk back to the locker room. When he exited a couple minutes later, Christian was sitting on a padded examination table listening as Dom briefed him on his upcoming fight while tapping up his hands and wrists

"How ya guys going?" Shawn asked as he approached.

"What the hell kept ya?" Dom asked with a side glance before going back to Christian. "Now, remember kid, watch out for his left. On a good night, that left can stop a tank. Ya hear me?"

Christian nodded. "Yeah Dom. Watch out for his left. I'll remember that."

"Good to see you again, too," Shawn sarcastically commented. "How come you guys didn't work my corner?"

"Didn't I tell ya I wanted ta come back here to talk to Christian about his fight?"

"I thought you meant after the fight was over."

"Looks like ya thought wrong."

"Don't the judges or boxing commission or somebody want the boxer to have somebody in their corner in case anything happens?"

"How the hell would I know? I always wanted to stay neutral with the judges. And I associate with the commission only when I have ta. Too many damn politics," Dom replied while looking one last time at Christian's taped hands. "And, besides, your fight only lasted about fifteen seconds."

"Twelve."

"Twelve what?"

"It lasted twelve seconds, not fifteen," Shawn corrected.

"Now's not the time fer ya ta be a smartass," Dom told him irritably with a look. "And if ya're jokin' ta sound clever or intelligent, that job's taken."

"Yeah? By who, you?" Shawn asked while shifting his weight onto his left leg while putting his hands on his hips.

"No, not me, ya blockhead!" Dom jerked his head towards Christian. "That position is currently held by yer brother here. I would have thought all these years ya two spent with each other that some of his smarts might have rubbed off on ya. But, once again, ya proved me wrong. Now, I want ta get back ta what we were doin' before ya interrupted us."

"Don't you want to know how I won?"

"We already know how you won."

"You do?"

"Yeah, by knockout." Dom shot him an irritated look. "If you don't mind, we're a little busy here."

"Yeah, but I just wanted to tell you how I did it, though." With this, Shawn was a little taken back by Dom's indifference on this. Granted, Dom didn't shower you with hugs and kisses, but he always said something to you. He never ignored you like he was doing to him just then.

"No offense, kid, but I can't talk right now," Dom said. "I'm tryin' ta prep Christian for his fight. Mind if we talk later 'bout your fight?"

"No, I don't mind; I didn't mean to bother you two. I was gonna take a shower anyway," Shawn told him before walking towards the showers.

"Now, remember kid," Dom said while going back to Christian. "Keep your head down and your arms up."

"Sure, Dom. Head down and arms up to protect me. Yeah, yeah, I know all that."

"Ya do, huh?"

"Yes, Dom. You've beat that into me all the time at the gym."

"But if my senile mind is up to par, what happened to you during your last fight?"

"You can't expect me to have known that cheap-assed shot was going to happen," Christian protested in his defense with a scowl on his face.

"Ya should have. It happens all the time."

"Thanks for telling me."

"If ya had done what I've been tellin' ya all these months, then that wouldn't have happened," Dom told him with a combination scowl and smile. "Maybe ya'll remember that during this fight?"

Christian returned his mentor's scowl. "I doubt I'll forget, especially with you there."

"What did I say 'bout his left again?"

"Watch out for it. It could stop a tank on a good day."

"Good boy." Dom patted Christian's shoulder. "This guy has some speed and a mean left. Other than that, I wouldn't worry too much 'bout him. It might take ya a round or two ta feel him out, then a couple more after that ta wear him down. I wanna see how long ya can last tonight. Alright?"

"Yeah, sure Dom."

"Don't be in any type of hurry out there and, by all means, take yer time. Though it is a six-rounder, don't be in a hurry ta knock his ass out. The way ya two fight tonight, points will work in our advantage rather than his. Understood?"

"Yeah, understood Dom."

"Alright, I'll shut up now. I let ya be now until it's time. If ya need me, I'll be talkin' ta your brother 'bout his fight," Dom told him as Christian sat there in silence before he hobbled off to the showers.

***

"Yo, man, I can't believe you didn't knock that chump out last night," Shawn complained the next day as he sparred with Christian.

"Dom didn't want me to," Christian told him while either blocking or dodging a series of punches before countering with a string of his own.

"Do you always do what he tells ya?"

"Not all the time, but when it comes to boxing, I try if I can."

"You know what that's called, dude? That's called 'brown nosing' and you've been doing it your whole life. You outta try experimenting on occasion to see what you can do. There's nothing more satisfying than seeing the daze in your opponents face as he's tyin' ta get up after you've landed a first rate uppercut to his jaw; kinda like this...!" Shawn told him while exploding an uppercut of his own to send Christian back into the ropes.

While looking around in astonishment, Christian soon made a little come back of his own as he began bobbing and weaving while sending Shawn into defensive mode. While Christian poked and jabbed, he started dancing around while peppering Shawn with punches. He soon got Shawn in the corner with an array of jabs and body shots. Christian soon backed off a little to dance around the ring for a moment or two.

"I think I will once I get more experience," he told Shawn once he caught his breath.

"More experience?" Shawn asked while coming out of the corner and out of his defensive posture while smiling at him. "How much more do you think ya need?"

Christian didn't answer. Rather, he just smiled and shrugged as he stopped dancing.

"C'mon, bro. Let's hit the showers," Shawn told him while draping an arm around him before heading out of the ring to walk towards the locker room.

Later that evening, when Christian was coming out of a nearby corner store with various items he had purchased, Shawn caught up with him after spending the last hour and a half working out.

Their attires were as vastly different as their personalities. Shawn wore a tank top, sweatpants, and sandals. Christian, meanwhile, wore shorts, a sweatshirt, and hiking boots. The only things they had there were similar were that they both carried a bag. However, even in this case, their bags were as different as their attires: Christian's grocery bag to Shawn's gym bag.

"Dude, why the hell are you wearing those things on a day like today?" Shawn asked while pointing at his boots.

"I went out hiking a little while ago," was the reply as they proceeded to walk back to their apartment together.

"Couldn't you have worn sneakers?"

"Yeah, I could *have*," Christian said, not sure what the importance was while shrugging it off. "So, how was your workout today?"

"Went good. My legs feel a little rubbery, though."

"Oh, you worked them hard today?"

"Yeah, a little more than I should of."

Christian smiled slyly. "Not your fault. You were probably trying to show off to some gorgeous, yet slightly unintelligent college sorority chick. That, or you were trying to show up some beefcake who was training for his next competition."

"Listen here, *brother*," Shawn said while doing a bad Hulk Hogan impersonation. "It wasn't like that at all, *brother*! The Shawnster doesn't need weights to impress the ladies, dude!"

"That wasn't what I heard, *brother*," Christian told him while giving Shawn a thumbs up and sarcastic smile.

"So, huh-hum, what'cha get?" Shawn asked with a clear of the throat while looking inside Christian's grocery bag.

"Usual stuff; milk, bread, cereal, yogurt."

"Did ya get nothin' good?"

Christian didn't respond. He merely kept walking with Shawn next to him. After a few minutes in silence, Shawn spotted an attractive young woman coming the other way towards them. As she approached, Shawn started to walk in an arrogant, confident swagger while making eye contact with her before saying hi. She responded with a shy smile and salutation of her own as they exchanged looks in passing.

"Christ, dude," Christian muttered under his breath. "Do you always have to do that?"

"Do what?"

173

"You know damn well what I'm talking about. That," Christian told him while flipping a thumb and quick nod towards the woman they just passed.

"You jealous?" Shawn asked while turning to watch the woman vanish into the crowd behind them.

"Jealous of what exactly?"

"What do you mean of what? You serious? Jealous of me, you dip shit!"

"Jealous of you?" Christian asked. This happened to be one of the times where he honestly couldn't tell if Shawn was being serious or if he was just joking. He assumed a little of both. "No, I'm not jealous of you."

"You know, I really wish you'd show me a bit more respect."

"What the hell are you talking about?"

"Never mind. It's not worth it." Shawn shook his head slightly as they finally reached the door to their apartment building.

Shawn immediately reached into his pants pocket to pull out his keys and unlocked the front door. He bound up the stairs two at a time with Christian close behind. At the top of the landing, he reached for their apartment's door while trying to open it. To his surprise, it was locked.

"Goddamn it, Beeker! Why the hell do you always have to lock the damn door?" he complained while unlocking it. "No one's going to come in."

"If you want, I can tape a sign on the door saying that it's unlocked," Christian suggested while they walked into their apartment. "Better yet, why don't I leave the door wide open?"

"That's not what I'm saying, bro. I'm just saying that you don't *always* have to lock it. It is ok to leave it unlocked every now and then."

"I know. I am sorry," Christian said. "It's just out of habit."

"You know who you remind me of?" Shawn asked him. "Remember that guy Brad I told you about?"

Christian thought for a moment while going to the kitchen with the groceries. "I'm not sure. Would you refresh my memory?"

"He's this guy I knew at that restaurant I worked at. He was from L.A. and had been here in New York like five years or so. He's so in the habit of locking everything he has up, which goes so far as to pull his car in the garage, close the garage door, then lock his car and turn its alarm on; even when he's going into his house for a brief moment."

"That is a little extreme, I'll give you that," Christian said before checking the answering machine when he noticed they had a new message.

"*You have one new message*," the answering machine stated in a dull, monotone voice when Christian hit the play button. "Hi boys, it's your mother. Just calling to see how my boys are and to see if you have any plans this weekend. Give me a call when you get this, ok? Thanks. Love you. Bye."

The message ended with the sound of their mother hanging up as the voice on the machine told them when she called. Christian immediately picked up the phone to call her back. Shawn, meanwhile, took off his sandals and threw them in the general direction of the door. The phone rang three times before being answered by their mom.

"Hi, Mom. How's it going?" Christian asked before pausing to let her respond. "You know me, Mom. I'm fine as usual. And Shawn is also doing fine." Pausing again, he watched Shawn open a window before going into the kitchen for a drink of water. "Well, we've been busy working and all. We just got home and got the message you left. You wanted us to call?" Again, another pause. "Yeah, sure. I'll be there. I have to work at the restaurant that day, though, but I should be done around 4:30 or so. If you want, we can either schedule it for 6:30 or so, or I can give you a call when I get home." Pause. "Ok, 6:30 it is. I'll let you know as soon as I can if I'll be late. As for Shawn," Christian said while hesitating and glancing over to him. Shawn, having been listening to the conversation, immediately made quick hand motions across his throat. "He's in the shower at the moment but I'll let him know as soon as I can. I'm sure he'll come as well, but he may have other plans." He stopped talking suddenly when his mom interrupted while shaking his head a few times. "Mom, don't worry, I'll ask him. I can't very easily ask him now. I will as soon as he gets out of the shower. Promise. Mom, it's alright. I'll tell him. And, yes, we love you too. I'll talk to you later, ok? Bye for now and I'll see you Sunday." With that, Christian hung up as soon as he could while letting out a long sigh of relief.

"What did she want you to ask me?" Shawn casually asked.

"Wants to know if you'll come over Sunday for dinner."

"Are you going?"

"Have you ever known me to pass up one of her meals?" Christian scoffed. "Of course I'm going. How 'bout you?"

"I'm not sure yet." Shawn shrugged. "I may be busy at the gym."

"Busy at the gym? Aren't they closed Sunday's?"

"Dom's gym is closed on Sunday's, but I wanted to go to the Y to work out."

"You gonna be there all day?" Christian smiled at him.

"I'm not sure when I'll get there. All I know is that I'll be there sometime that day for a couple of hours."

"While you're deciding that, just keep in mind that dinner is set for 6:30 pm. Now, with that over with," Christian said with a hint of satisfaction, "I'm going down to Mike's. You wanna come?"

"I think I'll go," Shawn told him while taking off his sweaty tank top, "but I want to take a shower first."

"While you're doing that, I think I'll jog on down to see if Jake and Terry are there," Christian announced as a mild laugh escaped him as he reached the door.

Eyeing him suspiciously, Shawn asked, "Why's that?"

"So I can play some pool with them before you show up."

"What's that supposed to me?" asked Shawn defensively.

"C'mon, man. Do you really have to ask that?" Christian laughed heartedly at his brother's expense. "Once you're there, you won't let anyone else play until you're done. God help anyone else who might actually want to play."

"Oh, go fuck off!" Shawn said with a glare before laughing and waving his arms at him. He soon turned to walk the hallway to the bathroom.

Christian, continuing to laugh at Shawn's expense, trotted down the stairs and stopped long enough at the bottom to check for mail and to wave to some of the guys in Dom's gym. After doing this, he walked out the door before having a nice walk over to Mike's.

Fifteen minutes later, Christian crossed the street to approach a local bar with a neon-lit sign above the door that read *Mike's Place*. *Mike's Place* was a bar on the bottom floor of a six-story building; the top five were apartment buildings. Upon entry, he greeted the bald beefcake they liked to call a bouncer.

"Morning, Josh," Christian said when the bouncer turned towards him. "How's it going?"

"Mornin'? What the hell da ya mean by mornin'?!" the bouncer glared at him. "Last time I checked it passed being morning 'bout seven hours ago."

"Good to see you're doing well." Christian smiled while slapping Josh on one of his meaty shoulders. "How's the wife doing?"

"Wife's fine." Josh shrugged.

"And how are my kids doing?"

"What'd'cha just ask?!" Josh demanded while rising to his full height and talking a step forward towards Christian.

"Oh, I just asked how you're kids were doing, that's all," Christian told him with a smile and shrug.

"Yeah. That's what I thought you said," Josh stated while walking up to him before glaring down at him square in the eye. "*My* kids are fine."

"Good, good. Glad to hear."

"Now, listen here, jackass! Did you come here tonight to try and piss me off or did ya come here for something else?"

"I just thought a couple of games of pool sounded good."

"You might have to wait a bit," the bouncer told him while finally physically relaxing for the first time during their conversation. "Jake and Terry have been at it the last half hour or so."

"Oh, good, they are here. I was hoping they'd be here."

"Yeah? Why's that?"

"So I could play some pool with them."

"What about me?"

Slightly confused by the question, Christian asked, "What about you?"

"You wanna play pool with Jake and Terry but not with me?"

"That's not what I said."

"Well, that's how it sounded!" Josh sternly told him before a broad smile was revealed on his face, one that went from ear to ear.

"Goddamn it, Josh." Christian sighed with great relief. "I thought you were being serious."

"Hell no, I wasn't being serious! If I was, I would'a knocked your damn head off, son!" he announced with his usual stern voice and half smile.

Christian, not knowing how to respond, simply stood there smiling at him.

"Hey, I saw your fight last night," revealed Josh.

"It was on TV?" Christian asked as a look of disbelief came over his face.

"How the hell would I know if it was on TV? I was there, ya jackass."

"You were? How come you didn't say anything?"

"How could I of? Besides, I was with a couple of buddies of mine."

"So, what did you think? Did I do ok?" Christian asked with a small sign of excitement.

"The only thing I thought was why ya held back." Josh pushed his right shoulder. "How come you just didn't waste that chump?"

"Dom didn't want me to. He wants me to be able to last more than a couple of rounds."

Smiling, Josh asks, "Oh, you mean he wants someone whose fights last longer than your brother's?"

"Yeah, I think so. But it seems like if I want to be an overall decent fighter, I'll need to last past the third anyway," Christian told him while feeling like he needed some type of explanation so as not to insult Shawn. "Anyway, I won't keep you. I'll let you get back to beating up the bad guys, picking your nose, or whatever it is that you do when you're here."

"Alright, I'll talk to you later, Chris." Josh patted Christian on the back while he walked back inside.

With that, Christian had to smile. He had to smile because he liked Josh. Josh was a solid, thick, former professional wrestler who, when he had to, wouldn't take crap from anybody or anything. Though he was a 6'3", 250 pound wall of muscle, hops, and malt, he was in reality a really nice and personable guy. He had moved to upstate New York because his wife's parents were ill and needed full-time care. He took this job as a bouncer mainly to get out of the house and, ironically, was paid with alcohol since he had enough money saved from his wrestling days.

While walking into the bar, Christian waved to Jake and Terry who were playing pool in the back. Mike, the bartender, exchanged a smile as Christian sat on the bar in front of him.

"You want your usual?" Mike asked him before receiving a nod in the affirmative. He then made a triple Pepsi on the rocks before sliding down the bar and easily slid into Christian's hand.

Mike Lowry was the operator of the bar and had also owned it the last twelve years after inheriting it from his father. He still had his linebacker build from college, though it came with an additional twenty pounds. Christian could say that Mike was honestly one of the nicest guys he had ever met. Though he could be a bit of a hard-ass at times, he couldn't remember ever seeing him upset.

"How ya doin', Chris?" Mike asked while watching his customer gulp down half his soda.

"Oh, not bad, Mikey," Christian told him when he was done with his soda, but not before letting out a wall shaking belch. "Doing pretty good. How about yourself?"

"Same here." Mike smiled. "Are you aware that this place is a bar? That we serve other things here besides Pepsi?"

"Really?" Christian feigned surprise. "You actually serve stuff here besides that? Wow. After all this time that I've been coming here, the only thing I thought you guys offered was soda. Well, I'll be. You learn something new every day, don't you?"

Mike stood there while cleaning the bar as the two of them had a good laugh with Christian before going off to help some people who had just sat at the other end of the bar.

With soda in hand, Christian swung around on the stool, placed his back against the bar, and scanned the room. The bar itself wasn't anything special, nor did it have anything extraordinary about it. It was an average local bar with a heavy metal flare to it. It had numerous tables scattered throughout and several booths lined the walls.

The back third was slightly elevated and enclosed with a half-wooden rail fence. In his area, there were two dart boards on the wall, one of which was being used; a vacant pin ball machine; and three pool tables. A number of round, raised tables with bar stools lined the walls. The bar also had a handful of TV's hanging on the walls which had on the weather channel, local news broadcasts, and various sports shows. The center piece, though, was the extremely large big-screen TV on the wall above the actual bar itself for the really big sporting events.

After another moment of looking around, Christian noticed Terry waving him over to the table he was playing pool at. Waving back, he got up and walked over to Terry and Jake.

"Hey guys, what's going on?"

"Took ya long enough to come over," Terry sarcastically commented while following through on the cue stick. It connected with the cue ball to send it rolling across the table to knock the ten ball in the corner pocket.

"Chris." Jake nodded while chalking up his stick.

"I was happy to watch from the bar, really." Christian shrugged. "Besides, I didn't want to intrude without being invited."

"Not being invited?" Terry asked with skepticism while glancing at him. "Man, you don't need to feel like you can't come over here without being invited. Hell, your brother does it all the time."

"Well, that's him. With me, I don't really like people bothering me without a reason or an invitation. Since I had neither...," Christian explained politely as he left his comment open to interpretation before drinking more of his soda.

"Speaking of your brother, where's he at anyway?" Jake asked while walking to the table after a failed shot attempted by Terry.

"He's back at the apartment getting all pretty for his appearance here in a little bit."

Nodding his head when he heard this, Jake acknowledged that his curiosity had been fulfilled.

Jake and Terry were another pair of guys that Christian liked. Like Josh, they both were quite definitely a different breed of people when compared to Christian.

Terry was an auto mechanic for as long as Christian knew him and often wondered if he'd done anything else besides working on cars. For being in his mid-fifties, Terry was in really good shape for his age. He was a little taller than Josh, standing about 6'4", though not nearly as thick. His attire stayed mostly the same whenever Christian saw him, wearing some sort of t-shirt or long-sleeved button up shirt with the sleeves rolled up; black leather vest; blue jeans with a black leather belt; and either a pair of work cowboy boots or steel-toed boots, both black. Christian couldn't remember when his shoulder-length dirty blonde, curly hair had ever been combed; or if he ever had anything more, or less, than his half-filled in scraggly beard. Of the two, Terry definitely was the more vocal one. As far as Christian knew, he was never married.

Jake, on the other hand, spoke more with non-vocal forms of communication. When he did speak, there was no need for him to repeat himself. He spoke in a solid and clear, yet calming, voice and always to the point. Unlike most people that Christian had met who ask question and assume you know what they're talking about, Jake's questions were directed and worded around the answer he wanted. Though Terry and Josh were about five to six inches taller than Christian, Jake was a monster, even next to them. He stood just short of an astounding seven feet tall. For a living, Christian never heard what he did but he did know his main hobby, outside of playing pool with Terry, was motorcycles. His wife, Samantha, was a physical fitness trainer, had whims that were indulged by Jake at trying to keep their household in the best physical shape they were able to be in. Attire wise, the only think that stayed consistent was his long, dark brown ponytail; comfortable looking leather pants; and size seventeen black work boots. Of the two, Christian liked Jake more even though he couldn't place his finger on the reason. He simply did.

"Hey man, you know what'll happen if I sink this one?" Terry laughed while looking over at Jake.

"You don't need to remind me," Jake answered.

"Worried."

"No.

"Why not?"

"You won't make it."

"What's going on?" Christian asked. "What happens if you make it?"

"If I make the eight ball," Terry told him with a chuckle, "good-ole Jake here has to pick up our beer tab."

"What if you don't make it?"

"It's not necessarily if I make it," Terry said while doing down to line up the cue ball with the eight before pointing to the side pocket, to which Jake nodded. "Whoever loses this game is responsible for picking up the tab. And, as you can see, I only have the eight ball left whereas Jake, sadly, still has five balls left." He then went quiet long enough to take the shot. Even though it was close, the eight ball bounced off the corner of the pocket rather than being sunk. "Shit!" he shouted in anger.

Without acknowledging the close, yet missed, shot in anyway except for a slight smile, Jake proceeded to sink his remaining five balls, as well as the eight, on four consecutive shots.

"Looks like you're buying," Jake softly said while finishing his mug of beer before grabbing their two empty pitchers from a nearby table.

"But I don't have the money!" Terry told him in disbelief.

"You should have thought about that before making the wager." Jake smiled softly while walking to the bar for refills.

"What am I supposed to do?" Terry asked to Jake's silent back. "I can't believe it. He beat me. He actually beat me."

"Why can't you believe it?" Christian asked him.

"What?"

"Why are you surprised that he beat you?"

"Because I always beat him," Terry answered while standing there in shock while counting what money he had in his wallet. "He never wins."

"You should give him more credit than you do."

"At what, playing pool?" Terry asked while getting a nod from Christian. "Why? I told you. I always win."

"I've played him before. He really *is* quite good," the pugilist said in their friend's defense.

"Then why doesn't he try to win, then?" Terry questioned while obviously not wanting to believe what he just heard. "That's the name of the game, right? To win?"

"Let me put it to you this way. If Jake actually tried to beat you, he most likely would every time. If he did, would you continually play him knowing that you'd lose?"

"Hell no, I wouldn't!"

"Well, there you are," Christian told him while pausing long enough for it to sink in. "Jake knows that about you. I know because he's told me. He's willing to lose to you because you playing pool with him is more important than him winning."

"So you tryin' to tell me there's more important things than winning?"

"Yeah, 'fraid so, bubby." Christian smiled with a nod.

"Then why didn't he do his usual thing by losing to me if winning isn't that important?"

"Maybe to humble you? Maybe to make you think twice before you write checks your butt may not be able to cash? Or, knowing him, it was for the free beer you so generously agreed to pay?"

"So he hustled me?" Terry asked as his look of confusion still covered his face.

Christian nodded. "Looks that way."

About the time Jake came back with the newly refilled pitchers of beer, Shawn was just outside the bar's entrance. For a brief moment, Christian thought Shawn was trying to pick a fight with Josh, but let it go when he noticed Josh had a mischievous grin on his face before grabbing

Shawn by the collar and waist before proceeding to hay bale toss him further into the bar. A few people at the counter turned to see what the commotion was about but, when they saw it wasn't anything serious, went soon back to their drinks and conversations.

"Yeah, you keep on walking, Josh," Shawn said in safety while pointing to the bouncer. "If you weren't on the clock, I'd show you a thing or two."

Hearing this, Josh stepped back inside the bar to check the time. He soon folded his arms before saying, "I'll be going on break in about twenty minutes. If your scrawny little ass is still up for it, we can meet out back in the alley. How's that sound, little man?"

"Nah, that's alright." Shawn laughed while going to the bar for a drink. "I wouldn't want to tire you out. Besides, I'll be busy by then."

Christian wasn't able to hear how Josh responded since he had already walked back to the front door, but waited until Shawn came over after getting his beer before asking about it.

"I was just trying to keep him on his toes," was all Shawn had to say on the subject.

"You'd better be careful and not bite off more than you can chew with him," Christian warned.

"What are you saying, bro?! That I can't take care of myself?" Shawn asked with a look. "Or are you sayin' I can't take Josh?"

"I'm not saying any of those. All I'm saying is that Josh is one of the few people you shouldn't try and antagonize," Christian politely explained while trying to figure out what had gotten into his brother. "He has enough of his own problems at him with his in-laws."

Before Shawn was able to respond, they overheard Terry ask how he was going to pay for all they beer they had already ordered.

"Why don't you put it on your tab?" Jake asked while breaking a freshly racked set of balls.

The conversation ended there when Terry finally realized that it looked like he would be stuck covering the bill after all.

Christian stayed just long enough after that to get two games of pool in, one with Jake and one with Terry, before Shawn elbowed him out of the way to take his spot. Feeling that Shawn was in some sort of foul mood, Christian took his leave to a nearby table after getting a refill on his soda. During this time, he noticed that Shawn was already on his third beer. Without wanting to find out exactly what type of mood Shawn was in, or even one he'd be in if he kept up with the beer, Christian left the bar for a walk in the cool evening before returning home for the night.

Before he left *Mike's Place*, however, he noticed a stocky older gentleman, one well-dressed in expensive clothing, sitting in a corner booth and smoking a cigar. Though the smoke covered the man's face, Christian felt like he should have known who he was while also swearing that the stranger was watching both him and Shawn at the same time. Christian soon shrugged off this mysterious feeling before leaving to enter the cool evening.

Chapter 18

"Hello Mom, hey Dad," Christian said when arriving at his parents' home that Sunday for dinner. He soon bent over to kiss him mom on the forehead. "How are you two doing?"

"Your father and I are doing just fine, dear," his mom answered while returning his kiss. "It's so good to see you. It's been awhile since you've come for a visit. And, Christian, what happened to your face?"

"I, er, banged it work, Mom. It's nothing serious."

"It looks horrible," Sally informed him while taking a closer look at her son. "Did Shawn come too?"

"No, Shawn didn't come. There were some things he wanted to do. He said he may show up later."

"Ah, that's too bad. I really wanted to see him."

"Are you surprised?" David asked from his spot at the table while hiding behind that day's newspaper. "He hardly ever comes over. And, when he does, it's usually when he wants something or to brag about himself."

"David, that's not nice to say. But, no, I'm not surprised. Disappointed is more like it, but not surprised." Sally scowled with a long sigh before pulling herself in a better mood before walking back into the kitchen. "Why don't you have a seat in your usual spot, ok sweetie? Supper's almost ready."

As Christian did what his mother wanted, he noticed the kitchen table was set for four.

"Hey Dad, no need to get up," he remarked sarcastically while pulling back his chair.

"Don't worry, I wasn't," his father commented from behind his raised newspaper.

From where Christian sat, the paper covered the majority of Christian's father with the exception of his hands and the top of his now balding head. His legs were crossed as his top foot moved.

"Everything smells good, Mom. What'cha making?"

'Never you mind, dear. It'll ruin the surprise," Sally told him while stirring some gravy before giving the rest a taste test.

"Did Dad help you at all?" Christian asked with a slight smile.

"In a way I did," David answered in her stead.

"How's that, Dad?"

"I stayed out of her way."

"Glad to hear you're taking an active role in things. Good for you, especially at your age," Christian sarcastically complimented as his smile got bigger while waiting for his father's response.

The response never came. He waited while his dad simply turned the page of his paper, unruffled it, and merely kept on reading as he hid behind the black and white veil between them. Knowing his dad, Christian surmised that his dad was simply ignoring him.

"So, dear, how was work today?" Sally asked from the stove.

"It was a typical Sunday," he replied while putting his cheek on his hand, whose elbow was planted on the table. "Breakfast was slow until eleven or so, and then we got hit with the church people once services got out. The last hour of breakfast and first one of lunch were really busy."

"Have you gotten any more cooks yet?"

"No, not yet," Christian told her. "I think we should have at least two more for the place to run smoother. But what do I know? The company wouldn't want to spend any more money for labor than they would have too, not even if their lives depended on it."

"Didn't you have an interview somewhere this week?" his mother asked.

"Yeah, it was on Wednesday over at Bourbon-N-Ribeye."

"Really? Doing what?"

"Dishwasher."

"Doing dishes?" she asked with a puzzled look. "Do you really want to be doing that?"

"Not really, but the job will be easier and I'd be making a little bit more there than I am now," Christian explained. "After a month, I'd get a review and, if I do well enough, I'll be getting a little raise. If all goes well, that is. Besides, I could always work into other things there eventually, whereas where I am now, chances are I'll only be cooking."

"Well, I hope you get it then," his mother commented positively.

"Me too. Looks like it'll be a better job all around for me."

"Are you still working at the gym?" his dad asked while moving onto the last page of his business section.

"Yes, I'm still there."

"Oh, dear, I really wish you'd leave that place. The thought of you being around all that violence really bothers me," his mom worried. She had a tendency to do this, especially when it came to him being at Dom's.

"You don't really need to worry, Mom. The job's only temporary," Christian told her while getting up to help his mom bring the food over to the dinner table. He hoped his lie was believable, at least temporarily, until he came up with something else to tell her about it.

As usual, his mom fixed more than enough food. To this day, Christian still wondered why she did it, but always received the same answer: because she wants to. She fixed her usual, massive amounts of mashed potatoes and gravy, stuffing, mashed squash, banana bread, string beans, cabbage salad, cornbread, a big pot roast, and, for desert, both cherry and apple pies.

"Mom, you always seem to out due yourself." Christian found himself salivating at the aroma while placing the now full steaming bowls of food on the table. "This all looks wonderful."

"Why, thank-you dear. I hope you like it. Do you think I made enough?" She chuckled once she became aware of the sheer volume of food she once again made.

His father, meanwhile, had finished his paper and was now in the process of getting both him and Sally cups of freshly brewed coffee.

"Want any coffee, Chris?" he asked his son.

"No thanks, Dad. I'm all set."

"You know, you ought to come over more, Chris," David told him while coming back to the table. "Do you know why I say that?"

"Ah, no Dad, I don't. Why should I come over more?" Christian was already in the process of filling his plate up with food when he asked that.

"So I can have meals like this more often," his dad told him dryly before looking over to his wife from the corner of his eye.

"If you want more meals like this, it's alright with me to teach you a thing or two about cooking," retorted Sally with a soft and pleasant smile. "I've always wondered what kind of meal you'd have made."

"Nay, that's alright."

"Why's that, Dad?"

"Because it's woman's work."

"You know, Dad, I might have to agree with Mom on this," Christian told him. "You might actually make a pretty decent cook."

"As it turns out, I'm too busy to be picking up any new hobbies at the moment, with my wood making and the Lion's club and all," David informed him while accepting the bowl of potatoes from Sally before eyeing his son over the top of his glasses. "Besides, I still say cooking is woman's work."

"Does that make me a woman for being a cook at work?" Christian asked with a smile. "Besides, a lot of the world's best chefs are men."

"He's got a point there, dear," Sally commented.

"If they, or you for that matter, want to learn a woman's job, so be it. The more power to you, but not me. I don't want to learn it. Much too busy."

"Geez, Dad, you seem to be getting a little defensive. You alright?" Christian seemed to be taking enjoyment out of his father's aggravation. "If you really didn't want to learn how to cook, that's all you had to say. We'd understand, right Mom?"

David, who was growing impatient with his son's incessant picking, looked at him again from over the top of his glasses. This time, however, for a much longer period of time.

"Are you trying to aggravate me for any particular reason?" he asked while seeing his son reveal a broad smile that was followed by a well-drawn out laugh. His irrigation quickly passed when he realized Christian was purposely trying to provoke him before laughing softly himself. "You're getting pretty good at that. I think you've been hanging around Shawn a little too much."

"I don't have a choice with that. I do *live* with him, you know."

"That is true," David said while his eyebrows creased above his eyes. "Speaking of Shawn, how's business going at the gym?"

"Real good. Been picking up lately; it's been a bit busier."

"Do you really have to work there?" his mother asked him.

"No, I don't have to work there but as long as I do, I don't have to pay rent on the apartment."

"Why's that?" his father instinctually asked.

"Dom, the guy who owns the gym also owns the whole building. To him, I'm working for my rent. As long as I work for him and also live upstairs, he considers us even."

"Is that legal?"

"I don't see why not, but the rent actually comes out of my paycheck," Christian explained. "I guess the rent *is* my paycheck."

While looking as this son, David slowly inquired, "Is that where you hurt your nose?"

Christian nodded. "One of the perks from working there is that I can use the facilities when I'm not working."

"Oh, Christian," Sally chastised. "You said you hurt it at work."

"He did say that," her husband slyly commented, "though he didn't say which job he hurt it at."

186

"How did you really hurt it, sweetie?"

"I was getting a boxing lesson when I failed to block a punch," Christian lied after momentarily searching for an answer. "Broke my nose."

"You aren't going to follow Shawn's example, are you?" his father questioned him.

"Not fulltime if that's what you mean," Christian said. "Do it just to learn how to box."

"Enough about boxing and the gym. I don't want it spoiling dinner," Sally told them very matter-of-factly while moving her hair out of her eyes while adjusting her glasses. She definitely did not want to talk about it anymore. "So, how's Miho doing?"

"Miho's doing just fine," replied Christian. "You know she went back home for a visit for two weeks, right?"

"Oh, that's right dear. When will she be back?"

"Friday night, I think. She said she'd let me know the time when to pick her up. Classes start Monday from spring break and she wanted to be back in time to get ready."

"What part of Japan is she from again?" David asked. "It's not Tokyo, is it?"

"No, not Tokyo. She's from a suburb of Kyoto. That's a city about 300 miles southwest of Tokyo."

"How big is it?"

"Tokyo or Kyoto?"

"The second one, the one that she lives by."

"Kyoto has about a million and a half people there, not including the surrounding suburbs," Christian told him.

"That's a lot of people," his mom commented.

"That's nothing compared to Tokyo, though. I think I have around nine mill or so."

"You know, you should bring her over her more," she said with an approving smile."Your father and I would like to see her a little more often."

"Think this might be the one?" his father asked.

"You shouldn't ask that, dear," Sally told him.

"Why not? It's a legitimate question." David smiled while leaning back in his chair. "Besides, I really like her. He'd be a fool to let her go. So, is this the one?"

"I don't know, maybe," Christian said while trying to avoid the question. "We both have some things we want to do before we even thing about that. I can't really say for sure now."

"What's there to say? Either she is or she isn't."

"Dear, he already answered your question. You're beginning to embarrass him," Sally said while coming to her son's aide before giving herself a little bit more mashed potatoes. "Speaking of which, is Shawn seeing anyone?"

Christian merely laughed at that. "If that's what you want to call it. Shawn goes through spurts which I like to call flavors of the week. That seems to aggravate him when I say that, but it's basically true. He does have three or four he rotates through depending on his mood. I only know their first names, but only one can I associate with a face. He seems to like to cycle his way around them with various others in between. So, in a manner of speaking, he's seeing quite a few people but none too seriously."

"That's too bad," Sally said disapprovingly. "I hope he finds someone he can settle down with at some point."

"We all do, but I don't think he will anytime soon," David injected after drinking some coffee. "Not by choice anyway. With all due respect to him, I don't think Shawn is ready, or will be ready, for quite some time for any serious relationship. If he does get one anytime soon, it'll either be because he suddenly got a massive dose of maturity when he gets some poor girl pregnant. In either case, that's none of my business. On a different note, I think you out did yourself today, dear. Too bad Shawn isn't here to share it with us."

"That's why I made extra, so Christian could take it home with him," Sally informed him. "Knowing him, he'll eat everything you take home without leaving anything extra for his brother."

As the Eaton's ate the rest of their meal, their thoughts and comments changed throughout their various conversations. They remained conversing well after supper was ate and the dishes were washed.

Christian left well after dark that night with plenty of leftovers to satisfy both him and Shawn for a couple of days. When he arrived home, Shawn was sitting at the table reading.

"Hey Shawn, how's it going?" he asked while going to the kitchen to put the food away.

"Yo, Beeker. What's shakin', bacon?"

"Oh, you know, just living the dream."

"No, I don't know, that's why I asked. And what dream would that be?"

"The dream of being full from a very filling home cooked meal, a meal which came with plenty of leftovers," Christian said with slyly while showing off the containers of food he had brought home in a humorous fashion.

Smiling, Shawn says, "Oh, good. But didn't you bring back any for yourself?"

"Any what?"

"Leftovers."

"Of course I did. Why?"

"Never mind. Forget it." Shawn laughed while shaking his head before going back to the article. He soon pointed to it multiple times. "Hey, it says here that Duke Snyder has another guy going for a title again this week. Also says that six of the top ten contenders he represents in one manner or another. Can you believe that?"

"Duke Snyder?" Christian questioned while searching for the name recognition. In the process of doing that, he finished putting the food away before coming to sit at the table next to Shawn. "I can't place his name. Who is he?"

"You know, the white man's Don King?"

"Oh, him?"

"Can you believe that, though? He has six contenders, not including that jackoff challenging his week. He also has some butt-fuck who went for the WBA or whatever title a couple of months back. So, basically, eight of the top twelve he represents."

"Just out of curiosity, who wrote that article? I'm wondering if his name can be trusted."

"Ahhh, let's see." Shawn leaned over the article to search for the author's name. "Oh, Dave Mercer."

"Oh ok. He's pretty good about getting the facts. He's been around since we were teenagers," Christian commented. "He may like to over exaggerate or dramatize some things, but overall his facts are usually pretty sound. By the way, what weight classes are Snyder's contenders in?"

"All heavyweights, but still," Shawn told him while laying his paper down to look around the room while searching for what to say next. "That's eight more than what Dom has, you know that?"

"Well, actually seven more," corrected Christian.

"Seven? Who's the guy that we have?"

"You know, Billy what's-his-name. The one that likes to pose like Rob Van Dam?"

"Oh, no no no," Shawn said while holding up his hand. "Ole Billy Boy's gone."

"Really? Where to?"

"Jumped ship. He's one of Duke's elite eight now."

"No shit? Son of a bitch," muttered Christian while nibbling on his lower lip. "When?"

"He's been gone a month now, six weeks tops. Where the hell've you been?"

"I was wondering why I hadn't seen him in a while. I guess that explains it."

"Yeah think?" Shawn sarcastically asked.

"Occasionally it seems I do. You know, that's a real bummer."

"Bummer? I'm glad that jackass is gone."

"Well, me too to be honest. But consider what that might have meant to the gym and the other guys knowing that we had a contender there with us."

"I know, man, I hear yeah. But, hey, it was his decision. But I don't really blame him, though, for leaving us that is."

"Really? Why?"

"He felt that Dom wasn't the person to actually take him to a belt, and I'm starting to agree with him."

"I'm not following you."

"You wouldn't because you're still relatively new," Shawn told him. "Dom's the type who'll train a good all-around fighter, but when he has someone who's really good or actually has something, he doesn't follow up."

"Do you know why that is?"

"I don't know but he does tend to give some cock-and-bull story about them not being ready yet; but I don't really believe that, though. Maybe he doesn't know what to do. Maybe he's never really had anybody that was good enough to be a contender. Maybe he chokes. Hell, it could be any number of reasons."

"What if Dom's right? About them not being ready yet?"

"C'mon, man! He had a guy a few years back who jumped ship and, when he did, became a contender within a matter of months. Then there's Bill who left a month ago and now is in contention with good ole Duke. And what about me, huh?!"

Confused from the question, Christian asks, "What about you?"

"Hell, I could beat any of these chumps, these paper champions," Shawn told him with a hint of bitterness and anger. "They're just what you call a transitional champion, just until I get there."

"Oh, really?" Christian asked with a smile.

"Yeah, really," Shawn quickly shot back. "How long have I been boxing for, huh, Beeker?"

"I don't know. What, six or seven years?"

"Yeah, exactly! And how many times have I lost in these six to seven years?"

190

"Oh, man." Christian sighed. "I honestly can't remember the last time you lost."

"That's because I haven't. Not once in almost seven years," Shawn told him bluntly. "When I was an amateur I didn't lose and I kept up that tradition after turning pro. I have a combined record of 38-0 in just under seven years. 38-0 and I still haven't had a title shot yet. I haven't even been considered a contender. Can you believe that shit?"

"Talk to Dom. See what he can do."

"I have talked to Dom! Multiple times. Last week in fact."

"What'd he say?"

"What do you think he said? He told me I wasn't ready yet. Not ready?! Can you believe that? With a record of 38-0, most, in fact, by knockout, and I'm not ready?! Though I've been bugging him, begging for months now it seems like for a shot, he still says I'm not quite ready."

"And how long have you been pro now for?"

"About four and a half years."

"And what's your record since you've turned pro?"

Doing a quick count with his fingers, Shawn soon said, "Something like 25-0."

"And most of those came via knockout?"

"Well, yeah! Have you ever known me to last any longer than I have to?"

Christian had to laugh at that. "That is true. The ultimate one-minute man, huh?"

"Oh, fuck off, man!" Shawn said hotly with a scowl.

While sitting back looking for any logical explanation as for Shawn's lack of a title run, Christian soon asked, "What were the quality of your opponents like?"

"You were there. Weren't you paying attention?" Shawn sarcastically asked.

"Let me rephrase that question," Christian said with a little annoyance. He was annoyed because, times like now, he felt like Shawn purposely tried to make him feel like he should have known something when he didn't. He often felt that Shawn actually enjoyed belittling him, but, like the other times, Christian let it pass. "In your opinion, how do you feel the quality of your opponents have been?"

"Considering I've knocked most of them out by the fifth, I'd say they were pretty fuckin' shitty!"

"That's probably why you haven't had a title shot yet or even been a contender for that matter. Because your opponents haven't been that good. If you have had a history of facing good opponents, or at least good quality ones of late, you'd be in better contention than you are now."

"How would I be able to get better guys to knock-out?"

"You want me to tell you, honestly?"

"Yeah, that's why I asked you, wasn't it?"

"I think if you were to listen to Dom and not try to knockout everyone you face as soon as you can, you may get better caliber opponents. Being knocked-out in the eighth is one thing, but being knocked-out in the first or second is embarrassing. Almost anyone in the business is in it because they enjoy it and don't want to see themselves, or their boxers, being embarrassed. A lot of people that Dom works with, those who he tries to set fights up for us don't want to be embarrassed. It's easier for him to get matches for us if we wait a couple extra rounds before we open a can of whoop ass. There have been plenty of fights Dom could have had for you if it wasn't for this. Even the ones he has got have been hard for him to get."

"You mean for me to fight your style of fight?" he asked while getting a little hot headed.

"That's not what I'm saying..."

"Then what are you saying, huh?! That I'm fighting all wrong?!" Shawn hotly interrupted before Christian could finish.

"If you let me finish, I'll tell you," Christian said before pausing briefly to see if Shawn would attempt to interrupt him again.

Shawn, though ready for a heated argument, actually surprised Christian by not saying something else. Instead, he simply nodded for Christian to continue.

"What I was trying to say was," continued Christian, "was if you could wait, say to the fourth of fifth round, before you knock them out, you may be surprised to find that you might be going up against people that are better ranked fighters. That's all I was trying to say. Just wait a couple extra rounds, that's it. That and maybe try to be a little bit more patient."

"I've spent the last six years being patient, bro. I've been wanting my piece of the pie for a while now and I'm not sure how much longer I can wait for it."

"You could do what Bill did and jump ship," Christian joked with a laugh.

"I've thought about that, I really have," Shawn said with a good amount of candidacy. "That's really not a bad idea."

"Dude, I was joking about that."

"I know, and I really like to see some return for my effort."

"Speaking of that, you wanna go down and spar a little? That might help burn off some of your frustrations."

Shawn blinked his eyes in confusion when he heard this. "But the gym's closed."

"So?" Christian grinned. "We have keys, don't we?"

"That is true. We do, don't we?"

They exchanged looks with each other before getting up to go downstairs. On their way down, a thought came to Christian.

"Oh, a day or so ago I saw the obit for Mrs. Deeley in the paper. I've been meaning to tell you but it slipped my mind."

"How'd she die?"

Christian thought for an answer. "Stroke, I think. I hope Mr. Deeley's going to take her passing alright."

"I wouldn't worry too much about him." Shawn laughed.

"What's that?"

"Because he's dead, dude. Cancer ate his ass out a year or so ago."

"Ah, man! Really? That's too bad," Christian sadly said. "If I had known, I would have gone to his funeral."

"You did know, you jackass. I told you myself."

"You did? Where the hell was I?"

"Beats the hell outta me, bro, but I definitely told you."

"Is that store of theirs still around? If it is, who's running it now?"

"I think I heard that they sold it to their daughter and her husband about five years ago," Shawn told him.

"That's good; at least it's still in the family."

At that moment, they reached the door to the gym at the bottom of the stairs. They soon went inside to spar for the next ninety minutes.

Chapter 19

"You know, Shawn, I'm really starting to hate this," Christian told his brother early that next week as they ran down an alley with a number of guys in hot pursuit.

"That's because you have no sense of adventure." Shawn laughed while following Christian onto a dumpster before going over its adjacent wall.

"Is that what this is called? Running from some guy and four of his buddies after you try feeling up his girlfriend to be a *sense* of adventure? Christian asked while turning to notice the five guys still in pursuit of them as they cleared the wall. "If that's your idea of an adventure, then you would be correct in that statement."

"How was I to know he was her boyfriend?" Shawn asked in his defense.

"Probably by the way they were groping each other."

"You can never tell that, man," Shawn informed him as they finally came out into the street to find a parade in progress. "For all we know, she could have been a really friendly person."

Nodding to the parade, Christian made an attempt to blend it with it. "She didn't seem that friendly when she slapped you."

"That is true." Shawn looked thoughtfully to his brother while following him. "That would explain why that guy and his butt buddies got pissed."

"Speaking of which, watch out." Christian pointed to the alley they just came from to reveal the five who were in hot pursuit of them. "There they are."

"I see them. Let's duck down a little, bro."

They stayed in the parade for a several minutes to make sure they were safe. A man in the parade next to them soon gave them a look of recognition.

"It's good to see you two here," the stranger said to them. "In the parade, that is."

"Yeah, we like doing these types of things every now and then," Christian explained while not knowing what else to say.

"Oh, really?" the stranger asked with slightly more enthusiasm than they had anticipated. "Are you two officially coming out?"

Christian looked at him in a puzzled, eye scrunching manner for a moment. "Coming out of what? We've been outside for a couple of hours now."

"Oh, come on now. Don't play dumb with me," the stranger said with a certain airiness that got Shawn thinking. "It's ok for you to admit it, especially here among friends."

Shawn, meanwhile, started to look around the other people in the parade to discover that the vast majority of them were men, most of whom were holding hands with each other. Several of the women were seen partnered up with other women. Once guessing what sort of parade they found themselves in, he turned to their new friend, whose name was still a mystery, with a smile on his face.

"No, I'm afraid I'm not, coming out that is. But he is, though." Shawn pointed to Christian. "He asked me to come support him during this troubling time for him."

"Oh, that's so wonderful!" the stranger said with an over expressed joy as his hands came to his face while smiling to Christian. "I'm *so* very glad to hear that. If there's anything we can do to make your transition easier, let me know, ok?" He pulled a business card from his shirt pocket before handing it to them.

"Gee, thanks, um...Fred," Christian said while reading the card. It stated that their new found friend was Fred Stevens, a local councilor of sorts at a local charitable organization. "I'll keep you in mind. I really do appreciate it."

"Actually, all my friends call me Freddie. And as for my help," he informed Christian with a friendly, well-placed hand on his shoulder, "don't mention it. That's what friends are for, right? I'm a counselor in town who helps handle matters like this."

"Yeah, hopefully you'll hear from me soon," Christian said more out of pacification than out of pure seriousness. Meanwhile, he noticed Shawn was looking away while trying to hide a combination smile and chuckle, before noticing Dom's gym up the road. "Well, we'd like to stay longer, but we promised someone that we'd meet him over at the gym."

"I'm sorry to hear you're leaving so soon and, yes, if all goes well, we'll talk about this little manner in a couple of days." Freddie shook hands with them before seeing his two new friends may their way through the crowd and on towards Dom's gym.

Once they were out of range, Christian sighed as Shawn started laughing. "Man, am I glad that's over with."

"Hey, I hear ya," Shawn stated while glancing around behind them to make sure they weren't being followed or no one was looking.

"Are your friends still with us?" Christian asked while looking around as well.

"No, it seems like we lost them."

"Good," he said while looking at Shawn in frustration. "And, while it's still fresh in my head, what the hell was that about?"

"I told you, brother, I didn't realize she was taken," he snapped back with heavy sarcasm as they neared the gym before going in. They stopped briefly as Christian checked the mail. "And, for the record, how was I supposed to know those four other gorillas were there with him?"

"No, dude, that's not what I meant." Christian closed the mailbox as he and Shawn turned to enter the gym. "I meant with the parade. Why the hell did you make that guy think I was gay, huh?"

Hearing this, Shawn burst out laughing while tears started forming in his eyes. "Sorry about that. I couldn't help myself. It seemed like a good idea at the time and I just had to go with it."

"Thanks. I sure hope I don't run into dear old Freddie anytime soon."

"Run into? Don't you mean bend into?" Shawn asked with wide eyes while throwing a few mock jabs of his elbow.

"You're one sick bastard, you know that?" Christian said while shaking his head.

Meanwhile, Dom's voice was heard throughout the gym. "Get yer left up!" the old man yelled. "For Christ's sake, get yer goddamn left up ta protect yer face! Stop that jab of his!"

"Who the hell is that that Dom's yelling at?" Christian asked as they stopped to watch their elderly trainer yell at some guy he's never seen before. The new guy was sparring with Dave, an experienced boxer Dom has to test various fighters with.

"Shouldn't you know?" Shawn asked with obvious sarcasm. "You're the one who helps him with the books, right?"

"If I knew, I wouldn't have asked," retorted Chris walking to the ring.

Shawn, meanwhile, stood there watching for a moment longer before turning to locker room.

"Hey. Dom," Christian said while stopping next to his elderly mentor. "Who's your new prodigy?"

"Name's Nick Greenwood," the short spitfire answered. "Been here 'bout a week or so; up from Atlanta area. Time, time! Hey, Nick, come over here, will ya?"

Nice did what was asked of him. "Yeah, boss."

"What the hell was that? What the hell was you doin' in there?" Dom growled while scowling up at Nick.

"I thought I was sparring, boss."

"No, not that!" Dom yelled. "The other thing, besides sparring. What was ya doin'? Or, should I say, what wasn't ya doin'?"

"I don't follow, boss."

"Ya weren't breathin' in there."

"I'm going to have to disagree with you on that point, boss."

"Every time Dave goes ta hit ya, ya hold yer breath," Dom told him while calming down. "Stop doin' that, ya hear? Ya'll tire yerself out faster that way. Instead, exhale when ya anticipate the punch. It'll hurt less."

"Yeah, sure boss. Breathe out, I got it," Nick said as he started bouncing lightly on his feet while making quick jabs in front of him.

"Alright, kid. Now get back in there and show me what ya got," Dom told him before walking towards a bench that was at ringside and sitting on it.

Nice was a young guy in his late teens, maybe early twenties tops. Though he seemed to have a lot of heart, Christian thought he didn't have a clue. He was around 5'8" and about 150 pounds soaking wet. Outside of a massive amount of heart, it looked like he had the potential for quite a bit of speed to him but that was pretty much it.

"What the hell happened ta ya, kid?" Dom asked Christian when he saw his shirt was all sweaty. When he didn't get an answer right away, he repeated himself. "Hey, Chris, what happened ta ya?"

"Huh, what?" Christian dumbly asked when he finally realized that Dom was talking to him. "Oh, nothing. I was just out running with Shawn."

"Ya were out runnin'? With Shawn?" Dom asked with some reluctance while looking over Christian who answered him with a nod. "Ya were runnin' with Shawn in yer street clothes? Was it from anythin' in particular or was it for fun?"

Christian's expression immediately became serous as his eyes sparkled from the humor in that. "Now, why would you ask a question like that?"

"Yeah, just what I thought, kid. So, while we're on it, what the hell ya still doin' out here? Why ain't ya in the locker room gettin' changed?"

"Yes, sir. Sorry, sir. I'm on it," Christian told him as he started jogging in place before running off towards the lockers to get ready for his training.

.

197

Chapter 20

Christian's skills improved immensely over the next year under the watchful eye of Dominic. He absorbed any tidbit of information he could like a sponge. The more he learned, the more he trained. As a result, anyone would swear he'd been training at least twice as long as he had been. The only problem he still had was the naïve mentality he had towards boxing, but would be corrected with more in-ring experience. Dom was pleased with his progress and, as a result, placed him in quite a few more fights that year.

Shawn, on the other hand, was much more reluctant to Dom's way of training than Chris was. He preferred to listen to Dom if he felt the instructions would benefit his way of fighting; and he was bound and determined to knockout his opponents as quickly as possible. Occasionally, Christian would wonder why Shawn would have Dom in his corner if he wasn't going to listen to him, but hadn't found the answer important enough yet to ask.

At one point Shawn had approached Dom about why he hadn't had any title offers yet. The only answer Dom gave was, "Who says ya ain't had any?" This resulted in an argument to which Christian had never heard. They exchanged blows from Dom's inability to trust him; to Shawn's linear and one dimensional way of thinking; to Dom's love affair with people who does what he wants, when he wants; to Shawn's unlearnable, macho attitude. Ultimately, this led to an understanding that if Shawn could go at least six rounds in his next six fights, then Dom would have a title shot waiting for him. Reluctantly, Shawn agreed and, to everyone's amazement, kept his end of the bargain.

In correlation to Shawn's "next six matches," Christian was placed on the same undercards all six times.

"Hey, kid, what this make ya, 8-0?" Dom asked while counting his fingers as while walking back to the locker room after Christian's fight.

"9-0," he answered with a smile. "Though I feel bad for the other guy."

Shawn quickly shot him a look. "You feel bad for him? What the hell for?"

"I thought it was a bit sudden for the ref to call it. I didn't hit him all that much," Christian explained while a little taken back by the whole ordeal.

"You peppered him for almost the entire eight rounds the fight was scheduled for," Shawn told him with some confusion in his voice. "In another minute or so, the fight would'a been over anyway and you would'a won on points."

"He wasn't that bad; still had some life in him."

"I'm surprised the ref waited that long," Dom commented.

"Why's that?"

"His right eye was swollen pretty much shut by the seventh."

"Still," Christian said before thinking in silence before replying. "Just the feeling of winning by knockout when I was trying to go the distance doesn't seem right."

"You didn't win by knockout," Dom corrected him in his usual growl.

" I didn't? Will all due respect, I don't remember winning by decision."

"What good-ole Gramps here is saying, you dickhead, is that you won by technical knockout," Shawn told him while casually looking over to his brother before looking down the hall. "You *technically* knocked him out but apparently the ref didn't want to wait that long for you to do so."

"But the round was going to be over in another minute or so," Christian protested. "He wasn't going down in that time."

"*We* know that but the ref didn't. He didn't want to take the chance of him getting any worse than he already was," Dom told his confused pupil while patting him on the back. "Don't beat yourself up over it. Ya did good, kid. This was the first time this had happened to ya, but it won't be the last."

"Yeah, I know, but it doesn't feel right, though." Christian sighed with reluctance while looking down at Dom with a sheepish smile.

"Will you stop worrying about that bastard you just beat?" Shawn voiced with heavy irritation. "A win is a win! Don't be worryin' about how you get it; just be happy you weren't on the receiving end. You can't always get the win that you're lookin' for, so just be happy with the win that you got. Alright?!"

"I guess you're right"

"You guess I'm right?! Bloody fuckin' hell!" Shawn grumbled with a shake of his head as they finally made it through the door to their locker room. When they did enter, Shawn's demeanor changed to that of a little child on Christmas Eve. He soon started dancing around with enthusiasm while pumping his fists towards Dom.

"Hey, kid, come here and have a seat, will ya?" Dom told Christian, who obediently sat down on a medicine table. Dom promptly took off his gloves before picking up a pair of shears to cut the tape that was on Christian's hands and wrists.

Christian, meanwhile, gave Shawn, who was still dancing around, an inquisitive look. "What's got into you? Why are you so happy?"

"This is it, Beeker. This is it!"

"This is what?"

"My title shot."

"Title shot? You finally got a title shot?"

"Well, no, not exactly," he said while not breaking stride in his dancing. "Remember that deal Dom and I had, the one where I fight six straight fights and go at least to the sixth in all of them? Well, today was fight number six, brother. And they all went to the sixth."

"So, Champ, what are you going for then?" Christian asked.

"The belt, you moron!" he exclaimed as he stopped dancing to stare at him.

"What I meant was, which one? What belt will you be a contender for?"

"Pick your initials. WBC, IBF, whatever," Shawn told him while resuming to dance around before doing a bad Ric Flair impersonation. "I can almost taste it. The electricity is in the air. Whooooo!"

"Hey, settle down, kid. Don't put all your eggs in one basket," Dom informed him.

Hearing that, Shawn stopped dancing to look sharply at the old man. "What's that supposed to mean? We had a deal and I kept my end of it. Are you backin' out of it?"

"Don't worry about it. Ya'll get your title shot, that's what I meant." Dom finished taking the tape off of Christian's hands before giving him a once over. "Just cool yer engines and trust I'll keep my end of it, ok?"

Shawn merely looked at him and grunted before going back to throwing punches in the air.

It didn't take Dom long to put Shawn in a title fight though it was hardly what Shawn was looking for. The North American title was held by some guy with a hard to pronounce name that Shawn had already beat the crap out of once before.

"I can't believe you put me in this bullshit title fight. I deserve better," complained Shawn in the locker room as Dom taped up his hands and wrists.

"Ya deserve what I say ya deserve," Dom gruffly told him. "Try and go a few rounds with him, and I'll see what I can do."

"Speaking of that, why the hell am I still doin' these eight-rounder's?"

"What ya mean? You've had a few ten-rounders."

"Yeah, a few. Why aren't all my fights at least ten rounds?"

"Ya're right, they should be, but it's kinda hard to find very many good ten-rounders when ya don't choose to last past the second."

"In case you forgot, the last six I had all went well past the second."

"Yeah, because ya wanted a title fight. If it was up to ya, they'd've went ta the second at the latest," Dom said with a glance over to Christian, who was reading some textbook in the corner. "Prove ta me tonight that ya can go a couple rounds again and I'll do my best to put ya in more ten-rounders, ok?"

Shawn frowned irritably. "I don't have much choice in the matter, now do I?"

While hearing his trainer and brother bicker with each other, Christian broke out with a laugh that drew the looks from both Dominic and Shawn.

Scowling, Shawn asks, "What the hell're you laughing at?"

"Oh, just this, what I'm reading," Christian life while pointing to his book. "This chapter that I'm on is funny."

"One of your old college textbooks is funny? Which one is it?" Shawn asked with raised eyebrows to look at the book's cover after Christian moved it for him to see better. "Genetics? Readin' a genetics textbook is funny?"

Christian merely shrugged at this. "Well, yeah. It was either this or one on horse reproduction. That one's not as funny."

"Really? For a minute there I thought you were laughing at me."

Before Christian was able to respond, a knock was heard on the door. It was opened thereafter to reveal a man in a suit.

"Five minutes, guys. Five minutes."

"Almost time. Ya ready?" Dom asked Shawn.

"What do you think? I've been waiting for a title shot for like seven years now," the cocky pugilist answered rudely with a type of depressed sarcasm. "Though this wasn't what I had in mind, it'll have to do. For now. And, speaking of which, why the hell did it have to be in Atlantic City? Couldn't you have booked it any further from home?"

"The only other spot that we could have been was Vegas," Dom told him while giving Shawn the once over one more time. "Out of those two, I choose the locale that was closer ta home. I figured ya wouldn't have wanted ta travel all the way to Vegas when Atlantic City was closer. Other than these two, there weren't no other options."

"You should have asked. I might have wanted Vegas," Shawn complained.

"Ya would'a choose Vegas?" Dom asked with a twinkle in his eye as Shawn slightly shrugged. "Ya might've choose Vegas but, knowing ya, ya wouldn't have liked it."

"How would you know? You didn't ask."

"I've been to Vegas." Dom eyed him. "All that's there is a few main drags with lots of buildings condensed around them. That's it. It's set out in the middle of nowhere with nothing but desert ta see."

"Really? That's Vegas?" A confused Shawn asked by what he just heard.

Dom smiled at this. "'fraid so. Why don't ya ask yer brother here if ya don't believe me."

"Dom's right about Las Vegas," Christian agree.

"How would you know? You've never been there."

"Remember that class I had I college a few years ago? That desert environmental one? Where I actually spent a week out in the desert?"

"Nope."

"That week that we were out, we went to some desert out in Nevada. Nothing but desert as far as the eye could see," Christian informed him. "No matter where you looked, there weren't any signs of humans at all."

"And how the hell does that trip of yours have anything to do with Vegas?"

"When we were out there, the only thing that was in any way human was a road here or there. One day in particular, about a mile or so down the road, we could see a lot of these big, well lit building in the distance. They were all crammed together in a space too small for them. That ended up being Vegas."

"Really? Huh. Who would have thought that?" Shawn said after hearing this. "Sounds like I would have been bored off my ass if we went out there. But, on the other hand, you two do realize what's *legal* out there, don't you?"

"Yeah, kid, we do. We took that into consideration as well." Dom swatted Shawn's head. "I wasn't going ta take the change of gettin' ya infected with anything that didn't involve boxin'."

After thinking for a moment, Shawn looked at them with a broad smile on his face. "But we're in Atlantic City. That's probably legal here too, isn't it?"

"Probably, but don't ya worry 'bout that. Ya don't need any of that," Dom told him just as the same well-dressed man popped his head into the locker room again to announce that it was time for the fight. "Ok, kiddo, this is it. Let's go."

"Cool." Shawn got up, tied his robe around him, put his hood up, and started dancingly slightly. "Let's get this over with."

Seconds later, Shawn, Dom, and Christian left the locker room and walked down the hall for the fight. The fight itself sent how they expected it would go as they walked back to the locker room less than fifteen minutes later. The fight itself ended via knockout twenty-two seconds into the second round.

"I hope ya're happy with yourself," Dom complained while giving Shawn the evil eye. "Ya never do what I tell ya. I tell ya these things for a reason and they just go in one ear and out the other."

"Listen, Dom. You did say you wanted this to go a couple of rounds and it did. Now you're sayin' I don't listen?" Shawn disagreed. "But I guess in a way I could have ended it better than I did."

"How much better da ya think ya could have ended it?" inquired Dom.

A smiled crossed Shawn's face as he thought of the possibilities. "I could have completely unloaded on him and took him out a minute into the first. Man that would have felt great!"

"You think so? Even though he was one of the better fighters you've faced?" Christian asked while trying hard to hide his sarcasm.

"Hells yeah, I'm being serious!" Shawn laughed while loosening up for the first time. "It felt great when I did unload on him at the end of the first and on into the second. Just think what I could of done if I didn't have to carry him that whole first round. If my hands were untied, who knows what I could of done."

"None of us are doubtin' what ya could'a done, but I still wanted it ta go a couple of rounds. And I thank-thee for listenin' to me on at least that one small request." Dom shook his head while approaching the locker room before opening the door and walked in. "I just wished ya would'a went at least another full round before ya knocked him out. But considerin' ya did curb yer impulses to win in the first, I guess I'm lucky ya actually listened ta me." He sighed with another shake of the head. "So, I have to ask. How's it feel ta me be new North American Light Heavyweight Champion?"

"Dude, really?" Shawn smiled broadly while sighing with relief. "It feels great! I hope this'll finally jump start my career and people actually start taking notice."

"I'm sure it will."

"By the way, that's a nice belt," complimented Christian while looking at Shawn's newly acquired acquisition.

Shawn looked briefly at the belt in his hands before putting it around his waist. "Yeah, not really. So, be honest guys, I make this junk look good, don't I? Better than that jerkoff did that I just beat."

Chris and Dom exchanged a brief look with each other before Dom pointed to the bench while clearing his throat. Shawn immediately sat down so his gloves and tape could be taken off.

"Ya're a vain, arrogant bastard, ya know that?" Dom told him with a slight smile. "Why don't ya be quiet long enough so your brother can take off yer things? Speaking of that, would ya like the ring doctor ta come check ya out ta make sure ya're alright? Ya know, if something happened ta ya ta make ya this arrogant, we could take care of it right away."

"What I want is to get the hell outta here so I can show off my belt," Shawn informed them.

"Then sit still and shut up so we can finish." Dom patted him on the head.

Within a half hour later, the three of them were walking out the arena's back door to go back to their hotel.

"So, Dom, we're thinking about going out to check out the city. You want to come?" Christian inquired as he and his brother looked to their elderly mentor.

"Nah, not tonight. One of my programs is on tonight, one that I hadn't seen in a while. Kinda wanna go back ta the hotel ta watch it."

"Tel us tomorrow what happened on *The Golden Girls*, ok Dom?" mocked Shawn.

"Ya bein' serious? Ya think I sit around watchin' a show about a bunch of old women?"

"Just thought you would'a wanted to watch a show with a bunch of younger ladies there, Dom. I know I would," Shawn egged him on with a smile. "It might help get you feeling young again."

Dom, who was in mid-stride as they walked to the car, stopped to stare at his new champ who was laughing openly at his expense. "At least you finally are laughing at me to my face rather than behind my back. Get your asses in the car, will ya two?" Dom glared while pointing to their vehicle.

Christian and Shawn did what they were told and, after dropping Dom off at their hotel, they soon were off cruising the streets of Atlantic City searching for adventures they could put themselves into.

Chapter 21

Over the next several months, things went well for both Christian and Shawn.

Christian took that dishwashing position at the fine dining restaurant in lieu of the cooking position he had at the diner. He lost most of the remaining body fat he had been carrying around for most of his life and had replaced it with lean muscle. Meanwhile, his boxing skills had improved immensely under the watchful eye of Dom. Like his younger years, he absorbed information much the same as a sponge did water and he yearned or more.

Even though he'd been in the boxing realm for a mere two years, he gained roughly the same amount of Shawn had since childhood. He had went to college right after high school but soon became foolish with money and credit cards. Now knowing what else to do, he dropped out after two years in an attempt to pay off what bills he had. That was when he got into boxing.

At first it started off small, beginning with getting an office position at the gym Shawn worked out in. This eventually let him into the ring when he was able to receive lessons for free. When it became known that he had a natural talent for it, he began pursuing it on a more regular basis.

This, in turn, seemed to anger Shawn to the point of jealousy because, up until then, boxing had been his world, not Christian's. Shawn was hurt, betrayed really, when Dom turned his ever attentive eye to his "much weaker" and often "foolish" brother rather than on him, like he had the previous several years. Shawn felt that since Christian was able to do anything he would set his mind to, why on earth would he want to become a boxer? Besides, didn't Christian realize that that position, the one of a boxer, was already filled by his brother? Shawn often thought, 'How dare he take something that was mine and mine alone!"

But, then again, Shawn never did have what anyone would call a normal way of thinking or even a normal childhood for that matter. As a result of his family, he learned to turn to the only things that made them happy whenever they didn't get what they wanted or didn't get what they felt they deserved, which was pretty much on a daily occurrence. They would indulged themselves in the finer arts of drug education. Shawn's father's drug of choice was alcohol and denial; while his mother's was heroin and depression. Shawn seemed to embrace all forms of these, heavily we might add, starting in his teenage years.

If David wasn't already on a first name basis with Shawn's principal, he would have been long before Shawn dropped out of high school. David also came to know a few members of the local law enforcement personally during this same period, but not as well as well as his adopted son had.

When it seemed like Shawn had somewhat out grown a couple of his less than healthy habits, he was able to be persuaded by Christian to go back to get his G.E.D.. Shawn had already decided to be connected, in one form or another, with boxing and, as a result, he felt like going for this G.E.D. would just get in his way. He felt no need, or inclination, to why he would ever need it, but did it to stop being pestered by his brother over it.

After Christian's college years was when Shawn moved into the apartment above Dom's gym. He was offered the other bedroom in the same apartment before soon accepting the offer because he did want to move out on his own, but not completely on his own, and this seemed to be a happy medium. That was two years ago, a few months before catching Dom's eye.

More times than not, Christian would come home late after work on account that Shawn liked having private moments with an unnamed women he'd recently met. During times like these, Christian would spend at the local library and talk with its maintenance man who he knew during school or he'd go over to Miho's place. Miho had an apartment not far from the college he had met her at. The relationship that he had with her seemed to innerve Shawn a great deal. To Shawn, he couldn't believe that any sensible white American man would be attracted to anyone else who wasn't either white or American, but he soon would dismiss it because Christian was far from being sensible.

There were other reasons, of course, as to why he didn't approve of their relationship. First off, Shawn felt that she knew too much about Christian. To him, no one should know that much about anyone. If they don't know much about you, then they can't use that information against you. And, second, she was smart. Shawn felt that she was as smart, if not smarter, than Christian was. No woman would ever have either of those advantages over Shawn. But, then again, he was thinking why Christian would allow such an unnatural thing like that to happen. And as soon as he realized it, he felt alright again because Christian had always been the weakest one of the bunch. He'd get what was coming to him as a result of this soon enough and, when that happened, Shawn would be prepared to be the first one to dish out a well deserved "I told you so."

A few days after rationalizing the fact that Christian would be screwed over by having Miho there longer than what Shawn deemed necessary, the two of them went over to Mike's for a few drinks.

"So, Shawn," Mike started as he got both Shawn and Christian refills on their drinks, "this was what, your third title defense?"

"My *third*? Where the hell've you been, man? It was my tenth!" Shawn declared with an indication of ill temper in his voice while looking up at Mike before pounding a fist down on the bar. With his other hand, he took his refill of beer that was given to him and drank about half of it in one gulp.

Christian, meanwhile, was sitting next to Shawn while reading a newspaper as he took the refill on his soda. "Thanks, Mike," he said without looking up. "It says here that there's still that bad drought going on out west. It's been kicking their butts for about four months now. The wild fires that have stemmed as a result have been giving them hell as well," he told them before Shawn quickly turned to glare at him.

"How in the hell can you talk about a think like that now?!" he demanded while continuing to glare at his brother.

Times like this, Christian enjoyed getting Shawn riled and the easiest way to do it was to talk about something irrelevant to what he wanted to talk about. In this case, a drought and wildfires on the other side of the country.

"What do you mean?" Christian asked mildly while glancing up from his paper to look at his brother.

"Don't give me that shit!" Shawn spread his hands out while glancing back and forth between Christian and Mike a couple of times before focusing back onto Christian. "A minute ago we were talkin' about boxing, then all of a sudden you just changed the subject to start talkin' 'bout draughts and fires and shit that don't concern me, or you for that matter."

"For the record, when you said that *we* were talking about boxing, I wasn't part of the 'we' that you were talking about," Christian informed him while flipping through the pages of his newspaper while reaching for his soda to sip on. "As a matter of fact, it wasn't even a we per se. With all intense purposes, it was you who was talking about it while Mike injected an occasional comment or question about it while I sat back to listen."

"The point I was tryin' to make, you moron, we were talkin' 'bout boxing, not some drought or fire or any other bullshit that's thousands of miles away from here and we'll probably never go 'cuz we're stuck in this fuckin' dump for the rest of our miserable existence!" Shawn exploded while exhaling a sigh of aggravation.

"I'll try to keep that in mind next time," Christian dryly commented before starting to read an article that drew his interest."

"Keep what in mind?"

"That no one's allowed to talk about anything else but what you're talking about when they're around you." Christian smiled.

"Oh, fuck you!" Shawn shot him a glare before straightening himself on his stool and gulping down the rest of his beer.

"Nah, not now. I might take you up on that later if that's ok," Christian told him while finishing his article.

"Hey, Mike. Can we get a refill over here?" a familiar voice said to Chris' right as the sound of an empty beer pitcher was heard striking the bar.

"Sure thing," Mike said with a not while walking over to pick up the pitcher. "What'cha you having?"

"Labatt's if you still have any," the voice replied.

While Mike was filling the pitcher, Christian looked over to see the source of the voice next to him. It was Terry. He stood a couple feet from him while looking down to him.

"I was wondering how long I was going to stand here before you looked at me," Terry said.

"I was going to eventually," Christian replied while pointing to his newspaper. "I just wanted to finish the article I was reading first."

"I'm sure. Oh, by the way, we saw your title fight the other day," Terry told him while giving Mike a few folded dollar bills in exchange for the filled pitcher.

"You did, really?" Christian asked with a little excitement as Terry nodded he had. From the corner of his eye, Christian noticed that when he asked this, Shawn rolled his eyes in an over exaggerated manner while letting out a loud sigh.

Terry gave Shawn a fleeting stare before turning back to Christian.

"You weren't there, were you?" Christian inquired.

"Nah; Mike had it on the big screen. HBO."

"What did you think of it?"

"Thought it was a little long," Terry explained. "We thought that it should have been over by the eighth, but knowing that old man you have working for you, he was probably telling you to take it as long as you could." With this, he seemed to be talking with genuine honesty. "Other than that, we liked it a lot. Which belt was it for again?"

"The WBO cruiserweight championship."

"WBO, nice," repeated Terry. "That's a good belt to have, Chris."

"It's ok. Not one of the top three, but it is the fourth."

"Just ok? What are you talking about?" Terry question while embarrassing Christian. "C'mon Chris, really? That's a world title, man! It's more than just ok."

"Hey, Terry," Shawn called out to him. "Since you saw his fight, did you see mine?"

"Are you referring to that short-lived play fight that barely lasted two rounds? The one if someone blinked or sneezed they'd have missed it?" Terry asked as Shawn smiled back cockily while nodding his head. "Yeah, I saw it."

"It was great, wasn't it?" Shawn questioned while sitting there smiling his cocky grin. He adjusted his shirt in a suave and sophisticated manner.

"Well, that's a manner of opinion. If people like short, one-sided fights, then yeah, it was great." Terry laughed. "But if you're like me or Mike who like to watch a good fight unfold over a number of rounds, then yours was way too short."

"What are you talking about, you fool? I gave the people what they wanted to see."

"You did, huh? What exactly did you give them?"

"I gave them a fight with no question who the winner was. It was short, to the point, and didn't last long enough to be boring like other people we know," Shawn emotionally replied while pounding the bar and looking at Christian. "That's what people want to see. They wanna see someone get the shit kicked outta them. They wanna see blood. They wanna see a good, clean, fast knockout. They don't wanna see some boring ass fight that lasts twelve rounds, where the douche bag winner gets awarded the fight because he simply has more points than the other."

"Hey, Destroyer!" Jake interrupted while walking over to them from the pool table he was at. "I thought it was a helluva fight. I'll take a good, bloody KO anytime over that pussy footing, dancing fairy shit your brother thinks is boxing."

"You see now here's a man who knows when he's seen a boxing match," Shawn said with exhilaration after receiving the compliment from the big man. "Jake, that's why you're the man!"

"Then why was his fight the second to the last fight of the card?" Terry asked while pointing to Christian. "If they came to see you more than they came to see him, then your fight would have been later on in the card than his. Right?"

"Dude, just because his fight was later in the card doesn't mean that more people wanted to see him more than me. Where do you get off talkin' to me like that?" Shawn demanded as his eyes flared with anger.

"Oh, geez, I'm sorry. I assumed that the later on the card the match was than the more important it was. I didn't realize the opposite was true," Terry dryly told him while making eye contact with Shawn before letting out a light hearted laugh.

"You tryin' to insult me?" Shawn demanded while glaring at Terry with now threatening eyes. "You think you're funny?"

"Take it easy, Shawn," Christian said while trying to neutralize the situation. "Terry was just joking around with you. He didn't mean anything by it."

"Better not if he knew what was good for him," retorted Shawn while turning back around on his stool.

"So, um, our matches were on HBO?" Christian asked Terry.

"That's what he said, wasn't it?" Shawn rudely questioned before sighing again.

"You alright over there, Shawn?" Terry asked him.

"Yeah, great! Why wouldn't I be?" he answered while finishing his beer before waving the now empty mug towards Mike to refill.

"Honestly?" Terry asked which drew Shawn's attention. "Why I asked was because I figured you might be a little upset, that's all."

"Now why would I be upset?"

"Oooo, I don't know. I just thought you might be a little upset, possibly a little jealous too, if someone else around here got themselves a title shot," Terry told him while exchanging a silent, yet brief, look with Shawn

"Me, jealous? Of what, Christian getting himself a title? You think I'd actually be jealous of him?"

"I don't know, maybe you're right." Terry shrugged before taking a sip of beer from his pitcher. "Since you already have yourself a title, there really is no point you being jealous over your brother's new prize."

"If you have something to say, Terry, then just come out and say it!" Shawn locked eyes with him while standing up. "But don't you say I'm jealous of him when you don't know what the fuck you're talkin' 'bout."

"Well, I'm glad to see you're not jealous," Terry told him with a smile while turning to walk back to his table. "Maybe you'd better tell him why you're upset about it."

While he was walking back to his table with Jake, Christian looked over to see Shawn brewing about something over a freshly refilled mug of beer. Unsure of what to say or even if he should say anything, he took his soda before spinning on his stool to face out into the bar.

For a Wednesday, he noticed, it wasn't all that busy. Most of who was there were regulars like him. On the TVs Mike had on the usual channels; ESPN, FOX, CNN, the Weather Channel, and some sitcom. One the big screen, the birds were playing a game of baseball - Blue Jays at Orioles. He noticed that Jake and Terry started a game of pool just when two other guys wrapped up their game and left.

"Anything you want to talk about?' Christian asked while stretching a little before leaning back against the bar.

"No" was the reply.

Nodding, Christian got up to walk over to the jukebox to see what songs they had. After a minute or two of looking, he put enough change in the slot for two songs: *Crazy* and *Against The Wind* by Patsy Cline and Bob Seger respectively, before going back to his stool.

"It isn't fair," Shawn whined while turning to look at Christian.

"What's not fair?" he calmly asked after noticing Shawn had looked around the bar and back to him a couple of times. From the corner of his eye, he could tell Shawn was having a hard time figuring out what he wanted to say, a trait that rarely eluded him in the past.

"That Dom gave you a title before me!"

"I don't understand, Shawn. You got your title like a year and a half ago while I got mine this past week."

"Wha...are you tryin' to be funny?" Shawn asked in astonishment and wide-eyed wonder. "You can't seriously think my North American Championship is any type of title, right? The only reason why I got that was because Dom wanted to shut me up about getting a title. Instead of a real one, one to be proud of, he gave me that bullshit title for some second-rate has-been or for some guy who can't possibly get anything else. Let me tell you this, bucko," he continued while pointing his finger down at the bar, "I ain't either! Dom knows I can't say anything now to him about getting a shot when I've got that."

"What's wrong with it?" Christian asked him. "Doesn't that mean you're the best in North America?"

"Yeah, in North America. But what exactly is North America? Its three countries; the United States, Canada, and Mexico. Whoopty-fuckin'-do da!" Shawn sarcastically commented while rolling his eyes and waving a finger in the air. "Anyone that's worth a damn wouldn't be going for that title! You know why?"

"Ah, I'm not sure. Why wouldn't they?"

Pausing briefly to lean forward on his stool, Shawn soon answered. "It's because they'd be challenging for titles that had initials to it, like you did last week. You know, with all due respect to you and all, Beeker, but that title that you won should have been mine!"

"How could it have been?" Christian asked while scrunching his nose after smelling the beer on his brother's breath. "We're in totally different weight classes."

"Yo man, that's not what I meant, you knuckle-head! What I meant was that I should'a been goin' for the WBO belt, for my own weight class, not you in yours!"

"Ah, I see," Christian said while finally realizing what his brother was trying to tell him. He paused briefly to look up and to position himself better so he could face Shawn before speaking again. "So is this why you've been sort of in a bad mood the last week or so? You're upset that you either didn't get another title shot or because you feel the title I have is more prestigious or important than the one you have?"

"The reason why I'm upset is because you got a title shot before I did!" Shawn yelled while slamming his open left hand down on the bar while glaring at Christian. "There, I said it. Are you happy now?!"

A couple of the guys at the end of the bar stopped what they were doing before turning to stare at them for a few seconds before going back to their conversation they were in the middle of.

"How could I have gotten a title shot first when you already had a title when I got a shot?" Christian asked while turning away from Shawn so he wouldn't see him smile at this.

"Dude, I already told you once before but since you haven't been able to grasp the idea of what I've been tellin' ya. I'll repeat it one more time for you to understand," Shawn said slowly and deliberately while leaning towards Christian a little bit more.

Christian, meanwhile, mirrored his brother's movement by leaning forward to look at him.

"Yes, I got a title before you," Shawn continued slowly and just above a whisper. "But it's some bullshit title that's for people who are still new to the business, or are some second-rate fighter, or for some has-been asshole that's never had much of a career, and they all take this title that I currently hold so they have something they can take home to show-off to their grandkiddies

211

about. I ain't any of these. I deserve more and I expect better. This title is mainly just for North American, three countries, that's it. Think I'll face any worthy opponents if they ain't from around here? I say fuck no! You know why?"

Christian shook his head mockingly while having his eyes extremely wide in an exaggerated fashion.

"Because they ain't from around here," Shawn told him. "That, or if there's any good quality from North America, they wouldn't want to challenge for some second-rate bullshit title when there's others out there that mean a helluva lot more, like the one you just got for instance."

"I agree with you, Shawn," Christian agreed with a nod. "You should have had a title or two by now, a better one on top of your current title that is. But to understand that, you'll have to ask yourself why you haven't."

"I already have, bro! I ask myself that question every time I step inside that ring."

"And what answer have you come up with?"

"That Dom doesn't want me to have one."

"Why do you think that?"

"Isn't it obvious, dude?"

"Not to me it's not."

"He's holding me back," Shawn told him while his anger rose with the volume of his voice. "He's trying to keep me from fulfilling my potential. That's what it is!"

"Do you really believe that?"

"You're goddamn right I do!"

"Well, that's one way of looking at it."

"One way? There aren't any other ways!"

"Holding back your career is one possibility. I'll give you that." Christian shrugged. "Another is maybe he's trying to give you a title shot as a reward for listening to him."

"Bein' brainwashed is more like it!" Shawn scoffed. "I ain't nobody's puppet."

"That wasn't what I meant, Shawn. What I meant was that it's his job to train us to be better boxers. He feels that your ability to last more than a couple of rounds will make you better because there are things or a certain way of thinking that you don't get if it doesn't last past the second," Christian explained before drinking the rest of the soda in his glass. "Another reason for him wanting you to go longer than you usually do is because it's getting extremely difficult for him to find you guys to fight. They simply don't want to be in the ring with you. If he runs out of guys for you to fight, you'd be out of a job."

212

"I told you why he can't find guys to fight me," Shawn said while once again revealing his cocky smile. "It's because they're all afraid of me."

"You're right, they are," Christian confirmed with a shrug. "They're afraid you'll embarrass them. A lot of those quality guys you want to face don't want to be publicly humiliated. As a result, most of who you faced had nothing to lose if you knock them out early. I know that earlier Dom had turned down title offers for you because he said either you weren't ready or you refused to listen to him. But when he set you up for that title shot that you had, you had to go a certain number or rounds for a certain number of fights. He wanted to see how badly you really wanted it, or if you were simply all talk and full of hot air. In a sense, he was testing you; seeing if you'd actually listen to him for you to get what you wanted. Turns out you would.

"When you did listen, both of you got what you wanted," Christian continued to explain. "And when you did listen to him for those six fights, you actually became a better fighter. But once you won your title and started fighting your old way again, making sure the fights were as short as possible, you've been upset with Dom for not doing much for you. It's as much your fault as it is his. The people who hold the belts you want to challenge for, maybe their managers or promoters don't them to face you. Maybe the phone's stopped ringing the way you feel it should."

At this point, Christian paused long enough for what he just said to sink into Shawn's head while he got a refill on his soda.

"Or, maybe like you said," Christian continued soon thereafter, "he's holding you back. But, if my memory serves me correctly, please correct me if it doesn't, you got a title shot when you started listening to him; just like I did last week. But what the hell do I know?" He shrugged at that before drinking his soda.

"What do you think I should do then?" Shawn asked with a great amount of sincerity in his voice.

"It's not really my place to say what you should do, but my first gut instinct is for you to start listening to him. You can try talking to him and work out some sort of compromise but considering you've tried that in the past and it didn't work then, I doubt that'll work now," Christian said before thinking of any other possibilities. "Or, you could just keep doing what you've been doing. But, if you do this, I doubt you'll get any more title shots. In that case, you might want to start scoping out other managers or promoters to jump ship to. If you did that, however, would you have as much fun as you do now? Well, on the other hand," Christian commented with a smile, "whether or not you still do have fun is subject to interpretation."

"Gee, thanks you asshole." Shawn laughed before swallowing the rest of the beer he had before getting a refill from Mike. "It feels good for someone to say that without wanting to crawl up inside my ass to nibble on my lower intestines."

"In any event, try pressing Dom on this until you actually find out why you haven't been given another title opportunity," Christian supported. "In the meanwhile, it might be a good idea if you did go shopping around. If you do, see if they'll agree to put you in a title shot within a reasonable amount of time of you hiring them. Getting that perk established early on, especially if it's in writing, would be a good thing."

"That sounds like a really good idea, Beeker." Shawn nodded while turning to lean against the counter. While watching the various people coming and going into the barroom, he added, "I might just go that."

Just then, Josh strolled in to stop briefly to see who was at the bar. When noticing Christian and Shawn, he continued on over to them.

"I'm surprised to see you girls are still up," he said to them. "I would have thought it was past your bed time."

While looking at his watch, Christian said, "It's only 8:30."

"My point exactly. Isn't it a little late for you girls to be up?" Josh asked dryly before having a smile appear on his face.

"Hey, Josh. How've you been?" Christian asked while returning the smile and extended a hand which Josh immediately took to shake. "Good to see you."

"Been better," Josh grumped. "Mother-in-law's been bitchin' up a storm all day because the garbage man didn't come this morning to pick up her half a bag of trash."

"Don't the garbage guys come on Tuesdays around here?" Shawn asked him.

"Yep."

Christian looked at Josh with a confused look when he heard this. "Doesn't she know that today's Wednesday?"

"She understands the trash comes on Tuesdays but she thinks today is Tuesday," Josh mumbled with a heavy sigh while rubbing the back of his bald head. "After five minutes of tryin' to tell her different, I got so fed up with her shit that I left. She was still carrying on when the door closed between them. Other than wanting to strangle her with her tongue, I'm fine. How you two been?"

"I'm doing well, thanks man," Christian answered immediately.

Meanwhile, Josh turned to Shawn to wait for an answer that never came.

"What? You not talkin' to me today?" Josh asked him.

Shawn smiled. "No, no, I was. I was just figuring out how to word something."

"Just come out and say it already. I don't have all damn day."

"I was just going to say that this is an unpleasant surprise, seeing you that is, Josh. Just the sight of you makes my blood curdle."

While glaring at the pugilist customer, the bald bouncer tells him, "If that's how you feel, you can just take your scrawny little ass and go to Hell if you don't like it."

"You know, if you don't have anything else to say to us, Josh, we'll talk to you later." Shawn turned his back to Josh in a vain attempt to cover his gaping smile while drinking his beer. "Our drinks are getting warm."

"Listen here, jackass," Josh stated sternly while taking a step forward. "I came over here to see if you wanted to play a round or two of pool. But since it looks like you don't, I guess I'll just have to ask your brother."

Hearing this, Shawn whipped around on his stool to face him. "Yo, hey, hang on a second there. I never said I didn't wanna play pool. Have you ever known me to turn down a game of pool?"

"But you haven't said you did, either."

"You offering?"

"What would you say if I was?"

"I'd probably ask if you were paying if you were offering."

"Of course I would, you jackass," Josh told him while being a little taken back by the question. "I wouldn't expect you to pay if I was offering! Just like I wouldn't expect to pay if you were offering. So, what's it gonna be? You playing or am I going to put my boot up your ass before asking your brother instead?"

"If you're paying," Shawn said while itching the back of his head while deciding what to do before standing to look at him. "I guess I'd have no choice but to accept."

"Took you long enough for a simple yes," the bouncer said before ordering a beer from Mike.

Once Josh and Shawn had their beers in hand, they pounded fists while making their way to the pool tables while saying hello to the other regulars there.

Christian had stayed and watched them play three rounds before paying for his drinks and walked out into the night. Right then, he had the desire to see his friend Miho before he called it a night. So, before either of them did, he walked back to his apartment to call her. To his delight, he was in his car on his way to see her within an hour after leaving the bar.

Chapter 22

"Alright, Nick. Remember to keep your hands up to protect your head," Christian told him while lazily throwing some punches towards Nick's face.

"Yes, Chris," a slightly agitated Nick replied while either dodging Christian's swings or slapping them away. "And keep my chin tucked, right? You forget Dom likes to repeat himself."

"He does tend to do that, doesn't he?" Christian smiled. "I guess some of his little quirks are beginning to rub off on me. Speaking of Dom, where is that little old man?"

Nick bobbed and weaved a string of Christian's punches before retaliating with some of his own. "Shawn wanted to talk to him about something. They've been in his office for a while."

Glancing towards the back corner of the gym where Dom's office was, Christian asks, "How long ago was this?"

"About 15, 20 minutes now."

"Hey, don't forget, try and lay in a couple good jabs more often when you get a chance," Christian commented while looking back to Nick. "Helps to let me know you're still there. Besides, you might get lucky with one of those shots."

"You mean it could be a knockout punch?"

"It could, but it could daze or confuse them as well." Christian threw a few more punches as Nick tried to counter them with a number of his own punches. "But it'd be more to keep your opponent's guard up and could slow his ass down a little if he happens to get on a roll."

"Yeah, yeah, ok," Nick said while jabbing in between Christian's attempts to swat his his head.

While glancing back to the office with no luck of looking in, Christian questioned, "Do you know what Shawn wanted to talk to him about?"

"Oh, sorry, talk to who again?" Nick asked all confused like while stopping slightly to focus on Christian with a weird expression.

"Don't be stopping, don't be stopping!" Christian chastised while jabbing Nick in the face, who immediately went into self-defense mode while blocking and dodging the in-coming punches but not before two or three found their mark. "Do you know why Shawn wanted to talk to Dom?"

"Ah, no, not exactly." Nick inserted a few jabs when he could. "But Shawn did say that it had something to do with business."

"Alright. Thanks," Christian replied while finishing up the series of punches he was in the middle of. When he was done, he stopped to wipe the beads of sweat from his brow while looking at Nick. "That's it for now. What you do you say about a little break?"

"Sure." Nick shrugged while copying Christian's brow wiping while catching his breath. "A break sounds good."

With that Christian excited the ring to walk to a nearby bench to where he had his things. He took off his gloves, grabbed his towel, and wiped his head and neck. After this, he removed a bottle of water from his bad to drink.

Following suit, Nick came to sit down on the bench next to Chris while taking his gloves as well.

"Hey, you did pretty well in your first fight," Christian complimented while drinking more water.

While looking suspiciously at him, Nick asked, "You trying to be funny?"

"No. Why do you ask?"

"Because I lost. Why would you say I did good when I lost?"

"Listen." Christian cleared his throat while sitting down next to him. "You don't, or in your case, didn't need to win to look good. Your form was decent. You kept your hands up for the most part. I didn't think you threw enough punches, especially when you countered, but it was your first fight. Though you did lose, you lost by decision. You held your own."

"Held my own? What are you talking about? I got knocked down twice!"

"Yes, but you got up twice. That shows heart," Christian said firmly as he poked Nick on his shoulder. "You could have easily stayed down, especially that second time you got dropped. A lot of new people probably would have stayed down, but not you. You got up to finish the fight. Anyone can lose one fight; it's what you do afterwards that matters. Got me?"

A smile crossed Nick's face while hearing this. "Yeah, I got ya."

A few moments later, yells were heard coming from Dom's office before the door was thrown open as Shawn strode quickly through with brooding eyes. While ignoring all around him, he stormed through the gym.

Meanwhile, Dom came to stand about six feet outside his office door to watch him go. "If ya wanna play games with me ya selfish little bastard, ya'd better be prepared ta finish what ya start!" he shouted to a nonresponsive Shawn.

Continuing to walk across the gym, Shawn made his way to the door. Christian, meanwhile, got up to walk towards him to see what the problem was. Shawn merely bumped shoulder with him as he kept walking, went through the gym's door, and let the door slam behind him. The various people who were in the gym had all stopped what they were doing by now to see what was unfolding while Dom waved his hands, turned, and went back into his office.

"Hey, Nick. I'm going to talk with Dom for a few minutes," Christian told him while taking a step or two towards the office while pointing to it.

"Oh, yeah. Go ahead, Chris," Nick called out. "What do you want me to do until you get back?"

Christian shrugged. "Surprise me. A few good ideas would be to jump rope, use the speed bag, or shadow box. Hell, you could do pushups or sit-ups if you wanted. Any of those sounds good. And if you have anything else you want to do, feel free to go ahead and do that."

Giving double thumbs up, Nick went off to the corner to do some training.

Soon thereafter, Christian entered Dom's office to find him leaning against one of the tables while looking out into the gym.

"Hey Dom, you alright?"

Simply waving his hand before moving to pour himself a cup of coffee from a coffee maker on a table by the wall, Dom said, "What the hell's gotten into that kid?"

"I'm not quite sure." Christian opened one of the office's blinds slightly. "What happened?"

"He got upset because I haven't been able to give him another title shot," growled Dom foully while turning his back to Christian while looking out the window.

"Haven't been able to?" Christian repeated with a slight smile while walking to stand next to his aging teacher. "As in you couldn't or you wouldn't?"

"What's the difference?" Dom eyed his young pupil.

Returning the look, Christian answered, "One means you weren't able to no matter what he did; whereas the other you could have if you wanted to, but either turned it down or ignored it for whatever reason."

Dom, continuing to gaze up at him, broke eye contact to look back out into the gym. Looking around, stopped briefly on each person who was training. He soon let out an irritated sigh.

"You know, when he came here almost ten years ago, he had so many problems, so much anger. I actually turned him down quite a few times before finally accepting him," the elderly man said before hanging his head to think.

"Wha...you didn't take Shawn the first time he came here?" Christian was more than a little surprised when he heard that.

Dom shook his head in the negative.

"Geez, the way he told it, you were happy as hell to have him."

"He would, wouldn't he?" Dom more than laughed a little before going silent. "It took six or eight months of him constantly comin' here, hangin' 'round, and always gettin' in the way before I finally allowed him to train. But, since I don't let no high school dropouts train here, that was a double whammy for him, you see. But there was something in his eyes then. I had to see what he was made of. I finally gave in and said I would train him, but only if he went back to get his G.E.D. I insisted on seein' his progress. If he failed anythin' or didn't finish on time, then he was out. It was all up to him; no consequences to me."

Christian laughed. "At this time, I know I was pestering him about going back to finish school. I always thought he did it just to shut me up. Funny he never said what the real reason was."

"Of course he wouldn't. His pride wouldn't let him. What reason did he tell ya, fer goin' fer his equivalency?

"Either to get girls, or that the girls would be impressed, or some variation of that."

"Hmph. Sounds like him."

"Da you remember how he did?" Christian asked. "How were his grades?"

"Not great, but I've seen worse. But then all I asked was that he pass everythin', which he did. I just needed ta know what he was made of. If he was willin' ta do that, I thought he could do almost anythin'."

"How much of his background did he tell you?"

"Not much. Really the only think he told me was to call his parents if he ever got hurt," Dom answered. "It wasn't until a few months later when his P.O. came in did I actually find out more. What I heard didn't surprise me. Drug rehab, A.A., anger management, jail. Hell, most of the people here have been through at least one of those at some point."

"Not me. I've never been nor do I plan to," corrected Christian while shaking his head.

"Hell, kid, ya're considered a saint around here. If I didn't know ya, I'd wonder what a guy like ya was doin' in a joint like this."

"Thanks, Dom. That'll probably be the only compliment I'll ever get from you," Christian sarcastically said with a smile while shooting a glance to Dom before they both let out a friendly laugh. They soon quieted down while Christian folded his arms while leaning against the window. "His brother's death was hard on him. Did you hear about that?"

"Yeah, I a little. Didn't get too much info about that, though."

"He got killed in prison a year or so before you met him. He went in before Shawn and I even met," Christian told him just above a whisper as his eyes went into a distant stare. "Daryl, Shawn's brother, and one of his friends went out looking for a good time one day before deciding that it'd be fun to rob this old man on his way out of the local bank. When the old man resisted, they beat him to a pulp. He may have also got stabbed, I think. I had his granddaughter in my fifth grade teacher. He eventually died from the injuries. I don't know if they both were convicted or just Daryl, but I know he had spent quite a few years inside. Rumor has it he irritated some of the wrong people before being found face down in the shower; a shank had been shoved up in his ribs a number of times.

"Shawn had already been caught up in a variety of drugs on him before this, but his brother's death seemed to jump start the problem you mentioned earlier. What exactly got him into boxing or your gym, I haven't the foggiest idea." Christian paused for a moment to think if there was anything else he had wanted to add. "Oh, by the way, do you know that he's bipolar?"

219

"Bi-what?" Dom asked roughly with a confused look. "What the hell is that, kid?"

"It's a mental disorder, formerly called maniac-depression, or something along those lines," Christian explained while looking at Dom, who clearly had no idea what he was talking about. "It's basically a chemical imbalance, either having too much or too little of the stuff to stabilize you. In a normal person, their emotions are pretty stable; but with a person who has bipolar, their emotions are much more extreme. So, if they're in a good mood, then they're really in a great mood. If they're in a bad mood, then you should consider not being around them."

Dom grunted. "That explains a lot. How long has he been like this?"

"I think he was diagnosed a year or so after our grandfather died. I know he was taking some kind of medicine for it, but stopped a while ago."

"Why the hell would he do that?"

"Why did he get off his medicine?" Christian asked while Dom nodded. "Beats me. He said he didn't need them anymore. I think he likes it when he's maniac."

"Maybe he doesn't. Maybe he's cured, kid."

"No, he's not cured," Christian disagreed. "Once you have it, you have it for life."

While standing there in silence for a number of minutes while looking out into the gym, Dom cleared his throat. He soon started to speak before going silent again. He soon changed him mind before breaking the silence.

"Your brother had a lot of knowledge when he first got here, most of which he learned from your grandfather. That's not including the wealth of knowledge he picked up from all those Y's he's worked at. On top of being a natural athlete, he was years beyond what I thought he'd be.

"The only thing he needed was the structure, the discipline," Dom told him. "If he had a person that could harness those, they'd be able ta turn him inta the next Joe Louis. He really had no finesse, Shawn that is. He didn't or couldn't think multidimensional. It was always full steam ahead with him. I needed ta get him ta think outside the box of being a brawling, street fighter for him ta be a better, more rounded fighter. Granted, he learned, but only when he thought it was necessary to get what he wanted.

"It took me a couple of years before he actually started listenin' ta me; even then it felt like he did it just ta shut me up," Dom continued. "When I did leave him alone, he just went back ta doin' it his way. Granted, the needed ta keep who he was intact, but ta shut people out who was tryin' ta help isn't the answer. He always had ta da it his way, the cool way, the hard way. Always been stubborn and hard headed. Could never tell him anythin'. I don't think it ever occurred ta him that askin' fer help and cooperation were strengths, too," he said softly. "Ya're right about him not listenin'. God forbid he actually listened ta anyone. I think that the only way he could learn was for him just ta simply do it himself. Still is ta a certain extent, but a bit better."

"He's always been like that, even as a child," Christian laughed. He soon got thinking and went back to their previous topic. "So, um, what about this title shot he's been bugging you for?"

"Oh no, not you too!" Dom grumbled irritably while shooting Christian a glare.

"You needn't worry about me, Dom," Christian assured him, which brought a skeptical look from the little old man next to him. "I just wanted to get your side of the story first. Knowing Shawn, I'll hear about this later and didn't want to hear the story secondhand. His side could be altered once his emotions were able to set in."

"I have ta tell ya that ya have ta look at a title shot like a reward. Ya try and go ta a certain point and if ya get ta it, or even if ya get close, ya get rewarded with a title shot. Some wait longer than others, but ya get my point."

"But there are a lot of titles out there. Can't you somehow put him in some kind of title fight?"

"He already has a title."

"I meant another title."

"Don't ya think one needs ta earn a shot instead of bein' given one?"

"Don't you think a record of 42-0, with most coming by knockout, warrants a decent shot?"

"That's a good record but he still has ta earn it like everyone else," Dom stubbornly insisted. "He still has things ta learn."

"Like what?" Christian asked while drawing a look from Dom. "What does Shawn still need to learn that he hasn't already to a title shot?"

"Ya sure are persistent, kid, I'll give ya that." Dom grunted while clenching his fist. "But, ta answer your question, I'll tell ya. Patience. He needs ta learn that. He needs ta learn how to fight consistently longer than two or three rounds. If he meets a really good, well-balanced fighter, Shawn would be sucking wind by the fourth, the fifth if he's lucky." He slowly glanced up to Christian with a sly smile before going back to looking out the window.

Noticing Dom's subtle mannerisms, Christian asked, "You mean someone like me?"

"I didn't say that, but that ain't a bad idea, kid, now that I think 'bout it."

Laughing while looking out into the gym, Christian noticed that Nick had shifted gears as he went to do some shadow boxing. "What else does Shawn need to do for you?"

"He needs ta start trustin' me and doin' more of what I ask."

"Will he be ready then?"

"Perhaps, but I don't know if the title shots will come 'round again."

"He's had title shots that you never told him?" gasped Christian.

"Yeah, some more than once."

"Why'd you turn them down?"

"Who says I turned them down?" the old man asked with a hard look.

Christian smiled mildly. "Are you telling me that Shawn himself turned them down?"

"Don't be a wiseass, kid. I'm not in the mood!"

"Hmph. That's what I thought. It wouldn't be like him to pass up a title. His ego wouldn't allow that," commented Christian while looking down at Dom.

After remaining silent for a short time, Dom said barely more than a whisper, "Ya know, when he first was offered title shots, I turned them down because I didn't feel he was ready yet. Though he was quite good, he was still quite green when it came to professional boxin'. He was more of a brawler, a street fighter. It's ok if you're like that here, but this is still boxin'. As he got older and matured, his skills improved a great deal but he never curbed his hunger for a quick knockout. That, combined with his ego, is the reasons why I turned down those titles. If you're going to be champ, people expect you to act like one. I was afraid people would get sick of his antics. I also thought his ego would get the better of him once becoming champ. If he learned ta balance out some his other qualities, that would have been more appealing in the long run without him actually losin' who he was as a fighter. Now I can't get a title shot ta save his life. No one wants ta put their man in the ring with him; too afraid ta be humiliated."

"Do you think he's unstoppable? That no one can beat him?

"No, it's not that," Dom replied. "It's more ta do with the idea that most of Shawn's fights, more than half of them, have not gone past the third round. That, combined with what title he does hole, many consider that either a waste of time or one for beginners. Many don't want ta take the chance of their fighter losing ta a bottom-level champ, one who doesn't care about the welfare of his opponents. The manager's job is ta protect and take care of his fighter; or they should anyway."

"If you got him the title he has now, can't you get him something else, something better?"

"The only reason I was able to get him that was because he showed he could go a number of rounds for a number of fights. Other than that, what he has is just some bullshit title that no real competition would want ta fight for. And the other title shots have all run dry."

"He told me the same thing about it, why he had it, and why he doesn't face anyone decent."

"For once we're in agreement." Dom laughed. "Things were starting ta look good for him, picking up, up until that title match that is. Now you can barely tell him anythin'."

As Dom was saying this, Curly Kowalski walked in to start wandering through the gym. He took his time to speak to a number of boxers he knew. Curly was a middle-aged, eccentric manager who seemed like he can't get anything done, though he was enjoyable to have around due to his uniqueness and massive amount of boxing knowledge. He was about 55, wore glasses, sloughed at the shoulders, and stumbled occasionally when he walked. Today, like most times Christian saw him, he wore a cap of some minor league baseball team to cover his balking head. What hair he did have left was grayish-white. Christian liked him for numerous reasons, but mostly for his sense of humor and was easy to talk to; but he did seem to irritate the hell out of Dom. He irritated him without even trying to, while not knowing he did so, because of his eccentricities and of his unorthodox style of working. He's periodically managed some of Dom's talent; quite a bit in the past but not so much of late.

Once he made his rounds, Curly approached young Nick Greenwood to introduce himself. He thought what Nick would think once he got an idea about him.

"What are you going to do?" Christian asked Dom as his thoughts drifted back.

"Don't know," the old man answered while knocking on the window to wave Curly on over.

"What are your options?"

"If he continues doin' things his way, I don't know if I have any," Dom told him as Curly made his way over. "He does have his title and most likely will keep it a while. Maybe change weight class. Other than that, I honestly don't know."

"Hey Dom, hey brother," Curly said when he entered the office as he and Christian mocked saluted each other. He then went over to shake hands with Dom. "What's up?"

"I wanted ta ask ya for some advice." Dom folded his arms before raising one of them up ta rest on the side of his face. "I've got a problem with one of my fighters, ya see, and I'm not sure what ta do 'bout it. I thought ya might be able ta help."

"Sure. I'll give it my best shot." Curly shrugged with a wave of the hand as he focused his attention on Dom.

Christian, meanwhile, went over to sit in Dom's chair behind his desk. He spun around on it a couple of times before bringing it to a halt. He then made himself comfortable while preparing to listen to what Dom was about to say.

Meanwhile, Dom gave Curly a condensed and abridged version of the conversation he had had with Christian minutes before.

"If there's a way ya could put Mr. Calloway in some sort of title shot, I'd say put him against some guy he couldn't possibly beat; or, at least, go almost the whole fight with in order to win," Curly told him. He soon paused with an hmmm while thinking about it some more. "What if he changes weight class?"

"That's a possibility, though I'd have ta move him up," Dom told him. "If I moved him down a notch, he'd be killin' guys faster than he is now."

"Then move him up."

"Well, I had thought that, but I don't really know."

Curly looked at Dom. "Why don't you know? Or, should I ask, what about it don't you like?"

Dom flicked a thumb and nodded towards Christian. "I've already got him in that weight class above him and he's already doin' really well in it. I don't want him gettin' distracted by Shawn's jealous tendencies, or the irritation of having to set matching up by both of them being in the same class. I'd rather not have Shawn try and make him do so good so his ego isn't bruised."

"You mean Shawn would want Chris not to do as well if they were in the same class?" Curly was slightly confused when he asked that.

Dom shrugged slightly.

"Why would he do that?"

"'cause Shawn brought Christian into boxin', ya see," Dom said in a soft, gruff voice. "All Shawn wants ta do is fight; it's in his blood. He doesn't have the opportunities that Chris here has, though. This is all he knows, whereas his brother has a few other things he's done with his life and has come into boxin' only recently."

Dom paused briefly as he looked at Curly, who was digesting this, before glancing at this student behind his desk. Christian was looking back at him.

"Now, how do ya think Shawn would feel if Christian, who he brought in and who's been in the business only a couple years, is now pickin' up the sport faster than he did and is as good as him in a much shorter time span? Now, take in account that Chris has a title that is of more importance than what Shawn has. Then throw in his temper, ego, jealousy, and the fact that they live and train together. Take all of that and put them in the same weight class. What do you think will happen? I don't know what Shan will do, but I'd rather not find out."

When Dom finished, all three men were silent while they thought of a plan. Dom, with his arms crossed, looked out into the gym; Curly, standing next to him, looked on while in thought.

Christian, meanwhile, continued to sit lazily in Dom's old, worn office chair as he spun every so often on it before letting his eyes fall upon the few dozen or so framed pictures scattered on the walls. Many of them were of some fighter or promoter, most of which with Dom. Off to the side and behind Dom's desk, there was an old, run down bookshelf filled with artifacts and other boxing memorabilia Dom had collected over his forty plus years in the business. Christian was so focused at looking at each individual thing on the bookshelf that he forgot he was waiting for someone to start talking again. He jumped slightly when Curly finally spoke.

"Are you able to get Christian another title shot soon?" he asked.

"I told ya before he wasn't...wha...Christian?" Dom sputtered while quickly turning to face Curly. "If ya meant Shawn, I told ya the answer to that before. The answer is no."

"Yes, you did say that earlier, but I meant Christian," Curly said calmly before pointing to the fighter behind the desk. "Are you able to get him another title shot?"

Blinking several time, a confused look crossed the old man's face. "S'pose I could in a couple fights if things work out. Why?"

"I've an idea with what you could do with your troubled fighter," Curly stated while taking a step closer. He wet his lips multiple times while rubbing his fingers together. "Try to get Christian another title, preferably something better and more prestigious than the belt he has now, say, maybe the IBF. It can be any of the top three ones, probably not the WBA just yet, but something above what he has. I'd recommend you put him in a title match that you know he'd win. While you're doing that, try to keep trying to push Shawn for another type of title. Then, at some point, after Christian wins his second, yet more important, title, have him and Shawn go up against each other."

"What do ya mean go up against each other?" Dom asked in an amazed, shocked manner. "Ya mean in the ring?"

"Does Fred Flintstone go 'Yabba-dabba-do'?" Curly shrugged.

"Are ya tellin' me that ya want me ta work towards getting Christian another title and then, after he wins said title, ta put him in a match against Shawn?"

Curly nodded with a smile. "Why, yes, that's exactly what I'm saying."

Christian, meanwhile, had his attention shift back to the two men by the window by this point. He was wondering why Curly brought this up but decided to let Dom do the talking for the two of them before he intervened.

"Why would I do a screwball thing like that?" Dom inquisitively asked, genuinely interested in what Curly would say.

At this, Curly's eyes got wider. "Think about it. You have two of your better fighters, if not your two best, both undefeated and both polar opposites of each other; both in a sense best friends, both brothers, and both with a title. The real main difference in them is that people don't want to put their fighters in the ring with Shawn; whereas that's not the case with Christian."

"What would the point be?" Dom pressed. His voice and mannerisms suggested he was confused now and honestly didn't know what Curly was even suggesting.

"Have it be for fun," Curly told him.

By now, Christian felt he was beginning to understand where this was going as his wheels began turning; whereas Dom still looked confused.

"Exhibition," he said. "I think Curly's proposing this to be some sort of an exhibition match between us."

Hearing this, Curly's eyes lit up as he smiled. "Precisely!" was all he said while looking at Dom.

"Not to repeat myself, but why would I do some hair brained idea like that?" Dom asked while being more confused and agitated than before.

"Good publicity. Publicize it as something like, the Light Heavyweight North American Champion against the reigning WBO and IBF cruiserweight champion," Curly said while using his hands to

225

form a make believe marquee sign in the air. "Have it go the distance; preferably end in a draw. I know this guy who writes for the Tribune. I may be able to persuade him to write a glowing review of each on their performances. I might ask him to focus more on Shawn who went the distance with his heavier counterpart with the better quality gold. That could be what you guys need to have enough attention drawn to him to garner some type of title shot. If not, the publicity alone would be worth it."

"That *is* a possibility," Dom commented before going silent again to think about it. After a few moments to himself, he turned to Christian. "Hey, kid, what do ya thing 'bout this?"

"Fine with me." He shrugged. "But I'd like Shawn to hear this first before we make any final decisions, though."

"Oh, no, no, no. We'd never do a thing like this without talking to him first," Curly assured him with. "If it materialized into anything, would you have any problems with it?"

At this, Christian got up before walking over to look out the window by Curly and Dom. He sighed briefly when he saw young Nick Greenwood having a hard time at his shadow boxing before pursing his lips with a groan.

"The only problem I have with this," he said, "is that I don't want Shawn going ape shit or ballistic on me like he so frequently does to his opponents. Other than that, it might actually be fun. Moreover, it looks like I forgot to show Nick something. If neither of you mind, I'd like to go do that now." When neither Dom nor Curly objected to that, Christian went to the office door. "Hey, Curly, will you tell your lady friend hello for me?"

"Only if you tell the same to yours for me," Curly replied with a finger point to him.

"Hey, Dom. If you don't mind," Christian said before leaving the office. "I'll come by later on when it isn't as busy to do some office work."

"Yeah, kid, that's fine. Whatever ya want," the old man told him as his student turned to leave. "Oh, kid. It might be best if ya don't mention any of this to your brother; at least not until we know exactly what we'll be doin'."

"That's alright with me." Christian shrugged while giving him a thumbs-up before leaving the office to walk over to Nick.

On his way over, and during his time trying to teach Nick the finer art of shadow boxing, Christian got thinking back to the conversation he had with Dom and Curly in the office. The thought of having a match with Shawn, exhibition or not, made him nervous because he didn't quite trust him in the ring. For all he knew, Shawn could do anything to anyone for a win. Christian thought if they all slept on it, the conversation they just had would somehow be gone by morning, though the remark of a possible title shot in the near future he hoped would somehow not be included in that disappearance. Only time would eventually be able to answer any of this.

Chapter 23

"Alright, kid, ya ready?" Dom asked while taping up Christian's up hands.

"I think so but, whether I actually am or not, I'm about to find out."

"That's true. Ya will, won't'cha?" Dom asked with a broad smile. "Be careful of this guy out there. He was WBC heavyweight champ a few years back. Got sick with somethin' and took a few months, maybe a year, off. When he came back, he dropped weight. He's been tryin' to put on what he lost, but although he's lost enough weight to drop in class, he hasn't lost much punchin' power."

"The guy's a chump," Shawn remarked from the corner he was hiding in while concealed behind a Superman comic.

"Ya think they all are," Dom shot back with a glare.

"Well, ain't they?"

Just then, Curly walked into the dressing room "Good news, guys. My friend Dave is here and I just got done talking to him."

"Who?"

"You know, Dave Mercer? That sport columnist I told you I knew from the Tribune?" he replied. "He said that if Chris does well enough, he'll try to write a really good review about him."

"You came in here ta tell us that?" Dom scowled.

"I thought you'd have wanted to know he was willing to help you; especially with the fight you guys have planned," Curly asked in his defense.

"What fight?" Shawn quickly asked while looking at them from around his comic.

"C'mon and get outta here, will ya Curly?" Dom asked with obvious irritation. "Can't you see we're busy here?"

"What fight?!" Shawn repeated slightly louder than before.

"Never mind about that, Shawn," Dom told him. "It's just a little side thing I'm workin' on."

There was a knock at the door just then before being opened as a man in a suit looked in at them before saying, "It's time."

"Ok kiddo, this is it," Dom told Christian. "Let's go find out if you're ready."

Nodding, Christian stood up before holding out his hands so Dom could put on, and lace up, his gloves.

"Ya walkin' out with us?" Dom asked Curly.

"No, not tonight. I have a fighter of mine walking around here somewhere that I want to talk with."

"How'd your guy do in his fight?"

"Not as well as I hoped, but he won," Curly told him while looking at the door. "And I do believe this is where I'll part ways. Gentlemen."

When he was done, he shook hands with Dom, gave Christian a mock salute, and nodded to Shawn before leaving.

Within minutes of leaving the locker room, the ring announcer made his way to the middle of the ring.

"Good evening, ladies and gentlemen, and welcome to the main event of the evening," he announced while his voice echoed throughout the arena. "This next bout is for the IBF cruiserweight championship of the world. To my right in the blue corner, weighing in at 189 and a half pounds, wearing blue trunks with white trim, he is the challenger and current WBO cruiserweight champion, Christiiiaaannn Eeeaaatttooonnn!!!"

Christian danced from his corner out about a third the way, raised his arm in acknowledgement of the crowd's cheers, before turning to his corner. Shawn, meanwhile, helped him take his robe off once he got back.

"And his opponent, in the red corner, weighing in at an even 186 pounds, wearing black trunks with gold trim, he is the reigning IBF cruiserweight champion, Douglas 'The Shooting' Ssstttaaarrrrr!!!"

The pop that Star got when his name was called was intense. It was louder and longer than what Christian had ever heard. He himself had gotten some decent pops in the past, but they mainly were after a well-fought fight. Shawn also got really good ones as well, but, again, those were at the end of his fights. However, neither of them was close to what this guy got; at the beginning of the match nonetheless.

Star came out a few feet out of his corner, bounced slightly while shifting his weight from one foot to the other multiple times while staring at Christian. The stare made Christian uncomfortable. The stare was unwavering; eyes unblinking. It lasted only a couple of seconds before Star turned to walk back to his corner.

Just then, a thought occurred to Christian.

"Hey Dom. Why's he nicknamed 'The Shooting'?" he casually asked. "Is it because it goes with his last name?"

Before Dom was able to answer, the ref signaled each fighter to the center of the ring, each with their manager. Once centered in the middle of the ring, the ref explained the rules of the match and what to be expected. The two fighters touched gloves when the ref was done, then went back to their corner.

"When he was a heavyweight," Dom said as Chris turned to face his opponent while getting ready for the bell to signal the start of the fight. "A number of his opponents said he would shoot a straight or jab in so fast that they didn't see it comin'. Some of them who weren't fast enough to block 'em claimed to see stars for a little bit afterwards."

Shawn, meanwhile, let out a little laugh before patting Christian on the back.

"Wha...wha...what?" Chris stuttered. "Are you s-s-serious?"

"Good luck in there, you dickhead." Shawn laughed. "Try not to get your head knocked off."

As soon as Christian heard that, the bell rang out to start round one.

Christian soon found out that what Dom had said about the former heavyweight champ was true. His punches both were fast and hard. On a couple of occasions in that first round he got blinded for a second or two by either a well-placed or badly blocked punch.

He was somewhat irritated by the fact that Dom had waited until the start of the fight to tell him about his opponent's strength, and even more frustrated by the fact that if he hadn't inquired about his nickname, Dom most likely would not have mentioned it.

When the first round was over, Christian went back to his corner happy to be alive. Shawn brought out his stool to sit on as Dom entered to look at him.

"What the hell ya doin' out there?!" Dom yelled.

"O-o-once I f-f-figure th-th-that out, I'll l-l-let you know," Christian stuttered while gasping for breath.

"You did horrible out there!" Dom leaned in to look at his fighter's face before rubbing Vaseline on Chris' cheeks and eyes.

Shawn gave him water while saying, "Hey, bro, I think your face blocked more punches than your arms did."

"Ya need ta start blockin' those punches of his," Dom growled. "You ain't like Shawn! Yer head ain't full of cement and can take any shot possible and still pull a victory outta yer ass. Ya gotta protect that melon of yers! Ya've gotta keep from havin' all its innards scrambled up. Ya hear me?!"

"If I had known the scouting report on this guy more than three seconds before the fight," Christian said with a laugh, "I might be doing a little better."

"That's not completely my fault," Dom told him. "Ya should'a done your own scoutin' report."

"Great!" muttered Christian. "So it's my fault?"

"It's too late now ta be assignin' blame," Dom stated with a scowl. "Ya've always been a fighter that was able ta adapt. Now, get yer ass out there and adapt. Adapt, block, and run. Ya hear me?!"

"Wh-wh-what? You want me to run?"

"Run, dance 'round him, whatever ya have ta do ta keep that melon of yers from gettin' bruised." Dom wrapped his knuckles on Christian's forehead multiple times. "The only thing this guy has on ya is punchin' power; the rest is yers. Use that ta your advantage. Run 'round him and dance to yer heart's content. Throw in jabs. Just tire his ass out. It'll take a few rounds but once ya do, he's yours."

"Yeah, sure Dom," Christian said while standing up.

Shawn put in his mouthpiece before taking away his stool.

"Now, get out there and do what ya came ta get paid for," Dom told him while climbing out of the ring.

Round two continued the onslaught of punishment Christian received from the first. Rounds three and four weren't as bad, but still bad enough. Five was a slow one; each fighter more interested in taking it easy than trying to damage one another. Christian was doing this more to say out of reach of Star's punches than anything else. He thought Star was not as aggressive that round so he could rest up for the next round. Unfortunately, for Chris, he was right on for that point. During round six, the Shooting Star seemed to be throwing whatever he had left in the tank. The round was almost all offense on Doug's part and almost all defenses on the part of Christian. The bell that eventually signaled the end of that round was a welcomed relief Christian badly desired while stumbling back to his corner.

"I don't know what ta say, I really don't." Dom shook his head as Christian pretty much collapsed onto the stool.

"Don't say anythin' then," Shawn told him while removing mouthpiece before giving him water.

"Don't say anythin'?" Dom questioned. "He's gettin' his ass kicked and his head knocked off. He's being beaten to a pulp and ya don't want me ta say anythin'?"

"He's not doing that bad out there, Dom," Shawn told him while sponging off his brother's face.

"His face is beginnin' ta look like roast beef!" Dom commented while working at trying to fix a cut above Christian's swollen right eye.

"I look that bad?" Christian asked while gasping for breath.

"If we had some bread and mayo, we could turn your face into a nice sandwich," Shawn told him.

"C'mon kid, talk ta me," Dom said with concern in his voice. "What's goin' on out there?"

"I've got some good news, I think," Christian told him.

"Yeah, what's that?"

"He's finally starting to get tired."

"And ya ain't? How do ya know that?"

"His punches don't hurt that much."

"Maybe your face is just goin' numb. Ever think of that?" Shawn asked with a sarcastic tone.

"Maybe. But he's slowing up a little; breathing heavier."

"Ya'd better hurry up and do somethin' because ya're losing on points," Dom told him while finishing his work on him. "The fight's half over. Not only are ya gettin' yer ass kicked, but ya'll probably loose on points if ya do manage ta make it ta the end. So I hope ya really do know what ya're doin' out there. Hopefully ya still have some reserve in the tank ya can pull from."

"Thanks for the boost of confidence, Dom. Do either of you have any advice?"

"Don't get knocked down," Shawn told him which drew a scowl.

"If ya do get knocked down, the fight'll probably be called," Dom informed him.

"Thanks," Chris said dryly. "Anything else?"

"Just protect that melon of yours," Dom called out when round seven sounded.

Rounds seven and eight were pretty even; and Christian, for the first time during the match, had two back-to-back rounds that he seemed to make any headway. He kept talking to Star when he could, saying anything that came to mind whether it was a joke, comment, or even the local weather predictions. He said them whether they made sense or not. He thought he might be slightly delirious from all the headshots, but since his talking didn't seem not to be working, he kept it up. The eighth round was the first round Christian finally saw any type of swelling or welting on Star's face. This brought a smile to his face.

When he was walking back to his corner at the end of that round, clinging to dear life and thankful to be alive, disappointment soon ran through him when Dom wouldn't let him sit down in between rounds. He wouldn't even let Shawn bring the stool in.

"What's going on, Dom?" he asked while leaning heavily against the padded ring post, exhausted.

"Don't be leanin' against that! C'mon stand up!" Dom firmly told him.

"Wha...what?"

"I said stand up! No slouching!" the grizzled trainer repeated. "And shake yer head back and forth like ya don't like what I'm sayin'. C'mon kid, do what I say!"

Though Christian had no idea what the point of this was, he did what he was told. He stood up to shake his head but propped his arms on the ropes to help alleviate some of his weight.

"Right now, good ole Mr. Star is over in his corner gaspin' for air and wonderin' why, after eight solid rounds of him beatin' the hell outta ya, ya ain't ready to drop yet." Dom smiled. "He's most likely askin' his crew why you're standin'. And ya shakin' your head at me is probably confusin' the hell outta him. Think what types of things are goin' through his mind when he sees this?"

Shawn, meanwhile, worked diligently on Christian, sponging him down, giving him water, and anything he could do to make him more comfortable.

"Alright kid, what's goin' on out there?" Dom asked.

"I see three of him," Christian told him in between gasps of breaths while shaking his head.

"Hit the one in the middle," Shawn said with a shrug while wiping off Christian's face with a towel.

Dom quickly agreed. "Yeah, kid, hit the one in the middle. You're doin' good out there. You're still behind on points but you're catchin' up. A couple more rounds like this and he's yours."

"I don't know if I can go that much more, Dom," Christian said as Dom got out of the ring.

While putting Christian's mouthpiece back in, Shawn tells him, "Hey bro, I've been meaning to ask you somethin'."

"Wha…what?"

"You're favorite constellation. What is it?"

"Uh, I don't know. Maybe Orion. Why?"

"I was wondering if that's what you're seein' right now." Shawn laughed while climbing out of the ring.

"No, not seeing 'im at all."

Shawn smiled. "Be careful, bro, or else the Shooting Star will help you see him this next round."

"C'mon, Shawn! Get serious. This ain't no time ta act like a kid!" Dom chastised him while shooting him a glare.

"Sorry boss; sorry bro. But in all seriousness," Shawn said while looking to Christian while pointing to his brother's boot. "You're left boot's untied."

Believing him, Christian did a half look, half-bending over to examine his boots. While discovering that both boots were securely laced, but before he could situate himself properly, the bell sounded to start the ninth.

The round went much better than what Christian had expected and Doug Star was breathing heavier and his punches a little softer. Doug seemed tired and threw less and his mind seemed to be slowly leaving him, but Christian still felt slightly cautious.

As the round progressed, Christian, for the first time in the fight, felt comfortable to open up to start fighting his type of fight. However, he felt it maybe a little too late for him. He started dancing more, throwing more jabs, and getting hit less.

When he went back to his corner at the end of that round, Dom, again, refused to let him sit. He also was a bit more expressive with his arm movements and acted like he was yelling at him while, in reality, he was telling Christian to shake his head while telling him "No!"

As Christian did what he was told, he looked across the ring to discover that his opponent was watching them, wide eyed, bewildered, and confused. Christian tried not to smile when he told Dom and Shawn this.

"Good. Good!" Dom practically yelled. "We've got him right where we want him. If ya can take care of him this round, take his ass out. Ok?"

"I'll do my best, Dom." Christian started to feel himself finally getting his second wind.

The tenth round was more in favor of Christian than the round before and he was trying to loosen Star up enough for a knockout in the twelfth, the eleventh if he was lucky. At the end of the tenth, he had to laugh out of sure frustration out of Dom's refusal to let him sit down for the third straight time. At that point, Christian made his mind up to go for the victory that next round just so he was able to relax rather than taking the chance of standing in the corner yet again. Just when Dom was in the middle of throwing him orders, the ref came over with an announcement.

"Hey guys," he said while making his approach. "Just to let you know, the fight's over. It's being called…"

"Bein' called?!" exploded Dom before the ref could finish. "On what grounds?!"

"Forfeit."

"Like hell I'm going to quit, especially now!" Christian angrily told the ref.

"Not you, numbskull. Your opponent," the ref told him.

"Who, what?"

"What are ya talkin' 'bout, ref?" Dom asked.

"Your opponent is forfeiting. He refuses to leave his corner," the ref answered while looking to Christian. "It looks like your boy broke his spirits. It's over."

"Why I'll be," was all any of them had to say, which, ironically, was said by Shawn.

The three of them turned to see Doug Star on his stool with his face in his hands while being surrounded by his crew and the ring doctor.

The ring announcer made his way to center stage to caught the microphone on the decent down to make the official call.

"This bout has been called on grounds of a forfeit," he announced in a clear voice as it echoed through the crowd. "The winner, by technical knockout, and new IBF cruiserweight champion of the WWOOORRRRLLLLDDDDD, Christian EEAATTTTOOOONNNN!!"

While still overwhelmed by the decision, Christian raised his arm in victory while Shawn brought the stool in for him to finally collapse on. While in the process of sitting on it, Christian soon found himself being hauled back to his feet as Dom grabbed by the arm.

"What the hell are you doin', kid?!" the little old man demanded.

"Sitting down."

"Not now ya ain't," Dom told him while pulling Christian out onto the ring floor. "Ya're goin' ta go over there and hug that guy, touch gloves with him, or do whatever the hell ya gotta do ta make him feel better. Ya two had one helluva fight and he's gotta feel like a pile of crap with how it ended. So, be a good spirit by waddlin' yer beaten ass over there. He deserves yer respect and we owe him that much."

"Alright, Dom. I just hope I make it that far," he replied while walking over. He soon found it was harder than it seemed. "Shit, my legs feel like Jell-O right now."

Later on in the locker room while Christian's cut above his eye was being stitched up, Shawn had his brother's newly acquired belt around his waist while pretending like he was the newly crowned champion while dancing around with his arms held high. After a few minutes of this, he finally took the belt off to have a closer look at it.

"Man, this is a nice belt; good quality. I can't believe how much better it is than mine," he commented to no one in particular. "Hey, Dom, when did you say I was goin' to get myself one of these again? I forgot."

"I didn't. We didn't discuss it," Dom replied while packing Christian's belongings together. "However, now isn't the time to talk about it."

"What do you mean now isn't the time?!" Shawn asked while turning to face him.

"Just what I told ya. Now isn't the time."

"You holdin' me back is really starting to irritate my chapped ass..." Shawn started before being interrupted by a knock on the door.

"No visitors!" Dom yelled.

To his dismay, the door opened as Curly Kowalski walked in before closing the door being him. He seemed to be in a very good mood as he approached.

Dom continued to grumble while watching the unwanted visitor approach. "I'm glad ya listened ta what I say."

Curly ignored the comment while walking up to Christian to shake his hand.

"Hey there, brother. By the look of your face, I hope this was worth it," he said while bending over to take a better look at it. "How you doing, buddy?"

"Sir," the ring doctor said while giving him an evil eye. "Will you please move out of my light?"

"Oh, sorry," Curly apologized while stepping back a little without taking his eyes off of Chris' face. "How do you feel there, Champ?"

"How do you think he feels?" Shawn interrupted while waving the belt towards them. "He's the new fuckin' IBF champ! What's that tell ya?"

While ignoring his brother, Christian stiffened and groaned in pain from an accidental jab by the doctor before finally responding to Curly's question. "Other than my face being numb, I feel alright."

"Sorry about that, son," apologized the doctor.

"No problem, Doc," Christian assured him. "Hey, Curly, why don't you ask me in the morning if you're still wondering then."

"I think I may just do that," Curly told him. "By the way, my friend Dave and some of his colleagues are outside wanting a word with the new champ here, if that's ok with you."

"Hells yeah he wants to talk with the press!" Shawn stated while frothing at the mouth at the chance of being around the press.

"I don't really care, Curly." Christian sighed. "I kind of want to get going home once the doctor here is done putting my face back together. If they won't take too long, sure, I'll see them."

"What the hell ya mean ya don't care if ya talk with the press?!" Shawn asked while walking over before standing in front of Christian. "Are ya fuckin' crazy?"

"Please, Mr. Calloway," the doctor calmly said while turning to look at Shawn. "I'm almost done with Mr. Eaton here and I'll need as much light as I can until then. Thank-you."

"What are ya, fuckin' blind?" Shawn snapped while glaring at him. "There's plenty of light in here for you to use."

"I think what the good doctor mean is, that the light that's behind you is the one he's been using to stitch me up with," Christian mentioned mildly. "You may be blocking it somewhat from him."

"Why didn't he just say so?" Shawn complained while continuing to glare at the doctor.

235

"Mr. Calloway, I am right here next to you in case you didn't see me," the doctor said neutrally rather than looking at him. He continued to attend to Christian's eye. "You could simple have addressed me personally rather than pretend I wasn't here. Now, if you will, would you take a step or two in any direction of your choosing? Please and thank-you."

Standing there while his anger was beginning to get the best of them, it took Dom to come over for Shawn to move.

"Ok Shawn, that's enough," the fiery trainer told his hotheaded pupil before walking towards the door. "Just get out of his light for a couple more minutes, will ya? It won't hurt you to cooperate every now and then."

"Where you going, Dom?" Christian asked as he watched him walk to the door before opening it.

"Out for a little walk," he told him as the noise from the hall filtered into the room.

"When will you be back?"

"When your friends leave."

"My who?"

"Your friends." Dom smiled while finally walking through the door before flicking his thumb down the corridor. He then turned right and promptly disappeared.

When he was out of sight, about a dozen or so journalist and other news crew personal came from the left of the door and promptly entered. They all seemed to file in around Christian with their pens and pads out, and their microphones and cameras in his face. Everyone seemed to want his attention as flashes started going off which blinded him somewhat.

"Whoa, whoa, whoa guys!" Christian shouted while trying to yell over the noise. "Take a number and have a seat! Please be patient for a few more minutes while the doctor here finishes stitching my face back together. Once he's done, I'll talk with all of you but not until then. Alright?"

The news crew didn't do what they were asked at first until Shawn elbowed his way in between them while forcing them back.

"Maybe you all are deaf," he bluntly told them. "Maybe you guys don't hear all that well. Or maybe, just maybe, you are choosing to ignore his request. In any event, let me repeat what he said. In blunt, laymen's terms, get away from him, chill the hell out, and sit your asses down over there by the benches! He'll be with you as soon as the doctor is done with him. If any of you don't like this small request, then you can all get the hell out!"

Surprisingly, the crowd did what they were told but not before taking a few snapshots of Shawn in the process. After thinking about what he did and a look from Christian, he decided to go over to talk with them. His brother thought he might actually go over to apologize but soon realized that that wasn't the case. When Shawn did go over, he introduced himself as the current North American Light Heavyweight Champion and future world champion. Even though this caused a laugh or two out of awkwardness, it did cause, in hindsight, Shawn to talk and show off more. This, in turn, led to an informal question-and-answer session between him and the reporters before one parted the group to approach Christian. This loner ended up approaching, and talking to, Curly above all people.

"Hello Curly, how's it going?" the stranger asked while extending a hand which Curly immediately took to shake.

"Not too bad, Dave. How 'bout yourself?" Curly replied before turning towards Christian to introduce them. "Christian, I'd like you to meet a friend of mine, Dave Mercer."

"So you're that sports columnist Curly dislikes so much, huh?" Christian asked with a smile while he and Dave shook hands.

The columnist return the smile with a pleasant expression. "The one in the same. Good to meet you finally, Champ. How are you feeling?"

"Chris is doing just fine," he told him with a light frown at being called champ.

"All done," the doctor informed him while straightening up. He proceeded to walk to the sink to remove his gloves and to wash his hands. He came back, took a pad from his bag, and wrote a prescription on it before tearing it off and handing it to Christian. "You probably won't need these, but here's a prescription for some antibiotics for that cut of yours. Better be safe than sorry."

"Thank-you, Doc," Christian told him while shaking his hand. "I really appreciate it."

"No problem. I would have been done sooner if my light didn't keep being blocked," he commented before receiving a glare and the middle finger form Shawn. After they exchanged annoyed looks with each other, the doctor packed his bag. "Congratulations on your victory, son. That was one helluva fight."

"Thanks, Doc. You take it easy," Christian said while watching him excused himself and leave the room. Meanwhile, Christian turned his attention back to Curly and Dave who were waiting patiently for him.

Dave seemed to be a very pleasant sort of guy that gave the impression he could bullshit with the best of them. He stood roughly six feet tall and had an average 190 pound built. He had dark hair, dark eyes, and a dark, well-trimmed goatee. His eyes and smile showed that he had a side to him that was humorous and childlike, but, on the other hand, could make or break you with what he wrote in the papers about you. With this in mind, Christian decided to play their first meeting safe.

For the first few minutes of their conversation, Christian, Dave, and Curly talked about some family affairs they had going on, as well as a few things they each wanted to do in the near future. When they got past all the pleasantries, the conversation seem to shift to more of a professional tone.

"I just wanted to tell you, Champ," Dave said as his eyes twinkled, "that that was one helluva performance that you gave out there. It was just like that Ali-Frasier fight back in the '70s. Yo did know you were the underdog in this bout, right?"

Blinking in confusion when he heard that, Chris was totally taken off guard. "Ah, really? I didn't know that. But, in all honesty, I don't really pay that much attention to the hype of what critics say about my fights."

"Are you aware that you were behind on points when he gave up?" Dave asked, who's question was quickly answered by a shake of the boxer's head, while taking out his pad and pencil. "Yeah, you were catching up to him, though. Even if you two went the distance, it looked like you would have had at best a draw. Do you have any comment for me on that, Champ?"

"Just that I'm surprised he quit," Christian told him honesty while trying to figure out what else to say. "He still had some life left in him. His punches didn't hurt as bad at the end as compared to the beginning. I don't think I would have been able to knock him down at all the remaining couple rounds of the fight, although I was trying to."

"Wow! A modest champ," Mercer complimented while scribbling on his notepad. "Not a trait is very popular these days, especially among champions."

"If you want to speak with a modest champ, go on over there and talk with Shawn Calloway for a few minutes. He'll most likely show you the real meaning of modesty," Chris dryly told him while pointing to his brother who was still entertaining the journalists. The remark drew a laugh from Curly and a confused look from Dave.

"Hey, Chris, why don't you go on over and relieve Shawn from his standup routine?" Curly slyly asked. "They did come to ask a certain champ some questions, though I doubt he wasn't the champ they had in mind."

"I suppose you're right, Curly," the cruiserweight told him while groaning as he stood.

"Hey, let me ask you two one question," Dave said with pencil in hand. "What's this rumor that I've heard about there being some sort of exhibition match between Christian here and Mr. Calloway? Something about you agreeing to fight him to help give his name as a boxer more credibility? Is there any truth in any of this?"

"Do the Yankees wear pinstripes?" Curly quickly asked while exchanging looks with his writer friend.

"Mr. Mercer, I can't confirm or deny anything at this present time about any such rumors that you may, or may not, have heard. And Curly," Christian said while shifting his attention, "didn't you mean to say another one of your favorite saying?"

While looking at him as he tried to figure out what he meant, Curly asked, "Which saying would that be?"

"Didn't you mean to say, 'What's the last two letters of Fresno spell?' And, Mr. Mercer," Christian said while shifting his attention back to the columnist, "to be honest, it's just a rumor.

None of us have actually talked about that. But, once we do, if we ever do, you'll be the first one we talk to."

Christian was saying that mostly to try and change the subject in fear that Shawn might over hear them. He didn't want his brother hearing about this rumored exhibition match of theirs, if they were in reality going to have it, by anyone other than him and Dom.

"That's nice of you, Champ, but you don't need to do that on my account." Dave was obviously complimented by the gesture Christian had just given him.

"Maybe if there was any truth in this rumor of yours. Also, perhaps you may be the journalist that gets more inside information, if that is true, mind you." Christian smiled slightly as the three of them slowly made their way over near Shawn. "Oh, before I forget, I wanted to thank-you for that nice review that you wrote about me from my first fight."

"I wrote one for you?" the reporter asked with a confused look, which signaled that he had forgotten about it.

"Yes, you did."

"I'm sorry, but I honestly don't remember writing that."

"That's ok; I most likely wouldn't have remembered myself. I just wanted to thank-you regardless."

Mercer smiled at that. "In that case, you're most welcome."

"If you excuse me," Christian said while staring to walk towards Shawn. "I'd better get over there to relieve them from my brother's antics."

"That you should," Dave agreed while watching the new IBF champion walk over to Shawn and the reporters.

When Christian was seen by them as being ready to talk to them now, they almost immediately got up and started ignoring Shawn as they focused almost all of their attention on the new champ. Once Shawn got the hint that they no longer wanted anything to do with him, he went to his corner chair to sulk and brook while trying to finish his Superman comic he started before his brother's fight. He grumbled the whole way through.

Chapter 24

Early one morning a few months later, Christian made his way up the stairs to his apartment to see an attractive young woman came out and close the door behind her. Standing on top of the landing, she ran her hands through her bleach blonde hair before soon moving them to adjust her denim miniskirt, one Christian thought wasn't long enough to be considered mini. While reaching into her purse, she pulled out a bottle of perfume to put some on. She stood about 5'7", had a slender build, and could not be more than 110 pounds soaking wet.

Though Christian found her to be physically attractive, he knew she was his type. She looked cheap and easy. He was not sure if it was because of her bleached blond hair with about half an inch of dark roots showing, the heavy use of makeup on her face, or the over use of that cheap, sweet perfume she just layered on. It may have even been the quantity of jewelry she was wearing, an amount that would rival Mr. T; her revealing blouse not leaving any enough to one's imagination. Or it may have been her skirt barely concealing anything should she bend over; the streaks on her legs from her tan-in-a-can; or her difficulty maneuvering in her high heels, both of which were peeling black plastic.

While she started down the stairs, Christian thought he'd better help her rather than see her fall from stumbling. She finally was able to manage the stairs after three or four attempts before noticing him for first time. He was prepared at that point to just say hello while walking past, but instead slowed when her unfocusing eyes focused upon him.

"Hey there, handsome," she greeted with words that slightly slurred together. Her cheap perfume slightly masked the smell of cheap booze and cigarettes. "Don't I know you from somewhere?"

"I'm sorry, ma'am, but I don't think so."

"You sure?" she pressed while trying to place her hand on his chest to rub but not before putting it on his shoulder to steady herself. "I'm almost positive we've had some fun together."

"Oh, I believe I would have remembered if we'd ever met." Christian smiled while casually taking her hand off of him.

"Well, if you have a few minutes now, how would you like to have some fun? Don't worry; I'll make it worth your while," she said while showing off her body before being caught by Christian so she wouldn't fall.

While trying to stabilize her, he tells her, "I'm flattered by the offer, ma'am, but I'm really quite busy this morning."

"If not now, I'm free later on, handsome," she said with a not very subtle smile and wink. "Why don't we meet up later on for a little rendezvous to work up a little sweat? What do ya think 'bout that?"

"Well, even though that's very tempting, really, it is," Christian stated as politely as possible while trying not to cringe from her smell. "However, I don't think my girlfriend wouldn't like that very much."

"She doesn't have to find out. I won't tell," she purred while looking as coy as possible.

"I don't know," he said a bit more firm. "Like I said before, I'm awfully busy today. Why don't I help you down the stairs before I get going?"

"That's real nice of you, a real gentleman," she stated with a slight airiness. "I can manage myself. If you change your mind about that rendezvous, don't hesitate to look me up."

Taking a step or two further up the stairs, Christian turned to watch her go as she turned her back to him. "Yes ma'am. I'll let you know."

"Ma'am. I like that," she told him. "You're the only guy to ever call me that. If you knew me, you wouldn't be calling me that."

"Just trying to be polite," he explained.

Christian stood where he was to watch her stumble her way down the rest of the stairs and walk out the door below. Shaking his head while letting out a long, slow whistle, he turned to finally enter his apartment.

Moments later, the smells in the apartment, he noticed, were no better than that of the young lady he'd just met. The pungent smells were strong and lingering while giving the impression of a party shared by two the night before. The apartment was a complete mess and needed to be cleaned as Christian attempted to clear a path through the room's debris on his way to his room. The noise he was making must have woken Shawn because he soon heard movement coming from his bedroom.

"Hey, baby-girl, did you come back for a reply of last night?" Shawn asked before appearing in the hall while wearing nothing but a pair of boxer briefs.

"No, I'm afraid not, honey," Christian replied.

"Oh. It's you," Shawn flatly said while walking over to stand in Christian's bedroom door.

"If you're talking about baby-girl, I passed her on the way up," Christian stated before looking at Shawn. "That wasn't Candy, was it?"

"Nah, someone else. What are you doin' here so early?"

While nodding to the two boxes he was pulling out of his closet. "Just came to get the last of my things."

"I thought you were all moved out last week?"

"Yeah, me too," he said while putting them on his bed. "But there were these last few things that I forgot to grab. I had some time now so I thought I'd come and get them."

"Where's your place again?"

"A few miles from Mom's and Dad's place; more out in the country though."

241

"Is she movin' in with you?"

"Who, baby-girl?" Christian asked in shocked confusion.

"Not her, damn it!" Shawn irritable stated. "You know damn well who I'm talkin' 'bout."

"If you mean Miho, we haven't discussed it."

Shawn scoffed. "I can't believe you'd want her there over me."

"Like I said before, she and I haven't discussed her moving in with me. Besides, I did ask if you wanted a room there. You turned me down." Christian looked over to him. "Quite rudely if I remember."

"What the hell you talkin' 'bout, bro? You never asked me."

"Yes, I did."

"When?"

While rubbing his forehead to think for an answer, Christian soon said, "Thursday of last week. Though you may have been a little drunk or hung-over when I did; but I did ask."

"That describes most of last week for me."

Christian smiled. "Actually that narrows down most weeks for you, doesn't it?"

"Oh, shut the hell up before I knock your ass out!"

"You outta come by one evening. Stay for dinner and a movie or something," Christian offered while sorting through his boxes.

"Sounds like a plan, man."

"So, how was your night last night?" Christian slyly asked with a grin.

"Better than yours." Shawn shrugged with a rude, cocky tone. "Couldn't you tell by what you saw leavin'?"

"Hmmm." Christian tried to think of what to say. "How much did last night cost, if you don't mind me asking?"

"What makes you think I paid for that? You think I, Shawn Calloway, actually has to pay for a woman to spend the night with me?"

"You tell me," Christian responded with another smile. "Anyway, it was just a feeling I had, that's all."

"A feeling, huh?" Shawn asked while seeing his brother shrug before rubbing his face. "Oh, hey, I saw you on TV again last night."

"I wasn't on TV last night. I was out bowling with Larry and his team."

"That's not what I meant, you ass! It was one of your fuckin' commercials."

"Which one was it for?"

"I don't know. I was a little busy plowing the sidewalk," Shawn said with a cocky swagger before doing some hip thrusts towards Christian. "It was one of those sneaker commercials you did."

"Oh, that one." Christian laughed. "I'm a little embarrassed by that one."

"Well, you should be; it was fuckin' stupid," Shawn told him while looking around his brother's now empty bedroom. "How many different endorsements do you have now?"

"Five now, I think," he replied. When he was done with his belongs, Christian put the tops back onto his boxes, stacked them one top of the other, picked them up, and walked into the living room with Shawn following him. He put the boxes by the door before going into the kitchen for a drink. To his distaste, there was about two cases worth of empty beer bottles scattered throughout, a number of which he had to kick aside so he wouldn't step on any. When he had his fill of water, he walked back to the apartment's door to grab his boxes.

"I don't believe you got a place of your own, dude," Shawn told him while putting on a shirt and pair of shorts.

"Why's that?"

"It's not right, that's why," his brother complained. "I always thought I'd be the one to get a spot first, not you."

"You did."

"What're ya talkin' 'bout, your moron? You're the one who bought the house!"

"But you were the one who got a spot of your own first," Christian reminded him while opening the door before walking out. "I moved in with you, if you don't remember. In order for me to have done that, you would have had a spot of your own first."

"That's not what I meant, you dickhead!" Shawn followed him down the stairs. "What I meant was I thought I'd be the one movin' outta this shit hone first, not you!"

"Why haven't you yet?"

"I don't have the money."

"If you weren't spending it all on beer, pool, or women, you might have had a nice little spot of your own by now," Christian said with a wide grin. He then walked out onto the sidewalk with Shawn close behind.

243

"If I had the endorsements like you, I would'a moved out a long time ago," retorted Shawn defensively while approaching a Dodge pickup, one which Christian put his boxes in the bed of. "When the hell did you get this?"

"Last week."

"What was wrong with your car?"

"Nothing."

"Why'd you get this then?"

"I don't know." Christian shrugged. "I guess I wanted a change."

"You still have your car?"

"No. I gave it to Miho."

"You gave it to her?" Shawn asked in a shocked tone while his eyes got big. "Why didn't you ask me if I wanted it?"

"Because you've said on numerous occasions you didn't like it. Something to the effect that 'there was no power to it, and that only an old fart would be seen drivin' it'," Chris replied while trying to do his best impersonation of his brother.

"That's true, but I still would'a taken it," Shawn admitted while still being insulted he wasn't asked. "It's better than the car I have now."

"But you don't have a car."

"My point exactly!" Shawn nodded while spreading his arms out. "Besides, does she even know how to drive?"

"What kind of asinine question is that? Of course she does!"

"It's a legit question," Shawn said in his defense. "I wasn't sure if they were allowed to drive where she comes from."

"It's like it is here, Shawn. Most adults in Japan know how to drive." Christian was a little baffled by Shawn's statements but not completely surprised.

"Even the women?"

"I'm not really sure where you've been getting your information on world events, but, yes Shawn, even the women over there drive." Christian pursed his lips while slightly shaking his head.

"Dude, that reminds me. What do you see in her anyway?" Shawn suddenly asking in a serious tone.

Confused, Christian asked, "What do you mean?"

"What I mean is why her? What do you see in her? What's wrong with someone who's white *and* American?"

"Well, for starters, I like and trust her," replied Christian. At that moment, he found himself getting a little irritated by his brother's questions. "Secondly, I enjoy being around her and I like talking with her."

"Whatever, dude," Shawn said abruptly while turning to go back inside. "I'm goin' back to bed "

"Hey," Christian called out while climbing into his truck. Shawn stopped at the door to turn and look at him. "Will you be at the gym later?"

Shrugging, Shawn opened the door and walked inside to leave Christian outside to interpret that any way he want to.

Later that week when Christian and Shawn were at the gym training, Dom came out of his office.

"Hey, kid," he said while approaching Christian. "Go get your bonehead brother and the two of ya meet me in my office." He turned and walked away before Christian could reply.

After finishing up his set on the weight machine he was using, he found Shawn working a speed bag like there was no tomorrow.

"Hey, Shawn," Christian said while walking up to him. "Dom wants to see us in his office about something."

Shawn sped up on his punches. "What the hell is it this time?"

Shrugging, Christian answered, "I don't know but he seems to want us in there pronto."

While finishing his set with a power punch, Shawn picked up a towel to wipe the sweat from his face and neck.

"Alright, brother. Let's go," he said while he and Christian walked to Dom's office.

While entering, they found Dom sitting behind his desk while talking to someone on the phone. He waved them in while motioning them to close the door behind them. They did what they were told before sitting in the chairs in front of his desk and made themselves comfortable. By the sounds of the phone conversation, Dom was trying to set a fight up for a couple of his fighters in the upcoming weeks. When he did get done, Dom slammed the phone down in conjunction with a heavy sigh.

"Goddamn promoters!" he growled. "All they are is a bunch of money hungry, greedy bastards. No good bunch of filthy yaks. Don't let me catch either of ya considerin' becomin' one, if ya know what's good for ya!"

245

"Is this why you interrupted out workout; to tell us not to become promoters?" Shawn asked while being a little agitated thinking this could actually be the reason.

"No, it isn't the reason. If ya stay quiet long enough I'll tell ya why." Dom got up ta start pacing the room. "I just wanted ta tell ya two kids that I scheduled a fight for ya two in a couple weeks. I want the both of ya two ta be on the top of your game."

"Better be a title fight," mumbled Shawn.

"No, it ain't a title fight. It's an exhibition match."

"Wait. What? An exhibition match?" Shawn confusingly asked. "You scheduled me in a lousy exhibition match?"

"Actually, I scheduled the both of ya in one, as a matter of fact." Dom said while smiling and nodding as he and Christian exchanged looks with each other.

"Against who?" Shawn asked with a hint of agitation.

"Me," Christian told him while drawing a look from him.

"Oh, fuck off!" Shawn said while he looked dumbly at him.

"I think we'll be facing each other in this exhibition match," Christian told him with a slight laugh while rubbing his forehead with his fingers.

While focusing his attention to the man behind the desk, Shawn asks, "Dom, seriously, did you really schedule us in some sort of bullshit exhibition match or are you just messin' with us? And, who are we really gonna be facin'?"

"To answer your questions, yes and each other," Dom told him before sitting back down behind his desk.

Hearing that, Shawn looked back and forth between Dom and Christian. He soon eventually looked only at Christian while realizing this was no joke.

"Did you know about this?" he asked his brother. "Tell me you didn't know about this, bro."

"It was suggested before I won my last title," Christian slowly admitted while looking at the floor. "Since it was mentioned only in passing, I didn't think much about it."

"But you knew about it!" Shawn harshly accused. "You knew 'bout this and you didn't tell me about it?"

"Don't get upset with your brother, Shawn," Dom injected while coming to Christian's defense.

"Don't get upset? Why wouldn't I be upset?!"

"Like your brother said, he heard 'bout it only in passin'," retorted Dom. "There's no need to tell ya somethin' that at the time didn't mean a damn thing."

"It didn't mean anythin' then but it does now? What the hell?"? Shawn questioned. "What gives, Dom? It makes no sense!"

"Shawn, why don't you try to let Dom explain it for us," Christian said while looking to his brother. The look was returned with angry eyes. "I know as much about this as you do. If we let him talk, we'll both find out relatively quickly."

"Don't tell me what to do, you asshole! Old man, you'd better start makin' some sense," Shawn stated impatiently. "You've got five seconds or I'm outta here!"

"With a little persistence from your brother and Curly, I've been trying to get a title shot for ya, but nobody wanted to take the chance on embarrassing their fighter by putting them in the ring with ya," Dom said while leaning back and trying to relax. "One guy agreed, however how reluctantly, with one condition."

"Great!" Shawn rolled his eyes. "What guy and what's the condition?"

"You'd be going up against Jack Stratus if everythin' turns out ok and the cond…"

"Stratus?" Shawn asked with shock in his wide eyes. "Isn't he the WBO champ?"

"Yeah. So?"

"So? So?!" Shawn practically screamed back at Dom which drew confused, quizzical looks from both his trainer and brother. "Christian here holds that same title if you didn't know. The lesser of his belts need I remind you. Don't you see a problem with that?"

Both Dom and Christian each sat there looking blankly at Shawn before admitting that neither saw a problem.

"But why the WBO belt? That's practically the least important world title out there," Shawn told them. "Why not something better?"

"There weren't any others," Dom informed him. "He's the only one willin' ta let ya challenge. The guy who was goin' ta challenge Strauss backed out at the last minute for medical reasons. There seems ta be somethin' in ya that they liked, but I had ta put ya in some type of match ta show 'em ya can do more than steamroll over yer opponents."

"But why can't I challenge for something better? We all know I'm better than Christian. No offense, bro," Shawn quickly said while looking at him. "Why the WBO?"

"You ain't listening, kid! It's either this or nothin' at all!" Dom yelled with a growl. "If ya have a problem with it, let us know so we can do somethin' about it."

"The problem I have is with the belt," Shawn said as he took a deep breath while trying to calm himself down. "I want a better belt!"

"We all want better belts but none are bein' offered I tell ya!" Dom firmly shouted while slamming his fist onto his desk. "This could help lead ta other opportunities if ya weren't being so goddamned stubborn. Ya have ta get past whatever problem ya have with yer brother here and focus on what's bein' offered ta ya. If ya feel like he has had a better career in his short span as compared ta ya, ya have ta let that go. Ya have ta let go of whatever jealousy or resentment ya have against the opportunities he's gotten instead of ya. Those feelings of yers are blindin' ya ta what's really important!"

"And what's really important?" Shawn asked in a harsh, condescending tone.

"Shawn, I have a question," Christian softly said. "Do you really want a world title shot or not?"

Looking at him for a moment in shocked silence, Shawn soon snapped back at him. "What kind of dumbass question is that, huh? I haven't been carryin' on all this time 'bout a title if I didn't really want it! How could you, above anyone, ask me that?"

"Good." Christian smiled with a nod. "Now that we got that out of the way, we can focus on the issue at hand. Dom, would you mind if I say a few things?"

"Go ahead, kid," Dom told him with a wave of the hand.

"Alright, Shawn. Let's see if this makes any sense." Christian cleared his throat while looking up at the ceiling to word what he had on his mind. "A couple of weeks before I won the IBF title, you and Dom had that argument about you getting another title shot. Do you remember that?"

"How could I forget?" Shawn scoffed.

"Anyway, Curly came in shortly after you left and got talking with both Dom and me about any option he thought we could try to help get you another title," Christian explained. "Curly mentioned that I get another title, one that was better than the WBO belt I had at that time. Once I did that, if I could, and if you didn't have another belt to your liking by then, then you and I would have a match against each other, this so-called exhibition match. He also mentioned that our fight goes the distance, a draw if possible. He thought it be best if we both put in a well put performance, but not totally kill each other. He'd than have his friend, Dave Mercer, write up a good review for me, and a better one for you. The thought was for you to go up against me, a dual champion in a heavier class, and to actually go the distance with me. It couldn't help but give you a better, more credible name. On top of that, a well-known sports columnist had agreed to write a really good review on your performance should we go the distance. At the very least, think of the great publicity you'd get.

"So, Dom's been trying to use this match to your advantage and actually is able to give you a world title opportunity like you've been wanting," continued Christian. "Yeah, I'll still have another title of my own higher than the one you'd be challenging for, but so what? Dom and I are both willing to do this in order to give you a damn title shot. Though it may not be as prestigious as what you'd want, it's still in the top four. You can either graciously take this opportunity with a smile and "thank-you", or you can pass it up and wait quietly until another world title shot comes knocking on your door. I know you don't give a crap what I think or say, and I know you didn't ask me my thoughts on this, but I would highly suggest you do it but, whatever you do, don't be pissing and moaning about getting another shot, let alone demand one, if you don't accept this. Dom and I are getting extremely sick and tired of hearing you complain over and over about this and, as a result, we're both willing to do something to shut you up and give you what you want, which is another damn title opportunity.

"To put it mildly, are you willing to put aside whatever jealousy, resentment, anger, or anything else you have against me and the opportunities I've been given? Are you willing to accept what Dom's offering you to go for the WBO Light Heavyweight Championship? That's the question we're asking."

When Christian was done with his fairly lengthy speech, he and Dom sat quietly while waiting for Shawn to give them his answer. Christian, feeling both relieved and surprised at what he had said, sat patiently with his hands folded while looking down at the floor. Dom, on the other hand, had gotten up to go fix himself some coffee before going to look out into the gym.

Shawn, however, was sitting slightly slouched with his left hand on the left side of his face. His right hand, meanwhile, was bouncing rhythmically with his right knee while he steamed over what he had just heard. He was infuriated that they both insinuated that he was jealous of Christian; he couldn't believe they would any something like that to him. But, in hindsight, if this was his only chance to get his shot, he decided it would be best for him to accept their offer that was presented before him.

It was foreign to Shawn that a fight would be considered a good quality if it lasted more than four rounds and didn't end via knockout. He couldn't possibly fathom that after a set number of rounds, that one of the two would get their fight awarded to him because they happened to receive more points than the other. He began questioning whether or not he could actually follow through with what they offered. He was also bewildered that for once in his career, actually was considering putting his career into someone else's hands for him to get what he wanted. He didn't want to ask, let along get, help from anyone, especially help from either Christian or Dominic. He looked at one as his best friend, a brother; while the other, a mentor and father figure. Shawn also felt like he was selling out by going against what he truly believed in as a fighter in order to get what he wanted. He didn't compromise. Never. And how he hated going against what he believed in as both a person and a fighter. He never had never trusted anyone in his entire life, especially himself, and he surely wasn't about to start then.

Chapter 25

"Where the hell is he?!" Dom grumbled while pacing the locker room. He soon went out into the hall to look around in both directions. When he didn't see anything that satisfied him, he came back in to continue pacing. "Don't he realize Shawn can't do this without him in his corner?"

"Don't worry, Dom. He'll be here," Christian patiently said while he and Shawn warmed up in opposing corners. "He wouldn't jeopardize Shawn losing a match on account of him. He'll be here."

"Who the hell says I need his damn Polack ass in my corner anyway?" Shawn asked in between punches he was throwing to his shadow. "I can do this without him."

"The boxing commission says so, that's who," Dom shot over his shoulder while looking out into the hallway again. "Every fighter needs to have someone in their corner with them."

"Remember that one fight I had awhile back where you went back to prep ole Bozo here? It was one of his first fights and you left me hangin'?" Shawn pointed to Christian. "I didn't need a manager then but I do now? What's the deal, yo?"

"I'm surprised they didn't call that one," Dom admitted while coming back into the locker room to continue his pacing. "But since I knew most of the officials, I was taking the chance they wouldn't. Or at the very least I was hoping they'd at least wait until the first round was over before they did anything." He then walked back to the hall to look both ways before looking down at his watch. "Five minutes until fight time. Where the hell is he?!"

"I hope he's at some tanning salon," commented Shawn. "I don't wanna be blinded by the lights reflecting off that damn bald, white head of his."

"Here he is!" Dom announced while glaring down the hall. "Jesus Christ! Where the hell've ya been?!"

"Sorry, Dom," Curly's voice was heard as his footsteps were heard approaching. He was then seen following Dom into the locker room. "I got talking to some people I knew."

"Couldn't ya have done that later?" Dom asked sourly while squinting up at him before hobbling over to Christian.

"I always like making the rounds before the fight," Curly explained while approaching Shawn. "How you doing, Champ?"

"I'll be better once I knock this chump on his fat ass," Shawn replied while winking to Christian before focusing on what exactly Curly was wearing.

The balding manager was dressed in black dress shoes with tassels, nice black dress pants, a black leather belt with a silver buckle, and a gaudy, long-sleeved, black, button-up, silk shirt that had silver and white splotches over it as if he'd been painting. The top three buttons were unbuttoned to reveal a hairy, pale chest with two gold chains.

"Do you really expect me to go out there and have you in my corner while you're wearing a shirt like that?" Shawn rudely asked while pointing to Curly's attire.

"What's wrong with it?" he asked while pulling on his shirt a little to examine it. "Is it dirty?"

"Dirty? Dude, it's ugly as hell! That's what's wrong with it!"

"I wouldn't say that," Curly said in a hurt tone. "I know I've had my luck with the ladies whenever I've worn this."

"Dude, that's enough!" Shawn protested while raising his hands to his ears. "I don't wanna hear 'bout any of your adventures you've had with the woman folk. Thank-you very much!"

Curly smirked. "Hey, I was just getting to the good part."

"I don't care! I got the picture. Alright?!"

Just then, a well-dressed man came in to tell them that it was time for the fight. Dom and Curly took one last look over their respected boxers.

"Remember ya two, it's gotta go the distance," Dom reminded them once they got out into the hall. "In case if ya forgot, it's only a six rounder. It's alright ta hit each other just so long as ya don't kill each other. It's just an exhibition. Ya got that, Shawn?"

"Yeah, yeah, yeah. You sound like a broken record," Shawn mumbled while getting into a little jogging rhythm.

"Just makin' sure."

"While we're all here, I wanted to tell you who's here," Curly announced. "My friend Dave Mercer is. You two were one of the fights he was here to do a review on. Through him, I found out that Jack Stratus is also here with both is manager and trainer."

"That's good to know," Christian said while nailing Shawn in th arm with a jab. "You hear that? You're competition is here to check you out. Maybe I don't need to remind you that if they don't like what they see, they may not offer you your beloved title shot to ya."

"Keep it up, Cheesedick," retorted Shawn while still doing his half jogging, half trotting movement. "I wouldn't wanna have to lose control of a few of my punches out there an pummel your nerdy ass into the ground."

"Typical response from a guy who can't take a joke." Christian chuckled. "Go ahead if you want to, but that would almost guarantee you not getting your shot with Stratus."

"Hey, listen here, dickwad. I can take anything you throw my way!"

"I'm sure you can."

"Anytime, bookworm," Shawn said before looking over to Christian. "But what better way to show me what you got than in a boxing match, huh?"

251

"C'mon, Shawn, save your energy for the ring," Dom chastised.

"Oh, believe you me, I plan to." With that, Shawn smiled.

"Don't even think 'bout it," Dom growled. "Remember, he's not here t get in a pissin' contest with ya. If ya'd rather have that then his help fer that title shot against Stratus, ya'd better let him know now. If not, just cool yer engines and remember why we're here."

"Fine, have it your way. But keep in mind that the next fight's mine."

"Next fight? W-w-what do you mean by 'next fight'?" Christian asked while stuttering his words.

"Sounds like you're scared of me," taunted Shawn.

Rolling his eyes, Christian focused on the door that was roughly a dozen feet ahead of them. "Good luck out there, Shawn," he said with a smile before putting his gloved hand on Shawn's shoulder.

"Get your hand off of me, you faggot! Am I fightin' the IBF cruiserweight champion or a fuckin' chick?" he sarcastically taunted Christian with a smile.

"Now that would be embarrassing, wouldn't it?" Christian asked while they opened the doors that led to the arena.

"What's that?"

"That is fag is going to knock that scrawny ass of your out!" Christian smiled while leaping into the crowded arena.

All Shawn could do was tilt his head back slightly with a crooked smile upon it while following his brother to the ring.

The exhibition match they had agreed to do went on to be more of Christian's fight rather than Shawn's. It went that way mainly because Shawn had to reign himself in and resist the temptation of fighting the way he so desperately wanted to. In the fourth, Shawn finally got frustrated from not only holding back, but also from being constantly peppered by Christian's jabs and straights. Most time's when Shawn went in to give him a power punch or some combo to slow him down, Christian would see it coming and easily block or dodge it before countering with a combo of his own. In that round, he nailed Christian hard with a combo consisting of a body shot, hook, and an uppercut which sent his brother back against the ropes. When Shawn went in to give him another shot to the betty, Christian immediately tied him up.

"What the hell you doing?" Christian whispered in Shawn's ear.

"Sorry, bro, but I had to burn off some extra energy," his brother whispered back. "This pussy-footing around is irritating the holy fuck outta me!"

"I feel the same. Dom's telling me not to dance around as much. I don't mind if you do that just as long as you let me know ahead of time, alright? And don't worry, bub. Just two more rounds. Think you can make it?"

Before Shawn had a chance to respond, the ref came over to break them up.

"Alright guys, break it up," the ref said while pulling them apart. "People came to see a fight, not two guys hugging each other."

"Well, talk to you later," Christian said while braking the hold.

"Yup," was all Shawn said.

At the end of the sixth, each fighter stood in their respected corner with their managers next to them looking across the ring to each other. Christian was in high spirits because he had just fought a pretty decent match with his brother. Shawn, on the other hand, appeared nervous and anxious.

The ring announcer soon came center ring to announce the results. While grabbing the mic as is was lowered from the raptors, he cleared his throat before speaking into it.

"Ladies and gentlemen," he said while looking at the card he was handed moments earlier from the judges. His voice echoed throughout the building. "The winner, by unanimous decision, Chrriiissstttiiiaaannn Eeetttooonnnn!!!"

Christian came out of his corner to receive a warm applause from the crowd. Shawn, meanwhile, upon hearing the news of his loss, gritted his teeth and swore briefly while pounding his gloved fists together before seeing his brother coming over to him. They touched gloves as a hard, irritated look came into Shawn's eyes.

When Shawn and Curly finally made it to the locker room a few minutes later, Christian was already there getting his gloves and tape removed by Dom.

"Hey," Christian said when they walked in. "Good match."

"Yeah, for you."

"No, for the both of us. You'll be getting that title shot now."

"Weren't you supposed to let me win?" Shawn asked sorely while approaching.

"Not that I was aware of."

"You weren't?"

"If I was, no one told me," Christian told him. "What I thought I agreed to was to try to have a good match with you and to try to help you look good, regardless of who won."

"First of all, you don't need to make me look good. And, secondly, how was your winning on points supposed to help make me look good?" Shawn asked without getting an answer. "Fuck that! At least I'm still undefeated."

Christian laughed at that. "No you're not. I just beat you."

"Yeah, by decision in an exhibition match," Shawn reminded him. "A match that doesn't mean shit!"

"Maybe so, but I still beat you," he said with a smile.

"The next matchup will be mine. Mark my words, little man," Shawn stated as his temperature rose from his brother laughing at him.

While rolling his eyes, Christian shrugged. "Whatever you say, Shawn. Just don't beat the champ too badly."

By this point, Dom was already working on removing Shawn's gloves and tape. Christian got up, grabbed a towel and hygiene kit, and walked to the shower. Shawn, meanwhile, followed suit once he was all set. After they each went to the shower, Curly pulled Dom aside to ask a quick question.

"Hey, Dom, I've got a question for you. How are you able to manage Shawn out there?"

"What do ya mean?"

"What I mean is how do you get him to do what you want out there?" Curly asked. He adjusted his glasses before running his hand over his balding head as Dom looked up at him sternly. "During the fight, I was trying to tell him what he should do or coax him into something, but he just didn't seem to listen. I was just wondering what you do different."

"Well, I look at him like I would'a dog," Dom replied while shaking a small, wrinkled finger in the air. "A dog will walk all over ya, not respect ya, and ignore what ya say unless ya grab 'em by the ears, rough 'em up a little, and show 'em who's boss. If ya're firm and seem ta mean what'cha say, that dog'll listen and obey. That's how I look at Shawn. He's a lot of potential and raw talent, but he needs ta be corralled like a wild bronco. And like a wild bronco, he needs ta be broke and retrained to meet his fullness."

"How would I be able to do that? Make him listen to me, that is."

"I don't think ya'd be able ta," Dom told him honestly as Curly blinked a few times at him. "No offense, Curly, but that's not ya; ya're style I mean. Just like the way ya manage isn't my style. Yer style is more 'bout bein' equals with yer fighter. With Shawn's personality, I think ya'll be able ta, but I've been wrong before. Why do ya wanna know?"

"Oh, you know. Just wondering in case I manage him again, I just wanted to be prepared," Curly answered honestly with a shrug. "Besides, I was just curious how you were able to control him, is all."

"Who says I have any kind of control over him?" Dom asked with a wink. "Who says he's not doin' this to pacify me until he finds another crew more to his likin'?"

A moment or so later, Dave Mercer entered the locker room.

"Hi Curly, Dom," he said while approaching and shaking hands with them.

"Dave, what are you doing here, brother?" Curly asked him.

"Just wanted to tell you guys that I really enjoyed their match and you don't need to worry about that review of mine."

"Why don't you tell them that yourself?" Dom asked him in a tone that wasn't a question as it was a statement. "They're in the shower right now."

"I can't right now; I'm running late as it is," Dave informed him. "I've got to go meet up with some colleagues of mine. A couple of them were impressed as well and could probably be talked into giving both of your boys good reviews; The Times and Post to name a couple."

"I really appreciate ya doin' this for them and for me as well," Dom thanked him before reaching over to shake his hand again.

"Not a problem." Dave shook the offered hand before extending the same hand to Curly. While turning to leave, he says, "I still owe you a couple of favors, Curly. Take it easy."

"Take it easy, brother." Curly waved goodbye.

Dom nodded while watching Dave disappear around the corner.

To Dave's credit, he gave both Christian and Shawn excellent reviews with much more focus on Shawn. A few of Mercer's colleagues, as well a number of other papers, wrote glowing reviews for the exhibition match. To everyone's delight, Shawn's WBO title shot against reigning champion Jack Stratus was solidified.

Chapter 26

One afternoon a week before Shawn's big showdown with Stratus, he and Christian were out running. The day had been gray and dull. Clouds hung heavily and there was moistness in the air that suggested rain. They had already run eight miles and were on their way to their final two. Though Shawn was slightly damp with sweat, Christian's shirt looked like it had been through the storm that hadn't hit yet.

"Ya know there, Beeker, your shirt should be that wet only after the rains come."

"Yeah, I know." Christian laughed. "I'm sweating like James Brown."

"Livin' in America," Shawn sang while doing a little side two-step while trying to do his best James Brown impersonation. "WOW! Across the nation...!"

"You do realize that he had other songs besides that one, right?"

Shrugging, Shawn says, "Yeah, I know, but that's the only one from any of the *Rocky* movies."

"And do you know there are other movies out there besides Rocky?" Christian smiled at him.

"Yup, I know. There's also the *Rambo* movies, and *Over The Top, Predator, Commando, True Lies,* and..."

"And a whole slew of others out there that aren't the linear, testosterone-filled, macho, male way of thinking," Christian said while looking at his brother in jest. "Movies that actually have a plot, ones that are well-written, with good dialogue, which have various depths of the human emotion, and an overall good story. Ones that you can sit through without bombs going off, people swearing when they don't get their way, or nude scenes. Some of them you might actually like."

"I ain't sittin' through one of your borin' ass, tear jerkin', chick flicks, bro. No amount of money could pay me to do that."

"Those movies I'm talking about aren't chick flicks, man."

"You must be referring to your collection of Disney and Hallmark movies then, right?"

"No, I'm not talking about those, Cheesedick." Christian scoffed before laughing.

"Cheesedick? Who you callin' Cheesedick, Butterfingers?"

"I'm not calling anyone that. I was just quoting one of your one night stands that didn't quite last, um, one night," Christian said as serious as he could before soon letting loose a hearty laugh at his brother's expense.

"Listen, bro. If you're talkin' about that Russian chick, you can go fuck yourself. You hear me?" Shawn shot him a glare. "It was that vodka shit of hers. I'm sure she it was spiked with it something."

"The only thing that was spiked was you, I'm sure. Ha ha."

"Shut up, man! I was drunk then."

"Oh, so you admit your friend was, how do I put this, a little cheesy?" Christian laughed loudly at this. "Good ole Dick wouldn't salute the general?"

"Shut up, you bookworm! I was drunk. At least I can say I can get someone in the sack, unlike you!"

"That's true, but at least I don't need to get the person I'm with drunk for them to find me more attractive. Even a basic conversation, you know, one with words rather than grunts, is sometimes all you need. But, on the other hand, when are you ever sober?"

"Keep it up, limp dick, keep it up. I don't need any advice from a guy who's probably still a virgin, or, at most, has never had more than one woman in his life. If it was a woman."

"Fair enough, I'll give you that. But let me ask you this, if I may? How much do you usually spend for a woman to have sex with you? Or, should I ask, how much do you spend just for them to be around you? Do you actually pay them or do you merely just get them drunk? And what percentage of your lovers go to you willingly as compared to those that are persuaded with money or booze?"

"What in the hell are you talkin' about, bro? Do you even know?"

"Just what I thought." Christian laughed as they ended their run outside of Dom's gym. Heavy raindrops began to fall from the sky as they entered. Almost immediately Christian started humming *Raindrops Keep Falling On My Head*.

"Oh, listen bro, I wanted to tell you somethin'."

"Yeah? What's that?"

"I heard Wesley got released," Shawn told him only to get a confused look while watching his brother stumble at the news

"A-a-are you b-b-being serous?"

"'fraid so, bro." He shrugged. "I heard about it a day or so ago."

"Who t-t-told you that?"

"I have my sources, but it doesn't really matter who told me."

"I thought he got fifteen years. Didn't he?" Christian asked to which Shawn nodded. "But it's only been what, ten years?"

"Eleven, actually."

"Ok? So how'd he get out early?"

"Good behavior? Parole? Who the hell knows, bro. The point is he's out."

"You think he's stopped blaming me for what he did?" Christian asked with a worried expression.

"My same source says he's been askin' 'bout you."

"Great! That's just great!" exclaimed Christian as his anger rose. "Doesn't he realize I literally had nothing to do with him killing that guy?"

"Most likely, yeah."

"Then why's he still looking for me about this? He did his time. He's out. It's over. It's in the past. Why not just move on?"

"'cause he can't. He needs someone to blame," Shawn told him.

"Then blame himself," Christian retorted hotly. "I didn't do it. I had nothing to do with it!"

"I know, brother, I know. Some people just can't take the blame or responsibility," Shawn said. "They always need others to blame even if there aren't any others to blame."

Christian shook his head while he and his brother stopped outside of the door of Dom's gym. "Great. That's just great. Would you do me a favor for now? Would you please not mention this to Dom? I'm hoping this'll just blow over but, if it doesn't, I'd like to be the one to tell him in case if it comes here to the gym."

"My lips are sealed, bro." Shawn smiled while patting him on the shoulder. "You don't have to worry 'bout me."

Returning the smile, he said, "Thanks, Shawn. That means a lot."

Finally, when did they entered the gym, they noticed Dom wandering around giving pointers to a number of boxers. He soon looked up to see them walking over.

"Did ya guys get caught in the rain?" he asked while pointing to Christian's shirt and nodding towards the window.

"He did." Shawn flicked a thumb towards Christian.

Slightly confused, Dom asked, "Weren't ya both outside?"

Shrugging, Shawn confirmed, "Yeah."

"Then how did he get all wet and ya didn't?"

"You're going to have to ask James here that question," Shawn replied while slapping Christian on the shoulder. "While you're doing that, I'm gonna hit the showers."

"James who?" Dom asked while he and Christian watched Shawn walk towards the locker room.

"James Brown," Christian answered which drew a confused, quizzical look from his elderly mentor. "It's a long story."

"Oh," was all Dom said before nodding briefly while still not understanding what he was talking about. "So, kid, what did ya have planned for the rest of the day?"

"Well, I thought about finishing some of my paperwork here for you and then camp out in the library later on for a few hours. But as for right now, I might take Shawn's lead and shower first."

"Sounds good, kid. Might I suggest ya see what ya can do on that Jacobson account? That's been open a little long for my liking."

"Sure, Dom. That'll be my first priority."

"Thanks, kid," Dom said with a grateful tone before getting serious and focusing on his young apprentice. "What'ya mean ya'll be at the library for a couple of hours later? Won't they be near closing by the time ya get there?"

"Probably, but I'm friends with the cleaning guy there."

"What's that got to do with anythin'?"

Christian smiled. "He knows the spots for me to hideout in at the time they close. He lets me stay there as long as he's there if I don't cause any trouble."

"Don't they have cameras?"

"I don't know." Christian shrugged. "Maybe."

"Aren't ya worried about being there after hours? Ya could get in trouble."

"How long have I've been hanging around Shawn, bailing him out of trouble?" Christian asked while a smile while looking at Dom. "And I should be worried about being caught in a library reading a few books after hours?"

"Ya got a point there, kid." Dom returned the smile before getting serious again. "Now, go hit the showers! Ya've got work ta do. Get yer ass goin'!"

"Yes, sir!" Christian gave a quick, snappy salute before using the same hang to give Dom a thumbs up. He soon vanished in the locker room.

Chapter 27

"Hollywood Fred! What's shakin', bacon?" Larry asked when Christian entered the library later that night.

"Other than martinis, not too much, Catfish" he told his library cleaning friend. "How you doing?"

Catfish shrugged. "Oh, you know, you know."

"Actually, no I don't. That's why I asked." He smiled while approaching his friend Larry, the library's cleaning guy.

"Ah, just living the dream, my friend. Just living the dream."

"And what dream is that?"

"Well, it's more like a nightmare, really. I was just wondering how I'd be able to clean this joint up so I can finish reading that book I have stashed away in the basement," Larry responded while going back to his cart. While noticing he was short on supplies, he nodded in the direction he wanted to go while waving his hand to get Christian to follow. "C'mon, Hollywood. Take a walk with me."

"Where're we going?"

"Supply closet downstairs. I need to get some glass cleaner."

"This closet of yours, it wouldn't be anywhere near that hole of yours you hideout when reading?" inquired Christian when they were out of earshot of the librarians.

"Yo, H.F., what kinda fool do you think I am?" he asked with a slightly insulted tone to his voice. "You've got to give me more credit than that. I can hide myself very well when I want to, thank-you very much. Besides, that closet would be one of the first spots they'd check."

"They? They who?"

"The spooks of course."

"Do you mean 'spooks' or 'suits'?" Christian asked.

"Spooks, man, spooks! You know?   S-P-double O-K-S! Spooks! They know and see all. They're invisible, man, only showing themselves when they want to be seen. Usually they're white guys in dark suits and sunglasses with slicked back hair. When they do allow you to see 'em, they're often driving long S.U.V.s like a Tahoe or Suburban. Dark blue or black in color; one's that have the tinted windows to 'em," Catfish explained as they emerged in the downstairs hallway outside of an open supply closet. Larry, meanwhile, stopped abruptly when he saw this and started looking around with a weird, paranoid look in his eyes as if half-expecting to see someone or something.

Wondering what was going on, Christian asked, "Hey, Larry, you alright?"

"I was just wondering why the closet's open. Perhaps the person who opened it is still down here," he answered while looking inside the closet to see if anyone was there. "Could be one of those spooks I just told you about."

"Perhaps the person who left it open was you. You ever think of that?" Christian asked which drew the attention of Larry.

"Oh," he muttered while realizing that it was, in fact, he who had left it open for easier entry later. "Yeah, that's right. It was me, wasn't me?" He let out an embarrassed laugh before looking over at Christian. "I was just trying to see if you were paying attention. And, um, you passed. Good job, Hollywood."

"Well, you know Larry, it was a lucky guess on my part." Christian shrugged while returning his friend's look. "And considering those two black S.U.V.s with the tinted glass out in the parking lot, I figured that the least likely option was the funniest, and, henceforth, would make you laugh. But, sadly, I was wrong."

"Two S.U.V.s? Did you say you saw two of them?" Larry nervously asked while looking around suspiciously. "In the parking lot?"

"Actually I said there were two black S.U.V.s with tinted glass," corrected Christian as he tried to hide the smile that was trying to emerge on his face when he saw his friend's facial expression.

Larry's mouth opened and eye's went wide while he fumbled his words around before anything coherent came out. "Are you serious man? Are there really two of them out there?"

"No, Larry, I'm not. I was just joking with you. There aren't any S.U.V.s out there, black or otherwise." Christian finally burst out laughing at his friend's expense. "You can go check if you want."

"You son-of-a-bitch!" Larry exclaimed when he finally knew he had been had.

Christian, meanwhile, continued to laugh hard for a few more seconds before finally getting it out of his system.

"You done yet?" Larry asked with mocked irritation.

"Oh, yeah. All done," he replied while continuing to laugh.

"You sure?"

"Yeah, I'm sure," he informed as he stopped laughing.

"Good, because I didn't want to hear that dumb laugh of yours anymore," Larry bluntly stated before walking into the supply closet to grab the class cleaner he originally came to get as well as a few other things. He then started walking back towards the stairs with a "Let's go" escaping from his mouth.

When they got upstairs, Christian followed Larry back over to his chart he used to clean the library. Dumping his supplies onto it, he turned to Christian to say something.

"You know the drill. Do whatever you want but a few minutes before nine come get me. We'll then hide you in the supply closet downstairs. After everyone leaves, I'll let you out. Did you bring anything in with you?"

"Just a bad. It's over on one of the back tables." Christian pointed in the general direction.

"Just make sure you bring it with you. I wouldn't want to raise any red flags."

"Roger that." Christian agreed while giving his friend a thumbs-up. "Hey, by the way, how's your bowling team doing?"

"Oh, we're doing good, doing well in fact." Larry smiled with a nod. "We're still in first place and our season is about half over. If all goes well, we'll win league again this year. You outta come by more often to see the guys. We've improved a lot since the last time you came."

"Sure, I'll try to come Thursday if I can, but I doubt you've improved that much. The last time I saw you misfits play, you practically dominated the competition."

"That's true, we did. I was just trying to be modest, you know? I thought if I was better at being modest, I'd be a more well-balanced person. Know what I mean, Jellybean?" Larry asked while using both of his hands to make a few circles in front of him.

"When it comes to your bowling you're hardly that modest."

"That's true. I'm not, am I?" Larry laughed briefly before looking at his watch. "Whoa, look at the time! I'd better get my ass moving. I guess I'll see you a little bit before nine."

At that, he watched Larry go off with his cleaning cart before vanishing around the corner. Christian then went back to his corner table where he left his bag, sat down, and started reading a couple of science magazines he had brought with him.

Christian had known Larry "Catfish" Johnson for about ten years now, initially meeting him while in high school. Larry had dropped out after the eleventh grade to take care of his ailing dad. Christian was saddened by this fact not only because Larry was one of his few friends he had had during high school, but also because Larry was extremely smart. He had been head of their class and would have easily won the valedictorian title if he had stayed. Christian, being the salutatorian up until Larry left, consequently because valedictorian by default. Larry had been the only one in high school to ever really beat him in terms of grades, and Christian was upset he took the number one honor since he didn't feel like he rightfully deserved it. Larry was one of only a handful of students in his class to take both the SATs and ACTs during their junior year, but the only one to get a perfect score on both. Christian came close on both but was a few points away from doing so.

Larry was about 5'11" and weighed around 185 pounds. He had his head shaved but usually kept a few days growth on it. He often wore sunglasses with really big lenses, even when he didn't really need to. Christian would periodically say that if he had his head cleanly shaved, he would be the next Telly Salvalis.

Larry's dad finally got over whatever illness he had a few years back, but Larry still took care of him out of habit. As a result, Christian had been trying to get him to go back for his GED, but was finding it difficult to accomplish this.

He had been the cleaning man at their local library shortly after he quit school and had been there ever since. Though the pay wasn't that good, the fact that he received really good benefits and was able to read any of the library's material whenever he wanted made it worth his while to stay. He would often borrow countless books and hide them throughout the basement in spots that would be good for him to hideout at. Since he was extremely efficient at this job, he would often finish his work in half the time while the other half he would be reading the borrowed material somewhere in the basement.

About four years ago, a year or so before his dad got better, Larry formed a bowling team and have been in the local league ever since. There were a total of four of them on the team and they dubbed themselves *The Misfits*. They called themselves this more out of their different backgrounds than from actually being misfits. They had dominated their league ever since their genesis and never placed less than second during their tenure. The league had an average of fifteen teams each season, but changed periodically from thirteen to seventeen depending on the year and circumstances. The past three seasons the league met on Thursday evenings, which Larry took off of work for. He had gained the nickname 'Catfish' from a couple members in the league but how it came about, Christian didn't have a clue.

Just before nine, Christian packed his bag up and went to find Larry. Soon afterwards, he found himself hiding in the downstairs closet until everyone left. He was let out around 9:30 before soon returning to his corner table and spent the next few hours reading while also completing some paperwork he had brought with him from Dom's office.

That Thursday evening, as promised, Christian went down to the local bowling alley to watch Larry's team compete at league night.

"Hey, Jizmo. Long time no see, man!" Eric, one of Larry's teammates, said when he saw Christian approach.

"Hey, Cramselot. How've you been?" Christian replied while a shaking his hand.

"Not bad, not bad. How swingeth thy hammer with you?"

"It's going really well, Crammie. Thanks for asking."

"Hey, that's Sir Cramselot to you," Eric corrected with a smile.

"Oh, that's right. Sorry about that, *Sir* Cramselot."

"And don't forget it, ya hear?!"

"Yes, sir!" Christian said sarcastically with a mock salute.

263

"So, Jiz, did you come to help us win tonight?" asked Eric.

"No, not tonight," replied Christian. "Well, I did come as a spectator, one with plenty of moral support. Does that count?"

"We're actually short a guy. Roger wasn't able to make it and we haven't found a replacement yet."

"In that case, sure, I'll help you guys out. But I'll help only if it's ok with both Miggie and Larry."

"Hey, guys!" Eric yelled to his team. "Larry! Miggie! Is it alright with you two if Jizmo here fills in for Roger tonight?"

"Yeah, ok." Larry shrugged.

"Fine with me, too," Miggie said while in the process of putting a set of earphones on before waving to Christian. "How's it goin', Slim Fast?"

"Going well," Christian told him. "How about yourself?"

Miggie simply gave an 'ok' hand gesture while turning on his music.

Sitting in the middle of Miggie and Larry, in the spot where Eric usually sat, was an attractive brunette in her early 20s.

"So, Eric," Christian softly said while pointing to her. "New girlfriend?"

"Shh! Quiet!" he said under his breath while putting a finger quickly to his lips. "I've been with her on and off now for a while. She's more of a friend with kickass benefits than an actual girlfriend, if you know what I mean, bro. If you want, I could hook you up with her later on."

"Oh, she's one of *those*, huh?" Christian slyly asked with a smile that was reconfirmed by Eric. "You have good taste there, Crammie. She's attractive."

"If you think she's attractive here, fully clothed, you outta see her in the sack. Ha ha ha!" Eric laughed as a broad smile came over his face. When noticing she was looking their way, Eric smiled and waved. "C'mon, I'll introduce you two."

Her name ended up being Sophia, a person of Italian decent, but other than that, she was a mystery to Christian. Eric, on the other hand, was the head cook at the Bourbon-N-Ribeye, the restaurant Christian used to work occasionally at up until he won the IBF title. The few things Eric was interested in were professional wrestling, bowling, partying, and getting laid. He called himself Sir Cramselot, a reference to his sexual prowess, one that Christian was willing to take his word on rather than finding out through personal experience. He often jokingly equated this to a medieval knight with drawn sword and, therefore, slightly changed the name of Sir Lancelot, the knight from the Arthurian tales, with a sexual twist. He called Christian 'Jizmo', a slightly perverted modification of Gizmo, the hairy little creature from the movie *Gremlins*. Eric had overheard Christian doing an impersonation of Gizmo a couple times at work a while back and, as a result, christened him Jizmo as a way to carry on his sexual humor.

Miggie, the third man on the team, Christian had known in high school but more of an acquaintance than anything else. He was of Puerto Rican decent; having come here with his family at the age of five or six. He was a local rapper who wrote, produced, and performed all of his own material while having the dreams and ambitions of making it big. In his own right, he was more of a local celebrity than either Christian or Shawn, but without as many career opportunities of yet. He only recently got one or two of his current songs to be played by a local radio station.

"Hey, Hollywood," Larry called out when Christian came over. "If you were here ten minutes earlier, you would have seen one of your commercials on TV."

"Which one was it this time?" Christian asked with a certain amount of embarrassment. He was always a little embarrassed when someone told him they saw one of his commercials.

"The sneaker one."

"How many endorsements do you have?" inquired Eric.

"Five now, I think. Maybe four."

"How the hell do you *not* know?" Eric asked while being slightly surprised. He soon let out a muffled laugh. "If it was me, I'd know exactly how many I had and who I had them with. Hell, I'd be announcing them to the world whenever possible."

Christian laughed at that. "I can picture you doing that."

"Bet your ass I would!"

"Hollywood, before we start, you should go get your shoes to bowl with," Larry informed him while pointing up to the man behind the counter. "While you're doing that, I'll go take care of you substituting for Roger tonight."

"Oh, that's right. I forgot about the shoes. Thanks, Larry," Christian said while walking over to get his shoes.

"Not a problem, Hollywood. That's why I'm here," he said while making an almost suave-like pose. "By the way, on league night I'm Catfish, not Larry. Got it?"

"Yeah, ok. I'll remember that, Catfish."

League night that day turned out to be very successful for *The Misfits*. They ended up pulling out a close, and well fought, battle with three consecutive strikes on the last frame from none other than Larry 'Catfish' Johnson. For most of the match, they trailed their rivals, *The Outsiders*, but were always within twenty pins.

Christian enjoyed himself immensely that night and had agreed to be a substitute for them if he was available on the night they would need him. In return, he got them all tickets for his and Shawn's upcoming fight that next week, as well as transportation there and back again.

Chapter 28

"Mr. Calloway," a journalist called out while standing up in the crowd. "How does it feel to finally challenge for a world title this far into your career?"

"How do you think it feels?" Shawn responded from behind the table he was sitting at for the press conference. "I've been waiting for a title shot ever since I began fighting. It's long overdue if you ask me."

Christian, who sat on the opposite side of Dom that Shawn did, had to think that all press conferences were the same. He had one for each of his title fights, and honestly no need for them. He didn't like the idea of the reporters asking them questions that they've already asked multiple times before, and whose answers had been heard multiple times as well.

However, he did feel that these conferences gave each fighter and their crew the rare opportunity to gather as much information as they could on their opponent that the tapes they review would never give them. If they paid attention, this information was much like a poker game, making you think if your opponent was bluffing or not. But, regardless of that, you may be able to figure out your opponent's mood, mind frame, and what their game plan might be for your pending fight. And you always hoped your opponent was a talker because the more they talked, they more they gave away.

At times like this, Christian knew Jack Stratus would have the advantage going into his title defense against Shawn. By nature, Shawn couldn't help but demand being the center of attention, and where better to get attention than at a press conference? This being his first, Shawn was in his glory. He was able to tell the whole world in front of reporters, journalists, and TV cameras how bad he was, how he was the best in the world, and how he was going to beat Stratus in only a few short rounds.

Stratus, on the other hand, had been through a few more of these than Shawn had, only remained calm, cool, observant, and, above all, quiet the whole way through. He and Christian exchanged a few looks, smiles, and rolls of their eyes with each other when Shawn was rattling off what he'd do during the match. When Stratus was asked his game plan for his fight against Shawn, his reply was simple.

"Mr. Calloway has a great record, he's essentially unbeaten and most of his victories have been by way of knockout within four rounds. I just hope to wear him down and take him to the limit. I think this'll still be a good match," Stratus explained.

"A good match?" Shawn repeated back while scoffing heavily. He proceeded to look between Stratus and the audience multiple times with an over dramatic confused look upon his face. After doing this, Shawn stopped to glare at Stratus in a vain attempt of intimidation that didn't seem to work as well as he had hoped. "It's not gonna be a good match, brother. Do you know why? Because it's gonna be a god dammed massacre; a short, bloody, massacre, the kind of one which you have never experienced before. What do you say about that, Jack?"

Shawn continue to sit there and glare at Stratus who, in return, calmly looked back while cameras were flashing for a possible print in the following day's paper.

"I think you like to over exaggerate, Mr. Calloway," Jack finely told him in a soft, confident tone. "Unlike most of your other opponents, I neither am afraid nor intimidated by your tactics. I think you've beaten too many lower quality opponents with too soft of a chin for too long of a time, and you're at the point where you feel that you're scrawny little body is the next Mike Tyson. I also believe you feel that not only I, but the rest of the boxers you might someday face, are afraid of you or will lose in a very short time against you. You underestimate me, Mr. Calloway. You're not intimidating me. You do not frighten me. You're not going to have a quick and easy victory over me. You're a hell of a fighter, I'll give you that, and you very well may knock me out, but you're going to have to work for it. I am not going to just lay down before handing my belt over to you; the same belt I fought to wind and the belt I've fought so hard for so long just to hand it over to you without a hell of a fight. This old dog still has a few tricks. That's all I have to say about this."

"Really? Is that a threat?" Shawn asked over his growing anger while glaring at the ever calm Jack Stratus.

"I guess you'll have to wait until tomorrow night to find out, now won't you?"

After a few moments of tension on Shawn's part, a reporter rose and asked a question.

"Mr. Stratus, Todd Jones here from the Syracuse Herald. I have just one question," he said while drawing the champ's look and a nod. "Is there any truth in the rumor that neither you nor your manager wanted you to face Mr. Calloway? And the reason you changed your mind was as a result of his decision loss to his friend sitting by him, the IBF and WBO cruiserweight champion, Mr. Christian Eaton? Is there any truth in any of this?"

"Pretty much all of that is true," Jack confirmed with a smile. "You see, Mr. Calloway is a loose cannon. He's unable to follow any type of direction, even if that direction is beneficial to him. I and my team have received a series of phone calls from his manager who was willing to have an exhibition match in an attempt to help Mr. Calloway's career. We each reached an agreement, and that agreement was that if Mr. Calloway performed well in this exhibition match you just spoke of, if he was able to show he was more than a rabid killing machine and we liked what we saw, then we would accept their challenge to face us. That was mainly for what my what my team and I could see what else he had to offer. And here we are."

"Mr. Calloway, what are your thoughts on this?" Mr. Jones asked.

"My thoughts are that I don't have any," Shawn told him bluntly while looking briefly at Dom and Christian before looking back to Todd Jones. "I'm insulted by the fact that they actually thought they needed to do something in order to help my career. I didn't need any help from nobody."

"But you have to admit that, without them, you wouldn't be challenging for Mr. Stratus' title tomorrow night."

"Man, I don't have to admit nothin'," scoffed Shawn. "That bullshit exhibition match might have moved this fight up a few months, but that's it! Within a year I'd have been challenging for it regardless. Period. End of story."

"Then why did you accept it if you had it coming?"

"You know how long I've been asking for a title shot?" Shawn asked. "That was my way of getting this belt now instead of six months to a year down the road."

"But you weren't even a contender for it beforehand," Todd commented.

"Hey, Jones, I'd love to see how your smile would look without any teeth. If you don't wanna find out, I'd suggest you sit back down and shut up!" Shawn demanded while pointing to the reporter's chair.

"I'm just stating a fact, Mr. Calloway," the reporter told him.

At this point, Dom leaned in to put a hand on Shawn's forearm.

"C'mon, Shawn," he said softly. "No need for this. You don't need to be rude. He's just doin' his job."

"Do either of you two have anything else to add?" the reporter asked before sitting back down.

Stratus answered with a simple shake of the head.

"I think I'll speak for the both of us if no one minds," Shawn said while looking at Jack before continuing. "I just want everyone to know that tomorrow's main event will be the best short lived fight that this convention center, or the entire world for that matter, has ever seen. And I'm servin' notice to any jabroni with a world title that their time is up 'cuz it's time for Shawn Calloway to reach his potential. This is *my* time, *my* world, and everyone will respect me as they bow down and kiss my feet!"

Shortly thereafter, the press conference formally ended. Several minutes after that, Dom finally was able to ask Shawn a question in private as they walked out to their car.

"What the hell was ya doin' in there?"

"Just doin' my job," Shawn told him.

"Your job doesn't entail ya actin' like an ass!"

"It draws attention to the fight and has massive entertainment value," Shawn said before noticing that Dom was looking at him. "Someone always has to be the heel."

"There's no reasonin' with ya," Dom said, drawing a smile from his thick headed student.

The next night after Christian's IBF title defense, they were in their locker room getting ready for Shawn's own title match.

"Hey, Dom," Christian said from his corner chair. "No offense to Shawn or anyone, but I was just wondering why Shawn's fight was placed after mine on the card."

"Just the way the promoters set it up," Dom answered without breaking stride while pacing. "Why they did that I don't have a clue. Don't try and figure it out, kid, it's not worth it."

"Hey, bro, you should know by now that it was only a matter to time that my fights would be more important than yours," Shawn cockily informed him. "I'm just surprised that it took this long."

As Shawn was prancing around the room, Christian saw a TV mounted on the wall of the locker room.

"Why is this in here?" he asked while pointing to it.

"It's there to help the people in the room keep track of what's goin' on outside the room," Dom told him.

"What would be some examples of things they'd have on it?"

"Matches going on in the ring; interviews being conducted backstage; anythin' else that has anythin' to do with what's goin' on."

"Would either of you two mind if I turn it on to see what's playing?"

When neither Dom nor Shawn objected, Christian turned it on just in time to see someone introduce themselves as Sam Silverman, a sports reporter of sorts, who was wrapping up an interview with the champ Jack Stratus.

"...and now, I'm going to see if I can get a word with his challenger, Shawn Calloway," Sam said as he walked down the hall towards their locker room.

When Shawn heard that, he smiled and gloated immensely before going to the door to open it to await the arrival of the reporter. Dom, meanwhile, told him not to overdo it.

"Don't worry, old man. I know what I'm doin'."

"That's what I'm 'fraid of."

Just then, Shawn became very serious before going to a nearby bench, sat on it, and buried his face in his hands.

"What the hell ya doin', kid?" Dom asked him.

"If Stratus is gonna watch this, I want him to think I'm a little worried." Shawn smiled while tapping his temple with a finger. "It's called ring psychology. Now, do us all a favor and play along."

Christian shrugged while Shawn put his fact back into his hands just before Sam Silverman and his cameraman came in.

"We are here live in the back of the Silver Convention Center," Sam said to the cameras as they approached Shawn. "With me now is the challenger of tonight's main event, Shawn Calloway. I have to ask you, Shawn," he said while turning to face him. "How are you feeling now that the night has finally come for you to be challenging for the WBO light heavyweight championship of the world?"

"Fine," Shawn replied while still sitting on the bench with his face still buried in his hands.

"You're not at all worried about his fight?" Sam asked before putting his microphone down next to Shawn's head.

"No, I'm not."

"Not at all worried?" the reporter asked in a little more aggressive manner while trying to get some sort of a reaction.

"No, I'm not!" replied Shawn, this time a little louder.

"Shawn, you're not worried that your opponent is currently the undefeated WBO light heavyweight champion Jack Stratus?"

"Why would I be?" Shawn quickly retorted.

"He was quoted as saying he had a game plan for you tonight, one that will give him a victory in the later rounds. He's said in a previous interview that he doesn't sweat you; that you will suffer the same fate as his last twenty-two opponents," Sam told him. "Don't you have a retort?"

"A retort? You wanna know if I have a retort?" Shawn quickly asked while getting a nod from the reporter. "What the hell is a retort anyway?"

"Well, it's a form of a..."Sam started before being cut off.

"Shut up, fool! I know what a retort is," Shawn cut in as rudely as possible. "Let's take a look at the undefeated Jack Stratus for a minute, shall we? That guy's what, 6'2" and 175 pounds? Nice tan, goofy haircut, lazy eye, big ears, big nose, big ego, big head, and, sadly, no brains. Doesn't he know who I am? You know what you are, Stratus? A nothin'; a nobody. You're a wannabe tough guy. But you're gonna find out just like all the rest that I'm everything that I say I am. I'm the fastest, strongest, baddest, and a helluva lot better fighter than you could ever hope to be. Get a good look at this face, boy, 'cuz this is the last thing you're gonna see before I knock your ass out, chumpalicious! Now, get the hell outta here, Silverman, before I use you as my own personal punching bag! Beat it!"

"This is Sam Silverman and that was Shawn Calloway, the challenger for tonight's WBO light heavyweight championship. Now, back to you in the studio." Sam quickly vacated the room when the interview was over.

"We, um, apologize for those remarks, ladies and gentlemen," a broadcaster at ringside said once he came on the TV. We in no way condone those comments or actions made by Shawn Calloway. We're sure that there will be some repercussions resulting from that interview. With that said, let's give it up to the ring announcer for the start of the next fight."

The fight for the WBO light heavyweight championship turned out to be a long, hard fought battle as predicted by Jack Stratus rather than the short, one sided massacre Shawn bragged about.

"What are ya doin' out there?!" Dom yelled at Shawn as he came back to his corner after the end of the ninth round.

"Tryin' to win the fight. What the hell you doin'?"

"You're not doin' what we talked about!"

"Since when do I ever listen?" Shawn asked while trying to get his breath back. "Besides, you talked; I just listened."

"Sine ya have yer own method fer the fight, ya might as well tell me what the hell it is," Dom said while putting Vaseline on Shawn's face. "Don't be leavin' me in the dark."

"I've been talkin' to him out there. Tryin' to get in his head."

"Ya're doin' what out there?" Dom asked in a surprised tone.

"Talkin' to him. Tryin' to get him pissed off."

"Why are you doing that?" Christian asked. "Do you have a death wish?"

"If I piss him off, he'll try and knock me out," Shawn told him as Christian put his mouth guard back in. "Once he punches enough, he'll be more tired than he is now. When that happens, his ass is mine!"

"I hope ya know what you're doin', kid," injected Dom.

"Trust me," Shawn said as the bell signaled the start of the tenth round.

As the fight wore on, it appeared Shawn had the match in his grasps. Christian, meanwhile, stood next to the ring apron with Dom while looking through the crowd. There was still a very high energy radiating from them. Then, before he was finished observing the crowd, everyone around him exploded to their feet while erupting into a frenzy of cheers and screams. The noise was deafnifying as Christian covered his ears to muffle the sound.

"Down goes Calloway! Down goes Calloway!" Christian heard one of the announcers shout.

Feeling he was in a dream state brought on by the exuberant crowd, he didn't believe what he was hearing. Even though he looked into the ring to see Shawn face down, spread eagle, kissing the canvas, he honestly couldn't believe what he had just heard, let alone what he was currently seeing. He just didn't want to believe it. While still in his half denial trance, he sensed Dom was looking at him. Turning to look at his trainer, Christian saw a smile and wink appear on the wrinkled face before him.

"See? What'd I tell ya?"The old man seemed to chuckle somewhat while nodding towards the ring.

Eventually, Shawn got up at the count of eight. He looked as shaken, if not more so, for being knocked down as Christian was surprised. By his expression, Shawn obviously couldn't believe it either.

Straus, on the other hand, stood patiently in his corner without expression.

The ref asked if Shawn was ok, which simply got a nod from him. A few unheard questions came from the ref's lips before the fight continued. Shortly after Calloway and Stratus exchanged a handful of punches, the bell signaled the end of round ten.

While Shawn was in his corner being worked on, Dom was as talkative as his fighter was. Each remained silent as Shawn was patched up.

Round eleven began without any words being exchanged. That round was identical to the last in every detail except for the fact that it was Stratus, rather than Shawn, who got knocked down. The twelfth brought a knockdown of each fighter, but no knockout.

The fight ended at the end of the twelfth before going to the cards. Ultimately, Shawn won the match, as well as the belt, by a way he truly resented; he won on points.

A couple of months after winning the belt, he and Stratus hooked up again for a rematch. It was as tough and grueling as their first one, and was much more talked about. The rematch was so much like the original that even the ending was the same. Late in the twelfth, Shawn floored Stratus with what appeared to be a knockout with mere seconds left on the clock, but good ole Jack got up at the last possible moment. The bell sounded soon after he got to his feet to signal the end of the twelfth and the match. Once again, Shawn beat Stratus via decision to retain the WBO light heavyweight championship of the world. To Christian, his brother seemed a little flustered at the difficulty he had had against Jack Stratus, but you wouldn't have noticed it much by his elevated ego and cockiness.

"Will I be facing that goofy-looking bastard again?" Shawn asked in the locker room while laying down on the medicine table.

"If you're referring to Mr. Stratus, no, or at least not for a while," Dom waved his fingers in a 'come on' motion as a way for him to sit up.

Complying, Shawn swung his legs around over the edge while sitting up. "Good. There's no need to do a rubber match with him anyway. Oh, just to let you know, it's gonna feel great knowing that my hands have finally been untied."

"What the hell ya mean by untied, kid?" Dom asked while flicking a thumb to Shawn while looking at Christian. Almost immediately, Christian went to Shawn to remove his gloves and tape from his hands.

"Don't worry 'bout it, old man," Shawn told him. "You'll find out soon enough."

Shawn ended up defending the WBO championship consistently every few months while going back to his style of fighting just to piss off Dom. He knew that since he had a major title, he'd have people to face, better quality contenders, and more opportunities to make more money. He didn't care what Dom told him of not trying to go for a quick knockout because there would always be contenders for his belt and, as a result, he continued to think 'Why should I change?' He already got what he wanted by doing things his way so he didn't feel any great need to start doing anything different now.

He soon went on to defend his title against his personal favorite opponent, Lenny Couchmate. Previously, Shawn had made insulting cracks at Lenny's expense for a quick laugh. Couchmate had once been a good fighter in his prime, but that was ten years earlier when he held the WBO belt in a lighter weight class. He had been retired a number of years but was trying to make a comeback to pay off his debt. His charisma was really the only thing he still had going for him, but that was pretty much it. Shawn had the choice of facing another, higher ranked contender but choose Lenny as another way to make fun of him.

The match, on the same undercard as Christian's title defense for both of his belts, was at the Staples Center in Los Angeles. When Shawn learned that Sam Silverman was there and wanted an interview, a live one nonetheless, he couldn't pass up the chance to publicly poke fun at his opponent.

"Ladies and gentleman, Sam Silverman here. I am privileged to be here backstage of the Los Angeles Staples Center and, hopefully, I can bring an exclusive interview with the champ for tonight's second main event. I just interviewed the challenger, Lenny Couchmate, and I'm now standing outside the locker room of the reigning WBO light heavyweight champion, Shawn Calloway. I hope he's available for comment," Silverman said to his camera before turning to the locker room door next to him and knocked. He waited four or five seconds without an answer before knocking again. Without an answer the second time, he turned back to the camera to smile. "I'll just go on in to see if he's in there," he said before opening the door and walked in.

Shawn was seen sitting on a bench with his face buried in his hands.

"Mr. Calloway," Silverman called while approaching with his cameraman. "Do you have any comment before your title defense against Lenny Couchmate tonight? What about it, champ?"

"Go away," muttered Shawn.

"What was that, champ? I didn't catch that," Sam said while giving the camera a puzzled look before putting the microphone back down to Shawn's hands.

Hearing this, Shawn sprang up to glare that the reporter. "Maybe that's because I didn't throw anything for you to catch."

"What do you mean by 'throw'?"

"I'm gonna throw you through the door if you don't get outta my face!" Shawn said while pointing to the locker room door.

"But what about your opponent tonight? He was quoted as saying, 'that loud mouthed punk has lead pencils for feet and noodles for brains'," Sam read from a little notepad he held in his other hand before shifting the microphone over for Shawn's reply.

"What about Lenny? He's a fat, overweight, slow as hell, wannabe who couldn't lace my boots if he had taken a course in boot lacing, got an A in it, and got help from his teacher! And did he actually say that I have lead pencils for feet? Have you ever seen my feet?" Shawn asked while looking down to his feet, raising his right foot in the process for a closer look. "They're extremely beautiful; but not as pretty as my face, though! I'm gonna put Couchmate right back where he damn well belongs, right back on that damn couch of his, and there ain't a damn thing he can do 'bout it 'cept hope the remote doesn't get stuck in his fat, hairy ass. Now, get outta my face, Sammy!"

"Y-y-yes, s-sir," stuttered Silverman before returning the broadcast back to the ring announcers.

"We apologize for those remarks, ladies and gentlemen, for we are in fact live," the main ring announcer came on to state as the next pair of boxers were being introduced in the ring. "Let's bring it to our ring announcer for our next match."

Shawn was in a very good mood for the duration of the time they were in the locker room, as well as their trek to the ring for his fight. He, in all honestly, was hoping this would be the shortest match of his career but commented they wouldn't know if he would follow through with it until the bell sounded to start it.

The fight between Shawn and Lenny didn't even last two full rounds. The ref ended up calling it halfway through the second round on account of the three-knockdown rule; Lenny's fifth overall.

"Ya outta be goddamned ashamed of yerself!" Dom chastised once they reentered their locker room fifteen minutes later. "There was no need to publicly humiliate Leonard like that."

"I just wanted to show the man he had no business being in my ring." Shawn shrugged as Christian took off his gloves and tape. "He needed to be shown that he made a mistake on deciding to return to the ring. He should'a stayed retired."

"Who's ta say ya were the one ta do that, huh?"

"What's your problem, Dom?"

"That beatin' ya gave him was embarrassin' and uncalled fer. He's a former world champ!" Dom yelled while walking towards the bathroom. "I have a side note fer ya, Shawn. No matter what ya think, say, or do, that ain't your ring out there!"

"If not now, then when?!" Shawn yelled back as the bathroom door was heard slamming shut. While turning his head, he noticed Christian looking at him with a disapproving look. "What? What?!" he asked before Christian merely shook his head to go back on taking off Shawn's tape. "What's that look for?"

"Nothing," Christian answered with a sigh. "It wasn't anything."

"C'mon, man. What? Tell me."

"I was just thinking that it wouldn't hurt if you tried to appease Dom occasionally. It might actually shut his ass up." Christian looked at Shawn before sitting down next to him.

While taking the rest of the tape off of his own hands, Shawn firmly refused to accept what he heard. "I don't fight that way. Maybe Dom is the one who outta change, but not me. No sir!"

"Dom's been doing this for too long to change. I wouldn't be surprised if he threatens to drop you if you continue on like you are, to refuse to do what he asks."

"Why you sayin' that, bro?" Shawn quickly asked while throwing him a look. "Did he say somethin'? Do you know somethin' I don't?"

"No, I was just saying." Christian shrugged.

The two sat there in silence for a while longer before Shawn got up and headed for the shower.

Three days after Shawn's title defense against Lenny Couchmate, Christian approached Shawn in the gym with that day's sports section.

"Looks like your buddy's retiring again," he said while handing him the paper.

"Buddy? What the hell you blabberin' on about?" Shawn asked while taking the paper. He laughed soon after looking at it.

"Looks like the beating you gave Lenny the other day was too much for him." Christian chuckled while laying down to do a series of pushups.

"He should'a retired years ago," Shawn commented.

"He did retire years ago."

"He should'a stayed retired."

"Yeah, well, looks like he won't be getting into the ring anytime soon."

"I helped take care of that," Shawn said in between heavy, forceful grunts as he hit the heavy bag. "Y'all can thank me any time you want for that."

"Just to let you know, you might be waiting a while for that," Christian informed his brother while flipping over to start doing sit-ups.

"I outta get one from his wife at the very least."

"He's married?"

"I don't know but that's not the point, damn it!"

"Why one from her?"

"Because I saved her from becoming a widow, that's why!" Shawn stopped on the heavy bag long enough to catch his breath while glancing down at the paper. He soon focused on it before picking it up to start reading the article. "Or I could just accept this instead. Curly's friend, Dave, gave me a killer review. He said that 'that was one of the most dominating title defenses he'd seen in years'."

"Great! All the more wood to fuel your fiery ego." Christian laughed while finishing his sit-ups before lying flat on the floor.

"Shut up, man. I didn't ask you for a response." Shawn sighed while putting his hands on his hips. "That's it for me today, I think. I may go down to Mike's after I hit the showers. You wanna come?"

"Thanks but not tonight," Christian said while in the process of getting up before walking over to get a jump rope. "Dom wanted to do some training with me later."

Shrugging, Shawn started for the lockers. "Your loss."

"Hey, do me a favor and don't hit them very hard, ok?"

Turning to look at him with a confused look, Shawn asks, "Don't hit who too hard?"

"The showers," Christian answered dryly with a smile.

"Huh?"

"I'll see you later, bub." With that, Christian turned to watch his form in the mirror as he jumped rope.

Shawn, meanwhile, stood where he was momentarily wondering what his brother meant by that before turning to finish walking back to the locker room.

Chapter 29

Christian grunted while pounding the heavy bag with lefts and rights later that night. Sweat poured off his body as if standing under a hose.

"C'mon, kid! Don't hit it so hard. Ya got ta hit straighter and more precise than that!" yelled Dominic from the corner. "Remember, ya're a technical wizard, not a manila gorilla. We don't want ya breakin' yer damn wrists from punching someone wrong. Besides, yer a goddamn world champion, fer Christ's sake! Twice over. So start throwing punches that resemble that."

"Y-y-yes sir," Christian said while straightening his punches out on the bag.

Just then, Sly, Dom's utility man, called for Christian. "Hey, Chris! Telephone!"

"Thanks, Sly. I'll be right there," he replied back while stopping to take a few deep breaths. "Hey, Dom. I'll be r-r-right back."

"Hurry up, kid. I ain't runnin' a phone service here," grumbled the trainer while shaking his head.

Christian went to the phone on Dom's desk and picked it up. "Hello, Christian here. May I help you?" he said into it while listening for a few seconds. "Alright Josh, I'll be right there," he stated before hanging up and returning to the gym. "Dom, I'm s-s-s-sorry but I gotta go pick Shawn up."

"What?!" the foul tempted man questioned. "Ya're always savin' that kid from some kinds mess. What 'bout your trainin'?"

"I'll be in early in the morning, ok Dom?" Christian promised while grabbing a dry shirt from a nearby bench.

"Goddamn kids! They're always distracted with this, that, or some other bunch of crap. Bunch'a lazy asses, I tell ya! Ya hear me?!" Dom yelled out to Christian's back while watching his student exit the gym.

After about ten minutes of jogging, Christian crossed the street to approach *Mike's Place*. Slowing to a walk, he greeted Josh who was standing outside the door.

"Hey Josh. What's up?"

"Oh, same ole same ole, Chris. You know?" the beefy bouncer shrugged. "Listen, bro, your brother's in there and he's had a little too much to drink. Mike's a little busy to deal with him and I'm having problems watching both him and the door. Would you mind going in to take his ass home?"

"Yeah, sure Josh. No problem. Thanks for calling me." Christian stepped through the door before turning back to Josh. "Oh, hey, I've got a fight coming up in two weeks. I'll be going for the WBC belt. You coming?"

"Of course I am, you dickhead! I haven't missed one yet, have I? Now, do us all a favor and get your ass in there so you can get his outta here." Josh gave Christian a shove inside while a smirk came across his face.

While noticing Mike busy at the bar, currently in the process of getting several drinks at once, he inquired, "Hey, Mikey. Where's Shawn at?"

"Over there," he mumbled while nodding his head in the direction to the back of the bar. Beads of sweat were running down his forehead. It was unusually busy for a Wednesday night.

"Thanks." Christian turned and went in the general direction of the nod.

Shawn was easily found in the back area playing pool with an unbridled enthusiasm and cockiness, just short of being plain obnoxious. The regulars understood and loved Shawn, but the other customers where a bit uneasy. Though their distaste for Shawn was warranted, only the people that knew him knew his obnoxious cockiness got worse with the drink. Though he could get to the point of being a maniac, he wouldn't do anything without just cause. Christian waded through the crowd and was almost to his brother's table when Shawn turned and saw him.

"Hey, there brother. I'm glad you're here, man," he slurred before letting out a drunken laugh indicating he was about to say something he thought was hilarious. "I'm in the process of whipping Jake and Terry's ass at pool twice in a row; and with you here, we could make it thrice."

"You above all people should know that I'm not really that good at it," Christian replied while walking up to put an arm around his brother's shoulder. "And besides, we have to get up early tomorrow morning."

"Wha' the 'ell ya talkin' 'bout, bro? I ain't getting' up for shit tomorrow!" he said through unfocusing eyes and liquored breath.

"Yes, you do, Shawn. We have to train for my title shot in two weeks and your title defense in three, remember? You don't really want to take Michelle Gramia too lightly, do you?"

"What, that French faggot? He couldn't beat me if I gave him an openin' the size of his wife's pussy, which you and I both know is fuckin' huge! Ha!" By this point, he was almost on the brink of yelling when he said that. He also leaned on Christian so much, that Christian had to fight not only to balance him, but to keep standing as well.

"C'mon, Shawn, we gotta go. You're making a scene."

"I don't give a shit, or a rat's ass, what I'm makin'! If anyone don't like it, they can go and stuff it," he slurred before being grabbed by Christian right when he started to topple over. "Yo, Chris, don't be pushin' me, man. The condition I'm in, I may fall on my ass."

"Oh, sorry about that, Shawn. I don't know what got into me," Christian apologized with a chuckle while looking at both Jake and Terry, who found this equally amusing. "Anyway, Shawn, you're not really making any sense now. We gotta go. Help me out a little bit, ok? You're dragging your feet."

"Alright, I'm sorry, bro, I really am. You're so good to me, man, and I love ya for that. You know that?"

"I know, buddy, I know," Christian responded while noticing Shawn was looking at him for his response.

"I'm fuckin' serious, dude! I love ya. I really, really, *really* love ya, man! I love ya like a brother. And your family. I love your whole fuckin' family, too." For the first time, Shawn displayed a hint of modesty that was extremely rare coming from him. It usually showed itself only through a private and emotional connection or with the help from too much alcohol. In this case, most likely both.

"I know, Shawn. I really do." Christian was slightly embarrassed while trying desperately to drag him out of there while a look of irritation came over Shawn's face.

"Dude, I'm totally serious. I love ya. But not in a grab-you-from-behind sort of way but in a very brotherly, give me a nuggie and wedge sort of way."

"Uh, thanks Shawn. That was, um, very eloquently put," Christian told him while scrunching his face.

Just as Christian and Shawn were making their way to the door, eight tough, robust, incoherent, and fibrous looking guys walked in.

"Yo, Eaton, that you?!" yelled the leader.

Christian looked at him inquisitively. "Yeah. Who are you?"

"Ha, I thought that was you, lard-ass!"

"W-W-Wesley?" Christian asked with a shocked expression. He stopped while trying to prop Shawn up before leaning forward a little while squinting at the man confronting him. "Is that you?"

"Damn straight it is," Wesley answered while puffing himself up while pointing at him with a beefy hand. "I thought that was you walkin' in here. I'm here to get my revenge for you putting' me away a decade ago, boy!"

"Wesley, Wesley." Christian closed his eyes, shook his head, and let out a long, drawn out sigh. "Now just isn't a good time. May we finish this another time, say tomorrow?"

"Listen here, bitch! We're gonna finish this here and now, boy!" Wesley took two steps forwards while putting his hands on his abundant waistline.

"Look, asshole!" Shawn snapped while jumping to Christian's defense. "You're the one who decided it would be fun to kill a guy for his car because you thought it would look better

279

wrapped around a telephone pole. But, then again, you always were just as dumb as you look, you fuckin' prick!"

"Who are you too talk, Calloway?" Kyle asked while walking forward to stand just behind Wesley. "You went and proved everyone right be ending' up just like your old man. All that's left is for you to end up in a fuckin' gutter, half-naked, plastered, and cold as ice. Fuckin' trailer trash."

"What?! You dumb son-of-a-bitch! I'll rip your fuckin' throat out!" screamed Shawn while finally getting sober enough to make Christian try desperately to hold him back.

"C'mon, Shawn, not here! He's not w-w-worth it," Christian pleaded as Shawn turned to glare at him with high explosiveness. All he could do was look back with a calming glance.

"What's the matter, Eaton? You s-s-scared to f-f-face m-m-me?" Wesley mockingly antagonized him.

At this point, something seemed to switch inside Christian's head. Though he was nervous and didn't want to get into a fight, at that moment, everything that Wesley had dome to him all those years when they were children finally seemed to make sense to him. Because of this, a weird calmness came over him while turning to face his childhood nemesis. He propped Shawn up against a nearby table before taking several steps towards Wesley while knowing exactly what he was going to say.

"You know, Wesley. I've always been jealous of you," he said while walking calmly up to stare him right in the face. "I've always been jealous of you because you could do anything you wanted, to anyone whenever you wanted to, and seemingly always get away scot free without a trace of regret, remorse, or fear of ever getting caught.

"But when you got caught almost a dozen years ago, I finally felt happy for you. Happy that you might actually learn from all the bad things you've done to others by finally getting your act together. I hoped, prayed even, that jail would be the best thing for you; to scare you straight, if you will. I was hoping that would be a second chance for you, you see. A second chance for your poor, helpless parents who stood in that courtroom and cried their eyes out when they heard that verdict of voluntary manslaughter. The parents who saw you being led away in handcuffs, hoping against all hope you'd finally get your life straightened out. The parents who hoped their only son wouldn't turn out to be a full-fledged criminal.

"But, it seems that after all this time, you still haven't gotten it, have you?" Christian continued. "I never really understood why you've never liked me or why you picked on me excessively. But, seeing you here, now, I finally get it. I was the one person you wanted to be. Isn't it just a little sad to know that, even after all these years, you're still that same scared ten-year old boy whose life never amounted to crap no matter how hard you tried. And, you know something, Wesley?"

"Yeah? What's that?"

"I forgive you," Christian told him while seeing a shocked expression come over his nemesis's face while Wesley blinked in confusion. "After all you've done to me, after what you hoped to do to me here, now, I forgive you. You have a clean slate with me, here, now. Now, if you excuse me, I have to go. If you still want, or need, to finish whatever you came in here to finish with me, we will need to take care of it another time. I'm free for a little bit tomorrow morning. Incidentally, I never had anything to do with you killing that person twelve years ago, nothing to do with you being caught, nothing to do with you being convicted, and nothing to do with you spending eleven years in jail over it. You just simply need to let it go and to leave me alone about it."

When Christian was done talking, he calmly back up until he reached Shawn. All Wesley could do was look at him behind bewildered eyes and a gaping jaw. He soon snapped out of it and was about to say something when Shawn beat him to that.

"Listen, dickhead!" Shawn slurred while looking into Wesley's scared, childlike eyes. "You better get outta here before you get your ass handed to ya!"

For a moment, it looked like Wesley and his posse were about to make their move when Josh's voice became evident.

"Alright guys, break it up!" the bouncer bellowed in a deep, commanding voice while elbowing his way through the crowd before him. He soon planted himself solidly between Christian, who was holding Shawn back, and Wesley while giving The Hoods his full attention. While pointing a muscular arm towards the door, he said, "You guys better get the hell outta here if you want to remain healthy."

With that said, Josh simply glared at each of Wesley's cohorts before fixing his stare onto their heartless leader while sneering. The look he gave him was easily the harshest Christian had ever seen Josh wear. Even though Josh tried to look as stern as possible back, Christian had never seen Josh's eyes look so hard or anger-filled as they did at that moment.

Wesley, on the other hand, didn't see the same thing. He obviously hadn't learned anything, especially from his decade long prison term, about knowing when to call it quits when he was in over his head. He just looked back at Josh with a cocky smirk.

"Come on, boys, let's go. I hear the beer here tastes like his momma's panties anyway," Wesley cracked with a sarcastic laugh while nodding towards Josh.

Hearing this, the bouncer took a step towards him. "What the hell you just say?"

"Nothin' that ain't true." Wesley smirked. "I thought you above all people would have known that."

"Maybe you'd better say that again, if you don't mind," Josh told him with an intimidating glare. "My hearing in my right ear ain't so good."

"Josh! That's enough!" Mike yelled from behind the bar. "Step back."

Doing what he was told, Josh retreat a couple steps back while still looking at Wesley. As he turned to look at Christian and Shawn, Wesley spat a juicy wad right in his face. Josh slowly wiped the saliva off before cocking his head and exploding a right hand across Wesley's jaw. The sound the connection made set off a chain reaction better described as "all hell breaking loose."

281

Shawn pushed Christian aside before clocking Kyle square in the nose. He got a chair broken across his back for the effort.

Once Christian was able to regain control of himself, he got hold of Stan before kneeing him in the gut before following it up with a left hook that sent him across a nearby table.

Meanwhile, Jake and Terry, who had just finished their game of pool and last few swigs of beer, got into the mix. Christian couldn't help but find the humor in that, that it was only after they finished their game and beer did they get involved. Terry took a cue stick to a gang member's head before going after another thug. Jake elbowed someone in the face only to have two more come after him. This prompted him to feed one of them a size 17 boot, knocking them hard to the floor. The second he picked up to merely through against a nearby wall.

Bottle crashed, tables broke, and blood flew before Eric found himself face first through a window from a two-handed throw courtesy of a former wrestler. Christian saw Wesley on top of Shawn choking him before landing a forearm and elbow across Wesley's back. While rolling to a rough stop, Wesley found a broken bottle and was just about to use it on Christian when a gunshot rang out with a thunderous crack. The aftershocks stopped all in the bar like a still-frame photo to the point of hearing a pin drop. Mike, the man behind the bar and gun, quickly cocked the other barrel of his double-barrel while pointing it directly at Wesley with deadly accuracy.

"I suggest you get the hell outta my bar before I pump your guts full of lead!" he calmly informed the unwelcomed guests with a cool confidence and unwavering hands. Wesley took a step towards Christian with bottle in hand as Mike cleared his throat relatively loud. "Just give me a reason, asshole!"

Glaring at Mike, Wesley soon shot Christian an evil look while raising his broken bottle at him. "This ain't over, Eaton. We'll finish this the next time we meet. C'mon, boys! Let's go," he said while he and his cronies filed out into the streets to disappear.

When things seemed to quiet down a little after Wesley and his ignorant back of insubordinates had left, Christian carefully made his way over to his very excited brother.

"Hey, Shawn. We should think about get going ourselves, ok? We'll go out the back door, bud," he said while taking him by the shoulder to help lead him away. While passing the bar, Christian looked over to Mike. "I'm sorry about the mess, Mike. I'll come over in a day or so to help settle up with the damages with you."

"Yeah, man," Shawn slurred his apology. "Sorry, dude. And whatever he just said."

"Don't worry 'bout it, guys." Mike smiled while leaning his double-barrel against this shoulder. "This place needed a facelift anyway."

Christian returned the smile while Shawn nodded as they made their way to the back door. Before they got a third of the way there, a man hailed them from behind.

"Hey, you two," a voice called out to them. "Would you guys hang on for a second?"

As Christian and Shawn turned towards the voice, a tall, middle-aged man came out of the smoke-filled shadows. His table was a corner booth which had a glass of brown liquor on the rocks, most likely either bourbon or scotch, an ashtray with a lit cigar whose smoke rose up to hang a few feet above, and paperwork scattered everywhere else. The man himself was about 6'1", with a beefy 200-pound frame. He was dressed in a suit that fit his body well, but a suit that nonetheless was both too expensive and elegant to be seen in a spot like this. The well-dressed man walked with a confidence that hinted he was used to getting his way. His dark eyes brewed an unseen canny and intelligence that could bore a hole through steel. They were underlined with a cocky smile that spoke as elegantly as his suit should the situation call for it.

"Gentlemen. I just wanted to tell you what an impressive show you two just put on," he congratulatory said while reaching inside his jacket pocket to pull out a business card. It was Shawn who had accepted it while trying to read it through unfocusing eyes. "If you two ever wish to change management or promotion, you give me a call, alright?"

"Change management? Why would we do that?" Christian asked with a certain amount of surprise and paranoia. "We don't want to. We're perfectly fine just the way we are. And, besides, who the hell are you to be asking us that?"

"My deepest apologies, gentlemen," the stranger said while turning his attention from Shawn to Christian. Once their gaze met the other, he smiled slyly while extending a hand out. "Name's Snyder, Mr. Eaton. Pleasure to make your, and Mr. Calloway's, acquaintance."

"'Snyder'? Duke Snyder, the promoter?" A look of disapproval came over Christian's face. Without accepting the offered hand to shake, he took the card from Shawn to read instead.

"The one in the same, gentlemen," Dude answered with expressed enthusiasm while slightly bowing from being known. "That's the reason I'm here now, tonight."

"Come again, Mr. Snyder?"

"Please, please, call me Duke. What I meant was I came here tonight to offer you my services."

"Like I said before, Mr. Snyder," Christian said while gritting his teeth. "We don't need, nor do we want, to change management. Mr. Calloway and I are fine just the way we are."

"Yeah, sure you are. But what about your friend here," Duke pressed. "Is he fine? Maybe he may want to discuss business with me," Duke pressed.

"It's a pleasure to meet you, Mr. Snyder," Christian said while handing the business card back to him. "We're in a bit of a hurry and want to get home as soon as we can. Have a good evening."

When Christian was in the process of turning himself and Shawn around to continue their way to the back door, Duke cleared his throat.

"Why don't you let your friend speak for himself when he comes back to his senses?" he added with a stubborn tone. He walked to them before placing his card into Shawn's shirt pocket. "How's that? You be on your way and think about my offer, ok?"

"Again, we're not interested and it was a pleasure meeting you," repeated Christian with an emotionless smile before guiding Shawn the remaining distance to the door.

"Hey there, brother," Shawn slurred as they neared the door. "Who was ole fancy pants there?"

"Oh, that was just the Devil in sheep's clothing," Christian replied while glancing over his shoulder. Duke Snyder was back at his corner table, engulfed in shadows and smoke. He sat there watching them leave through the haze as he puffed on his cigar.

"Don't you mean a wolf in sheep's clothing?" Shawn asked with a stumble.

"Yeah, my mistake. Wolf in sheep's clothing," Christian told him while finally reaching for the door.

While exciting the building, they turned to make their way through the back alley. As they tried to get to the street from there, they didn't make it too far before Wesley crawled out of the shadows to stop them in their tracks.

"Yo, Eaton, I told you this wasn't over," he growled slowly while sliding a knife from a sheath he had attached to his belt. "I'm gonna carve you up, boy."

Christian, meanwhile, pushed Shawn into a pile of filled garbage bags before side stepping the forward thrust by his longtime nemesis. He easily blocked it with a knife-hand before following it up with an upward palm to Wesley's face. Wesley stepped back with a thud as he covered his now broken nose as his hands filled with blood. Christian kicked the knife aside and was about to make a move onto the now dazed and confused Wesley when Eric and Stan crept out of the woodworks to grab him from behind. Once Wesley got his bearings back, his two cohorts had Christian on the ground.

"Come on, Wes. Finish the job, man. You've been waiting for over a decade for this," Eric yelled with a nervous laugh.

"Wesley, Jesus Christ, man!" Christian said to him. "Are you guys being serous? I had nothing to do with that!"

"Like hell you didn't," he told him while looking down for the knife that was no longer there. "Where'd it go?"

"Yo, shithead," Shawn said with a sly grin while waving the knife around from his right hand. "Lookin' for this?"

As Wesley gasped in horror, Shawn jumped towards him before plunging the full length of the blade into Wesley's abdomen. While doing so, Shawn started wiggling it around in a saw-like motion back and forth until the knife seemed to move freely from one of Wesley's hips to the other. When Shawn finally removed it from him, Wesley's entrails flowed out of the now obvious, and gaping, wound.

Dropping to his knees, Wesley used both of his hand to cover his wound in a motherly fashion only to finally realize for the first time the extent of his injuries. While looking down, he let what entrails he held go while staring at his now bloodstained hands and clothing in horror.

"Hey, bro, I think you dropped something there." Shawn sneered over him with the knife ready for another attack.

Exhaling deeply, Wesley soon collapsed in the puddle of his own blood. Shawn towered over him with a bland stare before dropping the knife and spitting on his victim's face.

After seeing their leader fall, Eric and Stan did what they always had; they high tailed it out of there with their tails between their legs.

"Hey, Shawn," Christian said after getting to his feet and walking over to him. "Are you alright?"

"I am; he isn't," came Shawn's reply as red flashing lights filled the now blood drenched alleyway.

"Freeze, you mothers!" came an order as a handful of armed cops rand from around the corner with their guns unsheathed. "Put your hands up where we can see them!"

"Holy shit, bro," muttered Shawn as a look of fear and bewilderment came over his face while glancing towards his brother. "What the hell have I done?"

All Christian could do was stand there while raising his hands. The color of his face was washed away with the onset of surrounding police. Flashing red and white lights continued to fill the dark alleyway.

Chapter 30

Over the trees on a nearby hillside, a small town police station, one which didn't look like it had seen too much action, stood. There were a few parking spaces in front, one of which being for the handicapped, and about six or seven more in back. There were a handful of steps leading up to two sets of double doors; the first pulled out, the inner second pushed in. The front desk was off to the right where a middle-aged barrel of a woman named Rosalyn sat. To the direct left was the chief's office where a deputy sat behind his desk with his feet up while watching a small 15-inch TV/DVD combo. The phone on his desk rang.

"Police station," the deputy answered while pausing for a few seconds. "Hello, Mrs. Anderson. I'm sorry but, no, that is not an emergency. Yes – yes – yes, I understand, but you can't expect us to get your cat out of the tree every day. Mrs. Anderson, that's not our job. I suggest you keep him inside more often. No, no, no. Oooh, alright. If it'll quiet you down, I'll send somebody down but this'll be the last time. You understand? Yes ma'am, yes ma'am. Bye."

Hanging up, the deputy shook his head before going to watch the baseball game. When he went to pick up his coffee, it slipped out of his hand before spilling all over the desk. Panicking, he quickly removed any valuables from the immediate area he didn't want to get wet. While looking around for something to clean up the mess, he soon remembered towels in the janitorial closet. While walking there, he suddenly got a mischievous smirk when nearing the holding cells that currently housed Christian and Shawn.

"Hey, Calloway! Calloway, you awake?" the deputy demanded while drawing his nightstick. He soon started poking Shawn on the shoulder once he got close enough. "C'mon, wakie wakie!"

"Hmmmm," groaned Shawn. "What the fuck do you want?"

"Hey, moron, know what that three strike rule is?" the deputy asked with a cocky arrogance while jabbing his nightstick again into Shawn's shoulder. He chuckled while he spat a wad of tobacco loudly from his mouth. "Well, I just wanted to let you know that this is your third time you've been here this year. Come tomorrow when you see the chief, or the judge for that matter, they ain't gonna be too happy to see your sorry ass. As a matter of fact, when the chief gets here in the morning, I'll make sure to tell him what a model prisoner you've been. What'cha think 'bout that, huh Calloway?"

"I think you're an asshole," Shawn, whose face was in his hands, mumbled.

"What'd'ya say?" the deputy asked as a hard look came over his face.

"I said I think you're an unintellectual, hillbilly asshole."

"What'd'ya think you're tough or somethin'?" The deputy put his hands on his hips while leaning forward to look down at Shawn from the other side of the bars. "I saw your last fight. That Glass Jack dude you fought's a putz. My 84-yr old grammie could'a whooped his ass. You think you're such a tough guy because you knocked his sorry ass down a couple of times? Why don't you show me how tough you really are? I wanna find out how touch your constantly drunken ass really is, Calloway. I ain't scared - "

Before he was able to finish his sentence, a loud smack was heard, one that caused Christian to come back to reality from the nervous world he currently was in. The smack was the sound of flesh hitting steel bars. Apparently, while the deputy was trash talking Shawn, Shawn hopped up from his drunken stupor to punch the deputy in the face before grabbing him by his shirt's lapels to slam his face into the bars. The deputy fell like a ton of bricks while collapsing on the hard floor beneath him.

While standing over the deputy's unconscious body just long enough to glare down at him, Shawn pumped a clenched fist a time or two before going back to the bench he was sitting at moments before. He face immediately sank into welcoming hand and, within minutes, began to snore slightly.

"Shawn," Christian said from the opposite corner. "Shawn, wake up."

"What do you want?" he groaned.

"Do you know what you've done?"

"Yeah, I knocked his sorry ass out. Now I can get a little sleep."

"No, that's not what I meant. What I meant was, do you know what you've done?" Christian asked through a nervous tone. "Are you aware of the trouble you might be getting us into?"

"What do you mean?" Shawn asked with a confused matter while obviously not understanding the question being asked.

"You don't remember, do you?"

"Remember what?"

"You honestly don't?"

"Dude, I'm drunk. Well, hung over is more like it. Leave me alone."

"Shawn, please let's see if you can follow me here. Are you listening?"

"No, I'm sleepin'."

"Well, let me inform you of your actions from last night. You got drunk, again. Josh called me to help get you home, again. You started a fight, again. And, to top it off, you stuck a knife into somebody before disemboweling them. That's how you and I ended up here in this cell. Does any of this ring a bell?"

"What are you blabberin' on about?"

"Shawn, please pay attention uno memento. You," Christian emphasized while pointing to Shawn, "stabbed a guy," he continued while pointing to his abdomen, "in the stomach with a knife."

While finally looking up at Christian, Shawn shrugged. "So?"

287

"Wha…? So? He could be dead." Christian couldn't believe his brother's nonchalant reaction to this.

"Yeah. So what?"

"Are you kidding me? Dude, do you realize what this may mean? You could spend the rest of your life in jail. Don't you even care?"

Shawn shook his head. "No."

"No?"

"That's what I said, wasn't it?"

"What do you mean you don't care?"

"I don't give a flyin' rat's ass. I don't give a good goddamn rat's ass! I don't fuckin' care! Alright?! Now, get of my fuckin' ass! I've got a piss-ass headache at the moment and the last thing I need is some goody two shoes up my ass about something I don't even remember," Shawn hotly told him before putting his face back into his hands.

"You don't give a rat's ass, you say," Christian muttered while quieting down before shrugging his shoulders. "How can you not give a rat's ass? I'll tell you something right now. You better care what happens to you because what you do reflects not only on you, but also on me as well. And I don't want that kind of reputation."

Shawn raised his head to look him in the eye. "So, that's what this is about, isn't it? Your rep?! What people will think of you? Who fuckin' cares what people think?! Haven't you figured that out by now? Fuck everyone else! You can't depend on anyone for anything, let alone to save your ass, your life, or your goddamn reputation. That's what I've been saying for years now, dude! And if you haven't figured that out by now, then you can go fuck yourself, you fuckin' prick!"

"What did you say to me?" Christian asked while standing up.

"You fuckin' heard me, you pretty-boy Floyd," Shawn told him while meeting his gaze. "If you haven't figured it out by now that I don't give a damn what people think, then by all means, go crawl back to your mommy to suckle her titties 'cuz I have no further use for narrow minded vedge-heads such as yourself. Now, if you don't mind, I'm goin' back to sleep."

With that, Shawn put his hands back into his hands. He soon started snoring slightly. While finally resigning that Shawn wasn't in the mood to talk, Christian went back to his corner, sat down, and leaned against the wall behind him. He honestly couldn't think of a response to what he was just told, mostly due to the shock from it all.

Several hours later, the door opened to the police station and the familiar sound of a person coming in was heard over the snores of the dozing deputy. The person, who was out of view to both Christian and Shawn, walked with a familiar shuffle over to the deputy before standing

288

there in silence. Waiting to be acknowledged longer than he cared for, he cleared his throat after several moments that finally roused the snoring officer on duty.

Christian noticed that the deputy took a piece of paper from the stranger before him to look at it while muttering something to the visitor before finally getting up. He walked over to the cell they were in while unhooking the loop of keys on his belt loop. The stranger followed in close behind to reveal it was an exhausted com.

While the two men approached, the deputy let his keys clang onto the cell Christian and Shawn were housed in. The noise scared Shawn awake from a dead sleep.

"Rise and shine, ladies. You two have been bailed out."

"It's 'bout fuckin' time," Shawn said while standing and rubbing his eyes. "Who bailed us out?"

"I did," Dom informed him while walking up next to the officer.

While the deputy put the key in the lock to open the door, Dom stopped him. "Officer, before ya let them out, may I have a moment alone with 'em?"

The deputy merely shrugged while going back to his desk. He was vaguely heard saying "Let me know when you're done" as he walked away.

While waiting for him to leave, Dom soon turned to face his pupils in the cell before him. Christian noticed that even though the old man's eyes were heavily laden with sleep, there laid an underlining anger under them which he feared would show itself fairly soon.

"What the hell have ya two done now?!" Dom asked them. Instead of looking at both Christian and Shawn, the old man's eyes were locked only at Shawn.

"Yo, can you keep it down, man? The headache I have is a killer," Shawn grumbled through squinting eyes. While rubbing his temples he stumbled on over to the cell door. "Mind if we talk about this later? I wanna sleep off his hang over at home in bed instead of this shithole."

"This shithole is the bed that ya made, Shawn, so ya'd better get used ta the idea of sleepin' in it," Dom told him.

"What the hell is your problem, old man?!" Shawn asked defensively.

"What's my problem? What's my problem?!" Dom asked, slightly confused by the question, while making eye contact with the troubled young man before him. "My problem is bein' woken up ta come down here ta bail your ass out. Not only that, but I also have to bail Christian out, most likely as a result of ya I suspect."

"Hang on a sec, Dom!" Shawn said as his anger rose. "If he didn't want to be here, he should of thought about that before. It's not my fault he's here!"

"What'd'ya mean it's not your fault?" Dom demanded. "He went ta that damn bar ta take your drunken ass home and, next thing we know, both of ya are in jail."

"Like I said before, old man, it's not my fault!" yelled Shawn while walking over to the man before him while glaring down at him in the eye while puffing himself up.

"What the hell ya doin'?" Dom asked while glaring back. "Ya tryin' to intimidate me?"

"I don't need to try."

"You're so full of yourself it's comin' out your ears."

"What's that supposed to mean?"

"It means ya're so selfish and so concerned with yerself that ya can't see anythin' past yer own ego," Dom told him. "If ya didn't get stupid, neither ya nor Christian would be here. On top of that, I wouldn't be here fer that matter."

"Stupid? I ain't stupid, little man. I have more smarts than you could ever have," Shawn retorted angrily.

"Is that a fact?"

"Yeah, that's a fact."

"But I'm not the one in jail, now am I?" commented Dom while lowering his head while trying to comprehend what he was just told. "That makes sense now, all of it. If ya really are smarter than me, then ya had all of this planned out, didn't'cha?"

"All of what?"

"All of this," Dom said while looking around. "Getting drunk at Mike's, again. Knowing Christian would come down ta help ya home, again. While he was there, ya'd start another fight, again. Christian would have no choice but get involved in the fight ya started since he was there with ya. He couldn't very well ignore it, could he? Then, once Christian was able ta get ya outside, back on the way home, ya knew those idiots would try somthin'. Ya also planned on stabbin' that guy. This would lead ta ya and Christian's arrest, as well as me comin' down ta bail ya out. Planned all of this, didn't'cha? All of this was some elaborate plan that only ya can comprehend. Isn't that right?"

Shawn simply stood there in silence looking at him. Meanwhile, Christian wasn't sure if Shawn was biding his time before speaking of if he really didn't know what to say.

"If this was all some sort of an elaborate plan, than ya'd'a known that I was here just ta bail him out, not ya," Dom said as a soft grin came over his face.

"You wouldn't do that," Shawn softly said. "You haven't got it in ya."

"How the hell do ya know what I have in me, huh?!" the old spitfire asked. "Ya're so worried about ya and yer next title fight that ya don't know or care 'bout anythin' else. I outta leave ya in here until yer court date just ta knock yer egotistical ass down a peg or two!"

The silence between them was heavy as they sized each other up. Christian didn't think Dom would leave Shawn here if he could help it, but would do it to prove a point. It was ultimately up to Shawn if he wanted to get out.

"What's it gonna be, Shawn?" Dom asked while stuffing his old hands deep into his pockets. "Ya leavin' with your brother? Or are ya goin' ta spend the next few nights here, alone?"

"You wouldn't do it."

"Don't temp me. But, on the bright side, if I did leave ya here, ya might become real friendly with some trucker or whoever gets tossed in here, if ya get my drift." Dom grinned while looking up at Shawn before turning to Christian. "Alright, kid, looks like it'll just be ya and me leavin' here tonight. Officer," he called out to the deputy. "Will ya let him out, please?"

The deputy grunted while getting up, slightly irritated that he had to leave the TV show he was watching, but didn't say a thing.

Christian, meanwhile, nodded at the prospect of leaving while getting up before walking to the jail cell's door. While looking at Shawn, he said, "I guess I'll see you when you get out. Shouldn't be more than four or five days; just until your court date."

As the deputy was putting his key in the door to unlock it, that was when Shawn finally asked to be let out. Dom immediately asked the officer to stop before looking at Shawn.

"Before yer buddy here let's ya out, there's two things I need ta get off my chest." Dom softly cleared his throat. "First, if ya ever do anythin' stupid like this again, ya're on yer own. Ya won't be gettin' any more help from me. I'm too old and too sick of yer antics. Do it again and ya'll need ta find yourself a new gym to train at, a new person to train ya, and a new manager as well. Ya hear me?"

"Yeah, I hear ya," Shawn said slowly. "And what's the second thing?"

"I just wanted to tell ya two ta your face that I wished I was there when ya knocked those bums heads off," Dom said with a nod and a smile, coming of much more calm than expected. This revealed a softer side he rarely shown. "From what I heard, they had it comin'. Ya two did one helluva job and ya've had help backin' ya up, too. That's good. Havin' friends behind ya ta do that in a time like that's important."

Christian smiled and laughed softly while Shawn stood there a while longer looking down at the old man before frowning and shaking it off.

At that point, Dom motioned to the deputy to finally let the two out. A few minutes later, the three of them were walking out the front door before getting into Dom's car. They rode home in silence. Within an hour after that, Christian and Shawn each fell asleep in their own beds while wrapped blanketed in sounds and smells that the night had to offer.

Chapter 31

Early one morning a week after their jail experience, Shawn woke to the commotion to various noises coming from the gym below. Normally, Shawn wouldn't have thought that much about it, but when he looked at the time and discovered that it was just before seven in the morning, he got up to investigate. Since it was hours before the gym would actually be open, he was confused that people would actually be there without him knowing it.

Walking through his cluttered apartment, he pulled on a shirt before walking down the stairs. At the bottom of the stairs, shattered glass lay. While taking a closer look, Shawn noticed that both sets of doors, the one going out to the street and the one leading into the gym, each had been broke before each were forced open.

From inside the gym, noises of some sort were heard of a fight that seemed to involve multiple people. From the midst of it all, Dom's voice resonated over the rest.

"C'mon, ya bastards! Come and get me!" he yelled while the sounds of punches were heard, many finding their mark, which were soon followed by a number of moans and groans. "If ya came lookin' fer trouble, that's what ya found, ya bastards!"

"Watch out, Jonesy," one guy in the gym said to another. "This old timer is one tough old nut."

"I see that, Jimmie," Jonesy said before being hit again by Dom. He then seemed to gasp a little bit before releasing a yelp of pain. "Ow! That hurt, old man!"

"Yo, Jonesy, look at all that blood! I think he might'a broken your nose," Jimmie informed him before he himself began getting attacked by Dom. "C'mon, man. Take it easy. We don't wanna hurt ya."

"The three of ya break into my gym, attempt to vandalize it, then make this a three-on-one, and ya bastards don't wanna hurt me?!" Dom asked.

"Hang on guys, I got 'im," the third guy said just as Shawn entered the gym. The man came up behind Dom with a small dumbbell in hand before hitting him on the back of the head.

Dom immediately let out a groan before collapsing onto the floor unconscious.

"Dom!" Shawn yelled in a panic state, which immediately drew the attention of the three intruders.

"Hey, you said no one else would be here!" Jimmie exclaimed to the third guy, who was looking at a raging Shawn through terrified eyes.

Within a matter of seconds, Shawn went from the door to there the three young terrors were before opening a can of whoop ass on them. Shawn grabbed the first guy he came to, who was Jimmie, before pounding him with a few well-placed punches and pushing him hard against a weight machine. He soon moved onto the guy who had taken out Dom.

"Come here, you son-of-a-bitch!" Shawn demanded when he was within arm's length of the intruder. "Why don't you pick on somebody who can actually fight back?!"

The guy tried to run but, by then, it was too late. Shawn was on him like flies on crap as he threw him down on the floor before proceeding to beat the man within an inch of his life. At that point, Jonesy saw his chance to get away and didn't wait for another opening. He was gone in a blink of an eye.

When Shawn was finally able to let out his emotions and looked down at the guy's bloodied face, he was surprised at how good it felt. How good it was to finally release all of his anger, fear, and hatred, and to be able to beat a person's face in without care or compassion. What he did to them felt like a great burden had just been lifted from his chest. He felt like he had finally been released and was able to do whatever he had wanted. Shawn more of less wanted to kill the guy that had hurt Dom and would have if he didn't hear his elderly mentor groan slightly on the floor. Immediately stopping this assault on the man pinned beneath him, Shawn quickly went to his injured trainer.

"Dad! Dad, are you alright?" Shawn fearfully asked while shaking the old man in an attempt to wake him up. Shaking Dom, he found himself eight years old again after witnessing his father being attached by three younger men. "Hey, Dad! Dad, c'mon, Dad, talk to me."

"Huh, what?" Dom asked while moaning in a semiconscious state.

"Dad, I mean, Dom, try and stay awake. Try and stay awake, Dom," Shawn begged as tears filled his eyes before running down his cheeks.

To no avail, Dom slipped back into an unconscious state as Shawn go up to run to call for help.

***

Several hours later, Christian came into Dom's hospital room after hearing what had happened. He saw his brother sitting by the window as he somberly looked out it while ignoring all around him. Dom, meanwhile, was wide awake and throwing demands around like there was no tomorrow. The nurse, who was looking over him, told him that he should remain calm and still and would be released in the morning if all went well.

"I can be calm and still at home," Dom complained. "I don't know why I haf'ta stay here any longer than I have ta."

"Mr. Calavicci, you did receive a concussion and the doctor just wanted you to stay here for a bit longer for observation," the nurse informed him as politely as she could. "We just want to make sure you'll be alright before we send you home."

"I've had worse injuries than this in my day and I never went to the doctor, or hospital for that matter," he continued to grumble while giving her an irritated look. "So don't be blowing smoke up my ass with your medical jargon. Ya hear me? The next time ya come back ya'd better have my release form, signed and dated!" He shook a fist her as she left. "Ya hear me?! Signed and dated!"

"Dom, come on. You should be a little nicer to her and not be so hard on them," Christian chastised while looking at Dom's chart hanging at the foot of his bed. "They're here to help you. We all want to make sure you're going to be ok before you do get released."

"I'm fine. Why can't anyone see that, huh?" the elderly bedridden man demanded while waving his hands at the door. "Besides, all their job is is just guess work in a lab coat. That's it. I don't know why I had to come here in the first place."

"You came here because you got jumped by three guys, got wrapped upside your head with a dumbbell, got knocked unconscious, and got a concussion," Christian told him. "That's why they're here."

"I just don't know why I just couldn't have been taken home instead."

"Dom, Shawn was worried about you. You were hit pretty good and were going in and out of consciousness," Christian reminded him. "I would have done the same exact thing as he did if I was there. Besides, if he didn't do anything and you became worse than you are now, you would've been upset that he didn't do anything."

"I know, kid, I know. I'm sorry. I don't wanna be here, that's all I'm saying," Dom told him before pausing briefly as something came to his mind. "Besides, have ya ever had hospital food? That alone would kill ya."

Christian laughed. "It's probably better than that canned chili you eat all the time."

"And probably won't cause all those nasty smelling farts you normally have," Shawn commented from his corner chair.

Dom coughed as the three of them exchanged friendly looks with each other. Shawn soon got quiet again before looking back out the window. He sat there with a sullen look before anyone broke the silence.

"Hey Shawn, you alright?" Christian asked while going to him. "How are you doing from this?"

Continuing to look out the window in silence, Shawn didn't reply.

While posing the question differently, Christian soon asked, "What's going on inside that head of yours?"

Again, Shawn ignored the question while still staring out the window.

"Alright," was all Christian could say before turning away to sit in a chair at the foot of Dom's bed.

"He's been like that ever since I got my room, kid," Dom told him with a fair amount of tenderness that surprised even Christian. "Ya should'a seen 'im earlier, kid. He was givin' the staff hell about the so-called 'lack of attention' they was givin' me."

"I just wanted to make sure you were alright, Dom," Shawn quietly stated from his corner while looking over to them. "I'd appreciate if you didn't make fun of me because of it."

"Shawn, that's sweet." Christian smiled. "That sounds like you actually care about someone else, and Dom nonetheless. Who would have thought?"

Shawn shot him a disapproving glance. "I'm so glad you find this funny, bro. I really was scared back there this morning."

"Scared of what?"

"What do you mean of what? Of Dom being hurt, you ass!" Shawn glared at his brother who appeared to have a look of both surprise and disbelief on his face. "That's right, you heard me. I was scared! I thought Dom got hurt worse than he did. I thought he was going to die, possibly there in my arms. I couldn't help but think back when I was a kid, a time I was with my old man. Mom sent me out to try and find him, to try and bring him home, again. He was at his usual spot. I found him hunched over a bottle at a local bar.

"On the way home, he made a comment or two to a bunch of niggers and, in return, they beat the shit outta him. It was something like four-on-one. He didn't stand a fuckin' chance. He was lucky they didn't kill him. That then made me think of Daryl and how he was killed. When I saw those punks attacking Dom, and then when I held him in my arms while waiting for help to come, I couldn't help but think he was going to die before they got there. I lost my dad, Daryl, even Grandpa Joe. And then I was going to lose Dom. So, if you're going to make fun of me, you'd better get your facts straight before you do."

"Oh, geez, I'm sorry Shawn," Christian immediately said while regretting teasing him on the subject. "I didn't realize it was bothering you this much.

He looked at Shawn and considered what types of emotions and concerns he was showing was odd, even for him. Unfortunate for all of them, Christian never even thought that Shawn would actually express these thoughts or feelings, much less think them. As a result, he started feeling ashamed of himself to consider that Shawn was as cold and selfish as his outer shell suggested.

"I guess you don't know me as well as you thought you did, bro," Shawn told him before looking back out the window.

"No, it's not that. It's just I never knew you to be like this."

"Be like what?" asked Shawn hotly while looking back at him.

"Like anything bothered you."

"I guess you haven't been paying that much attention after all these years."

"Well, I guess I do have a hard time reading you," Christian admitted. "The only think I thought really bothered you was how soon you'd have your next title shot."

"What about the time I stuck up for you when Wesley and his little rat pack were comin' after you?" Shawn defensively asked while looking sharply again at him.

"What?" Christian answered in bewilderment. "You mean back when we were like 9?"

"But you remember." Shawn pointed at him. "So you can't say you don't know me not to care about anythin' and you'd better not forget it!"

"So, what're you saying? That things concern you other than getting another title? It's ok to admit it."

Shooting him a quizzical look, Shawn asked, "What the hell that mean?"

"It means exactly what it said it means." Christian shrugged. "Ever since I've known you, everything seemed to revolve, and evolve, around you. You've always seemed to be about yourself."

Shawn's temper rose and nostrils flared with that. He was a little surprised and taken back by the fact that he, his own brother, had said that to him. "How dare you say that to me! Don't you know who I am or what I've done for you all these years?"

"What the hell are you talking about, Shawn?" Christian asked completely taken by surprise by the accusation.

By the look on his brother's face, Shawn knew that Christian didn't have a clue as to what he had heard. Shawn also knew his brother had more insults directed for him.

"You come off as probably the most self-centered, selfish, and egotistical person I have ever known and to even think for a second that you care about what happened to Dom is laughable. You most likely care only because you still think he can get you more world championships. And, according to you, if Dom was out of the picture, you'd be have more world titles than you do already, if not all of them. Am I right or am I right?"

"You're wrong!" Shawn said with iron in his voice while standing, squaring himself, before glaring at his brother. "As smart as you are, don't pretend to think you know how I feel! You've known me almost my entire fuckin' life and that's the best psychoanalyst you can come up with? Just because you watch Oprah and Dr. Phil every fuckin' day doesn't make you an expert on humans or their emotions. Did I care that day when I was walkin' and saw a slightly porky geek gettin' harassed by the town bullies? Did I care when the voting committee saw fit to ridicule you when your rocket ship blew up when you were eleven? Or how 'bout when in gym class in tenth grade when you got kicked in the nuts by Tommy Callaghan and you pissed your pants? Who was it that got you to your locker, calmed you down, and then put Tommy right in the hospital for overnight observation? Do you know what it's like to be charged with manslaughter? Ooohh, that's right, you don't, do you? Well, I wonder why? Uh, nope, I take that back. I do know why. I killed a guy that's been pickin on you you're entire life. And now I could be facing 15-25. Why? Because I put someone else's needs ahead of mine!"

"Wha...what are you talking about?" Christian asked in dismay. "Those charges got virtually dropped. You just have to do community service for, what?, a five hundred hours or something to pacify the judge and you're in the clear."

"Yeah, I know, on grounds of self-defense. I was charged nonetheless, wasn't I?" Shawn asked while pointing to him. "And you got off without anything tarnishin' your squeaky clean record. But you know what? No more! From now on, all you so-called family that says they care about me can kiss my ass! Shawn Calloway's no longer doin' anymore favors for anybody. From now, you're on your damn own!"

"S-S-Shawn, I'm s-s-sorry," stuttered Christian. "I d-d-didn't know you felt like tha-"

"Save it, Chris," Shawn cut him off while stretching out an open hand. "Save it for somebody who gives a fuck because I don't. Not no more!"

With that, Shawn stormed out of the room.

"Shawn!" Christian called out while started to follow him.

"Let him go, kid, let him go," Dom told him.

Stopping in the hall to watch his brother leave, Christian soon let out a sigh of disappointment. He reentered Dom's room with a hung head.

"So, Dom, how are you really?" he asked while sitting down next to him. Christian honestly found himself at a loss for words and this was really the only thing he could think of to say.

Dom looked thoughtfully at his young pupil before replying. "I'm alright, kid. I'll live so ya don't have ta worry about my old ass."

Christian scoffed at that in jest. "Who says I was going to worry? I gave that up a long time ago." They both laughed over that before Christian got serious. "What happened this morning, Dom?"

The old man merely shrugged. "Ah, a couple of punks broke in and tried to vandalize the gym. That's all, kid."

"Do you know who they where?"

He shook his head. "Nah, but they've been in a couple of times before tryin' ta get me ta train 'em."

"Where you able to get their names?"

"Just their first names. I told the police when they were here earlier."

"Do you think they broke in to do whatever they planned to do because you wouldn't take them?"

Dom scowled while shooting Christian a mean, annoyed look. "Of course I do! I told ya. They're punks! I expected as much."

"How much damage did they do?"

"Not much. I came from out back soon after they started. Outside of the front doors, they used some dumbbells to break a few mirrors; they spray painted a few things on the walls; and tore open one of the heavy bags. A couple of the guys from the gym came in early and said they'd clean up the mess," Dom told him before going quiet. His eyes went distant while thinking about something. "Funny thing about the whole thing, kid, was what happened after I got my bell rung. As I lay there, for a moment, it felt like my son was there lookin' over me, protectin' me really."

Hearing this shocked Christian, almost flooring him. "You have a son? I didn't know you had any family."

"I don't anymore, kid, but for a moment it felt like he came back, like a guardian angel to help out his old man one last time."

"If you don't mind me asking, what happened to him, your son?"

"Steve, my son, was…taken from me many years ago. Along with his wife, Mary, and their daughter, Angela." Dom's voice was soft, barely audible, just above a whisper. He turned towards the window as his eyes narrowed. "A couple of kids were drunk, out celebrating one of their birthdays. They were out joyridin' before runnin' a red light. My son and his family were unfortunate enough to be going' through that same light when they did."

"I'm so sorry, Dom. I honestly didn't know." Christian sat there in silence, shaken by what he just heard.

"How would ya know, kid? It's been years since I spoke of it," Dom said without breaking his gaze from the window. "They were only a mile or two from home when it happened. They were returning home from havin' dinner with me." When he was saying this, he was getting choked up as he wiped tears from his eyes. This was not only the first time that Christian had ever heard this story, but it was also the first time he'd seen Dom cry. "What makes things hard for me is the fact that I delayed them at my place by showin' them a few things my fighters had won. If I didn't do that, they most likely would have made it home."

"That wasn't your fault, Dom. You couldn't have known what was going to happen."

"I know, kid, but just the thought of it, that it was me, is somethin' that won't ever leave me. Probably never will."

"Maybe his coming and being there with you is probably his way of saying it's not your time to go yet," Christian told him with a smile. "That it wasn't your fault, that he doesn't blame you, and that they'll see you when you do decide to roll over and croak."

All Dom could do then was turn to face him. A smile formed on his face while some trace amount of sadness still lingered in his eyes. "Yeah, I thought of that."

"So, what happened? When he was with you?"

"I was on the floor, goin' in and out, and I felt his presence there, guardin' me. He was talkin' to me, saying 'C'mon Dad, talk to me. Try and stay awake, Dad.' Before I passed out that last time, I tried to look up to see him, my son. Apparently that was when Shawn got there because he was the only one I saw. My son had stayed there long enough until Shawn answered."

Upon hearing that, Christian had a funny feeling that it was, in fact, Shawn who Dom mistook for his guarding angel, not his son, but wasn't about to reveal any of this to him. He soon changed the topic to professional matters, matters that would be affecting both of them in about a week or so.

"Since you're here now, what about my title shot next week?"

"Huh? What title shot?" Dom focused his eyes onto Christian as a perplexed look crossed his face.

"Next week I'm putting my WBO and IBF titles on the line against the WBC champ; belts for belt match. How am I supposed to win that without you in my corner?" he asked in a joyful manner while swatting the old man's foot.

"I forgot about that," Dom admitted. "Don't worry 'bout that, kid. I'll be outta here tomorrow, day after at the latest. You're prepared enough now to win it. All we need to do is fine tune some things beforehand. Hell, kid, we can do that the day of the fight. We'll talk 'bout it then."

"Sure, Dom. Anything you say."

At this point, Dom coughed before changing the subject. "So, kid, how's that lady friend of yours doin'?"

"Oh, Miho? She's doing fine."

"When ya two gettin' married?"

"We, um, haven't actually discussed that yet," Christian said in an awkward and embarrassed manner.

"Why the hell not?"

"We aren't ready yet."

"What the hell ya two kids waitin' on?"

"Well, for starters, she wants to finish college and get a job that's to her liking," Christian told him. "As for me, I don't know. I guess I'm just waiting for her to get in position for me to ask her."

"If ya leave it up to her, ya'll have a long wait, kid."

"Why's that, Dom?"

"'cause she's a woman, that's why! There's no tellin' what they're thinkin' or what they'll do. They change their mind on a whim." The feisty patient waved a gnarled hand in front of him. "If ya see a chance to marry her, take it. Ya hear me?!"

Christian smiled while rolling his eyes. "Yes Dom, I hear you. Loud and clear."

Dom scowled. "Don't patronize me, ya snivelin' punk! I'm bein' serious here. I'm lookin' out fer what's best for ya. Ya won't have boxin' the rest of yer life, but ya sure as hell can have her! I don't wanna haf'ta kick yer ass for makin' a stupid mistake by losin' a girl like her."

"So you like her?"

"What the hell ya think? I'm not tellin' ya any of this for my health. What's brother think 'bout her?"

Shrugging, Christian folded his arms while leaning back in his chair. "Who knows what he thinks? We don't talk much about her when we're together. He'd rather talk and brag about his cheap one-night stands. I've given up trying to add her into one of our conversations. I may be jumping out on a limb here, but I get the feeling he may be against the whole idea of me seeing her."

"He doesn't like her, kid?"

"I don't think it's that, but I do think it's the idea that I'm not seeing someone that's white or American. Not that he has problems with people of other colors, that's not what I'm saying. But to be actually dating someone of another color or from another country, he may not agree with that. But don't quote me on that. He's never actually said or did anything that would prove what I just said. If you could, would you not mention any of this to him? I don't want him to know I feel this way about him."

"Don't worry, kid." Dom smiled with a wink. "Your secret's safe with me."

Christian returned the smile. He stayed for about another hour or so before leaving. He had some things to do later on, including going to the bowling alley to see The Misfits.

Chapter 32

"...and Shawn walks in right when the third guy smacks Dom upside the head with one of the dumbbells," Christian said while telling the story of how Dom got hurt to The Misfits later that night at the bowling alley.

"What happened?" Larry asked while walking over to his ball. But, before Christian could respond, he rolled it towards the pins for a strike and walked back to the group.

"Shawn went nuts and beat the crap out of them. They high-tailed it out of there before he could do anything else to them."

"How's the old man doing?" Eric asked after he stopped kissing his lady friend long enough to ask his question and have some beer.

"Dom's fine." Christian chuckled. "He's staying the night up at the hospital and should be released a day or two."

"Is he alright, though?" Miggie asked after coming back from throwing his own strike, to now allow Eric his chance to perform.

"Yeah, he's fine. He's got a concussion from the blow, but other than that he's fine. When I went to see him today, he was his usual grumpy self. I think it'll take a lot more than that to actually hurt him physically."

"That's great to hear," Larry stated while waiting for his turn. "We're glad to hear he's doing fine. Oh, incidentally, Hollywood, you wanna bowl a turn?"

Christian shook his head while waving it off. "Nah, go ahead."

"You can bowl my turn if you want." Larry shrugged while pointing to his bowling ball.

"I'm not that good anyway. I wouldn't want to hurt your score by knocking down only like three," Christian politely refused.

"I don't know how it would hurt us," Larry told him while looking up at the score boards. "We're up by like forty and worst thing we had was a spare. At worse, we'll place second."

"Thanks, Larry, I'd feel bad if the reason you guys ended up second was because of me."

"Your loss," Larry said with a shrug before throwing a strike of his own. On his way back to his seat, he poked Christian on the shoulder. "By the way, how many times do I have to tell you that my name's Catfish here during league nights?"

"Oh, that's right. I don't know what came over me."

"That's alright, Hollywood. We forgive you, right guys?" Catfish asked, to which Miggie, Eric, and Eric's unnamed lady friend all said yes in their various ways. While looking back to Christian, Larry said with a smile, "Just make you sure you don't do it again."

"Oh, by the way, where's Roger?" Christian asked once he noticed that were there only three of them there bowling.

"He's no longer part of The Misfits."

"Really? Why?"

"His heart wasn't into it," Miggie told him after walking back from a spare.

"And he bowled like how old people fuck," Eric said while getting up to get his bowl. His comment drew a curious look from Christian before explaining it. "Slow and sloppy."

"We're all wondering how he knows that, but he has yet to tell us," Catfish said while drawing laughs or smiles from the other members of the group, but a scowl from Eric himself.

"Hey, what can I say," Eric eventually stated after a moment or so. "When you got it, you got it."

"So, thy hammer's still swinging quite well with you, Cramselot?" Christian asked with a smile.

"It's swinging quite well, Jizmo. And if you don't believe me, just ask Michelle here," he playfully said while kissing his now named companion on the neck.

"Eric, you shouldn't talk about that in public," she chastised playfully with an embarrassed laugh and blushed face.

"See? What I tell ya bitches?" Eric asked with a cocky smile and hearty laugh while looking around to the other three in the group who all either shook their heads or laughed.

"Hey, Miggie, how's your rapping coming?" Christian asked when Mig came back from his turn at bowling.

"It's going good, Slim Fast!" He nodded before drinking the rest of what little water he had in his cup. "I just finished a demo today as a matter of fact."

"That's great! How many song's it have?"

"This one about thirteen or so."

"That's right," Catfish interrupted as his eyes widened while pointing to Christian. "Miggie Smalls here is a celebrity. He had one of his songs playing on the radio."

"Congrats, Mig," Christian said while drawing an embarrassed look from the group's rapper. "What song was it?"

"The song was *My Sweet Home* but they haven't actually picked it up yet. I have a friend who's a DJ a night or two a week at a local station. He plays it there when he can to help me out," the rapper said. "He's been doing it for about a month now."

"That's great. Good for you, Miggie."

"Thanks, Slim Fast. I really do appreciate that."

Eric finished his beer. "If you appreciate it, maybe you could tell me why you call him that."

"Someone told me he used to drink that shit back in high school." Miggie shrugged. "I guess the name stuck."

"I think it was me who told you that," Larry admitted.

"That's funny." Christian laughed. "I haven't had Slim Fast since leaving high school, if you can believe that. But I can't believe something like that came up, Catfish, without a little help."

"No, I don't believe it would, Hollywood. And I do believe you are correct that it wouldn't without some help." Larry smiled.

Before they got any further in their conversation, Christian noticed a staggering Shawn emerging from the crowd while stumbling his way on over to them.

"Hi ya, fellas," Shawn said while slurring his words together. He almost missed his step that led down to them, but thanks for the accompanying railing and a little help from Christian, he quickly regained his balance before quickly getting in the way. "Ladies, the party can now begin! God almighty has finally arrived."

"Shawn, are you drunk again?" inquired Christian though the answer was obvious.

"Of course I am, Cheesedick. You've seen me drunk enough times to not even have to ask," Shawn told him as his eyes tried to focus on the five people in front of him before seeing Michelle for the first time. "Aren't any of you Neanderthals going to introduce me to this lovely young lady?"

"Shawn, this is my friend Michelle," Eric introduced them. "Michelle, this is Christian's brother."

"Nice to meet you," she politely said but, by her reaction, she didn't entirely mean it.

"That's what they all tell me," Shawn cockily told her while trying to strut and show off but soon stopped to keep from falling over.

"Sorry? Who tells you what?" Michelle asked while looking briefly to Eric who also didn't know what Shawn was talking about.

"That's what all the lady's say when they meet me, that it's nice to meet me." Shawn swaggered closer to her. As he did get closer, the stench of alcohol flowed off of him. He soon pointed to Eric while asking, "So, Baby Girl, this your husband?"

"No."

"Boyfriend?"

"Why do you want to know?"

"Whatever he is to you, he sure as hell not half the man I am," Shawn told her.

"He's man enough for me."

"Yeah, sure he is." Shawn laughed. "Why don't you stop by my place later so I can show you what a *real* man is."

"Come on, Shawn. That's enough," Christian told him as they exchanged looks with each other.

"What do ya mean, bro?" Shawn slurred his words when he asked that while trying to focus his eyes. "I've only just begun."

"You're drunk and in the middle of a bowling alley."

"Bowling? What the fuck are ya talkin' 'bout?!" he confusingly asked before looking around the alley. For the first time, he seemed to see and hear the people surrounding them. A number of other people not involved in their group were looking and pointing to Shawn as they wondered what he was doing. "And where the fuck did all these goddamn weirdoes come from?"

"Shawn, it's Thursday. Bowling league night. Don't you remember?" asked Christian while walking over to him. They're in the middle of one of their meets."

"Are you sayin' I can't be here?" Shawn asked him. "Is that what you're sayin'?"

"No, Shawn, I'm not saying that at all."

"Then what are you sayin', bro?"

"What I'm saying is if we want to be here, then we shouldn't be in their way."

With that, Shawn and Christian stood looking at each other in silence. The silence between them made Christian uncomfortable because he wasn't sure what Shawn would try to do. Most likely he wouldn't do anything, but given he was currently drunk, he couldn't be too sure.

Meanwhile, Larry and Miggie each were able to get up for their turn bowling. When it came to Eric's turn, Shawn took this as a chance to fill the void the bowler had left next to Michelle. Upon doing so, inappropriate and attempted come-ons followed suit.

After taking his turn bowling, Eric finally saw Michelle trying to get Shawn's hands and lips off of her. He immediately went over to give her a pair of helping hands

"Hey man, but what the hell do you think you're doing?" he demanded before picking Shawn up off of the seat and pushing him away.

Michelle and Miggie just sat where they were while watching the scene before them unfold. Larry, meanwhile, shrugged it off momentarily so he could bowl. Christian, on the other hand, positioned himself in a way where he could keep Shawn at bay in case if anything did happen.

While finally regaining his balance and adjusting his clothes, Shawn staggered over to Eric. "Bro, you just made the worse mistake of your life by puttin' your hands on me," he said while slurring his words. "Don't you know who I am, boy? Don't you know what a person like me could do to a person like you? I'd fuck you up without even tryin'."

"And that gives you the right to be all over my girl?!" Eric demanded while spreading his arms out and glaring at the drunken boxer before him. "Why don't you go home and sober up, man?"

A number of people by now who weren't watching before had stopped to watch the scene before them unfold.

Christian did his best to step in front of his brother to try and talk some sense into him. "Shawn, come on, man. It's late. We'd better get going."

"I don't know where we're goin' to go but I was gonna go over and teach this asshole a thing or two about who I am. Put some respect in him," Shawn stated while attempting to move around a resisting Christian. "Maybe even put the fear of God in him."

"Remember Shawn, we've got to pick Dom up tomorrow from the hospital. We also have to get ready for my title shot next week," Christian reminded him. "If we got in trouble with Eric or his girl tonight, how are we going to do either? Don't you think that you, Shawn Calloway, could do better than these two? What do you say?"

"What I say is fuck Dom! He's better off in that hospital. He's been hurting my career more than he's been helpin' it. And now you want me to help him? And now that you mention it, I'm better than these two. And as for your title shot," Shawn said with disbelief while making eye contact and fingering himself in his chest, "What 'bout my title shot?! What about me? Where's mine?!"

"What title shot?"

"Exactly! I don't have any!" Shawn's slurred words had an acidic tone to them as his body staggered. "Duke said if I enlisted him to help me, he'd get me a major world title shot within six months, tops!"

"Duke?" Christian looked at him behind confused eyes before realizing what his brother was talking about. "Don't tell me you were talking to him."

"I called him today. I found one of his cards in my shirt pocket."

Before anything else was said or done, the alley's manager on duty came over with a uniformed police officer to inquire what was going on.

"My brother and I were just leaving," Christian told them.

"Like hell I am!" Shawn protested. "I'm stayin' right where I am. Besides, this lovely lady and me weren't quite done yet."

"Mr. Calloway, I'm going to have to ask you to leave with me," informed the officer him.

"How do you know my name?"

"We've all seen you around enough to know your name," the officer told him. "Come on, let's go. If you leave on your own accord in the next twenty seconds, it'll save us all a lot of grief."

"And if I don't?" Shawn glared at the officer.

"Then I'll be forced to help you outside so I can place you under arrest."

"On what grounds?"

"For starters, drunken disorderly and trespassing," answered the officer while walking over to stand next to Shawn ad Christian. "And possibly even harassment if this young lady chooses to press charges."

"And if I do leave like you want?"

"You don't get arrested and you can go anywhere you want."

"Anywhere I want?" Shawn asked him.

"Anywhere within reason. Anywhere but here." The cop, who obviously was sick of playing games with Shawn, looked down at his watch. "Time's up, Mr. Calloway. Are you leaving by yourself or am I will I be helping you?"

"Alright, friend." Shawn smiled as both of his hands came up to face level and waved. "No need to get pushy. I was only funnin'. I was just about to leave when you showed up."

"I'll walk you out just to make sure." He pointed to the front door before following Shawn and Christian to it.

When they were outside, the officer spoke to Shawn briefly before asking if he needed a ride anywhere. Rudely, Shawn turned him down before abruptly walking off. Alone.

After a few minutes standing just outside the door, Christian watched his brother walk away while wondering what the matter with him was. He soon went back inside to go back to The Misfits, who had already started playing again. He tried to apologize for Shawn's behavior but was quickly interrupted by Eric.

"Hey, Jiz," he said, "it should be Shawn apologizing for what he did, not you. We don't hold you responsible for his actions."

Hearing that really did make Christian feel better and so did when the rest of the group confirm what Eric had just told him. He stayed there until their meet was over and helped *The Misfits* celebrate after another decisive win.

Chapter 33

"Hey, Dom, have you seen Shawn at all?" Christian asked several days later when he entered the gym's office.

Dom, who had been going through some papers and such in one of the office's filing cabinets, turned his head briefly to answer.

"No, I haven't'. Hey, kid, do ya know where Miller's file is?"

"It's in the cabinet to your left." Christian pointed to it. "Top drawer, the one labeled L-Z."

"How long have these been like this?" Dom asked. He signaled the organization of each of the gym's boxers alphabetically in two drawers in that one particular cabinet.

"I don't know; month maybe."

"Really?" Where've I been, kid?" Dom asked while drawing the wanted file.

"I don't know, but you were here when I was doing it."

Dom simply grunted while flipping through Ted Miller's folder before stopping on a piece of paper to read. "Miller was right. He hasn't had a fight in a while. Do you think he's ready for one?"

While thinking for the answer to that, Christian asked, "Which one's Miller? Short, feisty guy with a lot of energy?"

Dom nodded.

"I think he'd do alright in another fight."

"Still needs a bit more confidence if you ask me," muttered Dom.

Christian shrugged. "Try and put him in a fight with someone you know he can beat."

Dom muttered to himself while debating which managers to call, he soon picked up the phone to start dialing numbers. After about ten minutes or so, he hung up with a fight scheduled for Ted.

"So, Dom, the reason I came in here was because I haven't seen Shawn for a couple of days," Christian said. "It doesn't appear that he's been at his apartment and he hasn't returned any of my texts or calls. Do you think he'll be around for my fight in a couple of days?"

"He's been a little tied up the last couple of days, kid," Dom replied in an off-beat manner from behind his desk while sifting through a mob of papers he had on his desk. "I wouldn't really expect him to be in our corner come fight time."

"What makes you say that? He's never missed one of my fights."

"The fact that he's in jail, that's why." Dom looked at his pupil briefly with a scowl before going back to his papers.

"J-j-jail? How long has he been there for?"

"he got himself arrested Thursday night."

"W-w-what for? What'd he do?"

"He beat those hooligans up that broke in here last week."

"He's been in jail since Thursday?"

"That's what I said, ain't it?" Dom shot him a glare.

"Why didn't you tell me?"

"I didn't want ya to go down there and bail him out, that's why."

"Why wouldn't you have wanted me to do that?"

"We've bailed him outta trouble long enough," Dom told him. "It's time fer him to deal with his problems on his own. I told him the last time I bailed him out, when ya was with him, that that was it. I wasn't helpin' him anymore. He's on his own!"

"Yeah, I guess you're right," Christian somberly agreed. "You still should have told me."

"What would ya 'a done if I had?" Dom smiled.

Christian shook his head. "Probably went down to bail him out if I could."

"See? And that's why I didn't tell ya, for that exact reason," Dom hastily responded. "You would'a went down, bailed his ass out, and then where'd we be? Huh? If he's old enough to have a job, vote, drink, smoke, and enlist, then he's old enough to take care of himself. And he can start that by gettin' himself outta trouble." When Dom finished saying his fill, he finally noticed that Christian wasn't wearing any practice gear. "Why ain't ya dressed for practice? Where're ya gloves?"

"I wasn't expecting to practice right now; I came in looking for Shawn. My gear's at home."

"Well, go home and get 'em! Ya still need a lot of work fer yer title match. Ya've been slackin' off lately."

"Slacking off? Have you ever known me to slack off?" Christian asked while feigning insult. "While you were in the hospital, didn't you tell me that I was basically ready?"

"If I did, it was probably the meds they had in me talkin'. I wasn't myself."

"What about Shawn?"

"What 'bout im'? He's a big boy. Now, go and get changed!"

"Sure, alight Dom." Christian turned to leave before stopping to ask him another question. "Who's going to be in my corner with us if not Shawn?"

"I already got someone, if that's ok with ya," Dom said before pointing to the door. "Now get your ass movin'!"

"Yes, sir. Right away, Dom." Christian said while starting to jog out the front door.

Twenty minutes later, he walked into his house to the sound of his phone ringing. When he answered it, an operator informed him that someone was trying to call collect. It was Shawn.

"Yo, Beeker!" Shawn called out from the other end. "It's 'bout time you answered fuckin' phone. Where ya been?!"

"I just walked in. Where've you been?"

"I'm in jail, man! I need ya to get your ass down here to bail mine out!"

"I don't know about that, Shawn."

"What don't you know 'bout it?"

"I'm a little low on money. And, besides, Dom said he didn't want me to bail you out."

"Oh, fuck Dom!" yelled Shawn. "You need to get me outta here!"

"Well, I'm not sure I should. If seems like you've been there more often of late."

"Goddamn it, bro! Dom has you so fuckin' brainwashed that you can't take a piss without his ok," Shawn told him hotly, making Christian pull the phone away slightly.

"Ok, let me ask you this," Christian said when he felt it was safe for him to talk. "Why do you need to get bailed out? Meaning, what did you do to warrant you being placed in a position of being bailed out of jail?"

"That's not the point!"

"So, you got in trouble again and you want me to bail you out?"

"Of all the times I've helped you out, the least you can do is get me outta here."

"That's true, but still. I'm not sure if I should. Dom might get..."

"I don't care what Dom thinks! I'm goin' crazy down here," Shawn stated bluntly with heavy frustration. "I don't belong here! I've already been here a couple of days and my court appearance isn't for another three. If I have'ta spend another day in this god forsaken place, I'm gonna go more crazy than I already am! C'mon, man, help me out!"

"Alright, alright. I'll see what I can do." Christian sighed while looking around his living room before noticing his checkbook on the coffee table. "How much is your bail?"

"Two grand."

"Two grand?!" he gasped while balking at the price before mumbling a little to himself. "Jesus Christ! What the hell'd you do?"

"C'mon, man! You know I'd bail your ass out in a heartbeat if the roles were reversed."

"I know you would, and I'm sorry, but two grand?" Christian shook his head while figuring whether or not he could swing it. When he figured he could, he finally gave in. "Alright, I'll be there. If I do this, just make sure you show up to court, all right? I want my money back!"

"Dude, trust me, will ya?! Why would I fuck ya over like that?"

"And not a word about this to Dom, alright?" Christian told him. "I've got enough to worry about than to listen to him over this."

"No worries there, bro," Shawn told him. "I don't want to listen to his shit, either."

"Alright, hang tight. I'm not promising anything, but I'll see what I can do. Either way, I'll be there as soon as I can even if it is for a visit."

"I ain't going anywhere," Shawn said before hanging up.

Christian hung up and left his house minutes later with checkbook and boxing attire in hand.

Roughly an hour later, Christian parked outside the jail Shawn was at. While doing so, he noticed a long black limo parked there taking up four or five parking spots. He initially thought it was weird seeing a limo outside a jail but soon ignored it as the moment passed.

While walking to the main entrance, Christian heard a couple of voices talking to each other. Normally he wouldn't have looked, but this time he casually glanced over to see who the voices came from.

The voices came from three men, all of whom were walking towards the limo. The man on the left was very large. He stood about 6'8", had short reddish-brown hair, a thick reddish goatee, and was in excellent shape. He didn't have very much body fat on him and seemed to have the right amount of muscle for his build, or so thought Christian. The man in the middle was Duke Snyder and was dressed in all he wonder and splendor that a man of his talents could afford. He was in the process of trying to sell such services to the third man of the group, who was none other than Shawn, who was listening intently at was being said. Since Christian was not able to hear what the conversation entailed, he moved closer while trying to have some amount of cover behind the other cars in the lot.

"You really should consider switching sides, Mr. Calloway," Dude said confidentially while looking Shawn in the eye. "I'd be able to make it worth your while if you did so."

"What could you give me that I haven't got already?" Shawn asked.

Duke merely smiled to this. "Whatever your heart desires."

"I have to admit, Mr. Snyder, that mine desires quite a bit."

"Please, please, call me Duke," he said with a fake smile while spreading his arms in a friendly gesture. "And for your desires, what do they include? Money? Women? How about fast cars or big houses? Maybe even a worthy world championship or two?"

"C'mon, man, be serious," Shawn told him while being a little in awe at the possibilities of that he was just told. "Don't tease me like that."

"Do I look like I was teasing, Mr. Calloway?" Duke asked sternly. "Don't insult me with this bad comedy of yours."

There was a moment of silence between them as they looked each other over. The beefcake, who apparently worked for Duke, placed himself next to his boss while adjusting his sunglasses, folded his arms, and looked down at Shawn.

"So you can really get those for me if I did decide to change management?" inquired Shawn.

"That what Boss said," the giant said in a slow manner that was heavily laden with a thick Russian-like accent.

"Easy, Igor. Mr. Calloway didn't mean any offense," Duke told him calmly. He stopped walking before turn look to Shawn. "To answer your question, yes. Yes you could. If you enlist my services, that is. I can assure you you'd have your shot at any of those items I've mentioned, if not most of them within the first year of securing my talents."

"I didn't mean any offense, Duke, but after all these years with Dom, it seems like I should have seen a bit more than what I have, especially during the last couple of years," Shawn explained with some reservation and suspicion. "Why should I believe that you'd be able to get these things for me more quickly than he could?"

"Let me ask you this: do you feel like Mr. Calivicci is managing you the best way he can? Is he putting you in the matches against the competition you know you should be in the ring against?" Duke slyly asked before pausing briefly to let these questions sink into Shawn's head. In addition, he turned while putting his arm around Shawn's shoulders before starting to walk again towards their limo. "And are you telling me that you, with your obvious talents and many years of loyal service, are only worthy of the WBO title while maintaining a mid-card-like status? Hmmm, is this what you're attempting to tell me?"

"Well, Dom has said I still need some work."

"Do you believe that or do you think he's just trying to change and mold you to his type of fighter?" Duke smiled. "You're not some guy who's a technical masterpiece. You are the next Mike Tyson and Marvin Haggler. The reason why you haven't peaked, or reached your apex, yet with him is that you do not fight his style of match. If you team with me, you'll be able to fight the way you want; you'll fight your style of fighting. As a result, I can guarantee you'll make more money this first year with me that is more than your last five combined. You'll also have the best of everything, no one who I represent is seen as second class. No one. You hear me? No one! And that means having the best women, cars, houses, and, above all, a world championship belt around your waist you'd be proud of."

"Championship gold, huh?" Shawn asked while a smile came across his face as he thought of the possibilities. "Which one?"

"Anyone you want. Hell, all of them," Duke confidentially told him while spreading his arms. "But, in all honesty, you deserve nothing less than the WBA belt, the most prestigious belt out there. Just think about that, being called 'the new WBA champion of the world, Shawn Calloway!' I can get that for you, but only if you come to my side."

Shawn smiled before nodding his head as he let those words fill his head. "I like the sound of that."

"And WBA gold is something that none of Mr. Calivicci's students have ever won, let alone challenged for. Not even your brother."

"Hey, you leave him outta this!" Shawn hotly shot before calming down as fast as he said that. "He'll get there soon enough."

"He might," agreed Duke. "But should he get there before you? After all those long, hard, loyal years you strived to be the best. After bringing your brother in, helping him, do you think he deserves that more than you, let alone before? That just wouldn't be fair. Wouldn't you agree?"

"What if he wanted to come over with me to your side?" Shawn asked. "Would you take him as well?"

"Why are you so concerned with him?" Duke seemed genuinely surprised by the question.

"He's my brother," Shawn explained with slight irritation. "We've been through a lot together. I wouldn't want to leave him behind if he wanted to come with me."

"Speaking of Mr. Eaton, where is he?" Duke asked while looking around in an exaggerated way. It was obvious he was not expecting to see him. "I don't see him anywhere. You called Mr. Calivicci to help you out but he merely tossed you aside. You even called your brother looking for help, but, alas, he didn't follow through the one time you needed him. So, given that, why would yo want me to help your brother out when he hasn't come to help you?"

"It wasn't his fault, man," Shawn defensively said while looking hard at the promoter before him. "He would'a been here if he could."

"Really?" Duke asked while Shawn said yes. "Whose fault is it? What prevented him from being here?"

"Christian was just doing what Dom told him to. He didn't want to come because he didn't want to upset the old man."

Duke scoffed at that before laughing slightly. "Surely you can't be serious?"

Igor also laughed at this but soon quit when Duke did.

"Your brother's a grown man," continued the promoter. "He's able to make decisions for himself. He does not need Mr. Calavicci's approval for anything. The simple fact of the matter is that your brother bailed on you when you finally needed his help with something. And so did Mr. Calavicci."

"I know my brother," Shawn stated firmly. "He'd be here if he could."

"Are you sure he's not in the process of letting you go?"

"What the hell do you mean by that?"

"When you and I spoke previously, you implied that you had Mr. Calivicci's attention until your brother seemed to show promise. At that point, he began focusing more him and less on you. Sounds almost like you're being replaced," Duke informed him. "Maybe your brother's doing the same thing with you. He's replacing you with someone else."

Shawn shook his head. "No, I don't buy that."

Duke stepped closer to him while lowering his voice. "Think about it for a moment. You've helped your brother his whole life. You got him into boxing and you helped him along, helped develop him. Since he's easier to control, I can see why Mr. Calavicci favored him, especially in recent times. Nevertheless, knowing that your brother is successful, you know, with his titles, endorsements, money, new house, and all, why does he need you now? What can you offer him? Think about it. His actions seem to suggest he doesn't feel like he needs you as much anymore. Seems like he acquiring this trait from your beloved manager. They both seemed to need you until something better comes along."

"You're wrong!" Shawn said but, this time, with a little hesitation.

Duke smiled. "Am I? You don't sound too sure of yourself. And what do you have to prove me otherwise?"

"I know him and you don't."

"Aah, that's right. You've mentioned that already."

At that moment, Christian had enough of listening to their conversation. He backtracked to his truck before opening its door and slamming it shut in hopes it would give the impression he just got there. After that, he walked towards the door of the jail before turning to look at the three men while acting as if he was seeing them for the first time.

"Hey Shawn, there you are." Christian drew the looks from the three men as he walked over to them. "Sorry I'm late; traffic was a bear."

"What are you doin' here?" Shawn asked him.

"Came to bail him out. But seeing that you're already outside, I guess I won't have to after all."

"Dom agreed to this?"

"Ah, no, not exactly. I didn't tell him I was coming." Christian shrugged.

"Mr. Eaton," Duke announced while walking up to him while extending a hand to shake, "glad you could finally make it. We were just talking about you."

"Really? Nothing bad I hope." Christian attempted it as a joke while accepting Duke's hand with a cautious eye.

Duke threw him a smile. "I guess that's a matter of opinion."

"That's what I thought," Christian told him with a neutral look.

"You just get here, Mr. Eaton?" Duke asked while looking at him before glancing at the cars behind Christian.

Standing there momentarily, Christian and Duke looked at each other while still having their hands locked together.

"So, may I assume we're indebted to you for Shawn's release?" Christian finally asked, breaking the silence.

"If you mean was I the one who bailed your brother out, then yes, yes I did," Duke said smoothly while still holding Christian's hand. "But I wouldn't say that you're indebted to me."

"But is my brother?" Christian asked. "Is he indebted to you?"

"I wouldn't say that."

"What would you say, Mr. Snyder?" Christian noticed that, after he asked that, Duke didn't seem to want to answer it. "I'm fairly sure Shawn would like to know if he is or isn't as well. It seems to be a fairly simple question."

"Then you are a simple fool," Igor stated in his slow, Russian-think tone. "Boss doesn't need to explain himself to you."

"Whoa, dude. I'm sorry," Christian said while finally breaking his handshake with Duke before offering it to Igor. "I didn't see you there, bub. I'm Christian. What's your name?"

"None of your business," the giant told him as he remained steadfast without accepting the offered hand to shake.

"Igor, be nice. Mr. Eaton was just trying to be polite. Accept the handshake," Duke said to him before turning back to Christian. "I'm sorry, but Igor here hasn't quite learned the formalities of America yet."

314

"That's ok." Christian shrugged as Igor finally accepted his handshake. Once he was able to, Christian released his hand from the giant's firm grasp to shake it a little. "That's a hell of a handshake you got there, Igor. I'd hate to see what it'd be like if you wanted to do it harder. "So, Igor, are you German?" he asked knowing full well he wasn't.

"Me? German? Ha!" He genuinely seemed insulted by that. "Igor is Russian. Where you trying to be funny, little man?"

"No, I wasn't. My apologies about that, Chief. Didn't mean any harm." Christian harmlessly smiled before looking back to Duke. "So, Mr. Snyder, what brings you this way?"

"If it wasn't obvious, I came here to bail your brother out of jail."

"You called him?" Christian asked Shawn. "To bail you out?"

"No!" Shawn answered. "I thought it was you who bailed me out."

"If you don't mind me asking, Mr. Snyder," Christian said, "why'd you help him out?"

"Couldn't I have done this simply as a token of friendship?" Duke replied innocently with a smile.

"Yes, you could have," agreed Chris suspiciously. "But what are you hoping to gain from this?"

"Mr. Eaton, you aren't implying that I have an underlining or ulterior motive for being here, are you?" the promoter firmly asked as his eyes grew darker.

"I don't know, maybe. What do you say to that?"

There was another momentary pause between the two of them before Shawn cleared his throat.

"So, um, Chris, mind if we get outta here?"

Duke answered for him. "Mr. Calloway, if you would like, I could give you a ride anywhere you want," he offered while pointing to his limo.

With that, Igor immediately went to the limo's back door and opened it while waiting for them to climb in.

"Thanks, but I think I'll go with my brother instead," Shawn told him with a surprising amount of politeness in his voice.

"Whatever you'd like." Duke nodded before turning to walk to his car. While in the process of climbing into the back seat, he stopped to straighten himself out. "Mr. Calloway, maybe we could get together the next day or so to finish going over the details of our conversation. I would highly enjoy that if we did."

"I'm gonna be busy this next week or so," Shawn told him.

"Really? Doing what exactly?" persisted the promoter.

315

"Helping my brother here win his title match in a couple of days." Shawn pointed to Christian when he said that. "Then I have to get ready for my court date."

"Oh, that's right, that's right. I forgot all about Mr. Eaton's title shot," Duke said while looking at Christian. "This is what, the third world title you're going for?"

Christian didn't respond. He just silently stared at him.

"Well, good luck with that," Duke said with a fake smile before turning to Shawn. "Mr. Calloway, I do look forward to finishing our conversation sometime soon at your earliest convenience."

Nodding simply to that, Shawn turned to walk towards Christian's truck.

Christian stood there for a moment or two longer locking eyes with the promoter before watching him finish climbing in the back of his limo. He then followed his brother to his truck.

"May I ask what that was about?" he asked Shawn while flicking a thumb towards Snyder's limo who, by then, was pulling out of the jail's parking lot.

"Nothin', bro. That was nothin'," his brother told him. "Hey, thanks for comin'. Man, I can't wait to get back home."

"I hear you, bub." Christian went silent to look briefly at Shawn. "You sure there isn't anything else you'd like to say?"

"Yeah, I'm positive, man. All I wanna do is to get home." With that, a glint came into Shawn's eyes. "The person I wanna talk to isn't gonna like what I have to say to 'im."

They left it at that as they soon climbed into Christian's truck and exited the parking lot.

Chapter 34

Christian had been sparring with Mitch for about fifteen minutes when Shawn came into the gym. He walked with a purpose as his eyes scanned the gym. Christian, who had gotten back to the gym about a half hour earlier from picking him up at the jail. All he got out of Shawn was that he wanted to go up to his apartment to shower and get something to eat but would be down later on once he was ready.

By the way Shawn was walking, Christian knew his brother hadn't come to train. He came for some other purpose. Something in his eye suggested that whatever his reasons were, they'd been brewing for a while. Though he didn't know exactly why he was there or what the matter was, he assumed it had something to do with the conversation Shawn had had earlier in the day with Duke Snyder.

"Have any of you seen Dom?" Shawn asked a couple of guys near the water fountain.

"No, sorry," was their response while going back to their conversation.

Eventually, another new guy, Richie, said that Dom was in his office.

Christian kept sparring as Shawn made his rounds asking about Dom. After being verified by a number of other boxers that the gym's owner was in his office, Shawn walked in that general direction. When he got there, he entered without knocking.

A minute after Shawn disappeared into the office, Dom hobbled out to scan the gym. When his eyes fell onto the ring, he yelled, "Christian!" The force of his voice seemed to shake the building. "My office. Pronto!"

"O-o-kay, Dom," he said while he and Mitch stopped sparring. The two men touched gloves with each other before Christian climbed out of the ring.

The tension in the office when he got there was already thick, and most of that was coming off of Shawn, who was standing in the middle of the room with his arms crossed and glaring at Dom. Dom, on the other hand, was pacing back and forth while running his hand over his face.

"You wanted to see me, Dom?" Christian asked when he entered.

"What the hell was ya thinkin', kid?!" Dom growled while shooting him a glare that could stop a clock.

Taking a moment to figure out how to respond, Christian simply decided to play it stupid for the time being. "I'm sorry, Dom, but I'm not sure what you're talking about."

"Don't give me that crap! Ya know exactly what I mean."

"I'm afraid I don't." Christian looked to Shawn hoping he'd help him out but, when it was evident he wouldn't, looked back to Dom soon thereafter. Meanwhile, he began moving his fingers in circular motions next to his head before saying, "It would seem like I have a blank spot, Dom. If you could help me…"

"A blank spot? It's more like a damn hole in yer head, kid!" Dom yelled. "Did I not tell ya earlier today ta not help yer brother out?"

"Oh. That?" questioned Christian innocently while seemingly invoke more of a glare from Dom.

"Yeah. That! What'ya think I meant?"

"All I did was give him a ride home."

"A right home?" Dom asked in conjunction to having a confused look rise upon his face. "Didn't ya bail his ass out?"

Christian shook his head while finally taking off his headgear and gloves. "No. Shawn called when I was home getting my stuff. He asked for a ride. When I got there, he was already outside."

"So ya sayin' it wasn't ya who bailed his ass out?" Dom pointed to Shawn while obviously not quite believing what he heard.

"I may have if wasn't already bailed out. But, to answer your question, no, I didn't bail him out."

"See? I told you he didn't!" Shawn said through gritted teeth while shaking his head. "You never listen to me."

"Who bailed ya out, then?"

"Who says anyone bailed me out? Maybe I bailed myself out."

"No, ya didn't, kid," Dom told him.

"What makes you say that?"

"Because ya called me to bail ya out, that's why." Dom scowled. "If ya were able to bail your ass out but just needed a ride, ya would'a simply asked for a ride. So who bailed ya out?"

"What's it to ya, old man? Weren't you the one who said that you were done helpin' me? If that's true, why should you give a damn who helped me?"

"Knowing the type of people who most likely *did* help ya, there might be trouble. As long as ya train here and are under my management, I don't want any trouble here as a result of this mysterious third party."

"If it bothers you so much, I can always leave. I know someone who's appreciate representing a person of my talents."

"Yeah, ya do? And who might that be?"

"The same person who bailed me out, that's who," Shawn said while drawing a baffled look from Dom. "He also said if I went over to his side, I wouldn't have to worry about anythin' again."

"What the hell ya talkin' 'bout, kid?"

"What I'm talkin' about is the shit you haven't been able to give me," Shawn told him as his anger rose while walking over to him. "Things such as money, endorsements, and championship gold."

"Ya already got a championship."

"Yeah, I do, but you know what? It's a piece of crap. It's a third-rate championship belt in comparison to the three above it. I deserve better than what I have after all these years of bustin' my ass for you. Hell, Christian already had two world titles before I got my first one. Both of his are better than what I have. It ain't fair! At the very least, I deserve at least what he got!" Shawn looked at Dom while pointing to his brother who was still standing in the doorway.

At that moment, Christian slowly turned around to start walking out of the office while pulling the door closed behind him.

"Hey!" Dom quickly shot while looking at him. "Where the hell ya goin'?"

"Back out to spar with Mitch."

"No ya ain't. Get your ass back in here and close the door," Dom told him. When Christian did what he told him, he turned back to Shawn. "So what are ya sayin'? Ya wanna change management?"

"If I don't start seein' results from you, then yeah, yeah I do."

"And what results do ya want?"

"Isn't it obvious?!" demanded Shawn without getting from Dom. "I want more championship gold and I want endorsements. I want to be on at least equal grounds with my brother; not beneath him. The guy who bailed me out said he'd be able to get me a WBA title shot in under a year, guaranteed, and the endorsements would soon follow. I'm pretty sure Christian would be welcomed over there as well."

Christian was taken totally off guard when he heard this. "Hey, hey, hey Shawn. I never said I was going over with you."

"What?" Dom shot him a look. "Ya knew about this before, kid? Ya know who bailed 'im out?"

"Yes. He was in the parking lot talking to him when I got there."

"Who is this man? He sounds like a goddamn savior to me."

Sighing, Christian looked to his brother before saying, "You might as well tell him, Shawn. There's no reason not to."

"If you have to know," Shawn said while finally giving in. "It was Duke Snyder who bailed me out. He's the one who could guarantee those things for me."

"What?!" Dom suspiciously asked. "Why the hell did he bail your ass out? And how did he know ya was in jail?"

"I don't know either but, unlike you, he helped me out and is willing to help me out more if I want him to."

"I guess that'll make you happy, won't it?" Dom said with a grin. "When ya plannin' on leavin'?"

"I was waitin' to hear if you'd be able to do somethin' for me before I make my mind up," Shawn told him.

"If ya mean would I be able ta give ya more gold around yer waist," Dom said while raising his eyebrows, "I think my answer will be the same as it's been the last hundred times ya've asked. And as fer those endorsements ya're so hungry fer, we ain't responsible to 'em, managers that is. They come and search ya out."

"As long as I have the belts I currently have, do you really think I'll get any endorsements? Do you?"

Grinning still, Dom cleared his throat before speaking his mind. "Perhaps ya're missin' the point, kid. The company who pays ya fer an endorsement have ta feel that ya're a good, visible image for their product. If they think ya can sell it, then they'll approach ya. If not, then ya're outta luck."

"Guys, I've an idea," Christian said before waiting for the two of them to look at him before he continued. "If Shawn feels like we're screwing him over, the why don't we boost him to cruiserweight and have him challenge me for my titles?"

The idea seemed to please Shawn as a broad smile came upon his face. For the first time since entering the office, Shawn actually seemed to relax some. Dom, meanwhile, intervened to shoot the idea down.

"What kind of hair brained idea is that, kid?" Dom asked which was answered only with a shrug from Chris and a smirk from Shawn. Dom proceeded to look between the two young men before him before continuing. "What the hell is goin' on here? Did ya pressure 'im into this?" he asked Shawn while pointing a bony finger at Christian. "Did ya make 'im feel sorry for ya?"

"No, Dom, it wasn't like that," Christian told him.

"Then what's it like? He's always tryin' to talk ya into one thing or another."

"Well, I feel like I do sort of owe him something from the help he's given me over the years," Christian said while Dom continued glaring at him. Shawn, meanwhile, nodded his head. "Even if I don't owe him anything, he's going to be jumping ship to go over to Duke's side if we don't do something."

"What are ya sayin', kid?"

"What I'm saying is to give him a chance." Christian shrugged. "I'm not saying he had to win the match or anything. I'm not even suggesting that he try to lose. All I'm saying is that it sounds like Shawn doesn't necessarily need you or us to give him a title but if we're willing to put him in a title match against a worthy opponent, then I think that'll make him little bit happy. I know it would me. I don't think that it necessarily has to be against the WBA champ; the WBC or IBF champs may be enough. I don't know. But I think Shawn just needs to know that we or, more specifically, you trust him enough to actually put him in that situation. That's why I'm suggesting you boost him up and put him against me for my titles."

"But we already did that, remember?" Dom told him.

"It looks like Shawn'll do what good old Billy-what's-his-name did a while back," Christian said while drawing a blank look from Dom. "We had a fighter a while back named Billy, a cocky young guy who liked to pose. He wanted a title shot and when you wouldn't give him one, he went over to Duke's side. Six weeks after that, he was a contender to a world championship. If there's something more or anything else that's stopping you from giving Shawn his shot, maybe he should know what it is or you may find Snyder acquired another one of our boxers."

Shawn and Dom looked at him in silence when he got done.

With that, Shawn looked to Dom to say, "What's it going to be, Dom? You gonna help me out or do I have to go look for it elsewhere?"

"Like I told ya when ya was in jail, kid, I'm done helpin' ya out until ya get your act together," Dom bluntly told him.

"What do you mean by that?!"

"What I mean is I don't trust ya enough to respect this business or the history of this sport!" Dom almost yelled at him. "If you're in this title fight you so badly want, I need to know ya won't insult us all with your damn antics!"

"What the hell has gotten into you?! Respect the industry?" Shawn blinked his eyes in dumbfoundness. "Have you lost what little mind you have left?"

"So ya haven't learnt nothin' since ya've been here, have ya?" Dom was finally slowly realizing that, while speaking to Shawn, his words weren't sinking in nor would they as long as he had him there as a student. "Ya don't know nothin' 'bout integrity, respect, honor, or anythin' else that comes with bein' a champ!"

"What in the world are you jabberin' on about, old man?!" Shawn asked while not talking his eyes off him. "I love and respect everythin' that goes along with bein' a champion."

"Yeah? And what might that be?"

"Obviously you've never been in the position to either be a champ or have any of your students be one if you have to ask me that," Shawn told him with a glint in his eye as the two of them glared at each other. "But if you must know, what I want and respect are the things that only

321

being a world champion can give me. And those are fame, respect, women, certain privileges that goes along with that, and all the publicity I want!"

"Is that why ya got into this business? 'cause you're greedy?"

"As a matter of fact it was, but greedy for respect the most! I want people to get out of my way when I walk down the street. I want people to say, 'there goes Shawn Calloway, the world champ.' You can't get respect like that unless you got the gold."

"Ya still have a lot to learn 'bout this sport, kid." Dom sighed while hanging his head. "Ali would'a loved to have a chance to face ya. All ya are is a white man's version of Liston."

"If you want to compare me to anybody, compare me to Tyson, old man!"

"Yeah, compare you to a convicted rapist," Dom mocked. "But the only thing different between ya and Tyson is he was able to be trained."

"You sure about that, Dom?" Christian asked with a smile. "That woman he raped probably wouldn't say he got much training."

"What's it gonna be, Dom?" Shawn asked while totally ignoring Christian.

"Like I said before, ya got yourself inta this mess, now ya're gonna have ta get yerself outta it," Dom told him while waving his hands before turning to walk away. "Come talk ta me after it's done and ya're grown up some."

"What 'bout all those years of loyal service I've given you?!"

"The only thing ya was loyal to was your own greed!" Dom shouted before looking through some papers that littered the top of his desk. "The only reason ya never left or threatened to leave is 'cause no one was able ta offer ya what ya wanted. Now that ya do have someone," Dom paused long enough to look over Shawn a time or two, "ya come here to try and bully me into givin' ya what ya want or ya threaten to leave. Ya should know me better than that. I can't give ya title fights!"

"And why's that?"

"Either because ya ain't a ranked contender for any of the belts or 'cause ya'd embarrass the sport! Don't'cha get it? I ain't gonna have some greedy student of mine destroy the business I've spent my whole life in just so ya can get a little respect on the street from some easily impressed 16-yr old. I don't need that responsibility or hassle! Not at my age."

"What about Duke, huh?" asked his hotheaded student. "He's able to do it for me, someone he doesn't even know. How is it he's able to do that when you're not?"

"'cause he doesn't give a damn 'bout ya, kid. Ya're just another payday fer him. And even if ya might not be a contender or somethin', that won't stop him from bribin' some promoter or official to book ya in a match. All he cares 'bout is the bottom line. The only thing that calls his name is money. Once ya wear out ya're welcome, he'll discard ya like yesterday's newspaper."

"So you sayin' he's got connections that you don't?"

"I'm saying he's willing to use his connection to his advantage to line his wallet," the old man growled. "I'm sorry, kid, but if I have ta persuade or bribe some guy ta give ya a title shot, that's goin' against everythin' I stand fer. If ya wanna get a shot the honest way, then, by all means, I can help ya. But, if ya wanna take the easy way ta the top, I'm sure ya still have Snyder's number lyin' 'round."

"Then that's it, then?" Shawn softly asked while he and Dom exchanged silent looks. "After all these years, this is how it's gonna end?"

"No one's endin' this but ya, kid. I'm just refusin' ta help ya out," Dom said while looking over Shawn for a moment. "I can't afford to bail ya out every time ya get into trouble. Maybe your friend Snyder can, but I can't. Now, if that's the only reason why ya came here, ya'll have ta excuse me. I've got work ta do and ya're brother's got ta get ready for his upcomin' fight." And, just like that, Dom turned his back on Shawn to ruffle through a stack of papers.

Realizing that that was the end of the conversation, Shawn walked to the office door. While opening it to walk out, Christian followed suit, closing the door behind him.

"Hey, Shawn, wait up," he called out.

Stopping where he was before turning to face him, Shawn's eyes brewed with anger.

"Hey, I got thinking about what you said in there. What if I was able to setup a match for us to face each other?" Christian told him. "How would that sound to you?"

"You heard ole Adolf in there," his brother replied while pointing towards the office. "He won't go for it."

"We could always get Curly to help us out."

"Great! One extreme to another," complained Shawn while squinting his face. "We go from Hitler to one of the Three Stooges."

"Come on, Shawn. They aren't that bad." Christian laughed while putting his headgear back on. "After I win the WBC belt, you and I can go against each other again. Either for my belts or as another exhibition match. If you do challenge for my belts, you'll need to gain some weight, however, to move up in class. Whether you do or not, think of the publicity this could garner. The last fight was a lame six-rounder. But, this time, we make it a 12-rounder if you'd like. Have your hands untied this time around, but, you know, don't try to kill me. Granted, you may not be a contender, but maybe we can work around that and have you challenge all the same. I'm not sure how that would work, though. If you don't, it'll still be a better fight than before."

"Are you really willin' to do this?" Shawn skeptically asked while raising his eyebrows at him. "I don't think Dom will approve."

"Like you said before, I owe you. This could also be the final exam for Dom to see if he'll keep his word and not help you or if we'll see that he'll come around. If he doesn't, we both know that Duke's around if you'd need him." Christian shrugged before putting his gloves back on.

"Thanks, Beeker. This means a lot to me."

"No problem. But, just to be on the safe side, maybe you'd better talk to Duke to see what he can do for you just in case. Make it a little more legit and all."

"Yeah, maybe I'll do that," Shawn said before turning to leave.

"Hey, before you go, you're still going to be in my corner next week?"

"I can't believe you have to ask me that, bro." Shawn looked at him with an insulted expression came over his face. "Have you ever known me to miss any of your matches?"

"Yeah, I know, but Dom didn't expect you to be there. He apparently got someone else just in case," Christian told him with a shrug. "So I'll see you at ringside, then?"

"Yeah," was all Shawn said before turning to leave.

Christian did notice that once Shawn passed through the gym door, that he made a right to go outside instead of a left to go back up to his apartment. He assumed his brother was going down to *Mike's Place* for an evening of alcohol consumption and a few racks of pool with Jake and Terry. When this thought passed, Christian approached Mitch to see if he wanted to continue sparring with him.

Chapter 35

"And now for tonight's main event!" the ring announcer called as his voice echoed throughout the arena. "It is a your cruiserweight match of the evening and it is for the WBO, WBC, and IBF cruiserweight championships of the world! On my left, in the blue corner, weighing in at 189 pounds and wearing white trunks with gold trim, he is the reigning WBO and IBF cruiserweight champion, Christian Eaton!"

The crowd gave a good applause for Christian as he bounced out of his corner. Raising a gloved fist, he smiled to the crowd. The pop that he got during his introduction had gotten better his last several fights and he seemed to notice that it drove Shawn a little crazy. While going back to his corner, he noticed two of the three members of *The Misfits* at ringside with a vacant chair in the middle of them. Miggie was sitting in the left chair while off in his own little world as usual while listening to music from the headphones. Eric, in the right chair, had his arm around a woman Christian had never seen before; he was kissing her neck as she smiled. The seat between them was empty but, moments later, Larry appeared while carrying an armload of food and beverages for the group. All of them waved except for Larry, who simply nodded to instead.

On the other side of the ring, Christian noticed Duke Snyder sitting. And he wasn't alone. On one side of him was Igor, the human wall of muscle, while, one the other side, sat a gorgeous blonde. The blonde wore an extremely revealing dress with sparkles over it and a fur coat. He and Duke exchanged a brief nod while Igor only glared at him. The blonde, on the other hand, appeared to be as ditsy and stupid as she was pretty.

"I see your friends came to see you fight," Shawn said while acknowledging The Misfits.

Nodding towards Duke, Christian said, "Yours came too."

"And his opponent," the announcer continued, "weighing in at an even 181 pounds, wearing black with silver trim, he is the reigning WBC cruiserweight champion, Kevin 'The Knight' Ryder!"

The reaction from the crowd was moderate but Christian thought the response he got was a bit louder. Ryder came out with a trot of his own while holding his gloved fists in front of hm. His trainer came up behind him to remove his robe. A well-worn belt was soon exposed underneath.

Christian, meanwhile, had help removing his robe from Shawn. Once his robe was out of the way, Dom removed both of the belts he was currently wearing.

"Hey, bro, aren't you excited about being here tonight?" Shawn asked.

"Actually, I'm quite nervous," Christian admitted.

"Nervous? What the hell for? You should be ecstatic!"

"I'm nervous because this is the biggest fight of my career to date," Christian explained. "And why should I ecstatic?"

"Dude, don't you know where you're at?"

"Yeah. We're at the Glenns Falls Civic Center. So what?"

"So what?! I seriously cannot believe you, dude. You're unbelievable, man. You know that, right?" While getting a blank stare from his brother, Shawn continued. "Not only is Hacksaw Jim Duncan from Glenns Falls, which reminds me, we should try and see where he lived here, but this arena is where Tyson beat Burdick to win the WBC heavyweight championship to become the world's youngest heavyweight champion in history," he said with an excited look upon his face. "You have a chance to win that same belt here tonight, and I can't believe you had no idea! Unbelievable, man. You truly are unbelievable."

A short time thereafter, the ref called both fighters to center stage to explain the rules and what's to be expected of them. When that was done, he ordered the boxers to touch gloves and to proceed back to their respected corners.

"Recommendations?" Christian asked from his corner while waiting on the bell.

"You forgot already?" Dom asked in shock. "Didn't we go over this in the locker room?"

He didn't forget. Christian was just saying that on purpose to get Dom going. Dom had informed him that Ryder wasn't great in any one area but was really good at everything. He had speed, power, boxing knowledge, good instincts, excellent stamina, and, above all, a rock solid chin. He could easily go the entire match and not lose any of these attributes. The only thing Christian had on him was weight, out-weighing him by seven and a half pounds. Dom, as usual, told him to cover his noggin, to keep dancing, and try to sting and blind him with his jabs whenever possible. Surprisingly, Dom instructed him to damage Ryder whenever he could.

However, Dom said that Ryder's biggest weakness may have been the fact that he was a relatively new champion, having won the belt via tournament only seven months previously. He defended it successfully only once about four months previously to the runner-up of that same tournament and was eager to make a name for himself as a champ. Dom also informed him that it wasn't hard for him to put their name into challenge for the title if they were willing to put their belts on the line as well. The 'winner take all' mindset appealed to him, which made it easier to secure Christian another title shot.

Dom instructed Christian to take his time, blind Ryder with head shots before attacking his body. If the opportunity arose during the match to get a knockout, then to take it. They ignored Shawn when he commented, almost in a questioning manner, of Dom essentially untying Christian's hands, but Christian knew that his hands weren't exactly tied. To Christian, his hands were untied just for this one fight because it was necessary to win. Yet, he had done something that Shawn hadn't done yet – completely gained Dom's trust.

"No, I didn't forget," Christian told him with a smile. "I just wanted to see what you'd say."

"What're ya askin' me fer again?" Dom growled. "Get in 'ere and take care of 'im!"

To Christian's dissatisfaction, the fight went the entire twelve rounds in what was as well fought battle as he had ever been in. Dom's comment of Ryder having a rock solid chin turned out to be very true. Multiple times Christian went to go for the KO, thinking the fight was going to be over relatively soon, only to have his punches be absorbed before Ryder retaliated with his own string of combos. The closest he came to a knockout was a knockdown in the fourth and tenth. Almost immediately after doing down, Ryder got right back up again while allowing the ref to do a standing eight count.

When the smoke was cleared at the end, Christian not only won the fight via split decision, but the third world championship as well. Christian and Ryder touched gloves before hugging each other at the end after the decision was made. Ryder graciously accepted a rematch Christian had offered with a nod before going back to his corner.

In the hall on the way to the locker room, Dom recapped the match by telling his now three-time world champion what he liked and disliked. This was when Shawn interrupted to ask the question that had been on his mind since before the fight began.

"So, Chris, now that you won the match, when can I challenge for your titles?"

Hearing this, all Christian could do was slow to a crawl while closing his eyes, hung his head, and groan. He was hoping Shawn would have waited until he had spoken with Dom but, unfortunately, patience was never one of Shawn's virtues.

"Hey, kid, what's he talkin' 'bout?" Dom asked as he hobbled over to him. "Don't tell me ya ok'd a title match with him even though ya know how I feel 'bout that. On top of that, did ya forget that I'm still your manager and ya can't do anythin' without my ok first?"

"No, Dom, I didn't forget."

Dom glared at him. "No ta which question? No ya didn't tell 'im or no ya didn't forget?"

"No to both of them."

"What do you mean by 'no', bro?!" Shawn asked while staring at him. "Didn't you promise me you'd give me a title shot after you won that damn belt tonight?"

"Tell me ya didn't, kid," Dom pleaded. "Please, tell me ya didn't!"

"Not exactly."

"What'cha mean by 'not exactly'?"

"Last week I had asked Shawn for his thoughts on whether I was able to set a matchup for us to again," Christian said when they entered the locker room. "I don't recall it being specifically for a title shot for you, Shawn, but at the very least a good amount of publicity. Am I wrong?"

Shawn, while sitting in a nearby chair, stared at him. He watched his brother sit down on the table as Dom started taking off his gloves and tape.

Shawn glared at him. "You son-of-a-bitch. You tricked me!"

"How'd I trick you?"

"You made me think I'd be able to get a title shot against your ass!"

"Whether or not you get to challenge for my titles, you'd at the very least get really good publicity which, in turn, will help move you in better contention."

"You mean like last time?"

"Correct."

"You can't actually be saying that the reason I got a shot at all was because of you. Is that what you're saying?!" he demanded.

"Shawn, I'm now saying that at all. You're blowing it way out of proportion."

"Me blowing it outta proportion?" Shawn asked as his anger rose. "You're the one who guaranteed me a shot, damn it! Now you're backin' out? You owe me, bro. You fuckin' owe me!" He stood while pointing at him.

"C'mon, Shawn." Dom looked at while finishing up with Christian. "Now's not the time ta be talkin'. If ya two want ta amuse yourselves with another fight, go ahead. But it ain't gonna be for his titles and I won't be involved."

"Why not?" Shawn quickly asked.

"Why not?" Dom turned to face him.

"Yeah."

"You wanna know why not?!"

"I wanna know!"

"I'll tell ya why not!" Dom yelled while hobbling over to him. "Ya didn't earn 'em! I keep tellin' ya that! Ya're always tryin' ta make him do things for ya because ya think he owes ya everythin', just like we all do! We *all* owe ya somethin', don't we? Well, ya gotta start don' things for yourself if ya want those shots. Besides, ya ain't even in the same weight class as he is."

"I'll gain the weight then. No big deal." Shawn shrugged while looking down at Dom. "And what do ya mean I didn't earn it? Look at my record. Shouldn't that answer that?!"

"That don't mean a damn thing! And don't be tryin' ta bully him into givin' up what he's earned."

"He owes me, Dom!"

"He doesn't owe ya shit! Stop tryin' ta take advantage of him! Besides, ya ain't even a contender for his belts. Ya can't challenge unless ya're a contender."

"Then put me in some contention matches. You're my manager, so mange me!" exclaimed Shawn without drawing a reaction from the old man before him. "It's not that hard, Dom. Just do the damn job I'm payin' you for and let me worry 'bout the rest. You able to do that?!"

"Why should I? Why should I spend my time and energy into someone who's just a greedy, little punk with no respect for anyone or anythin' else but his own ass? What would I get outta it?"

"What would you get outta it? What the hell do you mean by that?" Shawn's confused, exasperated expression was priceless. "Dom, you'll be gettin' a shit load of money! You'll be in the main events, on TV. Shit, you might even be on ESPN."

"Ya think that's why I'm in the business, kid? To be on TV?" Dom asked his young, arrogant student before going quiet to merely look up at him. "Sure, all 'em are nice, and I hope to get a little bit of those before I die, but da ya really think that that is what drives me? Da ya?"

Shawn shrugged. "Well, yeah. What else is there?"

"Ya just don't get it , da ya kid?"

"What are you talkin' 'bout, Dom? What am I supposed to get? I'm a boxer. This is what I do for a livin'! I'm here to be the best!"

"And what is that, ta be the best? Huh?" Dom asked shrewdly.

"Tell me you're not being serious with that question."

"I know, kid, I know. I don't know what's gotten inta me." Dom smiled innocently. "But, still, since I asked, why don't ya amuse me, huh?"

"Being the best means you're the champ! And not just a champ, but *thee* champ. The undisputed one!" answered Shawn while using his hands to help emphasize what he was saying. "Being the best also means you're making the best money and have the best endorsements. It means being in the main events, being the one who highlights all the events or, at least, the most profile ones. Being the best brings respect. You can get whatever you want when you want simply by being the best. That's why I got into this business, to be the best, and I am going to get it with or without you!"

Dom lowered his head and rubbed his chin. "That sounds real interestin', kid. And how da ya propose ta da that, on becomin' the best? How do ya plan on gettin' all that ya just described?"

"By beating everyone out there. That's how!"

Dom winked. "But how are ya supposed ta da that, kid?"

"What do you mean?"

"Ya think ya're so smart when ya're really just stupid. How are ya supposed ta get in these matches on yer way to greatness?" Dom asked his baffled pupil who didn't fully understand. "Yer manager has ta arrange and setup fights fer ya."

At that moment, Shawn eyes widened and mouth opened as he finally grasped what Dom was talking about. Stepping back, he looked at him. "You're not gonna do anything for me, are you?"

"For what ya're willing ta offer, I've done all I can do," Dom told him while turning his back while waving in irritation. He then went back to Christian to look at his face "Ya need ta change yer attitude and start listenin' ta me if ya want ta get what ya want. Ya need ta learn the art of compromise and humility if ya want ta get anywhere."

At this point, the ring doctor made his appearance in their locker room.

"How's your kid doing, Dom?" he asked while sitting his bag on the table next to Christian.

Dom told him, "Seems ta be doin' ok, Ralph. If ya want ta know, why don't ya ask him yourself?"

"Hey Doc, he's fine," Shawn interrupted. "He's always fine. He's so worried about not getting hit that I'm surprised he even got into this sport anyway."

"If you two don't mind, why don't I hear from the person I came to see. If that is alright," Dr. Ralph said while examining Christian.

"I'm alright, Doc," his patient informed him.

"Anything wrong with you? Anything feel weird or funny?"

"Well, I don't see out my left eye very well, but that may be on account of being hit too many times there."

"Gee, ya think?" Shawn sarcastically asked.

"Shawn, please stop it," Christian told him.

"Stop what?"

"Stop interrupting and stop being annoying," Christian said while continuing to be examined.

"Are you now tellin' me what to do?"

"No, Shawn, I'm not," he told him while his irritation was beginning to rise before looking at his brother. "But the doctor can't do his job if you keep butting in. Now, if you please, have a seat and be quiet for a few minutes."

"Fine, have it your way, boss." Shawn gave up while sitting down in disgust.

"I'm sorry about that, Doc," Christian apologized.

"No problem. Is there anything else you want to tell me? Or anything else I should know about?"

"Well, my head hurts a little, sort of tingly."

"What do you mean by 'tingly'?"

"It's like the sensation you feel when your arm or leg goes asleep. Tingly like that."

"How long as it felt like this?"

"The last couple of rounds, I think. Maybe a little before that."

"It's probably nothing, but if you still have it in the morning, please call my office to schedule an appointment," Dr. Ralph told him while take a business card out of his jacket pocket to give to him. "Anything else?"

"No, Doc. That's about it."

"In that case, I think I'll show myself out." He smiled while extending an open hand.

Christian accepted the offered hand to shake.

Ralph soon broke the hold before going to Dom to shake his hand. "Good to see you again, Dom. You take care of that fight for me."

"Ya know I will, Ralph. It was good seein' ya too. And how's that wife of yours doin'?"

"Martha's fine, just fine. You should stop by one of these nights for dinner. We miss having you."

Dom nodded. "I'd like that. It's been a long time. Maybe I can take a rain check for next month?"

"Next month it is. We look forward to having you then," Ralph told him with a smile and a nod. He then picked up his bag before walking to the door. In the process, he looked at both Christian and Shawn while smiling briefly at each of them. "Gentlemen," he stated before taking his leave.

As soon as the locker room's door was closed, Shawn got up to walk over to Dom. "So, are you gonna arrange anymore title fights for me or am I gonna do it myself?"

"Take care of yer problems first then get back to me," Dom told him. "That's my answer; take it or leave it."

"I don't have any problems, Dom," Shawn told him.

Dom merely looked at him. "Ya don't? I distinctly remember ya bein' thrown in jail for fightin'."

"Those charges were dropped."

"Not those, ya idiot! The charges against those three hoodlums last week."

"That? Surely you can't be serious! They deserved that."

"I don't care if they did! Maybe they did, but that wasn't fer ya ta decide."

"That's not fair, Dom! It really isn't, you know? I did that for you," Shawn said in his defense.

"Ya did not do that for me. Ya did that fer yourself and ta make yourself feel better!"

"Dom, what the hell do you have against me anyway?" asked Shawn when he was failing to comprehend where the current conversation was going.

"Ya know, kid, ya probably have the best physical talent I've seen in all of my years since I started trainin'. What ya have is almost limitless," Dom explained. What he said brought a smile to Shawn's face as a glow came in his eyes. "However, the thing that's holdin' ya back is that gray blob in between your ears. Ya limit yer possibilities 'cause ya think it's cool and macho ta act the way ya do. If ya explore the mental aspect of boxin', ya'd be like a Haggler rather than yer hero Tyson; possibly more like Robinson. But fer some reason ya refuse. Ya won't even try. Ya're careless as a result. If ya're up against a person like ya, but someone who can actually think, like your brother, ya wouldn't stand a chance. They'd dance around ya 'til the cows come home, wait 'til ya're exhausted, then let ya have it. They'd embarrass the hell outta ya."

"You saying I can't beat Christian?"

"I'm saying ya can't beat a guy like your brother! And, concernin' him," Dom said, "I don't think he'd try ta win on account ya havin' 'im believe ya're the best damn thing that ever happened ta 'im. And also because he wouldn't want ta hurt ya. Anyone else would have ya fer dinner."

"Then I should be grateful that he doesn't have that killer instinct like I do."

"Ha! Maybe he's never had a reason ta have that. Ever think of that?" Dom asked while pointing a finger at Shawn's chest.

"What about my rematch against him?" Shawn asked while pointing to Christian, who was in the process of rounding the corner to the showers. Water was soon heard in the next room.

"What 'bout it?"

"I still want it!"

"Like I told ya before, that's between ya and him, but it ain't gonna be fer his titles. But whatever ya two decide, leave me the hell outta it," Dom growled before turning away. He then proceeded to open the door and walk out into the hall. The door closed behind him.

Shawn lagged behind in the locker room while sitting down heavily in a chair before putting his face in his hands. As he sat there, he couldn't help but think what had he done so wrong to be treated this way. He was a great fighter, wasn't he? Better than all those he had faced, even Christian he thought. He may not have done everything Dom had wanted, but his results more than made up for it. Didn't they? And this was the thanks he was getting? A career, a legacy really, that wasn't amounting to anything with a manager who cared more about his brother; his own brother that he himself brought in. He'd show them!

At that moment, Shawn finally made his mind up that he was going to be the best in the business no matter what. He was going to do it with or without Dom's help. If Dom didn't like it, Shawn decided he'd simply move on to greener pastures. He'd tell him that age old cliché about it being strictly business. Once he came to that realization, he heard the shower turn off to signal that Christian was done. While wanting to capitalize on his new found decision, he approached Christian to re-ask a certain question.

"Hey bro, I know we've already talked about this before, but I want to know if you were being serious about something."

"Yeah, what's that?" Christian asked while drying off.

"Were you really serious about us having that rematch?"

"From what I can recall, I was."

"Would you actually go through with it if Dom didn't want any part of it?"

"If it's a rematch, give me a time and a place and I'll be there."

"Would you have a problem with me challenging?"

"I would if I'd lose Dom as my manager," Christian told him while looking at his brother. "But, if I weren't to lose him, we wouldn't be able to arrange the fight ourselves."

"What if I took care of everything and the only thing you'd need to do was to show up?"

Shrugging, Christian said, "Let me know when that happens, ok? But, you know, Shawn, in order for you to challenge for my titles, not only would you have to make weight, but you'd also have to be in contention."

"What sort of bullshit is that?!" Shawn demanded. "You can agree to face anyone who isn't."

"That's true, I can," Christian agreed. "But in order for the titles to be on the line, the people behind them have to sanction the match. If they don't, then that title won't be on the line for you. But, besides, it wouldn't really be fair if you just jumped up in class to challenge me without actually earning your spot."

"Dude, you fuckin' owe me!"

"Fair enough, but weren't you carrying on to Dom about things not being fair?"

"That was different."

"Why?"

"It just is, that's why."

"Once you're a contender, or you are able to get the people behind my belts to agree for you to challenge, I won't mind having you challenge. That's fair, isn't it?" Christian asked him. "But, if you aren't in contention, don't make weight, or whatnot, it wouldn't be fair for those that have met all criteria to challenge only to have you jump ahead of the line. If that's the case, it looks like you won't be able to get what you want this time."

"And what is that?"

"To beat the crap out of me, to humiliate me, to prove you're the better man, and to take my belts from me." Christian shrugged with a laugh.

"I don't have to beat the shit outta you."

"Oh, but you do want to humiliate me? And take my belts?" Christian asked without getting a response. "If your hands were to be untied in this rematch of ours, do I have your word that you won't go ape shit on me?"

"All I have to say 'bout that is that I'm not gonna fight like I did last time."

"I wouldn't expect you to, but I also want to know that you won't try and destroy me right from the start like you do with every other opponent you face."

Shawn pursed his lips before shaking his head. "Still, I should'a won last time, plain and simple."

"You're still feeling a little resentful over that? About losing to me?"

"Hell ya, I am!" Shawn stated while stomping the floor with his foot. "You don't know how pissed I was on account that I lost!"

"Pissed about losing in general or pissed about losing to me?" Christian asked him with more of a smile as Shawn just looked at him while refusing to answer. "As long as you meet all the requirements on your end, Shawn, I don't care if we have a rematch, either for my belts or not. However, I still want to know that you won't be trying to kill me out there."

"I can't guarantee a thing but I'll do my best not to," he admitted honestly with a shrug.

"Fair enough," Christian stood to start getting dressed. While walking out to the locker room with his towel around his waist, he noticed Dom wasn't there. "Where's the old man?"

"He went out for a walk. He'll be back later," Shawn told him while pointing towards the door. "Speaking of that, I'm gonna go check out the local scenery here."

"What scenery?"

He feigned irritation with a grin. "The girls, man! Didn't you see the babes when we came in?"

Smiling, Christian said, "Try not to be too long. Dom might want to leave once he gets back."

"Yes, mother," his brother replied in a somewhat resentful tone before leaving the locker room.

Chapter 36

Over the next year, Christian had been busy. He won many minor championships of his weight class including the European, Asian, and Australian titles. By the time his rematch against Shawn came around, he would go on to also win the African, North American, and South American titles to unify the continents. He thought it would be fun to try to unify all of them together simply to hear what he would be called after doing so.

Dom, on the other hand, did it mainly to spite Shawn while trying to hint that there were other titles to be proud of other than just the major world championships.

Shawn had been talking more with Duke and his various associates for several of those months. Duke was ever more persistent of Shawn to leave Dom and to take him on to represent him, but Shawn decide he'd make his mind up after his rematch with his brother just so he could see how things panned out. Shawn himself had had a number of fights during this timeframe, easily defending his North American and WBO titles. During which time, Christian noticed that his brother was becoming much more aggressive in the ring and seemed to enjoy it greatly.

Dom finally seemed to give up on Shawn, often going without saying two words to him between rounds. The less Dom said the more aggressive and careless Shawn became. Dom would occasionally voice his disapproval, but would stop soon thereafter. Christian wasn't sure if it was because Shawn simply wasn't listening or because Dom was sick of saying the same thing over and over again. Perhaps it was a little of each.

Shawn obviously did not have, or see, a problem with his increasing aggressiveness. Often being called ruthless and bloodthirsty by members of the media just seemed to stoke his ego all the more. Whatever gap there was between Dom and Shawn before only grew those proceeding months. Christian suspected it was Duke's influence and his ever-subtle seed planting inside Shawn's head. He kept making requests, more like demands, to move up in weight class to face better opponents and each time Dom shot it down.

Dom, however, kept insisting that Shawn wanted to move up in weight more to challenge Christian for his belts than anything else. That, or to go for the WBA title, the more prestigious belt and only major one Christian had yet to win. In private, Dom expressed these views to Christian while feeling that if Shawn were able to get this, not only would it be the last important title Christian had to get, but that in and of itself ranked higher than any of his other belts. As a result, Shawn could than pull rank.

When the day for their rematch finally did come, Christian was saddened by the fact that Dom was sticking to his word. He was, as he mentioned time and time again, not having anything to do with it. Christian understood why, not blaming him for anything, but was saddened nonetheless. He happened to get Curly to manage him and Tony, one of Dom's guys, to be his cut man and Nick Greenwood to be his spit man.

Shawn, meanwhile, had a couple men who worked for Duke, one of which was Jackie Collins, a well-known manager, to represent him. Duke, as well as Igor and a couple of others in his entourage, sat in the front row near Shawn's corner. To this, Christian commented to Curly that he figured this cemented the writing on the wall. Curly's only response was, "What writing?"

Since Christian and Shawn had different locker rooms, a rarity when they both fought on the same card, they spoke only briefly before the match. When they did, Christian was surprised at how assured, boisterous, and cocky Shawn was.

"Hey, Beeker," he called out when they saw each other in the back hall. "How do ya feel 'bout being here?"

"That depends on how our match goes. I'll tell you afterwards."

"That's not what I fuckin' meant, you retard! Dude, don't you know where we're at?"

"Yeah, we're at the RPI Field house in Troy, New York," Christian told him.

"Yeah, exactly! Aren't you excited about that?"

He shook his head. "No. Should I be?"

"This is where Tyson won his seventeenth fight to earn his seventeenth straight victory by knockout, that's why!"

"Ah, ok?" Christian simply stared at him blankly. "Why would that be exciting?"

"Because in that very ring," Shawn said while pointing in the direction of the ring, "Tyson past Rocky Marciano's record of consecutive knockouts to begin a career by a man who would later become heavyweight champ!"

"I highly doubt it was that very ring."

"You know what I meant, asshole!" retorted Shawn sourly.

That was the highlight of their pre-fight conversations.

Later on, while looking across the ring to Shawn as they waited for the bell to sound the beginning of their bout, Christian was nervous. He was nervous because he wasn't sure how Shawn was going to fight. He knew that the harder he fought, Shawn would probably go crazy on him. He understood that this was a boxing match and the objective was to beat your opponent, but, to him, there was a difference between beating your opponent and *beating* your opponent.

Another thing that made Christian question Shawn's mental state was his entrance. For the first time during any of his entrances, Shawn actually played music while he came to the ring. AC/DC's *Back in Black* was heard over the house speakers when he walked over. Christian had heard of fighters occasionally doing this, and for them do to so showed a certain amount of arrogance. He felt that this shouldn't have surprised as much as it had.

Unlike the first match between them, Shawn's hands were untied this match and he was not afraid to throw down. Christian actually was surprised that he was fighting like this, but understood why. He was, however, glad that Shawn was not going crazy on him like he had on his other opponents. The first round went well except for two low blows from Shawn's end. The ref chastised him on the second of the two. Both Curly and Dom established early on that

336

Christian would have to be ready for any type of matchup against Shawn; that he would have to go into the fight as if he was putting his titles on the line against someone other than his brother.

Round two picked up where the first left off. Though both of them were exchanging blows, the main difference was that Shawn appeared to be hitting Christian to wear him down for an eventual knockout; whereas Christian went into his technical defensiveness while dancing around Shawn. This irritated the hell out of Shawn, who at times would try to cut the ring off and pepper him with a few hard shots in an effort to slow him down. Christian would easily block or evade them while moving around to sting his brother with a few jabs. Soon after this, Shawn once again was warned about his low blows.

The third round had a good amount of scoring by both fighters. Since Christian was a little more skilled in the art of blocking and more in the way of eluding, the points favored him. He continued putting the pressure on Shawn the remainder of the fight, dancing around and hitting him with jabs just to irritate him. He knew Shawn liked having a straight fight rather than have to dance around all the time, and thought this would be a good way to aggravate him to the point where he would not be able to think. Shawn wouldn't know how to handle himself at that point and, as a result, would try desperately to knock him out. If Christian evaded his punches well enough, Shawn would have spent all of his energy within the first few rounds. Once he got to that point, Christian knew he would have him.

Near the end of that round, Shawn tangled up Christian's arms so he would stop being hit. At that point, Christian knew his plan was working since Shawn hated doing that. Shawn felt that any boxer who tangled up with their opponent was either over-matched, under prepared, or some combination of the two.

"What the hell ya doin', bro?" Shawn asked while breathing heavily.

"I thought I was fighting you. What are you doing?"

"Stop it, will you?"

"Stop what?" Christian asked innocently.

"Stop hitting me so much. That's what!"

"Why?" Chris snickered.

"So I can win."

"If you want to win, you're going to have to earn it."

"But you won last time. This match is mine."

Before Christian could respond, the ref was there to break them up. "C'mon guys, break it up."

"I can't, ref," Christian told him. "He won't let go of me."

"If you don't want to lose by disqualification," the ref sternly said while looking at Shawn, "you'll break the hold."

"Anythin' you say, ref," Shawn responded while doing what he was told.

"Pull that stuff again and you'll lose a point," the ref told him while holding up a finger.

Shawn didn't respond. Rather, he and Christian went back to fighting once the ref signaled them to. Once they did, Shawn did a combo targeting his brother's body. One of which hit its mark, while the other two shots were below the belt, causing Christian to bend over and kneel to one knee. Shawn then hit Christian with a right hook across the face before being stopped by the ref.

"That's it! That'll cost you one point!" The ref held up one finger before turning to the judges. He then instructed them to remove one point from Shawn's score care for that round. While looking back to Shawn, the ref said, "Do any of that crap again and you're disqualified!"

"Oooh," was all Shawn said while shaking his glove and pretending to be scared.

Once Christian felt safe, he rose. When fully to his feet, the bell sounded to signal the end of round three.

"I've got him!" Christian stated happily when he sat down in his corner. "I've won the match."

"How do you know?" Curly asked while removing Christian's mouth guard.

"He feels I should lose to him on account I won our last match up. He's frustrated because I'm fighting back instead of letting him win. He's also beginning to fight dirty."

"He's scared," Tony commented while giving Chris a drink of water, who soon spat it back out into their pail.

"Any recommendations, you guys?"

"What do the middle two letters of snow spell?" Curly answered while taking one last look over Christian. "Only think I can say is for you to turn up the heat."

"Sure thing, Curly." Christian smiled."I was already planning that."

In both the fourth and fifth rounds, Christian did indeed turn up the heat. By the sixth, Christian had frustrated Shawn to the point that not only was his brother hastily throwing punches and exhausting himself in the process, but he was also fighting dirtier and more aggressive.

He seemed to be hitting his brother with everything he had at full strength, evidentially trying for a knockout. This took Christian completely off guard, momentarily confusing him while going back into defense mode. In the process, Christian was hit with two low blows. Seeing this, the ref called the match before awarding it to Christian via disqualification.

"What?!" Shawn yelled at the ref. "You can't be serious!"

"I am serious!" the ref yelled back. "I warned you earlier about that shit!"

"You were being serious?" Shawn asked while looking at the ref with a confused look. He carried on for a little bit more before going back to his corner. At one point, he glared over to Christian who was simply smiling back at him.

They stayed in their corners until after the ring announcer came to announce the result of the match. After it became official, Christian noticed that Duke was in Shawn's corner shaking hands with him. It appeared the promoter was complimenting his brother on his performance. Shawn seemed to disagree while pointing to the ref, but Duke simply put his hand on Shawn's shoulder while telling him it was ok. What was ok Christian hadn't a clue, but assumed that Shawn's sudden burst of aggression in that last round was as a result of Snyder. Christian decided to ask him about it once he got him alone. However, he wouldn't have to wait too long since Shawn came looking for him shortly after getting backstage.

"Hey Shawn, what the hell was that all about?" Christian demanded as Shawn entered his locker room. The doctor, who had been stitching a cut on his face asked him to be still. "Sorry, Doc," he said before looking back to Shawn. "Well?"

"What was what about?" he asked innocently with a smile.

"Come on, Shawn. Don't patronize me. Did Duke put you up to that?"

"What if he did? So what?"

"What do you mean by 'so what'?"

"What I mean was who cares? You were supposed to let me win this one."

"I was? Why?"

"Because you won last time."

"So what if I won last time?"

"Dude, really?" Shawn asked in a shocked manner. "Since you won last time, then that meant I'd win this time around."

"Like I told you before, wins are earned, not given," Christian told him. "That doesn't give you the right to throw a temper tantrum like an eight-year old and go crazy on your opponent if you actually have to try to win."

"Oh, what, you're now an expert on maturity?"

"What?" Christian asked in wide wonder. "You know, I can't believe we're actually having this conversation. Listen, I don't want to talk about this right now. Would you mind if we talked about this tomorrow at the gym?"

"Have it your way, bro." Shawn turned while walking to the door. He stopped when he reached for the doorknob. "By the way, I won't need a ride home. I'll be going with Duke."

"Ok. See you later, then."

Shawn left without saying anything else. The doctor finished tending to Christian's cut without further interruptions.

Two days later, Christian was talking to Dom about his rematch the night before.

"...I don't know. He just went crazy on me that last round."

"Any idea why, kid?"

"Actually, I have two," Christian told him while rubbing the stitching above his eye. "The first, to me, was because I was fighting back and not letting him win without a fight. That was *really* annoying him. The other was because I think Snyder put him up to it. I can't prove it, but it's just a feeling I have."

"Was that what your brother said?"

"Not in so many words, but that was the indication that I got. Shawn didn't deny it when I asked him about it afterwards. But, on the other hand, he didn't confirm it either."

"What else did he say, kid?"

"That's about it." Christian shrugged. "He felt that I should have let him win because I won our last match up; and a vague confirmation of Duke's involvement."

"What the hell's gotten into him?" Dom asked. "What happened afterwards?"

"You mean after the fight?" Christian asked, to which Dom nodded. "We spoke briefly before he left with Duke."

"Have ya seen him since?"

"No."

"If ya do, tell 'im I wanna have a talk with 'im. That's no way fer 'im ta act, in the ring or out."

Christian, who was leaning against the wall looking out the window, saw Shawn strut into the gym then before making the rounds. "It looks like I won't have to," he said while pointing out to the gym. "It appears like you'll be getting your wish sooner than expected."

As Dom followed Christian's finger, his face became stern once he saw what his student was pointing to.

By Shawn's mannerisms and broad grin, he seemed to be in a far better mood than the last time Christian, or Dom for that matter, had seen him. He was prancing around the gym in some new, expensive looking clothes. A number of the fighters who were training soon stopped to either look or point to him. When Shawn saw this, he didn't have any shame in showing off his apparent new possessions at a moment's notice.

Seeing this, Dom got up and walked to his office's door. "Shawn! Get your ass in here. Now!"

Complying with the order, Shawn strutted his way over. "Greetings, gents," he said with a short bow.

"Ya feel ok?" Dom asked while closing the door behind him.

"I'm feeling splendid," Shawn answered in a very upbeat, cocky way. "Was there something you wanted to see me about, Mr. Dominic?"

Dom walked to behind his desk while pointing to a chair in the process. "Yeah, there was. Have a seat, Shawn."

"What?" Shawn asked was the smile ran away from his face.

"I said sit down!"

Christian, who was leaning against one of the windows, squinted his eyes as his body tensed from the surprise at the loudness of the old man's voice.

"Yeah, sure Dom." Shawn shrugged while sitting. "You don't look so good, old man. You look like you're wound tighter than a cheap watch."

"The reason I don't look so good is because of ya, kid," Dom told him before he and Shawn stared at each other. "I brought ya in here ta give ya a chance ta explain yourself."

"Explain myself? Are you being serious? Explain myself for what exactly?"

Hearing this, Dom simply growled. "I *am* serious. What'd'ya have ta say fer yerself?"

"If it's any of your concern, I came here to see the guys," Shawn said while spreading his hands out before smiling arrogantly at Dom. His hands soon came down to fix his clothes. "I also came in to show off my new clothes."

"Speaking of yer clothes, where'd ya get them?"

"From a store, of course."

"They look expensive."

"They do, don't they?"

"I don't mean to pry, kid, but where'd ya get the money for 'em?"

"What's it to ya, old man?"

"I'm asking mainly 'cause it ain't a secret what ya tend ta spend yer money on." Dom looked at him. "There's also an implication that ya don't like ta save it fer a rainy day. If ya got the money from an outside source that could cause trouble fer me, I'd like ta know 'bout it."

"I don't really think I need to tell you that," Shawn replied. "This is just another way for you to try and control me, just like you've been doing ever since I got here."

"Fine, have it your way, kid. Just forget about it."

"I think I will," he said while standing up. "If that's it, I've got to get going. I'm meeting Duke for lunch."

Hearing this, Dom cleared his throat. "Speaking of Duke, is he the reason for all of this?"

"All of what?"

"This," Dom told him while waving his hands at Shawn. "Your clothes, your attitude, this new you or whatever the hell this is."

"Maybe. Maybe not."

"Ta be honest, that might explain why ya've been actin' more of a jerk lately." Dom got up to walk over to Shawn. "That would also explain yer increased aggression in the ring and ya goin' nuts on yer brother two nights ago."

"Hey, man, he deserved what I gave him," Shawn said while pointing to Christian.

"He deserved it?" Dom asked in a shocked manner. "He deserved all those cheap low blows? He deserved ya goin' crazy on him in that last round?"

"Actually, he deserved a lot more than that but that, damn ref stopped the fight before I was able to give him the rest of it."

"Ya could'a hurt him!" Dom yelled.

"So?! Maybe he deserved that as well?"

"Why, huh? Why'd he deserve that?"

"'cause that fight was mine. Mine!"

"What'cha talkin' 'bout, kid?"

"Our first fight he won, so that meant that the next I'd win. But he wasn't fightin' fair. He wasn't lettin' me win!"

"He wasn't supposed to let ya win, kid! If ya wanted ta win, then ya should'a earned it rather than takin' the easy way out. If the ref hadn't of called it, ya could'a hurt 'im and fer what? One more victory?"

"Hey, he owes me, little man!" Shawn yelled while getting in Dom's face.

"He doesn't owe ya anythin'!" Dom responded while not backing down from his younger and much bigger visitor. "You're ego's been blown so far outta proportion that ya lost track of what's

342

really important. Are ya really willin' ta hurt your own brother because ya think he owes ya somethin'?"

"You don't understand, Dom, so don't even stand there and try to lecture me 'bout something you know nothing about!"

"I know nothin' about this, ya say." The old man paused briefly to look at Shawn. "Let me tell ya what I do know. I know that yer brother is probably one of yer few friends, if not yer only one. And he probably had been the only one ya could count on yer entire life. Ya came into this business either because ya couldn't do anythin' else or ya wouldn't try. Ya brought yer brother in a few years later, who was in between jobs and needed money. Ya thought trainin' 'im here would shape 'im up so he wouldn't be as much of an embarrassment to you. Hell, ya probably also brought 'im here so ya could talk 'bout 'im behind his back as ya showed the other guys what ya had ta live with. Ya never worried he'd be in it as long as he has probably 'cause ya figured he doesn't have the mind set and 'cause he has the potential ta be anythin' he wants. Ya had nothin' ta worry 'bout.

"But once it looked like he was becomin' serious 'bout this," Dom continued, "serious 'bout bein' a boxer, ya became nervous. Though the wasn't in as peak physical conditioning as ya were, he learned quickly and absorbed any bit of trainin' he could. He was intelligent and was able to adapt ta any style he needed ta. He began to define his style with a way ya thought wasn't macho or manly enough. He didn't go fer the knockout, yet he was showin' promise of bein' a good fighter.

"People started ta take notice of 'im and less of ya. He started gettin' title shots, which he won, and endorsements. He had money the bank, he bought a house, he moved out on ya. He got a new vehicle and gave his old one ta his girlfriend rather than to ya.

"As for his girlfriend," Dom said, "he actually found one woman he's happy with. He found someone who cares 'bout him for who he is rather than for how tough and macho he acts, or for the 'mount of alcohol he can drink, or for the 'mount of money he'd be willin' to give her fer sex.

"He's also not the rebel ya strive ta be. He's not afraid ta be one of the boys so the team can succeed. He doesn't need ta show off or brag or get any titles fer him ta feel better about himself or fer people ta like him. Ya became jealous, maybe even envious, 'cause he's achieved more than ya have in a much shorter period of time. Sure, ya brought 'im in the business but he's gettin' all the rewards that ya feel ya should have gotten instead.

"Then, when ya two had your rematch two nights ago, that was your one chance ta shift things back ta your side. All ya needed was a win over 'im and ya'd have it. But, sadly fer ya, he fought back. He wasn't 'fraid of ya. He wasn't goin' ta lie down and cower so ya could beat the victory outta him. He forced ya ta earn it like ya did all yer other fights. How could he do this ta ya? Didn't he realize he owes ya? Owes ya for his very existence? Ya probably felt confusion at first that then turned to rage. Ya tried ta tell him ta stop fightin', ta let ya win. But when that didn't work, ya started cheating', fightin' dirty. Ya knew ya wouldn't last in the later rounds against him and ya knew he knew. Ya both knew the further the match went, the more it went ta his favor."

Dom paused long enough to look at Shawn while allowing him time to correct anything that he had just said to him. When the pugilist remained silent, he continued.

343

"When ya realized things weren't goin' yer way, ya may have gotten word from Snyder ta unleash whatever ya had left on 'im, that it'll be ok, and ta go fer it. Ya probably thought, 'Snyder is tellin' me this, a top promoter with several contenders and champions under 'im, then it must be ok.'

"That was probably the first time someone actually said ya could fight the way ya wanted ta with no regards ta your opponents health. So ya did it and ya enjoyed every moment of it. The thing that ya found most frustratin' was when the ref called the match ta award it ta yer brother. Ya probably thought how is that possible when he owed ya when Snyder said it was ok. Ya probably felt that he stole another victory from ya. Later on, after the match, ya had a little bit of hope. Duke still wanted ta talk ta ya, even though ya lost doing' what he said. He offered ya a ride home. Hell, he might'a had a big ole party in your honor; a party with lots of alcohol, lots of broads, and ya'd be able to get yer fill of both. Ta show his appreciation and that he hadn't lost any of his faith in ya, he most likely even bought ya some new clothes and gave ya money. When ya came in here a few minutes ago, ya probably came here ta tell us that ya're under new management, ya know, sorta like a store that got bought out. And ya, ya snot-nosed little brat, ya have the gull and audacity ta tell *me* I don't know what I'm talkin' 'bout?!"

When Dom was finally done with his monologue, he gave Shawn a solid poke on his left shoulder to send an extra point home.

Upon doing that, it enraged the young man before him to the point that he hadn't been since childhood. In this brief moment, whatever line of fabric that held Shawn's emotions in check finally broke. Shawn's eyes went wild and crazy while he grabbed Dom by the scruff of the his shirt collar before forcing him backwards. He pinned him on his desk while hunching over him, leaving only a few inches of room between them.

"Don't you ever touch me like that again! You hear me?!" Shawn shouted as saliva spat from his mouth like a rabid dog. "And who in the *hell* you think you are to be tellin' me shit like that, huh? You tellin' me how I should act?! You, a fuckin' nobody, a goddamn has been?! Don't be tellin' me what to do! Don't you dare do that!"

Seeing this, Christian sprang from where he was by the window to intervene. He was a couple seconds behind, being shortly delayed from the shock at what he was seeing. He was able to get in between the two of them as he tried to push Shawn back. When he and Shawn made eye contact, Christian knew at that moment that the Shawn he had known was no longer there. Another entity was now in possession of his body.

"Come on, Shawn! Get back!" he yell while continuing to push and pull him off of Dom. "Shawn, goddamn it, let him go!"

When it appeared Shawn wasn't going to let Dom go, Christian kneed his brother in the groin, which finally broke his brother's grip, before pushing him away. The push was harder than he had anticipated, a push that sent Shawn over a chair behind him. Immediately getting up, Shawn grabbed Christian to throw him against a nearby wall. He was making his way towards him when Tony and Mitch charged in through the door and quickly subdued him.

"You just made the worst mistake of your life, bro!" Shawn said while glaring at Christian. "You've fucked with me for the last time!"

"Shawn, settle your scrawny, white ass down," Mitch said after they got him on the floor. "We don't want to have to hurt you."

"If you know what's good for you," Shawn said to him. "You'd get your fuckin' black ass off of me. Now!"

Without hesitation, Mitch punched Shawn across the face, which immediately drew blood.

"I'd listen to him if I were you, Shawn," Tony said while maneuvering one of Shawn's arms behind him.

"As for you, Tony," snarled Shawn, "you'd better not even consider packing my ass like you do the rest of your boyfriends."

Just then, Sly, Dom's utility and maintenance man, ran into the office.

"What's going on?" he asked. "Is anyone hurt?"

"We're alright," Dom told him shortly while finally being able to adjust himself to a more suitable manner. "We're alright."

"What happened?" Sly again asked.

"Shawn and I just had a disagreement, that's all."

"A disagreement?" Tony asked while looking at him.

Mitch seemed to laugh briefly at this. "It sounded more like World War III had begun."

"It would have been if you guys didn't come in," Chris told him.

"Dom, want me to call the police?" asked Sly.

"Thanks, but that won't be necessary," Dom looked to the now restrained young man on the office floor. "Will it, Shawn?"

Shawn didn't bother to answer that.

"This is the last time, Shawn," Dom said while kneeling down next to him. "I've warned ya 'bout this. This is the last time I'm helpin' ya out. Don't come back until ya've gotten yer problems and priorities taken care of." When he said that, there was a brief look between them before Dom looked to both Tony and Mitch. "Oh guys, let him go. Be sure ta show him the way out."

When Tony and Mitch were in the process of dragging Shawn towards the office door after hauling him to his feet, Dom waddled over to them.

"Hey, kid. If ya come in here again lookin' for trouble," Dom said coldly before flicking a thumb to the guys around them. "I'm givin' each of these guys the ok to call the police on ya. Now, get the hell outta my gym!"

With that, Shawn was forcibly escorted out of the gym. After seeing him thrown out the front door and onto the sidewalk, Christian helped pick up the office. They did so in silence while everybody else went back to work.

Coincidentally, however, Shawn wasn't seen or heard from for the rest of the week. He came in that next Monday to inform Dom that he was firing him as both his manager and trainer.

"I also wanna tell you that I got Duke to promote me, and I just hired Jackie Collins today as a manager," he smugly said as Dom listened on in silence. "He found me a spot to stay at until I'm able to get myself somethin'."

"When will ya be movin' out from upstairs?"

"This week."

"Sooner the better."

Shawn smiled. "You know, that's one of the few things we've ever agreed on."

"Is that all?" Dom quietly asked.

Blinking his eyes, Shawn responded. "What?"

"I've got work ta do here, kid. So, if ya don't mind, is that all?"

"I do have one more thing," Shawn said in his now usual cocky demeanor. "Duke just wanted me to tell you to watch out. He has a few things for me to do in my weight class but, once I do those, he's gonna move me up in weight so I can challenge for Christian's titles."

"Fat chance that'll happen," Dom retorted flatly.

"Unlike you, Dom, Duke's connections he ain't afraid to use."

There was a moment of silence before Dom stood up to walk over to Shawn. "Kid, answer me one thing, will ya? All this can't be 'cause ya just didn't get more title shots."

"You just don't get it, do you Dom?" Shawn looked around before finally looking back to the old man square in the eye. "You just didn't trust me enough to ever push me. If you trusted me enough to do that, none of this would'a happened. All I can say is that it's just mind over matter from now on. Mind over matter. I don't mind 'cause neither you, or any of this, matters anymore. That's what's goin' on inside my head," he said while tapping a finger to his temple. "Have I answered all your petty little questions yet?"

"If you're finished, do us a favor and get the hell outta my place!"

"As you wish," Shawn coolly replied with a smile before leaving.

To his credit, Shawn kept his word and moved out of the apartment above Dom's gym that week, officially cementing the end of a relationship that was over thirteen years in the making.

Chapter 37

"Hollywood Fred!" Catfish said when Christian entered the library later that week. "What's happening', my brother from another mother?"

"Not too much, Larry. How've you been?"

"Oh, you know, just livin' the dream." He shrugged. "I've also been rollin' on down the highway so life won't pass me by."

"Wha-what? What the hell're you talking about, Larry?"

"Oh, nothing. The radio was just playing some old Jim Croce songs about an hour ago. That was a line from one of his songs. I kinda liked it so I thought I'd borrow it to see how it sounded."

"Did it sound good at all?"

"Not bad." Catfish shrugged again. "I may need to say it a few more times to see if it fits me or not. So, anyway, what are you doing here, Hollywood?"

"Well, I thought I might do some reading for a little bit if that's alright with you."

"It's alright with me just so long as we follow the same game plan as we've done in the past."

"I was planning on that," Christian informed him with a smile.

"Excellent! I'll see you around nine or so."

"Nine it is," confirmed Chris. "When we get together then so I can hide, I want to tell you want happened at the gym a couple of days ago."

"I can't wait. But, if you excuse me, I have some things I need to get to."

"Yeah, go ahead, Larry," Chris told him. "I'll be in my usual spot until then."

Christian, in fact, did go back to his usual table that he always sat at. On his way over, he got a well-worn copy of *The Autobiography of Charles Darwin* off of a nearby shelf. He had been intrigued with Darwin ever since his school boy days when he used to make his science fair projects. He had leafed through a copy of this book when he was a boy but discarded it shortly thereafter because he wasn't able to fully comprehend it. However, the image of Darwin on the cover, one which showed a very thick, all white beard, a receding hair line into a heavily creased forehead, and sad, thoughtful eyes etched itself into the back of Christian's mind. An image that had left a lasting impression on him.

What eventually got him to try and reread the book so many years later was because he happened to see it one night at the library. Upon seeing it, old memories long thought dead came back to life along with a renewed sense of belonging he had many years previously had.

This, eventually, led him to reading and rereading it multiple times thereafter. That night he planned to finish reading it for the fourth time since first discovering it there. He thoroughly enjoyed one chapter I particular, on which laid the foundations to *The Origin of Species*. This chapter, henceforth, was entitled *The Foundations of The Origin of Species*. A few pages within this chapter, Darwin explained that he had read, and also heard about rather early in life, the book that his deceased grandfather had written, one entitled *Zoonomia*, whose views were similar to that of Darwin himself. He confessed the probability that that influenced his later works and findings, even though his own views were different from that of his grandfather's.

Upon finishing the book that night, Christian reflected back on his life and wondered what his life would have been like if he hadn't been drawn into boxing. Would he have gone back to college? Would he have continued on in his restaurant jobs? Would he have found a new path? He even began to think what he would want to do after he got out of boxing. Granted, he knew that he wouldn't be in it for the rest of his life, but he never actually thought about it until then. What was he going to do? The answer that he eventually came up with was that he honestly didn't know. As he sat there befuddled while trying to contemplate the situation he found himself in, he noticed Larry making his way over to him.

"You still reading that?" Catfish asked while acknowledging the book. "I'd've thought you'd've finished that ages ago."

"I did," admitted Christian. "I liked it so much that I had to reread it."

"It took you this long to read it twice?"

"Actually I read it four times."

"You read that damn thing four times?" Larry asked in amusement.

Christian nodded.

"Did you read anything else in between each time?"

Christian shook his head.

"Do you plan on reading it another time?"

"Eventually, but not anytime soon," Christian stated while shaking his head again.

"Why that book? Why not read something more modern?"

"Remember those science fairs we had back in school? The ones where we made things for?"

Larry nodded.

"I remember reading this a little back then. I guess times just catching up to me; making me wish I had followed that longer in my life rather than boxing."

"Do you regret getting into boxing?" Larry asked while sitting across from him.

"No." He shook his head. When answering, Christian realized he was telling the truth. "Just that I wished I kept up that science part for when I eventually did get out of the sport."

"It's never too late, you know."

"Never too late for what?"

"To change; to go back and bring it back into your life."

"You serious?" Christian asked in a dismayed tone.

"Well, yeah." Larry nodded, which, to Christian, seemed like a polite way of saying 'Well, duh!' "Do you actually plan on fighting for the rest of your life?"

"No, actually I don't."

"What do you plan on doing then, once you get out?"

"I don't know."

"Well, there you go then." Larry shrugged.

"Are you suggesting that I get back into science or whatever?"

"Yeah, more of whatever though, but yeah," admitted Catfish. "Did you have anything else you were going towards or had wanted to."

"Actually, I haven't even thought about it until now."

"Maybe you should," Larry told him. "You just said that you don't plan on being a fighter for the rest of your life. You also said that you wished you kept up with science. So, I'd suggest you finish up with what you have to do with boxing, then get the hell out while you can and get something in the science field, or whatever the hell field you choose."

Christian blinked his eyes a couple of times in confusion. "But I'd need a degree to do that. Remember, I didn't finish college."

"Then go back," Larry told him bluntly. "I'm sure you have enough money set aside to help you for a little while at least. Miho's working, isn't she?"

Christian nodded.

"You two don't plan on breaking up anytime soon, are you?"

"Not that I know of."

"I'm assuming she's support you and back up whatever you did decide about going back to finish school. Am I right?"

"I've gotten that impression from her as well."

"Then what the hell are you waiting for then, a sign?" Larry laughed.

Christian didn't answer. He just sat there and looked across the table to his friend.

"You don't really want to be a dropout like me, do you?"

"Just like you can always go back and get your G.E.D."

"Just like you can always go back and finish college," Larry said while looking at his pugilistic friend. "I'd bet you'd be happier with yourself once you did do that. I know I would be."

"You'd be happier if I went back to college?"

"Yeah, as a matter of fact, I would."

Christian smiled. "Why's that?"

"So that I know you wouldn't be a dropout like me. And that you wouldn't be wasting what brains and smarts you have in the ring."

"I don't know," Christian softly said.

"Goddamn it, Hollywood! You've been getting on my ass for how long now to finish school but when the tables are turned on you, you end up making excuses!" Catfish looked at him with frustration in his voice. "What's up with that?"

"Nothing's up," Christian quickly retorted while having what Larry said sink in before answering a bit more slowly and quietly. "I'm not making excuses."

"You are so," Larry shot back. "I'll make you a deal, one that you would call a win-win situation."

Hearing this, Christian's attention got peaked. "I'm listening."

"If you consider going back to finish college after you get out of boxing, I'll consider going for my G.E.D." He faintly smiled with that. "If you actually do go back to college, I'll enroll myself in some night classes for my exam. What do you say to that, huh, Hollywood?"

Smiling, Christian replied with a "I'll consider it."

"That's it, then. We both agree to consider on going back to school. Agreed?" Larry smiled while extending a hand for Christian to shake.

Accepting the hand almost at once, Christian nodded. "Agreed."

"Then when it looks like you're close to getting outta boxing, I'll start nagging your ass about college like you're been nagging mine," Catfish told him while shooting his friend a glare. A thought crossed his mind then. "Speaking of your boxing, your last several fights the crowd reaction has gotten pretty intense; especially the last two you got us tickets for."

"I hadn't noticed but now that you mention it," Christian said while thinking about what he was

350

just told. "It has been pretty noisy in the ring as well."

"You're becoming quite the fan favorite."

Christian reluctantly agreed. "So it seems."

He was always embarrassed when he was talking about himself is ways like they were presently for some reason. He never quite felt comfortable being the center of attention, a trait, he thought, was never in short supply when dealing with Shawn.

As if reading his mind, Larry asked, "How's your brother's reaction to your so-called pop?"

"He says that they're cheering because of him."

Larry smiled. "Think he's jealous? The pops that you're getting are actually better than his now."

"I think so, maybe a little," admitted Christian. "But I doubt he'll come out and say so."

"Oh, not to change the subject," Catfish injected while rubbing his forehead. "The guys and I wanted to ask if you'd want to help us out tomorrow. We're short a person for league night."

"I'd love to but, unfortunately, I already have plans," Christian reluctantly told him. "My parents and Miho are coming over for dinner, otherwise I would. I'm sorry."

"That's ok. Just thought I'd ask," Larry told him. "How've your parents doing, anyway?"

"They're doing the same. You outta come by, when you can, to see them. I know they'd like seeing you again. It's been a while since you've been over."

"I highly doubt I'd be able to make it tomorrow for a visit. Would you take a rain check?"

"Rain check it is."

"Oh, shit!" Catfish stated when he noticed the time before pushing himself up out of his chair. "I'm late for a very important date. I should have been back to work eons ago. See what happens when I get you talking? Once that happens, you don't shut up!"

"Oh, be quiet and go back to work, will ya?" Christian laughed while shaking his head.

"Remember," Larry said while pointing to his visitor, "we're both going back to school this decade. And I still owe you that rain check."

"Yep."

"And let me know when you need me to let you out. If you can't find me, I'm probably hiding somewhere in the basement"

Then, just like that, Larry was gone. Moments later his cleaning cart was heard squeaking its way down the hall.

Christian stayed for another hour or so before retiring. His friend had given him a lot to think about, especially on things he could look forward to after boxing. Though he felt Miho would support any decision he'd make on this matter, he still wanted her opinion on it. On his way home, he hoped she'd still up so he could ask her.

***

"I don't know. Shawn just went crazy on Dom," Christian told his parents that next night during dinner. "I'm not sure what would have happened if Tony and Mitch didn't show up."

"What's gotten into him?" his mother asked while shaking her head. "It's as if we don't know him anymore."

"Are you telling us that we actually *did* know him?" her husband injected.

"Are you suggesting we never did?" she quickly asked back.

"I'm just saying there's more to him then he shows. Sometimes I think that my dad was the only one who ever really got to know him. Even then, I still have my suspicions," David explained while looking at his son. "That's probably what you'll have to look forward to if you keep up in that damn sport of yours. If you keep taking those head shots, you'll end up a nut case like that brother of yours."

"Have you given any thought about doing something else, dear?" his mother asked him. "Obviously you've been able to afford a house from the earnings you make; and I'm sure you've saved a little up. How much longer do you plan on taking that kind of abuse?"

"I'm not sure, Mom," he answered honestly. "There's still a few more things I'd like to do before finally getting out."

"Like what, being turned into a vegetable?" his father asked dryly.

"I agree with your father," Sally said. "It's barbaric and senseless. There's no need to take that kind of punishment, especially you; you could have been anything you put your mind to!"

"You should listen to your parents," Miho said softly from her seat. She hadn't said much since dinner started, and apparently felt this was a good spot to start. "There is no need to be in it any longer than you have to."

"Very well put," Sally complimented with a smile, which sstirred a smile from Miho. "You should listen to your friend here, Christian. She makes a good point. Very good in fact."

"Yes, mother," he responded sarcastically which drew a comical look from both of the women at the table. "But, to be honest, there were a few things I wanted to do first. I honestly never thought I'd be in it as long as I have, let alone do what I've done."

"What more do you need to do?" he father asked.

"Well, I sort of would like to get that last belt to unify my weight class before defending them

352

against the last few contenders," Christian told him. "Other than that, that's pretty much it."

"So, you'd retire if, and when, you did that?" David inquired.

"I don't think I'd actually *retire*, but I would get out of boxing, if that's what you mean."

"What would you do when you got out?" his mother asked while sipping her tea.

"He should go back to college and get his degree," Miho answered in his stead.

"Yes, I should," agreed Christian. "I've always felt sort of bad about not finishing college. Maybe with the money I get I'll pay off what I have left of my student loans and go back to finish."

"You should," Miho told him firmly.

"Yes, Miho." Christian rolled his eyes while sighing heavily.

"Don't be mean to her," his father chastised. "She's looking out for you. Besides, I sort of like her. I'd hate to think you'll lose her if you decide to stay in that sport of yours a little too long."

Rather than responding, Christian only looked at his father.

"Ok, boys. Enough about boxing," Sally told them in a tone that formally ended their current conversation. "So, dear, was there some reason why Shawn didn't come to dinner tonight?"

"I didn't ask him."

"Why not?"

"I didn't really want him here," Christian answered bluntly. "He's still upset about Dom overlooking him all these years and I didn't want him to bring any of those grudges with him tonight. Besides, I think he's still a little upset, jealous, or whatever that I have this place. He seems to feel that he should have been the one to get a place first rather than me."

"Are you serious?" David asked him.

He nodded. "I think so."

"He's upset because you moved out of that apartment first?"

"Silly, isn't it?"

"Has he ever been here yet?" asked his mother.

"No, he hasn't."

"Have you asked him to visit?"

"Several times."

"And why hasn't he?"

"Like I said, I think he's still a little upset I moved out first." Christian laughed. "I think he'd feel like I was rubbing it in if he comes over."

"That can't be the only reason," his mother said.

"It's not," Miho quietly responded, which drew quizzical looks from both of Christian's parents. "I may be another reason for his absence."

"Whatever do you mean?" asked Sally while not knowing the full meaning of that statement.

"Mom, maybe you haven't noticed, but Shawn seems to have a little problem with people who aren't white Americans, if you get my drift."

"Are you saying that Shawn, someone that your father and I have raised, is a racist?" She sounded shocked and hurt by that, as well as a number of other emotions, right then. Her facial expressions complimented her tone.

"You're never noticed?" her husband dryly asked her.

"In all honesty, no, I never have," she finally admitted before turning back to her son and Miho. "Are you serious? You aren't making this up, are you?"

"Yes, Mom, I'm serious. And, no, we're not making it up."

"Did you know about this?" she asked Miho.

"I suspected," she told her.

"Oh my, that could put a damper on things." Sally bit her lip before continuing. "Did Shawn come out and say that he didn't like you?"

"No." Christian shook his head. "Well, not in so many words but the implication was there,"

"The way your father and I raised the two of you, I'm surprised to hear that, dear. I truly am." She shook her head several times before going back to ear her dinner.

"He's Bruce's son, alright," David injected.

"So, dear, are you all moved in now?" Sally asked Miho with a smile.

"Oh, no, not yet," she told her with a confused look. Miho was confused because, even though she had been occasionally staying there with Christian for the last few months, she hadn't actually moved in and she knew that Sally knew this fact.

"How do you like it here?"

"It's very nice. Thank-you."

"Is it anything like the houses where you come from in Japan?"

"Um, no." Miho shook her head. "It's bigger and more spacious here. A lot of yard here too as compared to there. And it's very American; nothing like Japanese homes."

"Do you miss Japan much?"

"Oh, yes I do," she replied before getting somewhat fidgety. "Of course I'm not saying bad things about America. America is a very nice country, plenty of opportunities, but I miss home."

"Of course, dear. We understand. It's quite natural to miss one's home," Sally told her in a very motherly fashion. "Do you have any plans on going back?"

"I do want to go back at some point, but I'm not sure exactly when. That will depend on what I'm involved with over here, you see," Miho replied while briefly looking to Christian before blushing slightly.

David and Sally caught that personal look that she threw their son before they looked at each other with a smile. Christian, on the other hand, was off in another world and hadn't been following that bit of the conversation too closely.

"At least one person hasn't changed much," David stated while getting some coffee. His comment drew a baffled look from his son. "Never mind," was all he told him while laughing and shaking his head. "Speaking of someone not changing much, what's going on with your brother?"

"What do you mean, Dad?"

"A year or two ago, that whole thing with Wesley," he explained. "What happened with that?"

"Oh, that." Christian laughed. "The chargers were eventually dropped due to self-defense. He did do a ton of community service is all I really know. I hadn't heard anything about it since."

"What charges were those again?"

"I want to say it was some sort of manslaughter, but Shawn likes to say it was second-degree murder," Christian told her. "I think he was just saying that since it sounded worse. Better for his ego to inflate the charges, the whole tough guy thing. But I don't really believe much of what he says these days."

"Now, who did he kill again, dear?"

"Wesley, that heavy kid who had that little gang of trouble makers when we were kids," Christian told her. "They liked to try and beat the hell out of me every chance they could."

"That's who I thought, but for some reason I thought I heard it may not have been. Didn't Shawn stab him or something?"

"Yeah," her son confirmed. "He gutted him like a fish."

His mom shuttered at the image.

David, on the other hand, lowered his head while shaking it. "That's a lovely image. Thanks for putting that in my head, especially when I'm trying to eat."

"Sorry about that, Dad."

"You'd better be." He smiled.

"Dear, this Wesley guy that Shawn did this to," Sally said. "Was he the same one that was blaming you for the trouble he got in a long time ago?"

"Yeah, that's him."

"How much time did he end up doing?"

"Just over eleven years."

"And what exactly did he do to get that much?"

"Oh, I don't remember exactly," Christian vaguely said while wanting to change the subject.

"Anyway, perhaps we should leave such things in the past where they belong?" Sally suggested while wiping her mouth off with her napkin. Everyone at the table seemed to agree with that. "So, do you see much of your brother these days?"

"Not so much now, no."

"I don't think you should be around him anymore than you have to," Miho told him.

"Who, Shawn" Christian asked while seeing her nod to him. "Why's that?"

"Because he a bad influence and he into all kind of trouble," she told him. "Not to mention he did try to hurt Mr. Dom. He keep getting arrested is another thing. The list goes on. All he cares about is himself. I wouldn't be surprised if he pulls you down just to elevate his ego. Just cut him loose. Let him go. He may be the death of you one day!"

When hearing this, all Christian could do was lean back in his chair and look at her. He honestly couldn't disagree with anything she had just said. In fact, he agreed with most of it.

"Don't try and say I wrong. Me not wrong. Not about this," she shot at him with a look."

"Maybe you're right."

"Maybe?" She looked at him while scrunching her eyebrows.

"Perhaps maybe isn't the best choice of words there, son," David commented with a smile.

"Perhaps maybe you're right," Christian reluctantly agreed while looking at his girlfriend. "In all honesty, my life has been better these last two years or so since I moved out, mainly because he's not there, but he has helped me out a lot of little ways over the years."

"But these little ways, have they equaled all the negatives he's laid on you in that same time frame?" Miho asked him seriously.

"Good point." Christian looked at her with a smile. "Man, you really don't like him, do you?"

"He has not done anything to warrant me to," she told him bluntly. "He's rude, crass, blunt, mean, spiteful, egotistical, a drunk, a druggie, a bully, and very jealous. On top of that, he will use anyone he can to further himself anyway possible. Since I'm looking at him from the outside, I don't have the luxury of seeing him the same way you three do. My way consists of two things: a list of pros and a list of cons. Unfortunate for him, the list of cons greatly outweighs the pros."

"I hate to agree with you, but you do have a valid point." Christian sighed while feeling bad about saying that. He still felt an underlining loyalty to his brother, although he knew he shouldn't. "And I think he'll become much worse than he has been. Duke is so unscrupulous and money hungry, he'll exploit Shawn every way he can. And while he's doing that, he'll be boosting Shawn's already inflated ego up even further so that it's stretching at the seams. He'll never leave until Duke uses him for every penny he's worth. And considering how Shawn is about keeping his finances in order, he'll be as broke at the end of his career as he is now. Shawn'll think that it'll be him playing Duke when in reality it's the other way around. Duke will always be ten steps ahead of him."

"If it's ok with you," Sally said with a little iron in her jaw. "I'm sure we can talk about something other than Wesley, Shawn, or anything else along these lines. I was hoping we'd have a nice meal here tonight."

"That's alright with me, Mom," Christian said.

And by the way both David and Miho looked, they also agree on this point. They soon changed the subject to something more positive as they carried on with dinner.

After dinner, Sally helped Christian and Miho clear the table and do the dishes. David, meanwhile, turned on some game he'd wanted to watch. After that, they all went for a walk around the neighborhood.

Christian's house was a modest ranch-style home set on an acre plot of land roughly five miles from his parents place. He had been there almost two years and, during which time, Miho had lived with him. Also during this same time, Shawn not once had come visit. He always seemed to have some excuse as to why he couldn't. Christian decided to quit trying; he simply labeled the subject as a lost cause.

During those two years of living with Miho, Christian spoke of marriage but was denied as long as he stayed in boxing. She informed him that she didn't want to start a family with that in their lives. She said she wouldn't have any problems with it after he quit the sport, but also stated she didn't want him to quit prematurely because of her. Miho did, however, assure him that if things kept up between them as they had been, she would stick by him; but he alone would have to choose when he was done with that barbaric sport he called a job.

Chapter 38

The next year both Christian and Shawn each enjoyed success in their respected careers. Christian received a few more enforcement contracts, while making occasional appearances on TV. With the money he was generating, he began making generous contributions to several charities; children's centers, schools, hospitals, and shelters, both homeless and animal. He even bought some parcels of land to be donated. They were used for playgrounds for children and another hangout spots. A couple other locations he donated were also used for shelters.

Miho had officially moved in with Christian before becoming engaged a few months after that. Shortly after his engagement, Christian defended his minor belts a few more times before forfeiting them to allow the newer, younger guys a chance to go for them. This made him happy because it freed up quite a bit of time to allow him to face bigger opponents for his top three belts, the WBO, WBC, and IBF world championships.

After giving up the smaller belts, he pleaded with Dom to face other top contenders so he could eventually challenge for the WBA title. To his amazement, Dom agreed only if he would win the belt when the chance presented itself. To him, this could have been Christian's only chance to go for it and he didn't want to pass it up. With this, he felt Dom agreed for two reasons: first, because he's come a long way as a fighter and that this could be his reward and, second, it may very well have been Dom's way of sticking it to Shawn. Whatever the reason, Christian wasn't going to say anything about it. He didn't care just so long as he got a chance. For him, the idea was to put his titles on the line to unify all of them to crown an undisputed champion.

Meanwhile, Shawn had moved to Manhattan where he lived in a luxurious apartment that Duke set up for him. Duke was able to eventually put him in some high profile fights against the top contenders in his weight class, all of which Shawn won with various levels of difficulty. These wins put him in contention for the IBF light heavyweight championship a few months later. The fight didn't even go two rounds, practically ending shortly after it had begun. The IBF champ didn't stand a chance. It would have been over a full round sooner if Shawn hadn't wasted a good amount of time playing with him.

He fought some more fights against more top guys while still defending his belts. He eventually went up against the WBC champ, Daniel 'Greased' Lightning. Unfortunately for Shawn, he seemed to underestimate the champ slightly. He bragged that the fight would be over by the end of the second round; it went on to end near the end of the fourth.

Shawn's wishes seemed to be coming true at a much faster rate than he had planned. Within a year of leaving Dom, he won both the WBC and IBF titles in his weight class. These, combined with the WBO belt from before, gave him the right to say that he equaled Christian. He received a couple of minor endorsements with a promising chance for more.

On top of the belts and endorsements, he now had a good amount of money to help afford his less than ethical and unhealthy habits whenever and wherever he wanted. Since joining Duke, he felt he was around women that he actually deserved to be around. This meant instead of being with a $10 hooker, he how had four digit escorts. Everything with Duke was top of the line and top notched. He was promise that the rewards would keep coming just as long as the wins were, and Shawn wasn't planning on losing anytime soon.

In other news, *The Misfits* finally found a permanent replacement for Roger, and had, again, finished first in their league. Christian joked that it took them long enough. Larry was still working at the library while reading countless books in his various hideouts almost as fast as he was borrowing them. Eric was still cooking at the Bourbon-N-Ribeye but now was enjoying a recent promotion as kitchen manager. His countless supply of girlfriends almost rivaled Shawn's, but not quite. Miggie, on the other hand, received a record contract from a small, independent company downstate. He seemed to work twice as much as before, but this time he was able to hear a few more of his songs on the radio as a result.

With the increasing publicity that Christian had received, he was still slightly embarrassed whenever someone would recognize him in public. His increased popularity was still strange to him but, as a result, his fights drew more people which, in turn, drew more money.

As a result of his earnings, Dom was able to fix up his building while making needed repairs to both the gym and the upstairs apartments. He seemed to have gone crazy updating the basic items such as windows, heating and cooling, and the walls and floor, but left some things the same such as the office and the gym without a ceiling.

Young Nick Greenwood was coming along quite well in his junior middleweight division. He had quite a few amateur matches before turning pro. He won his first pro fight via six round decision.

Christian was soon picking up a variety of charity work as well as working as an occasional boxing analyst for ESPN when he had the chance. Not only did this help him learn a lot of various contenders that, but he also could secretly keep track of Shawn's career.

He was impressed with the talent Shawn was now facing under the direction of Duke. He was facing practically every contender there was out there, as well as anyone who wanted to challenge for his titles. Shawn's 'new' style of fighting was one of the first things Christian noticed about him. It was as if his hands were now completely untied and he was able to fight anyway he wanted. He felt that Shawn was now more of a combination of Marvin Haggler and Mike Tyson of his weight class. With his new aggressive fighting style, the going concern was that he would be completely spend and wasted if his fights went past the fifth round, the very same prediction that Dom had made several times before. Whether that was actually true or not, no one know because none of his fights ever went beyond that.

A few months into that same year, Shawn left an irritating message on Christian's phone. "Hey, bro. How's it going? I have a fight coming up this week, one which I'll easily win, mind you. And guess what I'll get as a result of that win? I'll get a shot at the WBA title, something that seems to have eluded even you. And, once I've gotten that, do you know what they'll be calling me? I'll give you a hint. It's the name of the person who has the WBA, WBC, IBF, and WBO world championships. Oh, that's right, you wouldn't know, would you? Ha, ha, ha, ha! I'll be called the undisputed champion of the world! That's something you'll never be called. If you want, I could give you a job once I get that so you're closer to greatness. Maybe I could have you shine my shoes, polish my belts, or something more fitting to a person of your talents. Hell, you could even be my driver if you want. What'cha say? There could even be a few other perks added in that I haven't even thought of yet. Don't worry, I'll even give your sweet little Jap friend a job. She could be my cook, but she'll have to learn to cook American food, not that damn slop she fixes you. I'll end this call by saying I'm glad you got a job as that goofy boxing analyst. You wanna know why? So I can see the look on your face once I get the WBA title while also getting crowned the undisputed championship! Ha, ha! So long, loser!"

And, sure enough, Shawn was telling the truth. He, in fact, did have a match that would put him in contention for the WBA title should he win. Not only did he win such a match, but he was in contention for named world title scheduled for four months later. Christian received another message from Shawn an hour or so after he won merely to rub it in. Shawn did his best to act all cocky and superior towards him because he now could officially claim he was the better fighter. He ended the message with a 'see you in the ring' comment that puzzled Christian.

Christian hadn't had time to worry, let alone think, about what Shawn meant by that on account of his busy schedule. Those same several months he fought five times against tough, top ranked contenders for his titles. Secretly, Dom made sure that one or two of those challengers were also top contenders for the WBA cruiserweight championship.

When he watched Shawn's fight against the WBA light heavyweight champ, Paddy McMurphy, the bout to unify the world titles of that weight class, he was sure that Shawn had gained a good amount of muscle since his last fight only a couple of months before. The fight commentator verified this when he announced the weight of both fighters. Paddy was down a couple of pounds to 172, whereas Shawn was up to the limit of 175.

Though Shawn bragged that he'd knock the champ out within the first three rounds, the fight itself was anything but short. The fight drew out for all to see, and was by far Shawn's best fight to date. The fight was a battle, taking its toll on both men involved. Although McMurphy was knocked down three times over those twelve rounds, the most surprising thing to Christian happened during the eleventh. For the second time in his career, Shawn got knocked down. Even though he could have gotten up by the count of three, Shawn decided to roll over to a knee to rest a little longer before getting up at the count of eight.

When the smoke cleared at the end of the twelfth, and at the end of a well-fought split decision, Shawn emerged victorious as both the new WBA and undisputed light heavyweight champion of the world. Shortly following the match, he left another rude message on Christian's phone to rub in what he had accomplished only a short time before.

Shawn spent the next couple of weeks doing interviews and a number of talk shows bragging he was the best fighter to step in the ring today and was, in his not so humble opinion, the best ever. He seemed to have gotten it all – world titles, fame, fortune, respect, endorsements, and women. After this time in question, he did one last talk show saying that he was going to do something that no champ had done in his generation: he was going to defend his belts once a month against the top four contenders. After that, he was going to spend his time training so he could go after the cruiserweight championships.

To his word, Shawn did what he had said. His first three defenses were three of the top four contenders, but his fourth was a much anticipated rematch against Paddy McMurphy, which went to the eighth. Shawn won them all by way of knockout.

At a press conference shortly after his rematch with McMurphy, Shawn publically dropped his belts while announcing at the same time he was moving up in class to the cruiserweight division.

"Mr. Calloway," one reporter said to him. "Why are you resigning your belts now, so soon after unifying them? And why are you moving up in weight?"

"Yo, man, don't you get it?" Shawn asked with attitude. "I'm undefeated and I've done all I can do in this weight class. I've won all the belts, unified them together, and beat all the top guys. What more is there for me to do? I did my job here and it's time I set my sights on unifying the cruiserweight belts while I'm still young, and pretty, enough to do so."

"Mr. Calloway, technically you're not undefeated," the same reporter injected. "You do have two loses at the hands of your brother, the cruiserweight champion, Christian Eaton. With this in mind, does this mean there'll be a third matchup between you two? Possibly for the titles?"

"Why're you bringin' that up, fool?" Shawn hotly retorted. "Those don't count! They were exhibition matches. Besides, if they do count, no light heavyweight ever beat me. So, in a sense, I *am* undefeated. And as for my has been brother, I'll deal with him when I get the chance."

The ever present Duke Snyder, being the opportunist that he was, stood to inject a comment when Shawn was done talking.

"For the record," he announced before looking to Shawn briefly before turning his attention back to the reporters. "I give you the next undisputed cruiserweight champion of the world, Shawn Calloway! Come on, Shawn, stand up," Duke said while tugging on Shawn's shoulder. At this moment, Shawn got up to smile at the camera. "Shawn Calloway, ladies and gentlemen, cruiserweight champion of the world!"

***

Over the next year as Shawn was making his mark as a cruiserweight, Christian defended his belts while allowing his fame and fortune to branch out into other areas. When he had time, he found himself doing various charitable organizations, TV guest appearances, gave interviews for a wide range of shows and magazines, and tried his hand at training a little at Dom's gym.

He finally paid off his student loans a year or so back, and had been thinking about going back since then but hadn't seriously considered it until recently. Though he most likely wouldn't do anything until he finally stepped out of the ring, he felt the more time the thought about it, the better prepared he'd be when he finally decided one way or the other. He had narrowed his choices down to a handful, but similar, in the wildlife sciences and nature oriented majors.

"Why the hell are ya thinkin' 'bout goin' back ta college now, kid?" Dom asked one day at the gym. "Especially when ya're in the middle of twenty other things?"

"I'm not actually considering going back now. I wanted to finish up some things first before I do," Christian told him while Dom watched him train. "Besides, I'm only like ten classes away from getting my degree and I'd like to get that while my head is still able to think."

"But why this wildlife stuff? Why not accountin' or business?"

"Accounting is too boring for me, and I do business here." He shrugged. "The wildlife stuff interests me, would keep me outside. Maybe work in a zoo or something."

"So ya'd rather clean up shit all damn day? Days that could be rainin', or be too damn hot or cold?" Dom questioned. "With accountin', ya stay in a nice office all day; an office that's air-conditioned in the summer and heated in the winter."

"Could you do that Dom? Sit in an office all day crunching numbers?"

"We're not talkin' 'bout me, kid; we're talkin' 'bout ya," Dom said with a scowl which drew a frown from his fighter. "Why now?"

"Like I said, I wanted to do this while I still have a brain that I can use rather than a three-pound pile of mush," Christian told him while he stopped jumping rope. He then walked over to sit next to his elderly mentor. "I've been in this business for quite a few years now and I'm at the top of my game. I got into this business because I wanted to learn how to defend myself and maybe make a little money on the side. I've achieved more than I ever thought I would and I owe most of that to you, Dom. The rest, I guess, I owe to Shawn.

"However," he continued, "I don't want to end up being one of those guys where boxing is the only thing they have because they can't do anything else. I also want to be able to choose when I leave the business rather than being forced out. I guess that's why I'm doing it. The business has been very good to me and I've taken to it very naturally. It's opened up other doors I can go down if I choose to. On the other hand, I'd like to try and amend anything I can with Shawn once I do get out."

"Is this why ya're doin' this, 'cause of Shawn?"

"You mean wanting to quit boxing?" Christian asked while receiving a nod from Dom. "No, well, a little I guess. This is all he has, he can't do anything else. He might say that he could, but I doubt it. If the roles were reversed, I think I'd be a little upset. If this was all I could do and I brought him in to help him out, then next think I know, he's achieved much more without even wanting it. I'd feel even more resentful if he was able to do anything he wanted before even coming in. So, maybe by me getting out could help him a little as well."

"What 'bout Miho? Has she influenced you at all?"

"A little bit, I suppose."

"Does she want ya ta quit the business?"

"She doe, but says she wants me to leave when I'm ready to. I know she doesn't want me getting hurt. I'd like to enjoy life after boxing and I want to enjoy it with her. If I stay in too long, I don't want to end up a vegetable or like Ali. I also wouldn't want her leaving me on account I didn't know when to quit or that I wasn't home enough."

"Ya love her, don't ya, kid?" Dom asked while they made eye contact. "It's ok, kid, ya don't have ta answer. I can see it in your eyes. How much longer do ya think you'll be in the business for?"

"I don't know if I'll ever truly leave, but as a boxer in the ring, I'm not sure. Maybe a year?" Christian sighed while thinking for a better answer.

"How long ya been thinkin' 'bout this?"

"My friend Larry was the one who first approached me about this."

"He did? When?"

"Oh, I'm not sure. A year back, maybe?" Christian thought. "I do know it was one of those nights I went to the library to read. We sort of have an understanding. He'd go back to get his G.E.D. if I go back to finish college." He laughed. "He dropped out of high school to take care of his sick dad. Now, years later, he said he didn't want me to end up like him, a dropout. He agreed to go back if I did. But it wasn't until a few months ago did I actually start seriously thinking about it. My parents and Miho have helped me alone, I have to admit."

"Have ya thought how ya might want ta go out?" Dom asked.

"A little." Christian chuckled while looking down to the floor before itching his leg.

"What, kid? What was ya thinkin'?"

"I kind of liked what Shawn did after he unified the belts."

"Ya mean have a press conference where ya drop the belts and retire?"

"Well, if I could. That is if I still have the belts when I do quit." Christian laughed at that. "And if I could, I'd like to have my retirement match against Shawn."

"What?!" Dom exclaimed while a little taken back with what he just heard. "Are ya bein' serious, kid? Against him?"

"Yeah, I guess I am."

"What the hell has gotten in that head of yours? Ya say ya wanna get out while ya still have a brain, but with what ya just said makes me wonder if ya already lost it!"

"I know it sounds crazy."

"Yeah, ya're right." Dom smiled. "It does sound crazy."

"But I've been thinking about it and that's what I'd like to do. That is, if you'll let me."

"Let's just say that ya get your wish, kid, and get ta face yer brother in this so-called retirement match. Ya think he'll fight ya just like he did the first time ya two met? I don't think so." Dom looked at Christian before shaking his head. "I'd say it'd be more like that last round of that second fight ya two had. He's beyond the point of needin' yer help and with Duke there at his side, anythin' is possible. He now see's ya as an obstacle; something ta conquer to get what he wants. You're in his way, kid. He doesn't care 'bout either of us in that way anymore. All he cares 'bout now is championship gold and money and everything else that comes with it. I'd bet money that, 'cause of this, Shawn'll want ta take ya out as soon as he could just ta prove ta everyone, 'pecially ta himself, that he truly is better than ya."

Pausing long enough to point a finger at Christian, Dom said, "He'd do it ta prove ta everyone in the whole world that ya're no match for him, 'pecially in a match where he's able ta win yer belts in the process. Just be careful what ya wish fer, kid, 'cause ya just may get it."

"But do you think Shawn will actually do that? Go ape shit on me?"

Dom nodded. "Ya shouldn't be so naïve, 'pecially when it comes ta boxin' and yer brother. Ya know him. He's selfish, and wants what he wants now. But if he's in a match with a promoter and manager tellin' him things like he's the greatest or fer him not ta hold anythin' back, do ya actually think with his personality and ego that he'll really take it easy on ya because of the history ya two have with each other?"

Christian sighed while thinking about what Dom just told him and the possibility whether Shawn would do it that way or not. "Maybe you're right, Dom. I do sound a little naïve, don't I?"

"Did ya change your mind about it, then?"

"No, I'd still would like to face him."

"Why, kid?"

"I'd like to prove to myself whether or not I can really beat him. I know it sounds crazy, but if I can, I'd like to get out that way."

"Ya're right, kid," Dom said before a smile rose on his face. "It does sound crazy."

"I thought so too. I know you didn't really want us fighting that last time, but if he and I have a rubber match, I'd want you in my corner."

"I can't really say fer sure, kid."

"Why's that?"

"I'm just too old, kid. I'm real old. I've got a bad ticker." He continued to smile while tapping his chest. "I could go at any minute. Any amount of excitement could set me off. Besides, there might be a good race down at the track that day."

"Well, then I guess you got in the wrong profession if you're afraid of getting any excitement in your life."

"I think ya got me with that, kid."

"So, will you do it? That is, hypothetically speaking, if this match was to happen and you hadn't keeled over by then, would you manage me during it? One last time?"

"Ya don't have ta ask me that, kid. Of course I will," Dom softly told him as they exchange another look. "So, honestly, what d'ya think ya'd do once ya do get out?"

"I don't know; maybe join the circus or something."

"A circus? Boy, you've taken more of a beatin' than I thought." Dom laughed before a thought came to mind. "Speaking of circuses, has your brother left you anymore messages?"

Christian nodded. "They were mainly just him rubbing in his recent accomplishments, the money he's making, the women, whatever. He left one the other day saying I'd better not lose my belts anytime soon until he comes to collect. I sometimes wonder what's going on in that head of his."

"Not much, kid. I'm sure at times ya can hear the wind movin' 'round in there if ya get close enough, kinda like those shells ya find on the beach," Dom expressed before letting out a light hearted laugh.

The two of them sat there for another minute or so until Dom got serious.

"If ya want to retire and still be champ, ya won't be doin' it sittin' on your ass," Dom barked at him. "C'mon, get up, you lazy bum! Give me twenty more minutes of dancin' with your partner!"

"Yes, sir!" Christian jumped up as a smile came across his face. He grabbed his jump rope in the process. "Right away, Dom."

Sitting there for another minute so glaring at him, Dom's expression soon softened to reveal a warm smile. He soon left before wandering around to give pointers to some other students that were also there training that day.

Over the next couple of months while defending his titles, doing his endorsement deals, and whatnot, Shawn was slowly climbing the ranks for better and better contention for the WBA cruiserweight title Then, on the evening of April 1st, Shawn got his shot to go up against Max Browning for that very title. Max Browning was a hard-hitting Italian southpaw from the Bronx. He won the belt just over a year before from a no-named underdog after a six-round blood bath.

Christian had invited Dom over to his house to watch the fight on HBO. He tried to talk Miho into watching the fight as well, but she simply refused before leaving to visit some friends. He wasn't sure if it was the actual boxing aspect or whether it was Shawn which turned her off to it, but he suspected it may have been a combination of the two.

Shawn, during interviews as well as the press conference that covered his match, stated in an array of ways how he was going to punish the champ over the course of the fight before taking what was rightfully his. Max, on the other hand, wasn't as flamboyant with his responses as was Shawn; instead, he simply said it would be a fight for the ages.

"C'mon, Browning! Knock his damn head off!" Dom yelled periodically during the match when it looked like Max was on a roll. Even though there was no clear favorite to win the bout, it was clear that Dom did not want Shawn to win under any circumstances. All day leading to the match, as well as during it, Dom made references to suggest this multiple times.

As Max predicted, the fight was a war between two fighters with iron wills and rock chins. They spared no expense at the cost of their own well-being. Also, as promised, Shawn pushed himself to the limit for the duration of the fight to torture Browning, who seamlessly absorbed the punishment as if he had a thirst for it. The fight went back and forth with no clue as to who was going to win. This was probably the first fight of Shawn's that Christian had seen and not felt that he was going to win. This clearly was the best fight of his career and could quite possibly be the first he could potentially legitimately loose.

Also, as foretold, Shawn began sucking wind by the seventh round. Obviously he hadn't taken his endurance training serious of late. Fortunately for him, Browning appeared to be in the same shape in that department as he was.

The fight went to near the end of the eleventh round before being called by the ref. Shawn was awarded the victory, and the WBA cruiserweight championship, via technical knockout. Even though Dom was yelling and swearing at the television, Christian was secretly happy for Shawn. Not only was he happy that Shawn won, but also happy because of the possibility of facing him in his retirement match to unify the belts, hopefully later that year.

The crowd went wild as Shawn jumped up and down in his corner. He held his newly won title above his head for all to see. At this point the announcer came over to him, microphone in hand, to ask him a few questions.

"Shawn Calloway, how does it feel to be the new cruiserweight champion of the world so soon after becoming a cruiserweight yourself?"

"How do ya think it feels? It feels great!" exclaimed Shawn. "I am king of the world; right where I should be!"

"And what are your plans for the future?"

"To win, man! I intend on keeping my winning streak alive and well, as well as going after the other belts to become the next undisputed cruiserweight champion of the world!" Shawn flowed with excessive cockiness when he said this. "But as for right now it's time for me to leave. I've got to get ready for a night of partying! Ha ha!"

"There you have it, folks," the announcer said while looking at the TV camera. Shawn, on the other hand, forced his way back to his corner where Jackie Collins, Duke Snyder, and the other members of their team as they begun to move out of view. "Those words from Shawn Calloway, the new WBA cruiserweight champion of the world, who only a few short months ago became a cruiserweight himself. He has traveled far in such a short span, and we wish him the best."

"Ha! Like hell we do!" Dom voices upon hearing the announcer's words.

Before anything else was said, Duke came back into view on the television while coming over to the announcer and stood next to him while waiting to be acknowledged. Finally, after several seconds, he was finally greeted by the announcer.

"Duke Snyder," the announcer said. "May I get your thoughts on the fight?"

"Well, sir, I'll tell you this," Duke said in all his splendor. "We just witnessed a truly remarkable match where the true victor prevailed. However, if you want to hear more about this magnificent fight, tune into our press conference we're planning for tomorrow night. Thank-you." He smiled before waving to the crowd. He soon exited the ring.

Within ten minutes after the fight ended, Christian's phone rang while he and Dom were reminiscing about the fight. He answered it on the second ring.

"Yo, Beeker!" Shawn's voice was heard saying form the other end of Christian's phone. "Did you see my fight?"

"Of course I did; Dom too. He's here now," Christian told him. "Congratulations on your win."

"Thanks!" As Shawn was speaking, Christian noticed how hard it was to hear him. Coming from Shawn's end where voices of people echoing through what seemed to either be a hallway or locker room. "I'm just callin' to see how you're doin'."

"You actually called to see how I was doing?"

"Yeah. Would I lie to you?"

"I don't think so, but by the way you've been acting lately, that's probably not the only reason why you called. You most likely called to rub in the fact of what title you just won."

"Maybe I did. Maybe I called to say that this is the closest you'll ever get to it." Shawn confirmed. "Finally, after all these years, I finally got the most prestigious belt, the only one you haven't got yet. Me! Not you. I also am offering you a spot over here with me because this may be the last chance you'll be in the presence of greatness. What'cha say, bro?"

"Thanks, Shawn, I really appreciate the offer, but I think I'll take my chances with Dom, if that's ok with you."

"You're makin' a big mistake, pal."

"Am I?"

"Yeah, a big one. Just like when you put your hands on me at Dom's during our disagreement."

"Hey, that was your fault, Shawn, not mine."

"What the fuck you talkin' 'bout?"

"If you called to brag or to get me going, it's not going to work," Christian informed him smoothly. "I'm happy with what I've achieved and I don't feel bitter about it. If that's all, I'm going to get going now. And, again, congratulations on our win."

And, with that, Christian hung up without giving his brother a chance to respond.

Chapter 39

The press conference that next night that Duke spoke about of merely was just there to congratulate Shawn on how great he was, as well as an ass-kissing session guised as a Q-and-A session.

"This, ladies and gentlemen," Duke stated while standing up next to Shawn, "is not only the present of this great sport, but is also the future as well. Today you know him as the WBA cruiserweight champ, but tomorrow you'll call him the undisputed champion. For the second time, if I might add."

"Mr. Snyder." Sam Silverstein stood up. "Are you saying that you already have a date setup between your man and Christian Eaton?"

"Not yet, but I assure you it's only a matter of time," the flashy promoter confidently assure with a feigned laugh.

"Has Mr. Eaton agreed to this match to unify the titles?"

"We haven't the opportunity to discuss this with him, yet," Duke smoothly answered with a nervous laugh while briefly looking over to Shawn. "But given their history, I'm sure we can come to some sort of agreement on such an historic matter."

"Mr. Snyder, Mr. Calloway." Another reporter rose while taking his turn. "Any comment on the fact that both of the fights that Mr. Calloway has had with Eaton he lost? Those two fights, incidentally, are also the only two fights that he's lost professionally."

"Hey, man! That's all in the past, brother!" Shawn stood while pointing to the reporter with a glare in his eyes. When Duke put a hand on his shoulder, Shawn realized what he was doing before quickly calming himself down in a vain attempt to act as if nothing was wrong. He took promptly took his seat with an air of importance. "That's water over the bridge. You know the sayin', or at least you should, third time's a charm. Right? Those two fights we had don't mean a thing. They weren't for anythin'. Just exhibition bouts. I'm eager to get in the ring with him a third time to setting this once and for all."

"Now, Mr. Calloway," the same unnamed reporter said. "You seem very confident in yourself, but you're relatively new to this weight class while Mr. Eaton's spent his entire career in it. He's also the undefeated, reigning IBF, WBC, and WBO world cruiserweight champion. Not only that, but both of your losses, exhibition or not, are against him. I'm curious why you're so eager to get back in the ring with him."

"Because I'm the best, that's why!" Shawn seemed to almost shout at him while at the same time attempting to control himself. "I've always been the best and he knows it. He's been avoiding me. He's afraid of me. He knows I'm best. Always has. If, when, he gets in the ring with me again, all of you will see I ain't lyin'! I was the better of us then, just like I am now. Y'all see."

"Technically you're not the best, Mr. Calloway," the reporter pressed. "Both of your losses are against the undefeated Christian Eaton. Based on this alone, you're claiming to being the best or better than him is not valid. Would you like to change your stance on being the best or, at the very least, being better than him?"

"The truth of the matter is that in both of those fights I had against him, my hands were tied," Shawn tried to explain as calmly as he could. "Now that my hands are untied to allow me to fight my way of fighting, you'll see soon enough who the better man is."

The reporter smiled upon hearing this. "Ah, that explains it, then. Your hands were tied. I see. But your hands didn't seem to be all that tied in your last bout against him. Didn't you get disqualified from too many low blows?"

Once this question was asked, Christian, who had been watching the press conference at home with Dom, stopped paying attention. Shawn was angry and resentful, while not wanting to wait to get into the ring with him again to settle an old debt that only he felt that they had with each other.

"That goddamn kid!" Dom grumbled for like the twentieth time when it was over.

"Hey Dom, you alright?" Chris dryly asked him.

"I can't believe your brother," the old man muttered. "The gall that he has ta think that he can have a press conference just so he can publically challenge ya is a crock of shit. Pardon my language, kid."

"Maybe he feels if he'd be publically embarrassing me by doing it this way; it'd be almost easier to call me out."

"I got thinkin' 'bout him, kid." Dom leaned in to tell him. "No offense to ya or your family, but the way he's been actin', 'pecially since working with Duke, seems like he's tryin' to hide who he is. It seems like he came from a place somewhere between nowhere and goodbye; a place that raised only poor, white trash. No matter how hard he tries to get away, that place always seems to be right around the next corner."

Dom paused here to reflect on something. "People know what boxin' is. See, people love violence. They'll slow down at a car accident to see the dead lyin' 'round, and those same people come to see the fights. Shawn's one 'em, but he took it a step further. He wants to be the one to inflict the violence. Boxin' isn't 'bout the violence. Well, it is, kid, but it's more 'bout respect."

"Respect?" questioned Christian.

"Yeah, gettin' it for yourself while takin' it from the other guy."

The next day, Christian and Dom each received a photo of Shawn wearing his new belt. He signed it with 'thought you might like this because this'll be the closest you'll ever get to it!'

***

May of that next year, Christian held a press conference of his own. Dom was there as well, being seen sitting next to him at the conference table.

369

"Ok, guys, before we proceed to the Q-and-A part of this, I just wanted to tell you why I requested this," Christian stated to various reporters and journalists. "What you may or may not know, I have been in talks with my manager here, Mr. Calavicci," he said while acknowledging Dom, "for some time about my retirement from boxing. You know, to get out while I still have a fair amount of my brain and facilities left. The reason for this decision is that I've achieved pretty much all that I can achieve in the ring.

"And, in addition, I'd been wanting to go back to college and focus on that finally," Christian continued. "The business has been very good to me and I've achieved more in these last few years than I ever imagined possible. The multiple titles I've won, my endorsements, and other things have been a dream come true. I've decided to be in the ring for a couple more months, but I can't get any more specific than that. I'm sorry. I wanted to allow other contenders I haven't faced yet to challenge for my titles. If I'm lucky enough to still have my titles after that, I wanted to be in one last match, a retirement match if you will, for the WBA championship. It has always been a dream of mine to unify the belts, and that's really the only dream I haven't achieved yet in this great sport of ours. I'm hoping to achieve this by the end of August, Halloween at the very latest. Now that I've said that, we can start the questions if you'd like."

With that, the bombardment began. He and Dom were there for almost an hour and a half answering a whole slew of things that were presented to them.

As promised, Christian faced the remainder of the top contenders for each of his belts by the end of August. At which point, Dom and Duke sat down to talk about the fight to unify the titles. The highlights of the talk wasn't if it would happen, but when, where, and the split.

In the end, the fight between Christian and Shawn, the one to unify the cruiserweight titles and to crown a new undisputed cruiserweight champion, would take place on Halloween and be set in Las Vegas. Though Dom wanted the split to be 60-40 in Christian's favor, he accepted a 50-50 split to shut both Duke and Shawn up. In the end, it wasn't about a 10% bigger paycheck.

The Saturday before their final showdown, Christina talked Dom into going down to Mike's for one last hurrah.

"Thanks for coming to share a retirement drink with me, Dom."

"Don't ya have ta be retired first, kid, before I can do that?" Dom asked while accepting a cold, frosty mug of beer from Mike.

"He's got a point there, Chris," Mike said while slyly passing over a triple Pepsi on the rocks to the champ.

"Thanks, Mike," Christian said in a tone and look that caused Mile to wonder if he was being thanked for his comment or the drink he served.

"You're welcome," he told him while assuming it was a combination of the two.

After taking a big gulp of soda, Christian noticed Terry was coming over to them while Jake took his turn at their pool table.

"Hey, old man," Terry said to Dom while the trainer gulped down half his beer in one hearty gulp. "I thought you quit drinking."

"Everyone has to drink," Dom bluntly told him. "We'd all die if we didn't."

"I mean stopped drinking alcohol."

"Looks like you thought wrong."

"Looks that way," Terry confirmed as they exchanged a brief, yet silent, look with each other. The look conveyed more than a brief conversation would.

"Glad to see you haven't changed," Terry told him.

"Did ya think I would?"

"I wasn't too sure."

"After all those years ya trained at my gym, ya thought old age might mellow or change my ass somehow?"

"One can always hope," Terry confessed with a smile. "Stupid to think that, wasn't it?"

"No, just wishful thinkin'."

"Terry y-y-you trained at Dom's gym?" Christian stuttered.

"Of course."

"In boxing?"

"No, ballet." Terry said with a straight face. "Really?"

"Have ya known me ta train anythin' else but boxin', kid?" Dom growled.

"No, I guess I haven't."

"Alright then."

"Terry, when did you train there?"

"Oh, geez. You had to ask me that, didn't you?" Terry said while stopping to think. "I think I started like twenty years ago or so. What do you say, Dom? When was I there?"

"Twenty two years, actually," corrected Dom.

Terry shrugged at that. "Close enough."

"When did you stop?" inquired Christian.

"A couple of years before you started."

"If you don't mind me asking, what made you get out?"

"My parents got sick and I wanted to be there more for them," Terry told him. "I could only afford one of at that time. Even though Dom was willing to help me with paying him, I felt funny going there for free, if you know what I mean."

Before Christian was able to respond, Jake yelled over to Terry.

"Hey, Terry!" he called. "Your turn."

Hearing this, Dom turned to Christian with a glint in his eye while nodding and flicking a thumb to Jake's table.

"What'd'ya say, kid?" He smiled. "Wanna join them?"

"Sure." Christian shrugged while returning the smile. "Why not?"

With that, the boxer and trainer, with drinks in hand, followed Terry back to his table Jake was waiting at.

They stayed there for a few more hours playing pool, having drinks, and listening to Terry complain occasionally whenever Jake decided to run the table.

***

As usual, there was a press conference to cover the event. Christian reinforced the idea that this would be his last match, win, lose, or draw. Shawn, on the other hand, bragged of how bad he was and how Christian had been avoiding a real challenge by avoiding him.

When asked what they expected during the course of the fight, Christian responded by saying he'd try to give it his all in an effort to retire undefeated. Shawn, in his trademark fashion, promised a short fight what would end in a bloody knockout. He then proceeded to say that Christian wasn't a champ but, in reality, was at best a transitional champion, one made out of paper.

"I just want to repeat myself by tellin' all you morons that I'm a bad, bad man," Shawn stated while repeatedly pointing to the crowd. "I'm the baddest man on the planet ad I'm going to reinforce this tomorrow night."

"How bad are you, Champ?" Duke asked.

"I'm so bad, I snack on danger and dine on death!"

"And what else, Champ?"

"I'm so bad I fart thunder and crap lightning."

"The truth of the matter, folks," Duke informed the crowd while standing up with microphone in hand. "The truth is that this," he said while pointing to Shawn, "is the best boxer, hell, the best fighter, in the world today. And the truth of the matter is that he'll prove it once again tomorrow night when he takes out Christian Eaton in a decisive, one-sided victory to unify the belts to become the newest, and best, undisputed cruiserweight champion of the world!"

Shawn sat there while cockily nodded his head with an arrogant expression.

"And what is the truth, Mr. Snyder?" Dom asked.

"I just told you what it is," he replied.

"What I meant was, what is 'truth'?" Dom asked before pausing briefly. "Is it what you believe or is it what you've been told?"

Duke smiled slyly at him. "It's both, Mr. Calavicci. I *am* telling you all the truth. Tomorrow night Mr. Calloway will make you believe it. Take it any way you want to but, I assure you, I am not lying, nor am I mistaken, in any shape or form about this."

"But ya fail ta address the matter of what it means ta be the best," Dom pressed. "I'd like ya ta tell us what bein' the best is."

"If I did that, then we wouldn't have time for the rest of the questions that these kind people here may have," Duke told him before turning to the press. "Shall we continue with the questions?"

And the questions did continue. After several were asked and answered, they received one that irritated Shawn.

"Mr. Eaton, Mr. Calloway," Sam Silverman said while standing. "What is your exact relationship to each other?"

"We're brothers," Christian told him.

"Like hell we are!" Shawn declared while shooting him a glare. "We are of no relation!"

"What are you talking about, Shawn? We *are* brothers."

"Why? Because a piece of paper says so?" Shawn asked him. "Yeah, ok, fine. I'll admit it. We're brothers, but only because you're parents adopted me after…"

"After what, Mr. Calloway?" Silverman pressed. "After your parents died? Is that what you were about to say?"

"Who told you that?!" Shawn asked in a demanding fashion.

"I looked it up," Sam replied. "The report I read was that the Eaton's adopted you because your parents had died and whatever relatives you had left didn't want anything to do with you."

"That's a lie!"

"To which part?"

"That we're brothers. We're anything but," Shawn scoffed. "How could we remotely be related? We don't act like brothers, we don't look like brothers, we don't even have the same parents."

"Then what are we, Shawn?" Christian asked him. "Best friends?"

"We most certainly are not!"

"I see," pondered Christian. "Then why did we hang around each other all these years since childhood? Even as adults, you helped bring me into boxing. You let me live with you above the very gym we trained at together. Why would you do that for me if we aren't brothers or friends? Why did you do any of that for me, then?"

Shawn shot him a glare. "Because I felt sorry for you. You're a disgrace!"

"Then why are you threatening to hurt me like you are?"

"Because I am. I just wanted you to be prepared."

"Why? Why are you going to hurt me, Shawn? And, tell me, why do you want to warn me of this so-called danger you say I'll be in tomorrow night?"

"Because you have what I want. Don't you get it?!"

"Are my titles the only things that I have that you want?"

"What's that supposed to mean" Shawn asked him.

"You know what it means," Christian told him.

They looked at each other for several moments while pictures of them were taken. Duke soon cleared his throat to allow the questions to continue.

Christian didn't know how much of what Shawn said he actually meant, but Dom said not to worry about it on account of Duke had his Shawn's mind so twisted that he didn't know if he was coming or going. Dom also pleasantly joked with Christian that if he ever turned into a controlling, unscrupulous person like Duke, then for him to put him out of his misery. Christian jokingly agreed.

Afterwards, Dom told Christian to keep his guard up during the fight because Duke would have gotten it into Shawn's head to destroy him, that he was the reason why Shawn hadn't achieved much success until he changed management. Dom also voiced that he should be careful on the account that Shawn might actually believe that and would want this fight for blood, vengeance, satisfaction, and to prove the world that Christian was nothing. It might also have been to prove that Shawn could beat him without a doubt and to hopefully end their feud once and for all.

"So, you're saying Shawn wants to destroy me?" Christian asked with a smirk.

"As a matter of fact, kid, I am," Dom said, also with a smile. "But remember to be careful out there, kid."

"What do you want me to do other than being careful?"

"I want ya to push his ass, push him ta the limit," Dom growled. "Unlike him, I want ya do ta what ya've done before. I want ya ta shut him up. I want ya ta dance around him and sting him with your greased lightnin' jabs! And, above all, don't stoop down ta his level and fight dirty! I want ya ta win, yes, but I want ya ta fight clean and legal. Ya hear me?"

Christian looked at him before answering. "I hear you, Dom."

"And if ya get a chance ta knock his arrogant ass out, go fer it." The old man pointed at his student.

"Sure, Dom. You don't have to worry about me." Christian smiled while patting Dom on the head. "I'll do my best."

"I know ya will, kid. I know ya will," Dom said while returning the smile. "Ya know, kid, but I'm proud of ya. I really am. Win, lose, or draw, I just wanted ta say that ya've been my best student ta date. Ya stickin' with me all these years I really do appreciate."

"I feel the same way, Dom."

When they were done there, they went for a short walk afterwards before stopping briefly at the ring where the big showdown would take place the next evening. They looked at it for a few minutes before walking back to Dom's hotel room. They said their good nights and wished each other well. Dom turned in for the night while Christian went to check out the sights of Vegas.

***

"...and now for our main event," the ring announcer said the next night at the start of their title fight. "This is our main event and is for the WBA, IBF, WBC, and WBO cruiserweight championships of the world! And the winner shall be declared the new undisputed cruiserweight champion of the world!" His voice rang out as the crowd erupted in an explosion of cheers.

"To my left, weighing in at an even 190 pounds, wearing black trunks with gold trim, he is the reigning WBA cruiserweight champion of the world. Shawn Calloway!"

Shawn bounced out of his corner with an arrogant posture while glaring at Christian.

"And his opponent, to my right, weighing in at 189 and one-quarter pounds, he is the reigning IBF, WBC, and WBO cruiserweight champion of the world. He is Christian Eaton!"

The crowd cheered long and hard as Christian came out of his corner to wave to them. The ovation seemed to last and last with no hint of stopping.

Moments later, they were drawn to the center of the ring as the ref instructed them on the rules of the match. Both Christian and Shawn stared at each other silently while ignoring what the ref was saying.

"You'll be broken," Shawn stated coldly.

"We'll see," responded Christian with a brief nod.

Unfortunately for Christian, when he would eventually wake up, he would not be able to remember the fight nor would he remember any of the days leading up to it.

Part III

Loyalty

"Where do anyone's loyalties truly lie?"

Chapter 40

Christian woke to find himself lying on a cot-like bed in what appeared to be a hospital room. It was softly lit and had beige walls. A blue curtain separated his cot from the one to his left. The only thing that moved on him were his eyes.

"Man," he thought while lying there. "Where am I? How did I get here? And why does my head hurt?"

Slowly, he finally began to look around. To his right, Dom was hunched over on a chair sleeping. In the far right corner, he noticed his clothes were neatly folded on a chair. Looking down, he noticed he was dressed in a blue hospital gown. An IV was hooked to his left arm.

To his dismay, he had no idea how he got to this predicament or why he was there. He understood there was a reason for him being there, that he needed medical attention, but as for what that reasoning was, he hadn't a clue. While in the process of sitting up, a nurse came into the room.

"Hey, you'd better not get up just yet," she softly, yet firmly, told him before putting a hand on his shoulder.

Nodding, Christian laid back down. While doing so, his head pounded heavily, causing him to let out a moan.

"You're finally awake," she said with a smile. "How're you feeling?"

"My head hurts."

"I should say," she replied while checking his vitals. She soon put a thermometer in his mouth before grabbing the chart at the foot of his bed. When the thermometer beeped, she took it out and wrote down his temperature. "You took quite a beating. Your temperature is now down to normal."

Confused, Christian looked at her with a puzzled look. "Why am I here?"

"You don't remember?"

"No," he answered while shaking his head. "If I did, I wouldn't have asked. When I woke up, I was here, lying in bed with an IV plugged into me."

Pausing a beat before responding, the nurse finally said, "You were in a really bad fight."

"I was in a fight?!" he quickly asked her while unable to believe what he was just told. His question drew a nod from the nurse. "When?"

Glancing at the chart in her hands before putting it back on the foot of the bed, she replied, "You came in two nights ago by helicopter. The fight was before that. You've been in a coma since you arrived."

"When will I be able to get out of here?"

She smiled. "Not for a couple more days. You might be out by the end of the week, the weekend tops. The doctor wanted you here for a little while for observation."

Christian moaned when hearing this. "This there anyway I can get out of here sooner? I've got a big match coming up in a couple of days and I've got to get ready for it."

"'fraid not. Remember, doctor's orders," she sweetly told him while tapping his feet. "You took quite a beating. Just be thankful you're alive."

"Yeah. You're right," Christian told her, hoping that would placate her, while rubbing his head again.

"While I'm here, is there anything you'd like?"

"Yeah. Burger, fries, and a milkshake. I'm hungry."

The nurse smiled when she heard that. "I don't think I can get that for you."

"How about some pizza, then? With barbeque wings?" Christian looked at her with a smile. "Don't worry, I'll share."

"I'll go down to the kitchen to see if they have any leftovers," she told him. "But they may not have anything you'd want."

"If you can, that'll be great," Christian said while finally feeling somewhat better at the prospect of filling his stomach. "Just so long as it's real food; not that processed crap that you have to read the box it comes in just to know what you're eating."

"Oh, I wouldn't worry too much about that," she explained. "The food's pretty good here."

"So you've eaten it here?"

"Well, no. I'm just repeating what I've heard."

"Ah, ok. At least you're honest."

"I have to finish my rounds first, but I'll be back when I can." She smiled. "If you need anything, just push the button there on your cord, alright?"

"No problem. And no worries, either. Take your time; I'm not going anywhere," he told her with a smile as she turned to leave. "Hey, there is one more thing. What is your name?"

"It's Sarah."

"Nice to meet you. Mine's Christian."

"I know." She smiled while she left.

Laying there for a moment longer after Sarah left, a smile appeared on Christian's face before hearing a familiar voice.

"Have a nice nap?" the voice said, causing Christian to jump slightly. Evidentially Dom had woken up from his nap.

"Not sure," he admitted while turning his head towards his old friend.

"Prob'bly because of the nurse." The old man laughed. "She was cute."

"No, it wasn't because of her. My head hurts. I think I slept too long; my head always seems to hurt when I do that."

"I don't think it's 'cause of that, kid," Dom said with a chuckle. "Ya took one helluva beatin'."

Christian sighed when he heard that. "So I heard. It looks like the fight's going to be postponed. I won't be able to get out of here until later on this week."

"What ya talkin' 'bout, kid?" questioned the kind old man. "We got no fight ta worry 'bout postponin'. Ya're retired, kid."

Shocked, Christian couldn't believe he was hearing his trainer right. He merely looked at him while trying to determine what was going on. "Yeah we do. The one against Shawn. You know, the one to unify the titles?"

"The one against Shawn? Hey, kid, ya ok? Did ya take one too many head shots or somethin'?" Dom asked while mirroring his student's confused expression. "Kid, I'm not sure how ta put it ta ya, but that fight you're talkin' 'bout was three days ago. That's the reason you're here."

"Wha...wha...what?" Christian asked in a shocked manner while being very disturbed at what he was told.

"Have ya ever known me ta lie ta ya, kid?"

"No, I guess I haven't," Christian said softy while laying his head back down. He soon found himself staring up at the ceiling while letting out a sigh of disbelief. "How'd we do?"

"We lost, kid. Fifth-round knockout." Surprisingly, Dom had a certain amount of tenderness in his voice when telling him that.

"Was the fight fairly even or was it lopsided?"

"It started off even but it quickly turned to his advantage." While saying this, Dom intently looked as his pupil to read his facial expressions. "He did quite a number on ya in that last round. Ya don't remember any of this, do ya, kid?"

"No, I don't remember any of it."

"Sarah the nurse did say ya were in a fight. Didn't that ring any bells?"

"No, it didn't." Christian shook his head. "I just figured it was as a result Shawn put me in."

"As a manner of speakin', it was, kid," Dom said with a soft chuckle. "What's the last thing that ya remember?"

"Ah, I think you and me down at *Mike's Place*."

"Kid, that was last weekend."

"And it's the last thing that I remember," Christian told him before going quiet. "How'd Shawn take it, beating me I mean."

Dom scoffed at that. "How da ya think? He was prancin' around like he just won the damn lottery. There was a news conference dealin' with him unifying the belts. Whatever shame or humility he had left was completely gone by then. He was trashin' ya, trashin' me, trashin' anythin' he could. He was buildin' himself up like the greatest thing ever made. Snyder was there next to him verifyin' every word he said. It was disgustin', kid. Just downright disgustin'!"

Christian continued to lie in bed while staring up at the ceiling. Soon afterwards, he laughed as something came to his mind. "Hmmm. At least he won the watch, unified the belts, and has the knowledge that I'm now out of the way."

"But ya could always make a comeback, kid," Dom slyly said. "Ya know, a one-match comeback? Ya challenge Shawn ta a rematch, win back the belts, and then retire again. That would really piss him off. Not only did he loose ta ya, again, but when ya do retire again, the championships will be broken up again. He'll have ta win 'em all over again if he wants 'em. Ta see the look on his face would be priceless."

"Yeah, a Kodak moment. Right, Dom?" Christian laughed.

Dom simply smiled in agreement.

"So, Dom, tell me something. How long have you been here? At the hospital that is. Really?"

"Oh, not that long. I was here for a bit when you checked in. I just got here a couple of hours ago."

"Where are we?"

"Vegas, kid. We're in Vegas."

"At least now I can say I've been here. But did I enjoy myself while I was here? I don't remember." Christian laughed while looking to his elderly visitor. "And you know you don't have to be here if you don't want to be. You can go home anytime you want to."

"I know, kid, but I like it here. I think it's the air." Dom smiled. "Oh, before I forget, some doctor saw ya when ya first got here and took some x-rays or something of your head. He said ya have somethin', some medical jargon. Don't be surprised if he comes tomorrow ta talk with ya."

"What's his name?"

"What's who's name?"

"The doctor you're talking about, the one who saw me."

Dom shrugged. "I don't know."

As predicted, Christian had a visit from the doctor who initially saw him when he first arrived at the hospital, paid him a visit that next day.

"Hello Mr. Eaton, I'm Dr. Greene," he said while approaching Christian's bed before picking up the chart at the foot of the bed to read it. "How are you feeling today?"

"You can call me Christian if you'd like. And to answer your question, I'm not sure. My head still hurts, but I otherwise feel fine."

Greene nodded at that while looking at Christian. He soon put the chart back on the end of the bed. "What I'd like to do is to take you down to get a CT scan so we can see what we can see."

"Didn't you already do one when I first came in?"

"Yes but you were unconscious then. I just wanted to see if anything has changed between then and now, especially when you're now awake."

Christian agreed. He soon was transferred to a wheelchair and wheeled down the corridor to be examined. Greene walked next to him while looking over his medical records once again.

"Incidentally, I've heard you may have some amnesia," he commented.

"So it seems."

"What's the last thing you can remember?"

"Going to a local bar with my trainer back in upstate New York."

"That elderly man that was there with you?"

"Yes, that's him," confirmed Christian. "He said that that happened last weekend, us going to the bar that is."

"He's been right by your side ever since you got here." Greene smiled. "Did you know that?"

"No, I didn't. He said he was here briefly when I first arrived, a couple of hours yesterday, and a little bit today."

"I think he was just trying to downplay it." Greene smiled. "From what I've heard, he's only left your side only to eat and to relieve himself. Also, do you remember anything else since this past weekend?"

"I remember dreaming of water."

"Did you get wet?" The doctor smiled.

"No," Christian told him. "I didn't get wet."

The CT scans, as well as some x-rays and an MRI Greene wanted took some time, but the doctor wanted to make sure all the bases were covered. When the results were done, Dom wheeled Christian into Greene's office.

"Mr. Calivicci, have a sit if you'd like," Greene told Dom as he pointing to a chair before offering a reassuring smile to the both of them. "I've got some news."

The doctor proceeded to take an x-ray out of Christian's file and put it on a wall-mounted device to light it up. It showed a scan of his brain, from the top looking down on it, showing both of his hemispheres. He noticed right away that it didn't look quite normal. In the middle of his brain, running vertical from top to bottom was a noticeable blackness, almost like a hole.

"The good news is that I know what this is," Greene told him while pointing to such blackness. "The bad news is that it's called a cavuum septi pellucidi. In layman's terms, it means that you..."

"...have a hole in my brain's septum," Christian said while finishing the doctor's sentence.

"Precisely," Greene confirmed with a sad smile. "Have you heard of this before?"

"I've read about it briefly when I was in college, but that was years ago," Christian told him with a sigh. "Because of this, what do I have the privilege of looking forward to?"

"Long term, it could lead to various forms of dementias. These dementias, worst-case scenario, could be both progressive and degenerative. Another possibility is Parkinson's, blood clots, or even a stroke. If you were to get such clots, this could lead to another type of dementia known as vascular dementia. You may have also heard it called multi-infract dementia. Same thing. By looking at your test results, and hearing what type of match you were in that caused this, you're a good candidate for dementia Pugilistica, which is also known as boxer's dementia. It's also been loosely associated with schizophrenia, PTSD, traumatic brain injury, as well as antisocial personality disorder."

"Is there any way I can find out for sure whether or not I'll get any of these?"

"Afraid not," the doctor replied. "The only way is to just wait it out and see if you develop anything."

"What time frame would I have to look forward to before any symptoms begin to surface?"

"Typically five to ten years. Maybe sooner, maybe longer, all depends on severity."

"Is there anything that can be done to make sure this doesn't happen or to help prevent something?"

"Just the basic stuff. Try to lead a good, healthy life; have annual check-ups if you aren't already; and get checked out if anything weird starts happening. Alzheimer's patients take drugs to slow down their symptoms that you could try. Other than that, I'm afraid not," Greene told him bleakly. "But I most likely am getting ahead of myself. Most likely, nothing will happen. I just want to take precaution now just so you know what may happen. For majority of individuals, CSP produces no ill effects. Also, feel free to get a second or third opinion."

Sitting there in silence, Christian found himself getting slightly depressed as the information-sunk in. "So there's no sure why to know if I'll get any of these problems or symptoms, right?"

"Sadly, no, there isn't," Greene informed him before turning optimistic. "But the good part of it is that we've made excellent advancement in the field of medicine. If and when the times comes when you do start showing symptoms, the advances would most likely have by then multiple several times over. The treatment will be much better than what it is now."

"I have a question, Doc," Dom said while moving closer. He had been sitting patiently next to Christian while taking everything in before finally saying anything. "He seems not to have any memory from anything after last weekend up until the time he woke up. Would he get any of this back?"

"I don't know," Greene admitted with a shrug. "Amnesia is a tricky thing. It may all come totally back, or just bits and pieces may, or simply none of it. There's no way to know for sure."

"Could it get worse, his amnesia that is?"

"Worse as in being progressive or degenerative?" Greene asked before going silent to think of an answer. "There's a good chance that the answer is no, but there's still a very small chance. As for right now, I wouldn't really worry about it until any noticeable abnormalities do start to appear in his memory. My gut feeling is no until then."

"Any finally recommendations or advice, Doctor?" Chris asked.

"The best thing I can say is not to worry about anything until something comes up." The doctor shrugged. "I'm not saying to literally not worry about anything. Please, worry a little, but don't obsess over it. Just live your life the best you can. Have fun. Be healthy. Other than that, I've got nothing."

"All right," Christian said with a nervous laugh. "With that in mind, I hope you don't mind me saying that after I get released, I hope the next time we ever see each other again is under more sociable situations."

Greene laughed at that. "No, not at all. I don't mind in the slightest. I hope that'll be the case as well."

With that said, Christian stayed at the Las Vegas hospital until Friday before Greene finally agreed to release him the next morning. He and Dom went home within hours after that.

The first couple of days of being home brought plenty of visitors. Obviously there were David, Sally, and Dom who virtually saw or spoke to him almost daily, but there also visits from Curly, several boxers from Dom's gym, and The Misfits.

When he was able enough, Christian took a day for himself to go to his local library. There, he surfed the internet for a number of hours to find out what he could as to what he may go through in the years to come. Not only did he get a number of printouts concerning dementia and its possible symptoms, but also that to Dementia Pugilistica, post-traumatic dementia, punch-drunk syndrome, Parkinson's, and another form known as early-onset dementia. This last one, he was surprised to read, was merely a term used to cover a range of diseases affecting memory and thinking in people under the age of sixty-five.

Christian was somewhat saddened to read that if he did get dementia, that the dementia itself wasn't as easy to diagnose as a simple cold, nor would it be treated as such. Dementia itself was a far more advanced and had many more forms than what he had anticipated. He found that it wasn't a disease but, rather, a set of symptoms of a brain disorder that got worse over time. Along with that, the patient would lose their memory as well as other mental functions.

Parkinson's disease, on the other hand, was something he could very well get. This would give his body trouble over time rather than his mind. While he was at it, he got a number of printouts concerning amnesia, Alzheimer's, vascular dementia, and anything else related to the hole he had in his brain.

All in all, he was pleased with what he had found out that day. He left with a nice little stack of printouts to read later. That night at dinner, he told Miho about his day at the library as well as showing her what he got. They discussed the many nights that proceeded that about what to expect. Of course, along the way he informed his parents about what he had potentially could look forward to. Out of respect, Miho did the same by telling her parents on Christian's situation. Given this, he found himself very lucky and fortunate to have support and blessings from each side.

Christian soon discovered that he adjusted well to life without boxing. Outside of periodically visiting the gym to see Dom and a few of the other guys, boxing was now in the past for him. He tried several times to get in contact with Shawn, but he never was actually able to talk with him. He even left a number of messages for him. None of them were ever returned.

Shawn, Christian noticed, seemed to have done much better in his boxing career as compared to his personal life. He had number of run-ins with the law in forms of drunken bar brawls, a DWI or two, and a number of charges of possession. Duke, to his credit, kept Shawn busy in the ring so that he didn't have time to get into trouble outside of it, but whatever trouble Shawn did get himself into only seemed to raise his market value.

When Christian recovered from his retirement match, and after he had his final bills taken care of, he enrolled himself back into the college he was at before. A year later, and a month after finding out he got accepted into graduate school, he walked up on stage during his college's commencement to receive his bachelor's degree.

A week after graduating, Christian and Miho married. Even though they wanted a small ceremony, one without publicity, it still made the local news as well as ESPN. The month following their wedding, they traveled the U.S. as part of their honeymoon. This was something Miho had suggested since neither of them have ever actually seen the United States. Sure, he traveled it when he was boxing, but never to sightsee.

After the month was over, they traveled to Miho's hometown of Kyoto, Japan and were also wed there. Even though Christian knew he wasn't able to hold dual citizenship in Japan like he could in America, he nonetheless questioned whether marrying a Japanese citizen would make him one. This wedding here was for the benefit of Miho's family and friends, whereas the one they had in New York was for Christian's side. Here, they stated with Miho's parents for a few days before doing some sightseeing in the northern part of the country. They both got home in early August roughly two weeks before Christian's graduate classes started.

The beginning of the following July marked a big time for both Christian and Miho as they celebrated the birth of their first child, a daughter. They decided to name her Asako, which was the middle name of Miho's mother, who was pleased and honored by the gesture.

Graduate school proved a little more challenging for Christian, mainly because not only did he have more challenging work to do, but he was now a parent with all the responsibilities that went along with it. He received his master's that following Christmas, although he would not officially get the degree until the commencement that next May. Even though he had found it more difficult to do as well as he had before, he still managed to make the dean's list all three semesters that it took him, though just barely for two of them.

That January, a month after completing his master's, he started teaching at a local college in their natural resources department. He worked only part-time so he could be home to take care of Asako while Miho herself went to graduate school. The summer that Asako turned two, Christian would also start working at the local zoo where he would lecture on specific topics, as well as at two nature centers where he would lead guided tours.

Miho graduated that following May, six weeks before Asako's third birthday, with a master's in journalism. She took some minor jobs at a number of newspapers before finding a job to her liking at a major magazine in Manhattan that fall. The three of them moved downstate into an apartment before buying a nice home right across the border in New Jersey. They decided on this given their money would go further south of the border rather than in the city itself. The house and land they got were in a rural suburb in the northern part of the state. They easily could have bought four of these houses to equal the price that that same house would have cost in or around the city.

The sacrifice they made in driving time was trivial to what they gained in exchange: a house compared to an apartment; a few acres of land in a safe neighborhood compared to a small parcel at best with higher crime rates. It was hard for Christian to leave his home in upstate New York but, in the end, he though a good home was more than lumber, concrete, and sheetrock.

While Miho was working full-time at her magazine as an assistant editor, Christian got two part-time jobs which suited his desires. One was at the Bronx Zoo where he worked multiple jobs including assistant keeper in the primate exhibit, bird handler, educational tour guide, and as a banquet and function organizer. His other job was as a teacher at a local community college close to home. These two jobs offered him the ability to do the things he wanted to do after boxing, yet he still had enough time at home with his family.

In October of the following year, three months after Asako's fourth birthday, the Eaton's celebrated again with the arrival of their second child, a son, who they named Dominic after Christian's former trainer and manager. David and Sally had come down to spend a week to help out; marking only the second time they've been to Christian's and Miho's New Jersey home, and the first to last more than two days. David left for home that weekend claiming the plant would go under if he was away any more. Sally, being the ever-loving mother, stayed another week to "make sure things were in order before leaving."

The Eaton's easily slipped back into their happy, content life they've made for themselves soon after Dominic's birth. Sally went back to life with David; Miho went back to work from maternity leave; and Asako was enrolled into pre-school that eventually turned into kindergarten.

At this stage of their lives, Christian and Miho had everything they needed and desired. Outside of an occasional endorsement that Christian did, boxing was far in the past and they adjusted well without it while still living off the rewards from it. They were as content as people could be and they planned to live happily ever after with each other. Or so they thought.

Chapter 41

The next several years went by without incident as problems eluded the Eaton's. They were living a dream come true while being blanketed by happiness in stress-free times. Their children had grown quite a bit. Miho accepted a promotion at work. Christian still maintained his part-time teaching position while being a full-time dad and periodically worked on an on-call basis at their local zoo.

The only thing that should have bothered them was Christian's memory. He had always had a good memory, almost to the point of being photographic, but little things were initially overlooked and easily pushed aside. The problem he found he was beginning to have, or seemed to be developing to a certain extent, was forgetfulness. Of course he was getting older and had been a boxer for a number of years, so he generally ignored it.

His forgetfulness started off small, such as not being able to locate his keys or wallet, before gradually increasing to forgetting an occasional appointment or what time to pick the kids up from school. Once he forgot he drove to the local store only to have Miho ask him where the car was after walking home. She laughed when he told her he didn't know. When he did go back for it, he practically walked around the parking lot multiple times before finally locating his car. And he found it not because he remembered where it was, but because he finally saw it by itself after several cars around it had left.

His memory stayed like this for a year or two longer before it started playing a nasty trick on him: he forgot the names of his children. It wasn't one of those momentary lapses or brain farts as some would call it, but a genuine honest-to-God forgot-what-their-names-were moment. This went on for a better part of a week before he finally told Miho.

"Hun," he said after coming into their bedroom while she was getting ready for bed.

"Hmmm?" She turned her head with a smile as he sat on the bed.

"I don't mean to make you nervous or anything, but something's been bothering me for a few days," he said while rubbing his forehead. "What are the kids' names again?"

She continued to look at him. She briefly turned to adjust her pajamas before looking back. While noticing her husband still had the same confused look on his face, she laughed slightly while her eyes studied him, almost waiting for him to confess to some joke.

When the confession didn't come, she finally asked, "You are joking?"

He shook his head. "No, I'm not. I've been trying to remember all week what they were." After saying that, he looked at her with eyes that reinforced that he was, in fact, being serious.

Letting out a brief sigh when the realization hit her that he was being honest with her, Miho walked over to sit on the bed next to him. She took his hand in the process.

"Our girl's name is Asako, which is also my mom's middle name," she explained before pausing to let Christian absorb this. He did so by saying her name a two or three times. "And Dominic is our son."

"Dominic," he repeated before his eyes lit up. "Oh, like my old trainer?"

"Hai," she answered in Japanese with a quick nod. "You wanted him named after him, remember?"

"That does sound like something I'd do."

With this, a thought came to Miho. "A few months ago when you came back for the store without the car, did you really forget it or were you joking?"

"No, I was serious," he somberly answered while looking down to his lap. "I found it only because I saw it by itself rather than actually remembering where I parked it."

"The doctors did say you might have some problems. Maybe it's time you get checked out."

"No, not yet." Christian shook his head. "I'd like to see if it gets worse a before I do."

While looking at him in silence, Miho finally said, "Don't wait too long."

"I won't." He smiled before leaning in to kiss her forehead.

While climbing into bed, Miho found herself posing her husband another question. "Is this the only time you've forgotten something?"

"No, but it's always been small stuff before, like where are the keys, my wallet, that sort of thing."

"And the car and the kids names?" she asked with a giggle.

"Yeah. You'll let me know if you notice anything weird or different with me, won't you?"

"Only if you tell me if you forget more, ok?"

He agreed with a nod. He leaned in to once again kiss her forehead before getting up to leave the room.

"You coming to bed soon?" Miho asked him.

"I will shortly," he answered while turning to her. "I wanted to do some paperwork before I did."

"Don't take too long."

"I won't."

"Are we still going to New York next weekend?" she asked while rolling over.

"What's that?" he asked with a smile before leaving the room.

That next weekend they did indeed go to upstate New York for two reasons. The main one was to spend time with David and Sally at their place; she had been asking both Christian and Miho to bring the family up one weekend so they could have the chance to see them all again. The other reason was to see Dom. It had been awhile since he had seen Dom and felt pleased to have a chance to go back to spend some time, though only a little, at his old stomping grounds.

"Oh, hello, hello," Sally said cheerfully after opening the door to reveal Christian, Miho, Asako, and Dominic. "Come in, come in. It's so good to see you again. Oh, before we go any further, come here," she told them while bending down to hug and kiss Asako. When she tried to do that with Dominic, he pulled away before she could finish with a yuck. Sally smiled at that before giving Miho a hug. "How are you doing, honey?"

"I'm fine, Mrs. Eaton-san," Miho softly answered while returning the hug.

Sally chuckled. "After all this time, I still haven't gotten used to being called missus by members of my own family."

Asako was smiling while standing there looking up at her grandmother. Dominic, meanwhile, was getting antsy before going off to start exploring.

"Dom," Christian called out. "Before you start exploring too much, why don't you come over here and say hello to your grandmother."

Like a typical boy, Dominic continued as he was without acknowledging his father.

"Dominic," Christian said a bit more firm. "We're waiting."

"Ah, Dad," the boy whined while walking over to his grandmother. "Hi Grandma," Dominic said once he got to her.

"Hi, sweetie." Sally smiled while bending over to kiss his forehead. "Did you have a nice trip up?"

"It was alright," he answered while starting to look around again.

"Just alright? What was wrong with it?"

"It took, like, *forever*, Grandma!"

"Yeah, it took around four hours," his father said with a sarcastic smile while rubbing his son's head.

"Hey, where's Gramps?!" Dominic shouted while pulling away and taking off to complete his exploration he started moments before.

Christian sighed heavily while closing his eyes. Miho, meanwhile, just laughed.

"Was he driving you crazy on the way up?" Sally inquired with a smile.

"You've no idea how much torture he put us through, Mom."

"It could be worse," his mom told him. "Your father and I had Shawn to raise. We never knew when he'd be home or what shape he'd be in when he did."

391

"But you had Grandpa to help out for a while there," Christian reminded her.

"For the first couple of years your grandfather was there to help, but after he left, especially during his teenage years, he was almost uncontrollable."

"Was he really that bad?" Miho asked.

"He was quite similar to how he is now," Christian confirmed with a smile.

"Oh, my," Miho exclaimed as a hand went to her mouth. "I hope Dominic won't get like that."

"As far as I can tell, you don't have anything to worry about," her mother-in-law told her. "He'll turn out just fine."

"I hope so."

"Grandma?" Asako said while looking up at her.

"Yes, honey?"

"Where do I get to sleep?"

"You know where it is, silly. You've been there before," Sally said while drawing an embarrassed laugh from her granddaughter. "It's up at the top of the stairs and to the right."

"May I go up there?"

"If you want."

Smiling, Asako started towards the stairs.

"Hey, Asako," Christian said to her. "What do you say to your grandmother?"

She stopped before turning to look at him blankly.

"What do you tell her for letting you go up there?" he repeated.

"Oh." She giggled from embarrassment. "Thank-you, Grandma."

"You're welcome, dear," Sally warmly said as Asako continued upstairs.

"Hey, don't forget to take your bags with you," Christian told her.

Asako, with a sigh, did what was asked of her before disappearing around the corner. Once she was gone, a bewildered expression came over her father's face.

"Hey, Mom. You still have my old room?" he asked his mother. "Even after all these years?"

"Of course, dear," Sally told him. "We weren't going to remove it from the rest of the house just because you move out, sweetie."

Hearing this, Christian shook his head while smiling. "That's not what I meant, Mom. Of course you weren't going to remove it from the rest of the house. I was just surprised that you still had my old room setup as a bedroom after I *did* leave."

"Of course, dear. What else would we have it as?"

While laughing, Christian answered. "Well, considering Dad turned Shawn's old room into his office and Grandpa's apartment back into a storage room, I wasn't so sure what my old room would be now."

"I'm sorry, Christian, that's not entirely correct," his mother said while looking around. "Your grandfather's apartment isn't completely a storage area. It still has the bathroom, kitchenette, bed, and dresser."

"Close enough," her son muttered.

"Well, since you're all here, would you two like to put your things away now or would you like to wait until later?"

"If it's ok with you two," Miho quietly said while looking them, "I'd like to put our things away first."

Christian shrugged. "Fine by me."

"Ok, kids. Have at it," Sally said while bending to pick up Dominic's bag before taking it up to her son's old room.

Meanwhile, Christian and Miho took their belongings out to the old apartment above the garage. The apartment, for the most part, looked how he remembered it but now was filled with boxes and other things his father had put up there over the years. If it was left up to his dad, Grandpa Joe's apartment would had been completely converted over to storage years ago but his mom intervened because she wanted it left as a spare bedroom. They compromised and the result was what Miho and Christian saw before them.

Grandpa Joe's bed, dresser, heavy bag, and speed bad were where they had been before but every space in between was filled with boxes. After about a fifteen minutes, Christian and Miho had moved enough things around to the point where they could move more comfortably.

As they explored, Christian was amazed to notice the plumbing still worked in the bathroom. While coming out, he saw Miho was trying her hand at the speed bag. After several failed attempts, she moved to the well-worn heavy bag next to it. She gave it a few pushes to judge its weight and movability before giving it a couple of uncoordinated punches.

"You'd better be careful," he told her while coming over.

"With what?"

"With how you're hitting it."

"What's wrong with how I hit?" she asked before punching the bag two more times.

"Might break your wrists with those punches," he informed her while walking up behind her. He soon found his hands on her waist as he pulled her towards him so he could kiss her neck.

"That tickles." She laughed before moving her head so he could do it again. "What's wrong with my hitting?" she repeated.

"Your hands weren't straight with your arms. They could roll over on themselves and break your wrists."

Holding up her arms, she said, "Show me."

Taking her hands to make a proper fist, he demonstrated. "You have to keep your punches straight."

After a few punches that were a little better, Miho asked, "Is this the bag you learned to box with?"

"It is."

"Did he help train you, your grandfather?"

"No. Shawn did."

"Shawn?" she asked in a slightly confused tone like she didn't hear him correctly.

"Hm-hmm," he confirmed before kissing her neck again.

"I thought your grandfather trained you," Miho said while turning around to face her husband.

"No; he trained Shawn," Christian corrected before kissing her.

"And Shawn trained you?"

"If that's what you want to call it."

"Huh?" She blinked a couple of times while looking at him.

This part of the conversation was one of the things in their relationship that actually bothered Christian and he was sure it bothered her as well, though they both had accepted it. The problem dealt with the slight language barrier that they still had, though it had gotten thinner over the years. The biggest thing with each of their languages was each other's slang they had used which did not translate or carry over very well, if at all.

"Shawn never really had the mentality, communication skills, or the patience to be a very good trainer. That, mixed with his short attention span and ability to become frustrated if I didn't understand hindered him as well."

"So it was Dom who trained you?"

"Yes, well, trained better and for a much longer duration." Christian kissed her yet again. "I already had the basic fundamentals down when I went to Dom's but it wasn't until after I'd been with him for awhile did everything begin falling together."

"I'm glad you don't do that anymore," she softly told him as they touched their foreheads together.

"Yeah, me too."

"Are you still having problems with your memory?" she asked in Japanese.

In English he replied, "Every now and then, but nothing serious."

"Maybe you should go to the doctor," commented Miho, this time in English.

"No, not just yet," Christian told her in Japanese.

"Why not?"

"The doctors said I might experience some problems with my memory, that it would be just a side effect from the fight."

"Don't you mean 'fights'?" she corrected with a smile.

"That's true," he admitted with his own smile. "All the matches I've been in could have contributed to my symptoms. But it was from that last match that put it over the edge."

"Have you seen or heard from Shawn since that last fight?" Miho asked in Japanese.

"No," he said as sadness came over his face. "The closest I've gotten was that mean, spiteful message he left on our machine after that last fight. I've seen him on TV a number of times, though."

"Maybe you should call him."

"I tried contacting him a few times with no luck. I never got through and, as far as I know, he never tried to contact me. I gave up trying."

"Maybe you could try again."

"You want me to contact Shawn?" Christian asked in shocked dismay as she giggled and kissed my nose. "I don't know his phone number."

"Isn't that why we have a phone book, no?"

"Yeah, I know. I should look it up," he admitted before having a thought cross my mind. "Besides, I didn't think you liked him."

"He is your brother," she firmly stated.

395

"He is family."

"Adoptive brother to be specific. And you're more family to me than he's been these last several years."

"He still is family," she repeated a bit more firm. "You do this, before it too late!"

"Yes, dear," he said in Japanese with a smile and small laugh.

"Don't make fun of me."

"I will if you want me to. Don't you know me by now?"

With that, he lowered himself just enough to put his arms around her waist, picked her up, and twirled her around several times. She laughed as he did so before hearing a voice from the stairs.

"Daddy, are you up there?" the voice called as the sound of footsteps came up the stairs. Dominic's head soon appeared in the doorway. When he saw his father twirling his mom around, his face showed an expression of both shock and surprise. "Oh, gross!"

"C'mon, put me down," Miho chastised with a smile who poking him on the forehead with a finger. "Not in front of the children."

"Not in front of the children?" Christian mocked her with a laugh. He tried to hide his smile before looking at his son. "Hey Squirt. What'ya need?"

"Grandpa wants you."

"Oh, he does, does he?" Christian asked while putting his wife down before walking over to his son. He soon picked him up and twirled him in the air a number of times.

"Yes he does," Dominic called out while laughing uncontrollably.

"You should be more careful with him," Miho chastised.

"Yes, dear," responded Christian before looking at his son. "Ok, off we go to find Grandpa. Where's he at?"

"Downstairs."

"Downstairs in the garage?"

"No, silly. Downstairs in the basement," giggled Dominic as his father bounced him in his arms as they walked down to the garage.

"Oh, *downstairs* downstairs."

Miho followed.

His dad's corner was basically the same as it had been since his childhood. There were a couple of electrical saws, a band and a table, which had sawdust on them; a work bench with tools hanging on the wall above it; an anvil amongst the metal-working tools, a blow torch with its accompanying mask on the wall above it; a bunch of lumber and metal products he had neatly stacked against the wall which were organized by size and shape; and a couple of cabinets filled neatly with miscellaneous items. On the floor were a number of boxes pulled out which he normally kept hidden under the table.

"C'mon you good for nothin', son-of-a-bitch!" David grumbled as he monkeyed around with the boxes.

Christian had stopped at the bottom of the stairs, Dominic still in his arms, to watch his father struggle with the boxes and some supplies he was trying to move around. Sitting in a metal folding chair, Christian watched his father to see how long it would take him to notice them. When placing Dominic on his lap, Miho, who came down behind them, started to walk over to her father-in-law before being pulled back by Christian. He soon put a finger to his lips as a gesture to be quiet. Smiling quickly, she returned to sit on her husband's other knee. They continued to watch David from this spot for another minute or so as he struggled with this work, constantly grumbling while doing so.

"Well, I'll be. These little bastards all fit in here easily the last time. C'mon, get in there will ya?!" David muttered. He soon stopped what he was doing to stand and look at it. He rubbed his lower back with one hand while wiping the sweat off of his brow. Soon, he became agitated again as he looked around and began muttering to himself. "In all the god-damned times that I need that son of mine, he chooses to ignore me. What in the hell is...," he started before noticing his three visitors watching him. While blinking in confusion when he saw them smiling at him, he said, "How long have you three been there?"

Smiling broadly, Christian said, "Long enough to have a good laugh at your expense."

Miho and Dominic each laughed at this before he hopped off of his father's lap and ran to greet his grandfather.

"Didn't I call for you about ten minutes ago?" David asked them.

"Ten? It was more like five," responded Christian. "Besides, Dominic got lost."

"Got lost going to the garage?" David asked with a hard look before loosening up and laughed. Times like this, he could be upset or chastise them for not coming when he asked. But seeing them laugh openly, both at his expense while his grandson tugged playfully at his arm, couldn't keep him irrigated for very long. "Whatever. How long were you going to sit there before you decided to help me?"

"Not sure."

"I wanted to help but he said no," Miho playfully said while slapping Christian's chest.

"I wanted to see how long it took before you noticed us."

397

Standing there motionless for a minute longer in silence, David merely looked at his grinning son. He soon shook his head before speaking, "While you're down here, do you mind helping me out for a few minutes?"

"I'm not sure. We might be busy."

"When you're done having fun, I wanted help moving some of my boxes and tools around," David told them while waving a hand in the general direction of what he was talking about. "I was hoping to have it done by dinner."

"Didn't I help you with this the last time we came up?"

David scoffed. "That was six months ago. I wanted to rearrange it and take some things out that I have stored."

"Alright," his son told him while indicating to Miho he wished to get up.

Acknowledging, Miho got up to allow her husband to follow suit. The two of them walked over to where David and Dominic where.

"Where do you want me to start, Pops?"

Sighing, his father looked at the mess he had before him. "Well, I just want to take whatever boxes I haven't pulled out yet, see what exactly I have in them, and take out what I'll need. Then put back what I don't need."

"What are you working on?" Miho asked him.

"Sally pointed out a coffee table somewhere that she liked. I hope to make her one similar to it for Christmas."

"Aren't you worried she'll come down here and find out what you're up to?"

"No. she hardly comes over here and, when she does, she probably won't notice."

"Grandpa, may I help?" Dominic asked.

"I don't care." David shrugged his shoulders. "Just don't touch the saws, ok?"

"Yes, Grandpa."

"If you do, you're going upstairs," Christian informed his son.

"Hey, where's that daughter of yours?" David asked.

"She's helping Sally-san in the kitchen," Miho told him.

"Helping or getting in the way?" responded her father-in-law with a smile.

With that, Miho smiled before taking her leave. She left the two younger Eaton males to help the elder one in the basement for the next half hour until they were called for dinner.

On the way upstairs, Christian popped his head into Shawn's old room. It looked the same other than the fact it didn't have any of Shawn's things in it. He knew that his parents were going to turn it into a sort of combination study and den, but thought they'd at least keep the bed and dresser that he didn't want when he moved out. David had his desk in the corner with a filing cabinet next to it. On the wall adjacent to it, he installed a nice bookshelf within which was filled with a variety of how-to, sewing, knitting, and other similar books. In the opposite corner of the desk, Sally had her sewing machine and knitting supplies.

"What happened to Shawn's bed and dresser?" Christian asked.

"Gave them to a family up the road," his father answered while flicking his thumb in the general direction. "They needed something for their son. We know them through church; good people. Not much money but they're happy and appreciate what they have. We didn't need them considering we still have your stuff as well as your grandfather's. They've helped us out with some things in the past, and letting them have them was the least we could do; though I did need to fix them up first."

"They helped you out with a few things?" Christian questioned while looking at his father. "I've never known you to get help from anyone unless you needed something. May I ask what they helped you out with?"

"Oh, you know, things," he said in a nonchalant manner while shrugging. "They weren't really important; just small things really. But they were hard pressed. They're worth it, I thought. Besides, we didn't need them."

"I like what you did to it," Christian complimented. "How long has it been now?"

"Five or six years."

"That bookshelf which you made in the wall is nice. How long did it take you to do that?"

"Oh, on and off for about three months though it could have been completed in a couple of days."

"Did you know Shawn was in a movie a year or so ago?" Christian asked him.

"I saw trailers for it, but I didn't know that much about it."

Christian laughed. "Those trailers had all the best parts. It was a low-budget action flick. He was the only known person in it, if you can call him known. I took the kids to see it."

Just then, Dominic wiggled his way in between them as he popped his head in the room. "Whose bedroom is this?"

"No one's now," David told him while rubbing his head. "It was your uncle Shawn's."

"I have an uncle?"

"Yes, you do."

"Have I ever seen him?"

"Remember that movie I took you and your sister to see about a year or so ago?"

Dominic nodded.

"Well, the main guy in that is your uncle."

"Oh, but have I ever actually seen him?"

"No."

"Then how could I have an uncle if I've never seen him?"

"It's a long story, kiddo."

"Oh."

"When was the last time you've heard from Shawn?" David asked.

"That last fight," Christian said softly. "That day was the last time I've actually seen him, but when I got home that next week he had left a couple rude messages for me. How 'bout you?"

"It's been awhile, a couple years at least." David rubbed his cheek while thinking for an answer. "Got to ask your mother on that; she'd know."

"I have tried getting in touch with him over the last few years, but never had any luck," Christian told his father. "I've sent him a few letters telling him what's been going on, Christmas cards, that sort of thing. I even sent him a few pictures of all of us in case he forgot what we looked like. That didn't do any good either."

"What's going on with that brother of yours?"

"I don't know but, whatever it is, he's no longer here."

"Where is he? Did he move from that Manhattan apartment of his?"

"No, he's still there. That's not what I meant, though," corrected Christian. "What I was talking about was him and his personality change, especially during the last few months we saw each other. It's like his body was still there but his brain was a galaxy away. Felt like he was somewhere between nowhere and goodbye."

"Do you know what he's been up to?"

"He dropped his cruiserweight belts after beating all he could before moving up in class to heavyweight. With the amount of weight and muscle he's put on in such a short amount of time, I'm sure he was taking something."

"Steroids?" his dad asked him.

"Maybe. Who knows?"

"That doesn't surprise me, especially after those experimental years he had as a teenager."

"What makes you so sure he's over that phase?" Christian asked with a sly smile.

"I don't." David scoffed. "While we're at it, I don't want you calling me or your mother saying he was found face down in a gutter like his old man was. You hear me?"

"Don't worry. I'll sugar coat it for both of you."

"You'd better if you know what's good for you," David told him while thinking of something. "Oh, is he still being controlled by that money hungry promoter? What was his name again?"

"Duke Snyder and yes he is."

"There was an article in some sports magazine I read a couple of years back about him, this Snyder character that is," David said. "It wasn't written in a flattery way if you get my drift. A few of his former fighters commented that he didn't give them their fair share of the earnings but they couldn't do anything about it on account of the contract they had signed."

"I heard that too."

"What about Shawn? Do you think he's getting his fair share?"

"I doubt it," Christian told him. "As long as he keeps winning, he'll keep making money, though probably only just enough to support all his nasty habits and not much more."

"You know, after all these years and how we've tried to raise him, I've still no idea what thoughts go through that head of his."

"I don't think he even knows."

"What the hell is wrong with him?"

Christian shrugged. "I think he's hungry for power, money, respect, fame, and anything else he can get."

They both stood there in silence not knowing what to say. After a few moments of this, David rubbed his stomach.

"While we're still young, we'd better go on up to eat while the food's still hot," his told his son.

"I'm all for that," Christian said while a smile appeared on his face. He soon picked up his son before running up the basement stairs two at a time.

Dinner that night closely resembled what you might find laid out for a holiday feast. Sally had fines a pork roast, mashed potatoes, dressing, corn, banana bread, cranberries, cabbage salad, and lots of gravy. She had also made apple pie, chocolate cake, and chocolate-chip cookies for desert. There was enough food made for everyone to get full twice over not only for that day, but easily for the next two as well.

"Geez, Mom, you still make more than is enough, don't you?" Christian asked near the end of the meal while leaning back and patting his stomach approvingly.

"I don't mind. I actually enjoy it." She smiled. "I'd rather make too much than having too little. Though, if you wish, I'll be glad to cut back the amount I make next time."

"You better not say yes to that, damn it," David told his son with stern eyes. "It's not very often that I have a meal this good. I don't intend on widening the distance between them anymore than they are on account you think that it's a good idea."

"Oh, will you stop that?" Sally asked while throwing her husband a disapproving glance. "That's not true. If it was, there's nothing preventing you from making a dinner like this. I think I might actually enjoy having a meal like this without the many hours preparing it."

"Since you put it that way, these meals aren't spaced all that badly," he dryly said while going back to eating his food.

Dessert soon came which then faded into the adults talking amongst themselves. Asako and Dominic excused themselves at this time to go play outside.

"Miho tells me you're having some problems with your memory," Sally said once the children left, which drew a delayed silence from the other three as she and Christian exchanged a brief look. Even if he denied it, the look between them was all the answer she needed.

"I have had some small problems, but nothing to worry about yet," he admitted in a way to downplay the situation.

"Small?" Miho asked with a smile. "What about the time you forgot you drove to the store? You ended up leaving the car there while walking back."

"Honest mistake. Could have happened to anyone."

"What about that week that you forgot the kids names? You were calling them these weird names hoping they'd correct you at some point?"

"There are days I don't even remember my own name," David commented.

"Dear, there are days you think Gerald Ford's still in office," Sally told him while sipping her coffee.

"Well, yeah, you've got a point there." David smiled.

"So, dear, how long have you been having problems with your memory?" Sally asked Christian.

Thinking for an answer, Christian soon replied. "Off and on for a few months now. Maybe a year."

"How come you haven't said anything?"

"It hasn't really bothered me enough to actually notice." He shrugged. "Until recently that is."

"Forgetting your car and kids names didn't raise any red flags?" his father asked him.

Shrugging, Christian said, "Well, those two were the exceptions. Mainly it's been the keys or my wallet, minor appointments, things like that."

"Have you talked to your doctor about it get" his mom asked.

"I did get checked out seven or eight years ago after that last fight," Christian said while looking around the table. "I'll probably go and get checked out if it gets worse."

"Don't wait too long. The sooner you go, the sooner they can find what may be wrong and the sooner they can help you."

"Yes, Mother," Christian said with a frustrated sigh.

"Don't get upset with her," Miho told him while rubbing his forearm. "She's only trying to help."

"Double trouble, huh?" David smiled while looking at his son.

Christian, returning the look, shook his head. Sally, meanwhile, simply smiled upon hearing that. Miho, not quite understanding the joke due to there still being some language barrier left when it came to American humor, just sat there looking between them.

"While you're up here, were you going to visit the old gym and Dom at all?" Sally asked her son.

"I thought about going tomorrow for a couple of hours or so," Christian confirmed.

"Where you going with him?" David asked his daughter-in-law.

"No, I do not think so," she quietly answered.

"Smart lady," Sally commented with a slight smile.

"Why do you think I married her?" Christian asked while getting an embarrassed look from his wife.

When they were done with the cleanup of the meal, Christian, Miho, and Sally took a walk around the neighborhood. Not only were they doing this to enjoy the nice weather they were having, but also so Sally and Christian could reminisce about what had happened in the area over the years. Miho enjoyed hearing the history of the Eaton's neighborhood as well as the stories Sally told of Christian's and Shawn's childhood.

They also tried to locate Asako and Dominic who seemed to be off enjoying themselves elsewhere in the area. Of the three, Miho was the only one worried when they hadn't spotted the children during their walk. Christian wasn't worried at all while commenting they just found a good spot to play, most likely with some neighbor's children.

Asako and Dominic, in fact, had been playing with some neighbor's children but, when they were found, were in Christian's old tree house playing with some toys they had found in the garage. What gave their location away was a light from a tree house window, which actually was coming from one of David's old lanterns. When questioned about this, Asako reassured them that their grandfather was the one that had hauled the toys out for them and was also the one who lit the lantern. She also told them that both her and her brother were told to be careful by this same grandfather.

"You two don't stay out too late, alright?" Christian told them while going down the tree house's ladder. "If you need any help with the lantern, come and get one of us. Ok?"

"Yes, Dad," each child said in unison as he went in for the night.

Chapter 42

"C'mon kid, get your hands up! Don't be lettin' 'hem bounce off that noggin of yours," Dom yelled at what seemed to be a new recruit. "Ya head is the best thing ya got. If ya continue using' it ta block with, ya should consider early retirement. Ya hear me?"

"Yes sir, Mr. Calavicci," the trainee quickly responded.

"Another thing that ya should keep up is your movement," Dom growled while pointing to the trainee's feet. "It's great that ya can block, but's it's better if ya can move the hell outta the way!"

Christian couldn't help but laugh at this mostly because Dom was treating the kid just as he'd been treated when he first started out. As he looked around the gym, he noticed that it looked the same, yet a little cleaner, as when he was last there. The walls had been painted and parts of the wooden floor had been replaced. Some of the older speed bags had been replaced, while a couple of the newer heavy bags had a fresh supply of duct tape around them.

While wandering the gym, Christian inspected everything as he went. Most of the old flyers and posters had been replaced by newer ones. All the pictures Dom had on the walls with his students over the years were still isolated together on the wall by the office and had some new ones mixed in. One picture in particular caught his eye, one which surprised him. This prompted him to go over to investigate. It was a picture of Christian with Dom and Shawn the night he won the WBO cruiserweight championship. He still had to laugh every time he saw it. Even though the picture was taken minutes after they got back to the locker room on the night he won his first world title, a night that was his, but he couldn't help but smile while remembering Shawn did his best to dominate the photo they had together. Neither Christian and Dom could hardly be seen as a result.

Why Dom chose that picture and how long it'd been there, Christian didn't know. He surmised Shawn had put it there some time ago, sometime before he parted ways. He also assumed that Dom knew about it all this time and simply chose not to take it down on. In any event, he wasn't going to ask. When he saw a chance, Christian went over to talk with his former mentor.

"Hey Dom. How have you been doing, old man?" Christian asked with a broad smile while reaching out to shake his hand.

" 'Old man'?" Dom glared at him while refusing to shake his hand. "That's something you'll never be if ya continue callin' me that."

"Getting a little touchy with age, aren't you, Dom? Don't most people mellow out in their golden years?"

"I ain't like most people, kid."

"So I've noticed."

"What the hell ya doin' here?"

"I just came for a visit."

"Came ta visit or came ta insult me?" growled the feisty old man.

"Came for a visit." Christian smiled broadly. "I have no reason to insult you at the moment. I was in town and I thought I'd stop by to see how you're doing."

"The air's still going in and out, kid. That's all that matters, right?" Dom asked. After a moment, he soon smiled for the first time during that conversation. "Hey, kid, did I ever tell ya the reasonin' ta why I'm still alive?"

"Was it because heaven or hell doesn't' want you yet?"

"C'mon, kid. I'm bein' serious here. Do ya know why?"

"Ah, no, Dom. I don't know why. I don't think you've ever told me. Why are you still alive?"

"To save money on funeral expenses. Ha!" Dom exclaimed with a hearty laugh.

Christian smiled while shaking his head. "I'd have thought that a guy like you would have had that taken care of long ago. You know, take the grandkids to some cemetery in the nice part of town, wander around before coming to you. They point and read your headstone: *Dominic Calavicci. Born 556 BC. Died N/A.* And you'll tell them, 'Kids, here's where my wrinkly ass will be buried once I decide to go over to the other side. And once I'm buried, I'll be buried upside down so everyone else can just kiss my ass', or something to that matter."

"Ya did, huh? Ya really thought I'd do that?"

"As a matter of fact I did."

"There's one problem with that, kid."

"Yeah? What's that?"

"I ain't got no grandkids."

"I know. I was just saying when you eventually to get some."

With that said, there was a momentary pause between them as they looked at each. They soon smiled as Dom finally accepted Christian's handshake before embracing in a hug.

"How've you been, Dom?"

"Been good, kid. Been real good. How've ya been?"

"Good good." Christian smiled. "I've also been good."

"And your family?"

"They've been fine as well. Thank-you."

"How's your mind doin'?"

"Ah, it's alright. Could be worse, though."

"Any problems with it yet?"

"Some, but nothing serious. Just minor details."

"You'll go get checked out if there was, wouldn't ya?"

Christian chuckled at that. "Yes. And if I didn't, Miho herself would drag me to the doctor."

"I can picture her doin' that." Dom smiled with a nod. "I noticed ya makin' the rounds before comin' over."

"Uh-huh." Chris nodded.

"Miss any of the action around here at all?"

"I miss being here at the gym, the guys, the training. I don't miss much else, though."

"Hey, kid, while you're here, I'd like ya to meet my new cruiserweight prospect," Dom said while acknowledging a well buy guy in the ring. "Kid, this here is Jackie Nash. Jackie, this here's Christian Eaton. He's a former student of mine."

"Oh, yes sir. I knew who he was when I saw him walk in," Jackie told him in a very excited manner as he tried pulling off his glove. After doing so, he then leaned over the top rope to extend his now gloveless hand to Christian. "I've been a big fan of yours since I was a kid and followed your career. I'm a local boy myself."

"Really? Where're you from?"

"Down off of Maple."

"Ok, ok. I know where that is," Christian told him. "That's not too far where I grew up. That's right down by Deeley's, right?"

"Oh, yes sir, that's correct. Right down by Deeley's," Jackie answered who seemed pleased that Christian knew where it was. He soon bounced away while putting his glove back on before continuing his training in the ring.

Jackie, being a young, good looking black man around 20 or 21 years old who seemed to have a lot of potential at first sight. He seemed like an overall good, young man whose eyes still had that twinkle in them that hadn't been faded with age or harsh living. He was about the same height as Christian though a little leaner, but had a bit more muscle on his frame. He was one of only a handful or so of non-while people training at the gym. That wasn't because Dom had a resistance to someone who wasn't white but, rather, was because the area was predominantly occupied by white residents.

After staying for a few more minutes, Christian told Dom the thought he'd go home on account of there were a few things he needed to do. The two of them shook hands with this while saying they'd stay in touch. Before leaving for home, Christian took a walk around the gym one last time before heading out.

When he finally got home, he discovered the door was locked.

"That's weird. I didn't think I locked the door," he thought to himself while reaching into his pocket for his keys. He tried to open the door before him, but each time his keys wouldn't unlock it. "Now why on earth don't any of these work? I wonder if Shawn's playing a joke on me and had the locks changed again."

While putting his keys away, Christian started knocking on the door .

"Shawn! Come on, man. Open the door, will ya?"

After several tried, he was about to give up and, right when he was to walk back downstairs to Dom's gym, the door to his former apartment opened to reveal Nick Greenwood on the other side.

"Yo, Chris! Long time no see, man," he quickly said as a huge smile appeared on his face. "What'cha doin' up here?"

"I'm trying to get in," Christian told him while walking back to the apartment door. "What's going on here? Did Shawn put you up to this?"

"Did Shawn put me up to what?" Nick asked, clearly confused. "What're you talkin' about?"

"What do you mean what am I talking about? I'm talking about the changed lock on the door and you acting like you don't know what I'm talking about. Did Shawn put you up to this? Where is he? Is he inside? Hey...," Christian said while pointing to inside the apartment when he noticed it for the first time. Everything inside clearly was not what Christian had there when he lived there with Shawn. The carpets were new, the walls were painted a different color, and the furniture was all wrong. "What did you guys do in there? Where's all our stuff?"

"I don't know what guys you're talkin' 'bout, dude, but the apartment was like this when I moved in," Nick told him. He stepped aside to open the door more so Christian could look inside better. "As for all your stuff, you and Shawn took it with you guys when you two moved out. All this stuff's mine."

There was an awkward momentary silence between them as Christian stepped forward to look further in. The whole living room had been over. He creamy beige coloring of the walls looked nice; better than when he lived there. The ceiling had a new light. The cheap, third-rate furniture that Shawn had when he moved in was now replaced by a better quality, second-rate set. The beer bottles that had once littered the floor was now replaced with occasional closes and magazines ranging from cars to heavy metal music to Playboy. The once desolate walls were now replaced with posters of similar topics as their companion magazines beneath them.

"Would you mind if I had a look around inside?" he asked Nick. "I just want to be sure about something."

"Sure about what?"

"What you're saying is really true or not."

"Yeah, sure, if you want to," Nick told him while inviting his unannounced visitor in. His expression suggested he still didn't know what was going on.

"Thank-you," Christian said while entering.

He started exploring the small, two bedroom apartment with the same surprise and amazement while walking down the hall. This was his apartment yet it wasn't. The rooms were where he remembered them to be, then the overall look had totally changed. There were new floors in the kitchen, new paint and wallpaper throughout. There was even a new vanity set in the bathroom.

As far as the furniture went, it was basically the same throughout as it was in the living room. None of it was what he and Shawn ever had and all was a better version. Christian soon came back into the living room to face a still confused Nick Greenwood. He honestly wasn't sure what to say due to still being in shock himself.

"How long have you been living here for, Nick?" he soon asked.

"I moved in when Shawn left."

"Right after or was there some time lapse?"

"Dom had to remodel it first, as you can see," Nick told him while waving across the room. "Shawn did leave it in really bad shape. I moved in 'bout a week or so later."

"Was that when the lock on the door was replaced?"

"I don't know about that, but I assume so." Nick paused to look at him. "Why would you still have a key here after all this time? Wouldn't'cha have given it back to Dom when you moved out?"

"Yes, I would have. Good point."

"So that key you were using wouldn't have worked regardless if the lock was new or not."

"Unless I made a copy." Christian shook his head while rubbing his eyes. "I don't know."

Shrugging his shoulders, Nick smiled before saying, "I wouldn't have put it past Shawn to make a copy for future use."

"I'm sorry, Nick," Chris apologized while making his way to the door. "I don't know what came over me."

"That's alright. One too many head shots." Nick shrugged again. "I should do what you did and get out before it's too late."

"It's never too late to think about it."

"I don't know how to do anything else, man." Nick sighed. "Besides, what could I get that paid nearly as well as me fightin', huh?"

"You do have a little bit of savings, don't you?"

"A little."

"You could always box for a little longer, say for a year or two. The money you earn from that could be put towards college, trade school, or some vocation training."

"I don't have the smarts like you do, man. This is all I know."

"How about training or managing?"

"Not enough know-how for that."

"Fair enough. I'd just hate to see you use whatever savings you have on medical bills later on. That wouldn't be too nice," Christian told him before offering Nick a hand to shake. "It's was good to see you again, and I'm sorry to have bothered you."

Nick smiled. "No problem, dude. The next time you wanna stop by, you don't need to make up some story to do so. Alright?"

"Uh, yeah, sure Nick. No more stories," Christian promised.

While descending the stairwell outside his former apartment, Christian still found the whole experience he just had with Nick highly confusing. He soon found himself back inside the gym wanting to talk to Dom about it, who he found in his office flipping through some boxing magazines. Dom looked up when he knocked.

"Couldn't stay away, could ya, kid?"

"Ah, no. Couldn't stay away." Christian cleared his throat. "May I come in?"

"Sure, kid. Pull up a chair while you're at it."

Christian did what he was instructed while sitting in a chair by the desk. "Thanks, Dom. Are you busy at the moment?"

"Nah. I just was goin' through some of these damn magazines I've had pilin' up," Dom said while sifting through a pile before dragging out a recent copy of *Boxer's Digest* before handing it to Christian. Shawn was the featured boxer on its cover. "He outta be happy 'bout that. He made the cover again."

"Geez, he's gotten big," Christian commented while looking at the cover. "I don't remember him being that big when we fought."

"That's because he's gotten a helluva lot bigger since ya two last fought. It's from all that crap that greedy manager of his been givin' him."

"Steroids?" Christian asked in surprise. "How long has he been on them?"

"Kid, what's the matter with ya?" Dom asked while looking up at him. "He's been on that stuff ever since I've known him."

"He has?"

"Yeah, kid. Ya're the one who told me 'bout it."

"Oh, yeah. That's right. I did, didn't I?" Christian lied awkwardly.

"Hey kid, ya didn't come here ta talk about Shawn's drug use, did ya?" Dom asked while looking at him suspiciously. He noticed his former pupil was sitting relatively uneasy in is chair.

"Ah, no I didn't, Dom."

"Thought not. What's on your mind, kid?"

"I'm wondering about my apartment upstairs."

"Your apartment?" Dom asked as a look of great confusion came upon his wrinkled face. "What 'bout it?"

"As far as you know, am I in the middle of a joke here? Is Shawn, Nick, or someone else messing with me that you know of?"

"How the hell would I know that, kid?" Dom quickly retorted while noticing his former apprentice still seemed nervous about something. He soon looked at him square in the face before asking, "Hey, kid, what's goin' on?"

"I was hoping you'd be able to tell me," Christian told him. "I just went to my apartment and the door was locked. I never lock it. And when I tried my key, it wouldn't. None of my keys would open it. I thought Shawn was playing a joke on me and changed it or something. Anyway, when I was knocking for him to let me in, Nick answered. When I asked him what was going on, he said that he moved in shortly after Shawn left. On top of that, the whole apartment had been remodeled and all of our stuff had been replaced, all of which Nick said was his. I check the whole apartment and everything's different. I'm just wondering what's going on here. What happened to the apartment and all of my stuff? Why is Nick saying he lives there now? I think I would have remembered Shawn leaving, the apartment getting a face lift, and Nick moving in. Dom, do you know anything about this?"

When Christian was finished, he found himself more agitated and confused than when he started.

"Kid, ya bein' serous here or are ya tryin' ta pull a fast one on me?"

"No, Dom. I'm being serious. What's going on?"

"Kid, everythin' Nick told ya is the truth," Dom stated while studying Christian carefully.

"W-w-what are you saying? Nick's my new roommate? When did this happen?! Where'd Shawn go to?"

"Kid, I don't know how ta tell ya this but you moved out a decade ago. Shawn followed suit 'bout a year or so after that."

"W-w-what? That can't be right. I've been gone from upstairs for ten years?" Christian asked in bewilderment while unable to accept what he was being told. "Well, w-w-where do I live now?"

"Kid, you and Miho live together with your family. Don't you remember?"

"That does sound familiar," Christian told him while calming down a little while starting to remember more of those first few years after leaving the gym. "That's right, I got that house down by my parents."

"Down by your parents?" Dom repeated. He was still slightly on edge. He still was studying him. "Kid, ya lived in Jersey now. Have been for awhile."

Hearing this, Christian's eyes widened as his face paled.

"Kid, have ya spoken ta yer doctor lately 'bout this?"

Christian thought before responding. "No, I don't think so."

"Maybe ya should. They did say ya could have problems with your memory as a result of that beatin' ya got from Shawn, right? Go make an appointment and see what they have to say."

Christian sat there in silence, taking what he was just told in while looking at his old mentor. "Ten years, you say?" he soon asked.

"Yeah, kid. A decade."

"Time flies." Christian let out a long whistle before getting up to shake his hand once again. "Thanks, Dom. I think it's time for me to leave."

"Where ya goin'?"

"Home," he said before closing his eyes and rubbing his forehead. "Er, no. I'm going to my parents' place. That's what I meant."

"Want me to call somebody to come pick ya up?" Dom asked while pointing to the phone.

"Thanks, Dom, but I'll be fine."

"Ya sure?"

"Yeah." Christian smiled before making his way to the door.

"Hey, kid," Dom called right when his former student was about to leave.

Christian stopped just short of the door to turn and look back at him. "Yeah?"

"Don't wait so long 'til ya visit the doctor. Ok?"

"I'll try not to."

"Or fer yer next visit either, ya hear?"

"I won't," Christian promised with a smile while giving Dom a mock salute before finally exciting the gym for his journey homeward.

Chapter 43

An hour later Christian arrived back at his parents' house a little more dazzled than when he left the gym. He went inside to the smells of supper being prepared. His dad was at the table in his usual place reading the newspaper. His mom doing her usual several checks of the food. Asako and Dominic were watching TV in the living room.

"Hi Mom, hey Dad," he said while entering the kitchen. "How're you two doing?"

"Fine dear," his mom replied. "How was your visit at the gym?"

"Not bad," he replied while looking around the kitchen and living room.

"That's nice, sweetie. Did you get a chance to talk with very many people while you were there? You were gone quite a while."

"Yes, Mom, I did. Where's Miho at?"

"She's up in your grandfather's apartment, dear."

"Thanks, Mom," Christian said while turning to leave.

"Don't take too long," Sally said to him while stirring dinner. "Food's almost done."

"We'll be down soon," he promised while leaving quickly before being delayed any further.

Miho was where his mom said she'd be. She was about to ask him how his day went but immediately hesitated upon seeing Christian's face.

"Honey, what's the matter?" she asked instead.

"I just wanted to tell you that I'm going to call the doctor when we get back."

"What happened?"

With that asked, Christian sat on the bed and proceeded to tell her what had happened at the gym. He left out no detail.

"Oh, hun, you must not have known what was going on," she said with a worried voice while rubbing his cheek. "Are you ok?"

"I'm not sure. It was like the last ten years were gone. I couldn't remember anything." He sighed heavily. "I forgot all about us and the kids. What made matters worse, I even went to our old house, you know, the spot we lived at before moving to Jersey? I went there thinking that that was home."

"What happened there?"

"Pretty much the same as at the apartment. I tried getting in but couldn't. I even rang the doorbell until someone answered. I'm glad that the people who bought it from us still lived

414

there. That gave me the excuse of saying I was in the neighborhood and wanted to see the old house. If they were someone else, I'm not really sure what I would've done. After that, I still had no idea where to go. I eventually make my way here for some help. I finally remembered everything when I saw the kids downstairs."

"Did you tell your parents anything?"

"No, not yet." Christian shook his head. "Once I remembered, I came looking for you."

"Maybe that was a good idea," confirmed Miho. "Maybe we shouldn't say anything of this until we know what's going on."

"I was thinking that as well." Christian flopped back on the bed to look up at the ceiling. "Hopefully I can get in this week."

"What about work?"

"I'm not too worried about that now. I can always schedule the appointment around it. If not, I can rearrange work for a couple of hours one day. It's really not a big deal there."

They were silent for a bit before Miho laid down next to him. "Don't worry too much about it," she reassured him. "We'll get through this."

"I hope so. I hope it won't be too bad," he told her before rolling towards his wife to stare at her in her eyes.

Sally came out then to call them down for dinner.

Neither Christian nor Miho spoke of this again that weekend. Luckily for all of them, nothing happened that needed them to talk about it.

***

Early that following Monday, Christian kept his word by making an appointment to see his doctor for later that week. What irritated him most was that his doctor's secretary scheduled just a mere office visit when he assumed there would have been more.

Dr. Timothy Levinstein seemed nice enough but he sometimes worked in a very eccentric manner which rubbed off on his employees. Christian often thought the kind doctor's Yamika was wound up a little too tight, that if he took it off his blood would finally be able to circulate in his head better, and ultimately give his brain a better supply of oxygen and other nutrients.

When Christian did call Monday to setup an appointment, he clearly told the secretary that he'd better have some tests done to his head as a precaution. He was told by the nitwitted receptionist that, "Let's let Dr. Levinstein decide if you need tests done, shall we? After all, that's why he's here, is it not?" What irritated him further was she said that in an ever nice, upbeat, uppity, condescending manner that made him want to reach through the phone, grab her by her tongue from the other side, bring it over to his end, and staple it to something so she could think about what she said. Better yet, he thought about sawing it off with a rusty, dull soup spoon while pouring salt over it in the process. This thought in particular exited his mind as fast as it entered it.

After voicing his problems and concerns to Levinstein, the kind doctor asked, "Why didn't you setup an appointment to have tests run?"

"I did but Carol, the lady who took my call, said to the effect that it was you who made that decision, not me."

"Well, yes, that is true. It is up to me, isn't it?" he asked while checking his schedule. "How's tomorrow morning at, say, 9:30 sound?"

"Both are good with me," Christian told him.

"Sorry? Both what are good?" the doctor asked Christian with confused eyes.

"Tomorrow morning and the appointment at 9:30 are both good for me."

"Oh, wonderful. I'll mark you down for then."

"Do I come here for them?"

Confused by the question, Levinstein asked, "Come here for what?"

"Do I come here for my exams or do I go elsewhere?" Christian asked while trying to conceal his rising irritation.

"Oh, you'll come here."

"So the tests I'll need will be done here?"

"No. You'll come here to fill out the required paperwork and then you'll go meet one of my associates at Community Hospital. The exams will be performed there."

"While I'm here now, may I do the paperwork rather than coming back in the morning? It'll save some time and, this way, I can just go right to the hospital in the morning."

"No. This paperwork is very specific. You'll need to do that before your tests can be done."

"If I do them now, today, wouldn't that mean I'm doing them *before* the tests are done, doctor?"

"Yes, but not *just* before."

"Ok, whatever." Christian gave up. Some things for him just weren't worth it. "I'll be here tomorrow to do the paperwork."

The next day, as scheduled, he went to Dr. Levingstein's office to fill out the necessary paperwork before going to Community Hospital. Dr. Ward, the one Christian was told to see, inquired why he was late for his 9:30 appointment. When he was told that it was because of the paperwork Dr. Levinstein needed just before Christian came up, Ward simply shook his head.

"You could have taken them with you yesterday and brought them here with you this morning," Ward told him while his head still shook.

Some of the tests they performed on Christian were x-rays, CT scans, M.R.I. scans, and vascular imaging studies. The latter was done to check for cerebrovascular disease, tumors, and hydrocephalus. They also did a couple of blood tests which they hoped would confirm or deny any nutritional deficiencies or hormone imbalances. They asked a lot of personal questions in the process, particularly about his family's health history.

He was there for several hours, dressed in an ugly greenish-beige gown with matching pants, lying on a cold metal table as the tube he was in swirled around him. He had gone through this a couple of times before and knew what to expect. He napped as the equipment whirled; his thoughts wandered as he considered the various scenarios.

The next day, he went to Dr. Ward's office to get the results of the tests. Christian could tell right away the news wasn't going to be as pleasant as he had hoped. Ward closed the door behind him before making his way to his desk. Sitting down, he started flipping through Christian's file.

"Ok. So, I have the results of your tests here," Ward announced while looking through the file in his hands. He drew out several x-rays from the folder, stood, and put them on the lit apparatus on the wall behind him. The x-rays showed a person's head and brain, their tabs were clearly labeled Eaton, Christian E. "Ok, this is you. The good news is that I believe I know what the problem is. The bad news is that I believe it's dementia pugilistica. It's also known as boxer's syndrome, boxer's dementia, and about a half dozen other names."

"You can tell that just by looking at the x-rays?" Christian asked while getting up to take a closer look at the images.

"Partially. The x-rays do suggest some brain injury you have had at one point, which seems to have happened some time ago; one that caused your cavuum septi pellucidi." Ward pointed to the black vertical hole that ran almost the entire length of Christian's brain. "With injuries like this, symptoms usually surface five to ten years later. These very symptoms are what you've been experiencing for a while now. Given the nature of these symptoms, which seem to be irregularity with your memory, some memory loss, things of this nature; combined with how you got this hole has led me to believe that you're in the early stages of dementia pugilistica."

"Could it be anything else?" Christian hopefully asked. "What I mean is, is this clear cut that what I have is this boxer's dementia? Or could I have something else?"

"Good point." Ward smiled before looking away in thought. "You could be showing signs of another type of dementia known as post-traumatic dementia, or PTD for short."

"What's the difference?"

"Dementia pugilistica is causes by head trauma, mostly you seem them in contact sports. Its more common symptoms are dementia and Parkinsonism, which appear many years later. People that are affected may also develop poor coordination, slurred speech, things like this.

417

"PTD, on the other hand, is very similar to that but usually also includes long-term memory problems. This is usually caused by a single traumatic brain injury. Other symptoms may vary depending on what part of the brain was injured."

"Could I potentially have both?"

"In reality, you could have either or both. Unfortunately, there won't be any way to tell which one you have until your symptoms develop further."

"So, Doc, what exactly is dementia pugilistica anyway?" Christian asked while walking back to his chair to sit down in.

"Well, as you can probably guess, the word pugilistica is just a fancy way of saying boxing," Ward said fairly straight forward. "I'm sure you've heard other boxers being referred to as a pugilist or a pug at one point, have you not?"

Christian nodded. "I have a few times."

"Now dementia is not a disease but, rather, a symptom of a progressive brain disorder in which a patient slowly loses their memory and other mental functions."

"If I in fact have this, what would I have to look forward to?" he asked Ward in a calm, yet concerned, voice.

"If you do, which I'm thinking you may, there could be other dementias, as well as Parkinsonism. You could get there in time as a result from these, as well as long-term memory loss from the PTD," Ward somberly answered. "There's also Huntington's, Parkinson's, Pick's, Alzheimer's, Creutzfeldt-Jakob, and a few other things, not to mention a similar syndrome called punch-drunk syndrome. If you get this, there would be a group of symptoms involving progressive dementia such as hand tremors and epilepsy.

"I'm sorry, but I'm getting ahead of myself. I'm not trying to scare you or give you nightmares over something that may never happen," Ward told him before going silent in thought. "The good news is that there has been really good advances in the field of brain injury and dementia."

"Is there a cure for any of this?"

"Not presently," Ward told him before becoming optimistic. "But there's more and more research coming in about this. Quite a few well-known boxers who have suffered with this include Joe Louis, Muhammad Ali, and the Quarry brothers, Jerry and Mike."

"What are my options?"

"First, I would greatly advice getting a second, if not a third, opinion. Please do not rely soully on my word, not when it comes to this. I wouldn't want you going through something you don't have to. I can give you a list of references you could use if you want, or you could choose someone else if you'd prefer that. Better yet, use someone on my list and one that isn't." Ward pulled out a list of doctors he used as references before highlighting four or five of them before handing it to Christian. "Here's the list of doctors we refer patients to with head trauma. The ones I marked are the ones I personally refer other to, but you are in no way required to. They're just a suggestion."

"Anything else I can do?"

"With your permission, I would like to put you on some experimental drugs until we can narrow down exactly what *is* wrong with you."

"Experimental?"

"Yes. The government's working on trying to get them passed by the FDA," Ward explained while filling out a number of prescription slips. "These are used to soothe agitation and aggression for people with A.D.."

" 'A.D.'?"

"Oh, sorry. Alzheimer's disease," Ward replied as he handed Christian the slips.

"I don't have Alzheimer's, do I?"

"Oh no, not presently you don't. But I'm hoping these could help to slow it down for you in case you do."

"What are these?" Christian asked while looking down at the three prescriptions he held in his hands.

"One is for Zyprexa; another is Seroquel; and the third is Risperdal," Ward told him. "They belong to a class of medications known as atypical antipsychotic. These drugs are used to treat schizophrenia and other psychoses."

"And they haven't been passed yet by the FDA?"

Ward shook his head. "No. Like I said, the government's still working on it."

"Huh." Christian shrugged. "It's worth a shot. What else?"

"Lead a good, healthy life. Come in for periodic check-ups. But, above all, tell your family," Dr. Ward suggested. "Do you think they'll be supportive of this?"

"I don't see why they wouldn't."

"Good, that's important. That right there could help influence what type of life you'll lead. Other than that, there's nothing else at the moment I can think of."

"Do you think I'll ever get better?"

"I doubt it. However, with what's out there and with technology being what it is, your future should definitely be much less bleak as it would have been ten years ago. Also, while you're at it, it may be a good idea to check out some clinics or other medical facilities that might specialize in dementia or injuries related to head trauma. These spots might offer you the most help since they're around it more, but it may also make you a little bit more crazy since you'll be around a higher concentration of people with mental disorders." Ward let out a chuckle with this. "This last comment I meant figuratively, not literally. But I am serious about you checking out other clinics or facilities, though."

"Thank-you, Doctor, and can do. That does sound like a good idea. If I can take what you've told me in, hopefully I won't have any more questions."

"Sure, go ahead. Take your time."

With that, Christian slowly recapped what Dr. Ward had told him during his visit there. After thinking and absorbing it all, he concluded that, for now, he was all set.

"I don't think I can think of any more questions for you at the moment, Doctor. Is there any way I could have one of your cards if you have any to spare, please?"

"Sure," the doctor replied while reaching over to pull a card out to give to him. "If you need to get ahold of me, that has everything you'll need, except for my home information, of course."

"Thanks, Doc." Christian put the card in one of his pockets as he got up. He extended a hand, one the doctor accepted, before saying, "Thanks for everything today. I'll call if I need anything or if I have any questions."

"You do that." Ward smiled at him. "Don't forget to check out with Vanessa before you leave, alright?"

"Roger that. I'll talk with you later," Christian told him before leaving.

On his way out of the hospital, Christian thought about what had happened to him the last week and what news he just received. While reflecting back, he decided that the outcome could have been a lot worse than it what it was already. Even before he fully left the hospital, he made his mind up to get in touch with Shawn one last time, if he could that was. He wanted to do this not only to tell Shawn what's been going on in his life, but also what may happen to him. If there was a chance he could lose his mind, he wanted to reestablish whatever relationship he could with him before his time ran out.

Within two weeks of seeing Dr. Ward, Christian took his recommendation by getting two additional opinions regarding his condition; one of which was on Ward's list of referrals, the other was not. Both diagnoses came back the same as what Ward had told him; and both for the time being agreed for Christian to discontinue taking the experimental medication prescribed. They stated that the side effects could be very harmful and that they needed some more testing before any conclusive results would be recorded. Aware of his possible outcome, Christian decided to continue taking the medications regardless.

Over the next several months, Christina memory dissipated a bit more than they had hoped. He had more exams done which only proved his brain had deteriorated since his initial checkup with Dr. Ward. His initial doctor, Dr. Weinstein, seemed inapt to Christian and, as a result, was able to get Ward to accept him as a new patient.

420

To Christian's distress, no matter what the doctors did for him, his condition didn't seem to improve any, much less stabilize. His coordination diminished slightly, his memory was worse than before, and every now and then his body would have mild tremors. The only thing his doctors suggested was look for a nurse that would come periodically for home checkups or to find a clinic he could go to for the short-run. In either case, Dr. Ward increased the dosage for his prescriptions.

Christian wanted to finish out the year before he took any action for the nurse, clinic, or any other option but, by October, his luck seemed to finally catch up with him. By then, his dementia had worsened, he started showing symptoms of other psychoses, and his medicine, no matter how high the dosage, didn't seem to work any.

What made matters worse, The New York Times printed an article in their October 12th edition, front page nonetheless, stating that the drugs Christian was taking "where no more effective than placebos for most patients, and put them at further risk of serious side effects." Apparently, the reason they hadn't been approved yet by the FDA was because the study was still going on and it hadn't yet been concluded. The week after reading this article, Christian made an appointment to see Dr. Ward to confront him about his medication.

"There's no way I would have known they wouldn't work, Mr. Eaton," Ward said in his defense. "Most things out there now aren't designed for someone of your parameters."

"What do you mean by someone of my parameters?"

"What I meant was, that most people who have dementia, or other forms of psychoses are much older that you. Rarely do we doctors treat anyone younger than someone in their early 50s; generally they're in their 60s at least. The only exceptions are a few who were deployed or in some kind of an accident. Hardly ever have we seen a young male with no history of mental illness, either personally or hereditary, to have your symptoms at such a young age. Even though there have been several boxers to come down with similar situations such as you, they were much older when they were treated and their symptoms developed more slowly over a longer period of time. You truly are one of a kind. I'm sorry if it seemed like I deceived you but that was not my intention."

"What were your intentions?" Christian asked almost like a demand.

"Since your symptoms weren't of the normal parameters, I thought taking those experimental drugs, ones that did have a positive effect on several people, would have some positive effect on you as well. Or, at the very least, slow your symptoms down enough to let us treat you more effectively."

"One question," Christian said while looking at him. "How do I get better?"

"You can't," Ward replied softly. "Like I've told you before, there is no cure for what you have."

Hearing this, Christian's heart sunk. "Will I die from this?"

"Eventually, given enough time I think you will," Ward answered honestly. "But when the time comes, there's a very good chance you won't know anything about it."

"Is there any hope for me at all?"

"You do have your age, time, and health on your side. There are other options if you want to try."

"What sort of options?"

"One would be to continue on the drugs which you're on now." Ward paused long enough for Christian to respond with a shake of his head. "Another, which really isn't an option, is not doing anything and wait to see where your dementia takes you."

"I agree with that. I'd rather not take that route if I can help it."

"You could have a nurse come into your home occasionally, say once or twice a month, to check you out. Maybe more if you'd want."

"I'd rather not do that just yet," Christian said with hesitation. "I'm not quite that bad yet. Besides, I don't really want my kids to see that if they don't have to yet."

"In that case, I'd say there are two other options. You can either come in every so often for checkups and treatments, like at a hospital or a clinic or there's electroshock treatment. This might help restart your brain in some ways, but that's almost a last resort," Ward told him. "The hospital would have more advanced equipment but it's more expensive and the wait will be longer for you. A clinic, on the other hand, is cheaper and you wouldn't have to wait. Usually at these clinics, a lot of them specialize in whatever treatment they do. The clinics therefore would have a staff where that's all they do. They don't have ten or more diseases or illnesses they have to know. The down side of these are they don't have a wide range of equipment; they just have what they need."

"Are there any of these clinics nearby?" Christian asked him.

"There's one in Manhattan and another in Long Island; these are the closest two. The one in Manhattan is by appointment only, whereas the Long Island one you would actually have to reside there for the duration of your treatment."

Christian was shocked when he heard this. "A clinic where you can actually live? Are they really that bad there?"

"Not necessarily." Ward quickly shook his head. "Most are elderly with various mental disorders; ones who either don't have any family to help care for them or their family just can't care for them for one reason or another. Only a small percentage of them are what an outside might actually call 'crazy'."

"Do these clinics have visitation for family?" Christian asked.

"I'll try and get some information on them for you."

"Thank-you, doctor. I would really appreciate that."

With that, Ward politely excused himself from his office to get the information he mentioned. He was gone only for a few minutes before reentering his office while carrying a number of brochures, applications for both clinics, and other miscellaneous things pertaining to them. Upon the transfer of named material, they shook hands.

"Thanks a lot for your help, Doc," Christian graciously said while flipping through his newly acquired paperwork. "This'll give my family and I a lot to think about. It'll take some time for us to look through this, though. We'll do our own research before coming up with a final answer. I'll keep in touch to let you know if, and when, we decide anything. Do you have my number in case you want to get ahold of me?"

"If it's in your file, then I do," Ward told him.

"It's in there. Thanks again. And I'm sorry how I came across to you earlier when I first got here. I didn't mean any offense or anything."

"No worries. It happens a lot, I have to admit." Ward smiled. "All part of the job."

"I'll talk to you later then." Christian offered him his hand once again to shake.

"Keep in touch," Ward replied while accepting the offered hand.

They soon broke their hold as Christian left the hospital. He had some new things on his mind, as well as other things, he wanted to discuss with Miho. Whatever they decided, he felt this decision was going to be one of the more important decisions of his life.

One his way home, the only thing he thought of was being home with Miho and the kids. He smiled as the thought of this as the sounds of the radio filled his head.

Chapter 44

Christian rode into Manhattan with Miho on her way to work a week following his appointment with Dr. Ward. He planned to spend the day checking out the clinic Ward had told him about there. If he had any time left over, he hoped to camp out at any library he came across to do some research and, if possible, get in contact with Shawn.

The clinic was on the east side of the city and upon first impression, it appeared updated, modernized, and a much more elaborate VA hospital whose main focus was mental illness. It appeared to have a lot of room, was very pleasing to the eye, and whose staff seemed to be knowledgeable, courteous, and professional. He spoke to some to some of the administrative and medical personnel and was pleased to find out that he didn't need to apply for admissions there. If he did decide to go here, he'd merely schedule his appointment on days Miho worked so he could just get a ride in with her.

After leaving the clinic, he made his way to the last known address of Shawn. He didn't think Shawn would actually still be there, but he figured it was worth a shot. As he had suspected, Shawn had moved a few years previously. After a couple of questions were asked and a few dollar bills changed hands, Christian soon found Shawn's current address. After heading that way, he found himself outside an expensive looking hotel.

"Pardon me," Christian said to a clerk behind the desk in the hotel's lobby. "Would you be able to tell me which room Shawn Calloway is in?"

"Of course," she said before clicking on her keyboard to bring up the requested information. "Here we are. He's in room 1248. Shall I phone ahead to let him know you're coming?"

"No, thanks. I was hoping to surprise him." Christian smiled while walked away. "Thanks."

"You're welcome. Have a nice day," she replied while going back to work.

While making his way up to the forty-eighth room of the twelfth floor, Christian couldn't help but be impressed with the quality and exquisite quality of the hotel.

"He's come a long way," he thought to himself. "Much better than where he's from. Better than Dom's apartment."

Shawn's door opened on the third knock to reveal an extremely attractive woman who was levels above anyone he'd seen Shawn hang around with before. Christian, pausing from hesitation upon seeing this, thought he was sent to the wrong room in error when she spoke.

"May I help you?" she said in a clear voice filled with confidence. Her eyes held the same confidence but also expressed loyalties that would change to the highest billfold. She had long, golden blonde hair; a size four body; a full C cup; and stood about 5'8". She wore only a nightshirt, which hung loosely down to just above her knees. She had flushed cheeks and eyes of the deepest blue. She soon repeated herself. "May I help you?"

Once his confusion past and tongue untied he said, "Oh, I'm sorry. I'm looking for Shawn. Is he available?"

"You don't look like a collector," she informed him with a smile.

"Uh, what?"

"You a collector? If you are, you don't look like one."

Christian smiled. "That's good to hear considering I'm not one."

"Good to know. I'd hate to see one of my best clients unable to perform for some time," she told him in a childlike manner. This woman, no matter her profession, intrigued him with what seemed to be humor. "You know, I wouldn't want all his money going to bailing him out of jail again or to any more medical bills."

"Oh, I'm sure it'll take quite a lot for him to stop performing, if you get my drift. Even if he couldn't, I'm sure he'd find a way to." Christian chuckled. "Besides, he's been getting in trouble for as long as I've known him. He still somehow manages smelling like a rose in the end."

"You seem to know him quite well, stranger."

"I should. He's my brother."

"You're his brother?" she questioned with raised eyebrows.

"Yes."

"I see. So, um, who are you really? And what do you want with him?" she asked while finally becoming serious.

"To answer your first question, again, I'm his brother." He sighed while looking around impatiently. "And for the second, I'd like to see him."

"His brother's dead," the woman said in a way indicating she didn't believe him.

"If you're talking about his brother Daryl, then you would be correct. Daryl was killed in jail. Obviously I'm not him."

"I wasn't aware he had another. He's never spoken of having more than one," she commented while looking Christian over. "You don't look like him."

"I'd be surprised if I did." He laughed which drew a confused look from her. "He's my adopted brother."

"And why are you looking for him?"

"I've told you already; I'd like to see him," Christian repeated while getting slightly irritated. He was becoming quite annoyed by the consistent questioning of the woman at the door's threshold. "Besides, do I really need a reason?"

"He doesn't like being disturbed this early in the morning."

425

Christian looked at his watch before pursing his lips. "It's almost noon."

"It's almost noon and he doesn't like being disturbed this early in the morning."

"So you've said," he replied as they made eye contact. "Listen, if you go and get him for me, I'll be outta here within five minutes, ten at the most. Ok? Hell, you can even frisk me and be with us to make sure I don't damage your best client."

"If I did I'd have'ta charge." She smiled slyly before turning back to the apartment. She waved him in with a single finger.

Obliging, Christian closed the door behind him while she went into another room. He heard her voice saying something, while another was heard moaning. Its source was from a man but whether it was Shawn, it was hard to tell. While she spoke to the moaning male, Christian took a look around at what was apparently Shawn's apartment or, in this case, hotel room.

The quality of the room matched everything else he saw up until that point. The room was not merely a single room, but three. The main living quarters was spacious with elegant furnishings. Christian was not only impressed with what he saw but also of Shawn's tastes. He was not aware that Shawn possessed such a trait. He thought that maybe his brother had always had them but never had the opportunity, or money, to express them.

While walking in from the door, he passed through a mini-hall which was lined with closets. In the corner to the left was a kitchenette. In the middle of the left wall was a door leading to a dark room, probably from a blind-covered window. Christian assumed this to be the bedroom. On the right was another door leading to the bathroom. The most noticeable thing that he saw, outside of pearl white tiles lining the floor, was a Jacuzzi for multiple people. Still wet, probably from the night before, several pairs of ladies lingerie were scattered about. In the corner of the right wall was a giant flat-screen television mounted directly onto the wall. It was complimented by a state-of-the-art home entertainment system. In the opposite corner was a mini-bar; empty whiskey and vodka bottles lined the floor around it. The wall straight ahead, opposite that of the door, really wasn't a wall but, rather, one giant window overlooking Manhattan.

Christian had been to the city several times before but had never seen it from this height. Fascinated by the view as he walked over to it. While doing so, he noticed a number of small bottles littering a neighboring coffee table. There were eight in all and all were prescriptions prescribed by different doctors. Six seemed to be some form or painkillers, a seventh was for Valium, an anti-anxiety, and the eight was Prozac, an antidepressant. Two of the prescriptions were of a dosage that together would knock a horse out. Christian was disappointed by this but not totally surprised. Shawn's habits seemed to have increased, expanded, and become more expensive. Only Shawn for sure knew if there were any more.

Just then, when he went back to overlooking the city, the woman's voice was heard again. This time, the same male groaned louder. The sound of a bed creaking implied someone was getting up, while a second woman's voice was heard over that. This explained the multiple sets of lingerie in the bathroom.

When Christian looked back to the bedroom door, Shawn emerged wearing nothing but a pair of boxer briefs. By the looks of it, he'd gained quite a bit of weight, most of which was muscle. The other bit seemed to be as a result of water. Christian guess him to be around 230 pounds, a far cry of 190 or so he struggled to get at for their third match. His hair was messed up, eyes were puffy, and his face sprouted about a week's worth of growth. His expression at first revealed shock and surprise when their eyes met, but quickly went to one of neutrality and indifference.

"Looky here. The prodigal son returns," Shawn commented sarcastically. "What the hell you doin' here?"

"Well, screw you too," Christian shot back. "I just wanted to thank-you for the Christmas cards you sent me the last year."

"I didn't send you no fuckin' card."

"Do you know him?" the blonde asked from the bedroom door.

"He's my brother," Shawn answered coolly while not taking his eyes off of him. "Used to be anyway."

"You said your brother died."

"I did and he did," Shawn told her while continuing to stare while coming about eight or nine feet out of the bedroom.

"What? That doesn't make any sense," the blonde told him.

"I said my brother did die because my brother did die," replied Shawn with a strong hint of anger in his voice while turning to look over his shoulder to her. "Does that explain it for you?"

"It does now."

"Good. Then why don't you go back to bed and keep Candy company? And, this time, don't start anything until I get in there. Understood?" The tone of his voice told Christian that that wasn't a request. The blonde soon disappeared into the darkness of the bedroom behind her as sounds of the bed moving soon followed. Shawn then turned his attention back to Christian. "What the fuck you doin' here?"

"How long have you been here now for?" Christian asked while indicating the hotel room.

"Awhile. How'd you find me?"

"It wasn't hard. I asked the right questions. What happened to your apartment?"

"Don't worry about it," Shawn bluntly told him. "That doesn't matter."

Christian surmised he had lost it somehow but kept it to himself.

"I saw your movie," Christian said instead in an effort to change the subject. "I took my kids to see it."

"Is that why you came? To tell me you and your half-breed kids saw my movie?"

"No."

"Then what do you want?"

"To see you."

"You wasted your time then. Don't wanna see you." Shawn turned around to start back towards the bedroom. "You saw me now, you can get out."

"Shawn, I want to talk with you," Christian pressed. "It's important."

Turning to face him, Shawn said, "Don't tell me. You want to borrow money, right?"

"No, I don't want to borrow money."

"Then you're looking for a woman or spot to stay? That chink woman of yours finally got sick of you before throwing your fagot ass out? And you came here looking for a spot to stay?"

"No, Shawn, Miho did not leave me. Nor did she throw me out. Nor do I need a spot to stay."

"So you need a girl to fuck?" Shawn pointed to the bedroom as a faint smile rose on his face. "I've got an extra."

Christian shook his head. "No. I don't need a girl to have sex with. "I'm married, remember?"

"So what if you're married? A lot of people screw around with someone they aren't married to."

"That's true, but I'm not one of them. I'm happily married to a woman I love. And what you just offered I can get for free at home. Call it one of the many fringe benefits of marriage."

"So you sayin' you and that chink are still together after all these years?" Shawn asked while turning around to look at him in amazement. "How's that even possible? Didn't she have any other choices to choose from?"

"Shawn, say anything you want about me but leave her out of this. You hear me?" Christian firmly told Shawn as they exchanged looks with each other. "Besides, I distinctly remember telling you on multiple occasions that if you want to be a racist, ignorant, bigot then you should get the right racial slur down to insult your intended target. Miho is not a chink."

"What the hell is she then, a gook?"

"Miho's Japanese for the umpteenth time," Christian patiently corrected. "A chink refers to one of Chinese decent and a gook is Vietnamese. To your racist mind, she'd be a Jap."

"What's the difference? They all look the same," Shawn said in a serious tone. "Besides, I still say you marred her because you couldn't get an American woman who'd want to fuck you."

At first, Christian didn't say anything. He remained silent for a moment while looking at his brother. "I didn't come here to correct your misused favorite racial slurs. I came here to talk. May I at least do that?"

"Get the fuck out, bro. I haven't got time for this shit!"

"What happened to you, Shawn? Huh?"

"What do ya mean?"

"This." Christian waved his hands at Shawn and to everything else. "Why are you like this? What happened?"

"Nothin' happened, man!" Shawn said while walking over to his unwanted guest. "This is the real me. This! Right here, right now. What you see is me. Do you know who made all of this possible? Do you? Duke. Duke made it possible for me to start living like I always knew I could and should. He got me away from that goofy-assed family of yours, away from that old ginnie trainer, and, above all, away from your fruity ass!"

"What about Grandpa Joe? What about him?"

"What about him?!" demanded Shawn. His breath at this range made Christian contort through several faces at once. It was heavily loaded with alcohol and smelled terrible.

"Duke didn't take you away from him."

Shawn simply waved his hands at him. "Old man Joe took a dirt nap way back when we were like ten. You know, I've had enough. Get the fuck out. Seriously, get out. I'm going back to bed," he said while pointing to the door. Afterwards he turned to walk back to his bedroom. "I'm hung-over and I went to bed around six this morning. Be a good little brother and lock the door behind you. Oh, and put the *Do Not Disturb* sign on the knob outside."

"Shawn, I came by to tell you that I'm sick."

"Then go to a fuckin' doctor, then," Shawn bluntly told him while disappearing into his blackened bedroom.

At this point, Christian found it extremely difficult to find the works he wanted to say. "I have been for a while now. This could be it for me."

After saying that, he stood in silence waiting for a response. Waiting for anything that suggested that Shawn had heard him. Nothing came. No response. No acknowledgment. Nothing.

"Shawn?" Christian called out with no response. "Alright, have it your way. I just thought you should know." With that, he walked towards the door to leave. He soon stopped short to turn back towards the bedroom. "Oh, before I forget, Mom and Dad wanted me to tell you that they want to hear from you one of these days, even if it's just a letter. Goodbye, Shawn."

When he was done talking, he finished walked towards the door. Just as he grabbed the Do Not Disturb sign while opening the door, he finally heard Shawn's voice from behind him.

"Dude, you being serious? You really sick, bro?" Shawn's voice, for the first time during that visit, hinted at an emotion that wasn't one of neutrality, anger, or ignorance. It seemed to have genuine care in it.

"Yeah, Shawn, I'm being serious. I really *am* sick," Christian told him while hanging the sign on the outside knob while entering the hallway. "You can read about it in the obits if you want. If you change your mind, which will probably be never, I'll talk to you later about this. See ya."

He pulled the door closed behind him to leave Shawn standing in the bedroom's doorway.

While on the way home a few hours later, Christian told Miho what he had seen at the clinic and what had happened that day between him and Shawn.

"It sounds like he finally is able to be the person he's always wanted to be," Christian stated with great disappointment. "Too bad that some people have to have all these expensive, bad things in their lives just to feel good. But once they do have them they're still miserable. I wish there was something I could do."

"With your brother, I don't think there's anything you can do," Miho told him. "Just try and worry about you and us."

"Maybe you're right. Maybe I should just forget about him."

She sighed at that. "Just think about it. But don't completely forget about him."

"On the upside, I'll be able to start going to this clinic here just as soon as I make an appointment. Hopefully early next week."

"Would you ride in with me?"

Smiling at her, Christian replied, "If you let me."

She smiled back.

"Also, if I didn't tell you," Christian added, "I did some research at the library today after I left Shawn's place."

"Oh?"

"looked back into what I have, or might have, or could get, and not much has changed since I looked a while back." He showed her some of the printouts he had on his lap. "I pretty much have the same things as diagnosed but some things are different in terms of treatment. I made some copies for us to look at over later if you'd like."

Miho turned to look briefly at them before going back to focus on driving. "We can look over them at home tonight if you want."

"Now, as for this clinic I went to today, I hope they'll be able to help me."

"We all do, honey," she told him in a very loving tone as a smile crossed her face. "We all do."

Chapter 45

Christian went to the Manhattan clinic periodically over the next three months and, in the meantime, his symptoms continued to get worse. The shakes and various tremors he had lasted longer. He also lost hours, if not days, from his memory on a more consistent basis.

He finished out that current semester at his college before going on an indefinite medical leave. He should have left earlier, leaving his duties to the various professors or teaching assistants in his department, but he wanted to finish out the entire semester before doing so. He also stopped volunteering at this zoo temporally for him to make the time for the clinic. His symptoms eventually made it so he was going to the clinic five days a week.

Soon after that, Christian's mental health got to the point where the clinic told him there wasn't anything more they could do to help him more than they have already. They recommended he go to the Long Island clinic to see if they could do something they currently couldn't, but left the final say up to him. They also said he could keep coming there to them if he so desired.

"Momma," Asako said to her mom shortly after Christian stopped working. "What's wrong with Daddy?"

"Well, honey, your dad is sick," Miho answered in Japanese while trying to word her answer both honestly and carefully.

"Daddy's sick?" she quickly asked in an almost demand-like fashion.

"Yes but it's not quite what you're thinking."

"He's going to be ok, right?" Asako, by this point, was able to read her mom well enough to know that there was something she wasn't telling her. She fought back tears, trying to control them, but ultimately couldn't.

Miho, meanwhile, went over and knelt down next to her. "Why don't the three of us, you, me, and your father, get together later today so we can talk about his. Ok? How's that sound?"

"But he's going to be ok, right?"

Miho replied, "We'll talk later tonight about this."

That night after dinner, as promised, Christian and Miho sat down with their daughter to tell her what was going on and what to expect. They also included Dominic in the conversation just so he would know as well. Obviously they were both scared and cried, but Christian had to laugh when Asako said, "That explains why Daddy's been acting weird for lately."

"You're not going away, are you, Daddy?" Asako asked after hearing about the clinic in Long Island.

"I don't know. Maybe."

"When will you be back?" Dominic asked.

"Well, I first have to be gone before I can come back, right?" Christian said with a smile. "But to answer your question, I'm not sure if I will be leaving. If I do, I'll be gone only as long as I have to be. Then, after that, I'll be home again."

The next day, Christian made an appointment for the following week to check out Forestry Park, the Long Island clinic. When the day came, Miho took the day off of work to take Christian there. At one point during the ride up, Christian took a newspaper article from his jacket pocket and began reading it.

"What's that?" Miho inquired when she saw this.

"It's an article about Shawn. I cut it out a day or so ago. I wanted to read it again. It appears he's been busy," Christian told her while laughing mildly to himself. "From what I've gathered from TV and the paper, these last few months he's been arrested for soliciting a prostitute who turned out to be an undercover cop; charged with D.U.I., twice; and has a number of visits by the police for domestic dispute and domestic abuse cases. I've always wondered what's gone through that head of his but I've always been able to take an educated guess. But since he joined Duke, my guesses are no longer educated."

"You should worry more about yourself than him," Miho told him. "It was always a matter of time when he would start living the way he wanted to. I'm surprised it took him this long. He always reminded me of that one book that you have."

"Which one?"

"I don't remember its name." Miho thought. "It's that famous old one of some doctor who changes into a bad guy."

"Do you mean Dr. Jekyll and Mr. Hyde?" Christian asked her.

"Uh-huh, that's it."

"I can see how you'd feel that way about him," Christian confessed while looking out the window. Up the road he noticed Forestry Park in the distance. "Here we are," he said while pointing to the drive.

Pulling in, Forestry Park was pleasant to the eye as they drove down a tree-lined drive. The combination birches and spruces which were used was a weird mixture to Christian and he was curious as to why they did this. However, he wasn't going to question their reasoning.

The lawn was green and well-manicured, which looked like a checkerboard pattern from its recent mowing. The grounds were quite a bit more spacious than what he had imagined and pleased him immensely.

The building itself was equally impressive, which looked to be roughly half the width of the yard by Christian's judgment. It appeared to be four stories, but the middle section where the entrance was looked like it might have another level above that. With this, he was unsure whether it was in fact five true stories or just four with a lot of wasted space. This middle portion had a nice marble flight of stairs leading up to the entrance, whose top step was big enough to allow several people to stand on it. The inner three sides were enclosed by the rest of the building, and three giant pillars where there to help support the overhang above it. The building itself was made of a weird substance, almost a combination of concrete and marble, but Christian was not able to identify what exactly. Each floor had several painless mirrored windows.

The drive itself rose at a slight incline until it stopped at a small parking lot to the right of the facilities. When they parked and were in the process of getting out of the car, Christian noticed a small pond in back that had a number of ducks and geese in and around it. There was a nice patio that ran from the pond to the back of the building. A number of residents were there enjoying the day; some sat on benches provided for them, others sat at available tables with their accompanying umbrella unfurled, while other still just walked around without any apparent idea of what they were doing.

While taking the walk that led to the front door, Christian caught sight of an elderly man in a wheelchair watching them. The brief instance that their eyes met, Christian swore the look the man gave him was one of recognition. Just before vanishing around the corner, the old man waved to him. Christian politely waved back. He normally wouldn't have thought anything of it, but what made this brief moment with a complete stranger standout was not only did the look he received was weird but also, for some odd reason, he could have sworn he had seen this man before though he couldn't place where. He soon shrugged it off as déjà vu thinking that old men were like boys: they all seemed to look alike.

"Hello and welcome to Forestry Park," the receptionist greeted when they entered.

"Thank-you," Christian replied. "We feel welcomed."

As the receptionist answered her ringing phone, he couldn't help but find her pleasantly attractive though not his type. She was in her late 30s with shoulder length, semi-straight, auburn colored hair. She wore a very nice, expensive looking suit over a fine beige blouse. He felt she wore a little too much makeup while finding her face a little too pale, lips too glossy, and cheeks having a bit too much rouge; a little less of each would have sufficed. Her eyes were that of the deepest green, ones he couldn't take his eyes off of.

Though he found her to be a real head turner, he couldn't decide why she wasn't his type. Maybe it was because she had too much of a professional look to her. He wasn't suggesting that Miho didn't look professional, especially when she dressed for the office, but this was different. Maybe it was her mannerisms she was giving off or the tone of her voice. He simply couldn't decide. When he was thinking about that, she finished her phone call before focusing her attention back to them which brought him out of his trance.

"Sorry about that," she stated in a pleasant, soft voice. "How may I help you?"

He was about to answer when he realized he honestly had no idea as to why they were there. He just looked at her blankly before giving Miho the same dumb look. Seeing this, she turned to the receptionist to respond.

"We have an appointment with Dr. Wellwood and are a little early. Our name is Eaton."

While looking at her appointment schedule before her, her eyes brightened when she found them. "Ah, yes, here you are. You are a tad early, but not bad. Why don't you have a seat and he'll be out shortly?"

"Thank-you," they told her before being directed towards a pair of chairs.

The interior matched Christian's perceptions of what it would look like from the outside. The furniture was high quality leather on sturdy frames, either black or brown in color. The furniture, which were a few night stands, a couple of coffee tables, and the desk the receptionist sat behind were all made from cherry and stained mahogany. As he looked at the arm of the couch he noticed the name *Stickley* etched into its wood. Thinking he remembered that name, he soon forgot what he was thinking about. Many serene and natural or wildlife looking paintings, mostly oil based, lined the walls.

A number of throw rugs, which appeared to be of an Asian origin, highlighted the floors but were mainly used as something to set the tables on. A number of what Christian referred to as indoor plants accented the corners and places where there were outlets on the walls. Several hanging plants were dispersed around the painless windows. For the most part, he wasn't sure if they were real or not but most of the hanging ones appeared so. The walls were neutral beige and the floor a standard hardwood.

While looking around, he noticed that he had never been there before. The more he looked the less he saw in way of familiarity and nothing gave him a clue as to why they were there. The only reason why he chose to stay was because Miho was sitting next to him. He continued to look around for clues as to what this place was while he thought why they were there. When he heard the receptionist answer the phone with the greeting of Forestry Park, he felt he should know what it meant nothing to him. Another minute went by as he wracked his brain over this before finally asking Miho about it.

"Where are we?"

"Forestry Park," she replied absent mindedly while continuing to stare off into space.

"No, sorry," Christian corrected which seemed to bring her back to reality. "What I mean was, where are we? Why are we here? What is this place?"

"Oh, that," she quickly answered in Japanese while blinking a few times. She realized he just had a memory lapse again. "We're in Long Island. This place that we're at is called Forestry Park and it's a clinic or medical facility of sorts for people who have brain injuries, but they mostly deal with things of your nature – dementia, Alzheimer's, that sort of thing. We're here to talk with someone to see if you could come stay here for treatment."

"You mean I'd stay here to live?" he asked in a shocked manner.

"Well, yes, in a way," she told him. "But nothing permanent."

"What about the clinic in Manhattan? Can't I go there?"

"You have, dear, for the last few months," she told him sweetly. She looked at him while patting his arm. "They said you've reached the point where your needs were more than what they could treat. They suggested you come here for the next stage."

"What's that, the next stage?"

"Either a full-time nurse or you staying at a clinic." Miho paused while smiling. "You don't remember any of this, do you?"

"I guess I do now." Christian blushed slightly. "I guess I forgot."

"It's ok." She patted his arm again.

"Thank-you." A smile came on his face before leaning over to kiss her forehead. "Have we been here long?"

"No. Not long."

A few minutes later, a tall, lean man in a white lab coat walked out with a clipboard in hand. He wore tan khakis, dark dress shoes, and a white dress shirt with a bluish tie.

"Mr. and Mrs. Eaton I presume?" he addressed them while extending a hand for them to shake.

"Yes," Miho answered as she rose.

"Do we know each other?" Christian asked politely while shaking the man's hand.

Miho smiled briefly at this.

"No, not yet we don't," the stranger told him. "I'm Dr. Wellwood. I run the dementia unit here at Forestry Park."

"I'm sorry. I guess I forgot why we were here," Christian said while looking at Miho. "Again."

"That's ok. It happens to the best of us," Wellwood told him with a pleasant smile.

Christian was happy neither of them made a big deal over his forgetfulness.

"Shall we go back to my office and talk?" the doctor asked while indicating the door he came through moments before. "Or if you'd rather talk out here..."

"No, your office is fine," Miho told him. "Thank-you, Doctor."

As Dr. Wellwood led them to his office, Christian couldn't help but notice the freedoms that the patients there seemed to have. They wandered the halls, almost at will, as they conversed with each other. Some sat in wheelchairs by windows, others with a cat in their laps, while others still seemed to dose in a hidden corner chair.

They past a fairly good sized room which seemed to be used for recreation. In which, there were a few televisions, a pool table, Ping-Pong table, and a various selection of board and card games. One patient was making coffee at a coffee maker.

"It appears that the patients here some to have quite a lot of freedom, Doc," commented Christian in both a surprised and approvingly manner.

"A lot of them do but not all, though," Dr. Wellwood replied in a pleasant manner. "We try to give them as much freedoms as we can as long as they're able to enjoy them and aren't a risk to others or to themselves."

"Are there any that you would withhold?" Christian asked.

"If you mean withhold patients, we try not to withhold them from anything that might, or could, help them in one manner or another. But, we still withhold certain freedoms or privileges if the patient is disorderly or risks injury to anyone," Wellwood answered in a soft, easy going manner.

As they continued walking Christian noticed that the expensive and exquisite look wasn't just limited to the exterior or lobby of the facilities. Everything what he considered to have seen behind-the-scenes was of the same quality.

"If our application is accepted, how much would it cost us?" Miho asked when they entered an elevator.

"That varies from person to person." Wellwood hit the second floor button when they entered. "You see, different people come here with different needs and situations. We try and determine what's expected from us to help treat them, if we can that is. If we can, we try to judge each patient individually and see where they fall in terms of medical care. We charge proportionately to the care needed. There isn't any set fee. Our prices are quite competitive to other facilities. You may find that we offer more here for what we charge than in other places."

"How are you able to do that?" Miho politely asked. "How are you able to have the same fees as other places but yet still have a better looking place with more liberties than most?"

Bowing his head, the doctor smiled slightly at this. "We get an occasional grant from the government that's very generous. These grants enable us to have the current resources while ensuring our patients aren't going broke to pay for it. Once we get to my office, we can talk more in detail about that."

The elevator opened. They exited while making a left down the hall until they reached Wellwood's office. While entering, Wellwood was last so he could close the door behind them. The office, though made as expensive as everything else, wasn't decorated or furnished to hint at his status here and was fairly spacious; probably given to him as a result of his position.

The doctor's desk was a solid, heavy wood, probably oak, which was finely made and stained relatively dark. It was neatly organized with very little clutter; everything had its proper place. There was an in-/out-box on the corner nearest to the door and a fairly good sized desk calendar centered almost perfectly. A couple of small framed pictures were in the corner opposite of the box – one was of the doctor with a woman; another of three teenagers, two boys and one girl;

and a third showing the five people from the two pictures in front of a rustic cabin in the middle of some far off forest. A plain gold band on Wellwood's left ring finger told them he was married and whose family members were probably the ones shown in the pictures. The three pictures were placed around the base of an expensive, yet simple looking brass lamp. In front of the desk calendar was a mug filled with pens and pencils.

On the wall behind the good doctor's desk was an oil painting of what looked like that of the cabin which was in the desk's picture. This one, however, was of a night scene of just the cabin with trees outlining the background, while the moon was coming over a mountainous ridge in its upper corner.

To its right hung three diplomas – one was a bachelor's in pre-med from Cornell University, a second being a masters in psychology from Yale, and the third was a doctorate in medicine from Harvard. A fourth piece, his medical license, hung with the diplomas. To the left of the cabin painting hung several certificates of appreciation from what appeared to be of various local organizations as well as from Forestry Park.

The only other decorations that were present was a coat rack next to the door which held a gray overcoat and a matching hat, a potted tree-like- plant in the opposite corner next to the window, filing cabinet whose drawers were labeled according to this patients last initials, and a night stand in the corner next to Wellwood's desk. The night stand had two shelves on it; the bottom one held a number of medical books, while the top had a fairly good sized framed picture of a group of men, some in Army class A uniforms. Dr. Wellwood was included among these men.

"Do you have friends in the military, Doctor?" Christian asked while acknowledging the picture.

"Well, sort of," Wellwood said softly with a smile. "That's a picture of the guys form my platoon when I was in."

"You were in the Army?"

"I served twenty years."

"You don't seem to have aged much," Christian told him with a sly smile while nodding to the picture.

"That was taken last summer. I served almost fifteen years ago...," the doctor said before breaking off his sentence when he noticed he allowed himself to be drawn into a joke that wasn't intended to go this far. He laughed while being slightly embarrassed. "Yeah, I haven't aged that much."

"May I ask how long it's been since you've been discharged?"

"Almost fifteen years. I enlisted as a field nurse after I got my bachelors. That was an experience." He laughed while rolling his eyes. "Since it was generally peacetime, I didn't get much practice being a nurse in the field so I tried a number of things in the medical area. I ultimately wanted to be a surgeon but that was before I found out my hands weren't nimble enough for it. I settled on being a nurse. To me, that was the next best thing."

"How'd you go from that to what you are now?" Chris inquired.

"They were looking for volunteers to help out with some psych patients," he said in an off-beat shrug. "I guess it stuck."

"So you became a doctor of mental illness as a result of volunteering at a psych ward while in the Army?"

"Yeah, I guess so," Wellwood replied with a chuckle, almost as if the realization of what was being said. "You know, I've never actually thought about it but, the more I do, I do believe that to be the case."

From that point on, the conversation turned to matters more at hand. Dr. Wellwood gave them a number of forms for them to fill out and to be mailed back at their convenience. In the material he included information on the various mental illness and disorders that they treated here at Forestry Park, a list of payment options, and another form that seemed to confuse Miho.

"What is this one for?" she asked while showing the form.

"That's a form to give to your insurance company."

"Will they pay for it?"

"They could." Wellwood shrugged. "A lot of times no, but that depends on who and what you have. They could pay for it all, only a portion of it, or they could reimburse you. Most of the time they won't pay for any of it. It's worth a shot, though. Worse comes to worse, you're out the time for you to fill that out and the cost of postage."

"What are our chances of getting accepted here?" Miho asked.

"That also depends, but mostly on the number of openings we have as well as what we feel we can do for you," the doctor told her. "But, to be honest, I think the list for the amount of space we have is too great."

The answer was clearly a disappointment to the Eaton's. They sat there in silence while exchanging looks with each other. Wellwood, meanwhile, smiled slightly.

"However," he continued, "the final acceptance ultimately goes through our director. Knowing the little man like I do, I'm sure he'll be more than happy to make an exception for you."

"Why?" asked Christian. "Why would he bump us up the list when there's plenty of people ahead of us in line?"

"Simple. It's a matter of publicity and marketability." He smiled before realizing his answer went over their heads. "He's always looking for as much publicity and press-coverage as possible. Our esteemed director won't take the chance to pass you up."

"You guys know who I am?" Christian was surprised by this.

"Of course, Mr. Eaton. In fact, I'm a big fan of yours."

"But why would your director do this? It can't all be about publicity."

"No, you're right," Wellwood honestly agreed. "He'll use the publicity of your name as one of our patients to help get a couple of grants he's been trying to get. He'll use the money to get some things done that's been on our list for a little while now.

"But don't think about being accepted here in terms of publicity and money," he continued. "You'll get into a top-notched facility for what you're looking for. The top in the northeast, one of the top two or three east of the Mississippi, and one of the top five in the country. But, essentially, you'd be correct in thinking your acceptance here would be publicity driven."

"Great," Christian sarcastically said with a heavy sigh while sloughing in his chair. "We came there thinking you'd be able to help us when, in fact, the opposite will be true."

"Please don't think like that, Mr. Eaton," Wellwood suggested with a smile. "Think of it more as a mutually compatible relationship. You'll be accepted into a top-notched facility, like I said, and, as a result, without even trying, you just being here will help us out tremendously by allowing us to better compete for money. This, in turn, would allow us to improve our facilities."

"But you guys are already one of the top five in the nation," Chris reminded him. "Wouldn't other clinics or facilities dealing in similar treatments benefit more by these grants than you? Is it that important the money comes here rather than to them?"

Wellwood shrugged. "It matters to our director."

"Hun, maybe we shouldn't let this influence our decision of us coming here," Miho softly told him. "Dr. Greene did refer you here, did he not? I don't think he'd have done so if he felt you couldn't have gotten the help we needed."

Before Christian could respond, the sound of footsteps pitter-pattering was heard coming down the hall. There was a knock at the door and, before Wellwood could respond, was opened to reveal a small, nervous man.

"Tom, have you seen this so-called new agenda that Hughes has sent us?" the visitor asked in a hyper, rushed manner while waving around a manila folder.

"Ah-hum, Doug." Wellwood cleared his throat while glancing to his potential patient.

"Seriously, have you seen it?" Doug continued to wave the folder, almost losing some of the paper contained within.

Doug, a slim man of about 5'8", acted like he had just drunk a pot of coffee. His complexion was slightly pale; apparently as a result from spending too much time inside. He had short reddish brown hair and green eyes. He was dressed in a safe, professional attire consisting of dark blue dress shoes, tan Dockers, a white button-up dress shirt, and a plain blue tie. Christian saw a wedding band and, as a result, assume he was married. He also assumed he was a doctor here from the while lab coat he was wearing.

439

"I mean, can you believe it?" Doug continued. "How can Hughes actually expect us to get everything he wants done with what little time we have? I mean, he's already pushing us to the brink, Tom. I just spoke with Sandy from personnel and they got a similar one earlier in the week. I understand we have a name to uphold here when we come to work, but some of us here have lives outside of these walls. I hardly see my family as it is and with this new proposed agenda, I'll see them even less!"

"Doug, I'm in the middle of a meeting here," Dr. Wellwood injected when he had a chance to. This seemed to draw a silent stare from his unexpected visitor.

Doug, at that moment, looked at both Christian and Miho as if seeing them for the first time. He glanced back to Wellwood for a moment before asking, "How did these two get in here?" He quickly looked back to the Eaton's before shifting his gaze to the floor. "I'm, um, sorry Tom. I didn't realize you had company."

"That's alright, Doug, but don't worry about it," Wellwood told him in an almost fatherly tone which seemed to calm his visitor a bit. "It happens to the best of us from time to time. Besides, you came at a good time. You'll have a chance to meet a potential patient of ours."

Squinting his eyes at what he was told, Doug focused back onto the Eaton's. He stared at them for a few moments before a look of recognition came upon his face.

"Oh my god. I-I don't believe it," he fumbled in a half shocked, half amazed voice. "Christian Eaton! My god! Is that you?" He stared at him in an exhilarated manner before stepping forward in a nervous attempt to shake his hand.

"How are you doing, sir?" Christian asked in an embarrassed manner while wishing to himself Doug would just leave him alone.

"Oh, I'm just wonderful! Just wonderful indeed," he responded in a manner quite the opposite of what he displayed a minute before. "I can't believe it's you. I really can't. I heard rumors that you might be stopping by but I assumed that's what they were, just rumors. But you know what they say about assuming, right?"

"Doug, would you mind giving him his hand back?" Wellwood asked with an amusing smile. "He still may need it to fill out some paperwork."

"Oh, sure, of course. I'm sorry, really I am," he said while quickly releasing Christian's hand. "I'm just excited that you're here. I cannot tell you how big of a fan I am of yours. It'll be great knowing that you'll be a patient here."

"I'm not really a patient yet," corrected Christian. "I still need to fill out the application and wait for a response."

"Really? You haven't been approved yet?" Doug asked with a confused look. "I thought that was why you're here now. But I wouldn't worry about that. Hughes will most definitely approve your application once you're done with it."

"Hughes is the director?" Miho asked.

"Yes he is. Have you met him?"

"The opportunity hasn't yet come up but the more I hear of him, the more I think I'd like him," Christian replied while drawing smiles from the others. He soon focused back onto Doug with a pained expression. "I'm sorry, but I seem to have forgotten what you are here."

"Oh, silly me," Doug fumbled. "I'm Doug Allen, one of the doctor's in the dementia wing. I thought I mentioned that already."

"You may have but I don't remember."

"What do you think of our place so far?" Doug asked. His mannerisms indicated he was still a little awe struck by being around Christian.

"We've only seen a small portion so far, but we like what we have seen," Miho told him.

"Before you leave, make sure you check out back," Doug told them. "We have a nice patio were we have cookouts occasionally. It connects to a little pond that's stocked with fish. There's also some resident ducks and geese that like being fed by the patients."

"We saw them on our way in," Miho informed them with a smile.

"One of the old men out there waved to me," Christian commented with a slight laugh.

A brief look between the two doctors took place then after hearing that comment by the former pugilist, but each remained silent while doing so. Though the look was both quick and non-verbal, Christian felt what was exchanged between the two was much more than simple eye contact. Sensing this, Dr. Allen coughed uncomfortably.

"Well, I'll let you guys get back to what you were doing before I interrupted," Doug said while going to the office door to open it. "I've still got some more complaining and mumbling to do about this new agenda." He waved his folder while saying that. "And it might be best if I did that in private. Sorry to bother you folks."

"It's no bother, Dr. Allen," Christian told him.

"I have to agree," Wellwood concurred. "Your comments about the new agenda, however, might be best worked out in an out of the way broom closet."

"I'll keep that in mind." Doug gave him a look before turning back to the Eaton's. "Good to finally meet you two."

"Good to meet you, too," the Eaton's said almost in unison.

At this point, Dr. Doug Allen finally made his exodus which allowed the other three to finally get back to business at hand. They were there for almost another hour while talking about the ins and outs of what could be expected if he ultimately got accepted there. Afterwards, Wellwood took them on a brief tour of the facilities.

"Doctor, what is your visitation policy?" Miho asked about halfway through.

"You may come whenever you'd want, just so long as who you're seeing isn't being treated for whatever it is when you do come," the doctor responded. "We'd rather you make an appointment as far in advance as possible so that we know, but we're fairly lax on that rule. We understand things change or come up at the last minute, but that might change if someone has a lot of unexpected visits on a consistent basis. However, if you wanted to, you could set the same day or time each week aside for visits if you wanted to. There is no time limit or curfew just as long as we know where you are, when you'll be back, where you're going, and so on."

"Would she be able to stay the weekend if she wanted?" Christian asked which caused Miho to blush slightly.

"We don't usually condone that but we could make an exception every now and then," Wellwood told him while taking the question in stride. "If you wanted to, you could be granted a pass to leave for the weekend if you wanted to go home or get away for a day or two."

"What type of restrictions is there with that?" Miho asked.

"Just let us know as far ahead as possible on the dates, where you think you may be going, when roughly when you'll be back. We usually approve most requests but the exception to that would be if we felt the patient wouldn't be able to leave, say, as a result of their health."

"Are there any spots to stay around here if I had anyone that wanted to stay during their visit?" Christian asked.

"We have a few in the area, but there is one in particular I'm quite fond of." Wellwood smiled with this. "The Jones family has a nice b-and-b on the outskirts of town."

" 'B-and-b'?" Miho asked, not quite understanding this.

"Bed and breakfast."

Twenty minutes after this the Eaton's tour ended as Dr. Wellwood showed them to the front door. Christian and Miho drove straight home, stopping only to get gas and something to eat. They had a lot to talk about on the return trip, most of which was positive. Whatever their decision, they agreed they wouldn't get anything better any closer to home. The last piece of the puzzle was to talk to Asako and Dominic about it.

Chapter 46

What Dr. Vincent Hughes lacked in physical stature he made up for it in everything else. Christian could almost hear Shawn ask, "I wonder what he's tryin' to compensate for?" when he stepped into Hughes' office.

The door to his office was wide open when Dr. Wellwood brought Christian there to introduce the newly moved-in patient with the clinic's director. They stepped just inside the doorway and scanned the apparent empty office before giving each other a baffled look.

His office, virtually quadruple that of what Dr. Wellwood's, took up most of the small fifth floor. His office was in the front half of the floor and had a nice view of the front yard and nearby village.

The back half of the fifth floor was left open and had an enclosed balcony that overlooked the floor below and patio outside. In the space next to the balcony that overlooked the floor below was an enormous crystalline chandelier, the only decoration of this floor, which fell below the base of the balcony. A stairwell was off the balcony, which led down to the bottom level, and in the corner was an elevator and restroom. All other furnishings and decorations resided within Hughes' office.

"Real expensive stuff," Christian thought when he entered. Everything in the office appeared top of the line. "Maybe too expensive." If Hughes had the money to line his office like this, Christian didn't want to think how he furnished his home, if he even had one that was. He was guessing that what everything might have been worth could have been equivalent to a small home.

As soon as Christian and Dr. Wellwood walked in, there was a stuffed grizzly bear standing on its hind legs in an attack position in the left corner; while in the right, a full suit of armor armed with a broad sword in one hand and a shield attached to its left forearm.

The front half of the office was carpeted in a high quality, very expensive Middle Eastern pattern and had a dark leather couch with matching chairs set around a similar colored coffee table. The first half of the right wall had three giant bookshelves that were all connected together and went from the floor up to the ceiling, standing between seven to eight feet tall, and had the same dark cherry coloration as the furniture. They were filled mostly with books that were all hardbound. A lot of these were bound in leather though most weren't. The spaces that weren't filled with books were filled with various knick-knacks, one in particular being a giant old-fashioned British warship in a bottle. To the left of the bookshelves was a giant, old-fashioned globe in a combination bronzy metal and wooden base.

The first half of the left wall was filled with pictures. These pictures started about waist high and continued all the way up to the ceiling. They were of different sizes and shapes, and didn't look to be in any particular order outside of trying to make them all fit in a neat, orderly fashion. They were mostly of Hughes with various so-called important people. One was with former President Bill Clinton and his wife, former Secretary of State and former New York senator, Hillary Clinton. Another was with Reverends Jesse Jackson and Al Sharpton. Another still was with Ted Kennedy. Thrown in were also those with entertainers such as Barbara Streisand and John Fogerty. There were a few other people that Christian did not recognize but mostly they were pictures of him

443

with guys on a golf course, yacht, or in a fancy restaurant. Others appeared to be Hughes on vacation somewhere outside the Taj Majal, Eiffel Tower, the Vatican, White House, and other similar places.

The back half of the office was the complete opposite. The flooring in this half, unlike the other, was of a high quality hardwood. The entire back wall were essentially one big window that allowed Hughes to overlook the front of the facilities and neighboring town. The back half of the left wall, unlike the other two, was divided into two parts - the top being a window, and the bottom being an almost full-sized bar

In the middle of the floor was an impressive looking desk that was filled with various folders, papers, a couple of books, and a number of foreign artifacts decorating it. Behind it was a black leather chair with a tall back. It was turned facing the window. Coming from it was a cloud of smoke. From what little aroma that had reached the door, the smoke came from a cigar. It smelled expensive. Other than the smoke, no other hint was given to suggest the room was occupied.

"Hughes, you in here?" Wellwood asked while knocking on the door.

"Of course I am, Thomas," an arrogant sounding voice came from behind the desk. The chair swiveled around to reveal Hughes, who was indeed puffing on a big, fat cigar. "Do you really think I'd abandon my post knowing full well you were bringing a famous celebrity into my midst?"

"I just wanted to be sure."

"Hold on a sec. I want to wrap up a call I have on hold first," Hughes told him while picking up his phone before hitting one of its many buttons. "Hey George, sorry to keep you waiting. I came to a decision about tonight. If you want to meet down at the yacht, say, 6:30, we can go from there. How's that sound?" He paused to wait for an answer. During this pause, Christian and Wellwood gave each other mixed looks while Tom rolled his eyes. "Ok, great. I'll see you then. Remember, 1830." Hughes hung up the phone before smiling.

Giving the impression of being as pompous and pretentious as his voice was filled with arrogance, Christian immediately didn't trust him. Regardless of what type of person he was, he didn't see, nor hear, anything in this brief exchange that would make him feel any different. He felt slightly ashamed of himself because he was raised with the philosophy that you don't judge a book by its cover, which was exactly what he was doing right then with Hughes.

Hughes' dark eyes seemed to penetrate Christian as they looked him over; his sneer-like grin matched everything else that Christian had seen. He had that aura of a person who eventually got everything he wanted and was someone you didn't want to be around when he didn't. Christian assumed Hughes had more enemies than acquaintances and more acquaintances than friends. He looked to be a person who seldom, if ever, let anyone know his true inner self. His expensive and elaborate tastes, as well as his desire to show them off, led Christian to believe he was used to being the center of much desired attention. Where the attention was good or bad was entirely up for debate.

"Christian Eaton," Hughes said after a long puff of his cigar. "It's such an honor to finely meet you."

The smoke, which was trapped inside him a moment before excited his mouth before practically engulfing his head in the process. Christian couldn't help but smile to himself while imagining the head of the devil superimposed over Hughes. The image of the director with a pair of horns, fangs, reddish eyes, and a red tint to his skin while being surrounded by smoke was somewhat amusing to him. Christian smiled briefly with the thought that the office they were in could be a secret entrance to Hades.

"The pleasure is all mine," Christian lied effortlessly in return.

When the smoke diminished slightly, Hughes rose to walk over to meet them. When he emerged from the remaining cloud and from around the desk, Christian was surprised at how short Hughes was. The director stood roughly 5'3" tall – with his shoes on. His shoes made the tap-tap-tapping sound as he walked on the hardwood beneath. Glancing down, Christian noticed that he wasn't actually wearing shoes. In fact, the sound came from a nice pair of cowboy boots with 3-inch heels.

Before he know it, the director had covered the distance between them in a matter of seconds. While accepting his handshake, Christian was surprised that Hughes much smaller hands provided a firmer grip than what he would have expected. Hughes seemed to sense this before giving the new patient a small smile when their eyes met.

"The good Dr. Wellwood here tells me you're all moved in," the director commented.

"Yes sir, I am."

"Please, there aren't any 'sirs' here, is there, Thomas?" Hughes tried sounding modest but failed. "We're very informal around here. You can call me good-ole Dr. Hughes and that'll be alright with me."

Christian smiled at that. "Dr. Hughes, huh? Yes, the informality here is quite refreshing."

This brought a moment between Hughes and Christian when they locked eyes, each with their own slight smile on their faces, before Hughes continued.

"When did you finished getting all settled in?"

"I think it may be some time before I'm *all* settled in, but I moved in yesterday," Christian explained.

"Did you have any help moving in?"

"Yes, sir, I did. My wife and kids helped me."

" 'Sir'," Hughes repeated with an arrogant smile before looking up to Dr. Wellwood, who easily stood a foot taller than he. "You see, Thomas, there are some people who still show respect to others."

"That's probably because he doesn't know you yet," the doctor commented light heartedly but the look they exchanged was anything but.

Turning back to Christian when the exchange was over, Hughes said, "How old are they, your family that is?"

"You had to ask me that, didn't you?" Christian asked in an embarrassed manner before thinking for the answer. "Well, let me see. My wife is five years older than me, so that would make her, what, 45? And I can't quite remember how old my kids are; but I think my daughter is about ten or eleven and she's four years older than our son."

Hearing this, Hughes waved it off while looking down at his watch for longer than he should have. The watch itself was had a diamond studded face attached to a wide, thick solid gold band.

"Well, I don't want to keep you," he said while looking back up. "I'm sure Thomas still needs you for a few more things today. Besides, it appears like it's time for lunch, wouldn't you say, Christian?"

"Honestly?" he asked the director as a puff of cigar smoke filled the space between them. "That maybe we shouldn't let a watch dictate when we're hungry."

With that, another fixed gaze between Christian and Hughes caused Wellwood to smile slightly. Hughes soon puffed his cigar before blowing the smoke directly into Christian's face to cause their look to break.

"Vincent, we should get going," Thomas commented with an uncomfortable cough.

"Of course. But, before you do," Hughes said while turning back for his desk. "Thomas, would you mind taking a picture of me with the champ here?"

"A picture?"

"Yes, Thomas, a picture. You do know how to use a camera, don't you?" the director asked in a condescending manner while opening a desk drawer while taking out a camera.

Wellwood simply ignored the question.

"I seem to still have room on my personal wall of fame for at least one more picture." Hughes indicated his wall of picture while looking at Christian. "That is, if you don't mind."

"No, not at all," he lied. "A picture would be great."

For the backdrop of the shot, Hughes wanted to use his filled bookshelf. "Why don't you make a fist and look like we're trying to hit each other? Shall we?" he asked while putting his fist near Christian's chin.

Christian complied as Wellwood took the picture.

"Oh, by the way," Hughes stated in an offhand manner. "When the picture comes back, would you mind signing it for me?"

"Oh, no. Not at all. I'd be happy to," Christian replied while not knowing what else to say.

"Now, Christian, not to cut this short, but I'll need to have you do a couple of things before we break for lunch," Thomas took a step or two towards the door while giving Hughes a questioning side glance.

"Go on ahead you two," Hughes told them with a nonchalant wave. "I'm sorry to have kept you two as long as I have."

"Not a problem, Vincent."

"Maybe we can continue our conversation at a more convenient time?" the director asked Christian.

"Sure. Why not?" he told him while internally cringing. "Besides, I'm not going anywhere."

Thomas and Christian left with that while not saying anything until they were secured within the safe confines of the elevator.

"So, what do you think of our director?" Wellwood asked once the elevator doors closed. A soft chuckle escaped his lips while a mild smile tried not to show itself.

Whistling while shaking his head, Christian shook his head. "I'm not sure. Interesting to say the least. He's not very tall, is he? Even with those boots of his he's still short."

"You noticed that too, huh?" Tom finally laughed. This was the first time that Christian had ever seen or heard the quiet doctor do this. "I think that's why he's so *tall* in other areas, to help make up for his lack of physical stature."

"Speaking of that, how's he reach the books at top of those bookshelves of his? I didn't see a ladder or anything in there."

"They aren't real. Those top books are just a fancy cover over some type of backing."

"For a minute there, I thought he was trying to compensate for something else," Christian dryly commented.

Wellwood smiled. "Let's hope neither of us has the chance to find out."

***

"Who the hell are you?!" an elderly man demanded when Christian entered his room.

"Evening, Lloyd," Christian said while ignoring the question as he continued past his roommate to go to his own bed.

"Why the hell you sayin' it's evening when it's early afternoon?! Can't you tell time?"

"Not very well I can't," replied Christian. "Maybe with your help I'll improve in a timely fashion."

"Don't patronize me, you snot-nosed little punk! Don't you know who I am?!" Lloyd demanded of him.

Sitting on his bed, Christian took off his shoes while drawing a quizzical look from Lloyd. "I only know three things about you. You're a white American male; you're name's Lloyd; and we're currently roommates with each other."

"Is that all you know?"

"About you, yes it is. What else is there?" Christian asked dryly.

"Well, let me tell you what." Lloyd's temper clearly rose with his. "I was a full-bird Colonel for the US Marine Corps! I enlisted in the Corps right out of high school and I started off as a rifleman before moving to their paratrooper unit. I had three tours in Korea and seven in Vietnam. That's ten tours, you condescending little prick! Ten! And all ten I volunteered for. I won the Purple Heart seven out of those ten; the naval cross three times; and was a Congressional Medal of Honor recipient. I've been in countless battles and killed many men; many with my bare hands," Lloyd stated while flexing his hands. "After Vietnam, I got my commission and began work in M.I. – that's military intelligence to you! Intelligence/counter-intelligence was my specialty. As a result, I dealt mainly with secret, top secret, and classified assignments, shit the average Joe Blow wouldn't even dream about! Many lives lived and died on what decisions we made. I loved it! I wanted to die a Marine!"

"What's that old saying, 'once a Marine, always a Marine'?"

Lloyd scoffed. "That's not what I meant, you arrogant little bastard! I wasted to die while still in the Corps. That's what I wanted." His voice trailed off at this last part.

"Why didn't you, stay in that is?"

"They forced me out, that's why! It wasn't my decision." He went quiet for a moment, his eyes going distance while looking up at the ceiling. "They stopped trusting my word, my decisions. I don't blame them really; I would'a done the same thing if I were in their shoes."

"What made them not trust you anymore?"

"It was that green shit they dropped on us over there in 'Nam. After we breathed it in, it got to our heads," Lloyd said while tapping the side of his head. "Of course there isn't any evidence what I'm saying is true. Just the ramblings of some crazy, old coot but I tell ya it's true! We started seeing and hearing things a few months later. Shell shock, battle fatigue, or whatever the hell they're calling it now is what they said it was. But it wasn't!" He pounded the edge of his bed with a fist. "I know guys that had had that, but this was different. Our symptoms just didn't matchup.

"It wasn't until years later when guys started dropping like flies did they start to take notice. The ones that were left were brought in for tests disguised as a physical or some other bullshit excuse. Some of us who were left had brains like Swiss cheese, holes throughout our memory;

while others it was more like mashed potatoes. For a lot of us, everything just ran in together. I was different. It took longer to affect me."

"When did you start showing signs?"

"About a year ago."

"A year ago?" Christian questioned. "Vietnam was like 40, 45 years ago."

"Yeah. What's your point?"

"Wouldn't that green stuff you breathed in have affected you then when everyone else was? Why did it take you so long to show signs of it?"

"Are ya saying I'm lying?" Lloyd demanded with a glare.

"No, of course not."

"You're just like everyone else. Can't see what's right in front of you, can ya?"

"I'm not saying that," Christian said in his defense. "I was just suggesting that maybe you didn't get hit with enough of that stuff to have those awful things happen to you. Is it possible you managed to survive that? Is it possible that this thing that you have is not related to that in any way?"

"Hell no, it's not possible," his roommate stubbornly answered while relaxing somewhat. "I don't even know why I talked to you about this. You're like all the rest."

"I can't speak for everybody else, but I freely admit I'm totally ignorant on this subject," Christian admitted with a shrug. "I'm not saying I'm stupid or that I don't believe you. It's just that I don't' know anything about this. If you want to talk about it, maybe my youth, total lack of military experience, and relative subject ignorance might be a nice change for you."

Lloyd eyed him for a moment before asking, "Ya think so?"

"Beats the hell outta me, Captain, but I can't think of a better way to pass the time here, especially since we're roommates and all."

"Colonel," Lloyd corrected. "I was a colonel, not a captain!"

"I remember. I did that just to see what you'd say." Christian smiled while laying down in his bed before going to sleep.

The following morning, Christian woke to the gently nudging of Dr. Allen.

"Oh, good golly. You are alive," he said in the same hyper tone he had when they met previously in Wellwood's office.

"Don't worry, Doc. It'll be a while before I kick off."

"Well, that's good to hear. Real good to hear. I haven't gotten your autograph yet for my kids," Allen said with a smile. "Wouldn't want you kicking off until then."

"It's on my application, as well as a dozen other forms for this joint. You can always make a copy of one of those if you like." Christian rolled up in bed before rubbing the sand from his eyes.

"So, you adjusting ok to everything here alright?" Allen asked while giving Christian some pills to take. He moved on then to this patient's vitals.

"I guess I am. I miss my family, though," Christian told him while pointing to some pictures on a nearby window sill.

After Doug recorded the numbers, he went over to look at them. "May I?" he asked while bending slightly towards them. He picked them up after getting approval. "Oh, they are adorable. Just adorable. Your wife, Korean?"

"Japanese."

"Ah. How old are they, if you don't mind me asking?"

"Miho, my wife, is like 45 or somewhere around there, and the kids," Christian sighed while rubbing his forehead while trying to remember. "Asako, our daughter, is around ten I think. Dominic is four years younger than her. Their ages may be on the back of the pictures, though. I'm not sure."

"How are they taking this, you being here and all?"

"I'm not really sure. Miho has always been strong and wouldn't complain. She wants me to stay as long as I need to. I think it's hard for her to be the only one now taking care of the kids."

"That's understandable," Dr. Allen said while putting down the pictures. "That's why I'm here now."

"Why? Has something happened to them?" Christian shot out when he heard that.

"Oh, no, no. Goodness no. It's nothing like that," he quickly answered while waving his hands. "Later today, I wanted to borrow you for a little while. I wanted to ask you some questions for your file and also to get some updated C/T scans, MRIs, other similar things. The questions are basic, just to see what you've noticed with your memory, things you find you're having trouble remembering. I've been meaning to do this since you got here but I hadn't a chance until now."

"I've got nothing else planned." Christian shrugged while getting out of bed before stretching. "Do I have time to leave a urine same and shower before I start?"

"Of course. I've got some things to do in the meantime. Just stop

by my office when you're all set and we can go from there."

An hour later, as promised, Christian met with Dr. Allen. The rest of the morning they completed the tests Doug had told him about. Afterwards, he went back to his room to find Lloyd, who was still in bed, glaring at him.

"Ah, Christ! You still here? I thought Allen came by to sign your release form."

"Sorry to disappoint."

"Shit! When will your good for nothin' ass be outta my way 'round here?"

"Sorry to be the bearer of bad news, but my good for nothing ass will be here until I'm ready to leave." Christian smiled at him.

"I don't suppose that'll be anytime soon, will it?"

"'fraid not," Christian told him while sitting on his bed.

"Damn," Lloyd complained while laying back down.

"Hey, Lloyd. I got a question for you."

"That's Colonel Anderson to you!"

"Sorry, sir," Christian said with a smile. "Colonel, are you saying I'm in your way here?"

"That's what I said. Got a problem with that?"

"No, sir, I don't. But how could I be in your way if you never get out of bed?"

Lloyd ignored the question before rolling over.

Looking out their window, Christian sat on his bed before letting his eyes fall to the pictures of his family. Picking up one that was a group shot of the four of them, he sat there looking at it.

"What's that?" demanded Lloyd.

"A picture of me and my family."

"Ha! Family!" Lloyd scoffed as his bed creaked from him moving around. "They're overrated."

"What's overrated?"

"Families."

"Mine isn't."

"You're still young and filled with idealistic thoughts. Live awhile. In time, you'll see I'm right. But while I'm at it, there's somethin' I gotta tell you, kid, something I've learned through experience."

451

"Yeah, what's that?" Christian asked while lying down on his bed. This was a time he found himself wishing Lloyd would just shut up and go to sleep.

"You, at your age, you're missing out on the best thing possible; something my old, chapped ass will never get again. And that thing is pussy!"

Christian practically sat up when he heard that. He was already on the verge of falling asleep when the comment brought him back to reality. That, mixed with the intensity of his roommate's voice, made him come awake in a confused state.

"Wha...huh? What was that?"

"You heard me! You, at your age, need to get as much pussy as you can," Lloyd repeated. "Pussy of all sorts, and I'm not talkin' 'bout that old scabby shit we've got around here. The exception would be Rita, that is, if you're into dark meat. If I were you, I'd go for that young meat 'cause that's the best. It's still in its prime and hasn't been stretched out that much yet."

"You talk like you've experienced it," Christian dryly commented.

"Of course I have! How else would I know what I'm talking about?"

"I haven't a clue, Lloyd."

"Keep in mind, stay away from that fresh meat under eighteen. That shit's jail bait and not worth it! If you do nail any jail bait, make sure you don't get caught. That or make absolutely sure it's pure and good enough to do three-to-five over. Remember that, kid. I wouldn't want you to get in any trouble for taking my advice," Lloyd said in a very self-assured, cocky manner. "Speaking of not getting into trouble, make sure you shrink wrap your dick with a condom before you hammer that nail home. Wouldn't want you picking up any stowaways. I've heard HIV is a bitch to get rid of. It also helps to prevent knocking up that young lady, if you know what I mean."

"Lloyd, I'm married!" protested Christian. "I can't do that."

"So what if you are? That hasn't stopped people before from screwing around on their spouse."

"That's true. I'll keep that in mind. Thanks for the advice, Lloyd," Christian told him before turning is back onto his eccentric roommate before drifting off into the dream world.

"Anytime, kid. That's what I'm here for," was the last things Lloyd said before he himself fell soundly asleep.

As Christian lay there on his bed with the picture still in his hand, he began to understand somewhat why Lloyd seemed so miserable. Maybe it necessarily wasn't him per se but, rather, it could have been Lloyd's own family or lack thereof. To be honest, Christian didn't know that much about him. He felt it wasn't any of his business and that Lloyd would reveal things when he was ready to. But, on the other hand, Christian did want to know more about him but was somewhat reluctant to ask. He just didn't want to touch upon any subjects that might be sensitive. Only time will tell.

Looking back to the picture in his hands, he thought of the last time he saw his family; it was the day they all came up to help him move into Forestry Park. He and Miho didn't speak much on the drive up, just being in the company of the other was all that mattered to them. Asako and Dominic were grumping about one thing or another, which ultimately led to them arguing. Christian smiled at this; happy that occasions like that were really the only times their children did fight. It wasn't until they started bringing what luggage he had up to his room did they truly understand the importance of their trip.

"But why, Papa?!" Asako demanded of him as tears streamed down her face. "Why are you staying?"

"It's only for a little while, baby," he told her while kneeling in front of her. He soon began wiping the tears off of the face of his crying daughter. Taking a tissue from his pocket, he gave it to her. "Here, blow your nose."

She did what she was told.

"How long you staying, Daddy?" Dominic asked.

"I don't know. A while, I suppose. As long as it takes."

"What's wrong with you, Papa?"

"Remember what we talked about? I have problems inside my head," Christian told her while taping his forehead in the process. "Remember all those times I was acting weird or when I forgot your names? Well, if I don't come here for help, those problems will get worse."

"Weren't you playing around then, Papa?" Asako asked him.

"No, I wasn't playing, sweetie."

"Maybe you don't really need to come here. Maybe it won't really get worse. If we just play make believe it'll just go away," she asked with not much confidence.

"No, honey, it won't go away," he said while trying to console her. "My mind will keep getting worse and worse until I won't know you or your brother. Even your mom I'll forget."

"It won't ever get better, Daddy?" Dominic asked while starting to tear up himself.

Christian wasn't able to answer that. All he could do was look at him in silence. Unfortunately, the look h gave spoke volumes. The shock, horror, and bewilderment that came into his son's face was something he would never forget. Dominic's eyes widened, mouth dropped, and all color left his cheeks before his eyes squinted before a wail of sorrow escaped him. The reaction almost immediately rubbed off onto Asako who quickly followed suit. He picked them both up, one in each arm, and let them cry on his shoulders until their eyes finally dried up.

While looking past his children's heads to Miho, his eyes fell upon her face on the picture his hand still grasped. He soon fell asleep with her as his last waking thought.

Chapter 47

He woke a few hours later to find his picture had fallen onto the floor next to his bed. As he put it back on the sill, the clock next to his other pictures read 3:15p. While getting up to stretch, he noticed that other than him, the room was empty. Christian had mixed feelings about not seeing Lloyd there. On one hand he was glad because he didn't want to listen to him complain about something but, on the other hand, he did want some company.

He soon found himself leaving his room intent on exploring. He planned on first seeing who was in the rec room at the end of the hall and proceeded that way. When he got there, he found the room was empty. At that point, he decided to explore the facilities. Though he knew the overall layout, he wanted to keep busy and getting a lay of the land was a good start.

While exploring, he soon found that it was more extensive than he previously thought. Though it looked like a simple rectangular shape from the outside, one with some basic hallways within, he soon found the opposite was true. The inside was, in fact, a number of hallways and narrow stairways that connected one area to another. The more he explored, the more he saw.

The first floor was essentially divided into three parts. The entire front half was for non-medical, non-resident areas such as administrative, personal, human resources, payroll, and billing. The back left corner was walled off for an employees' lounge that medical and non-medical personal alike used. In the lounge someone was cleaning a fairly large aquarium against one of the walls. The lounge itself only took up mostly a third of the back half. The other two-thirds was reserved for the cafeteria and dining hall for the residents. A number of them, as well as a few nurses, sat in their own little groups as they talked over coffee.

The second and third floors were divided pretty much in half; not so much front to back as they were left to right. The middle of the two floors was reserved for two fairly large elevators. Each one was big enough to fit two beds side-by-side with a little room left over. The staircase and chandelier that were on the fifth floor was visible outside the elevator on the fourth floor. An elaborate, metal railing ensured no one would fall over should they get too close.

The second, Christian's floor, was reserved mostly for mental illness and disease but also had a number of people that didn't quite fit this criteria. He couldn't figure out exactly what specifically the third floor had or if it actually had one. It looked like a combination geriatrics, cardiac, and miscellaneous units all in one. Both of these floors had their own nursing staff and two doctors assigned to them. As he watched them work, he was impressed at the laid back, yet tight run, shift they ran.

The basement itself was divided in half. On one side, the equipment which was needed for the daily operations was housed. There were two backup generators, multiple water heaters, and their very own fully staffed, fully equipped laundromat. The other half was purely for medical purposes. Here was a couple of examination rooms, another for C/T scans, MRIs, x-rays, things of this nature, as well as a fairly good sized rehabilitation room they chose to call a 'center' instead. In the rehabilitation center, a couple of nurses were working with an elderly couple. The man was on the treadmill while the woman was on a bench doing leg exercises.

Christian stopped long enough to see what was going on and exchanged a smile with the nurse attending to the man. When the turned, he nearly ran into Dave, the burly janitor from the second floor.

"What'ya doin' down here, Chris?" he asked dryly. A twinkle in his eye appeared ever so slightly. He stopped the cart of freshly cleaned and folded bed sheets he was pushing to wait for an answer.

"Nothing. Just looking around."

"Which is it? Nothin' or just lookin'?" Dave smiled. "You can't be doing nothin' if you're lookin'."

"I guess I'm just looking."

"Checking out the local scenery? Doesn't that ring on your finger mean you're married?" David asked while pointing to Christian's wedding band.

"What? You think I was…?" Christian left the question open while pointing to the nurse. This brought a mischievous grin onto the janitor's face. "Oh, no, no, no. I think you misunderstand."

"Did I?"

"Yes."

"So, you're down here in the basement, with hardly anyone around, looking into a room where a young, attractive nurse is working and you're telling me I misunderstood your intentions?"

Christian stood there in silence as the thought implied dawned on him. Though it did put him in a rather precarious position, one which he couldn't prove one way or another, he began stuttering his works together in an attempt to explain.

To this, David finally laughed. "There's no need for that, Chris. I was only teasing you. There's nothing wrong with looking. Hell, a woman like that would make me stop to look."

Chris merely shook his head and laughed. He was embarrassed that he let himself get drawn into this joke that was now clearly obvious. While finally able to compose himself, he noticed Dave's chart of bed sheets.

"Didn't you already bring up a load of sheets this morning?" he asked.

"Yeah, but this is for third floor," Dave replied while fingering his beard. "They're a little shorthanded today. They had a call-in."

"That would explain it." Christian nodded. "As for me, I'm down here wandering around seeing what they have. I'm a little bored."

"It can get boring here for you guys," Dave admitted. "You should go up to the rec room on two. A number of the older guys usually are playing cards up there."

"That sounds pretty good. I may just do that," he told him. "But it was empty when I was up there a few minutes ago."

"Watch out for Walt, if you do," Dave warned. "He's been known not to play all that fair."

"I'll keep that in mind."

"Now, if you'll excuse me, I have to get back to work," Dave said lightly while moving to the elevator and pushed its call button. "If I'm gone too long, they may think I'm making moves on that pretty little nurse in there. Just don't take too long yourself. Someone might think the same about you."

The bearded janitor smiled before completely disappearing in the elevator.

Christian continued smiling at him little while shaking his head. He soon departed himself before finding the stairs to jog up two at a time. When he got to the second floor, he decided to go back to the rec room to see if anyone was there yet.

"Where do you think you're going, Mr. Eaton?" Rita, the head nurse of the floor, asked from behind the nurses' station when he was in the process of passing.

"Down the hall," he retorted while pointing in the general direction.

"I can see that," she said hotly.

"Why did you ask then?"

She stared in silence before responding. "Are you gettin' fresh with me, Mr. Eaton?"

While shaking his head, Christian said, "Ah, no, ma'am."

"Good." She scoffed as her head bobbed while her hands went to her hips. She soon pointed a finger at him. "I axed you a question if memory serves me correctly."

"And I answered it, if memory serves me correctly. But feel free not to believe me, I am a dementia patient after all."

Standing there in silence while looking at each other, they waited to see who would break first. Head nurse Rita's attempt to drill a hole through his head before Christian got a whiff of something that he hadn't smelled in a very long time.

"Is that fried chicken?" he asked while moving closer to the nurses' station. "With mashed potatoes?"

"What if it is?" Her head bobbed slightly when she answered.

"Is it yours?" he asked while seeing the plate of steaming food from behind the counter.

"What you askin'?"

"I'm asking whether that fried chicken with mashed potatoes is yours or not."

"Are you askin' me that because I'm black?" Rita's head really started bobbing at this point.

456

"Ah, no."

"You smell fried chicken and automatically think it's the black girl's? Right? That what you sayin', white boy?"

"For starters, I didn't assume, imply, or say anything. I merely asked. Secondly, you're the only black person here from what I've seen. Thirdly, you're not a girl. You're a woman. Fourthly, and lastly, I smelled some good smelling fried chicken and, since you're the only other person I'm seeing here, I asked if it was yours. Even if you were a 90-year old Brazilian man, I still would have asked you."

"Do 90-year old Brazilian men eat fried chicken?"

"I wouldn't know. I was just making a point."

"But you would know if a middle-aged, black American woman would. Is that it? You're stereotyping my kind?"

"I wouldn't say any of that."

"What would you say then, saltine?"

"I'd say it was nice talking with you but I don't want to lie," Christian told her while looking at her. Rita seemed to blink at what she heard. But, since you're not answering one way or another whether this chicken is in fact yours," he continued while making a move to reach over the counter to grab a piece of chicken. "I'll assume it's not. With that being true, you then won't mind me eating some of it before I get out of your way and stop pissing you off. It would be a shame to waste such good food."

Before he could grab it, Rita smacked his and to cause him to jerk it back from its sting.

"To answer your two questions, yes and yes."

"Yes and yes what?" Christian asked blankly.

"Yes the chicken and potatoes are mine. Yes you have some."

Smiling at this, Christian quickly grabbed a chicken leg before he took a hearty bite. His mouth salivated at it while moaning.

"This is delicious," he complimented.

"Of course it is," she said very matter of factly. "It's my mama's receipt."

"I don't remember my mom's fried chicken tasting this good."

"Is your mama black?" Rita asked in between mouthfuls.

"No."

"That explains it. Only a black woman would make fried chicken like my mama can."

"Wait. A minute ago you accused me of stereotyping blacks for liking fried chicken."

"Firstly, I didn't accuse you. If I had, you'd be dead," she said in a very stately manner which caused Christian to almost choke with a laugh. "Secondly, I haven't met a white person yet who could make fried chicken like we can."

"So you eat a lot of fried chicken with us white folk?"

"As a matter of fact, I don't."

"Why's that?"

"Is your dementia worse than anticipated or did you just choose to ignore what I just said?" she asked while staring at him. "Did I *not* tell you only a black person can make friend chicken the way it ought to be?"

"Now would be a perfect time to thank-you for your chicken and leave before this conversation gets worse than it already is," Christian told her while finishing his chicken and throwing its bones in the trash. "So, thank-you for the chicken. It was nice chatting with you, Ms. Rita."

Before he had a chance to leave, Rita's glare quickly faded into a warm smile. "You know, white boy? You're alright in my book. You're alright."

"Gee, thanks, Rita. You're alright too," Christian told her while being totally confused by her. He honestly had no idea what to think or how to take her. Was she messing with him? Was she being serious? He just didn't know. "Oh, by the way, do you know where Lloyd's at?"

"Lloyd who?"

"You know, Lloyd my roommate? The grumpy old bastard?"

"Honey, with all due respect, that doesn't narrow it down all that much. That describes most of the men around here," Rita told him. "If they ain't a grumpy old bastard, then they're a DOM."

" 'DOM'?"

"Dirty old man."

"The Lloyd I'm talking about, he doesn't seem to walk right. His legs seem to be paralyzed."

"Oh, you mean Mr. Anderson. That's your roommate?" she asked in wonder before scoffing loudly.

"Ah, yeah. Why?"

"Your scrawny little white ass is braver than I thought," she said while eyeing him. "That man definitely *is* a grumpy old bastard. Capital G, O, *and* B with that. I think they broke the mold when they made him."

458

"He can't be that bad."

"Honey, I've been here a long, long time and I can't remember any other patient that's come in here that's been as miserable as he is. Just give it time; you'll see the light soon enough," she told him as a thrill-like laugh while waving her hands at him. "To answer your question, he's in therapy at the moment."

"What happened to him? Why can't he walk?"

"He was in some sort of accident a number of years ago," Rita explained. "He's been crippled the entire time I've known him."

"Don't you mean physically handicapped?" Christian asked with a smile.

"Honey, crippled is crippled no matter what you want to call it."

"What happened to him? Why is he the way he is, so mean and everything?"

"I think it was as result of the shit his old ass was in."

"What stuff?"

"Oh, come on. You tellin' me he hasn't told you any of those old war stories of his?"

"Those are real?"

She nodded while looking at him suspiciously. "They all are, and then, some from what I'm told."

"Well, I'll be. I thought he was just making it up for attention."

"No, not those he's not. Maybe he is about other things, but definitely not those. The shrink here really had helped him out."

"How did they get him out of our room?"

"They used his wheelchair."

"He has a wheelchair?" Christian question. "He's never had one since I've been here."

"That's because they took it away from a couple of days before you arrived."

"Is that legal?" Christian asked but immediately regretted doing so. Rita glared at him so intently that he thought his head was going to explode.

"Honey, that man was hell on wheels. Now he's just hell. When he had that damn chair of his, he'd be racing up and down every hallway here every damn day. Up and down, down and up," she told him while using her arms to emphasize what he was saying. "He'd be knocking over nurses, patients, or whatever got in his way. Even run over things that weren't in his way. Mr. Beckman suffered a broken hip and leg, as well as receiving a concussion from the head-on with your roommate."

459

"Did he come out at the last minute or something, Mr. Beckman that is?"

"He was sitting in his chair against the wall. On the other side of the hall. There was nothing blocking Mr. Anderson's view."

"Lloyd ran into him on purpose?"

"Weren't you listenin' to me at all, Saltine? Of course he did."

"Why?"

"Because Beckman beat him at cards."

"Seriously? Over a lost card game?"

Rita's head started bobbing again with that. "That's what I said, whitey. We took his chair away from him for safety of the others, as well as his."

"Why for his safety?"

"Some of the older gentlemen were talking about gangin' up on him during the night one time. Dr. Allen and I walked by when they were working out the finishing touches."

"You have to admit it is sort of funny." Christian laughed.

"I don't have to admit nothin' and I wouldn't have been laughin' if I got fired or sued by some patient's family that got hurt by him."

"No, I guess you wouldn't."

"I'm still surprised you've lasted this long with him."

"He's not that bad."

"Not that bad, you say. You've been his roommate the longest since he got here a year ago."

Confused by this, Christian said, "I haven't even been here three weeks yet."

"Two weeks to the day used to be the record until you showed up. The record now falls to you, though the guy that had it previously died. If he didn't, God knows when he would'a left."

"How many roommates has he had?"

"A lot."

"How many is that?"

"Honey, let me put it to you this way. He's been here about a year and the longest person to be his roommate, excluding present company of course, has been two weeks. Do the math and the answer is 'a lot'."

460

"I hope he's not this way to his family."

"We *are* his family, honey. What family he has left want nothin' to do with him." Rita shrugged as the nurses' station phone rang. She answered it before looking back to Christian. "As a matter of fact, I'm looking at him now," she said into the phone. "Ok, I'll let him know." After hanging up, she looked at Christian. "Dr. Allen wants to see you down in the basement."

"I just came from there. What's he want?"

"He didn't say and, as you heard, I didn't ask. Guess you're gonna find out, now won't you?"

***

"I'm sorry you had to come down here," Dr. Allen apologized when Christian entered one of the basement's room a couple of minutes later. "Please, close the door behind you. When you're done, strip down to your shorts and have a seat on the bench, please."

"That's alright. I was bored anyway," Christian said while doing what he was asked. Allen soon started listening to his hear. "I was just talking to Nurse Rita about Lloyd."

"Lloyd?" Dr. Allen repeated back in a confused tone.

"Mr. Anderson. He's my roommate."

"Oh, him," he said with a chuckle while jotting down Christian's heart rate. "Thinking of changing rooms yet?"

"Not enough to actually follow through on it. Is he always like that or did I just catch him on a bad month?"

"Don't mind him. It just takes him, um, awhile to open up to people he doesn't know."

"Awhile?" Christian asked sarcastically with raised eyebrows. "I've been here just under three weeks and every time I walk in our room he asks, 'You still here? Haven't discharged you yet?'"

"That's just his way of joking. Give him time," Allen suggested while starting to take Christian's blood pressure. "Try not to be so critical of him. You're new, after all. He actually likes you."

"Is that what he said?"

"Well, ah, no. Not exactly." Doug nervously write down Christian's blood pressure readings.

"Then how do you know he likes me then?"

"You're still his roommate," Allen replied while stuffing a thermometer in under Christian's tongue.

"Why am I here, Doc?"

"Because I forgot to take these down this morning," he told him while closing Christian's mouth

461

with his hand. "Keep your mouth closed. It won't get a read properly with your jaw's flapping."

After that, Dr. Allen put a plastic clip on the end of one of Christian's fingers.

"What's that for?"

"Are you choosing to ignore me or did you forget what I said already?"

"Wha...?"

"Keep your mouth shut, please," Dr. Allen repeated while removing the thermometer and writing that reading down. "As for what this thing on your finger does, it helps tell us what your blood oxygen level is. You should know this already; I do it each time you come into my office."

"I guess I forgot."

"I guess that's alright." Allen smiled while looking at Christian's reading he just took. "Perfect. Looks like everything's normal, Mr. Eaton. Yes indeedie. Fine, fine, fine."

"Please, will you call me Christian?" he asked with obvious embarrassment. "I'm still not used to being called mister."

"Of course. I know just what you mean. I'm the same way," Allen said in a nervous tone while looking around. "I still can't get used to being called doctor."

"How long have you been a doctor for?"

"Oh, gee whiz, you had to ask me that, didn't you?" Allen paused to think. "I just turned fifty this year and I graduated med school when I was twenty-five. Geez, has it been that long?"

"Twenty-five years you've been a doctor and you still not used to being called that yet?"

"You have to understand, Mr. Eaton, er, Christian, that before I came here, all my patients called me Doug. It was never Dr. Allen."

"But yet you go by Dr. Allen here? Why?"

"It's that director of ours," he answered with an insinuated scoff.

"Hughes?"

"That's Dr. Hughes to you and everybody else. Good golly, I swear that man's soul would turn over in his grave if he wasn't called anything other than *Dr.* Hughes or some other variation of it," Allen said in contempt as his eyes widened. "He wants us to show a higher level of professionalism here. He doesn't want us to associate with the patients as equals. He wants us to be above you guys, almost like a superior figure."

"What's wrong with that?" Christian asked which drew a startled look from the doctor before him. "You guys, as well as the nurses, in a sense do control what we do here."

Dr. Allen seemed genuinely surprised when he heard this. For a moment he was speechless and much more nervous than Christian had previously seen him.

"Well, yes, that much is true, I'll give you that," he finally confessed. "That is the responsibility we chose upon accepting our jobs here, just like those are the concessions you as a patient chose to concede when you came here for treatment. But to outright imply or assume that the medical staff is higher up the food chain or the list of importance merely by what our diplomas say is outrageous! I'm no better than you or anyone else for that matter. And to treat us as such I find insulting. Truly, I do!"

"Why insulting?"

"Why? Why?! Surely you can't be serious?" Dr. Allen asked in wide-eyed wonder at this. Christian smiled while thinking of that classic line from the movie *Airplane!*. "We're here doing this job because we want to make a difference. We want to do something that helps people or put a smile on someone's face. We try our darndest to promote a healthier, fuller life. We're in the trenches with you guys. We get pissed on, shit on, burped on, puked on, spit on, spat at, sneezed on, coughed all over, and whatever else you can think of and that arrogant little piss-ant has the audacity to demand that we go by 'doctor this' or 'nurse that' because we're so much better than the people we choose to let soil us? But you won't ever see his short little legs down here with us lessers, not as long as he could get one of his $50,000 suits slightly tarnished."

"Do you think he's trying to compensate for something?" asked Christian dryly.

Dr. Allen blinked several times at this while not comprehending the question asked. "Is who trying to compensate for what?"

"Do you think your buddy Hughes'…"

"Dr. Hughes," Allen corrected.

"…over-bearing, arrogant, pompous, pretentious, pomp and circumstance attitude is his way of trying to over compensate for his obvious lack of height, especially when it comes to, say, his fifth appendage?" Christian asked as smoothly and dryly as possible. He briefly glanced down to his lap before quickly reconnecting eye contact to the doctor before him.

Hearing this, it finally seemed to sink in what exactly was being inferred between them.

"You know, that thought has never occurred to me. And, by golly, I think you just hit the nail on the head," Allen honestly admitted almost as if a light bulb went off in his head. "I've been trying so hard to do my job in a way that pleased him that I never really thought about why he acts the way he does. Even now, after all these years of him improving the facilities to what it's become, and the associations with all those high profile people that he has, what you just said explains a lot. But, with all his accomplishs, why would he still have that need to prove himself?"

"Maybe some habits are hard to break?"

"Maybe you're right. Oh, speaking of habits, have you been able to get in contact with your brother yet?"

"No, not yet," Christian confessed. "I gave up on that."

"Did you write him that letter yet that you said you wanted to write him?"

"Not yet, at least I don't think I did. I think I forgot about it."

"Speaking of your brother, have you had a chance to read that article on him in today's paper?"

Christian shook his head. "I didn't know anything about it."

"Maybe you should, read it that is." Allen laughed slightly. "We should still have a copy or two of today's paper up in the rec room. That is, if old Myrtle hasn't used it to line her litter box yet."

"We're allowed to have pets here?" Christian asked with a certain amount of surprise.

"No, though we do let the patients some liberties that we shouldn't," Allen told him. "Myrtle, one of the dementia patients from the opposite wing than you, still thinks that her cat lives here with her. She doesn't remember that he died going on twelve years ago now. The only cats we have here are our resident ones."

"Doesn't she ever wonder why the litter never gets dirty?"

"Oh, it does, though we aren't sure who does it." Allen paused to think. "Every now and then there'll be a wet spot in it or someone will bury pieces of chocolates to continue the illusion that ole Fluffy is still very much alive. But, to be honest, I hope the staff isn't doing that. That would be wrong for us to do that. We could get in a heap of trouble if we did."

"With that in mind, maybe I'd better get up there before the paper's gone," Christian said as a smile rose on his face while getting up.

"First, you'll need to get dressed," Allen reminded him.

"Oh, yeah. I can't walk around here half naked, can I?" Christian laughed while getting dressed.

"You can but if Crazy Betty sees you, you'd have wished you stayed dressed," Allen told him while shuttering with fright. "Fortunately for you, Crazy Betty inhabits the halls of third floor."

"Thank for the info, Doc," Christian said while walking to the door.

"Please, please, call me Doug."

"Sure thing, Doug, but only if you call me Christian." He shrugged.

"Oh, by golly, that's fair enough. Now get outta here, will ya?"

"Take it easy, Dougie."

"Oh, I will. Yes indeedie," Allen told him as Christian left. "You take care of yourself as well."

Chapter 48

"*Shawn Calloway wins IBF Heavyweight Championship,*" the headline boldly stated when Christian opened that day's paper to the sports section. "In a shocking turn of events, 5-1 underdog Shawn Calloway defeated reigning IBF heavyweight champion Larry Holiday with a decisive eighth round knockout. Despite being a relative newcomer to the weight division and being knocked down in the second, Calloway was determined to prove he was as good as his mouth had boasted him to be…"

Christian read with slight amusement before skimming a few paragraphs to the end to read a quote from Duke Snyder. "Not since Evander Holyfield has a boxer unified the cruiserweight and heavyweight divisions. Mr. Calloway and I are determined to be the next to do so. "And not since Michael Spinks has someone who was the undisputed light-heavyweight champion went on to win a heavyweight championship which, coincidentally, is the same title Mr. Calloway has just won. And, I may add, when Mr. Calloway unifies this division, he would then have unified them in three different weight classes, a feat I'm doubtful has been accomplished by any one, if at all, in a long, long time."

"Hey, old timer, you done with that yet?" a voice called out before Christian could read anymore.

The question was not answered.

"Hey, old timer," the voice repeated. "I asked if you were done with that."

Christian looked up to see five elderly men around the table playing cards, poker by the looks of it, all of whom were currently looking at him.

"Yeah, you with the paper," one of them said after Christian looked over to them. The man had the same voice as the faceless speaker moments before. "You done with that paper yet?"

"No, not quite. Why?"

"We wanna read it sometime this century. We ain't gettin' any younger here, ya know? So you'd better hurry up and pass it 'round before Loony Myrtle comes lookin' for it."

"We don't want it lining a catless litter box before we get a chance to read it," a second man at the table stated.

"Sure, give me a minute to finish this article and the paper's all yours," Christian told them while going back to reading. Almost immediately after this, he heard the old men start arguing.

"Hey! What the hell ya doin'?!" the first man demanded.

"What?" the dealer asked.

"Don't be givin' me that shit! I saw what you did."

"Ernie, what'ya talkin' 'bout?"

465

"What I am talkin' about, Walt, is that your palming cards, skimming off the bottom, giving 'em a five finger discount!" Ernie hotly stated. "To put it more simple like, you're down right cheatin'! That's what I'm talkin' about!"

"I am not!" Walt defensively said while being slightly insulted by the accusation. "I have no reason to."

"Then roll up your sleeves and prove it."

"Guys," Walt said while looking around the table in hopes someone would stick up for him. No one did. "I wouldn't cheat all of you. Honest."

"Then you'd better prove it by rolling up your sleeves," Eddie, a third guy who sat next to Walt, said.

"No offense against you, Walt," Frank said while positioning himself better in a seat next to Ernie. "Even though we're just playing for matches, we would all feel better if we could trust the people we play against."

"Alright, alright," Walt finally said before withdrawing an ace and two kings from his left sleeve. "You got me."

"Is that all?" Eddie asked.

Hearing this, Walt sighed before revealing a second ace from his right sleeve.

"I knew it! Goddamn it, I knew it!" Ernie shouted while using his cane to stand up before taking a wobbly step towards the dealer. "I outta pop you right in the lip for trying to cheat us like that."

"Whoa, Ernie, take it easy!" Frank told him without getting up. "Doctor said you haven't quite recovered from your stroke just yet. For Christ's sake, do us all a favor and sit down before you fall down. The worse that would have happened is we all would be out a handful of matches."

"That's not the point, Frank, and you know it," Ernie stated before taking the advice of his friend and sat down. "The point is he was cheating and then lied to us about it."

"The point *is* we can always get more matches. Remember, Tom makes sure we all have a constant supply of them. Besides, he probably just forgot about it, right Walt?"

"How the hell do you forget you're cheatin' and lyin' to your friends?" Ernie questioned.

"Maybe you forgot all of us have Alzheimer's or some other form of dementia. With that in mind, it wouldn't be any of our faults if we forget anything, right?" Frank asked while looking at Walt, who nodded in agreement. "You see, guys, he just forgot about cheating and lying to us. All's forgiven amongst us old, two-timing friends."

Frank and Ernie sat there in silence while looking at each other for another moment or two before Ernie finally conceded.

"Alright, alright, you win," he told Frank. "If I'm gonna die soon, I wanna die on good standings with all of you."

"Hey, that's the spirit," Frank said before turning back to Walt. "Go ahead and finish dealing. Try not to cheat too much next time, alright?"

"Hey, George, thanks for backing me up," Ernie said to the unnamed fifth man of the group who was the only one of them not to have said anything.

"Not a problem," George responded dryly while looking at the hand that was dealt to him.

"Why didn't you attempt to seem interested?"

"You guys had it under control," he told him.

"Didn't you mind you could'a lost all your matches?" Eddie asked.

George shook his head. "Not at all."

"Why not?"

"Why should I? I don't smoke and I can just get more matches from Tom."

"It's hard playing cards with a cynic," Eddie commented as they finally continued the game they were playing moments earlier. "By the way, if Hughes ever hears you call any of his doctors by their first name, he'd shit a ton of bricks. You can call him Tom with us, but whenever that short little midget's around, make sure it's Dr. Wellwood, alright?"

Meanwhile, after the commotion from the five old men had settled down, Christian sat on a corner sofa to finish reading the paper. He hadn't read half of a current events article when there was whooping and hollering from the hall as the sound of something coming closer was heard.

"Oh, Christ! Say it ain't so!" Ernie demanded as the five card playing men looked up towards the door as the whooping and hollering got closer.

"It would appear that it *is* so," George retorted.

Just then, Lloyd shot past the door while being in what appeared to be a wheelchair. After flying past, a woman screamed from the general direction Lloyd went.

"I thought they took that damn chair away from him?" Frank asked.

"It appears they gave it back to him," George replied while laying his hand down to go out.

"I hope Myrtle got out of the way," Eddie wishfully said.

"You do?" Walt asked. "Why?"

"I find her conversations about her damn dead cat entertaining."

467

"It would appear you're the only one."

"Maybe, but at our age, anything that helps us take our minds off of that eventual dirt nap is always a positive thing."

"He's got a point there," Eddie agreed.

Down the hall, the same woman screamed again before a crash was heard. Nurse Rita was heard yelling at Lloyd by this point.

"Looks like he didn't miss that time," Eddie stated.

"It appears you are correct, Ed," stated Ernie

Christian went back to reading the paper as the guys continued playing cards. During an article Christian found himself engrossed in, one dealing with the minor, yet apparently major, differences with the Sunni and Shiite Muslims in Iraq, the five elderly gents started giggling and laughing up a storm as the aroma of cigars filled the room. Sure enough, when Christian focused his attention back onto them, all five of them were enjoying freshly lit cigars.

"Is smoking allowed here?" he asked with a certain amount of surprise.

"No, it's not," Frank told him.

"Yes it is," Eddie corrected with a sly smile.

"No, it *isn't*," Frank quickly retorted while shooting Eddie a look. "There isn't any smoking allowed here."

"It is if you go outside."

"In case if you forgot, we're not outside."

"No, I didn't forget."

"Why do you smoke in here when all of you acknowledge that we aren't allowed to?" Christian asked as a smile crossed his face.

"Because we can," Walt casually told him.

"But not all of us have acknowledged that we can't," commented Eddie. "Remember, we're dementia patients."

"Some more than others," George slyly said while glancing at Eddie.

"Hey!" he quickly shot back. "What's that supposed to mean?"

"Oh, nothing. Just making a statement, is all."

Ed feigned insult. "Not all of us have dementia or Alzheimer's here."

"What's your excuse then?"

"Rather not talk 'bout it."

"Rather not because you forgot?" George smiled.

Eddie glared at him. "At least I don't need to get an erection to wash my dick off."

"At least I can still *get* an erection."

The dirty jokes and name calling continued on for a few more minutes as Christian continued reading.

"Hey, hey Joe!" George called out a bit later as a tall, elderly man entered the room. "Pull up a chair. You're just in time to enjoy a fine cigar and a crappy game of poker. How's that sound?"

"That sounds good to me," Joe softly answered while making his way over to the table before sitting down next to George. He accepted a cigar before Frank reached over to light it for him."

When Christian heard Joe's voice, a ring of familiarity made his eyes jump from his newspaper to the newest, and seventh, member of the room. Christian remembered seeing Joe a couple of times before at Forestry Park and each time with the feeling of déjà vu. He was also the same man who waved to him when the day he and Miho came to check out the facilities: Joe was the one in the wheelchair near the duck pond. The only difference now was that Joe was walking rather than being confined to a the chair.

"How's the leg, Joe?" Walt asked him.

Joe puffed on his cigar a few times before saying anything. "This truly is a fine cigar," he acknowledged approvingly while studying it. "As for my leg, the leg's doing fine, Frank. Still a little stiff, but Wellwood said it's going to be just fine."

"Just to let you know, your buddy has his wheels back," George informed him while dealing out a fresh hand.

"Oh, dear God." Joe shook his head. "I thought they took that away from him."

"They did," Frank said. "Apparently they just gave them back. Just recently. He came whipping on down through a little while ago."

"Has he taken out anyone yet?"

"Sounded like he may have put Myrtle temporarily out of commission," Eddie replied while taking his turn. "Other than that, we dunno."

"If he did that job right, we'd be able to read the paper for more than an hour or so," Ernie stated. "I always hated it when she had to gimp that bony, wrinkly ass of hers down here to grab that day's paper for that damn litter box of hers. There *is* no cat! And, even if there were, she doesn't need to change that damn box every day. She can wait a day or two."

"You know what we outta do?" George's mischievous twinkle in his eye shown while asking that. "Get a cat and stuff it in a position where it's taking a crap. Not one of those little crappers but one of those nice, big, juicy loggers," he said while using his hands to gage the size of it. "Make it look like it's straining to get it out and put it in that damn box of hers. Then we all take bets on how long it'll take her to notice that the cat hasn't moved yet."

The whole table broke out in laughter at that. Two or three of them coughed and sputtered uncontrollably in the process.

"At least it'll give us some time to read the paper," remarked Walt.

Meanwhile, Christian couldn't take his eyes off of Joe. There was something very familiar about him, even though he couldn't figure it out. Their eyes met for a brief moment and Christian felt sure he noticed a hint of recognition in the old man's eyes, but it soon past when Joe nodded and turned back to the card game.

Christian sat there for a minute or two longer studying Joe. He took in every feature, every line, and every wrinkle he could while storing them away as best he could for future reference. He had never experienced déjà vu this extreme before in his life. The one time that he had, he couldn't remember anything about it. Even Joe's voice and name were familiar somehow but even those weren't enough to fit the pieces together. It was like something was drawn from his childhood somehow but whether it was his memory or his illness, something wouldn't let him remember. Maybe it was nothing but maybe, just maybe, it wasn't nothing. The feeling of recognition Christian had of this elderly man was something he couldn't shake and it frustrated him.

He soon gave up trying to figure it out while going back to his article. When he was done, he left the room to explore more of the facility. There was still almost an hour and a half left before dinner and, even though he had been there roughly three weeks and wandered around whenever possible, a lot of what he saw he forgot. He wanted to use as much of that to familiarize himself with what he hadn't already.

The only part of the facility that he hadn't already explored was outside. He went to his room and pulled an old gray wool sweater Miho had given him before venturing outside. The day was overcast, the sky was dimming, and a slight breeze was present. Even though it was December, it hadn't snowed yet. Flakes were threatening to show themselves, they still lacked the courage to fall.

The landscape of the yard looked like it was well manicured during the good weather. The drive, which was roughly a half-mile long, was lined alternately with red spruce and grey birch. The shrubbery that lined the front consisted of barberry, dogwood, spireas, and dwarf Scotch pine. A dual-layer privet-shrub fence lined the front yard by the road. The privet receded to a spruce and maple forest-like fence on both sides of the yard which extended the entire length of the yard before being met in the backyard. The total acreage of the yard Christian gauged to be five acres, but he wasn't sure if he was right on this or not.

Before too long, Christian made his way to the pond out back and sat on one of the benches the patio had to offer. The ducks that were there quacked loudly while invading the space around him. One was bold enough to come up to nibble on one of his shoelaces. The bulk of them were the domesticated white breed, as well as mallards, but there were also a few scoots mixed in. Canada geese also inhabited space amongst them.

Some type of torpedo-shaped goldfish, probably koi, swam freely in the pond. Some were at the surface nearest to him looking for food much the same as the ducks and geese were.

He sat there thinking for forty-five minutes under the darkening sky. For the amount of time that he had been there at Forestry Park, Christian didn't feel like he progressed as positively as he would have liked. His memory was stable thanks to the medicine and other treatments he was receiving, but he still could feel it slipping away. His head was occasionally tingly, like it was after he and Shawn fought that last time, but the sensation would visit more often now than it had and would stay longer during those visits. He believed that the only reason he stayed consistent was because of the help he was receiving there.

He missed his family immensely and desperately wanted to be back home with them, but also greatly feared that if he left to do so that he would lose what was left of his facilities and his memory would fade even faster and, as a result, would purge any memory he struggled to keep. Though he didn't want his children to see him like this, not seeing them at all caused him equal disparity.

Besides his present memories, he didn't want to lose those of his childhood. Of course he still remembered his mom, dad, and Shawn, he still found those memories were harder to retain. He wondered how his memories would fade and in what order. He feared that his last remaining thoughts would only be that from Forestry Park.

He also feared that he and Shawn wouldn't, or couldn't, reconcile their differences before he unofficially became brain dead. Even though Shawn ignored any type of reconnection Christian had attempted, Christian decided to write a letter that night to him to explain everything while not leaving anything out. He also decided to give Shawn an ultimatum: either come forward so they could try and reconcile or to stay away permanently like he had the last decade as total strangers. Christian would put everything onto Shawn's lap. He would make Shawn be the one to decide their status for he was done trying. He didn't want to die while still getting a response from him, but if he chose not to respond, Christian would then forget about him. Christian would choose that way until his brain took that option for him. After that, he would focus his attention on his family for they were all he had left.

While deciding on how to word the letter, a shuffling noise came from behind him. Christian turned to see Joe walking towards him with help from a cane.

"I'm sorry, I don't mean to scare you," Joe apologized.

"That's ok. You didn't scare me."

While looking at him, Christian got that déjà vu feeling all over again. There was just something behind Joe's eyes that suggested that they knew each other previously. He desperately tried to remember again where he knew this old man from, refusing to believe it was merely a simple case of confusion or déjà vu, but couldn't.

"Would I be intruding if I sat on the bench with you?" Joe asked as he nodded towards the vacant space next to Christian. In the same instance, he pulled out a plastic bag of crumbs from his jacket pocket. "I've got some old bread and cookies I know they'd like."

"No, not at all," Christian said while moving over to make more room on the bench.

"Thank-you." Joe sat down before opening his bag. "I've seen you around here the last few weeks."

"I've seen you too."

"When I first saw you, when you came with your wife, I thought you were coming here to visit someone," Joe softly told him while throwing a handful of crumbs onto the ground. The crumbs quickly disappeared after being attacked by the waterfowl. "I found out after that I was wrong. The more I saw you, the more I realized you're a resident here."

"I could be here on sabbatical," Christian commented dryly.

"That's true, but please forgive me if I say that I highly doubt that." Joe snickered before passing the bag of crumbs over to Christian. "Would you like some?"

"Sure. Why not?" He accepted a handful of the damaged food inside before spreading them about the ground near his feet. As he was wiping his hands free of crumby residue, he stopped as the thought about what Joe had said to him. "How did you know that woman I came here with was my wife?"

"I saw her with you in a few articles that I've read."

"What articles?"

"Ones in the newspapers and magazines," Joe explained while continuing to feed the ducks. "There were a few about you once you got hurt from boxing, as well as what you've been up to since getting out. They talked about your teaching, your charity work, things like that."

"You know who I am?" Christian questioned as a feeling of paranoia slowly crept inside him.

"Of course."

"How long have you know?"

"Ever since I first saw you."

"That's not what I meant," Christian told him. "How come you never said anything to me before now?"

Joe shrugged. "The opportunity never came up."

"How many others here know who I am?"

"Most of the people here do, but most of them know you only as 'the kid patient.' Very few of us know you as Christian Eaton, former cruiserweight boxing champion of the world."

"You seem to know more about me than I do you," Christian said while looking at his visitor suspiciously.

"What can I say? I'm a fan." Joe smiled before stopping briefly to think. "But you know more about me than you give yourself credit for, or at least you used to."

"I highly doubt that," Christian informed him as Joe shrugged. "How long have you been here?"

"About twenty, twenty-five years or so."

"Long time."

"It is indeed."

"Why'd you come here?"

"I was in a car accident about thirty years ago over in St. Louis. The results are the reason as to why I eventually came here."

They sat there in silence as Joe finished feeding his crumbs to the birds before looking at his watch.

"Dinner will be in another twenty minutes or so," him said before looking up at the sky. "Do you like the food here?"

"Not bad. I'd rather eat at home, though."

"Is your wife a good cook?"

"Yes she is, but I do most of the cooking, that is, when I was home."

Hearing this, Joe looked at him in silence. "I'm not surprised by that," he soon stated before looking back to the darkening sky.

"Though my mom is a better cook than the both of us."

"I agree with you on that."

"On what exactly?"

"Your mom has always been a good cook."

Christian looked sharply at the tall, elderly man sitting next to him when he heard this. He continued to observe every detail he could from the heavily creased face before him while trying to interpret what Joe meant by his comment.

"You knew my mother?" he soon asked.

"I did a long time ago, before I came here," Joe confirmed with a nod. "How's your brother Shawn doing?"

"How do you know about them?"

Smiling slightly, Joe shifted his position in silence. When it seemed like he wasn't going to answer the question, he spoke. "Have you spoken to him lately?"

"No. Only once since our last match."

Joe sounded surprised when he heard this. "Only once in all this time?"

"Yes."

"What happened?" The elderly man seemed to know the answer to this but asked merely out of politeness.

"We had a falling out." Christian shrugged. "He seemed to want his own identity, one that didn't involve me or my family. Once he got his current promoter, I guess that kind of sealed the deal."

"Do you think his promoter, this Duke Snyder, was a major influence in this?"

Christian thought briefly before answering. "Once they partnered up, I do. Before then, Shawn seemed to just be needing a little push to go in that direction. Either way, it didn't take too much coaxing at that point."

"Huh," Joe grunted while thinking about that. "Shawn had always had that independent, 'leave me alone' attitude, but I never thought he'd do this. Have your parents heard from him lately?"

"They've heard less from him than I have." Christian continued to stare at Joe. "So who are you? Really?" he blurted out before he know it had happened.

Turning to face Christian and meet his gaze, Joe said, "Don't I look familiar to you?"

"There is something vaguely familiar about you, though I can't place it."

Joe, meanwhile, looked back up to the sky while taking in a deep breath. "Does your dad still have that apartment above the garage?"

"Sort of. He wanted to turn it completely into a storage unit, but my mom wanted it left as a spare bedroom. They ended up compromising about that. How'd you know about that?"

With that, there was a long pause after the question was asked. Joe obviously was contemplating what to say. Finally, after what seemed an eternity to Christian, Joe seemed to have the words to answer it with.

Joe faced him to say, "Because I used to live there, in that apartment."

Christian's mouth dropped and eyes squinted when he heard that. "You couldn't have. My dad had that made for my, for my..."

He found himself unable to finish his sentence. He was afraid of what the words that came out would mean. As he continued to look at the old man next to him, the pieces of his scrambled memory seemed to finally fit back into place at that moment. He was about to speak, to acknowledge what this all could mean, but he found that he couldn't. How he hated the silence between them and the agony of what he knew was to be right.

"It looks like it may snow tonight," Joe commented while still looking at the sky.

The comment broke their uncomfortable silence as Christian jumped slightly. His face was now a ghostly white as he started to believe his thoughts and instincts.

"It can't be," he softly whispered. "It just can't be."

"On the contrary," Joe said while finally meeting Christian's gaze. "It does look like it'll snow sometime tonight. We're all times captives and hostages to eternity."

"I don't believe it. It's not possible."

"I've gotten pretty good at predicting the weather, especially with these knees of mine," the old man said while rubbing both of his knees. "When I say it's going to snow, it really *is* going to snow."

"N-n-no, n-n-not th-th-that," Christian gasped as tears started to fill his eyes. "Y-y-you really c-c-can't be m-m-my m-m-my…"

"Yes, Christian, I am." Joe sighed while finally answering and cementing the question at hand. "I am your grandfather."

Chapter 49

"G-G-Grandpa Joe, is th-th-that you?" Christian stuttered.

"Yes Christian, it's me."

"I th-th-thought you were d-d-dead."

"For while there it felt like I was. Then, it wasn't so much it felt like I was as opposed to I actually *did* want to die," Joe softly said before a sigh left his mouth. He went silent before staring at the birds around them. "But, as you can tell, I didn't. Die, that is. And I am so grateful that I hadn't."

Sitting there in silence, Christian was too shocked by the news he had just received. He simply stared ahead into the pond's water. He was not really seeing the water but, rather, looking through it. He honestly had no idea what to think, say, or feel.

"But why?" he finally blurted out. "Why were we told you were dead?"

"Because I was so close to death that no one expected me to survive."

"W-w-who else knows about this? Or am I the only ones not to know?"

"Your dad was the only other one who knew. Everyone else was in the same boat as you."

"So, just my dad knew?" Christian asked while still looking at his grandfather. "No one else did?"

"Well, there were the doctors and nurses, of course." Joe laughed awkwardly at this. "Some of my friends knew."

"Your friends? Why didn't they say anything to us about it? Did you tell them not to?" he almost demanded while receiving a slight nod from his grandfather.

Joe shook his head. "On the contrary, they thought you knew."

"How?"

"When they came to see me, a number of times your dad was there," Joe explained. "With him there, they assumed the rest of the family knew. They had no reason to question it."

"When was the decision made to tell us you were dead?" Christian asked him straight out. "Any why my dad? Why was he the only one to know?"

"When I was in the hospital," Joe started to explain before going silent, watching the waterfowl in the process. "Like I mentioned before, I was so close to death that no one thought I would make it out alive. Your dad got three or four opinions from some of the best doctors in Missouri, where I had that accident, and they all came back with the same answer. When I slipped into a coma, it just seemed to confirm what they had said. I had a living will made up beforehand stating I didn't want to be put on any type of life support. The doctors honored that and they all waited for me to die. I had your dad tell you guys I was dead or, at the very least, wouldn't last very long. I guess I chose the former.

"I ended up being comatose for a couple of years before waking up. The doctors assumed I'd be a vegetable if I ever did wake up. And I was for a good amount of time after that. Those first few months I was like that, not really sure what the hell was going on. I eventually went through therapy to help me regain my strength and, if possible, my speech."

"Couldn't you have let us know you were all right?" Christian asked him.

"In effect, I've never been right since," Joe told him while looking at him. "Like I said, I was in a coma for a number of years after the accident and a vegetable after waking up. The doctors still didn't think I'd be much more above that. Once I was pretty close to being back to normal, I thought it'd be best if we continued with the charades. I was planning on telling you guys at one point, but decided to wait when Shawn started getting into all that trouble when he was a teenager. I felt that was enough for you guys to handle at that time. I guess that gave me another excuse to hide from reality until I was able to accept myself for what I had become. I guess I still hadn't learned to deal, or live, with it. I had become the one thing I strove not to become – a coward. My body wasn't the same, my mind wasn't either. I'm not talking about my age; I know both of these recede over time, but they were already diminished beforehand."

"And you thought we couldn't accept you as a result of that?"

"Christian, as smart as you are, you just aren't listening to me." Joe looked at his grandson while setting his jaw. "I'm saying I couldn't accept myself for what had happened to me!"

"Why?"

Joe sighed while slightly shaking his head. "Maybe you don't get it. I was hoping you would, really, I was, but….," he said before going quiet while thinking how to word what he wanted to say. "Let's see if this makes sense. Alright? What I considered my strengths was mainly my body and what I could do physically. Just like your brain is your biggest asset. My body and physicality was mine. The one thing that really defined us was the same thing that was our ultimate downfall."

"We have other strengths than what you just mentioned," Christian told him.

"That's easy for you to say, you still have your strength to use but look at me! I can't even walk without this goddamn cane or with a damn limp!"

"But you can still walk, can't you?" Christian stated before pausing. "You can even remember your son's name, right? Me, well, I don't have a cane nor a limp, but ask me what my kids names are and I most likely couldn't tell you depending on the day. I even forgot how old they are. Miho had to give me this little flipbook with pictures of everyone in the family, as well as friends, and on the back it has their names and a little personal bio about them. My memory's at the point where I can't even remember my own family's name or any little detail about that I'd like to remember. "

Christian sighed before looking to the pond before them. A number of fish broke its surface, ripples permeated around them. "I think about when I'll eventually forget their faces, their laughter, and the sound of their voices. What scares me the most is when they come for a visit, all I'll ever see are the faces of strangers looking at me."

"Right now, can you tell me the names of your family?" Joe questioned him.

"Well, Miho is my wife. And for my kids," Christian said with a sigh before taking a deep breath and exhaling it loudly. He went silent while thinking for the answer. "I remember we named them after people we know. I named our son and Miho named our daughter. Oh, that's right, I named our son after my trainer. What was his name again?"

"Wasn't your trainer's name Dom?"

"Was it? Oh, that's right, it was. Our son's same is Dominic." Christian laughed from embarrassment at this. "As for our little girl, I'm not sure. All I know is you better not let her hear you call her little. She absolutely hates that."

"My lips are sealed." Joe went along while drawing his fingers across his lips as if closing an invisible zipper.

"As for her name, I want to say she got it from one of the females on Miho's side. An aunt or sister, somebody. No, wait, Miho got the name from her mother. Her mother's name is Yukiko, but that's not the name of our daughter but I do know it dealt with her mother."

"What the mother's middle name?"

"It's Asako. Oh, that's right," Christian said with a chuckle. "Our daughter's name is Asako. Incidentally, they're coming up for the weekend if you'd like to meet them."

"I'd love to but I wouldn't want them to know who I was just yet. Maybe once I got more comfortable with having a family, you can tell them then."

"That's alright. I'll have you meet them but we won't tell them who you really are to me. I'll most likely forget myself," Christian said with a laugh before looking sharply back to his grandfather. "Wait, how'd you know my trainer's name was Dom?"

"I followed your career, as well as Shawn's," Joe replied with a shrug. "Very closely."

"You did?" He was surprised to hear that but smiled as if given a very flattering compliment.

Joe nodded with this. "Yeah, from your first fight all the way 'til your last."

"The last fight was just after he broke apart from us and went on his own. I sure wish I knew that was going on with him. And I sure wish I could somehow, I don't know, get us back to being a family before I look all my...," Christian left that last comment open while waving his around the side of his head.

"Have you forgotten much?" his grandfather softly asked.

"I'm not sure. And I'm not sure if I'll even know if I forget something."

"Take plenty of pictures and write a lot of notes."

"Yeah, really," Christian agreed as he sat there in silence thinking about what his grandfather just said. "I hope it doesn't get to be that bad, but I doubt it. So, Grandpa, if you don't mind me asking, why exactly are you here?"

Hearing his, Joe laughed briefly at his grandson's straight forwardness but soon found himself answering the question. "It appears that during the car accident I was in many years ago, I developed some brain damage. They say it's in my brain's frontal lobe, but I don't know. I came here pretty much to hide myself away, but also just in case anything should surface with it."

Before either of them were able to add anything more to the conversation, the sound of someone walking behind them. They turned to see who was coming.

"There you two are," Nurse Rita said as she approached. "We've been looking all over for you. You should let someone know when you decide to wander outside."

"Neither of us wandered out here," Joe told here. "To wander sounds like walking aimlessly without thought. We both knew where we were going when we came out here."

Hearing this, Rita exchanged a hard glare with Joe before announcing it was time for supper. She then turned and left without waiting to hear for a response.

Christian and Joe sat there in silence for a few more minutes before Joe rose and announced he was going in to eat. Christian followed suit with him.

Dinner that night was like every other dinner Christian had had there. Here, you were part of one of two groups: one who couldn't wait on themselves and one that could. Christian was both fortunate and grateful to be currently in the latter, though he wasn't sure for how much longer.

If you weren't able to wait on yourself, such as people in wheelchairs or other severe handicaps, you would order your meal ahead of time, usually at dinner the previous night, and the staff would bring it out to you. If you were able to, however, you could still choose this option of you could opt for standing in line for your food, a line that Christian usually visited. The food in line wasn't any different to what the pre-ordered meals were, but the line gave an added freedom for the patients.

Outside of Christian's pork chops being a little tough and his mixed vegetables being a little rubbery, he enjoyed his meal. In fact, he enjoyed most of his meals there.

He and Grandpa Joe ate together as they occupied a corner table while talking about various things, mostly miscellaneous and personal subjects. Christian found that his memory was still as good as it used to be when it came to pulling specifics from past events such as dates and places. He also found that time seemed to slightly mix itself up within his head. An event that had happened a year ago was next to something that took place a decade earlier but, in his mind, they happened relatively close to each other. During their dinner conversation, Christian and Joe both acknowledged that they couldn't mend any fences, bury any hatches, or make up for lost time during one single conversation. They each felt, though, they were having a good start.

"Do you like the music?" Joe asked while pointing to an elderly man in the far corner of the cafeteria.

The man, who appeared to be in his 60s, was playing an acoustic guitar while singing into a microphone. The music he was playing was a cross of American folk and acoustic rock; it also had some country thrown into the mix.

"He's not bad," Christian said approvingly. "Why do you ask?"

"No reason." Joe shrugged. "He's comes here periodically. Some here don't really like his music, others do."

"I don't think I've seen him before. There was that one woman who comes a couple times a week."

"Oh, the one with the bright orange tan and overly white teeth? She was his replacement," Joe said with a twinkle in his eye while nodding to the guitar-playing singer. "Hughes said they weren't having him back because a couple of people here didn't really like him. He brought her in the next day or so."

"Did he really think she was better than this guy?" Christian scoffed. "She used to yodel when she sang and she didn't even know how to play. Besides, either her tan or teeth would blind anyone who looked at her."

"I concur. And so did Hughes."

"Then why did he bring her in then?"

Joe shrugged. "To stick it to the few who actually did complain. When the complainers heard her, they realized this guy was actually decent. Besides, he's a local guy, out near Oyster Bay, and is labeled as a sort of up-and-comer."

"But he's in his 60s."

"He does have a name around here in Long Island as a musician," Joe told him. "You have to understand Hughes. He won't pass up the opportunity to bring in a guy who may get a record contract. That way, he can brag that he found this guy or that he used to play here. That sort of thing."

"Is he always thinking about publicity?"

"Most of the time. He doesn't have much else, I don't think."

"What about family and friends?"

"What about them? I don't know, but I highly doubt if he has any or, if he does, he doesn't really care. He must but I've never seen or heard about them."

"Hmmm," Christian sighed while looking around the cafeteria. "What'll the guys from our floor have planned for tonight?"

"The usual bunch will probably be playing cards while a couple of others will be having a wheelchair race in the hallways."

"Wheelchair races?"

"You know, first guy to drive his wheelchair from point A to point B wins?" Joe smiled with a shrug. "Wheelchair races."

"Won't Rita get upset with them?"

"Of course she will, but she understands that we don't have anything else to do to keep occupied. As long as we follow the rules she established, everything will be fine."

"She established rules for these races?"

"Someone had to. She thought it be best if it was her so she could at least be able to control them better. It's worked so far."

"How long have they been doing these races?" Christian asked.

"Off and on for about a year."

"I haven't seen any since being here."

"Hughes ordered those to stop after your roommate ran over Beckman."

"From what I've heard, he wasn't run over during a race," Christian told him. "Lloyd went after him unprovoked, right?"

"Didn't matter."

"What makes you think they'll have the races tonight after Hughes said they couldn't?"

Joe smiled. "I heard some of the guys talking about it."

"That should be fun to see."

You should get involved if you like."

"They'll let me race?" Christian asked with some enthusiasm. "The idea does sound fun."

"Sure. Why not?" His grandfather shrugged. "Always looking for some fresh meat to join in."

Christian smiled. "I might just do that."

"You might have fun," Joe told him before sitting there a moment or two longer in silence. He soon got up and looked at his grandson. "I think I'll go back up. I want to see if they're still playing that damn game of theirs and, if they are, find out who's winning. Are you coming?"

"No, not just yet," Christian said while leaning back in his chair. He looked around while stretching. "I sort of want to let things settle first. I'll be up shortly."

"Suit yourself." Joe shrugged while picking up his tray of empty plates before leaving the cafeteria.

Christian continued sitting where he was for several more minutes while thinking about everything that's been happening of late. He soon got up, discarded his plates where they needed to go, and soon went up to the second floor's rec room.

Chapter 50

"Hi'ya, Christian," Dr. Allen said when they saw each other in the hall. "How ya been?"

"Been good considering. How're you doing, Doc?"

"Oh, I'm doing the same. And, please, call me Doug."

"No problem, ah, Doug. Also, aren't you here a little late?"

"A little. My wife's outta town for business and that gave me an excuse to stay late to finish up some things that I've been wanted to get done."

"And you needed her to be away for you to do that?" Christian asked him as a smile came over his face.

Dr. Allen merely smiled at this while not answering the question. Instead, he changed the subject. "I just saw your grandfather a minute or two ago."

"Yeah, he was going to the rec room to play cards or something. Hey, wait a sec. You know that he's my grandfather?"

"Oh, good golly yes," Allen confessed. "I've known for quite some time now."

"Why didn't you say anything about this to me before?"

"He asked me not to," he explained. "He didn't want us to say anythin until he was ready to tell you. I hope you understand, but I couldn't as a result of the doctor-patient confidentiality."

Christian sighed. "Oh, ok. It looks like I was the last to know."

"Don't be so hard on him," Doug told him. "He's wanted to tell you for some time now. How are you taking all of this?"

"How do you think? I just found out less than two hours ago that my grandfather, who I thought was dead for thirty years, is alive. I think it'll take me a little while to get used to this."

"Don't be so hard on him, he meant well. It's been difficult for him to keep this secret of his for as long as he had. If you need someone to talk to about this, my door's always open," Doug told him with a great amount of sincerity.

Christian thought about it before nodding his head. "Thanks, Doc. I'll keep that in mind. I may just take you up on that."

"Okie dokie." Allen said before looking at his watch. "Oh, geez, look at the time. I've been dawdling a little too long. I should get going. I'm almost done with some work and I wouldn't mind finishing it sometime tonight."

"Alright, I'll talk with you later." Christian extended a hand to him. Allen accepted the handshake while nodding with a smile. The two parted ways soon after as Doug went back to his office and Christian continued on to the rec room.

"Hey, Champ!" Eddie shouted when Christian entered the rec room.

"How you doing?" Christian replied in a horrible Italian accent while trying to do his best mobster impersonation. In the process, he noticed the usual group was there: Eddie, Ernie, Frank, George, and Walt. Grandpa Joe was also in with them. All were playing cards and all were smoking cigars. The room was heavily laden with smoke as the six men laughed amongst themselves as Frank dealt.

"What the hell was that?" asked Eddie.

"What was what?"

"That thing you just did. What the hell was that?"

"Oh, that?" Christian asked while realizing what exactly was being asked. "That was my Italian mobster impression."

"Is that what that was? I thought you were giving us your take of a dead fish."

"Was it that bad?" Christian smiled while sitting on the couch.

"Let me put it to you this way; if you do it again, you'll be sleepin' with 'em." retorted Eddie with a more authentic Italian accent and swagger. "Does that answer your question?"

"Perfectly," Christian told him while grabbing a section of that day's paper he hadn't already read.

"Aren't you done with that paper, Champ?" George asked.

"Aren't you done playing cards yet?" he asked in return.

"We haven't decided who the winner is yet. As soon as we know, we'll stop playing." George shrugged. "You can't expect us to stop playing before we know who the winner is, can you?"

"How long have you been playing this game of yours?"

"This particular game has been going on for four days," George stated before glancing down at his watch. "Nine hours, fourteen minutes, and twenty-eight seconds."

"You've been playing this card game for four days?"

"And nine hours, fourteen minutes, and now forty-two seconds."

"Whatever." Christian shook his head as he went back to his paper. "What I meant was that his one individual game's lasted over four days?"

"Yeah. What's your point?"

Christian sat there in silence while trying to figure out if they were being serious or not and, after deciding that they were, posed another question. "What's taking you guys so long?"

"So long at what?" Ernie asked.

"At finishing this one game of yours."

"We aren't in any hurry," Frank told him.

"That's fairly obvious," Christian dryly said while flipping through his paper.

"Son, at our age and with what problems we have, what the hell else do we have to worry about?" Walt asked him directly.

"Good point."

"What's that supposed to mean? Huh?!" Ernie demanded. "You telling us that we *don't* have anything else to do but play cards? Huh, is that it?"

"No, I didn't mean it like that at all," Christian said in his defense.

"Then how did you mean it? Tell me!"

"Ernie, take it easy," Joe said softly. "My grandson didn't mean anything by it."

"Like hell he didn't! He was trying to say..." Ernie stated hotly before cutting himself off. He found himself looking between Christian and Joe multiple times before finally focusing on the elder Eaton. "Grandson? This kid's your grandson?"

"He is," Joe answered with a smile.

"Well, I'll be." Ernie whistled while looking at Christian. "Sorry 'bout that, kid. I didn't realize Joe here was your granddaddy."

"What difference would that make if he was my grandfather or not?" Christian smiled slightly while looking at him.

Hearing this, Ernie sat there to think up a possible answer before shrugging. "I guess it doesn't much, kid, now does it?"

"Not to me it doesn't," Christian told him with a smile and shake of the head. He went back to reading his paper while ignoring the sounds the group of old men made, which only lasted a few minutes before the sounds of cans were heard cracking open.

"Damn it, Walt!" Ernie shouted. "Don't be gettin' the fuckin' foam from that on my cards! Ya hear me?"

"Sorry about that," Walt said apologetically.

"Don't be sorry. Just don't do it!"

Christian peered from around the paper to see Eddie finish passing cans of beer around to the other guys.

"Old Milwaukee Light?! What the hell is this shit?" George asked while looking at the can he held in his hand.

"Like you just said, it's Old Milwaukee Light," Eddie retorted sarcastically. "It's a type of beer, if you didn't know."

"I know what it is, you jackass!" George retorted irritably while setting his can of beer down on the table. "Why the hell do you have this pale, weak shit? Lemonade has more potency than this crap."

"My son got it for me," Eddie explained. "I get sick if I mix the better beer with my medication. But, seeing that you don't want it," he said while reaching across the table to take back the can of beer he had previously offered. "I think I'll just offer this to the kid over there, instead."

"Hey, hey, hey," George said while rising a little in his chair while his arms stretched out to take the beer back. "Pass that shit back on over here. There's no need to be hasty just yet," he told him while taking the beer back and sitting it down next to him. "If you want the kid to have one, you can give him one from that stash of yours."

Shrugging, Eddie reached into a small duffle bag at his feet that Christian didn't see while pulling out another can of beer. "You want one, kid?"

"No, thank-you," Christian politely refused while shaking his head. "Hey would you mind if I turned the news on?"

'The what?" Eddie asked after not being able to hear him from the laughter the other guys were giving off.

"I wanted to watch the news on TV. It that ok?"

"Yeah, sure kid, go ahead." Eddie waved to the TV before going back to his half-smoked cigar, can of warm beer, and card game at hand.

Christian turned on the television to hear the ending of the weather.

"...so expect the temperature to drop down into the low twenties tonight, and by morning we could have anywhere from six to eight inches of snow. Other than that, it'll be clear blue skies for the rest of the week. Back to you, Scott," the weatherman reported.

"Thank-you, Jacob," Scott said. The caption under him identified him as Scott Nelson, anchorman of the local television station. "If you're a boxing fan, you've probably heard of Shawn Calloway winning the IBF heavyweight championship last night in Las Vegas," he announced as a picture of Shawn came up on the screen, one that had been take when he was awarded the belt. "but you may not know is what happened in its aftermath. Calloway was placed in police custody early this morning after a DWI related car accident he was involved in."

As Christian focused on the TV, he noticed from the corner of his eye that Grandpa Joe was watching it as well.

"From what police have gathered, Calloway had spent the better part of the night celebrating his newly won championship when a challenge of sorts turned into a drag race. The race ended when Calloway lost control of his car before crashing into a tree a few miles from his hotel. When emergency vehicles arrived, they found a number of bags of uncontrolled substances, several bottles of prescription painkillers, and an opened bottle of alcohol in Calloway's possession. Other than appearing confuses and severally intoxicated, Calloway appeared otherwise unharmed. He was taken to a local hospital to be checked out before being released back to the police. He was ticketed for possession of an illegal substance, driving while under the influence, speeding, reckless driving, reckless endangerment, driving with an open container, as well as a number of other charges. This arrest was the most recent of a long list Calloway has had, including several domestic dispute charges spurring from his upper Manhattan apartment. Calloway was unavailable for comment.

"In local news, Forestry Park, the clinic and rehabilitation center outside of the city of Glen Cove, was awarded a check in the amount of $2.5 million. The money was awarded to them via government grant in which they had applied for. Forestry Park is one of the nation's leading facilities helping people with various types of mental illness such as Alzheimer's and other forms of dementia. They also specialize in physical ailments stemming from mental disorders. One of their current patients is none other than Christian Eaton, former WBC, IBF, and WBO cruiserweight boxing champion and, coincidentally, brother to current IBF heavyweight champion Shawn Calloway," Nelson announced with a smile.

When he heard his name being mentioned, Christian's internal body temperature shot up to what felt like twenty degrees warmer as he started sweating profusely. He had hoped his stay there would be kept to only a select few of his choosing, but now seemed he would no longer have that luxury. He glanced briefly to the men at the card table and saw that they were all staring at him while realizing for the first time who exactly he was. His cheeks flushed from both anger and embarrassment.

"The person who accepted the check," Scott the anchorman continued, "was none other than Dr. Vincent Hughes, esteemed director of Forestry Park. Here is Dr. Hughes as he accepted the check earlier today."

The screen then changed to show Hughes standing in front of Forestry Park with a couple of people around him. Surprisingly, he seemed as tall as everyone else was. Christian assumed this was because he was standing on a few of the higher steps to bring himself up to their level.

"Oh behalf of everyone here at Forestry Park," Hughes said humbly after accepting the check, "I am honored to accept this gracious grant and I am deeply humbled by the generosity of this gift. The money will go far to advance what we already have, as well as give our patients hope for a brighter future. On behalf of myself and my staff, I would like to say thank-you. In exchange for accepting this, I would like to say that we are having a pancake breakfast this weekend that will

487

be open to the public. Here, people will get to see what exactly we do as well as see where this check will go towards. In addition to that, former cruiserweight champion of the world Christian Eaton will be in attendance. He was very honored to volunteer his time to help us out and will be available free of charge to sign autographs and have pictures taken with the public to all that attend. The pancake breakfast will be both Saturday and Sunday, and tickets will be made available for purchase as of noon today. Once again, thank-you all for this most generous contribution."

Hughes then waved to whatever crowd there was before him as the TV went back to Scott Nelson. Christian immediately got up to turn off the television, swearing to himself as he did so. He knew his memory was getting bad, but he knew damn well he didn't volunteer for any publicity pancake breakfast that coming weekend. That weekend he had planned to spend entirely with Miho and the kids.

As turned to face the room, he noticed all six pair of eyes were on him. Grandpa Joe, however, was the only one of the group that didn't look surprised by what was just heard. The other five all looked at him with surprise and open amazement.

"Are you *really* Christian Eaton?" Eddie asked.

Not knowing what else to say, Christian simply nodded.

"The former cruiserweight boxing champion?"

"Seriously, Eddie? Weren't you the one who was just calling me champ a few minutes ago?"

"I call everyone that," Eddie told him. "That didn't mean I knew who you were."

"Funny how I never heard you call anyone else that before."

"Maybe you need to pay attention a little bit more."

"I pay attention just fine, thank-you very much," Christian told him while making his way to the door.

"Where ya goin', Champ?"

"I'm going to have chat with that midget director of ours."

"You probably will be waiting a little while if you do," Frank told him.

"Why's that?"

"He's not here," Frank replied while dealing a new hand. "He's been out all day celebrating, I think, from getting that grant of his."

"You mean that grant he got because of me? When will he be back?"

"Try tomorrow morning," Joe answered that. "He'll want to brag and prance around here with it."

"Alright, tomorrow morning it is." Christian left the room at that point before anyone else could talk to him. His temper had already risen higher than he had wanted it to.

"Have fun this weekend," George blurted out just after Christian left the room. The statement was followed by laugher that stopped almost immediately by something Grandpa Joe had said. Whatever he did say, it worked effectively and it was something Christian himself could not hear.

Christian wasn't sure why Hughes had said that he would be doing this publicity stint this weekend but, considering the director, anything was possible. What upset him the most was that Hughes publicly announced Christian's participation without asking him first. The more he thought about it, the more upset he got. He convinced himself that once he spoke with Hughes that next day everything would be cleared up. But, somehow, he didn't quite believe that would actually happen.

When he came close to the nurses' station, a loud burst of laughter was heard from somewhere about. While trying to find its source, Lloyd came flying around the corner in his wheelchair as he whipped it for a head-on collision with his much younger roommate. Even though Christian could have sidestepped him and his wheelchair, ducked into a side room, or made some other attempt to get out of the way, he chose not to. He was walking close enough to the wall for Lloyd to have more than enough room around him but Lloyd was bound and determined to run him over.

Christian simply stood where he was and waited. As Lloyd approached, Christian noticed a folding chair up against the wall. He picked it up and used it as a barrier between him and his pursuer; the chair's legs positioned so they would be the first things that Lloyd would hit.

It took Lloyd a couple of seconds of seeing Christian with the outstretched chair before realizing he wasn't backing down. He soon tried to slow himself down but, by then, it was too late. He ran chest first into the chair before toppling over onto his back. Once the threat had passed, Christian dropped the chair and used his hands to pick Lloyd up off of the floor and pinned him against the wall in one motion.

"What the hell do you think you're doing, huh?!" Christian demanded. "Trying to run me over with that damn chair of yours?!"

Lloyd was too scared at that moment to answer. All he could do was look at his younger counterpart through terrified eyes. As long as he had been terrorizing the halls, no one had objected the way his roommate was doing at that moment. While looking as Christian, what he had previously presumed was an easy-going pushover was now a person of extreme anger. Not only was he pinned fairly well against the wall but, after looking down, Lloyd noticed there was easily a two-foot gap between his feet and the floor.

"Answer me, will you?!" Christian demanded again as he soon began banging Lloyd against the wall.

Before an answer could be given, Rita came out of nowhere to try and break it up.

"Mr. Eaton, what do you think you're doing?!"

"What the hell does it look like I'm doing?" he replied without looking at her.

"It looks like you're about to put Mr. Anderson down before things get out of hand."

"Things have *already* gotten out of hand once Lloyd here got his damn chair back! Didn't it, Lloyd?" he asked while slamming his roommate against the wall again. "This miserable bastard ran over Myrtle earlier today and he just tried to run my ass over just now."

"Mr. Anderson, is this true?" Rita asked while looking at Lloyd.

He didn't answer. Instead, he chose to just stare at Christian.

"Lloyd! Is this true?" Rita asked again, this time with a great deal of authority in her voice.

The tone make Lloyd flinch a little bit. "Ah, yeah. Yeah, it's true. It's all true. Now, will you put me down?"

"Why should I, huh?" Christian asked him.

"Mr. Eaton, will you please put him down?"

"Only if he promises *not* to run over anyone again in that damn chair of his," Christian explained while he and Rita looked at Lloyd.

"Well? We're waiting, Mr. Anderson."

"You want me to promise that?" Lloyd asked while seeming to get back some of his rebellious personality.

"Yes, we do."

"Here's my promise, then." He smiled before spitting a big, juicy wad of saliva full into Christian's face.

Immediately after being spat on, Christian slammed Lloyd against the wall one last time before letting go. Lloyd fell the two feet onto the floor beneath. After landing, Christian kicked him twice squarely in the ribs, which he found extremely satisfying and seemed to take a heavy weight off of his chest.

With that, he turned to see the staff working that wing were all watching him. Sighing heavily, Christian used his sleeve to wipe the saliva off of his face. He desperately wanted to go somewhere where he could be alone. Alone and away from Forestry Park. Away from Lloyd. Away from Hughes. And away from anything and anyone Christian felt would make his calming down any slower than he wanted it to. He wanted to go somewhere to think about that day's events as well as what he'd write in this letter to Shawn.

"I'm going out for a walk," he soon informed Rita before turning his back and left the scene.

Chapter 51

Dear Shawn,

I hope this letter finds you well like all my previous ones have. I often wonder why I keep trying to contact you after all these years with no prevail. And, after every time, I never come up with a single, reasonable, sane reason to why you would ever respond back. Let me get to the point by saying I am writing to you today for two reasons.

First, I wanted to tell you that this will not only be my last letter to you, but it will also by my last attempt to contact you in any way. I am choosing to delete you from my life much the same way you did to me years ago only, this time, I am acknowledging the deletion as compared to you choosing to ignore it. It has been evident for quite some time that you did not want to associate with me, or the family that raised you, the one you grew up with. You replaced us with another kind of family, one that gives you money, drugs, alcohol, women, and any other vice you choose to consume your life. This letter is to let you know that you are free. Free from me, free from your adopted parents, and free from any other humiliation and embarrassment that we obviously have shamed you with. This is my final gift to you. You are finally free.

This brings me to my second point for writing you this letter. I wanted to tell you that I am sick and quite literally will be losing what mind I have left in the years, maybe even months, to come. I don't mean a sickness like the common flue but, rather, a sickness of mental illness – dementia. I briefly mentioned this when last we spoke.

It all started when I lost to you in our third fight, in my "retirement" match. But, when I think about it, it actually started before that when you felt you had to break away and prove yourself, or whenever it was, that got the ball rolling towards that last matchup between us.

Anyway, because of that last fight, the abuse and trauma I received caused my brain to have a large cavuum septum pellucdium. In laymen's terms, I have a hole in my brain; a transparent, thin partition between my brain's hemispheres. There was other brain damage because of this fight, but this was the most significant, serious, and damaging one.

This eventually led to me having dementia pugilistica or, to you, boxer's dementia. It is also called punch-drunk syndrome, as well as a handful of other names. I have been battling symptoms of these for several years now, even though I have never told you until now. I figured you simply wouldn't care at all. You are now the last person of the family, and whatever friends I have, for me to tell.

Since you have made it quite clear, crystal in fact, that you would rather choose to ignore any and all of my attempts to contacts you, I am now choosing to ignore you for as long as my memory allows me to remember you. I want to spend the rest of my life, or what life my mind chooses for me to have, thinking about the family that I have. That family that I do have, today, is Mom and Dad, of course, whom you've chosen to also delete from memory; Miho, whom you seemed to accept because she wasn't white or American; my children, Asako and Dominic, whom you've never met; and Grandpa Joe.

That's right, I wrote that correctly, and I didn't stutter. Grandpa Joe is alive, though not well, and is living here at the same facility as I am here in Long Island. Apparently there was some accident he was in that that doctors didn't expect him to survive. That's the reasoning behind it; or that's what he says anyway. I'll be speaking with Dad later tonight to confirm this since he's the only one who knew about it. Apparently Mom doesn't even know he was alive.

Grandpa's been here about twenty-five years or so, all that time at Forestry Park. Forestry Park is a combination clinic and facility dealing mainly with mental disabilities right outside of Glen Cove, Long Island.

I will end this letter now before it gets any longer than it has to be. Again, this will be the last time I ever contact you, though I wish it wasn't. The ball is now in your court. Any, and all, communications between us will be totally up to you from this point henceforth. I truly wish things were different between us these last dozen or more years, but it's a bed you yourself have made, and rather than it just being you sleeping in it, we all are. Rather than simply losing a family member, I look at this, instead, as losing a member while at the same time gaining another with Grandpa Joe. So, to me, I just replaced you with him. Who did you replace all of us with? Whoever they are must be very special an important to be able to replace us all. That, or your new family is able to offer you things more valuable than what we were able to. Either way, I honestly do not know what to say.

I wish you all the best and I truly hope Duke Snyder will be able to offer you all the things that we, Dom include, were unable to.

Your brother with love,

Christian->

When he was done with the letter, Christian read it over before putting it in an already addressed and stamped envelope. He planned on mailing it that next day after he had a chance to speak with Dr. Hughes. After taking care of this, he turned off the little light he had above his bed and went to sleep.

***

"Christian, it's so good to see you again," Vincent Hughes said while answering his office door on the third knock the next morning. He said it in a failed attempt to act genuinely pleased to see him. "Please, come in, come in. What brings you to this part of the facilities?" he asked while walking over to his sofa where he had a lit cigar and a glass of brown colored liquor on its accompanying coffee table. Next to them lay a couple of folders, ones he closed upon sitting.

"Well, I'll cut right to it. I know you're really busy and I don't want to keep you," Christian said in his own failed attempt at niceties. "I came by to apologize, Dr. Hughes."

"Pleas, call me Vincent. Like I mentioned during our first encounter, I like to have a very laid back atmosphere here," he said arrogantly while pointing to one of his chairs. "Care to have a seat?"

"No, thank-you though," he declined. "I'll only be a moment."

"As for this apology of yours, what have you done to feel that you need to offer me one?"

"I'm apologizing because I already had a previous engagement this weekend when I agreed to help you out during this pancake breakfast of yours," Christian said as calmly as he could, with as straight a face he could muster, while looking at Hughes.

The director's arrogant smile vanished. It was replaced by a look that showed the true nature of who he truly was. He coldly asks, "What do you mean you had a previous engagement?"

"I mean just that, I had a previous engagement," Christian repeated himself. "I've seen my family only once since I've been here and they're coming up this weekend."

"You're canceling on me?" Hughes demanded in a soft, yet stern voice.

"Yes, sir, it looks that way. I made a request with Janet in person last week, before you asked me for my, um, help. I forgot to tell you because of my memory. You can check with her if you like to verify I'm telling you the truth."

"You can't cancel on my. You promised to help me, damn it. You promised!"

"I never promised you anything," Christian calmly stated while shutting the office door that was still open. "You involved me without even asking me first. Besides, my family comes first."

"But, here you are, apologizing to me while trying to get out of responsibilities you said you would do."

"I saw you on television yesterday as you announced my involvement this weekend. Up until now, you and I never discussed this," Christian told him as the two men exchanged cold stares.

"Are you telling me you don't remember the conversation we had late last week where I asked you directly about this?" the director asked with raised eyebrows, hoping this would settle the conversation.

"If you had, I made my own plans on Tuesday to spend this weekend with my family, days before this alleged conversation of ours."

Hughes sighed briefly while hanging his head. "I'm sorry to hear this, I truly am. But I cannot permit you to cancel your responsibilities with me."

"Again, I never agreed to them. They are not my responsibilities. Never have been. You forced them upon me when you publically announced it. You got yourself into this."

"That's beside the point. If you forgot, you have brain injuries that led you to have a poor memory. In other words, your forgetful. That's not my problem."

"It will be if I no show this weekend." Christian smiled. "And what could happen to me? I'm a dementia patient. With a bad memory. Who forgets things very, very easily. While living at a facility who is supposed to make sure their forgetful residents are taken care of."

"Mr. Eaton, please, sit down," he said in a manner that suggested it was not a request.

"I prefer to stand, thank-you." Christian smiled faintly as Hughes shot a glare up at him.

"Now, Christian, excuse my bluntness when I say this," Hughes said as his face became a colder coloration than before. "But sit your ass down, now!"

"Why should I? Why is it so important to you?"

"Listen here, you little punk," he snarled while pointing a finger before catching himself on how he was acting before reverting back to how he was when Christian first arrived. "Christian, I'm sorry, I've been under a lot of stress lately, particularly with this government grant I received."

"Wow. What are you using this second grant for?" Christian asked in an awe struck tone as he finally sat down in feigned interest.

"Which second grant do you mean?"

"Well, we at Forestry Park received a grant the other day," he politely explained while leaning back in his chair. "Now you say that you yourself got a grant, one for yourself. What's this for?"

"The grant I was referring to was the one for us, here, at Forestry Park. They're one in the same," Hughes calmly stated.

"Hmmm. I see," Christian simply stated while he and Hughes sat in silence staring at each other. Christian's expression was giving off a warm smile in a vain attempt to melt away the icy glare the director had. After a beat or two, he soon stood before speaking again. "Now, if you will excuse me, that's all I came up for. I'm sorry to be bothering you again. I have to get going to mail a letter now."

"Christian, we aren't through yet," Hughes stated with a soft, yet hard, edge to his voice as his visitor made his way to the office's door.

"Sure we are. What else is there to talk about?"

"We still have much to talk about your involvement this weekend for our pancake breakfast. Don't you remember?"

"I remember clearly explaining to you that I will not in attendance this weekend," Christian calmly reminded him. He found it increasingly difficult to remain calm to such an antagonizing, small, little man. "I'll be away with my family. Did you forget already? Besides, I do not remember you asking me to help either you, or the clinic, out by doing any publicity stints you arranged without my consent."

"When you leave for a nice family weekend, where do you plan on living when it's over?" Hughes coyly asked with a trace of mock innocence.

Catching it, Christian looked at him with a mild smile while saying, "Why, I'll be staying here, of course, since that's what I'm paying you for."

"Well, it'll be a shame for you to come back here thinking you have a warm bed to sleep in and hot food to eat, only to find that your slot has been replaced," Hughes mildly explained. "If you do this and not attend the event, one which you personally have been advertised to be in attendance, you'll find yourself living on the streets. I wouldn't advice that since I heard the weather will be quite cold this coming week."

"Are you actually looking out for my best interest, Dr. Hughes?" Christian asked.

"Oh, fuck no! I don't give a damn about you!" Hughes shouted as his emotions finally got the better of him. "You're just a number to me. But you do have something that none of the other so-called patients have."

"Yeah? And what is that?"

"Marketability. A name that sells."

"What's that got to do with it?" Christian asked in a shocked tone. "I've been out of the spotlight for a decade."

"But you were popular. You touched a nerve with the common folk. You were one of them. They looked up to you."

"Yes, key word: looked. As in past tense. They aren't looking anymore at me. I'm passé, out dated, past my expiration date, or any other term you want to label me as."

"But you still can draw money."

"You'll throw me out over money you haven't even seen yet?"

"No, I'd throw you out over lost money."

"How can it be lost money?" Christian questioned. "It's a fundraiser. All the money you get is pure profit. And you just got two and a half million of *free* money."

"People have already bought tickets on account of you," Hughes explained. "If you're not there, they'll want a refund and there's no way I intend on doing that. That's why it'll be lost money."

"You should have thought about that before you volunteered my services without securing them first," he sternly said. "You made this bed. I suggest you sleep in it."

Hughes got up to walk over to him. "Aren't you forgetting something?" He puffed himself up while asking this as he looked Christian right in the eye.

"Not that I'm aware of," Christian replied; an answer that seemed to raise the eyebrows of the short director. "What am I forgetting?"

"You're forgetting that you owe me. You owe for your slot here." Hughes poked him in the chest.

"If seems like I always have at least one person who I owe," Christian muttered while shaking his

495

head. "I don't owe you anything."

"You don't, huh?"

Christian shook his head firmly. "No. You gave me this slot so you could use my name, and who I am, to brag to the US government, or whoever you had to brag to, in order to get that grant you so badly desired. That makes us even. So, with all due respect, I'd appreciate it if you stop threatening me, stop glaring at me, stop trying to bully me, and stop puffing yourself up to make your short little self any bigger than it can be. We both got what we wanted out of it and we simply should leave it at that."

Hughes shook a finger at him. "I don't think we will. You still owe me this weekend."

"I'm a dementia patient. I'll forget all about it."

"You won't if you still want to live here."

"The press and my lawyer would have a field day with this," Christian said with a smile while noticing the director getting slightly nervous. "Especially if I offered an exclusive to 60 Minutes, O'Reilly, or some other major news show."

"You wouldn't risk your spot here."

"And you wouldn't risk the negative publicity," Christian shot back. "All you had to do was ask. If you asked, I would have helped."

"Christian, please, think of yourself," Hughes reached out with his fake plea. "Think of what would happen if you don't do this."

"I *am* thinking of myself! I'd waste a weekend of not seeing my family to help a money-hungry vulture."

"Then what?" Hughes paused briefly to heighten the question. "You see your family and then what? You're on the street, looking for a new spot, and your family worry about your rising medical bills."

"There's other places for me to go. We have good medical insurance. We have money stashed away for a rainy day. I'm not telling them I sold them out to help you."

Hughes' tone quickly changed with this. He softened his approached before countering with something. "Maybe you don't have to, sell them out that is."

"What are you talking about, Vince?"

"We're advertising this as a pancake breakfast, right?"

"Yeah. So?"

"What time of day is breakfast usually?"

"In the morning. Where are you going with this?"

"Are you as blind as you are forgetful?" Hughes snapped "You come to the breakfast, do a little publicity stint, and then when it's over, wham!, you're outta here like a bat outta hell with your family right beside you. You'll be done by noon at the latest. You have my word."

"Your word doesn't hold much water for me."

"Hey, don't be a smartass! I can throw your ass out on the street if I wanted to," Hughes said while snapping his fingers.

"No you wouldn't. I'm more valuable to you as a patient here. And, besides, if you ever did, I could give an exclusive, with my lawyer of course, on national television." Christian snapped his own fingers in return. "Just like that if I wanted to."

"Hmmm." Hughes sighed while looking at the man before him. "Where do you and your family plan on staying this weekend?"

"Dr. Wellwood recommended this little bed-and-breakfast here in town."

"Ah, yes. I know just the spot." Hughes' his face brightened. "Your wife and kids'll love it."

Just then, a thought came to him. "How's this, Vince. If you tell my wife everything we basically just talked about, everything from how you involved me without my permission, the whole nine yards, I'll agree to help…"

"I'll do it," Hughes injected quickly before turning to run to his deck to pick up his phone. "What's her number again?"

"…and as reimbursement for my act of charity for helping you," Christian continued as if nothing had happened, drawing an agonizing look from Hughes. "I'd like you to tell her you'll reimburse us for what we were charged at this bed-and-breakfast. Then you'll tell her you'll never do this again without my written permission again. If you do that, and then actually follow through with it, I'll help you this weekend. How's that sound? Do we have a deal?"

"Surely you can't be serious?" Hughes questioned.

"It's a win-win situation." Christian shrugged. "You get what you want and had advertised, and we get a free room and board for the weekend. Or, if the opposite happens, I'd be looking for a place to stay as you read a letter from my attorney while watching me tell this whole story to O'Reilly."

Hughes continued to stare at him before finally relenting. He sighed while picking his phone back up while nodding to him. "What's her number again?"

***

After dinner that night, Christian called a number that was in a book next to his phone.

"Hello?" a woman's voice answered on the third ring.

"Hi, Mom," he said bubbly. "How's it going?"

"Oh, Christian! It's so good to hear from you," his mother said with excitement. "It's been such a long time since you called. We were beginning to worry."

"Yeah, I sort of lost track of time. Besides, I forget what your number was."

"Were you finally able to remember it?"

"No, I wasn't. I had to look it up," he admitted. "It's a little embarrassing to look up something you've had for how many years now?"

"Things happen, sweetie. I wouldn't worry too much about it. Just be grateful you've kept most of your memory up until now," Sally assured him. "Where are you now?"

"I'm in my room; just got back from dinner."

"How was it and what did you have?"

"They said it was pot roast but, from what I can remember, though it didn't look or taste anything like that. With the amount of money we spend a month to stay here, I thought the food'd be a little better."

"It wasn't up to your standards, I take it," Sally commented while hinting at a grin.

He scoffed before laughing. "No, not quite. They need to take lessons from you."

"I'm glad you still approve of my cooking," she said. "And how's your roommate? What's his name again?"

"His name's Lloyd and he's still as grumpy as ever," Christian told her while leaning over to look out his window. "I don't remember if I told you, but he can't walk. His legs were paralyzed from some sort of accident before coming here. Anyway, the wheelchair he had was taken away because he would run over people in the halls whenever he could. He just got it back a day or two ago, I think. I also think I upset him a little because I roughed him up after he tried to do that to me. He didn't seem to like that very much."

"I don't think he would. But maybe you shouldn't have done that, dear."

"Considering he's given one guy a broken leg, anther a concussion, ran over another within minutes of getting it back, and it doesn't look like he'll stop anytime soon, I got a little irritated. I wanted to make sure he wouldn't do that again."

"Has anything happened as a result?"

"Well, he's a little sore and had a few bruises." Christian chuckled. "I heard I may have broken a rib or two when I kicked him, but that was before they did any x-rays."

"How much trouble did you get in?"

"I'll pay for medical expenses, that's a given, but other than that I haven't heard. I doubt I will, though. Anyway, how have you and Dad been?"

"Oh, we're fine, dear, just fine," she answered cheerfully. "I'm in the process of making dinner."

"What're you making?"

"Just leftovers; potatoes, beans, meatloaf. Oh, that reminds me. Miho called last night."

"Really? What's she up to?"

"Not much. She just put the kids to bed when she called, about 9:30 or so."

"Wow, the kids were up that late?"

"I think some of the neighbor's kids were over playing games or something," Sally told him. "Apparently Asako did really well on her report card and this was her reward. Miho also mentioned coming to visit you this weekend."

"They are?" Christian asked before quickly remembering that they were. "Oh, that's right, they are. I forgot about that. I've some things on my mind the last couple of days."

"Is your memory getting worse?"

"Eh, it's ok, but that's a matter of opinion." He laughed. "Is it better if it goes slowly over time, where you know it's going and you wonder what'll go next? Or is it better if it goes all at once?"

"You have a point."

"Oh, before for I forget, may I speak with Dad? I wanted to talk to him about something."

"Of course, dear. Let me go get him."

"Thanks, Mom."

Christian sat there for a few moments thinking about how he was going to talk to his father about Grandpa Joe but his dad picked up before he could finally decide.

"Hello, son."

"Hi'ya, Dad. How's it going?"

"I'm well, thanks. Just working on a little project here before dinner. How's it going with you at that hospital of yours?"

"Not really sure how it's going, but I'm still alive."

"You haven't been in touch much this past month. Is everything alright?"

"Well, ah, not sure how to answer that, Dad," Christian replied while trying to pick and choose his words carefully.

"Is there a problem you want to talk about?" his father asked.

"Yeah, yeah there is. But, first, is Mom still on the phone?"

"No, it's just us. Would you like her to be put back on?"

"No, I just wanted to talk to you about it," Christian answered while there being a hesitation on both sides. "Well, it's not really a problem as it is a question about something."

"I think I know what you're going to ask and, first off, I'd like to say I'm sorry."

When Christian heard his day say that, he felt that was the evidence towards the first steps for his dad to admit that not only did he know Grandpa Joe was still alive, but that he was part of his cover-up. Still, Christian needed to hear his father say it, to admit to it before he took the plunge off the pirate's plank to ask the somewhat fatal question.

"You do?" he asked.

"Of course. You were going to ask why your mother and I haven't been down to see you," his father replied, which was one that had been on his mind but not on the immediate forefront. "We've been meaning to come down, but I've been backed up at work. I wanted to wait until after I got caught up a little bit more before we made the trip down. I'm sorry about the wait and we'll make it down for a visit just as soon as we can. I promise."

"That sounds great, Dad, and I'll hold you to your word," Christian responded while pausing. He wasn't sure if he should ask his dad now about his grandfather but, figured he'd forget about it if he didn't. He should just throw it out there and see what happens as a result. "But, to be honest, that wasn't why I called. I called to ask you about one of the other patients down here with me. I wanted to talk to you about it first without involving Mom. That way, you would be able to tell her whatever story you wanted to when you were ready to."

With that, a silence fell over both ends of the phone that felt very awkward and was the type of silence that could cut like a knife.

"Oh, that," David finally said after what seemed to be an eternity but, in reality, was only a few seconds. "So, um, how's your grandfather doing?"

"All things considered, he's doing fine," Christian told him while still being confused. He thought that if the roles were reversed, he wasn't sure how he would react to it. "How come you didn't tell us about this, Dad?"

"To be honest, I didn't think you would remember."

"How could I forget something like this?"

"Considering he left when you were like ten, I was hoping you'd naturally forget about him," his father admitted.

"Weren't you at all worried I'd know who he was when I got here?"

"That had crossed my mind, but I was hoping you wouldn't recognize him."

"To be honest, I didn't really. He did look familiar, but I couldn't for the life of me remember where," Christian told him. "I just figured it my was faulty wiring playing tricks on my again."

"That was another reason as to why I didn't tell you," David told him. "I was hoping your crappy memory wouldn't allow you to remember him."

"Yeah, that makes sense."

"So how'd you finally figure out it was him? Did you remember?"

"He looked familiar to me each time I saw him but I didn't know why. I just thought it was déjà vu or something. Two days ago we got talking outside by the duck pond here and he started saying things or commenting on stuff that only someone who knew us would know. After a few minutes of this it finally dawned on me. It was almost as if he wanted me to know who he was."

"Wait a second. Are you saying he approached you?" his father inquired. "That if it wasn't for him, then you might not have known who he was?"

"Yeah, pretty much," Christian told him. "Like you said before, he left when I was ten and I'm here due do a bad brain. With those two things, I very well may never have found out."

"Damn it all! He told me he wouldn't say anything," David grumbled.

"Have you been in contact with each other since I've been here?"

"Of course we have."

"Does Mom know about his?"

"Of course she doesn't. She'd skin me alive if she knew we were withholding this from you."

"Are you going to tell her?"

"Yes, but I was hoping you'd know first so it was easier for me to tell her."

"How do you think Mom will react to hearing that Grandpa's still alive?"

"Good, I hope. I think she'll be glad knowing in the end. I know she never likes living with lies. All we can do is ride this one out."

"Oh, that reminds me, Dad. What did you think when you first found out that I was coming here to stay, here where I'm at now?"

"Not much," he admitted. "From what I can remember, I don't think I even heard the name of it until recently. All I knew was that it was someplace in Long Island. I wasn't that worried you'd remember him and I was certain he wouldn't say anything to you. I wasn't even worried."

"What would have happened if you and Mom came down for a visit? How would you have seen me without risking him?"

"I don't know, but I would have figured something out."

"How would you have done that? We both live on the same floor."

"That would have been a little challenging," David admitted. "I probably would have taken you and your mother out to eat or something. Something, anything, would have been good as long as I was able to keep your mom from seeing him."

"From the impression I've gotten, I don't think he'd have done anything if you two came down."

After this, Christian and David changed subjects to other things. David told him about his various projects he was working on to things at work at the plant. Christian, meanwhile, told his father of Lloyd and the trouble he's been causing; the card playing guys in the rec room; and finally about his upcoming weekend while doing double duty as both family man and charity man. His father laughed at this, especially how Christian was able to get his bed-and-breakfast paid for.

"That's good that he's doing that for you," David said in reference to Hughes.

"He's just doing it to get the publicity. Anything for a buck."

"Well, just hang in there. It'll get better soon."

"I hope so, Dad, I hope so."

"It will," David said before pausing. "Now, not to cut this off, but you're mom's calling me for dinner. Do you want to talk to her again before I get off?"

"No, that's alright, but thanks," Christian replied. "Tell her I love her, would you, please?"

"Of course. And we love you too, son."

"I love you too, Dad."

"Well, we'll talk to you soon. Your mom and I will come down soon for a visit."

"You'd better. It'll be good to see you two again."

"We will. I should go now. Good-bye, son."

"Bye, Dad."

With that, both Christian and David hung up. David went to dinner in upstate New York with his wife; Christian, in Long Island, sat thinking on his bed. He looked out the window while doing so.

Chapter 52

That weekend passed without incident and Christian enjoyed seeing his family again. As promised, Dr. Hughes paid for their stay at the local bed-and-breakfast, as well as promising them 'free' entry to the pancake breakfast both days. Hughes seemed to be quite taken with Miho before soon being turned down coldly when she didn't return any of his advances. After he left, she called him something in Japanese that Christian wasn't sure what it meant. Her tone indicated that she wasn't impressed.

Also, as promised, Christian introduced Miho, Asako, and Dominic to Joe while failing to mention that Joe was in fact his grandfather. He wanted to scream it out but didn't on account he had given his word it wouldn't be revealed until Joe was comfortable with it.

Saturday after that initial pancake breakfast, they spend most of the day by the ocean. It was Asako's idea to go on account she had been learning about it in school and wanted to show off her new founded intelligence. Christian and Miho laughed when Dominic stated, "Will the Miss Know It All shut up and keep her self-proclaimed thoughts to herself?!" Christian had no idea why Dominic was talking like that, but Miho said Asako had been trying to teach him the proper way to talk.

In other news, Lloyd Anderson healed nicely from his encounter with Christian. Outside of covering the medical costs, no repercussions hung over the retired boxer's head. Strangely, Lloyd conceded to stop terrorizing other patients with his wheelchair; or at least temporarily.

That next week winter finally came to Long Island and to Forestry Park. Since going outside had been getting more and more restricted due to the colder temperatures, it was made even more limited due to the snow. Because of this, Christian found himself passing the time winning at wheelchair races, usually at Lloyd's experience. Christian, meanwhile, soon found that the only person that could beat him consistently at these races was Grandpa Joe. Jokingly he accused his grandfather of beating him only because Joe had more experience at using a wheelchair than he had.

He soon found himself teaming with Joe during races to make sure that Lloyd wouldn't win. Lloyd's competitive nature seemed to come out during times like these. When it became evident that he never had a chance to win during these times, his temper tantrums got tremendously worse the more he lost. As a result, Christian and Joe started letting him win on occasion to make sure he kept playing. This, in turn, allowed them to keep ganging up on him.

Christmas came later that month and Christian found himself going to his parents with Miho and the kids for a couple of days. Those few days were the happiest he had had in a long time and he jokingly commented that that might be the last Christmas he'd remember.

The day Christian and Miho packed to go home, David told him he wanted to show him some new things he had gotten for his workshop. It wasn't until after they got down there did his father pull out a good sized box wrapped with Christmas paper did he realize he was setup.

"I'm sorry I lied to you, but I don't have anything new down here," he confessed while handing Christian the box. "I wanted to know if you'd give this to your grandfather for me."

503

"Sure, of course I will, but why'd you have to bring me down here to ask me this?" he asked his dad. The look on his father's face was enough.

"Your mom made some cookies a day or so ago," David said with a shrug. "I stole a few of them to put in here. I didn't want to get in trouble if she knew I took them."

"That's obvious," Christian said sarcastically.

"Hey, don't be a wiseass! A matter like this is extremely delicate. I wouldn't want it to come out wrong," David retorted. "Have you told Miho and the kids yet?"

"No, not yet."

He smiled. "And why not?"

"Because Grandpa wanted to wait until he was more comfortable."

David pointed a finger at his son. "See, that's exactly what I'm doing. I'm waiting for a more comfortable opportunity here with me."

"The apple doesn't fall too far from the tree, I see."

"Hey, what did I say about being a wiseass, huh?"

Before an answer was be given, a voice from upstairs called out.

"Christian," Miho said, "we're ready to go."

"Be right there," he answered before looking at his dad. "Would you be able to distract Mom long enough for me to get this in the car?"

"Don't worry about that; I've got it covered," his father told him before going upstairs. Once there, he diverted Sally long enough so that Christian was able to get by without being seen with his package.

After coming back inside, he and his family said good-bye before his mom handed him a package of cookies.

"I'm sorry I didn't give you more," she apologized. "I thought I made more than I had."

Christian, Miho, and the kids left a few minutes after this for their long trek home. Since he wasn't due back to Forestry Park until the next day, they all went back to their New Jersey home for the night.

Being back home was a welcomed relief for Christian, even though it would be only for the night. It was pretty much how he remembered it and Miho had done a great job at keeping it up by herself. That night would be the last his utopia would run for and, to him, the best night he had had in a very long time.

The next evening when Miho and the kids dropped him off back at the clinic, he went up to his room to find it empty. Lloyd and all of his belongings were gone. He didn't find out the reasoning behind it until the next day: Lloyd had died a couple of days earlier from an apparent heart attack, which had happened sometime during the night. No one came to claim his body and, as a result, Hughes was complaining the whole time he would have to arrange for his services.

"Look on the bright side," Dr. Wellwood commented to him, "it'll be great publicity."

Over the next week before Lloyd's bed was filled, Christian lobbied for Grandpa Joe to be his roommate. With help from Drs. Wellwood and Allen, and Nurse Rita, Dr. Hughes granted permission for it and within two days after that, Christian had himself a new roommate. It was that night that Joe moved in did Christian bring out the package his dad wanted him to have.

"What's this?" Joe asked when seeing the package on his bed.

"Oh, that?" Christian asked. "It's a new car."

"A new car?"

"Yeah. It's one of those new compact ones," Christian added. "To think that technological advances would allow them to make a car that small nowadays."

"Remarkable," his grandfather commented while looking at his grandson before lifting the package. "To think that it has almost no weight. It must get great gas mileage."

Christian had to laugh at this. "To be honest, it's a little something my dad put together for you. I've no idea what's in it, though."

Quickly opening it, Joe found that inside were some of his favorite books that he had in his apartment many years ago, as well as current pictures of the whole family. There was also a bunch of Sally's cookies.

"My mom made some cookies when we went home for Christmas," Christian explained. "My dad grabbed a bunch of them to give to you. Speaking of that, when was the last time you saw my parents?"

"It's been a while, a week or two before you came here to live I last saw your dad, I think," Joe answered while rubbing his head. "But I've spoken to your dad a number of times on the phone and exchanged several letters with him since then. As for your mom," he sighed, "well, it's been a while."

"Since he knows I know about you, he may even show up or a visit every now and then."

"He might. I'd like to have them come for a visit. I'd like us to be a family again," Joe commented while looking through his belongings.

"So would I."

"I wouldn't want to wait much longer for my family to come back together." Joe sighed before pausing briefly as something crossed his mind. He smiled evilly while looking at his grandson. "Speaking of family, when you went home for Christmas, guess who dropped by to see you?"

"How would I know that?"

"It looked like your brother has had a change of heart."

"Shawn came here?" Christian asked in amazement. "Looking for me?"

"So it seemed."

"Well, what happened?"

"Just what I said. He came to pay you a visit when you went home. Is your memory that bad?"

"I heard you the first time."

"Then why'd you ask?" Joe continued to smile.

"What happened while he was here?" Christian asked while ignoring his grandfather's comment. "Why'd he come?"

Joe shrugged. "I'm not really sure; I only saw the back of him when he was leaving. He seemed to have gotten into a little argument with Rita about your whereabouts; then with Lloyd when he thought you were in here. There was a woman he was with who pretty much stopped him from doing anything he'd regret."

"He was with a woman who actually stopped him from doing something?" Christian whistled at that.

"It looked that way," Joe admitted. "She was real pretty, a sort of class attractiveness rather than those less-than-savory airhead types. She seemed European, French or Italian by her accent."

"Are you sure it was Shawn?" Christian still couldn't believe what he was hearing.

"That's the name he left Riga and it did look like him to me. Well, his back did anyway," Joe told him. "He said he'd stop by at some other point."

"Do you know why he stopped by?"

"No idea."

"Let's see if he does show back up. It'd be funny if we end up trading one pain in the ass with another."

"You mean Lloyd for Shawn?"

Christian nodded.

"Maybe he's not a pain in the ass anymore."

"That's fairly obvious since he's dead."

"I was talking about your brother, the one who's very much alive!"

"Just because you're not dead doesn't mean you're alive," retorted Christian.

"What I'm saying is that he's probably not the same person he's been the last decade or so," Grandpa Joe said foully. "Maybe he's changed."

"Shawn? Change? What drugs do Wellwood and Allen have you on? You're beginning to talk some pretty good nonsense."

"He came, apparently to see you, didn't you?"

"What's your point? That he changed?"

"Sure. Maybe he has."

"How can I trust that's who you saw?"

"I'm sure you have a picture of him lying around, right?"

"Somewhere I do," Christian confirmed.

"Take the picture to Rita and ask if he's the one who was looking for you that day."

"And what will that prove, whether or not that was really him?"

"It'll prove that it was him and that he's changed, even if that change may be small."

"What are we talking about here?" Christian asked him.

"That this was the first time he's tried to make contact with you since, when, the last fight you two fought?"

Shrugging, Christian said, "Something like that."

"Aren't you at all curious why?" Joe asked him. "Why now would he visit after all these years? And who was that woman with him, a woman who seemed to be giving him hell? When was the last time anyone did that to him without him getting defensive, argumentative, or any other pissed off attitude?"

"I never thought about it that way. You do have a point there."

"Of course I do." Joe smiled while looking at his grandson. "So, what are you gonna do about it then?"

"I'm not going to do anything. Let him wait it out like he's made us wait. He came for a reason and he's really impatient. If I don't do something, he'll come back for another visit."

As foretold by Christian, Shawn did make a return visit. When he was going back to his room after his morning treatments with Wellwood, he saw a familiar shape emerging from his doorway.

"It's about time you decided to show up," Shawn irritably grumbled as Christian neared. "I was about to leave. I was getting sick of waiting."

"You've waited over ten years to stop for a visit. A few more minutes wouldn't have really mattered," Christian said while walking past him and on into his room. In the process, he caught a whiff of a sweat smelling scent. "Are you wearing cologne?"

"Have you ever known me to wear that shit?" Shawn quickly asked.

"Outside of one that's beer scented, no I haven't."

"Then why in the hell would I start now?"

"I've no idea but I did smell a sweet fragrance when I passed you. For a moment I thought it was you," Christian explained as he sat on his bed before taking of his shoes.

"That would be from Francesca, the woman I'm with," Shawn softly said while looking around to see if anyone heard him, almost embarrassed by admitting that.

"Francesca, huh?" Christian asked while eyeing Shawn suspiciously with a smile. "That doesn't sound American at all."

"That's because she isn't, you asshole! She's European, I think."

"You think? Oh, how charming. I see this relationship has about as much conversation in it as a pair of mating rabbits."

"Hey, listen up! I've spoken more to her than my past eight or nine relationships combined!"

"That's saying something and to think she's still with you?" Christian laughed. "What's her malfunction?"

Shawn was about to protest before smiling himself.

"Do you want to sit?" Christian asked while pointing to a corner chair.

"If I wanted to sit, I would'a sat already."

"Suit yourself." Christian shrugged while remaining on his bed.

There were a few moments of uncomfortable silence between them before either of them spoke. During this silence, Shawn nervously rubbed his hands together before walking over to sit in a corner chair.

"So, Shawn, not to be rude, but is there any particular reason for this visit?" Christian finally asked.

"What? Can't I stop by to see my own brother?" Shawn asked with a smile as he tried to shrug as coolly as possible.

"After more than a decade and countless times I've tried to contact you, you now finally decide to visit? What's the real reason?"

Shawn seemed to fumble dumbly with his thoughts before speaking. "Seriously, dude, I came here to see ya."

"Really?" Christian looked at him with great reservation a few times while trying to gage whether or not he was telling the truth. He honestly wasn't sure if he was, but thought he should give him the benefit of the doubt for now. "So, outside of getting in trouble with the law, what have you been up to?"

"You've heard about my little run-ins with the law?" Shawn cockily asked, almost as if he was proud of that fact.

"It's almost impossible for a person who watches TV or reads the paper not to hear about it," Christian said dryly. "Besides, those little run-ins weren't exactly so little."

"Ah, man, what are you talkin' about? Those were peanuts next to things my ass is capable of doin'!"

"And you're still alive? Now that's a real surprise," Christian mocked. "Do you still live in that hotel or whatever it was when we saw each other last?"

"Oh, that dump? Hell no, I moved out. It didn't work out for me there."

"Why's that, too many complaints from other tenants about your late night visits by police?"

Shawn just sat there looking at his grinning brother before responding. "Real funny, asshole! As a matter of fact, no. I got myself a house a year or so ago. I'm living right outside of Manhattan."

"Geez, that must have cost you a pretty penny."

"Yeah, well, I can afford it." He shrugged in a cocky manner.

"You could if Duke set you up with it. How much longer can you afford it given your less-than-discreet habits?" Christian asked mildly while drawing a nasty look from Shawn.

"Yo, man, that's in the past. I'm trying to stay on the straight and narrow," Shawn said in a surprisingly serious manner.

"Really? You're actually trying to stay sober?" Christian asked with some suspicion.

"Something wrong with that?" Shawn's tenseness returned a little with this.

"No, nothing wrong with that. I'm glad. I'm just surprised by it, that's all," he admitted. "What's the occasion?"

"Occasion for what?"

"For you trying to be, and stay, sober?"

"What's the day?" Shawn asked him.

"January first. Why?"

"It's a new year. I might as well start my New Year's resolution."

"You're New Year's resolution is to be sober?"

"Well, yeah," Shawn admitted in a slightly nervous manner which made Christian suspect something or someone else was involved in helping him with this.

"And was another of those resolutions for the new year to come and see me?"

"As a matter of fact, it was."

"Was it a choice you made freely or did you have some outside influence in this matter?"

"Ah, you know." Shawn flustered with his words while getting slightly embarrassed. He did a combination nod of his head and flick of his thumb towards the hallway.

"I'm sorry, Shawn, but I'm not following," Christian told him as seriously as he could while also suspecting that it was Francesca who was behind it.

"You know what I'm talkin' 'bout, man!" Shawn stated bluntly as his brother continued to look at him. "Francesca!"

"Francesca who?"

"The hot chick I'm with."

"Oh, that's right. Francesca the hot foreign chick. I'm sorry, I forgot all about her," Christian said while waving his left hand towards his head. "You're going to have to forgive me, my memory's not as good as it used to be."

"So, is this problem with your head for real or were you just saying that so I would start coming around again?" Shawn asked with his own suspicions.

"What do you think? Do you actually think I'd lie to you about that?"

"I don't know. That's why I came."

Christian grinned. "Ah, so the truth is now revealed for behind the visit. And I thought this was just a social call."

"C'mon, man. Stop tryin' to bullshit me. I hate it when you play these fukin' mind games with me. Just tell me the damn truth!"

"You want the truth?"

"Yes."

"You want the truth?"

"I just told you I did."

"Have you ever seen the movie *A Few Good Men*?" Christian asked while thinking of the climactic scene in that movie.

"Wha...? What the hell does that have to do with anything?" Shawn, obviously confused, blinked several times.

Christian just let the moment pass. "If you want to talk about the truth, were have you been the last decade?"

"You know where I've been."

"I know where you lived if that's what you mean, but that's not what I meant." He paused long enough to look at him. The stared at each other as Christian contemplated if any of this was sinking in. "Where have you been? Why did you leave us? Why did you never keep in touch with any of us? What did we do to you for you to decide you'd be better off without us? And why, after all these years and failed attempts by me to contact you, did you chose now to make any kind of contact?"

The silence between them was deafnifying as Christian waited for an answer.

"You know why," Shawn finally said softly.

"No, I don't know why. Will you please just tell me?"

There was another awkward silence between them.

"The thing is that I'm here now and I wanted to see you," he finally told him as a thought came to mind. "That time when you came to see me at my hotel, you said you were sick. Were you really sick then?"

"Not as bad as I am now, but yes I was."

"And you knew all this time about whatever it is you have?"

"I've known ever since our last fight together, or at least I knew the potential it could get to."

"Why didn't you say anything?" Shawn demanded.

"I did, twice," Christian told him. "You never seemed to care enough to listen."

"I'm listening now."

"How long will you be here this time around?"

"What's that mean?"

"What it means is, what are your intentions? Why are you here? How long are you planning on staying?" Christian asked as his questions shot out. "I'm not saying I'm not glad to see you, I truly am, but I have to question your motives. If you're here for a visit to see whether or not I was telling you the truth, and then we'll never hear from you again, then you made a mistake by coming here. I have enough problems going on without having to worry about that. I'd rather spend what time I have left with the people who are willing to spend time with me than those who'd rather use me as a conversational piece at some party I'd never have any interest in."

"Are you saying you don't want me here?" Shawn asked in a defensive tone.

"No, Shawn, I'm not saying that at all." Christian sighed. "I'm just saying I don't want you here if this is a one-time deal or you don't intend on being here on a consistent basis. It's not fair to me or to my family if I'm worrying about a relationship with you that'll never happen. What I'm ultimately asking, I suppose, is why are you here? Do you want anything to do with me?"

"Is that it?" Shawn seemed shocked by the bluntness of that.

"Yes, that's it."

"Before I answer that, I'll need to ask you a question," Shawn said as a smirk rose on his face. "What the hell were you talkin' about in that last letter of yours when you said that Grandpa Joe was alive and living here?"

"I meant just that. That's true."

"Dude, he died from a car accident like twenty-five years ago."

"That's the story Dad told us."

"And that's the truth." Shawn got a little emotional with that. "You shouldn't be tellin' me that, bro. That was a mean, cruel joke."

"It would have been both mean and cruel if it *was* a joke," Christian admitted with a slight nod. "But I assure you it's no joke."

"Like hell it's not."

"I'm not laughing over here, am I?"

"Then where the hell is he? Huh?!"

"Downstairs. Most likely in therapy."

Shawn scoffed while rolling his eyes. "Oh, that's convenient!"

"There's nothing convenient about it. He'll be along shortly," Christian said while pointing to the bed and nightstand that was on the other half of the room. "There's his stuff if you don't believe me. Take a look if you want."

As Shawn followed Christian's finger to the other half of the room, his eyes widened slightly at the possibility it wasn't a joke. He soon got up to go over and investigate. There, on the extra nightstand, was a wide variety of pictures of the Eaton's, both new and old, some of which even included Shawn. There was even a number of Grandpa Joe's favorite books Shawn remembered going through as a child. He picked up some to leaf through to make sure he wasn't dreaming. Soon, he came across a picture of himself with Grandpa Joe. The picture was taking the Christmas he got his first pair of boxing gloves.

"Is this for real?" he asked, not really sure what to believe.

"You tell me, Shawn."

"C'mon, bro, be serious."

"I am."

"You could'a set this all up to make it look like he's alive."

"You're right, I could have," Christian admitted. "But if I did that, then where did I put the belongings of the person who I room with?"

"You could have hid them," Shawn told him while starting to look around for them. He left no place unsearched. "You knew I was coming back to visit so you set this all up to play with me."

Just then, Grandpa Joe hobbled into the doorway from wherever he was before stopping. He didn't enter the room nor did he say anything. He just watched and waited in silence until the time was right.

Shawn, meanwhile, didn't see him because his back was to him while he continued to search. Christian exchanged a look with his grandfather, but otherwise remained silent.

Ultimately, he focused back to Shawn with a shrug. "You're right, Shawn. I could be playing with you. But why would I?"

"I don't know! Maybe to get me to visit you. If that was it, then the game worked. I can't believe I fell for the idea that Grandpa was still alive. Goddamn it!" Shawn threw the pictures on the bed before slamming his head against the wall while trying desperately to hold back twenty-five plus years of tears.

At this point, Joe flicked his hand and nodded at Christian.

Taking the hint, Christian spoke. "Alright, Shawn, you win. All of this was a setup to get you to visit."

513

"I fuckin' knew it! Ha. I knew you were full of shit!" he said while straightening up to look at his brother. "I can't believe I fell for it."

"But first, would you do me a small favor that I'm having a problem with?" Christian said while holding up an index finger and thumb together to indicate that it was truly small before pointing to the door. "Would you mind telling me who, or what, that is? Ever since I got here, I kept seeing Grandpa and I thought he was real. Is that really him in the doorway or is it just an apparition?"

As Shawn turned towards the doorframe to look at the figure, he froze in helplessness. The longer he stared, the more he seemed to shake. After almost a full minute of this, Shawn finally conceded to the fact that Christian had been telling him the truth. Staring emotionally at the elderly figure before him, tears started to fill his eyes.

"Grandpa," he finally said as emotions cracked his voice. "Is that you?"

Chapter 53

"Of course it's me. Who else would it be?" Joe answered while stumbling into the room. He soon sat on his bed.

Christian continued to look at Shawn with a smile before turning to their grandfather. "How was therapy?"

"I think my leg will be better soon, but whatever Wellwood did to it," Joe replied while rubbing and extended his left knee a few times, "It feels better than it had been, but sure is a helluva lot stiffer."

"I did notice you gimping on your way in."

"I was doing no such thing!" his grandfather quickly retorted. "I most certainly was *not* gimping. I was walking perfectly."

"Alright, Gramps, whatever you say." Christian smiled before looking up at Shawn, who was still looking at Grandpa Joe in wide-eyed wonder. "So, Shawn, have you figured out exactly what is sitting on that bed over there?"

While Shawn was still looking at Grandpa Joe, but before he had a chance to answer, a very attractive woman appeared in the doorway. She stood about 5'7" and had long, straight, brown hair that hung loosely past her shoulders. A tan of the most golden brown Christian had ever seen colored her skin. Because of the jacket she was wearing, it was almost impossible to tell the overall shape of her but, to him, it didn't really matter. Her face, being more long than round, had a rounded chin, button nose, and high cheekbones. Her full lips slanted up in a slight smile while giving her an overall warm look. Her piercing eyes, being of the darkest brown, hinted at those that sees all as well as suggesting an intelligence of a higher quality.

"Shawn, I'm sorry it took me so long to get back," she said with a very obvious western European accent. "I got lost coming back. This place is *so* big!"

"Oh, just like me, right?" Shawn replied with a cocky swagger.

"You shouldn't brag, Tiny Tim. People might get the wrong impression," she sternly stated with glazed eyes before smiling.

Shawn stopped posing long enough to look at her dumbly before glancing back to Grandpa Joe. He tried to say something but nothing came out.

"Shawn, close your mouth, will ya?" Joe told him. "We don't want you killing any more flies that you have to. And, while you're at it, how long do you intend on being rude?"

"Huh?" Shawn asked with a dumb look.

"Are you going to introduce us to your friend or do we have to take the first steps?" Christian asked while getting up to walk over to his female friend who was still standing in the doorway. Along the way, he picked up the same sweet fragrance as he had smelled earlier, a sure sign that

515

it came from her. "I want to apologize for his lack of communication right now. He seems to have swallowed his own tongue from some recent news he wasn't exactly expecting. I'm Christian, Shawn's non-existent brother," he told her while extending a hand for her to shake.

She accepted it with a smile and a firmness he wasn't expecting. "It's so good to finally meet you. Shawn's told me so much about you."

"He has, has he?" Christian looked at Shawn. "Funny I can't say the same about you. He's never mentioned you from what I can remember. But, then again, we haven't spoken much the last few years. If I were to guess, however, you wouldn't by any chance be Francesca, would you?"

"Why yes, yes I am." She smiled at that to show off a great set of perfect looking teeth that twinkled in the light. Her accent was very apparent, but Christian wasn't exactly sure which dialect. He thought perhaps either Italian or Spanish. "How did you know my name if Shawn never mentioned me?"

"Well, my quick and intelligent brother only mentioned you by name alone," he answered while pointing to Shawn. "I regret to say that we were talking about other things when you arrived. If we had been talking about you, however, I have no doubt he would have mentioned how attractive you are. His taste in women definitely has improved since the time we spoke," Christian explained while reaching for a hand to kiss.

"Why, Chris, are you coming onto me?" she asked flirtatiously."

"Oh, hell no!" He quickly showed her his wedding ring. "I'm happily married."

"And you say you're Shawn's brother?"

"I'd been questioning that very thought for about ten years now but, regrettably, we are indeed."

"It's a shame," she cooed.

"What's that?"

"That one brother is so open about his masculinity and honest about his feelings while another is trying so hard to hide his," she said while trying to give Shawn a stern look before smiling. "There's always room for improvement if the same blood that created you also created him."

"I know." Christian nodded in agreement. "Shawn has always said the same thing. He always said I should open up more and not try so damn hard to hide things. As for the last point you just made, like Shawn has always said, we're not blood brothers; just adopted."

"Still, you should've picked up some things to let people know what exactly you're thinking. That is *so* much sexier. Wouldn't you say, Shawn?" she asked him with a twinkle in her eye before turning back to Christian. "So, are you a boxer too, like Shawn?"

"No, not like Shawn," Christian replied. "I'm a full-time patient here now."

"Really? You're a patient here?" she asked as a look of surprise came over her face. "What happened, if you don't mind me asking?"

"Well, I used to box a little a long time. I got hurt quite bad in my last match which, ah, caused some lingering effects," he tactfully said before soon waving it off with a shrug.

"Wasn't your last fight with…?" Francesca started to ask in a hushed manner while leaving it open before her eyes Shawn's.

Shawn remained silent to this. Christian merely looked at her while quietly nodding his head slightly.

"Oh, I see. That must be hard on your family."

"They manage well," Christian nervously replied while not really wanting to get into it further. He quickly changed the subject. "And what is it that you do?"

"That's confidential," she said seriously while finally taking off her coat. Christian couldn't help but see the hourglass figure that was hidden only moments before. He noticed she possessed a lean, yet athletic, physique with blue jeans and a sweater that showed off every curve and asset she possessed.

"Confidential? You mean you work for the government?" he questioned while trying to conceal the fact by how impressed he was with what some would call the "complete package" look that she possessed.

She scoffed when she heard that. "Oh, please! Do you know how much they pay?"

Christian found himself smiling. "Who do you work for, then? What do you do?"

"Corporate gigs," she said while a smile crossed her face and her hands showed off her body. "I'm a great help for finalizing deals."

"Oh, I'm sure you are," Christian expressed while his eyes took advantage of the offer that presented itself to him. He looked over her body as a smile of his own appeared.

"Hey there, bro. Don't you be checkin' out my girlfriend, ya hear?" Shawn sternly told him. "Just because we're brothers doesn't give you the right to check her out."

"Girlfriend?" Francesca questioned in both a shocked and delighted tone as her hand went up to her mouth.

"That's what I said, ain't it?" he demanded. "You're my girl! Now don't be gettin' all mushy on me because of that, ya hear?"

"Why, Shawn, I'm thoroughly impressed with you," Christian told him in a half-truth, half mocking tone. "I truly am. Not only did you grace us with your presence after all these years, but you also called me your brother *and* said she was your girlfriend, which seems to be a delightful surprise to her as well. You truly are mellowing and maturing in your old age. You know that, right?"

"Oh, fuck off, will ya?" Shawn retorted hotly as he smiled.

"Shawn, since I introduced myself to your friend…," Christian started.

"Girlfriend," corrected Shawn.

"…maybe you'd like to introduce the other person in the room?" Christian asked while looking at Grandpa Joe.

"Yes, Shawn, why don't you do that?" Francesca asked in a way that did not leave it open for debate.

With this, Shawn coughed uncomfortably. "Baby, I'd like you to meet Joe, our grandfather."

"Your grandfather?" she repeated in sincere confusion. "You told me your family was dead. Did you not?"

"I'm sorry, young lady," Joe said while looking up to her. He soon stood to stretch himself. "That was a big misunderstanding which I started a very long time ago. Please don't be too hard on my grandson for he just recently found out himself that I was still alive. Also, if none of you mind, why don't we go somewhere else more comfortable to talk; that is, if neither of you are in a hurry to leave? It's nearing lunch and I'm getting hungry."

They soon found themselves at a table in the cafeteria with fresh coffee in hand; Francesca was the odd one out of the group with her bottled water. None of the staff seemed to object serving two uninvited guests, but Christian and Joe were both told they would need to notify the cafeteria crew beforehand if they intended to have guests again.

"They came unexpectedly," Joe patiently told them, but their point was well taken.

The four of them occupied a table against the sidewall and sat there talking with each other for the next several hours. Christian told their visitors how he came to be at Forestry Park and what was wrong with him as well as his prognosis. Joe gave an overview of his life and the reason he'd been dead the last three decades. He and Christian seemed to embarrass Shawn as they told Francesca a brief biop of his life with them.

Francesca, as it turned out, was born and raised in Italy to French immigrants. She spent five years in Spain studying education before graduating and moving to New York City a couple of years back. Because of her background, she was fluent in both French and Italian, and near fluent in Spanish and English. She was currently looking for a job as an elementary school teacher while working as a model on the side to earn money.

Christian, through hearing this, was more than confused on how these two got together before finally asking.

"I'm sorry, but considering your backgrounds, but how in the hell did you two meet?" he asked. "It's not like you two share any of the same interests, mingle with the same crowd, or even visit the same establishments. There has to be some common connection between the two of you. That I'm just totally missing. What is it?"

"Well," she blushed while looking over to Shawn. The look she gave him made him blush as well. "He came up to me and the friends I was with and asked how much I would charge to spend the night with him. When I said he couldn't afford me, he pulled out a wad of $100 bills while asking if that would be enough." She laughed while turning a darker shade of red.

Shawn merely shook his head while covering his eyes with his hands.

"Well, that did it," she admitted. "I've heard a lot of pickup lines in my time but nothing that humorous. Anyone who was able to joke that way to me, I just had to talk with him."

"Are you sure he was joking?" Christian asked with a slight laugh but serious eyes. When his eyes met his brother's, he got a look that spoke volumes: Shawn, in fact, was not joking when he asked her that. He soon looked back to Francesca. "So how long have you two been together?"

"Almost a year now."

"I think that may be a personal record for you, Shawn," Christian said with an amused laugh.

"Man, what are you talkin' 'bout? You don't know anything 'bout me," Shawn told him.

"And whose fault is that?" Christian jokingly mocked.

Shawn apparently didn't like that question. He got all serious while glaring at him.

"Come on, Shawn," Francesca said to him. "He was just joking with you. Don't be getting all riled over something that doesn't mean anything."

"He was saying it was my fault he doesn't know me!"

She looked at him calmly. "And in truth, it is. Can you honestly say you never ignored him or your family the last several years? Did you respond to any of your brother's letters? The answer to both questions is no! The reason I made you come here is for you to try and reestablish whatever relationship you can with your brother before he loses all his marbles. You're the one who messed that up, but I'm the one who's going to fix it if you won't.

"You need to grow up and take some responsibility for the decisions and actions you've made," she continued. "If you truly do not want him, or the rest of your family, in your life now's the time for you to come clean and admit it like the man you so frequently claim to be. But, if you don't, you'll always be that scared little boy you've been trying so hard to forget. If you can't see that your bother and grandfather love you, your own family, then you're more blind and shallow than I thought you were. The best gift you can give them is the truth. They want you in their lives, but if you don't want them then you need to tell them. Don't insult their intelligence! You owe them that much."

"You think I owe them?" Shawn asked her coldly.

"With this, yes I do," she firmly told him while meeting his threatening gaze. "If you can't be honest with these people, those that love you, the people who raised you, then you'll never be honest with me and I *won't* allow that! There's no us if you can't be open and honest!"

"Are you done, woman?" demanded Shawn.

"For now, yes I am."

"Wait a second," Christian said while injecting himself into the conversation. "Are you saying you're the reason Shawn came here to see me, er, us?"

"Yes," she said with heartfelt honesty. "That's exactly what I'm saying."

"That's not true!" Shawn quickly denied. "You didn't make me do anything I don't want to do."

"Oh, really? So you came here of your own free will?" Francesca waited for a response to this, which never came. "If it wasn't for me getting on your case, you would *never* have come. So you need to be honest with yourself and to us about this."

"Fine, I'll be honest if that's what you want," Shawn sternly said before getting up. "We're leaving, now!" With that, he turned, walked out of the cafeteria, and left.

The remaining three sat there in a shocked silence while comprehending what just happened. Shawn, meanwhile, disappeared around the corner of the hall.

"You'd better hurry up before he leaves you here," Joe politely said while pointing towards the door.

"He won't leave without me if he knows what's good for him," she calmly told him while standing. "I'm sorry for that outburst of his. I don't know what came over him."

"Don't worry about it," Christian told her. "In fact, you're the first person I've ever seen talk to him that way without him hitting or yelling at. He must really like you for him not to do either of those to."

"Oh, he wanted to, he really did," she said while putting on her jacket. "But he knows I'd kick his ass if he ever tried. Besides, he knows I'm right. I'm always right."

"I'm sure you are," Joe commented with a smile.

She giggled before turning to leave. "Don't worry, you'll be hearing from us soon. It was nice meeting the two of you."

"Nice meeting you as well," Christian replied.

"Ditto," Joe said while watching her leave the cafeteria in Shawn's wake. "Spirited girl, isn't she?"

Christian laughed. "I have to admit I feel almost sorry for him once she gets him alone."

"Almost?" Joe eyed his grandson.

"Yeah, but not quite. Everything she did say was the truth and he needed to hear it. That and then some."

"Amen to that."

"With a hallelujah on top like a big fat cherry."

"Think we'll ever see them again?" Joe inquired.

"If she has any say about it, you can count on it."

"Yep, most definitely."

They sat there in comfortable silence the next several minutes while laughing and talking about their interesting visit.

"Well," Joe said while finally getting up. "I'm going up to the rec room to see if the guys are there yet."

"They probably have been for a while now."

"You coming?"

"In a bit. I'll be along soon." Christian nodded before stretching out. He stayed where he was for a few more minutes while laughing slightly at the way Shawn's spirited and so-called girlfriend had chewed him out.

Fifteen minutes later, Christian walked through the rec room's threshold and entered a very heated and aggressive game of five-card stud. Walt was thrown out of the game by that point, quite forcibly from what Christian had heard, for, above all reasons, cheating. The other guys wanted Christian to take his spot and, when he did, his grandfather finished telling them the story of Shawn and Francesca. All the other old timers at the table were eager for them to revisit, mostly so they could all lay their eyes on his golden European beauty, something they hadn't seen in years.

Over the rest of the winter, Shawn made periodic appearances at Forestry Park to see Christian. Many times he came with Francesca, but usually he came alone. It seemed he was trying to make amends with Christian after many years of neglect, thought Christian wondered if Shawn was doing it by choice or because he was felt he was being forced to by Francesca. In either case, Christian was just glad he was around. Progress was going slow between the three of them, Christian, Joe, and Shawn, and they all were taking their time at getting to know each other again.

David had visited three times, all without Sally. Joe, to this, complained that he wanted to see her but David insisted that she was too busy at home to make the trip.

And speaking of complaining, Shawn didn't seem to have a shortage of words concerning Francesca. Most weren't complementary, and always when she wasn't there. For as many faults he claimed that she had, not one of them was a good enough reason to leave her. When she did come with him, she always made it a point to keep him in line whenever possible. This would send Shawn up the wall, even at the slightest inclination. She seemed to enjoy giving him hell consistently, but whatever she said was the truth and she would never do it unless he needed to hear it; which was usually all the time.

A number of times during these moments that Shawn and Francesca would have, Nurse Rita would make herself known and threaten to escort them from the premises if they continued to keep up their disturbances. Occasionally she actually followed through on named threats, usually with the help from Dave the janitor and a few orderlies. Shawn and Francesca definitely had a love-hate relationship going strong between them.

Chapter 54

The last Friday of the New Year's second month, Christian got another unexpected visit from Shawn. Shawn was very much alone during this visit and was told point blank from Rita that, "Your visit will most certainly be a pleasant one or your white, honky ass can just turn right back around and leave." Since he knew she meant every bit of it and had adequate help to enforce it, he reluctantly gave his word that no trouble would occur during his visit.

"I'm surprised to see you here without your wife," Christian dryly commented as Shawn was waiting in his room when he returned from that morning's treatment.

"She's not my wife!" his brother hotly retorted. "Besides, she's at work right now and I wouldn't want you fantasizing over her if I did bring her."

"Why would I do that? If I'd fantasize over anyone, it'd be Miho. I'm surprised to see you here."

"It wasn't my idea," Shawn admitted. "She wouldn't stop crawlin' up my ass unless I agreed to come back."

"Be sure to thank her for me then, won't you?"

"It'll be the first thing outta my mouth." Shawn shook his head before looking around the room. "Where's Gramps?"

"Therapy," Christian said as he looked out his room's window before sitting on his bed. "That friend of yours is really spirited, if you don't mind me saying so."

"You noticed, huh?" Shawn rolled his eyes.

"I'm surprised to see you're with someone like her."

"You're not the only one. I don't know what it is about her but, whatever it is, I just can't get enough," he admitted. "And I'm not talkin' about just the sex. I mean, she's always on my ass if I do or say something she thinks is wrong. She knows it irritates the hell outta me but, still she keeps it up. She keeps it up and I keep going back for more. I'm starting to think this relationship is a mistake."

"Why do you say that?"

"Mostly because she's not like any of my other flings. She doesn't drink or do drugs. Forget about getting her drunk or stoned. She won't even have sex with someone unless she knows them well enough. And she gets mad as hell if I look at other women! What the hell is wrong with her?!"

"Who says anything is wrong with her?" Christian laughed.

"But how can anyone live so, so..."

"Clean?"

"Yes."

"Sober?"

"Yes!"

"Boring like?"

"Exactly!"

"How's that going for you?" Christian asked him. "Living a clean, sober, and boring life?"

Shawn smiled slightly. "It's going great."

"Is it?" Christian paused.

"It's so hard living like that without a little excitement thrown in, if you know what I mean."

"It's not so hard if you choose not to live like that."

"That's easy for you to say; you've never cared about any of that shit," Shawn told him. "I thought the mold was broke after they made you. Then we met that wife of yours. She's as straight as you are!"

"But she is older than I am. The mold that made me could have been used to make her first."

"That's true, it could have." Shawn smiled before thinking about something. "Did you know she wants me to give up drugs and alcohol now? Can you believe that?!"

"Who, Miho?"

"No, you fuckin' asshole. Francesca! She wants me to."

"How dare she?! Drugs and alcohol? They've been your closest, and best, friends since your teenage years," Christian mocked as Shawn stared at him. "What in the world is she thinking about when she asked that of you?"

"Dude, that's not funny, man! Do you know how hard it is to all of a sudden give up something you care about?"

"You're asking me a question like that?"

"Don't patronize me, you fuckin' prick!" growled Shawn while smiling for the first time that visit. "You've never had those in your life to matter."

"But I have had to give up my family when I came here. I'm losing my memory and I have no control over that so, you can say, I'm giving that up as well," he told him. "But, then again, they weren't as important as what she wants you to give up, right? What are you going to do, leave her because of this?"

"That's just it, I don't want to. For the first time in my life I've found a person who I can actually imagine being with," Shawn confessed. "Every time I come up with a valid reason to drop her ass to the curb, I end up naming two why I can't. On top of that she's such a hard-ass and won't do anything I tell her."

He shrugged. "Maybe that's a good thing. Maybe you should start listening to her. It might actually help."

"That's easy for you to say," Shawn abruptly told him. "Miho had your ass castrated after that first date of yours and has been controlling your balls ever since. She probably even has them in a baggie up in the freezer for all I know."

"Shawn, that's below the belt," he chastised as his brother gave him a stern look. "What have I told you about that? I distinctly remember telling you that you can say anything you want about me but I want you to leave Miho out if it. Alright?"

"Sure, fine. Whatever you want." Shawn dismissed it with a wave of the hand.

"While we're at it, I think it'd be a big mistake for you to leave Francesca, let alone think about it."

"But she's such a fuckin' bitch to me!" Shawn whined.

"She's a bitch because you deserve it, Shawn. Have you ever thought about that?" Christian's tone and firmness of his voice made him jump slightly. "You've got to get it through that thick skull of yours that she's trying to help you!"

Shawn rolled his eyes. "Oh, sure, tryin' to help you say. That'll be the day."

"Shawn, will you please stop being such an ignorant asshole? Stop talking long enough, open both your eyes, and actually see what she's at least trying to do for you."

"She's trying to change me into a different person all together!"

"You're right, Shawn, she is," Christian agreed. "But not totally different; just tweaking certain aspects. And you know what? You shouldn't fight it. Just go along with it. You might actually like the person you may become."

"You mean let her change me into someone completely different? Are you fuckin' nuts?"

"I am nuts, remember? Look where I live." Christian chuckled while acknowledging his room. "But not as much as you'll be if you don't start listening to either of us. Besides, are you actually happy with who you are and how you are at the present moment?"

"Maybe I am. So what?"

"You're happy with your drug habits? Your drunkenness? All those one-night stands and womanizing episodes you've had? Happy with having no one around in your life who likes you for who you are? How many people like you only because you're rich and famous?"

Shawn didn't answer any of these questions. Rather, he sat there looking at his brother while thinking about what he was just told.

"Please do not think I'm trying to criticize you," Christian told him.

"It sure sounds like you are."

"I *am* aware it's none of my business what you do."

"You're damn right it's not."

"But what would happen if you go on a drunken binge or overdose on some pain killers and end up in the hospital comatose?" Christian soon continued. "Who would be there if you woke up? Who'd take you home? Or, when you're an old man, well past your boxing prime, who'll keep you company, that is, if you're still alive? Do you really think you'll be able to pay someone to hang out with you? Please, Shawn, at least consider this. That's all I'm asking. If you truly don't want to change, then don't. I no longer care what you do. Really, I don't. I have more important things to worry about than you. You're the least of my problems."

Those last few words seem to sting Shawn. He soon shrugged it off, trying to act like it hadn't affected him, but clearly it had. "I wouldn't say I've become the person I wanted to be, but who can honestly say that? Huh?"

"What would you say, then?" Christian asked him softly. "Who did Shawn Calloway want to grow-up to become? Who does he want to be now?"

There was a long pause as Shawn struggled for the words. "I wanted to be like my father, my real one, but better."

"Well, it looks like you may achieved that very admirably. I hate to say it, but you've achieved your goal with flying colors. You passed with straight A's."

"I'm nothing like him!"

"Really? You're not?" Christian asked with raised eyebrows. "You're a drunk, just like. I'd say you're a junkie just like him, but it was your mom who was that, wasn't she? You most likely dominate and beat most, if not all, of your women, just like him. You have no known friends or family, just like him. And the ones you do have don't want anything to do with you, just like him. But you are in a sense a better version than he ever was if you consider being rich and famous better. You're great at your job, you clearly are. Was your dad? I'm not sure on this point. If you're not careful, you'll end up just like him.

"And if you don't start to change soon, you'll most likely find yourself face down in some dark, dingy, cold back alley one night with no money, no friends, and no family," Christian continued. "You may end up there from the drugs and alcohol you've let consume your life. Or it may be after some guy you pissed off shoves a knife in your belly. It's all up to you. You're the one who ultimately decides how and where you'll leave this world. I just hope my mind's completely gone by then so I don't have to witness.

"Also, if you do choose that type of exodus for yourself, will you just wait until Mom and Dad are dead first when that happens? They already lost you once and it'll tear them up if they have to lose you again. It's either that, which path you're heading down, or you can choose to go down another one, one that you so desperately want to ignore. This different route is the one Francesca seems to want to divert you down. It's all up to you."

"You don't know what you're asking of me," Shawn said very emotionally as tears filled his eyes. "She's so hard to live with and so hard to please."

"And she's the person you quite surprisingly fell in love with," Christian told him softly. "All you need is to accept and trust she's looking out for you. But that's hard to do if you're used to not trusting people. Please, try to accept it and tell her that. If you do that one small thing, you might be surprised at how happy you'll become. Don't let us down as you consistently have been. But, more importantly, don't let yourself down. You've been this way for far too long, and you've finally come to that crossroad in your life we all have to cross sooner or later. You'll soon need to make a choice before the choice makes you. If you do this for yourself, I assure you, you won't regret it."

"How can you be so damn sure of yourself?" Shawn asked while the tears from his face. "Will it be that easy?"

He shrugged at that. "Call it faith. Or a gut instinct. But making the choice is easy. It's following through on it that's the hard part. It'll get easier for you the more you do it. Now, if you don't mind, I'm going down to the rec room to play some cards. I'm going to be bringing you with me once you dry that face of yours."

"I'm not going."

"Yes you are," Christian insisted. "You need to stop feeling sorry for yourself and you need to be around honest people. I know just the people to help you with that. With any luck, they're there right now playing cards."

"Ok," Shawn finally agreed with a nod. He soon got up to follow Christian to the clinic's rec room.

Chapter 55

Overtime, the more Francesca encouraged Shawn's returned visits, the more he seemed to enjoy it. And the more he enjoyed it, the less encouragement he needed to continue.

"So, is this thing you and her have remotely serious?" Christian asked during one of his brother's visits as they drank coffee in the cafeteria.

While not wanting to answer the question, Shawn coughed.

"I'll take that as a yes."

"Now wait a damn minute! I in no way said yes to that particular question."

"But you didn't deny it either, now did you?"

"Well, maybe it is, but you didn't hear it from me. Alright?" Shawn pointed a finger at him. "You didn't hear it from me."

"Don't worry; she won't hear it from me." Christian laughed. "Besides, do you think I'll remember it long enough to tell her?"

"Maybe, maybe not. But in either case, you'd better not tell her."

"My lips are sealed. Let me ask you this, though," he said while considering his words. "If she knew your true intentions when you two first met, would you two still be together?"

"Are you fuckin' kiddin' me?! She wouldn't have given me the time of day."

"Who says she does now?"

"Keep it up, you mother, keep it up," Shawn told him while trying not to smile.

"Whatever you say, Champ. Anyway, this fight you have coming up next week, is it a title defense?"

"Of course it is. Duke wouldn't have it any other way."

"Is he even a contender for your belt?"

"No, but he *is* a top contender for the WBC belt. A win in this match would put the winner in a good spot to challenge for that belt hopefully later this year."

"Trying to unify the belts again?"

"What other reason would I have?"

"Have you given any thought to retiring?"

"What the hell are you babblin' on 'bout?" Is your mind so full of holes you forgot who I am? Of course I haven't thought about retirin'! Why the hell would I do a stupid thing like that?"

Coming back from refilling his coffee, Christian asked, "What else do you have to prove? Besides, I can think of two reasons why you should at least consider it: Francesca is one, and what happened to me is the second."

"First off, Francesca will like whatever I tell her and be happy about it."

Christian laughed when he heard that. "Oh, she will, will she?"

"Yes, she will! And if she doesn't, then she can go fuck off because I don't need her. She's just like everyone else – replaceable. And, secondly," Shawn said while shooting Christian a dirty look, "what happened to you won't ever happen to me."

"How do you know?"

"Because I do."

"Are you a soothsayer?"

Shawn blinked. "A what?"

"A soothsayer?" Christian repeated. "A psychic? A fortuneteller? Can you predict the future?"

"Of course I can, you prick," Shawn stated cockily. "I know and see all."

"So, what will be the outcome of our previous talking point then?"

"To answer your question, I'll be the next undisputed heavyweight champion of the world!" Shawn announced with all the cockiness he could muster. Meanwhile, he was pointing both of his thumbs to his chest.

"You seem to fail to understand what the word 'previous' means," Christian commented with a smile.

"What the hell are you talkin' 'bout, bro? I know exactly what I means."

"Boxing is our current talking point, not our previous. The previous would have been your relationship with Francesca. What do you foresee in the future for the two of you?"

"Yo, man, didn't I cover that for you already? She'll do what I want, when I want!"

"Yeah, sure she will. What army do you have at your disposal to make her do that?"

"Say what you want, cheese dick, but I'm the one with the woman at my side."

"Right." Christian looked at Shawn's empty ring finger before looking to his own wedding band. "But I'm the one wearing the ring. Funny I don't see one on you. Is it one of those new, invisible kinds?"

Shawn sighed. "Dude, you know I'm the not the marrying kind."

"Maybe you aren't, but you should tell her that before she puts anymore stock into this relationship of yours or whatever it is. It could save her a lot of heartaches and a few migraines."

"You think I can't handle her?"

"I wouldn't presume to tell you what you can or cannot handle." Christian smiled. "Without her, would we even be talking right now?"

Sitting in his chair opposite of him, Shawn started to squirm. "Alright, damn it. I'll give you that," he finally conceded. "But there isn't much else she influences me on."

"Not much else, huh?" Christian's smile widened as he leaned back in his stair. "I can't believe you actually have a girlfriend, one that you freely admit to."

"First off, she's not my girlfriend," Shawn stubbornly corrected. "She's just a friend with benefits. And, let me tell you, the benefits truly are some of the best I've ever had." He winked when he said this last remark.

"She's not your girlfriend?" he asked as Shawn shook his head. "You two act like a couple. You said she was your girlfriend the first day we met her. You let her talk to you and treat you like she's your girlfriend."

"Listen, bro, I'm only gonna tell you this once so you'd better listen up," Shawn told him while holding up a hand and looking directly into Christian's eye. "I ain't pussy whipped. Never have been, never will be. You got that?"

"Hey, whatever you say, Shawn." He smiled while hold up his hands.

"I'm only here because not only is she probably the hottest chick I've ever been with, but also because she's the best lay as well. So, with that in mind, don't presume to know anything about our relationship. I can drop her like a bad habit anytime I want."

"That may be awhile considering you enjoy having bad habits in your life," Christian commented. He enjoyed teasing his brother and he knew Shawn knew it as well. "Speaking of bad habits, how's Duke doing?"

"How the hell should I know?"

"You still work for him, don't you?"

"Hey, I work for myself! I work alone and you know that." Shawn point at him. "But, to answer your question, he looks and acts the same."

"Does that Russian tank still work as his hired muscle?"

"If you're talkin' about Igor, then, yes, he's still there." Shawn rolled his eyes at that. "Let me tell you this: that guy is strong as hell and will do anything his job calls for, but by goddamn he's fuckin' stupid! A box of rocks has more smarts than he does."

"Are you saying that in order for him to raise his I.Q. he'd have to stand on a chair?"

"Basically, yeah. Oh, that reminds me, the guys down at Mike's bar all said hi."

"What guys?" Christian asked with a slightly confused expression.

"Dude, you're joking, right?"

He shook his head.

"You're being serious?"

He nodded. "I am."

"I'm sorry, bro, I didn't realize," Shawn confessed. "I was talkin' 'bout Mike, Josh, Terry, and Jake."

"Who are they exactly?"

"Mike's the owner and main bartender there. Josh is his bouncer. Terry and Jake are a couple of locals we used to play pool with there."

"When did you last see them?"

"I went up a couple of weeks back for a visit."

Christian smiled at that. "Did this visit entail showing off your belt?"

"As a matter of fact, I left the title home," Shawn returned the smile as they looked at each other. "I couldn't very well show it off if it wasn't with me, now could I?"

"That surprises me that you went all the way up there and didn't bring the belt with you. What is the world coming to?" Christian joked. "Did you stop by the gym while you were up there?"

"What gym?"

"Dom's gym."

"Why the hell would I do a dumbass thing like that?"

"I don't know. Can't you give me any reasons?"

"I ain't got no reasons to go back to that dump." Shawn scoffed. "And, if I did, I wouldn't on account Dom ain't there no more."

"Why isn't he there? He didn't die, did he?" Christian asked while feeling a tremendous amount of remorse at the possibility that his old mentor died without knowing.

"No, the old man didn't die. At least I don't think he did," Shawn told him while thinking whether Dom actually did die. "He sold the gym to either Mitch or Tony a couple of years back."

"We should look Dom up one of these days."

"Feel free to do that if you want, but leave me the hell outta it."

"You could at least call or send him a letter," he pressed. "After all those years, that's the least you could do."

"I don't write letters and I hate talkin' on the phone. I only do it if I have to. I'd rather talk face to face, but that's one thing I ain't doing."

"I know he'd like to hear from you again."

"But I don't wanna hear from him. Don't you get it?" Shawn asked irritably while looking at him. "And if it isn't too much trouble, would you mind if we talked about something else?"

"No, I don't mind." Christian shrugged. "What would you like to talk about?"

With that, Shawn moved around nervously before saying, "No offense, but I've got to get outta this place. I'd better get going before the effects of this place rub off on me."

"None of what we have here is contagious," Christian told him while watching him stand. "But if you box any longer than you have to, this may be the life you have to look forward to."

"Don't even start with that, ok bro? I told you before that shit'll never happen to me. Besides, I'm not ready to retire. If you haven't noticed, I'm still in my prime. Tell Gramps I'm sorry I didn't come up to say good-bye to him but I think he'll understand."

"Only if you tell him next time." Christian smiled.

Shawn scoffed while pulling on his jacket before leaving.

Sitting there alone, Christian began thinking not only of the so-called relationship between Shawn and Francesca, debating on what exactly it was and how it could be classified, but also the real reasons Shawn had for visiting him. Granted, they appeared to be a couple, but Shawn had never allowed anyone to get this close to him, nor allow himself to be influenced by anything other thins his own instincts and desires. Was she the real, and only, reason behind his visits or did he have an ulterior motive? Whatever it was, Christian wasn't going to worry about it just yet. He felt he had more important things to worry about, one of which was his roommate who quite possibly could be up in their room right then. Deciding to finally leave the cafeteria, he went back to his room to ask Grandpa Joe on his opinion and advice on the matter with Shawn.

When he entered his room a few minutes later, he was surprised do see both his father and mother there with Grandpa Joe. He stopped in the doorway and didn't move for quite some time. Standing in silence, he scanned the faces in the room as he thought that it had been awhile since the four of them had actually shared the same room together. He wasn't sure how long he was here trying to figure that out when his grandfather spoke to him.

"Are you going to stand there all day being rude or are you going to come in at some point?" Joe asked him.

"I'm sorry but what was that?" Christian blankly asked while coming back to reality.

"I asked if you were coming in or not."

With that, Christian finally entered the room while going to his side of the room. "How was your treatment, Grandpa?"

"It was fine." Joe had a hint of hardness in his voice. "Where've you been?"

"I was visiting with Shawn."

"Shawn's here?" David asked.

"Was here. He left a few minutes ago, just before I came up," he told his dad before looking to his grandfather. "Before I forget, he wanted me to tell you he said good-bye."

"Why didn't he do it himself?"

"He said you'd understand," Christian answered while looking at his parents. "How are you two doing?"

"Fine, considering," his father said while nodding. "Finally got through the hard part."

Looking at him, Christian wasn't sure what to think. Even though he was happy to find out his grandfather was still alive after all these years, he couldn't imagine the situation his father had been in to keep this secret. He must have felt relieved, a giant weight being lifted off of him, when he finally admitted it to his wife.

With this, Christian turned to his mother. "How are you doing, Mom?"

"Oh, same as your father, I suppose, though I can't say for sure." She sniffed. "How are you doing, sweetie?"

"I'm good, Mom. Have you two been here long?"

"Got here about twenty minutes ago."

"Staying for dinner?"

"We haven't discussed that yet," his dad told him. "Hasn't had a chance to come up."

"I see." Christian looked at his mother again before going back to his dad, who seemed to nod in acknowledgement. "If I knew you two were coming down for a visit, I would have had Shawn come up. I'm sorry about that."

"Don't be. That's probably best he didn't come up," Joe told him.

"He's been coming around lately and I think he'll be back again for a visit."

"It seems his girlfriend is behind Shawn's sudden reemergence," Joe stated.

"Shawn has a girlfriend?" Sally asked in a surprised tone.

"If that's what you want to call it," Christian said while rubbing his face. "They act like they're a couple. He even called her his girlfriend the first day Grandpa and I met her. But today he insisted that she wasn't. I don't know what they are exactly, I don't even think they themselves know, but it's fairly obvious something's going on."

"Is she a nice girl?" Sally asked.

"She is."

"And *very* attractive," Joe added with a sly smile.

"So, Dad," Christian said with a slight cough. "What was the occasion for work sending you down here today?"

His father looked at him for a moment as a slight smile crossed his lips. "Today has nothing to do with work."

"Are you saying you actually took a day off of work to come for a visit?" Christian suspiciously asked. "Didn't you say a while back that you were really backed up there?"

"We aren't that backed up now and, besides, I had some time coming," David told him while getting serious after a side-glance from his wife. "We're actually here to see you and your grandfather."

"You're here to see the both of us. Or was I just a side note?" Christian smiled.

"Well, yes to both, but it's leaning more to the latter," his father admitted in a slightly uncomfortable manner.

"When did you tell Mom about Grandpa?"

"A couple of nights ago; after dinner," David answered.

"Yes, finally," his mom said with a certain amount of anger or bitterness, Christian couldn't tell which.

"She didn't quite believe me when I first told her, though. I had to call your grandfather so she could talk to him."

"How are you taking all of this, Mom?" Christian asked her.

"I'm not sure," she told him. "It's still all very overwhelming for me. I still can't believe it, after all these years."

"It was hard for me, too, when I found out," Christian said. "I'm still getting used to the idea myself."

"Idea?" his mom asked. "Don't you mean a lie?"

"That could be another way of looking at it." Christian looking awkwardly a\to his father.

"It's the only way," Sally firmly stated. "They choose to live behind a lie rather than face the problems they had. The old saying about how the family is the last to know doesn't seem to be a humorous cliché after all."

"No, I guess it doesn't," Christian softly agreed.

Everyone seemed to go quiet for several moments after that before Joe brought up the idea of going down to the cafeteria to talk over coffee. They agree but, before finally making their way down, Joe and Christian gave David and Sally a tour of Forestry Park. In the process, Joe introduced them to the five semi-permanent residents of their rec room. They also pointed out Myrtle, who was seen just before vanishing around a corner with a newspaper in hand.

During most of their visit, Sally was quiet. She kept to herself and hardly had anything to say. To Christian, her behavior and mannerisms were similar to those of one being in shock. She hinted at breaking from her cocoon near the end of the visit; and by the time she left with David, she appeared to pretty much be herself again. They ate dinner with Christian and Joe before going back to a motel they were staying at in nearby Oyster Bay.

"We'll see you tomorrow," Sally said after getting into their car. "We wanted to visit you two before we went home."

"Tomorrow?" Christian asked in both a surprised and humorous tone. "Dad, you actually took two days off of work? What in the world's come over you?"

"I only took one day off," his father calmly told him. "Tomorrow's Saturday."

"Oh, that's right, I forgot." He smiled while tapping his forehead. "That makes sense now. I don't remember the last time you ever took two days off in a row from work."

"That's because the last time I did was well before you were born," David sternly told him before giving his son a smile. "I was hoping for us to drive down tonight after I got out of work, but your mother wasn't having any of that. Now, if you two don't mind, we're leaving now."

"See you tomorrow," Grandpa Joe said to them.

"Yep" was all that was heard from the car as Christian and Joe waved goodbye to them. They stayed outside to watch the car disappear down the road before finally turning to go back inside.

"I'm glad that's over with," Joe grumbled as he and his grandson went inside.

"You're glad what's over?"

"I'm glad that your mom knows about me."

"I thought you meant the visit." Christian smiled.

"Well, that too, but her knowing was more important."

"All we need to do now is to make us all one big happy family again."

"Does that include Shawn?" Joe asked as a twinkly sparkled in his eye.

"Of course it does." Christian looked at him. "He's still part of the family, isn't he?"

"That's a matter of opinion. Rather subjective, don't you think?"

Christian shrugged. "That depends on who you ask. Hey, are you up for a few wheelchair races? Loser buys coffee?"

"Considering we get coffee for free here, that sounds like a novel idea." Joe grasped his grandson's shoulder. "Do you remember how I like my coffee?"

"How could I forget?" the younger Eaton retorted. "Do you remember how I like mine?"

"Of course I don't. When was the last time I actually had to buy you coffee?"

"It's been a while." Christian smiled. "But after today, I don't think you'll forget."

They both laughed at this while giving up to see if there were any wheelchairs laying around for them to use.

Chapter 56

The next several weeks seemed to melt away much the same as Christian's memory did. Though he would recognize people's faces, he began forgetting who people were.

While still visiting on occasion, Shawn would show up whenever he had the urge. On a few of such visits, he would stumble in on a moment between Christian and their parents; the first several were extremely awkward for all of them.

Christian was saddened when Miho and the kids weren't able to visit, usually because of the weather or her job. As a result, their names began to fade more and he'd have to look at his pictures to keep their memories alive.

During one of his parents' weekend visits in late February, Sally asked something that took Christian totally off guard.

"Before I forget, but do you have any plans today?"

"I don't think, but I may have forgotten if I had," he told her.

"Good. I wanted this to be a surprise when we saw you."

"You wanted what to be a surprise?"

"I called Miho a couple of days ago and told her that your father and I were coming down to see you today. I asked if they wanted to come as well. Anyway, they should be here anytime now."

"You telling me that all you guys are going to be here for the weekend?" Christian asked as a giant smile began appeared.

"That's what she's saying," David verified with his own smile.

Hearing this, Christian suddenly was filled with excitement at the thought of a soon to be two-day family reunion.

"While we're at it," Grandpa Joe chimed in, "I think this might be a good opportunity to let her and the rug-rats in on our little secret."

"Are you sure about that?" Christian asked as they all looked at him with some surprise. "You did say you wanted to wait a bit."

"Well, I had said that," Joe said before going silent. He sat where he was in silence, thinking. "But the longer I think about it, the more it feels right. Besides, the three of you know, so why shouldn't they?"

Roughly an hour later, Asako and Dominic came running around the corner and almost knocked over Christian as he emerged from the shower.

"Good Lord! What's your mom been feeding you?" He grunted with surprise at how much they had grown since last he saw them he bent to pick him them up. They laughed when he did that. "You each weight a ton. Speaking of your mother, where is she?"

"She got talking to some short guy downstairs," his daughter told him.

"Oh, good grief," Christian mumbled before putting them down. "Why don't you two go down to the rec room at the end of the hall? Your grandparents should be down there waiting for you two. While you're at it, tell Grandpa I may need his help."

"Help with what, Daddy?" asked Dominic.

"If that short guy your mom's talking to is who I think it is, I don't want him bothering her and I may need some help to get rid of him," Christian told him. "So, will you please go get him for me?"

He pointed in the direction they should go before leaving before they could respond. Walking briskly down the stairs that led to the lobby, he found Vincent Hughes talking with Miho. By her expression, she definitely didn't want to be alone with him. Hughes, apparently, was attempting to convince her to have a drink with him in his office, alone.

"There you are," Christian said while nearing the stairs bottom. Miho was immediately relieved when she saw him. Hughes, meanwhile, became visually irritated. "The kids said you were down here."

"I've been trying to come up for some time now." She gave Hughes a side-glance. "But I kept getting delayed."

"Hello, Dr. Hughes," Christian said cheerfully to the short man before him before hugging and kissing Miho. "What brings you here on a Saturday?"

"I have some paperwork to finish up for Monday," he smoothly replied as if his conversation with Miho was nonexistent. "I finished a little time ago and was just leaving when I saw your lovely wife come in."

With this, there was an obvious pause between them as Christian and Hughes looked at each other square in the eye. Hughes smiled slightly while doing so. Having never have been a jealous person, Christian found himself absolutely not wanting Hughes anywhere near his wife, which conflicted him. He had never wanted to tell, let alone demand, anyone from speaking to who they wanted, but he was willing to make an exception this one time.

"Now, if you excuse us, the rest of our family is upstairs and they're waiting." Christian's tone indicated he wasn't leaving it open for debate.

"But Miho was just about to come up to have a quick drink with me," the good doctor stated innocently.

"She never agreed to that."

"How would you know that?" Hughes asked defiantly.

"Because when I showed up, you were still trying to talk her into it," Christian told him. "Why would you still be trying to talk her into something you now say she already agreed to?"

"Perhaps you came a little too late to say for certain what exactly you thought you heard? Ever think of that?" Hughes countered.

"I never agreed to come up with you," Miho injected before her husband could respond. "Let me tell you right now that I do not wish to come to your office, I do not want a drink with you, and I do not want anything to do with you or your offer."

"Are you refusing any type of hospitality I have to offer?" Hughes coldly asked with an icy stare that was equally cold.

"That would be a yes, she is, Hughes," Christian answered in her stead.

"That's Dr. Hughes if you don't mind and, besides, I don't remember asking you." He turned his icy stare onto him. "I was asking her."

"That is a no," Miho told him firmly. "No offense, no drink, and no hospitality."

At that moment, Christian saw both his father and grandfather making their way down the staircase. Hughes, however, didn't on account that his back was turned towards them.

"Do us all a favor and stay away from her," Christian warned the facilities very short director. "None of us want any trouble that might come as a result of this."

"Are you threatening me, boy?" Hughes demanded hotly why jabbing a stubby finger into his young patient's chest.

"Take it any way you want to, but she doesn't want you around her. I don't want you around her."

"You'd better do what they say, Hughes," Joe told him, finally revealing his presence there.

Jumping from surprise, Hughes quickly turned to see both of the elder Eaton's quickly approaching from behind.

"I don't think you want your ass hit with a sexual harassment suit, do you?" David calmly asked.

"Think of all the bad publicity you'll get from that," Joe rubbed in with a smile. "Especially if your star patient here, the same one who helped get you that multi-million dollar government grant, were to show up on the evening news, with his lawyer nonetheless, while going public. A sexual harassment suit that would have the four of us testify for it." He paused long enough to smile at the now uncomfortable director. "I'm sure that little head of yours is smart enough to realize that the best course of action to do is to simply leave her alone."

Exchanging glances with Joe before looking at David, Miho, and Christian, Hughes saw the light to what was being said, quickly assessed the seriousness in their tone and mannerisms.

"Whatever you want," he said in an easygoing tone and relaxed manner. "Whatever you want."

"Now that we got that settled," Christian said while looking at Hughes from under his brow. He soon looked to Miho to say, "Shall we go upstairs?"

She nodded while she and the three generations of Eaton men left the now speechless Dr. Vincent Hughes standing alone at the foot of the stairs.

That weekend Christian thoroughly enjoyed his time with his family. The only downside was the revelation of Joe to Miho and the kids. Asako and Dominic weren't fazed one iota by it, but Miho had a very hard time comprehending what she was told. Through various explanations in various ways, she left that weekend more confused than when she first was told.

"You know I love you, don't you?" Christian asked her as she and the kids were getting ready to get into the car the next evening.

"If you think that's your way of trying to get me to come around this idea that he's been alive all these years, you're not doing a very good job at it," she told him from behind a scowl.

"But it is a start." He smiled softly before leaning in to kiss her on her forehead.

"We'll see." Miho went silent while looking away. She soon looked back before returning the kiss. "I'll try and come up again at least every other weekend."

"Only if you bring the kids up with you."

"Do you think I'd come up alone?" she asked very childlike.

"You shouldn't tempt me with such an awful idea." He smiled.

"Come on, Mommy," Dominic said from the car's backseat. "Are we going home or do you plan on us being in the car for the rest of the day?"

"If you don't like it, you could stay here with me until your mom comes back for you," Christian told his son while trying extremely hard not to smile.

Dominic quickly shook his head. "And be here with all these old people? No, thank-you!"

Christian shrugged. "We could stuff you in the trunk instead."

"Dad, be serious," Asako stated. "Can we go now, Mom? We're getting cold."

She nodded before opening the driver's side door. Pausing, she turned back to hug her husband once more. "I love you. Hang in there a bit longer. Try to avoid that director of yours."

He leaned in to kiss her. "I love you, too."

With that, she got in her car and started it. David and Sally came out with Grandpa Joe soon after.

"I would have thought you had been gone by now," David commented to his daughter-in-law.

"Sorry to disappoint you, David-san," Miho told him with a smile.

"Oh, you know how she is," Christian said with a smile. "She got talking my ear off and wouldn't stop jabberin' away. The kids practically froze to death."

Miho quickly silenced him with a look before smiling. She made her final goodbyes before finally leaving for home to northern New Jersey. Soon after, David and Sally also said their own goodbyes before heading northwest to central New York.

Winter finally broke in Long Island to bring the onset of spring. The warmer weather, returning birds, and spring blossoms were all a welcome gift. The Park arranged a variety of outings for the patients, their weekly cookouts often drew the most sheltered of all residents.

Miho kept her word and came up every other weekend with the children, but the visits soon became closer together with the onset of better weather. The weather also brought more visits by David and Sally, who would visit the same weekends as Miho and the kids would for a more family get-together.

Shawn, as usual, would show up when he wanted; sometimes during the other family members' visitations, most times not. Shawn also increased his visits there with the better weather, but not much more.

Chapter 57

One morning in early summer, Dr. Wellwood came into Christian's room to find him on his bed reading a book, one that he was almost done.

"Hey, Doc. If you're looking for my grandfather," Christian said while nodding towards Joe's bed. "he's somewhere else; therapy, I think."

"I didn't come to see him. I actually came to see you," Wellwood said with a soft smile. "What book are you reading?"

"I'm not sure. It's one of my grandfather's," Christian told him while looking at the cover. "*A Tale of Two Cities*. You ever hear of it?"

Wellwood expressed he had. "That's considered a classic; one of the 100 greatest, I do believe."

"It's not a bad book. I started it last night before I went to bed."

"You've read almost that entire book since last night?"

"Yes."

"Have you read it before?"

"I don't remember."

"Outside of enjoying the book, how're you doing?"

Christian shrugged. "Fine, I guess."

"Has your therapy and medication been giving you any problems?"

"Not that I can recall."

"If you notice anything unusual, be sure to let us know, ok?"

"Sure thing," Christian said while looking up at him. Staring at him, he found himself realizing the doctor's name escaped him. "I'm sorry, but what was your name again?"

"It's Wellwood. Thomas Wellwood."

"And what do you do here?"

"I'm one of the doctors on the dementia unit here."

"Oh, that's right. Sorry about that."

"That's ok," Wellwood assured him while exchanging smiles. "Before I forgot, the reason I'm here is that Dr. Hughes wanted to see you in his office about something."

"Ah, ok," Christian said while closing his book and getting up. "Who's this Hughes person again?"

"He's our director, the guy in charge. Would you like me to take you up there?"

Christian soon found himself being led to Hughes' office. The door, upon arrival, was open to show Hughes sitting on his couch while two men were sitting in the matching armchairs. One of these two was in his thirties and as big and solid as an oak. His eyes showed a lack of intelligence that equaled physical attributes. The other man appeared to be twice as old and whose eyes had the intelligence the first set lacked. Christian felt he should know these two strangers, but didn't. On the coffee table between them lay an ashtray with two lit cigars and three glass tumblers half full of brown liquor.

"Thank-you, Thomas, for bring Christian up," the man in the center said while getting up to walk over. He held out a hand for them to shake. "Christian, so good to see you again. Thanks for coming on such short notice. I trust I didn't catch you at a bad time."

"No, you didn't." He looked at the offered hand before taking it while shaking his head. "I was just doing a little reading is all."

"Great! Please, come in and have a seat." Hughes waved one of his hands eloquently towards his couch. "It's ok, Thomas. We'll send him down once we're done."

Wellwood, meanwhile, stood in the doorway while studying Hughes and his visitors. He clearly did not trust these men nor did he want to leave Christian alone with them. He soon nodded, however, before leaving.

"So, tell me, Christian, do you know who these two gentlemen with us are?" the director asked while indicating the two men with them.

Looking at them for a moment, Christian soon answered. "They look familiar but other than that, I don't know them. Are they new patients here?"

"No, they aren't patients here. Let me introduce my two newest friends to you," Hughes arrogantly stated while hold a hand up to men before them. "This is the world famous boxing promoter, Duke Snyder. The other gentleman is his business affiliate, Igor Fenderbov."

Christian's memory seemed to slowly come back to him as he sat on the couch. He continued to stare at them in silence for a moment to get his thoughts together.

"Chris, aren't you going to say anything to them?" Hughes asked after an extended pause.

"My apologies," Christian soon said. He continued to sit there wondering what was going on by this unexpected visit and why they had apparently come to see him. "This visit just took me by surprise. I was just taken off guard, is all."

"That's understandable considering," Duke said.

"Considering what?" Christian asked while not really sure what was meant.

"Considering that you didn't consider us being here," Duke slyly said while reaching for one of the cigars before him. Tapping off its ashes into the now half full ashtray. He smiled before puffing on it; its smoke soon engulfed his face after being released. Duke raised his eyebrows at Christian before soon winking through a bluish-gray cloud.

"So, what did you guys want?" Christian asked.

"How would you like to stay here free of charge for as long as you may need our facility?" Hughes asked while grasping his own cigar.

"I would say that'd be great if my insurance didn't already cover the bulk of it," Christian told him. "The rest is mere pocket change for me. Why do you ask?"

"What would happen if your insurance stopping covering you? Do you and your family have the resources for your continued stay?"

"My insurance would keep paying its end if I keep paying my monthly premium."

"What would happens if they stopped paying, or cancelled your policy, or something else came up," Hughes continued. "Then what?"

After looking at the director for a moment while taking the questions in, Christian soon found himself asking the director, "What's this about, Dr. Hughes?"

"What if there was a way you could do something that would keep you and your family financially satisfied for the rest of your life?"

Not wanting to be forced into these question, Christian once again asked, "What do you want?"

Duke cleared his throat before puffing on his cigar. "I came here to propose a compromise, a deal if you will."

"I'm not doing it," Christian quickly told him.

"But you haven't heard the offer yet," Hughes told him.

He firmly shook his head. "Doesn't matter. I'm not doing it. Was there anything else you wanted from me?"

"Would you consider fighting again, even for just one more match?" Duke asked as his penetrating eyes never left Christian.

"No, never," he retorted while shaking his head. "Why would you ask such a question?"

"Money. What else?" Duke shrugged. "It does make the world go 'round."

"I appreciate your thoughtfulness, but I'm retired."

"Like I said before," Duke said. "It'll only be one match. And from what Vincent told you, the financial rewards would be tremendous. You and your family would be set for life."

"We already are set for life," Christian told him with a harder edge to his voice. "I'm not going to risk what health I have left for money I don't need."

"You know, Mr. Eaton, I'm very disappointed in you." Duke sighed while hanging his head. "I really am. I wish you'd reconsider, truly I do."

"I'm sorry you feel that way but my answer is still no."

"Your brother will be very heartbroken when I tell him the bad news," informed Duke.

"Why would this be bad news for him?"

"Because he was going to be your opponent for this proposed match." Duke shrugged. "He really wanted to get back in the ring with you."

"Did he now?" he suspiciously asked as Duke nodded. The smoke from both cigars was beginning to burn his throat, his eyes began to water. "Tell me, why did he want to get back in the ring with me?"

"You know why," the promoter told him.

"No I don't, hence why I asked."

"Let's just say he wanted an opportunity to even the series between the two of you."

"Evening the series?" Christian finally was beginning to understand. He was surprised at how unsurprised he was at hearing this.

"That is correct, Mr. Eaton," Snyder continued. "He wanted an opportunity to even up the score between the two of you. It has something to do with him clearing his conscious."

"Funny he's never mentioned that to me."

"Of course he wouldn't. Why would he?"

"Hold on a second," Hughes injected while looking at Christian. "Are you saying you've spoken to your brother recently?"

"Yes, that's what I'm saying."

"When?"

"He's been coming here periodically to visit."

"When did he start these visits of his?"

Christian shrugged while thinking for an answer. "I don't know. Maybe the beginning of the year."

"Why didn't you say anything to me about it?" Hughes questioned.

"Considering he was coming to see me, it never crossed my mind that I should."

"Up until recently," Duke said, "how long as it been since you last spoke with your brother?"

"Only once since our last fight, I think."

"What was the stipulation of that one visit?"

"I don't remember," Christian admitted.

"So, one form of communication between you two in, what?, over ten years?" Duke asked as he leaned back in his chair to puff on his cigar. "Up until recently, he's made literally no attempt to contact you. Isn't this right, Mr. Eaton."

"From, what I can remember, yes, that's correct."

"Then, starting around the beginning of the year, he starts showing up out of the blue to start visiting you on a regular basis." Duke paused long enough for Christian to nod that this was also correct. "Didn't you find this a bit peculiar, especially given his track record?"

"I figured it was as a result of a letter I sent him just prior him showing up. I never gave it much thought," Christian told him.

"Did he give you a reason as to why he finally showed up after all this time?"

"The impression I got was that his girlfriend talked him into it," Christian told him. "She wanted him to start seeing me before my condition got worse than it already is."

"You mean the condition with your memory."

"Yes."

"And are you sure it was Shawn who told her about you?"

"Who else would it have been, then?"

Duke tilted his head to stare at Christian while puffing on his cigar. When their eyes met, what workable wheels in Christian's head that remained began turning as a suspicion began to grow.

"Are you saying you told her about me?" He asked while leaning back. "Were you the real reason behind them getting together, to use her to influence him? Is that what you're saying?"

"I'm merely suggesting that you don't really know what prompted your brother to start visiting."

"I see," pondered Christian. "I have been a little suspicious as to what his true intentions were."

"And do you really think his coming here was just for that piece of ass of his?" Duke scoffed. "Sure, she's a great looking girl and could produce a dish almost as great but, let's be honest here, shall we? Do you really think she's the only reason behind his visits? Think about it. Regardless of who told them about you, regardless of why they got together, and regardless of why he started coming around, this is still your brother we're talking about. He goes through women like we do toilet paper. Do you honestly think a guy like that would ever become pussy whipped? Please!

"Open your eyes, will you?" Duke continued. "At least open what's left of your mind to at least think about it. Knowing your brother the way that you and I both do, what do you think is the real underlining reason behind his sudden reemergence? Does he all of a sudden give a damn about his long lost, sick brother? Is he doing this for a great piece of ass? A great piece of foreign ass, I might add. Or could he merely be masking his true intentions for a chance, how shall I put this? To settle a debt between the two of you?"

Hearing this, Christian had to admit, at least to himself, that he was suspicious when Shawn first started coming around, but merely blamed that on Francesca's influence. Duke's words did strike a chord inside him as he. Maybe there was something more to it than that.

"You've brought up some very good points, Mr. Snyder, some of which I myself have suspected," Christian admitted. "I'll need some time to think about this.

Hughes' eyes simply lit up when he heard this while leaning forward in anticipation. "So you've changed your mind about the fight, then?"

"No, I haven't changed my mind." Christian shook his head while looking at the cigar-smoking director seated next to him. "How would you be involved in this exactly?"

Duke cleared his throat before Hughes was able to respond. Hughes, meanwhile, blow his cigar smoke into his young patient's face.

"Why don't we all sleep on this, shall we?" Duke asked. "We may all come to some type of agreement if we did that."

"I highly doubt that, Mr. Snyder," Christian said while turning his attention back to the promoter before him. "I've already given you my answer several times. I'm retired. I'm never setting foot inside a boxing ring again. That's my answer no matter how much sleep I get."

"I probably speak for all of us here when I say that that's very unfortunate, Mr. Eaton," Snyder stated with a hardness in his voice. "I thought we might come to an understanding that would be mutually beneficial to all of us."

"You have my heartfelt condolences. Now, if you don't need me anymore, there's a book in my room I'd like to finish." Christian said while standing while offering them a hand to shake. "Thanks again for the visit, Mr. Snyder. Igor."

Duke accepted it immediately with a fake smile. Igor, however, needed some coaxing. When he did, Christian thought he was going to lose his hand under the great pressure from the Russian.

"We'll be seeing you," Duke promised as Christian made his way to the door.

"My answer will be the same then as it is now," he replied before closing Hughes' office door behind him.

Chapter 58

"Where're you going?" Christian asked when he saw his grandfather leaving their room minutes later.

"If you must know, I was going for a walk," Joe replied while putting on a jacket.

"Mind if I tag along?"

"Not at all."

"Where we going?"

"Outside," Joe replied as they tackled the stairs together. "I thought about doing laps on the driveway before making the rounds to the pound."

Christian sighed heavily. "That sounds good."

Looking at him, his grandfather studies his expression before speaking. "What bug crawled up your ass today?"

"Not a bug," he responded. "A cockroach would be a better term. Well, two of them actually."

"You actually have enough room up there for the both of them?" Joe smiles slyly.

He looked at his grandfather while shaking his head before both started laughing .

"Would one of these cockroaches of yours be Hughes at all?"

Christian nodded. "And the other's Snyder."

Joe questionably looked at his grandson, but otherwise kept quiet.

Catching the look, Christian explained. "Dr. Wellwood came by the room while you were away to tell me that Dr. Hughes wanted to see me. When I got up there, Snyder was there with him. And so was Igor, Snyder's hired muscle."

"What did they want?"

"It sounded like they wanted me to have another match. Against Shawn, nonetheless."

"You serious?"

"Like a heart attack," Christian told him before going into detail of the meeting he had just gotten out of.

Joe seemed genuinely surprised by the whole ordeal as his grandson was. "And Shawn wants this match, you say?"

"I myself don't know but that's what Duke implied."

"Has Shawn ever mentioned this to you? Did he ever bring it up?"

"Not that I can remember."

"Just keep in mind that Hughes would do almost anything in his power to get good publicity."

"And Duke would do the same for money."

"Do you think that the reason behind Shawn's visit of late is for another match with you?"

"Ten years ago I would have said yes, but now, after all this time? I honestly don't know. If it is, why wait a decade?"

"You could always ask him the next time he stops by."

"I could." Christian sighed while thinking. "What do you think? Do you think Shawn's been coming around for another match?"

"Hard to say. I agree that he would have asked years ago and it does seem a little late now to go for it, but you are still alive. Has your brother been talking to you about fighting again? Has he tried getting you back in the ring?"

Christian shook his head. "No, not yet anyway."

"So, with this in mind," his grandfather started, "would you think that Shawn does in *fact* want this because of this implication? Or that Snyder is trying to throw a monkey wrench into the mix to try and setup something?"

"Hey, you know, I never thought about that."

"You see, just stepping back and looking at the evidence might be the best thing you need," Joe said while grasping his grandson's shoulder.

Several minutes later, Christian and Joe found themselves sitting by the duck pond in silence. They were there about fifteen minutes before Joe stated he was cold and was heading back inside. It wasn't until they got back to their room did they speak again.

After dinner, Christian gave *A Tale of Two Cities* back to Joe.

"Thanks for the book, Grandpa. I liked it."

"You're done with it already?" Joe asked while taking it.

"Yes, just finished it now. Do you have anything longer I could borrow?"

"How 'bout *War and Peace*? Have you read this?" Joe asked while taking that piece from his collection before passing it to his grandson.

Taking it, he said, "I'm not sure."

"You've read all my other books. By the time you finish reading this, someone over there will finally be able to get a loaf of bread."

Christian looked at him, obviously not getting what he meant. He shrugged it off before laying on his bed to start reading.

"Are you watching the fight tonight?" Joe soon asked him.

"What fight?"

"Shawn's fight. It's tonight."

"I wasn't aware he had one."

"You should." Joe laughed. "He's been commenting on it the last few times he's been here. He's going for the WBC title."

Christian was surprised when he heard this. "Tonight he is? Seriously?"

"That's what I said," his grandfather confirmed.

"How would I be able to watch it? I don't have tickets."

"For starters, you don't need tickets. Dr. Allen ordered it for us," Joe told him. "The guys and I, as well as a few others, were planning on watching it in the rec room."

"Won't Hughes be upset that Allen ordered it?"

"I don't see why considering Allen paid for it. Are you doing to come down later and watch it?"

"Sure, that sounds good. Where's he fighting?"

"I think Madison Square Garden."

"Damn!" Christian stated "If I'd remembered, I would have gotten us tickets for it."

"You still could, maybe."

"No, not now since we can watch it here for free."

"Suit yourself." Grandpa Joe shrugged before hobbling out of the room. "I'm going down to see if the card games are going on now. See you later. Oh, the fights starts at eight, alright?"

"Ok, thank-you. I'll see you then," Christian said while watching his grandfather leave.

Just as his grandfather had said, Dr. Allen did order the boxing event slated for eight o'clock, one that was being fought at the world's most famous arena; and one where the main event was for two world heavyweight championships. One of such championships was for Shawn's IBF title; the other was the WBC title, currently held by *The Iron* Will Jones. The winner of the match would be awarded both world championships.

When Christian got to the rec room just before eight, and was just beginning to fill up with patients and staff alike. By the time the main event rolled around, the rec room was by then a standing room only.

The fight in question was hard fought and drawn out. This, by far, was Shawn's most compatible opponent. Their style to each other was so similar that they could have been twins. To Christian, the only way one would win would be whoever wanted it more. Each fighter got knocked down once in the later rounds. The fight would go on to last the entire twelve rounds and would be ruled by split decision in Shawn's favor. Even the points were close, giving Shawn the match, and championships, by only one point. The reaction to the fight was at a peak during the fight itself; each fighter got an equal amount of cheers and boos. And when the decision at the end was called, the crowd's reaction was more intense than during the match itself.

"What the hell?!" yelled Ernie. "That bum didn't deserve that match! No offense to you, Christian. We all know he's your brother and all, but he still didn't deserve it."

"What the hell are you talkin' about, Ernie?" Eddie retorted. "He clearly whipped that guy's ass!"

Ernie and Eddie carried on with the insults and name calling for a few more minutes up until Duke was seen on TV walking to center stage. He spoke for what seemed to be twice what he should have while Shawn attempted to fight his way in to say something. Duke, very nonchalantly, pushed Shawn away while wrapping up what he was saying and ended the interview before Shawn was allowed to say anything about his newly won championship. He soon gave Duke an icy glare before going back to his corner, grabbed his robe, and left the ring.

Christian went back to his room soon after that with a smile on his face while thinking about Shawn's victory and recent championship gold. When getting back to his room, he laid on his bed while picking up his grandfather's book up off of the windowsill. He finished it two days later right before his parents walked in for a visit.

"Hey, Mom, Dad. What are you two doing here?" he asked while sitting up in bed.

"Can't we come by to see our son?" David responded with a smile.

"You actually took another day off of work to come visit?"

"Of course not! Today's Saturday."

Christian grinned. "You were beginning to worry me for a second there, Dad. I thought for a moment that you'd actually start using some of that massive amount of time you have coming to you."

"I'll have plenty of time to take that when I'd dead."

"Oh, by the way, did you watch the fight a couple of days ago?" Christian asked.

"What fight?" his mother inquired.

"Shawn's. He won the WBC belt."

"Didn't he have that already?" asked his dad.

"That was the IBF title. He has both of them now."

"Sweetie, where's your grandfather?" Sally asked.

"I think he's down in the rec room playing cards with some of the guys," Christian said while getting up. "Come on, I'll take you down there."

Sure enough, just like he had said, his grandfather was where he said he'd be. The three of them entered the rec room in the midst of a heated game, one that Joe was winning, and one that Ernie was horribly loosing.

"Geez, Ernie, looks like you'll be out of the game in another hand or two," George observed with a smile.

"Hey, mind your own damn business, why don't ya?" Ernie hotly shot with a glare.

"Ernie, why don't you just forget about it?" Eddie asked. "When you lose, what're you really loosin'? It's just a bunch of matches."

"That's easy for you to say. No one's ganging up on your ass!"

At this point, Christian and his parents went over to say hello as Walt dealt a new hand.

"Hey, what are you guys doing here?" Joe asked, obviously surprised to see them."

"We came for a visit," Sally told her father-in-law.

"Weren't you going to stop by next Saturday?"

"This *is* next Saturday," his son replied with a smile.

"Boy, time sure does fly when you're having fun, doesn't it?" Joe pondered.

"Has it been a good couple of weeks for you?" Sally asked him.

"Not bad overall. But I have to admit that that son of yours has had the best day since the last time you two visited."

"Why?" Sally asked as she and David looked at their son. "What happened?"

Christian merely shrugged at this.

"What?" Joe asked him. "You didn't tell them that that money hungry promoter came by to try to talk you into boxing again?"

"Son, is this true?" his father asked him.

"Sadly, it is," Christian confirmed.

"You told him no, I hope."

"Of course I did."

"Hey kid, why the hell did you tell him that for?" Walt asked. "Don't' you know what kind of money you'd've made?"

"I have other things to worry about than money at the moment."

"You should still just think about it," pressed Walt. "Besides, who's to say that you can't take a dive in the first or something?"

"Are you suggesting I agree to it only to blow the match for a payday?" Christian asked.

Shrugging, Walt said, "Yep, that 'bout sums it up."

"I'm not going to do that. It's unethical."

"Think of the publicity."

"Why don't you think about it?" Christian asked him.

"Because no one would pay to see my ass in the ring. Would you?" Walt asked with a smile. "Besides, I'd get my ass killed if I ever faced him."

"Son, did Duke Snyder come to ask you to do another fight with your brother?" David asked. "Was that behind his visit?"

"Yes, that's the reason," Christian told him. "Apparently there'd be big money in it."

"Does Shawn know about any of this?"

"I don't know. It's never come up."

"Is this why he's been coming around? For another match?"

Christian shrugged. "In all honesty, boxing hasn't come up much between us. But what little was mentioned never dealt with me getting back in the ring."

"Could he be biding his time?"

"You know how Shawn is. He's not exactly the most patient person in the world. If this was one of the main reasons for him to visit, it would have come up by now."

"I do have to agree with you on that," his father admitted.

"Me too," Sally added before pausing briefly. "But could he be coming around for altogether different reasons?"

"It looks like his girlfriend's a big part of that but, on the other hand, the possibility of him trying to get me back in the ring may also be there," Christian told her. "When it comes down to it, I don't really know the real reason behind his visits."

"Maybe you should ask him." David shrugged.

"Maybe I should."

"Hey, are ya three goin' to be standing there yapping all day or do you intend on doing something a little more constructive with your time?" Ernie asked them with a sour look upon his face. "I'm asking only because you're interfering with the game. If ya wanna talk here, we'll be more than happy to deal ya in. If not, would you do it elsewhere?"

"Charming fellow," David commented after they got out into the hall.

"If you think he's charming now, you should see him on days that he has a losing streak," Christian told him.

David and Sally stayed to visit with Christian and, eventually, Joe once he got done with his card game. They stayed long enough to eat dinner with them before going home.

Chapter 59

That next week Shawn and Francesca came by one afternoon for one of their periodic, unannounced visits.

"Hey hey, Beeker, how's it hanging?" he asked while entering Christian's room.

"Going well. How's it going with you?"

"Oh, you know, you know," he said in a very cocky manner while wigging his hips in a vulgar grinding motion at Francesca "Long and hairy and hard to carry."

"Wha...what?"

"Full of juice and ready for use. Ha ha!"

"You're absolutely disgustin, you know that?" Christian stated before laughing and shaking his head.

"You should hear him at home," Francesca told him.

"I can just imagine." Christian rolled his eyes.

"So, seriously bro, how's it goin'?"

Shrugging, Christian said, "Like I said, I'm going well."

"Where's old man Joe?" Shawn asked while pointing to his bed.

"Somewhere around," he replied with another shrug while getting up to put a book away he was reading. "Most likely down the hall playing cards."

"Yo, does he spend his entire time here playing cards?"

"No, not all the time. Sometimes he and a few of the other guys go in some hall and have occasional wheelchair races."

"Wheelchair races?" Shawn asked with a perplexed expression.

"You know, the first person to get from point A to point B while using a wheelchair wins?" Christian said with heavy sarcasm. "Wheelchair races."

Hearing this, Shawn started moving around with excitement while rubbing his hands together. "Think they'd let me in on one of those races?"

"I'm sure they would since you're almost as crazy as they are."

"Real funny, asshole. You're a real fuckin' comedian, you know that?"

"That trait does seem to run in the family." Christian told him was they looked at each other while smiling. "Speaking of family, you should have been here this past weekend. Mom and Dad came down for a visit. They seemed to have wanted to see you again for some strange reason."

"Maybe it's because I just have that sort of magnetic personality people are drawn to," Shawn arrogantly said while pointing to himself with a thumb.

"Maybe it's because you're their son and they wanted to see you again? Have you ever thought about that?" Francesca told him.

"That's life." Shawn shrugged before being whapped on the back of the head by her. "Ow! What was that for?"

"Your parents want to see you again and all you have to say is c'est la vie?"

"I didn't say whatever the hell you just said," he quickly told her. "I said that that was life."

"Shawn, c'est la vie is French for 'that's life'," Christian told him while giving Francesca a smile.

"It is?" he asked as both his brother and girlfriend nodded. "Listen, this ain't France. This is America, so speak fuckin' English, alright? I definitely do *not* wannabe pressing one for that shit. Anyway, the reason we stopped by was to see if ya wanted to come to a party I'm having at my place tonight."

"Is Grandpa invited?"

"I don't think he'd be interested in the type of party I'm having."

"And you think I would be?"

"Good point, but you may actually enjoy yourself a little more than he would."

"In that case, sure, I'll come," Christian told him. "As if I'll need to ask, but what'll this party of yours going to be like?"

"It'll be like what they say about life."

"Oh, that If is Life's middle name?"

"No, man! I don't know where ya come up with half the shit you do but, ya really gotta get that head of yours outta all those damn books. They ain't good for ya. This party will be a bitch, just like life, and tonight she's gonna be back in heat! Ha ha ha!"

"Shawn, that was just gross, man," Christian told him while shaking his head. "Totally and utterly gross."

"I have to agree with him." Francesca shook her head. "You should be ashamed of yourself."

Shawn laughed while pointing to his brother. "Don't you know it!"

"So, this party of yours won't be too crazy, will it?" Christian asked him.

"You may want to bring a pair of earplugs if you have any," Francesca advised him.

***

Later that night when they pulled into Shawn's drive, Christian was amazed at the size of the his house.

"Is your house big enough?" he asked.

Shawn merely laughed while shrugging it off with an air of cockiness.

"He's just trying to overcompensate for something," Francesca commented dryly while looking out the window as they parked.

Shawn quickly looked at her with the intent of saying something, but she got out of the car before she could.

As Christian emerged from the backseat, he realized his eyes were not deceiving him. Shawn's home was literally enormous and covered almost its entire yard. What little yard that was there, that which wasn't covered by the house or the drive, had some nice shrubs and low growing trees planted. In essence, what he currently had, he had very little lawn to mow, if he actually moved it himself.

In the drive just ahead of where they parked was a basketball hoop and free-throw line. Most of the remaining drive was filled with several vehicles including a Mercedes Benz, a Lexus, a Saab, Porches, and two Hummers, not including the BMW they had just driven up in.

"Are all these cars yours?" Christian asked.

"Most." Shawn shrugged. "The Saab, which is a shit car, and one of the Hummers isn't. The guys that own them should be inside setting up the party."

"You actually let them in your house when you're not here?"

"Sure. Why not?"

"Aren't you afraid they'd take anything?"

"You mean steal?" Shawn asked in a surprised tone as Christian nodded. "Not at all. I'll just buy whatever they took again if I want it bad enough. Besides, they know I'll break their arms off if I catch them doing it. Enough of this talk, alright? Let's go inside. I need a drink. While we're at it, I'll introduce you to the guys."

Christian felt that Shawn's house was just a grander scale of the hotel room he had seen years earlier. Everything was top of the line and very expensive. Many things, such as the furniture and some of the art, however, were not of Christian's style or taste.

While entering, three men were setting up what looked like was going to be one loud, long party. There was Miguel, a guy of Latino background; Robert, a slender but well-built black guy from Brooklyn; and his beefy cousin Charles. These last two, because of their sizes, reminded Christian of George and Lenny from Of Mice and Men. All three wore extremely oversized clothing and loads of gold jewelry. They also wanted to bang fists with each other rather than shake hands. That or bump chests with them.

"Hey, Charles! You know who this is?" Robert asked while indicating Christian.

"Just another white boy to me," his cousin told him. "Hope he brought some beer, man. I'm dehydrated as fuck."

"You're dehydrated because you drank too much damn beer, man! Don't you know nothin'?" Robert asked him. "You can just get a drink of water if you're so thirsty."

"You serious, bro? Water? Damn, man! What the hell do you think I am, a fish?" protested Charles. "I need some *real* substance here."

"Just like you'll need a real liver transplant if you keep it up.

But, never mind that," Robert said while going back to Christian. "This here's Shawn's brother, Christian Eaton, former cruiserweight champion of the world! Boy, I have to admit was he ever good. He was damn good for a whitey."

"For real?" Charles asked while looking Christian over.

Christian, meanwhile, merely shrugged it off.

"Word that," Robert replied while also looking at Christian. "So, Chris, what have you been up to since you left the ring?"

"Oh, this and that," he said while trying to be as vague as possible. "I was teaching some and worked in a zoo for a few years."

"That's cool. What do you do now?"

"I live over at Forestry Park."

"The mental spot in Long Island?" Miguel shot out when he heard this as Christian nodded. "What do you do there?"

"I live there. I'm a patient."

"For real? Whoa, sorry bro. We didn't know," Robert quickly apologized. His eyes got big while his hands came up in front of him.

"That's alright. Most people don't," Christian said in a tone indicating he wasn't upset at all over it. "It's not something I really want people to know. Things happen."

Over the next hour or so, roughly fifty people showed up for the so-called party and what a party it was. There was a D.J. playing a combination of rock and hip-hop, and Shawn entertained his friends at the bar. Several others played a shoot-them-up game on one of the many big screen TVs. Another big screen was on some sports channel that, incidentally, was talking about professional boxing.

After an hour of this, Christian went to go find Shawn to see how long the party would last for. After searching the house without any luck, one of the guests said Shawn might be outside. He was soon found shooting baskets out in the drive with only the house light to help aid him.

"With all the action inside," Christian said as he approached, "I'm surprised to see you out here."

"That's the way I like it." Shawn grabbed a rebound after a failed shot before making it on a layup. He then passed the ball to Christian.

"You like it what way?" he asked while making a jump shot.

"I like having the action inside. That way I can come out here for peace and quiet."

"You have a party with a bunch of your friends, who are all inside doing whatever it is that they're doing, and you want to be out here shooting baskets because that's where the peace and quiet is? Is that what you're telling me?"

Shawn shrugged at that. "Yeah, pretty much."

"You have a weird way of doing things." Christian laughed.

"Coming from you, that's saying something," Shawn joked back.

"I want to ask a question, something I've asked you once before, if you don't mind," Christian told him after making another shot.

"Shoot," Shawn said while grabbing the ball.

"I can't without the ball."

"I meant ask your damn question."

"Have you been thinking about retiring?"

"Are you serious, bro?" Shawn asked while taking the ball in for a layup. "I'm planning to be the next undisputed heavyweight champion."

"I mean after that, once you unify the belts and all. What then?"

"Then I intend on beating the crap outta whoever there is for me to beat the crap outta."

"What else do you have to prove?"

"Why this sudden urge on me getting out?"

"I just don't want what happened to me to happen to you."

"Like I told you before, bro," Shawn said as a cocky smile crossed his face. "I'm too good and too smart to let that happen to me."

"That's what I thought about me," pressed Christian. "Something could still happen."

"I'll consider retiring when you consider gettin' back in the ring."

"That reminds me. Duke and that tank of his came by to visit me about two weeks ago."

"Really? They did?" Shawn asked as he stopped dribbling. His suddenness to it allowed the ball to roll away from him.

"He wanted to know if I'd consider fighting one more time."

"You told him yes, I hope," Shawn said while finally coming back before going after the lost ball.

"On the contrary, I told him no."

"Why did you do a dumbass thing like that? Think of the money you could'a made."

"No offense to you at all, but I don't want to risk my health, or my life, just for a nice payday."

"Think about it," Shawn started to explain. "You train a little bit for six months or so just to get in the ring for forty-five minutes, fifty tops. Then you go back to that loony bin of yours with a whole lot more money in your back pocket."

"I've already got enough money. I don't need any more."

"We all need more money, bro. It's a fact of live."

"For some that may be true."

"Dude, you only live once," Shawn told him. "An opportunity like this probably won't come around again and you're turnin' it down not only because you don't want more money, but because you don't want to get hurt more? What the fuck's that about?"

Christian simply looked at his brother in silence. "What other reason would I have to get in the ring?"

"To prove you still can do it."

"Prove what to whom exactly?" Christian spread his arms while looking at Shawn.

"Don't you want to find out if you can get into that ring one more time?"

"No, I don't."

"Why not? Aren't you worried what other people will think?"

"No, not at all. I could care less what other people think," Christian told him. "But when you say other people, do you mean those not in my own little circle?"

"Are you really that shallow or are you just being selfish?" Shawn bluntly asked him.

"What are you talking about?"

Standing there in the driveway, Shawn tucked his ball under one arm before staring silently at Christian, who never did answer the question. As they stood looking at each other, they soon realized that the other knew the reason.

"Oh, so that's it. Huh?" Christian asked while finally breaking the silence between them. "You want to face me again, don't you?"

"What if I do?"

"Why? Why now after all these years? Why now when I have these problems going on inside my head?" Christian swallowed hard after asking that.

"You don't get it, do you bro?"

"No, I don't get it. I'm past my prime. I'm in not ring shape. Another fight would mess me up worse than I am already, maybe even kill me. Besides, why would I face you? You're an established fighter who's achieved so much more than I ever had."

"Are you saying that I haven't achieved as much as you outside the ring?" Shawn defensively asked.

"No, Shawn. You're reading too much into it."

"Am I?"

"Yes, you are."

"You're the one that has his personal life all together. Right? You're the one who has the wife and kids. You have the house in the suburbs. The one who's always stood by the family while I ran off to play with the Devil. Right?"

"No, Shawn. That's all wrong. Besides, I have nothing left in me, and nothing left to prove. I'm very happy with that. Boxing is in my past, and that's where it's going to stay. Period."

"You still owe me," Shawn harshly stated.

"Owe you for what exactly? I've owed you ever since you stuck up for me against Wesley thirty years ago when we were like eight."

"I didn't have to do that. Ya know that, right?" I could'a just kept on walkin' and let him beat the crap right outta ya."

"Yes, you could have but that doesn't mean I still owe you now, thirty years later," Christian earnestly responded. "You need to give it a rest and get over yourself. There's more important things to worry about than an old debt you think I still owe you."

"But people are talkin', man! Talkin' like I can't beat you."

"But you did beat me. In our last fight, remember? Have you forgotten that? You beat the snot out of me. You beat me to a bloody pulp. Not only did you beat me, but you became undisputed champ for the second time in your career, and you also made damn sure I wouldn't return to the ring!" Christian said while almost on the verge of yelling at him.

Hearing this, Shawn blinked his eyes in shock as if the words began to sink in. "Are you sayin' it's my fault you're like this?"

"I didn't have these problems *before* that last match of ours and the beating that you gave me did lead to what I have. So, in a manner of speaking, yes, Shawn, it *is* your fault," Christian told him bluntly. "But it's also my fault as well because I chose to get in the ring knowing you might do something like that. It's also my fault that I chose to be a boxer for all those years."

"You really don't get it, bro."

"Get what exactly? There's nothing left to get! You beat me. You beat the holy hell out of me. Just like you wanted. You unified the damn cruiserweight belts. Just like you wanted. You made sure I couldn't come out of retirement to steal whatever spot light you thought I was stealing from you. That pretty much sums it up. Did I forget anything, Shawn? Anything at all? Because if I did, then you would be right by your accusation that I just don't get it."

"All you said was true, bro. But you did forget one thing: you're still winning the series between us."

"What? You need to be at *least* even with me?" Christian asked as it finally seemed to be dawning on him.

"Shawn, is any of this true?" a voice was heard coming from behind them. When they turned towards the voice, Francesca emerged from the shadows. "Do you want to have another match with him just to satisfy some childish gripe that you have against him?"

"I refuse to have it on my record that someone has the advantage over me."

"What about Duke, then?" she asked.

"What 'bout him?"

"Are you telling us that he doesn't have an advantage over you?"

"Nobody has any type of advantage over me. You understand me? Nobody!" Shawn said in anger while stepping towards her.

Seeing this, Christian walked over to them to try to get in the middle while she held her ground.

"Shawn," he said, "did you come back into my life just to get me back in the ring again?"

"I wouldn't say that."

"What would you say, then?" Francesca asked him.

"That I did it to get you off my ass about seeing him," Shawn bluntly told her. "But the thought about evening the series was also another driving factor."

"You would risk killing your own brother just so you could say he wasn't better than you?" she asked in a confused and shocked manner. "You almost killed him that last time that now, that I think about it, you probably were trying to really hurt him as badly as you could, if not kill him."

Shawn shrugged that off. "I didn't, did I? He's a big boy, he was able to handle it. Besides, if I did kill him this time around, it's definitely better than then how he's currently living. Wouldn't you say?"

"I can't believe it, your own brother." She shook her head before slapping him across the face. The sound it made was a loud smack that rang in Christian's ears.

With that, Shawn's face got all red as his eyes flashed with anger. His jaw set as he pulled back a fist to hit her. Seeing this, Christian stepped in the middle of them to attempt to block the punch. However, he was far too slow and too far away from the boxing mindset to effectively block it. His lights went out when Shawn's clenched fish hit him squarely in the face.

Chapter 60

Christian woke to find himself lying on his bed while suffering from a tender jaw and a massive headache. Grandpa Joe was looking down at him with a look of concern.

"You're finally awake," he said with a smile.

"It would appear that I am," the younger Eaton replied while rolling over to sit on the edge of his bed. "What time is it?"

"It is just after eight o'clock tomorrow morning. If you weren't awake by the time I got back from breakfast, I was going to get you some help."

"Get me help for what?"

"From that shot you took from Shawn last night." Joe looked at his grandson with a worried look. "You do remember being hit by Shawn last night, don't you?"

"What the hell are you talking about, Grandpa? I haven't seen Shawn since our last fight."

"Christian, are you ok?"

"I'm fine. Why?"

"Because Shawn's been visiting us here since the new year. You went to his house last night for a party he was having. Chris, he knocked you out."

"Knocked me out? You mean he hit me?"

Grandpa Joe nodded. "Yes, and did he ever."

"Why did he do that?" Christian asked while rubbing the side of his face.

"According to Francesca, he was going to hit her instead. You seemed to have been the noble knight that stepped in to stop him. You were hit instead."

"Who's Francesca?"

"His girlfriend."

"Shawn has a girlfriend?! Since when?"

"Up until last night he had one. And for a while."

"Are you saying she dumped him because he hit me?" Christian laughed at the thought of that.

"And why did he hit you?"

"Because I got in the way of him hitting..."

"Precisely," Joe confirmed. "But she didn't leave him because you got hit, by accident mind you. He tried to hit her, after all, and would have succeeded admirably if you hadn't stepped in."

"Why can't I remember any of this?"

"You apparently have amnesia from the blow."

"Will I be able to remember any of this?"

"I don't know," his grandfather responded. "It's up to you, I guess."

"What do you mean?"

"Only you or, should I say, your brain will be able to get back the memories. Maybe you will, maybe you won't. Maybe it'll only come back in pieces."

Christian moaned while using both hands to rub his face. "My head hurts," he said while pulling his hands away.

"Do you want to see a nurse? Maybe Allen or Wellwood?"

"No, thank-you. I'll be fine."

"You sure?"

"Maybe I will in a little bit."

"What about after breakfast?" his grandfather suggested with a smile. "A good hearty breakfast might make you feel better."

"That does sound good." Christian nodded while standing up. He found himself almost toppling over as the room spun around him. "If I was at his party last night, and he's the one who knocked me out, then who brought me back?"

"Francesca."

"Have I met this alleged girlfriend before last night?"

"Many times."

"Is she nice or is she like all of his other flings?"

"She indeed is very nice, but I wouldn't know about any of his other, what did you call them?, flings?" Grandpa Joe said with a smile while walking to the hallway. "I've been here the last twenty years. And, as a result, I've never met other flings of his. But, if I were you, I wouldn't call her that to her face."

"If she broke up with him, what makes you think I'd ever have a chance to call her that to her face?"

"Because she's coming down the hall as we speak," Joe said while pointing to the stairs.

With this, Christian went out in the hall to see a highly exotic, extremely attractive woman walking their way, one who smiled when she saw them.

"Is that her?"

"It is indeed," his grandfather confirmed.

"Was she really his girlfriend or was she something else?"

"She seemed to be the real deal but I can't really say. You could ask her if you'd like." Joe laughed.

"No, that's alright. That sort of question may be a little insulting."

"Maybe just a little."

"Christian," Francesca said as she neared. She soon pushed her arms out to embrace him in a hug. "Are you alright?"

"I think so," he said while returning the hug.

"We were so worried about you."

"We? We who?"

"Shawn and myself."

"I see," Christian stated coolly. "You *and* Shawn were worried?"

"Yes."

"If he was so worried, where is he then?" Christian questioned. "Why didn't he come with you? Why didn't he help bring me back here last night?"

"That's a long story."

While standing there looking at her, Christian tried to figure out what nationality she was. Meanwhile, he completely forgot everything that had happened to him since waking up. He had no idea how he got out in the hall, why he was there, or why Grandpa Joe and this strange woman were looking at him.

"I'm sorry but I seem to have forgotten your name," he kindly admitted.

"Are you being serious?" she asked. "You don't know who I am?"

"I'm sorry but, no, I seem to have forgotten."

"I'm Francesca, Shawn's girlfriend," she told him with an awkward expression.

"Shawn's girlfriend? As in my brother Shawn?"

"Well, yes and no." She smiled. "Yes, I do mean your brother but, no, I'm not his girlfriend. Not anymore. Not after last night."

"Why? What happened last night?"

"What are you talking about, Christian? You don't remember him hitting you at his party?"

"I think you may be a little confused, ma'am," he tried to explain as politely as possible. "I couldn't have been at his party last night. I haven't seen him in years. Now that I think about it, I can't remember when I actually did see him last."

There was a pause between them as his words set into her head. The more they sank, the more she began to realize to what extent.

"Oh, Christian, I'm so sorry," she softly said. She patted his cheek as tears began to fill her eyes.

"Sorry about what? Are you ok?" He reached for her. "Do you want us to get you some help with anything?"

"No, I'll be alright. Thank-you, though," she answered while drying eyes. "I'm sorry to have bothered you so early. I should go."

"Alright. Thanks for stopping by." Christian's tone and mannerisms clearly indicated he had no clue as to what else to say. "Will you be back again?"

"I'm not sure. I will try to get your brother to stop by for a visit if I can," she informed him.

Christian smiled at the prospect. "I'd like that. Tell him it'll be good to see him again after so long."

At that, Francesca turned before quickly vanishing in the stairwell. When she was gone, Christian noticed his grandfather looking at him with an unusual expression.

"What?" he asked.

"Did you want to shower and change before breakfast this morning?" was all his grandfather could say in response.

"It's time for breakfast already? I can't believe that I overslept," Christian told him while looking down at his wrinkled clothing. "Did I sleep in my clothes again last night?"

Joe nodded his head to this.

"Mom's going to be upset if she finds out I did that again."

"If you hurry up and don't tell her, how's she going to find out?"

"You've got a point, Grandpa." Christian smiled before going back into their room. He took off his shirt before going to the bathroom for a shower.

Joe, meanwhile, stood where he was for a few moments while thinking what he had just witnessed. He felt bad for his grandson but, more importantly, felt sorrier for Miho, Asako, and Dominic. With this in mind, he considered there could be a chance he may have forgotten a good deal about them since last night. Only time will tell.

That following Monday brought an unplanned visit from Miho. Joe had called to tell her the situation of what had happened to Christian over that weekend. She had left the kids with a friend, took the day off of work, and came up to Forestry Park. She got there to discover Christian had lost more memory loss was more than she had expected. Joe informed her that Christian had in fact regained much of his memory from Shawn's party, though still had much to get back.

During her visit, Dr. Hughes and Duke Snyder entered Christian's room for a much unexpected, and very surprised, visit.

"What the hell do you two want?!" Joe demanded when they entered.

"Can't we come by to visit one of my favorite patients here?" Hughes asked in a highly condescending tone.

"Not without an ulterior motive." Joe scoffed while turning his back on the most unwelcomed visitors while sitting down on his bed.

Hughes and Snyder looked briefly at him before turning their attention to Christian, who stared blankly at them. Miho, sitting next to her husband, only looked suspiciously at the two unscrupulous men.

"Mrs. Eaton, this is quite a pleasant surprise to see you here," the director announced with a fake smile while walking over to her in an attempt to shake her hand.

"I'm sure it's more of a surprise for me to see you than you me," she responded. She did not accept the handshake. "Is there something that we can do for you?"

"The reason we're here was is because we wish to speak with your husband, Mrs. Eaton." Duke smiled while making his way further into the room.

"Just to let you know, the answer is no," she told them flatly.

"But you haven't heard the reason for our visit yet."

"I don't need to. You two have been coming around the last few months trying to get my husband back in the ring. And for what? More money? Again, the only think we have to say to that is no!"

"With all due respect, Mrs. Eaton, that's presumptuous to assume that that's why we came," Hughes said elegantly. "But if it were, we came to ask your husband, not you."

"Maybe you don't fully understand what I am saying." Miho's voice became hard as her eyes glazed over with more of an icy coldness than they were before. "No matter what you say, how you say it, or how much you promise us, the answer will always be no."

"I'm afraid you're the one who doesn't fully understand," Duke injected. "This fight would be worth millions for each party involved. In addition, we're not even saying he has to fight. All that we would require is a few publicity things such as photos, a press conference, that sort of thing. That's all. Then when the fight begins, all he has to do is take a dive in the first if he wanted to."

"You mean he would lose on purpose?" questioned Miho.

"That would be another way of looking at it." Duke smoothly smiled.

Joe scoffed behind them, drawing the attention of those in the room. "Sounds like the only way."

"No, sir!" Miho stated firmly. "I do *not* think we will accept what you have to offer."

"Maybe you should let your husband answer for himself," Hughes said while looking at his patient. What do you say, champ? How does one more match sound?"

"Oh, geez. I'm not sure," the former champ replied. "I don't think I should."

"Oh, come on, Mr. Eaton," Duke pressed him. "All we ask is you do one more match for us. That's all. And in exchange, we'll pay you no less than $5 million. How does that strike your fancy?"

"$5 million does sound good," Christian agreed.

"Honey," Miho said while putting a hand on his forearm. "Don't you remember what your doctors said? They said you shouldn't fight anymore."

Christian looked at her in a way to indicate he didn't have a clue as to what she was talking about.

"Now, Mrs. Eaton, you shouldn't believe everything that the doctor's tell you," Hughes told her. "They merely recommend that you husband doesn't fight. We're giving you a chance to earn more money than you can possibly use and to also keep your spot here at Forestry Park."

"Are you implying that you'd toss him out if he didn't do this?" Miho questioned while getting up to walk over and look Hughes in the eye. "You, above all people, know why he's here. Another fight could kill him and why? So you can line those deep pockets of yours a little more? No! I'm not having any part of this and neither is my husband! From not on, I would appreciate if it you two money hungry vultures leave us alone. If not, you'll be hearing from our lawyer."

"Is there any way we could get you to reconsider?" Snyder asked.

"Absolutely not!"

"That disappoints me, Mrs. Eaton. Truly, it does," Hughes told her while giving her an icy stare.

While returning the stare, Miho replied, "I'm sure it does in more ways than one. And you did say I shouldn't believe everything that the doctors tell us, isn't that right, *Dr.* Hughes?"

Pausing a beat, Hughes turned to leave the room. "Have a good day, *Mrs.* Eaton. Joe."

Duke stayed another moment longer to look at the three members of the Eaton family before also taking his leave.

Unfortunately for the Eaton's, the thoughts that Joe had had that day after Shawn's party soon became a reality over the next couple of months. When it seemed like all the Eaton's were on their way to becoming one big happy family, Christian's mind finally slipped past the point of no return. His memory went downhill and the first memories to go were essentially everything from his last fight with Shawn and beyond. Those twelve years quickly faded before totally vanishing and to never surface again.

The two that took it the hardest were Asako and Dominic. They honestly could not understand, or comprehend, why their own father would have no idea as to who they were. His eyes would verify this very point every time they would see him, and there was nothing anyone could do about it.

Chapter 61

Christian was soon diagnosed with Parkinson's and was eventually confined to a wheelchair; whose advancement was faster than what was anticipated. At times, his arms would be so weak that he would need help feeding himself.

During this time of declining health, Shawn's career had blossomed more than anyone could have possible imagined. He had more money than he could ever possibly spend, easily triple as many endorsements as Christian had had, and each time he got into trouble with the law only seemed to increase his price tag; all of which pleased the hell out him. However, that main thing that upset him was that Snyder controlled every aspect of his life, a life he worked really hard to get to. And what made him more upset was the fact that his brother was not able to comprehend the magnitude of his professional success he so desperately wanted him to see.

The only person that Shawn felt he had to compete against, or whose approval mattered the most, was unable to understand or see anything that he had achieved. And this fact alone caused him so much distraught and sleepless nights that he almost blamed his brother, his closest friend, of the failure that had always riddled his life. Almost. He chose to go confront his brother one weekend to express his dissatisfaction for Christian's failure on not applauding him on a successful career. In the back of his mind he knew his brother most likely wouldn't remember much after he left, yet Shawn still felt compelled to go anyway.

While climbing the stairs to the second floor of Forestry Park, Shawn almost knocked Grandpa Joe over as they rounded the corner. A girl in her early teenage years and a boy a few years younger, both of which Shawn didn't recognize, were with his grandfather.

Shawn and Joe simply looked at each other in stunned silence while neither wanted to be the one to speak first.

"Well, well," Joe said while giving his grandson a hard glare. "The prodigal son returns. What are you doing here?"

"What do you think? I came to see my brother," he answered while returning the glare.

"You have a lot of guts showing up here after what you did to him."

Before either of them could go any further, the young lady tugged at Joe's sleeve.

"Grandpa, who's he?" she politely asked.

"This is your uncle," her grandfather told her.

Asako's expression was one of surprise while alternating her gaze between Joe and Shawn. She soon focused to a speechless Shawn before asking, "You're Uncle Shawn?"

"Who the hell are you?" he asked in an almost demand-like manner.

"Shawn, don't you know your own family?" Joe asked as emotionless as possible, hoping to embarrass his grandson with his question. "This is your niece Asako. The young lad next to her is her brother, your nephew, Dominic."

When Shawn heard the boy's name, he sharply looked to his nephew. He was going to comment about the name, but chose not to instead. He merely shifted his gaze back to his grandfather.

"Where's Christian? I'd like to see him."

"He's in our room," Joe replied simply. "Miho's feeding him his lunch."

"You serious? Why the hell is she doin' that?" Shawn scoffed. "Man, she has him so pussy-whipped that he even needs her to feed him, for Christ's sake?"

"As a matter of fact, Shawn, Christian can't very well do much for himself these days. But, you'd have known that if you were around here more often."

"I came to speak with him, not to argue with you," Shawn stated.

"No one's stopping you," Joe told him. "May I assume you still know where he's staying?"

"Don't you know what they say 'bout assuming?" asked Shawn before sidestepping his grandfather and proceeded towards Christian's room.

Joe didn't respond. Instead, he warned his grandchildren. "Why don't we not come back for a few minutes? How about we go down to the cafeteria instead to see if we can't get some ice cream? How's that sound?"

"That sounds awesome, Grandpa," Asako told him.

"Why can't we go back to the room with Mom and Dad?" Dominic asked.

"I don't think Shawn wanted us there when he came to see your father," Joe informed him. "Besides, knowing your mother, she wouldn't either. So, how about that ice cream?"

When Shawn entered Christian's room, he found a slender, wheelchair-bound man sitting next to the window. Miho sat next to him while feeling him some sort of soup. He stopped just inside the door's threshold to watch and honestly couldn't believe what he was seeing. Shawn did a double take and, even then, would've swore he'd entered the wrong room if Miho hadn't have been there.

Since the last time Shawn had seen his brother, Christian had lost a tremendous amount of weight. His face was gaunt and both of his eyes, as well as his cheeks, were sunken. With the pasty white complexion he was now sporting, Shawn swore he looked almost skeleton-like. He was wearing a long-sleeved flannel shirt and had a thick wool blanket over his legs.

Miho soon looked up when she noticed him. As their eyes met, a look of surprise briefly lit up her face before it turned to anger. Outside of the look, she didn't acknowledge him. She went back to keep feeding her husband.

"Aren't you going to say hello?" Shawn asked in his typical cockiness.

Miho ignored the question.

"Aren't you gonna answer me?"

"What do you want, Shawn?" she asked coldly and flatly while finally turning to look at him.

"I've come to see my brother, if that's alright with you."

"And if it isn't?"

"I'm still gonna see him no matter what you think. He's still my flesh and blood, after all."

"That's funny." Miho smiled slightly as her eyebrows scrunched. Christian, meanwhile, still hadn't noticed Shawn.

"What's funny?" Shawn asked her.

"That you only seem to call him your brother or flesh and blood when you want something out of him," she told him. "Other than that, you've never seemed to want people to associate the term brother for the two of you."

Shawn stood where he was and found himself unable to respond the accusation as he realized that she was right.

"Listen, are you gonna do all his talkin' for him or do you mind givin' him back his tongue and balls long enough for me to say to him what I've come to say?"

Miho's eyes flashed red while glaring coldly to her brother-in-law. Pausing briefly she soon put the soup down before getting up to walk over to him. "What was that?!" she demanded.

"You heard me. I want you to give my brother his tongue and balls back so I can talk with him. Once I've said what I've come to say, you're free to take them back for as long as you want."

"I'm so happy I have your majesty's approval," Miho mocked while curtsied ever so slightly.

"Yo, woman, what the hell is your problem?!" Shawn demanded as he exchanged looks with her. "If you have somethin' to say, then just come out and say it."

"Do you really want me to tell you my problem? Do you really want me to come out and say what's on my mind?" Miho sharply asked while glaring up into Shawn's eyes.

Surprisingly, Shawn found himself groaning as he immediately wished he hadn't have said that. However, he knew it was far too late to take it back.

"The problem I have is you, Shawn," she informed him. "Did you come here to brag about yourself some more? Once you're all bragged out, do you intend on disappearing for a few more months, if not years, until you have something else to brag about? Is that why you're here?"

"Hey, woman, do you even know what you're talkin' 'bout?"

"Are you saying I'm wrong?" Miho held his gaze. "Are you?"

While looking at her a moment longer, Shawn soon realized that his internal balloon had burst. He let out a sigh before finally speaking.

"I guess I'm all bragged out," he finally admitted.

"Did you then finally have the guts to come here to challenge him to another fight? Is that it then?" She continued to glare hotly at a now silent Shawn. "When your henchmen Snyder and that vulture Hughes weren't able to get you what you wanted, you thought you should give it a try? How about it? Do you deny *that*?"

Remaining silent while studying her face, Shawn, uncharacteristically, decided to choose his words carefully.

"The thought had crossed my mind a time or two," he finally admitted. "But not for quite some time."

"Oh, is that so?" Miho questioned. "Please forgive me if I don't entirely believe, or trust, what you have to say, Mr. Calloway."

Shawn's eyes soon flashed a warning. "Listen here, I came to see my brother. Now, are you gonna get outta my way or not?"

"If I do, then what? Huh?" She tilted her head to look at him at a better angle. "You then leave for how many years without so much as a good-bye or a letter to tell us where you are or what you're up to?"

Shawn silently looked at her without answering.

"If that's it, then you're not seeing him. Don't waste my time and, what seems to be really more important is, don't waste yours either. You hear me? You can turn right around and never come back because we don't want you here!" Miho sternly told him as her anger rose even more.

"Is it really 'we' that don't want me here, or is it 'you' that doesn't?"

"I'll give you that," she admitted. "To be honest, I don't want you here. All those years when Christian tried so hard to get you back in his life, and time after time he kept getting disappointed and his heart broken because we were either an embarrassment to you in some way or simply not good enough. He could never understand why you refused not to want him or us in your life, or why you chose to torment him by not being in his."

She paused long enough to catch her breath while glancing over to her husband, who was blissfully sitting in his chair while looking out the window.

Shawn continued to watch her in silence.

"He's just on the verge of completely forgetting you for good, and I don't want him to remember you any more than he has to," she continued. "I cannot tell you how painful and hear wrenching it is for us to hear him talk about your next visit or to see that ray of hope in his eye at that possibility. No, sir! I won't have it nor will I. Nor will the rest of the family go through that because of your selfishness. You're going to have to make a choice, Shawn, and you're going to have to make it today."

"And what choice is that?" he inquired.

"You will either chose to be part not only of his family but ours as well, from this day forward *or* you chose to never come around here again. And I do mean *never* One or the other. That's it," Miho told him as her eyes seemed to soften for the first time since Shawn had arrived. "You can't keep popping in and out of our lives whenever you feel like it. Whatever you decide, it has to be a permanent thing. Make a choice and stick with it. Don't flip-flop."

"That's it?!" Shawn demanded. "That's the choice?"

"Yes. That's it."

"What the hell type of choice is that?! How can you expect me to make a decision like that?"

"You didn't seem to have a problem making it before," Miho answered with a smile. "What was it, eleven years you went without contacting us? Besides you almost killed him during that last fight you two had. And what you did to him at that party of yours that last time you saw him is what put him over the edge to what you see of him now. We're still paying for it. All of us except you." She paused to nod towards Christian. "In a sense, you did kill him that day; we just didn't know it yet. The gift of death that you gave him just took a little longer than you anticipated."

Shawn, who was done listening to the ultimatum given to him by his brother's wife, turned towards the door.

"If you leave now, I never want to see you again," Miho told him bluntly. "Ever!"

Stopping in the hall, Shawn stopped to contemplate the offer before him. Before he knew what happened, he nodded his head before simply walking away.

Seeing this, a tear came to Miho's eye for a brief instance. She quickly pulled herself together before returning to her husband. She sat next to him in her usual spot before giving him the rest of his now cold lunch.

"Was there someone just here, honey?" Christian asked as his wife sat next to him.

"It was just someone looking for a patient here," she told him. "I pointed him in the right direction."

"That was nice of you."

"I do my best." She smiled while patting his cheek. She soon leaned in to kiss his forehead.

Chapter 62

The following months Christian got a lot more use from that little book of pictures Miho had made up for him. In it, she had pictures of all the family members as well as close friends. On the back she wrote who was in the picture and what their relationship was to him. He used it so much that she ended up making him a new one.

The only people Christian seemed to recognize on sight were, outside of Miho, were his parents and his grandfather. Grandpa Joe, however, soon began to fade from his memory on account of the recent discovery he was still alive. Many times Christian would revert back to his old way of thinking that Joe was still considered dead. Slowly, his memory of his marriage began to erode until he believed they still lived together not far from his parents in upstate New York. During these times, he would often ask how his friend Catfish Johnson was doing as well as his team, The Misfits.

Shawn, for some reason, had taken a hiatus in visiting before finally returning.

"Hey, bro," he said one afternoon as he entered Christian's room.

"Oh hey...Shawn," Christian said from his chair by the window.

"What'ya doin'?"

"Just looking out the window. You know the view is a lot different from this window."

"What are ya talkin' 'bout, Beeker? Different from what?"

"Different from the other windows in the house."

Looking out the window to see if he could see any of the same differences that apparently Christian did, none were available.

"I'm sorry, bro," Shawn told him. "But I don't see anythin' different in this view. I also doubt it's changed much over the last couple of years since you've been here."

"I don't remember this window having a different view from the rest before. Besides, isn't this the first time you've been to my home?" he asked while looking up to Shawn.

"What're you talkin' 'bout? We're not at your house. Do you even know where you're at?"

They both exchanged looks with each other at that. By both the look on Christian's face and the expression in his eyes, Shawn knew that his brother had no idea what he was talking about.

"Anyway, I came to tell you something." Shawn cleared his throat in an attempt to change the subject. "I've got some bad news."

"Oh? What's that?"

"I found out yesterday that Dom died, bro," Shawn told him. "Heart attack from what I've heard. He apparently went in his sleep.

"Dom who?" questioned Christian.

"C'mon, bro, you can't be serious. Are you tellin' me that you don't know who Dom in?"

"Maybe if you describe him to me I might remember."

"You know, Dominic Calivicci? The little, old spit-fire who trained us for all those years?" Shawn explained as a look of revelation crossed his face. He was about to continue when he heard a voice.

"I wouldn't do that, Mr. Calloway," Nurse Rita said as she came into the room. She appeared to be there to give Christian some of his medication. "He doesn't know anybody nor does he know where he's at."

"What the hell you talkin' 'bout, Ratchet? He knows who I am," he told her. "And how long has he been like this?"

"These problems started the day after he went to some party over in Manhattan," the nurse answered while staring at Shawn with evil eyes before looking him over from head to toe. "Whatever he did there, accelerated his symptoms to what you see now. He can't remember anything new, and he forgets more than he can remember."

"He remembers me."

"That's because you're still part of his life that he does remember. But as far as his wife, children, and grandfather go, forget about it 'cause he already has. He has no memory of them, nor will he ever gonna no matter how many times we try to tell him. It'll only be a matter of time before he forgets you."

"He'll never forget me; I'm his brother," Shawn told her with a very arrogant and cocky swagger.

"Yeah, ok. Some brother you turned out to be," she retorted while giving Christian his medication before turning to leave. "Just like that party he was at."

***

Miho, David, and Sally soon met with Drs. Wellwood and Allen to discuss the options pertaining to Christian. The only one left available at that point was to keep him comfortable until he died which, based on his overall health, would be within a matter of months, a year at most.

Shortly after this prognosis, Grandpa Joe tripped over the wheelchair he eventually had to resort to one evening while getting ready for bed. During the fall, he hit his head on his nightstand, rendering him unconscious as a result. He stayed that way well after being taken to a nearby hospital where he died peacefully in the early hours of the next morning. This marked the second, and final, time he would be dead. The official cause of death was severe head trauma, but everyone knew it was simply from old age. David and Sally, along with Dr. Wellwood, came to Christian's room later that day to give him the news.

"Hi, Mom. Hi'ya, Dad," Christian said as they entered his room before staring blankly up at Dr. Wellwood. "Hello."

"Hello, Christian," his parents seemed to say almost in unison.

"We've got some bad news, honey," Sally said while sitting in a chair next to Christian. "We just wanted to tell you that your grandfather died this morning from that fall he had last night."

"Last night?" Christian asked while staring at her in confusion. "He didn't die from a fall last night. Don't you remember? He died in that car accident over in St. Louis."

"He didn't die in that, Christian," David told his son. "He's been your roommate here for the last couple of years."

"Roommate? The last time I saw him was when he went to St. Louis back when I was ten. How could he have been here with me?" Christian asked while looking around room. An expression of complete confusion crossed his face with every moment he looked. "Hey, this isn't my room! What happened to it? Where am I? What happened to my room?!"

"This is your room," Wellwood calmly told him.

"Then where's all my books, posters, and toys then?" Christian demanded. "And my telescope? What did you do with that?"

Hearing this, Christian's parents and doctor were silent.

"We're remodeling the house, Christian," David quickly lied. "We have all of your stuff in the basement. Your mother and I are in the process of bringing them back up here."

"Oh, ok," Christian said while being unaware of the awkward silence that fell on his visitors as they looked at him. "I forgot about the remodeling."

"So, honey," Sally said while reaching out to hold his hand. "Your grandfather's funeral is going to be this weekend. Will you be well enough to come to it?"

"I don't see why I wouldn't," he told her before looking out the window for several moments. When he turned back, he was surprised to see his parents and Wellwood looking at him. "Oh, Mom, Dad, what are you guys doing here?"

David groaned slightly as tears filled Sally's eyes. "We just came to tell you that your grandfather's funeral is this weekend."

"Who's he?" Christian asked while pointing to the good doctor.

"He was your grandfather's doctor," Sally replied in a half lie. "He wanted to see how we're doing since your grandfather passed away."

"Oh, that's nice of him," Christian told him almost absent minded like before turning to look back out the window.

When it looked like he wasn't going to acknowledge them anymore during their visit, Christian's three visitors quietly took their leave.

"Dr. Wellwood," David said once all three were well beyond his son's room. "How long will our son be like this?"

"I'm afraid it's permanent," Wellwood melancholy answered.

"Is there anything more that can be done?" Sally asked.

"Outside of keeping him happy and comfortable, I'm afraid not."

The next day, Shawn walked into Christian's room to find him sitting in his chair staring blankly out the window.

"Hi'ya, Beeker. How's it going?"

"I'm not sure," Christian told him. "I'm trying to figure out what that is out there."

"Well, let's take a gander, shall we?" Shawn bent to look out the window. "What are ya looking at?"

"That black thing out there," Christian said while pointing to his target.

"Could ya be a little more specific?" Shawn asked while looking in the general direction of Christian's pointing finger.

"The black thing down on the telephone wires. What is that?"

"The only black thing I see on the lines as a bird," Shawn told him with some confusion. "A crow to be more specific."

"Oh, is that what that is?" When the answer sank in, Christian looked up at Shawn as if seeing him for the first time to stare at him for a moment or two. "I'm sorry, but who are you?"

"You're joking, right?" asked Shawn thinking it was a joke. Christian's look of unfamiliarity proved it was no joke. "It's me, Shawn. You know, your brother?"

"Brother? I don't have a brother but I do remember knowing a kid named Shawn. I remember he stuck up for me once when I was little, but I don't have a brother."

"That was me, bro. That kid who stuck up for you was me."

"I remember him being a lot smaller."

"That's because that happened over thirty years ago."

"No, it couldn't have happened that long ago," corrected Christian as he shook his head. "It was much more recent than that, within the last couple years or so." Christian looked at Shawn again, this time with a more puzzled look than before. "Hey, are you my new roommate?"

Shawn sighed at this. "No, I'm not your new roommate."

"I remember my last roommate going somewhere. Are you a doctor here?"

"Yeah. Yeah, I'm a doctor," Shawn lied as he looked at him with sympathy in his eyes before turning to look out the window.

"You don't look like a doctor. You aren't dressed like one either," Christian said critically while he eyed Shawn's Superman shirt, faded blue jeans, and mud stained boots.

"I'm new here. And today is a dress-down day here."

"Oh, that's probably why." Christian shrugged mildly while going back to looking out the window.

"I just came to tell you that your grandfather died," Shawn softly told him after a few moments of silence.

Christian looked at Shawn and blinked confusingly at him. "My grandfather? I don't have a grandfather."

"That's because he died. Grandpa Joe died, Beeker."

"Where've you been?" Christian asked. "My grandfather died when I was ten."

"Yeah, yeah he did. His funeral's tomorrow. Your family wanted to know if you're going to it."

Christian didn't answer. He simply stared out the window.

"Hey, bud?" Shawn said while bending down to touch him on the shoulder. Christian flinched slightly in the process. "Are you going to it?"

"Going to what?" he asked while looking up at him.

"Grandpa Joe's funeral. It's tomorrow."

"If it's alright with my parents I probably will."

"I don't believe you'll have any problems there."

"Good. I wouldn't want to miss it." Christian smiled slightly while nodding his head. He then got serious while looking up to Shawn, again, seeing him for the first time. "Oh, hello. I'm sorry, but I seem to have forgotten your name."

"Hey, um, listen bro. I just came to tell you I finally took your advice that you gave me a few years ago," Shawn told him while receiving a blank stare in return. "I finally was able to make amends with Francesca about a year or so back. We'll be getting married in the spring."

"Oh, that's nice," Christian said absently. "Who's Francesca?"

"An old friend of mind." Shawn looked at him with melancholy in his eyes.

"I've heard that those are the best kinds of relationships."

"Yeah. Yeah they are. I'd like you to come to our wedding if you aren't busy that day."

"Sure, I'll come," Christian said as a look crossed his face. "If it's on a school night, my mom won't want me to stay out too late. She won't want me being too tired for school the next day. Will this be a problem?"

"I don't think you'll have to worry about that. I highly doubt it'll be on a school night," Shawn commented with a smile.

"How could you know that this far in advance?"

At that moment, Shawn finally realized that Christian, his brother, one of the few true friends he'd ever had, was gone and would never be back. Out in the hall, *Somewhere Over The Rainbow/What A Wonderful World* began playing on the radio. Shawn hung his head and cried softly. Christian ignorantly and blissfully went back to looking out the window as he ignored all around him.

***

The funeral for Grandpa Joe took place that next day. Overall, the funeral was as nice of one as the next as he was surrounded by close friends and family as they prepared for his final rest.

The attending Catholic priest, Father O'Malley, a childhood friend of Joe's, was vested in a black cope, and met the body of Joe at the foot of his flowered coved grave. He made the sight of the cross in the air.

"Come to Joseph's assistance, ye Saints of God. Come forth to meet him, ye Angels of the Lord, and receive his soul. We ask that you offer it in the sight of the Most High," O'Malley said while looking up to the sky above before continuing on in Latin. "In nomine Patris, et Filii, et Spiritus sancti. Amen. Introibo ad altare Dei. Ad Deum qui laetificat juvintutem meam."

Christian sat in the front row with his family – Miho, Asako, and Dominic were on his left, while Shawn and his parents were on his right. As he looked around, he saw many people that looked familiar such as Joe's old Army friends. Mike, Terry, Jake, and Josh were clustered together in the back. In another area, Larry, Miguel, and Eric stood. Christian felt like he should know these people but couldn't.

Father O'Malley, at this moment, told a story of when he and Joe had first met many years before.

The sun beat down on Christian's face as he looked up to the blue sky and white clouds above. After watching a number of birds fly by, he looked back to wonder what he was doing there. He understood he was at a funeral for somebody but, for the life of him, couldn't remember who it was for.

When the priest was done with his story, he looked down at the grave. "Misereatur tui omnipotens Deus, et dimissis peccatic tuis, perducatte ad vitam aeternam. Amen," he said as what appeared to be another part of the service before going silent to walk twice around the bier. The first time around he sprinkled the grave with holy water; the second, he incensed it. "And lead us not into temptation But deliver us from evil. From the gate of Hell. Deliver Joe's soul, O Lord. May he rest in peace. Amen."

As the priest made the final preparations for the funeral, Christian looked over to Shawn and said, "This is a nice funeral. Who's it for again?"

Epilogue

"All good things must come to an end."

As promised, Shawn and Francesca were married that spring. Contrary to popular belief, the ceremony was a small one in an out of the way church in an unnamed central New York town were only family and close friends attended. Much to Shawn's objection, the church was closed to any type of media.

As a wedding gift to his bride-to-be, Shawn had a retirement match the week before their big day. Win, lose, or draw, he promised that that would be his last boxing match of his professional career. It was the one he had wanted to unify the world heavyweight championships. He had trained hard on with what time he had and dedicated that match to Christian. He fulfilled his last, and final, boxing dream by being not only able to unify the heavyweight crowns via sixth round knockout, but was also able to say he did that in each of the weight classes he had fought.

He did not have as much time to celebrate the victory as he had wanted because he spent the better part of that next week preparing for the wedding. He held one last press conference that night before to publically drop his titles and to officially retire from professional boxing. He declared that, "I have closed one door in a very long chapter of my life and I hope to turn the page to a new chapter that's equally long."

The morning after the wedding, but prior to Shawn and Francesca departing for their honeymoon, they met up with the other members of the Eaton's to pay a visit to a nearby cemetery. Sally had planted some flowers the night before at Grandpa Joe's grave while having brought more then to plant. These flowers, however, were not for her father-in-laws headstone. They were, in fact, for Christian's who lay to his immediate left. Miho helped plant the flowers while David went to get some water. Shawn and Francesca looked on to watch as Asako and Dominic chased each other around. The family stayed for a several minutes to tell both Joe and Christian what was going on in their family.

One year later, Shawn and Francesca welcomed their first two children into the world as a healthy set of twin boys were delivered.

"What shall we name them?" Shawn asked while kneeling next to his wife.

"We've already discussed that I would name the girls and you the boys," she said with a smile while holding the two babies in her arms in the hospital bed. "But since they're both boys, there's only two names I can think of, if that's alright with you."

Quickly making eye contact with his wife, Shawn soon smiled at what he was being told. "Are you serious? Do you want to? Would it be ok, you think?"

"Sure. Why not?" she asked while returning the smile.

"That would be great!" he responded as a huge smile came onto his face. "That's a great idea. Christian and Joseph would be perfect names for them!"

Francesca returned the smile. "I agree they would be."

They soon kissed each other warmly before looking down at the joys they each had produced.

The End.